PENGUIN CLASSICS

THE PORTABLE CHARLES W. CHESNUTT

CHARLES WADDELL CHESNUTT (1858–1932) was born in Cleveland, Ohio, to parents who had emigrated from Fayetteville, North Carolina, to escape discrimination. Shortly after the Civil War the Chesnutt family returned to Fayetteville, where Charles received a basic education before becoming a schoolteacher and principal. Seeking better economic opportunities and dreaming of becoming an author, Chesnutt moved back to Cleveland in 1884, where he was admitted to the bar and established a thriving legal stenography business. The first African American to publish fiction in the *Atlantic Monthly*, Chesnutt secured a major Boston publisher for his first two books, *The Conjure Woman* (1899), a collection of tales told in dialect, and *The Wife of His Youth and Other Stories of the Color Line* (1899), which dealt primarily with the experience of middle-class African Americans. Launching a career as a full-time man of letters, Chesnutt published two widely reviewed novels, *The House Behind the Cedars* (1900), a story of "passing," and *The Marrow of Tradition* (1901), a study of a white supremacist takeover of a North Carolina city. In 1905, the third novel in Chesnutt's New South trilogy, *The Colonel's Dream* (1905), appeared to unenthusiastic reviews. Having resumed his business career, Chesnutt continued to write essays and fiction in defense of civil rights for African Americans, especially in the South. The National Association for the Advancement of Colored People celebrated his artistic leadership in the last decade of his life by awarding him its Spingarn Medal in 1928. His contributions to the development of realism and honesty in American race fiction place him among the m̶ and insightful writers of his time.

WILLIAM L. ANDREWS is E. Ma glish and Senior Associate Dean f the University of North Carolina of *The Literary Career of Charles Story: The First Century of Afro-American Autobiography, 1760–1865*. He is coeditor of *The Norton Anthology of African American Literature* (1997) and *The Oxford Companion to African*

American Literature (1997), and the general editor of *The Literature of the American South: A Norton Anthology* and *North American Slave Narratives: A Database and Electronic Text Library*. He has edited Chesnutt's *Conjure Tales and Stories of the Color Line* for Penguin Classics.

HENRY LOUIS GATES, JR., is Alphonse Fletcher University Professor and director of the W. E. B. Du Bois Institute for African and African American Research at Harvard University. He is editor in chief of the Oxford African American Studies Center. His most recent books are *America Behind the Color Line: Dialogues with African Americans* (Warner Books, 2004); *African American Lives,* coedited with Evelyn Brooks Higginbotham (Oxford University Press, 2004); and *The Annotated Uncle Tom's Cabin,* edited with Hollis Robbins (W. W. Norton, 2006). *Finding Oprah's Roots,* his latest book and documentary project, is a meditation on genetics, genealogy, and race published by Crown in February 2007. In 2006, Professor Gates wrote and produced the PBS documentary *African American Lives;* a four-hour sequel aired in February 2008. He also wrote and produced the documentaries *Wonders of the African World* (2000) and *America Beyond the Color Line* (2004) for the BBC and PBS, and authored the companion volumes to both series.

The Portable
Charles W. Chesnutt

Edited with an Introduction by
WILLIAM L. ANDREWS

General Editor
HENRY LOUIS GATES, JR.

PENGUIN BOOKS

PENGUIN BOOKS

Published by the Penguin Group

Penguin Group (USA) Inc., 375 Hudson Street, New York, New York 10014, U.S.A.

Penguin Group (Canada), 90 Eglinton Avenue East, Suite 700, Toronto, Ontario, Canada M4P 2Y3
(a division of Pearson Penguin Canada Inc.)

Penguin Books Ltd, 80 Strand, London WC2R 0RL, England

Penguin Ireland, 25 St Stephen's Green, Dublin 2, Ireland (a division of Penguin Books Ltd)

Penguin Group (Australia), 250 Camberwell Road, Camberwell, Victoria 3124, Australia
(a division of Pearson Australia Group Pty Ltd)

Penguin Books India Pvt Ltd, 11 Community Centre, Panchsheel Park, New Delhi - 110 017, India

Penguin Group (NZ), 67 Apollo Drive, Rosedale, North Shore 0632, New Zealand
(a division of Pearson New Zealand Ltd)

Penguin Books (South Africa) (Pty) Ltd, 24 Sturdee Avenue, Rosebank, Johannesburg 2196, South Africa

Penguin Books Ltd, Registered Offices:
80 Strand, London WC2R 0RL, England

First published in Penguin Books 2008

1   3   5   7   9   10   8   6   4   2

Introduction copyright © William L. Andrews, 2008
General Introduction copyright © Henry Louis Gates, Jr., 2008
Selection copyright © Penguin Group (USA) Inc., 2008
All rights reserved

Footnotes by William L. Andrews to "What Is a White Man?" from *The North Carolina Roots of African
American Literature: An Anthology* edited by William L. Andrews. Copyright © 2006 by the University of
North Carolina Press. Used by permission of the publisher. (www.uncpress.unc.edu)

ISBN 978-0-14-310534-3
CIP data available

Printed in the United States of America
Set in Adobe Postscript Sabon

Contents

THE PORTABLE
CHARLES W. CHESNUTT

I Short Stories

II Novel

III Essays

What Is an
African American Classic?

I have long nurtured a deep and abiding affection for the Penguin Classics, at least since I was an undergraduate at Yale. I used to imagine that my attraction for these books—grouped together, as a set, in some independent bookstores when I was a student, and perhaps even in some today—stemmed from the fact that my first-grade classmates, for some reason that I can't recall, were required to dress as penguins in our annual all-school pageant, and perform a collective side-to-side motion that our misguided teacher thought she could choreograph into something meant to pass for a "dance." Piedmont, West Virginia, in 1956, was a very long way from Penguin Nation, wherever that was supposed to be! But penguins we were determined to be, and we did our level best to avoid wounding each other with our orange-colored cardboard beaks while stomping out of rhythm in our matching orange, veined webbed feet. The whole scene was madness, one never to be repeated at the Davis Free School. But I never stopped loving penguins. And I have never stopped loving the very audacity of the idea of the Penguin Classics, an affordable, accessible library of the most important and compelling texts in the history of civilization, their black-and-white spines and covers and uniform type giving each text a comfortable, familiar feel, as if we have encountered it, or its cousins, before. I think of the Penguin Classics as the very best and most compelling in human thought, an Alexandrian library in paperback, enclosed in black and white.

I still gravitate to the Penguin Classics when killing time in an airport bookstore, deferring the slow torture of the security lines. Sometimes I even purchase two or three, fantasizing that I can speed-read one of the shorter titles, then make a dent in the longer one, vainly attempting to fill the holes in the liberal arts education that our degrees suggest we have, over the course of a plane ride! Mark Twain once quipped that a classic is "something that everybody wants to have read and nobody wants to read," and perhaps that applies to my airport purchasing habits. For my generation, these titles in the Penguin Classics form the canon—the canon of the texts that a truly well-educated person should have read, and read carefully and closely, at least once. For years I rued the absence of texts by black authors in this series, and longed to be able to make even a small contribution to the diversification of this astonishingly universal list. I watched with great pleasure as titles by African American and African authors began to appear, some two dozen over the past several years. So when Elda Rotor approached me about editing a series of African American classics and collections for Penguin's Portable Series, I eagerly accepted.

Thinking about the titles appropriate for inclusion in these series led me, inevitably, to think about what, for me, constitutes a "classic." And thinking about this led me, in turn, to the wealth of reflections on what defines a work of literature or philosophy somehow speaking to the human condition beyond time and place, a work somehow endlessly compelling, generation upon generation, a work whose author we don't have to look like to identify with, to feel at one with, as we find ourselves transported through the magic of a textual time machine; a work that refracts the image of ourselves that we project onto it, regardless of our ethnicity, our gender, our time, our place. This is what centuries of scholars and writers have meant when they use the word "classic," and—despite all that we know about the complex intersubjectivity of the production of meaning in the wondrous exchange between a reader and a text—it remains true that classic texts, even in the most conventional, conservative sense of the word "classic," do exist, and these books will continue to be read long after the generation the text reflects and defines, the generation of readers contemporary with the text's author, is dead and gone. Classic texts speak from their authors' graves, in their names, in their voices. As Italo Calvino once remarked, "A classic is a book that has never finished saying what it has to say."

Faulkner put this idea in an interesting way: "The aim of every artist is to arrest motion, which is life, by artificial means, and hold it fixed so that a hundred years later, when a stranger looks at it, it moves again since it is life." That, I am certain, must be the desire of every writer. But what about the reader? What makes a book a classic to a reader? Here, perhaps, Hemingway said it best: "All good books are alike in that they are truer than if they had really happened and after you are finished reading one you will feel that all that happened to you, and afterwards it belongs to you, the good and the bad, the ecstasy, the remorse and sorrow, the people and the places and how the weather was."

I have been reading black literature since I was fifteen, yanked into that dark discursive universe by an Episcopal priest at a church camp near my home in West Virginia in August of 1965, during the terrifying days of the Watts Riots in Los Angeles. Eventually, by fits and starts, studying the literature written by black authors became my avocation; ultimately, it has become my vocation. And, in my own way, I have tried to be an evangelist for it, to a readership larger than my own people, people who, as it were, look like these texts. Here, I am reminded of something W. S. Merwin said about the books he most loved: "Perhaps a classic is a work that one imagines should be common knowledge, but more and more often isn't."

I would say, of African and African American literature, that perhaps classic works by black writers are works that one imagines should be common knowledge among the broadest possible readership but that less and less are, as the teaching of reading to understand how words can create the worlds into which books can transport us yields to classroom instruction geared toward passing a state-authorized, standardized exam. All literary texts suffer from this wrongheaded approach to teaching, mind you; but it especially affects texts by people of color, and texts by women—texts still struggling, despite enormous gains over the last twenty years, to gain a solid foothold in anthologies and syllabi. For every anthology, every syllabus, every publishing series such as the Penguin Classics constitutes a distinct "canon," an implicit definition of all that is essential for a truly educated person to read.

James Baldwin, who has pride of place in my personal canon of African American authors since it was one of his books that that Episcopal priest gave me to read in that dreadful summer of 1965, argued that "the responsibility of a writer is to excavate the experience of the people who produced him." But surely Baldwin would have agreed with E. M. Forster that the books that we remember, the books that have truly influenced us, are those that "have gone a little further down our particular path than we have yet ourselves." Excavating the known is a worthy goal of the writer as cultural archaeologist; yet, at the same time, so is unveiling the unknown, the unarticulated yet shared experience of the colorless things that make us human: "something we have always known (or thought we knew)," as Calvino puts it, "but without knowing that this author said it first." We might think of the difference between Forster and Baldwin, on the one hand, and Calvino, on the other, as the difference between an author representing what has happened (Forster, Baldwin) in the history of a people whose stories, whose very history itself, has long been suppressed, and what could have happened (Calvino) in the atemporal realm of art. This is an important distinction when thinking about the nature of an African American classic—rather, when thinking about the nature of the texts that comprise the African American literary tradition or, for that matter, the texts in any underread tradition.

One of James Baldwin's most memorable essays, a subtle meditation on sexual preference, race, and gender, is entitled "Here Be Dragons." So much of traditional African American literature, even fiction and poetry—ostensibly at least once removed from direct statement—was meant to deal a fatal blow to the dragon of racism. For black writers since the eighteenth-century beginnings of the tradition, literature has been one more weapon—a very important weapon, mind you, but still one weapon among many—in the arsenal black people have drawn upon to fight against antiblack racism and for their equal rights before the law. Ted Joans, the black surrealist poet, called this sort of literature from the sixties' Black Arts movement "hand grenade poems." Of what possible use are the niceties of figuration when one must slay a dragon? I can hear you say give me the blunt weapon anytime! Problem is, it is more difficult than some writers seem to think to slay a dragon with a poem or a novel. Social problems persist; literature too tied to addressing those social problems tends to enter the historical archives, leaving the realm of the literary. Let me state bluntly what should be obvious: writers are read for how they write, not what they write about.

Frederick Douglass—for this generation of readers one of the most widely read writers—reflected on this matter even in the midst of one of his most fiery speeches addressing the ironies of the sons and daughters of slaves celebrating the Fourth of July while slavery continued unabated. In his now-classic essay "What Is to the Slave the Fourth of July" (1852), Douglass argued that an immediate, almost transparent form of discourse was demanded of black writers by the heated temper of the times, a discourse with an immediate end in mind: "At a time like this, scorching irony, not convincing argument, is needed. . . . a fiery stream of biting ridicule, blasting reproach, withering sarcasm, and stern rebuke. For it is not light that is needed, but fire; it is not the gentle shower, but thunder. We need the storm, the whirlwind, and the earthquake." Above all else, Douglass concludes, the rhetoric of the literature created by African Americans must, of necessity, be a purposeful rhetoric, its ends targeted at attacking the evils that afflict black people: "The feeling of the nation must be quickened; the conscience of the nation must be roused; the propriety of the nation must be startled; the hypocrisy of the nation must be exposed; and its crimes against God and man must be proclaimed and denounced." And perhaps this was so; nevertheless, we read Douglass's writings today in literature classes not so much for their content but to understand, and marvel at, his sublime mastery of words, words—to paraphrase Calvino—that never finish saying what it is they have to say, not because of their "message," but because of the language in which that message is inextricably enfolded.

There are as many ways to define a classic in the African American tradition as there are in any other tradition, and these ways are legion. So many essays have been published entitled "What Is a Classic?" that they could fill several large anthologies. And while no one can say explicitly why generations of readers return to read certain texts, just about everyone can agree that making a best-seller list in one's lifetime is most certainly not an index of fame or influence over time; the longevity of one's readership—of books about which one says "I am rereading," as Calvino puts it—on the other hand, most certainly is. So, the size of one's readership (through library use, Internet access, and sales) cumulatively is an interesting factor to consider; and because of series such as the Penguin Classics, we can gain a sense, for our purposes, of those texts written by authors in previous generations that have sustained sales—mostly for classroom use—long after their authors were dead.

There can be little doubt that *The Narrative of the Life of Frederick Douglass* (1845), *The Souls of Black Folk* (1903), by W. E. B. Du Bois, and *Their Eyes Were Watching God* (1937), by Zora Neale Hurston, are the three most classic of the black classics—again, as measured by consumption—while Langston Hughes's poetry, though not purchased as books in these large numbers, is accessed through the Internet as frequently as that of any other American poet, and indeed profoundly more so than most. Within Penguin's Portable Series list, the most popular individual titles, excluding Douglass's first slave narrative and Du Bois's *Souls*, are:

Up from Slavery (1903), Booker T. Washington
Autobiography of an Ex-Coloured Man (1912), James Weldon Johnson
God's Trombones (1926), James Weldon Johnson
Passing (1929), Nella Larsen
The Marrow of Tradition (1898), Charles W. Chesnutt
Incidents in the Life of a Slave Girl (1861), Harriet Jacobs
The Interesting Narrative (1789), Olaudah Equiano

The House Behind the Cedars (1900), Charles W. Chesnutt
My Bondage and My Freedom (1855), Frederick Douglass
Quicksand (1928), Nella Larsen

These titles form a canon of classics of African American literature, judged by classroom readership. If we add Jean Toomer's novel *Cane* (1922), arguably the first work of African American modernism, along with Douglass's first narrative, Du Bois's *The Souls,* and Hurston's *Their Eyes,* we would most certainly have included many of the touchstones of black literature published before 1940, when Richard Wright published *Native Son.*

Every teacher's syllabus constitutes a canon of sorts, and I teach these texts and a few others as the classics of the black canon. Why these particular texts? I can think of two reasons: First, these texts signify or riff upon each other, repeating, borrowing, and extending metaphors book to book, generation to generation. To take just a few examples, Equiano's eighteenth-century use of the trope of the talking book (an image found, remarkably, in five slave narratives published between 1770 and 1811) becomes, with Frederick Douglass, the representation of the quest for freedom as, necessarily, the quest for literacy, for a freedom larger than physical manumission; we might think of this as the representation of metaphysical manumission, of freedom and literacy—the literacy of great literature—inextricably intertwined. Douglass transformed the metaphor of the talking book into the trope of chiasmus, a repetition with a stinging reversal: "You have seen how a man becomes a slave, you will see how a slave becomes a man." Du Bois, with Douglass very much on his mind, transmuted chiasmus a half century later into the metaphor of duality or double consciousness, a necessary condition of living one's life, as he memorably put it, behind a "veil."

Du Bois's metaphor has a powerful legacy in twentieth-century black fiction: James Weldon Johnson, in *The Ex-Coloured Man,* literalizes the trope of double consciousness by depicting as his protagonist a man who, at will, can occupy two distinct racial spaces, one black, one white, and who moves seamlessly, if ruefully, between them; Toomer's *Cane* takes Du Bois's metaphor of duality for the inevitably split consciousness that every Negro must feel living in a country in which her or his status as a citizen is liminal at best, or has been erased at worst, and makes of this the metaphor for the human condition itself under modernity, a tellingly bold rhetorical gesture— one designed to make the Negro the metaphor of the human condition. And Hurston, in *Their Eyes*, extends Toomer's revision even further, depicting a character who can only gain her voice once she can name this condition of duality or double consciousness and then glide gracefully and lyrically between her two selves, an "inside" self and an "outside" one.

More recently, Alice Walker, in *The Color Purple*, signifies upon two aspects of the narrative strategy of *Their Eyes*: first, she revisits the theme of a young black woman finding her voice, depicting a protagonist who writes herself into being through letters addressed to God and to her sister, Nettie— letters that grow ever more sophisticated in their syntax and grammar and imagery as she comes to consciousness before our very eyes, letter to letter; and second, Walker riffs on Hurston's use of a vernacular-inflected free indirect discourse to show that black English has the capacity to serve as the medium for narrating a novel through the black dialect that forms a most pliable and expansive language in Celie's letters. Ralph Ellison makes Du Bois's metaphor of the veil a trope of blindness and life underground for his protagonist in *Invisible Man*, a protagonist who, as he types the story of his life from a hole underground, writes himself into being in the first person (in contradistinction to Richard Wright's protagonist, Bigger Thomas, whose reactive tale of fear and flight is told in the third person). Walker's novel also riffs on Ellison's claim for the revolutionary possibilities of writing the self into being, whereas Hurston's protagonist, Janie, speaks herself into being. Ellison himself signified multiply upon Richard Wright's *Native Son*, from the title to the use of the first-person bildungsroman to chart the coming to consciousness of a sensitive protagonist moving from blindness and an inability to do little more than react to his environment, to the insight gained by wresting control of his identity from social forces and strong individuals that would circumscribe and confine his life choices. Toni Morrison, master supernaturalist and perhaps the greatest black novelist of all, trumps Ellison's trope of blindness by returning over and over to the possibilities and limits of insight within worlds confined or circumscribed not by supraforces (à la Wright) but by the confines of the imagination and the ironies of individual and family history, signifying upon Faulkner, Woolf, and Márquez in the process. And Ishmael Reed, the father of black postmodernism and what we might think of as the hip-hop novel, the tradition's master parodist, signifies upon everybody and everything in the black literary tradition, from the slave narratives to the Harlem Renaissance to black nationalism and feminism.

This sort of literary signifying is what makes a literary tradition, well, a "tradition," rather than a simple list of books whose authors happen to have been born in the same country, share the same gender, or would be identified by their peers as belonging to this ethnic group or that. What makes these books special—"classic"—however, is something else. Each text has the uncanny capacity to take the seemingly mundane details of the day-to-day African American experience of its time and transmute those details and the characters' actions into something that transcends its ostensible subject's time and place, its specificity. These texts reveal the human universal through the African American particular: all true art, all classics, do this; this is what "art" is, a revelation of that which makes each of us sublimely human, rendered in the minute details of the actions and thoughts and feelings of a compelling character embedded in a time and place. But as soon as we find ourselves turning to a text for its anthropological or sociological data, we have left the realm of art; we have reduced the complexity of fiction or poetry to an essay, and this is not what imaginative literature is for. Richard Wright, at his best, did this, as did his signifying disciple Ralph Ellison; Louis Armstrong and Duke Ellington, Bessie Smith and Billie Holiday achieved this effect in music; Jacob Lawrence and Romare Bearden achieved it in the visual arts. And this is what Wole Soyinka does in his tragedies, what Toni Morrison does in her novels, what Derek Walcott does in his poetry. And while it is risky to name one's contemporaries in a list such as this, I think that Rita Dove and Jamaica Kincaid achieve this effect as well, as do Colson Whitehead and Edwidge Danticat, in a younger generation. (There are other writers whom I would include in this group had I the space.) By delving ever so deeply into the particularity of the African and African American experience, these authors manage, somehow, to come out the other side, making the race or the gender of their characters almost translucent, less important than the fact that they stand as aspects of ourselves beyond race or gender or time or place, precisely in the same magical way that Hamlet never remains for long stuck as a prince in a court in Denmark.

Each classic black text reveals to us, uncannily, subtly, how the Black Experience is inscribed, inextricably and indelibly, in the human experience, and how the human experience takes one of its myriad forms in blackface, as it were. Together, such texts also demonstrate, implicitly, that African American culture is one of the world's truly great and eternal cultures, as noble and as resplendent as any. And it is to publish such texts, written by African and African American authors, that Penguin has created this new series, which I have the pleasure of editing.

—HENRY LOUIS GATES, JR.

HENRY LOUIS GATES, JR., is general editor for a series of African American classics, including *The Portable Charles W. Chesnutt,* edited with an introduction by William L. Andrews, and *God's Trombones,* by James Weldon Johnson with a foreword by Maya Angelou.

Introduction

"I think I must write a book," Charles Waddell Chesnutt announced to his journal on May 29, 1880, after a long day in the classroom at the Colored Normal School of Fayetteville, North Carolina. "It has been my cherished dream," the twenty-one year-old teacher acknowledged, "and I feel an influence that I cannot resist calling me to the task. . . . I do not know but I am as well prepared as some other successful writers." Chesnutt then catalogued his qualifications with characteristic aplomb: "a fair knowledge of the classics, a speaking acquaintance with the modern languages, an intimate friendship with literature, etc., seven years' experience in the school room, two years of married life, and a habit of studying character." Besides, "fifteen years of life in the South, in one of the most eventful eras of its history; among a people whose life is rich in the elements of romance; under conditions calculated to stir one's soul to the very depths;—I think there is here a fund of experience, a supply of material, which a skillful per[son] could work up with tremendous effect."

Few aspiring writers have predicted as accurately as the young Chesnutt what the thematic crux of their mature work would be: "If I do write, I shall write for a purpose, a high, holy purpose. . . . The object of my writings would be not so much the elevation of the colored people as the elevation of the whites—for I consider the unjust spirit of caste which is so insidious as to pervade a whole nation, and so powerful as to subject a whole race and all connected with it to scorn and social ostracism—I consider this a barrier to the moral progress of the American people; and I would be one of the first to head

a determined, organized crusade against it." The role of literature in such a crusade would be to "lead [white] people out,
imperceptibly, unconsciously, step by step" to a point at which
they could begin to question and reconsider "the subtle almost
indefinable feeling of repulsion toward the negro, which is
common to most Americans." The ultimate goal was clear:
"social recognition and equality" for blacks in the United
States. The challenge Chesnutt envisioned for the African
American writer was to devise literary strategies that would
"open the way to the goal" without requiring a frontal assault
on the bastion of white racism. The defenses of the whites had
to be subverted so that "while amusing them," black writers
could "lead them on, imperceptibly, unconsciously, step by step
to the desired state of feeling." By employing such diversionary
arts, "we will find ourselves in their midst," Chesnutt predicted, "before they think it."

This mix of idealism and calculation, crusading zeal and prag-
matic craftiness helped make Charles Chesnutt the most widely
read and critically respected African American fiction writer of
his era. His short stories and novels were solicited and mar-
keted by some of the most prestigious publishers in the United
States. His fiction was reviewed more extensively and more
thoughtfully than any previously published by a black American. He made a name for himself initially as a local colorist
and practitioner of dialect tales set in the post-Reconstruction
South. But, as he noted many years after his literary career had
reached its apex, "My physical makeup was such that I knew
the psychology of people of mixed blood in so far as it differed
from that of other people, and most of my writings ran along
the color line. . . . It has more dramatic possibilities than life
within clearly defined and widely differentiated groups."

For these reasons, at the height of his fame, Chesnutt, whose
color and facial features barely distinguished him from those
privileged as white, championed people of color with whom he
most identified—namely, middle-class mixed-race persons like
him. Nevertheless, his fiction, particularly his last two novels,
also advocated for working-class blacks of the small-town

South, whom the author had come to know by growing up in eastern North Carolina. While his mixed-race protagonists often struggle with conflicted loyalties and unresolved aspirations, the most determined, outspoken, and spirited heroes in Chesnutt's fiction come from the ranks of the black yeomanry of the South.

Hungry for recognition and financial reward, Chesnutt tried his best to create fiction that would appeal to the general reader while earning the praise of critics and reviewers in the literary press. As his career progressed, he readily avowed a third ambition—that his stories and especially his novels would be taken seriously as thoughtful examinations of current racial problems. The goal of his second novel, *The Marrow of Tradition* (1901), as he confided to his cousin, was to address nothing less than "the whole race situation" in the South.

Unfortunately, a winning combination of sales, critical applause, and social relevance proved elusive for Chesnutt, as it did for even well-established white writers such as Mark Twain and William Dean Howells when they invited their readership to examine white privilege and prejudice in fiction. Most of Chesnutt's white readers preferred to ignore—or demanded cheerier resolutions of—the vexed issues he probed with growing incisiveness as his literary career evolved. Most literary critics, as well as editors and prospective publishers, wanted Chesnutt to endorse, not contest, the sentimental evasions that often passed for art in conventional American race fiction. Within three years of launching his career as a full-time man of letters in 1899, Chesnutt admitted to his friends that he had failed to win an audience sizable enough to realize his dream. Within a half century of his death, however, Chesnutt emerged from historical obscurity to attract the kind of readership he had strived to generate during his brief heyday. He is now recognized as a literary innovator of major achievement, whose mastery of his craft, particularly in the short story, placed his distinctive African American personal signature on American fiction at the turn of the twentieth century.

Charles Waddell Chesnutt was born in Cleveland, Ohio, on June 20, 1858. His parents, Andrew Jackson Chesnutt and Anne Maria Sampson Chesnutt, came from antebellum North Carolina's free Negro class. Chesnutt's paternal grandfather, Waddell (or Waddle) Cade, after whom Charles was named, was a prosperous white farmer and tobacco inspector who accumulated property in and around Fayetteville between 1805 and 1821. During the 1830s and 1840s Cade held the land in trust and eventually willed it to his white offspring by marriage and to the free mixed-race children whom he sired by Ann Chesnutt, his mistress and later his housekeeper. One product of this union, "Jack" Chesnutt, left home in the late 1850s and moved to Ohio. After serving in the Union Army as a teamster, Charles's father brought his family back to his home state in 1866 and set up a grocery store in Fayetteville on land provided him by his father. Charles grew up near the center of town in a cottage behind a bank of cedar trees, the house and the lot also gifts from Cade to his son. There in the house behind the cedars that he later memorialized in his first novel, Charles Chesnutt spent his boyhood.

A bookish, inquisitive boy, Charles worked in the family business and attended the Howard School, which his politically active father helped to found in 1867, until his mother's death in 1871. To help with family expenses, he then began teaching, first in Fayetteville and later in rural schools around Charlotte, North Carolina. Barely a teenager when his own formal schooling ended, Charles soon became an insatiable autodidact. On his own or with local tutors, he studied everything from the organ to shorthand. He was particularly devoted to the classics of English and European literature. In 1877 Chesnutt returned to Fayetteville to teach at the Howard School, established by the state of North Carolina for the training of black teachers. Three years later he was rewarded with an appointment to the principalship of the school. By this time he had married Susan Perry, the daughter of a comparatively well-to-do Fayetteville barber. Children soon followed, Ethel in 1879 and Helen Maria the next year. Yet the young father was far from satisfied with his accomplishments and status in

Fayetteville. Having spent his Christmas holidays with only
one invitation anywhere, Chesnutt summed up his predicament
in a journal entry on January 3, 1881: "I occupy here a position similar to that of Mahomet's Coffin. I am neither fish,
flesh, nor fowl—neither 'nigger,' white, nor 'buckrah.' Too
'stuck-up' for the colored folks, and, of course, not recognized
by the whites." But "these things I imagine I would escape
from, in some degree, if I lived in the North."

By the spring of 1881 Chesnutt had concluded that authorship was "the only thing I can do without capital, under my
present circumstances, except teach." He reckoned the "chance
of success" at barely "one out of a hundred." Nevertheless,
Chesnutt candidly admitted to his journal, "I want fame; I
want money; I want to raise my children in a different rank of
life from that I sprang from. In my present vocation I would
never accumulate a competency, with all the economy and prudence, and parsimony in the world. In law or medicine, I would
be compelled to wait half a lifetime to accomplish anything.
But literature pays the successful." In the North, Chesnutt
hoped, he would be judged by his ability alone. Racial and
color discrimination could be deflected by individual hard work
and perseverance.

After teaching himself a practical skill, stenography, Chesnutt resigned his position at the Howard School in the spring of
1883 and set out for New York City. He aimed to find employment "in some literary avocation, or something leading in that
direction," he promised his journal. He would be satisfied temporarily with the work he found as a reporter, but his long-
range goal was loftier. Ever since the publication of Albion
Tourgée's A Fool's Errand (1879), a best-selling novel about
racial turmoil during Reconstruction in North Carolina, Chesnutt had been convinced that he could do as well as Tourgée,
a transplanted white Ohioan, in writing about racial issues
in the South. The aspiring young author reasoned that if a Yankee carpetbagger with only short-term knowledge of Southern
African Americans could achieve such literary notoriety, then a
man of color like himself, who had an insider's view of the
same subject, could write at least as good a book about the

South. Gaining the kind of audience Tourgée had won would satisfy both Chesnutt's personal ambitions and his sense of moral responsibility to people of color in America.

After less than a year in New York, Chesnutt had earned enough money to move his family to Cleveland in the spring of 1884. There he settled his wife and their three children in comfortable quarters, passed the Ohio state bar, and set up what would become a profitable court reporting business. He soon made his first mature attempts to break into print. Beginning in 1885 with a sketch entitled "Uncle Peter's House," Chesnutt's name appeared repeatedly in the S. S. McClure newspaper syndicate, which published most of the humorous sketches and mildly sentimental or didactic squibs that Chesnutt wrote during his literary apprenticeship in the second half of the 1880s.

Through a friendship with George W. Cable, the most liberal white Southern literary figure of the time, Chesnutt also started contributing to the Open-Letter Club, a group of progressive Southerners who were interested in constructive solutions to the South's problems. Cable was instrumental in the publication of his protégé's first essay, "What Is a White Man?"—a thoroughly researched indictment of the South's arbitrary and contradictory laws governing the definition of race—in the *Independent* in 1889. When Cable asked Chesnutt to become his secretary, the young man was flattered, but his court reporting business was thriving, and his family responsibilities demanded more income than Cable could offer. Besides, Chesnutt had begun to taste real success as a short story writer for some of the best magazines in America.

In August 1887 the *Atlantic Monthly* printed Chesnutt's "The Goophered Grapevine," his first important work of fiction. Inspired by a voodoo tale told by his father-in-law's black gardener in Fayetteville, "The Goophered Grapevine" features a story of slave life in antebellum North Carolina embedded within a framing story from the present day. The frame introduces the reader to both a white Ohio businessman who explains that he has moved to North Carolina to set up a profitable business and an elderly mixed-race former slave who recounts for the businessman's edification a weird and wonderful folktale in Negro dialect. Uncle Julius McAdoo, the ex-slave raconteur, unveils for the *Atlantic*'s reader, as well as for his Midwestern interlocutor, the lore of "conjuration"— Southern African American folk beliefs and practices designed to harness supernatural powers for the protection and advantage of those who knew how to wield them. Julius's story of the weird and marvelous effects of conjure on a man and the grape vineyard to which he is vitally and tragically linked proves both an escapist trip into the past and, by the end of the story, an ironic education for the white businessman in the present. On one level "The Goophered Grapevine" appears to be part of the "plantation tradition" of late-nineteenth-century Southern literature, typified by the work of Joel Chandler Harris and Thomas Nelson Page, who made their fame retailing often-romanticized tales of the Old South told by nostalgic ex-slaves. But Chesnutt gave his readers a new kind of black storytelling protagonist—one who shrewdly adapts his recollections of the past to secure his economic advantage in the present, sometimes at the expense of John, the Ohio businessman, who, by the end of "The Goophered Grapevine," is so impressed by Julius that he takes the old black man into his employ.

Thomas Bailey Aldrich, the influential editor of the *Atlantic Monthly*, was sufficiently impressed by Uncle Julius and his tales to print two more in the next two years. The first, "Po' Sandy," kept to the formula of "The Goophered Grapevine" but added a feminine and somewhat sentimental dimension to both Julius's tale and John's framing narrative. To both John and his newly introduced wife, Annie, Julius imparts the story of the tragic love of an enslaved couple, Sandy and Tenie. Tenie is obliged to use her power as a conjurer to turn her husband into a tree in order to prevent his master from hiring him out for long stints as a laborer on neighboring farms. The death of Sandy, and Tenie's subsequent grief and guilt-induced madness, brings the tale to its end, leaving John and his wife to disagree about the true significance of what Julius has told them. John laughs the story off as "an absurdly impossible yarn," but Annie, both fascinated and moved by Tenie's plight, declares her sympathy with the widowed slave woman and recognizes that slavery was the ultimate cause of her pathetic end.

A year later, in October 1889, the *Atlantic* published "Dave's Neckliss," probably the most thoroughly tragic dialect story Chesnutt ever wrote. Recounted by Uncle Julius, the story of the humiliation, madness, and suicide of Dave, an exemplary slave preacher and community leader whom Julius claims to have known personally, has no leavening of conjure or fantasy to relieve the steadily downward movement of its plot. The reader witnesses, step by step, Dave's terrible regression into social alienation, self-objectification, and ignominious death. Perhaps readers of Chesnutt's own time also detected the subtle but eloquent commentary in the story on the destructive power of scapegoating. A particularly acute reader might have drawn a parallel between the ruinous effect of discrimination on Dave and the impact of racial prejudice on African Americans in the post-slavery era.

Chesnutt told Tourgée, with whom he had developed a correspondence, that "Dave's Neckliss" was "the best of the series" of dialect tales that he had published in the late 1880s. Nevertheless, Chesnutt opined in September 1889, "I think I have about used up the old Negro who serves as mouthpiece, and I shall drop him in future stories, as well as much of the dialect." Chesnutt was not dissatisfied with Uncle Julius as his entrée into the literary world, but he did not want to be known as solely a local color writer or purveyor of Negro dialect stories. "Dave's Neckliss" was designed "to get out of the realm of superstition [and] into the realm of feeling and passion," Chesnutt informed Tourgée. In the same letter, Chesnutt called attention to his newest story and was careful to distinguish it from the kind of writing he had been doing. "The Sheriff's Children" was another "southern story," but "it is not in dialect." It centered on "a tragic incident, not of slavery exactly, but showing the fruits of slavery." Appearing in the *Independent* in November 1889, "The Sheriff's Children" signaled the new direction in which the thirty-one-year-old author planned to move.

Set in Reconstruction North Carolina, the story shows how an incident of interracial sex and betrayal in prewar days comes to haunt a guilty Southern aristocrat when his vengeful, unacknowledged son returns to the land of his birth. Tragedy envelops the son and father at the story's conclusion, leaving the father, who is also the local sheriff, unable to atone for his sins of the past. The reader is left for the first time in Chesnutt's fiction with a disquieting moral dilemma to ponder. In its emphasis on the consequences of miscegenation—repression and denial, mob violence, and moral compromise—in Reconstruction North Carolina, "The Sheriff's Children" was the germ of much of Chesnutt's later fiction. "The Sheriff's Children" was also the first of many color-line stories that Chesnutt would write concerning the situation of mixed-race people in post–Civil War America. Both "The Sheriff's Children" and a longer story called "Rena Walden," which Chesnutt tried unsuccessfully to publish in the *Century* magazine in 1889, register the author's growing determination to explore the origins, aspirations, and social and psychological dilemmas of persons of mixed racial heritage in the South. However, the dismissive response of the *Century*'s editor to the first draft of "Rena Walden" showed Chesnutt that it would not be easy to place honest fictional portrayals of life along the color line in genteel literary magazines that catered to popular white taste.

From the fall of 1889 to the summer of 1891, Chesnutt spent most of his writing time revising "Rena Walden" at the behest of Cable and Richard Watson Gilder, editor of the *Century*. Cable was encouraging, but Gilder could not conceal his distaste for Rena, a near-white girl who struggles tragically against the caste system of a Southern town. Chesnutt detected more than a critique of his literary artistry in Gilder's pronouncement that the mixed-race characters on whom "Rena Walden" focuses evinced a "brutality" and "lack of mellowness" that made them simply *"uninteresting."* Stung by what he believed was Gilder's unabashed prejudice against mixed-race people— people like him—Chesnutt wondered how he could possibly accommodate himself to the demands of editors like Gilder. Wearily, he told Cable in the summer of 1890 that he could see no alternative but to "drop the attempt at realism" in stories like "The Sheriff's Children" and "Rena Walden" and go back to safer material. Cable counseled exactly the opposite, urging Chesnutt to write from conviction, not simply to please editors. The young writer took heart from his mentor's advice and devoted himself over the next six years to two projects, a novella called *Mandy Oxendine* and short fiction on various topics.

Conceived as early as 1893 and revised at least once before it was submitted to the *Atlantic Monthly* early in 1897, *Mandy Oxendine* was Chesnutt's first novel of "passing" (for white). The title character, as well as the young teacher who loves her, both chafe under the caste and color restrictions of a small North Carolina town. While Tom Lowery chooses education at a Negro college as his ticket to a better life, Mandy decides that passing for white is the only way she can escape classification with those she disparages as "'black an' ugly an' pore.'" The narrator of the story neither excuses nor denounces his heroine's ambitions. Though in the end Mandy's deception is exposed and she returns to Lowery, Chesnutt does not have her suffer for her socially proscribed behavior. Nor does he rule out the possibility that beyond the ending of this story Mandy and Tom Lowery may yet immerse themselves "in the great white world" in order to find "such a place as their talents and their virtues merited." Regardless, the narrator asserts at the end of the novel, "They deserve to be happy." In an age that stereotyped African American women as garrulous mammies or doomed mulattas, Mandy Oxendine's self-assertiveness, daring, and refusal to be deterred by the morality and conventions of the color line represent a striking literary experiment. The *Atlantic* did not accept the novella, and there is no evidence that Chesnutt tried to place it elsewhere. Instead, by the fall of 1897, Chesnutt tried to interest Aldrich's successor at the *Atlantic* in a book of short stories.

Walter Hines Page, not only the *Atlantic*'s editor but a senior member of the prestigious Houghton Mifflin publishing firm in Boston, replied to Chesnutt's inquiry by suggesting that "a skillfully selected list of your short stories might make a book."

Chesnutt quickly dispatched to Page twenty-two miscellaneous short stories and sketches for the editor's review. A North Carolina expatriate, like Chesnutt, of comparatively liberal bent, Page was struck by the distinctiveness of the three conjure stories—"The Goophered Grapevine," "Po' Sandy," and "The Conjurer's Revenge"—that Chesnutt had published almost a decade earlier. He advised Chesnutt to "produce five or six more" conjure stories in a similar vein. Despite the fact that he had written nothing of this nature for eight years, within a mere six weeks Chesnutt cranked out a half-dozen new conjure stories for his editor's inspection. Page liked enough of the new stories that in September 1898 he committed Houghton Mifflin to publishing Chesnutt's first book, a collection of seven conjure stories to be entitled *The Conjure Woman*.

Published in March 1899, *The Conjure Woman* was not a big commercial success, but it was favorably received by most reviewers, who recognized it as a dialect book with a difference. Although the vogue of dialect writing was waning, the wily Uncle Julius, the peculiar blend of realism and fantasy in his reminiscences, and the byplay between him and the whites who hear, judge, and record his tales all pleased Chesnutt's reviewers. Unlike most plantation fiction, which generally romanticized slavery and the slaveholders of the Old South, *The Conjure Woman* evoked a world of mean-spirited, penny-pinching masters so preoccupied with profit that they care little for the welfare or feelings of their slaves. Through the magic of conjuration, slaves in several stories in the volume successfully resist the power wielded by their would-be exploiters. But whether they win or lose these contests, the slaves' sometimes comic, at other times tragic, humanity is unmistakable, constituting a literary as well as ethical triumph for Chesnutt's portrayals of black people straining against bondage. Deploying universal folk motifs such as metamorphosis and the trickster figure (namely, Uncle Julius), Chesnutt added a depth to his literary adaptations of black folklore not found in the work of more famous white writers like Joel Chandler Harris. By pitting the white narrator of *The Conjure Woman*—the literal-minded John, to whom Julius is merely a reciter of quaint fairy tales—against Annie, who perceives darker, more disturbing truths beneath the beguiling surface of Julius's marvelous stories, Chesnutt's first book challenged the social and aesthetic premises on which genteel literary discourse about race had been established.

Soon after *The Conjure Woman* came out, word began to spread that this new voice of realism belonged to an African American. Chesnutt had not asked his publisher to feature his racial heritage in the advertising of *The Conjure Woman* because he wanted his work to be judged on its literary merits alone. Public curiosity about Chesnutt, along with the promising sales of his first book and the admiration expressed by several literary figures for "The Wife of His Youth," which the *Atlantic Monthly* published a few months before *The Conjure Woman,* convinced Houghton Mifflin to heed Chesnutt's suggestion that a second collection of his stories be published. Late in 1899, just in time for the Christmas trade, *The Wife of His Youth and Other Stories of the Color Line,* consisting of nine stories, appeared. On these two collections of stories, which contain almost all of Chesnutt's best short fiction between 1877 and 1899 ("Dave's Neckliss" excepted), Chesnutt's reputation as a short story writer ultimately rests.

The fundamental social issue, as well as the unifying theme, in most of the stories of *The Wife of His Youth* is miscegenation in the United States. The title story of the volume as well as another entitled "A Matter of Principle" analyze with both irony and pathos the aspirations and prejudices of light-skinned middle-class African Americans in "Groveland," Ohio. Many of Chesnutt's fictional models in these stories were people he knew from his own membership in the Cleveland Social Circle, an exclusive society of upwardly mobile mixed-race people who were reputed to discriminate against anyone with complexions darker than their own. "The Wife of His Youth" tells how a leader of the Groveland "Blue Vein Society" triumphs over his class and color prejudices by acknowledging, after decades of separation, his dark-skinned wife from his long-concealed slave past. In a less pathetic and more satirical case, Chesnutt deflates the racial pretensions of Cicero Clayton, the protagonist of "A Matter of Principle," by showing how his "principle" of dissociation from dark-skinned Negroes spoils his daughter's chance to marry a congressman. In 1930 Chesnutt confided to a critic: "I belonged to the 'Blue Vein Society,' and the characters in 'The Wife of His Youth' and 'A Matter of Principle' were my personal friends. I shared their sentiments to a degree, though I could see the comic side of them." Both stories reflect on color consciousness among African Americans with a balance of objectivity and irony unequaled—in fact, hardly attempted—in American race fiction up to Chesnutt's time.

Chesnutt's objective and often sympathetic treatment of mixed-race persons was greeted by his less responsive readers as a barely disguised brief for racial intermarriage. However, more than one story in *The Wife of His Youth* makes it clear that, while Chesnutt was in favor of the assimilation of people of color into the socioeconomic mainstream of American life, he believed that the most reliable means of accomplishing this was through African American dedication to the middle-class work ethic. This is in part the message of "Uncle Wellington's Wives," the longest story in *The Wife of His Youth*. Although Chesnutt sends Wellington back to his hardworking black Southern wife after his experimental marriage to a white woman in Ohio sours, other stories in his second collection show that Chesnutt did not believe that blacks who espouse traditional rugged individualism would exempt themselves from racial discrimination, particularly in the South. In "The Web of Circumstances" an aspiring former slave who tries to pull himself up by his bootstraps articulates a self-help philosophy in line with that of Booker T. Washington, but a combination of adverse circumstances, intraracial betrayal, and blatant white racism leaves the aspiring protagonist broken and hopeless at the end of the story.

In this story and in "The Sheriff's Children" Chesnutt acknowledged his increasingly pessimistic reaction to the rise of white supremacist attitudes and the eclipse of black opportunity in the "New South" of the 1890s. When the North Carolina expatriate surveyed the cancerous racism that threatened the entire social organism of the South, he could not adopt the pose of the urbane ironist that had let him write with comic imperturbability about the color consciousness of members of his own mixed-race class. The problems of the South demanded a stronger rhetorical reaction. Chesnutt would sentimentalize, sensationalize, even sermonize to force his readers to consider contemporary racial realities in the clarifying light of purely ethical considerations, unrefracted by custom, prejudice, or past traditions.

The Wife of His Youth did not sit particularly well with many reviewers, especially those from the South. Some critics, the respected William Dean Howells in particular, called Chesnutt a literary realist of the first order, but others were troubled by his concentration on such somber topics as segregation, mob violence, and, most obviously, interracial sex. Although his publishers were disappointed by the immediate sales of his second book, Chesnutt refused to look back. In the fall of 1899, with *The Wife of His Youth* on the verge of publication, he closed his prosperous court reporting business to pursue his lifelong dream, a career as a full-time author. With a comfortable middle-class style of life to maintain and two daughters enrolled at Smith College, Chesnutt, now forty-one years old, did not take this step lightly. Nevertheless, by living frugally on his savings and his modest royalties, he felt that he could afford to test the literary waters for two years to see if writing would keep him and his family afloat financially. The reputation that his short story collections had earned was starting to pay dividends in the form of readings and lectures. Moreover, the Boston publisher Small, Maynard and Company had asked Chesnutt to write a schoolroom biography of Frederick Douglass, which appeared in the publisher's Beacon Biographies series in 1900. None of his first three books would make much money, Chesnutt knew, but he thought them all useful in creating an audience for the novels he planned to publish soon.

In late 1899 Chesnutt sent a new novel-length version of his "Rena Walden" story to his editors at Houghton Mifflin. The product of ten years of thinking, revising, and expanding, this story and its heroine were probably closer to Chesnutt's heart than anything he ever wrote. Houghton Mifflin accepted the novel in March 1900, asking that it be published under the title *The House Behind the Cedars*. Chesnutt hoped that his first novel would identify him as a writer whose perspective on the color line allowed his readers to see through abstract social problems to what he called "the element of human interest involved." In a letter to his publishers, Chesnutt stated the plot of *The House Behind the Cedars* succinctly: it was "a story of a colored girl who passed for white." The first half of the novel describes the attempt of Rena Walden, product of an illicit union between an unnamed antebellum Southern gentleman and his light-skinned slave concubine Molly Walden, to assimilate into white upper-class society in a South Carolina town. Her brother, John, who has himself successfully passed into the white world, introduces his demure sister to George Tryon, a Carolina blueblood, who courts her fervently. After Tryon learns of Rena's background, however, she retreats to the black community of her hometown to become a country schoolteacher. Harassed by Tryon and a lecherous African American principal, Rena tries to take refuge in the safety of her mother's home but dies of fatigue and exposure.

Many late-nineteenth-century American fiction writers, pundits, and politicians discussed the prospect of racial intermixing as a consequence of the putative freedom extended to African Americans by the Fourteenth and Fifteenth Amendments of the Constitution. Chesnutt was virtually alone among novelists of his time in portraying racially mixed characters like John and Rena Walden as having a morally and socially defensible argument, if not a natural right, to be accepted as white. Such people as the Waldens, who were, like Chesnutt, seven-eighths white, were Negroes only by a "social fiction," Chesnutt declared in a series of articles on "The Future American," which he composed for the Boston *Transcript* in the late summer of 1900. As long as white bigotry barred deserving people of color from access to the American Dream, he maintained, aspiring men and women such as the Waldens would be obliged to take a clandestine route to dignity and opportunity across the color line.

Chesnutt did not write *The House Behind the Cedars* to advocate either crossing the color line or the racial intermarriage that John Walden seeks to engineer for his sister. Indeed, Chesnutt's novel largely conforms to convention in plotting tragic consequences for his heroine after her failed attempt to pass for white. At the same time, however, Chesnutt as narrator tries to make his readers aware of and responsive to the social, economic, and psychological reasons for the Waldens' effort to assimilate totally into mainstream American life. In pursuit of this aim, Chesnutt dispassionately details the antebellum conditions that foster the liaison between Molly Walden and her white lover and help determine the alien status of the "bright mulatto" class in post–Civil War "Patesville" (Fayetteville), the town in which the Waldens grow up. The story demonstrates why traditional racial stereotypes do not fit the Waldens and standard moral categories cannot be easily applied to their actions. Chesnutt did not try to idealize John Walden or his means-justify-the-ends morality. At the same time, the author refused to portray Rena's brother as contemptible or degenerate, as popular mythology often judged the mixed-blood. As a result, John Walden became one of the few convincingly portrayed mixed-race characters in late-nineteenth-century American fiction.

Rena has many affinities with the literary convention of the "tragic mulatta," but in Chesnutt's attempt to arouse sympathy for his heroine, he never lets her indulge in self-hatred over what too many whites would have judged facilely as her "tainted" blood. Chesnutt personally detested the implication of most American fiction dealing with mixed-race persons— namely, that people like him wanted to become white out of a poverty of self-respect owing to shame at having a mixed ancestry. Many years earlier, Chesnutt had decided not to pass for white, though he could have done so, because he was unwilling to deny his family or his past. Yet he knew other mixed-race people who had chosen the white world, and he could empathize with their agonizing choice. *The House Behind the Cedars* was his literary memorial to these people and to what he termed their courage as well as the often tragic outcome of their strivings.

Chesnutt's first novel had only a modest sales record, but critics and reviewers were generally satisfied with its restrained and judicious treatment of an often-sensationalized social question. Compared to contemporary novels of passing, *The House Behind the Cedars* was remarkably subdued and un-polemical. Its artfulness lay primarily in the disarming way in which mixed-race men and women and their social options were characterized. Perhaps the novel's concessions to literary clichés and popular sentiment, as well as to the "tragic mulatta" figure, were the price Chesnutt felt he had to pay to present his favorite literary child to the American reading public. Whatever faults may be attributed to the novel today, it was sufficiently well-received in its own day to encourage both Houghton Mifflin and the Harper & Brothers publishing firm to solicit a second novel from Chesnutt.

Convinced that the time was ripe for a novel on a major racial issue of immediate concern, Chesnutt was more than willing to oblige his publishers. For two years he had been gathering information about a nationally reported incident in Wilmington, North Carolina, in November 1898, when more than a score of black people had been killed during the overthrow of the town's government by a cadre of white supremacists. In February 1901 Chesnutt went to Wilmington and the Cape Fear region of North Carolina on a fact-finding mission. When he returned he felt he had enough material to write what he hoped would prove to be the *Uncle Tom's Cabin* of his generation.

In the fall of 1901 Houghton Mifflin published Chesnutt's magnum opus, *The Marrow of Tradition*. The novel incorporates his most probing analysis of the causes and effects of the racial and social conditions pervasive in the New South. The book also contains the largest and most diverse cast of characters, the most complicated plotting, and the most problematic themes to be found in a single work in Chesnutt's corpus. Invited by the Cleveland *World* to preview his new novel for his hometown readers, Chesnutt announced that *The Marrow of Tradition* "belongs in the category of purpose novels, inasmuch as it seeks to throw light upon the vexed moral and sociological problems which grow out of the presence, in our southern states, of two diverse races, in nearly equal numbers." The author then went on to define the theme of his book:

> Tradition made the white people masters, rulers, who absorbed all the power, the wealth, the honors of the community, and jealously guarded this monopoly, with which they claimed to be divinely endowed, by denying to those who were not of their caste the opportunity to acquire any of these desirable things.
>
> Tradition, on the other hand, made the negro a slave, an underling, existing by favor and not by right, his place the lowest in the social scale, to which, by the same divine warrant, he was hopelessly confined.
>
> The old order has passed away, but these opinions, deeply implanted in the consciousness of two races, still persist, and *The Marrow of Tradition* seeks to show the efforts of the people of a later generation to adjust themselves in this traditional atmosphere to the altered conditions of a new era.

The main thread of the novel's action knits together the lives of two families in the coastal city of "Wellington," North Carolina: the Carterets, who represent the New South leadership class, and the Millers, a mixed-race couple who embody Chesnutt's idea of the progressive New Negro. As editor of Wellington's white newspaper, Major Carteret pursues a policy of Negro defamation while conspiring with other reactionaries to take over the town's government. Dr. William Miller exerts quiet, largely apolitical leadership in the town where his father was once enslaved, but is overly confident that recent antagonism between the races is only a temporary hitch in steadily improving race relations in Wellington. Eventually the editor's machinations bring about a race riot in which the hospital Miller founded is destroyed and his son is killed. In the midst of the violent climax of the novel, Carteret is forced to humble himself to Miller by requesting the African American physician to save the white man's critically ill son. Indignant over the tragedy that Carteret and his henchmen have brought to his own family, Miller at first refuses Carteret's plea. Miller relents, however, after his wife Janet intercedes, having been moved to pity by the entreaties of her once disdainful white half-sister, Mrs. Olivia Carteret. At the end of the novel Miller puts vengeance aside and sets out to save the Carterets' child, affirming in the process his centrality to the healing of the societal wounds of Wellington.

Several subplots and a dozen significant characters in *The Marrow of Tradition* represent a wide spectrum of Southern racial opinion and class identity at the turn of the century. Appearing in the novel, Chesnutt assured the readers of the Cleveland *World,* are an old-fashioned black "mammy," a fawning "white man's nigger," an idealized old aristocrat and his loyal black retainer, a degenerate young Southern aristocrat, a brutal former Klan leader with political ambitions, a beautiful well-intentioned belle, a young Quaker-born Southern liberal, and a vengeful black street fighter. All play rather predictable parts in Chesnutt's drama of a New South that cannot, or will not, free itself of the bitter legacy of slavery and injustice. The most remarkable figure in this secondary cast of characters is Josh Green, a working-class leader who exhorts other black men, despite Miller's refusal to join them, to engage in a desperate, though doomed, resistance effort during the fiery conclusion of the novel. Green's heroic determination to defend his fellow blacks during the riot elicits Miller's admiration, but it does not change the doctor's conviction that the violence Green advocates cannot bring about lasting positive change. That Miller survives the riot to minister to the Carterets, who epitomize the white South's perverse fixation on tradition and privilege, may signal the author's endorsement of the doctor's forgiving accommodationism rather than the uncompromising resistance embodied in Josh Green.

Balancing figures like Miller and Green, each of whom has his strengths and limitations, within his cast of characters helped Chesnutt reinforce his argument that the turn-of-the-century

South symbolized by Wellington was poised at a historical watershed. A longtime optimist, Chesnutt had wanted to think that the wave of segregationist legislation that had swept the South in the 1890s would soon subside as whites and blacks evolved toward a higher level of civilization and a finer ideal of citizenship. But the white supremacist coup d'état in Wilmington forced Chesnutt to recognize that the post-Reconstruction South had lurched backward into the deadly embrace of its discredited racial traditions. In the writing of white Southern apologists like Thomas Nelson Page and Thomas Dixon, these old traditions—especially white supremacy and the aristocratic monopoly of power—were given a literary face-lift, so that unreconstructed Dixie could pose as the "redeemed" and "reconciled" New South. One of the major goals of Chesnutt's second novel was to tear away the New South's mask of progressivism. In an atmosphere of intimidation and violence, naked power politics, and ever-widening racial polarization, the South had little chance of reforming itself, Chesnutt believed, unless the national conscience could be galvanized in support of the region's embattled progressive forces. "There's time enough, but none to spare," Miller is told at the close of the novel as he enters the Carteret house, from which he had been previously barred, on his mission of mercy. This remark sums up *The Marrow of Tradition*'s urgent plea for moral action from white America.

Hoping for sales of twenty to thirty thousand copies, Chesnutt was disappointed to learn from his publisher that *The Marrow of Tradition* had sold fewer than five thousand copies in its first two months despite an energetic advertising campaign. Chesnutt had expected an outcry from Southern reviewers, but he did not anticipate the split opinion among their Northern counterparts, who could not agree on whether Chesnutt had been fair to the South. Some hailed him for his social realism, but others dismissed him as a bitter pessimist. Even a previously supportive William Dean Howells was disturbed by and ambivalent about the book. The fact that few complained about the novel's workmanship or the power of its message led Chesnutt to conclude that his subject matter and moral thesis were what had doomed the book. "I am beginning to suspect," he told his publisher, "that the public as a rule does not care for books in which the principal characters are colored people, or written with a striking sympathy with that race as contrasted to the white race." Heeding the advice of his friends that he should withdraw temporarily from the field of race-problem novels, Chesnutt decided in 1902 that it was time to reopen his court reporting business.

As he rebuilt his financial base, Chesnutt remained closely attentive to social justice issues centering on race, color, and political equality. He turned to articles, essays, and speeches as the most efficient means to speak directly to worsening racial conditions. Perhaps the most timely of his essays was "The Disfranchisement of the Negro," which appeared in *The Negro Problem: A Series of Articles by Representative American Negroes of To-day*, compiled by Booker T. Washington in 1903. In this landmark volume, whose contributors read like a who's who of African American political leadership, Washington and W. E. B. Du Bois argued their opposing solutions to the challenges facing black America: the Tuskegee plan of industrial education for the masses versus the Du Bois program of higher education for the African American "talented tenth." Refusing to endorse publicly either of these positions to the exclusion or detriment of the other, Chesnutt focused on the right to vote as the only lasting guarantee of black advancement.

In the fall of 1903 the lure of fiction induced Chesnutt to fashion a new novel centering on a love triangle among a group of white upper-class Bostonians. "Evelyn's Husband" may have been motivated by its author's frank desire for commercial success in a vein completely removed from the more problematic subjects of his earlier fiction. Whatever the motive for its creation, the manuscript had no appeal to the publishers to whom Chesnutt sent it. This put him in a dilemma. He had been able to publish two serious problem novels about the Southern racial situation, but they had not sold as he had hoped. Yet when he tried to write noncontroversial, mass-market fiction about white people in the North, he had not been able to attract a publisher. In the winter of 1903–4, therefore, Chesnutt decided to return to the short story, a form he knew well and one that had brought him his first recognition. The result was "Baxter's *Procrustes*," the author's best-crafted work of short fiction and the last story he published in the *Atlantic Monthly*.

Although "Baxter's *Procrustes*" deals solely with whites and has no ostensible racial concern, the story has much in common with the author's earlier conjure and color-line stories. Like Uncle Julius McAdoo, the enigmatic, dilettantish sometime-writer known only as Baxter is a con artist and a trickster. His victims are the members of the Bodleian Club, an all-male organization of well-heeled bibliophiles whose apparent love of literary classics is rooted in the dollar-consciousness that makes finely crafted books a wise investment. Baxter contrives a brilliant stratagem that exposes the misplaced priorities of his fellow Bodleians. In the process, Chesnutt satirizes the Bodleians' self-delusions in ways reminiscent of his mockery of the social pretensions of another exclusive society, the Groveland Blue Veins. Like the Blue Veins, the Bodleians were patterned on a social club in Cleveland to which Chesnutt belonged, though he was aware of the excesses and prejudices of its membership. Members of Cleveland's Rowfant Club, an all-white fraternity of upper-class book collectors, undoubtedly recognized themselves when they read "Baxter's *Procrustes*" in the June 1904 issue of the *Atlantic*. Two years earlier they had denied Chesnutt membership in their club because of the racial prejudice of a few of the Rowfanters. Chesnutt created Baxter to expose those who claimed to respect culture and humane letters but who actually cared much more for appearances. The tone of the story and its deft ironies show that it was conceived as a literary riposte, not an exercise in revenge. In 1910 Chesnutt accepted a second nomination for membership in the Rowfant Club, and he took an active part in the club in subsequent years.

In the spring of 1904 Chesnutt began to work again with Walter Hines Page—who had become a senior partner in the newly formed publishing house of Doubleday, Page—on a race-problem novel called *The Colonel's Dream*. With Page's advice and guidance, Chesnutt hoped to write a novel about the New South that could accomplish something positive on the social front while also restoring his literary reputation. In this new book Chesnutt tried to enhance the identification of the majority of his readership with his protagonist by making him a white man, an enlightened ex-Confederate officer who has made himself rich in Northern industry without losing his Southern sense of noblesse oblige. Colonel French's return to his native North Carolina for health reasons reveals the land of his birth languishing in a social and economic depression. Like many heroes of economic novels from the Progressive era, French optimistically sets about reforming the archaic, often exploitative systems of education and production in his region. Resistance mounts steadily from Bill Fetters, a corrupt power broker and economic kingpin whose control over blacks and poor whites has reduced both classes to virtual servitude. Ultimately, the colonel gives up his dream of reform in despair after violent acts of racist intimidation—including a lynching and the disinterring of a black man from a white cemetery—convince him that the people of his region are not yet civilized enough to accept the opportunities he would give them. French and a handful of other forward-looking Southerners, black as well as white, immigrate to the North at the end of the novel.

The Colonel's Dream is the final volume in what might now be termed Charles Chesnutt's New South trilogy. Each of the previously published novels tests out a means of alleviating the caste consciousness and social injustice that Chesnutt believed was endemic in the South. In The House Behind the Cedars, the individualistic strategies of the Waldens are shown to be risky, often self-defeating ways of gaining social rights and opportunities for African Americans. In The Marrow of Tradition, both violent resistance and diplomatic accommodation are weighed as alternative means of achieving justice for Southern blacks and progress for the region as a whole. At the end of this novel, neither alternative proves itself capable of halting the spread of institutionalized racial repression in the postwar South. The Colonel's Dream asks whether white philanthropy, cooperative enterprise, and the pursuit of enlightened self-interest among blacks and whites could raise the socioeconomic prospects of everyone in the New South, so as to create a climate in which racial justice might thrive. In articles, speeches, and letters, Chesnutt had subscribed to several of the colonel's programs for combating the social and economic ills of the New South. French sponsors an industrial school on the Tuskegee model, employs African Americans in the rebuilding of a textile mill, attacks black peonage in the courts, and tries to soothe white suspicions and fears with reasoned appeals to fair play and business pragmatism. Despite his moderate, well-intentioned progressivism, however, French ends up a loser mainly because he realizes too late that his piecemeal reforms in education, economics, and civil rights do not address the fundamental moral and intellectual blight of racism in the small-town South.

"The very standards of right and wrong had been confused by the race issue," French concludes. In response, nothing less than "a new body of thought must be built up" to counter the massive mythology of racism that had permeated Southern thought and institutions for centuries. Unfortunately, French does not know how to create this new thinking, nor does Chesnutt seem to have had a clear idea about how to do this either, except by writing novels like *The Colonel's Dream*. Nevertheless, this novel's analysis of the problems facing the New South has been borne out by subsequent historical investigation, which in turn identifies Chesnutt as a dedicated muckraker, one of the precursors of twentieth-century Southern realism. It is unlikely, however, that he took much comfort from the few reviewers who praised him for his honesty in recording the ugly facts of Southern mill-town life. Most of the critics who bothered to comment on the novel at all felt it was too unpleasant and pessimistic to recommend it to their readers. Consequently, much like Colonel French, Chesnutt in 1905 took his literary leave of the New South as he had done in life twenty years before.

After *The Colonel's Dream* Chesnutt involved himself in social and political activities that drew his attention and energy away from literature. He joined the Committee of Twelve for the Advancement of the Interests of the Negro Race, an early advocacy group designed to prepare speeches and circulate materials that would correct public misinterpretations of the African American cause. Membership in the Committee of Twelve, perceived by some as a tool of Booker T. Washington, did not prevent Chesnutt from serving on the central committee of the rival Niagara Movement, led by the more militant Du Bois and William Monroe Trotter. Chesnutt continued to stress both publicly and privately the necessity of predicating the reform of Southern racial conditions on the restoration of the suffrage to African Americans of that region. Chesnutt continued to foresee the ultimate solution to the American race problem in the amalgamation of blacks and whites into one undifferentiated race. Toward this end, he fought caste consciousness and color barriers wherever he found them, whether in anti-intermarriage laws, Cleveland settlement houses, army training practices in the South, or popular films such as *The Birth of a Nation* (1915).

In the decade that followed the publication of *The Colonel's Dream,* Chesnutt became an established civic leader in Cleveland. He joined the Chamber of Commerce and the City Club and presided over the Cleveland Council of Sociology. He also served on the General Committee of the National Association for the Advancement of Colored People (NAACP). His court reporting business flourished, enabling him to live affluently, travel abroad, and provide college educations to all four of his children. A mild stroke in June 1910 reduced Chesnutt's literary stamina, which may help to explain why only three minor short stories published locally in Cleveland and in the African American periodical press appeared during the decade following *The Colonel's Dream.*

The 1920s saw a revival of Chesnutt's enthusiasm for writing and some belated recognition of him for his pioneering literary labors at the turn of the century. In 1921 he wrote *Paul Marchand, F. M. C.,* a historical romance set in pre–Civil War New Orleans. In this story, the extremely light-skinned title character has been raised as a free man of color but discovers that he is, in fact, entirely white. The revelation compels him to decide whether to acknowledge his mixed-race wife and children or embrace the beautiful white woman promised him as heir to the fortunes of an old Creole family. Although *Paul Marchand* has a number of affinities with Chesnutt's earlier fiction, the novel had little in common with the social concerns of the Jazz Age and the literary priorities of Modernism, both of which would help to spawn the New Negro Renaissance in the 1920s. Unable to place *Paul Marchand,* Chesnutt was gratified by the Chicago *Defender*'s serialization of *The House Behind the Cedars* in 1922, which put that novel back into print for the first time in over fifteen years. As the decade wore on, Chesnutt kept his eye on the new Harlem school of writers, whom he welcomed in theory but often scolded in practice. When Du Bois, editor of the *Crisis* and an admirer of Chesnutt's fiction, asked him to respond to the question "The Negro in Art: How Shall He Be Portrayed?" the dean of African American writers responded that there should be no limitation on the matter or manner of race literature. But when Chesnutt read Claude McKay's risqué *Home to Harlem* (1928) and Wallace Thurman's satirical *The Blacker the Berry* (1929), he found much to condemn in their failure to portray what he called "the real romance, the worthy ambition, the broad humanity" of black folk in all social classes. With Du Bois and the poet William Stanley Braithwaite, Chesnutt fought a rearguard action in the late 1920s against the aesthetic and social iconoclasts of the New Negro Renaissance, failing to see the ways in which his writing had anticipated theirs.

At the end of the 1920s, Chesnutt created another novel extolling the virtues of an ostensibly mixed-race hero who, on discovering he is actually white, chooses to remain a Negro rather than compromise himself morally by accepting wealth and position in the more favored caste. But *The Quarry* in 1930 met the same fate as *Paul Marchand, F. M. C.* nine years earlier. Viewing Chesnutt's career from the perspective of these late manuscripts, the clear-sighted, often ironic analyst of the embryonic black middle class at the turn of the century may seem to have evolved by the late 1920s into a somewhat tunnel-visioned literary apologist for the entrenched black bourgeoisie. On the other hand, the fact that both *Paul Marchand, F. M. C.* and *The Quarry* found their way into print by the end of the twentieth century (1998 and 1999, respectively) suggests that Chesnutt's literary reputation is now so well established that even books that he could not publish in his own lifetime have become objects of appreciative study in twenty-first-century academe.

In 1928 the NAACP bestowed on Chesnutt its most distinguished award, the Spingarn Medal, for his "pioneer work as a literary artist depicting the life and struggles of Americans of Negro descent, and for his long and useful career as scholar, worker, and freeman of one of America's greatest cities." The next year Houghton Mifflin reprinted *The Conjure Woman* in a handsome deluxe edition that put Chesnutt back in print thirty years after he had first become an author. In 1932 the African American filmmaker Oscar Micheaux made *The House Behind the Cedars* into a film entitled *Veiled Aristocrats* that played for African American theater audiences around the country. Thus, when he died on November 15, 1932, Chesnutt was not the celebrated literary figure he had once wanted to be, but he was by no means forgotten or ignored, especially in black America, where his books had become classics. A year before his death, the seventy-three-year-old author reckoned some of the gains and losses of his artistic career in "Post-Bellum—Pre-Harlem," an essay in literary autobiography. Chesnutt accepted the fact that literary fashions had passed him by, but he took pride in pointing out how far African American literature and the attitude of the white literary world toward it had come since the days when he first broke into print. Although he was too modest to do so, Chesnutt could have claimed an important role in preparing the public mind in America for the advent of the New Negro author of the 1920s, for, in a basic sense, the new movement followed his precedent in unmasking the false poses and images of his era in order to refocus attention on racial realities in America.

Almost single-handedly, Charles W. Chesnutt established a truly African American literary tradition in the short story, if not in the novel. He was the first to make the broad range of African American experience his artistic bailiwick and to consider practically everything therein to be worthy of treatment.

Chesnutt not only surveyed the literary topography of African American life, he also assayed some of its richest sociopsychological veins. Because he was concerned with finding literary modes appropriate to his materials, he left to his successors examples of the uses of ironic distance in an African American fiction of manners, a precedent for a black magical realism, a concept of tragedy for a people once regarded as merely grotesque or pitiable, and a sense of the comic potential of the trickster figure from African American folklore. This was a rich artistic legacy that influenced such twentieth-century black writers as James Weldon Johnson, Nella Larsen, and Charles Johnson. In his own era, Chesnutt's achievement can be summed up succinctly: it was he who taught white America for the first time to respect a black fiction writer as a critical realist, even if it could not embrace him as a literary native son.

—WILLIAM L. ANDREWS

Suggestions for Further Reading

Andrews, William L. *The Literary Career of Charles W. Chesnutt.* Baton Rouge: Louisiana State University Press, 1980.
———. "William Dean Howells and Charles W. Chesnutt: Criticism and Race Fiction in the Age of Booker T. Washington." *American Literature* 48: 327–39 (November 1976).
Baldwin, Richard E. "The Art of *The Conjure Woman.*" *American Literature* 43: 385–98 (November 1971).
Bone, Robert. *Down Home: Pastoral Impulse in Afro-American Short Fiction.* New York: Putnam's, 1975.
Brodhead, Richard H., ed. *The Journals of Charles W. Chesnutt.* Durham, N.C.: Duke University Press, 1993.
Bruce, Dickson D., Jr. *Black American Writing from the Nadir: The Evolution of a Literary Tradition, 1877–1915.* Baton Rouge: Louisiana State University Press, 1989.
Chesnutt, Helen M. *Charles Waddell Chesnutt: Pioneer of the Color Line.* Chapel Hill: University of North Carolina Press, 1952.
Crisler, Jesse S., Robert C. Leitz, III, and Joseph R. McElrath, Jr., eds. *An Exemplary Citizen: Letters of Charles W. Chesnutt, 1906–1932.* Stanford, CA: Stanford University Press, 2002.
———. *Critical Essays on Charles W. Chesnutt.* Boston: G. K. Hall, 1999.
Duncan, Charles. *The Absent Man: The Narrative Craft of Charles W. Chesnutt.* Athens, OH: Ohio University Press, 1998.
Ellison, Curtis W., and E. W. Metcalf, Jr. *Charles W. Chesnutt: A Reference Guide.* Boston: G. K. Hall, 1977.

Ferguson, Sally Ann. "Rena Walden: Chesnutt's Failed 'Future American.'" *CLA Journal* 15: 74–82 (September 1982).

Gibson, Donald B. "Charles W. Chesnutt: The Anatomy of a Dream." In *Politics of Literary Expression: A Study of Major Black Writers*. Westport, CT: Greenwood, 1981, pp. 124–54.

Gleason, William. "Chestnutt's Piazza Tales: Architecture, Race, and Memory in the Conjure Stories." *American Quarterly* (51:1), 33–77 (1999).

Hemenway, Robert E. "'Baxter's Procrustes': Irony and Protest." *CLA Journal* 18: 172–85 (December 1974).

Howells, William Dean. "Mr. Charles W. Chesnutt's Stories." *Atlantic Monthly* 85: 699–701 (May 1900).

Keller, Frances Richardson. *An American Crusade: The Life of Charles W. Chesnutt*. Provo, UT: Brigham Young University Press, 1978.

Knadler, Stephen P. "Untragic Mulatto: Charles Chesnutt and the Discourse of Whiteness." *American Literary History* (8:3), 426–48 (1996).

McElrath, Joseph R., Jr. "Why Charles W. Chesnutt Is Not a Realist." *American Literary Realism* (32:2), 91–108 (2000).

McElrath, Joseph R., Jr., and Robert C. Leitz III, eds. *"To Be an Author": Letters of Charles W. Chesnutt, 1889–1905*. Princeton, NJ: Princeton University Press, 1997.

McElrath, Joseph R., Jr., Robert C. Leitz III, and Jesse S. Crisler, eds. *Charles W. Chesnutt: Essays and Speeches*. Stanford, CA: Stanford University Press, 1999.

McWilliams, Dean. *Charles W. Chesnutt and the Fictions of Race*. Athens, GA: University of Georgia Press, 2002.

———. "Charles Chesnutt and the Harlem Renaissance." *Soundings: An Interdisciplinary Journal* (80:4), 591–606 (1997).

Myers, Jeffrey. "Other Nature: Resistance to Ecological Hegemony in Charles W. Chesnutt's *The Conjure Woman*." *African American Review* (37:1), 5–20 (2003).

Petrie, Paul R. *Conscience and Purpose: Fiction and Social*

Consciousness in Howells, Jewett, Chesnutt, and Cather.
Tuscaloosa, AL: University of Alabama Press, 2005.

Pickens, Ernestine Williams. *Charles W. Chesnutt and the Progressive Movement.* New York: Pace University Press, 1994.

Posnock, Ross. *Color and Culture: Black Writers and the Making of the Modern Intellectual.* Cambridge, MA: Harvard University Press, 1998.

Render, Sylvia Lyons. *Charles W. Chesnutt.* Boston: Twayne, 1980.

Sedlack, Robert P. "The Evolution of Charles Chesnutt's *The House Behind the Cedars." CLA Journal* 19: 125–35 (December 1975).

Simmons, Ryan. *Chesnutt and Realism: A Study of the Novels.* Tuscaloosa, AL: University of Alabama Press, 2006.

Stepto, Robert B. "'The Simple but Intensely Human Inner Life of Slavery': Storytelling, Fiction and the Revision of History in Charles W. Chesnutt's 'Uncle Julius Stories.'" In *History and Tradition in Afro-American Literature,* edited by Gunther H. Lenz. Frankfurt, Germany: Campus, 1984, pp. 29–55.

Sundquist, Eric. J. *To Wake the Nations: Race in the Making of American Literature.* Cambridge, MA: Harvard University Press, 1993.

Thomas, Brooke. "Charles W. Chesnutt: Race and the Re-Negotiation of the Federal Contract." In *American Literary Realism and the Failed Promise of Contract,* edited by Brooke Thomas. Berkeley: University of California Press, 1997, pp. 156–90.

Wagner, Bryan. "Charles Chesnutt and the Epistemology of Racial Violence." *American Literature* (73:2), 311–37 (2001).

Wideman, John Edgar. "Charles Chesnutt and the WPA Narratives: The Oral and Literate Roots of Afro-American Literature." In *The Slave's Narrative,* edited by Charles W. Davis and Henry Louis Gates, Jr. New York: Oxford University Press, 1985, pp. 59–78.

Wilson, Matthew. *Whiteness in the Novels of Charles W. Chesnutt.* Jackson, MS: University Press of Mississippi, 2004.

Wonham, Henry B. "What Is a Black Author? A Review of Recent Charles Chesnutt Studies." *American Literary History* (18:4), 829–35 (2006).

A Note on the Texts

"The Goophered Grapevine," "Po' Sandy," "Mars Jeems's Nightmare," and "Sis' Becky's Pickaninny" are reprinted from the first edition of Chesnutt's *The Conjure Woman* (Boston: Houghton Mifflin, 1899). "The Wife of His Youth," "The Sheriff's Children," "A Matter of Principle," "The Passing of Grandison," "Uncle Wellington's Wives," and "The Web of Circumstance" are reprinted from the first edition of Chesnutt's *The Wife of His Youth and Other Stories of the Color Line* (Boston: Houghton Mifflin, 1899). "Dave's Neckliss" is reprinted from the first edition of the story, as published in the *Atlantic Monthly* 64 (October 1889), pp. 500–508. "Baxter's *Procrustes*" is reprinted from the first edition of the story, as published in the *Atlantic Monthly* 93 (June 1904), pp. 823–30. *The Marrow of Tradition* is reprinted from the first edition of the novel, published by Houghton Mifflin in 1901. "What Is a White Man?" is reprinted from William L. Andrews, ed., *The North Carolina Roots of African American Literature* (Chapel Hill: University of North Carolina Press, 2006), pp. 251–57. "The Disfranchisement of the Negro" is reprinted from the first edition of the essay, as published in Booker T. Washington et al., eds., *The Negro Problem: A Series of Articles by Representative American Negroes of To-day* (New York: James Pott, 1903), pp. 79–124. "Post-Bellum–Pre-Harlem" is reprinted from the first edition of the essay, as published in *Colophon* 2, no. 5 (1931).

The word "Negro" also appears uncapitalized in various texts in this volume, reflecting the lack of unanimity at the turn of the century among publishers as to whether the word should be capitalized or not.

A Note on the Texts

The Portable
Charles W. Chesnutt

I

SHORT STORIES

THE GOOPHERED
GRAPEVINE

Some years ago my wife was in poor health, and our family doctor, in whose skill and honesty I had implicit confidence, advised a change of climate. I shared, from an unprofessional standpoint, his opinion that the raw winds, the chill rains, and the violent changes of temperature that characterized the winters in the region of the Great Lakes tended to aggravate my wife's difficulty, and would undoubtedly shorten her life if she remained exposed to them. The doctor's advice was that we seek, not a temporary place of sojourn, but a permanent residence, in a warmer and more equable climate. I was engaged at the time in grape-culture in northern Ohio, and, as I liked the business and had given it much study, I decided to look for some other locality suitable for carrying it on. I thought of sunny France, of sleepy Spain, of Southern California, but there were objections to them all. It occurred to me that I might find what I wanted in some one of our own Southern States. It was a sufficient time after the war for conditions in the South to have become somewhat settled; and I was enough of a pioneer to start a new industry, if I could not find a place where grape-culture had been tried. I wrote to a cousin who had gone into the turpentine business in central North Carolina. He assured me, in response to my inquiries, that no better place could be found in the South than the State and neighborhood where he lived; the climate was perfect for health, and, in conjunction with the soil, ideal for grape-culture; labor was cheap, and land could be bought for a mere song. He gave us a cordial invitation to come and visit him while we looked into the matter. We accepted the invitation, and after several days of leisurely travel, the last hundred miles of which were up a river on a sidewheel steamer, we reached our destination, a quaint old town, which I shall call Patesville, because, for one reason, that is not its name. There was a red brick markethouse in the public square, with a tall tower, which held a four-faced clock that struck the hours, and from which there pealed out a curfew at nine o'clock. There were two or three hotels, a court-house, a jail, stores, offices, and all the appurtenances of a county seat and a commercial emporium; for while Patesville numbered only four or five thousand inhabitants, of all shades of complexion, it was one of the principal towns in North Carolina, and had a considerable trade in cotton and naval stores. This business activity was not immediately apparent to my unaccustomed eyes. Indeed, when I first saw the town, there brooded over it a calm that seemed almost sabbatic in its restfulness, though I learned later on that underneath its somnolent exterior the deeper currents of life—love and hatred, joy and despair, ambition and avarice, faith and friendship—flowed not less steadily than in livelier latitudes.

We found the weather delightful at that season, the end of summer, and were hospitably entertained. Our host was a man of means and evidently regarded our visit as a pleasure, and we were therefore correspondingly at our ease, and in a position to act with the coolness of judgment desirable in making so radical a change in our lives. My cousin placed a horse and buggy at our disposal, and himself acted as our guide until I became somewhat familiar with the country.

I found that grape-culture, while it had never been carried on to any great extent, was not entirely unknown in the neighborhood. Several planters thereabouts had attempted it on a commercial scale, in former years, with greater or less success; but like most Southern industries, it had felt the blight of war and had fallen into desuetude.

I went several times to look at a place that I thought might suit me. It was a plantation of considerable extent, that had formerly belonged to a wealthy man by the name of McAdoo. The estate had been for years involved in litigation between disputing heirs, during which period shiftless cultivation had well-nigh exhausted the soil. There had been a vineyard of some extent on the place, but it had not been attended to since the war, and had lapsed into utter neglect. The vines—here partly supported by decayed and broken-down trellises, there twining themselves among the branches of the slender saplings which had sprung up among them—grew in wild and un-pruned luxuriance, and the few scattered grapes they bore were the undisputed prey of the first comer. The site was admirably adapted to grape-raising; the soil, with a little attention, could not have been better; and with the native grape, the luscious scuppernong, as my main reliance in the beginning, I felt sure that I could introduce and cultivate successfully a number of other varieties.

One day I went over with my wife to show her the place. We drove out of the town over a long wooden bridge that spanned a spreading mill-pond, passed the long white-washed fence sur-rounding the county fair-ground, and struck into a road so sandy that the horse's feet sank to the fetlocks. Our route lay partly up hill and partly down, for we were in the sand-hill country; we drove past cultivated farms, and then by aban-doned fields grown up in scrub-oak and short-leaved pine, and once or twice through the solemn aisles of the virgin forest, where the tall pines, well-nigh meeting over the narrow road, shut out the sun, and wrapped us in cloistral solitude. Once, at a cross-roads, I was in doubt as to the turn to take, and we sat there waiting ten minutes—we had already caught some of the native infection of restfulness—for some human being to come along, who could direct us on our way. At length a little negro girl appeared, walking straight as an arrow, with a piggin full of water on her head. After a little patient investigation, nec-essary to overcome the child's shyness, we learned what we wished to know, and at the end of about five miles from the town reached our destination.

We drove between a pair of decayed gateposts—the gate it-self had long since disappeared—and up a straight sandy lane, between two lines of rotting rail fence, partly concealed by jimson-weeds and briers, to the open space where a dwelling-house had once stood, evidently a spacious mansion, if we might judge from the ruined chimneys that were still standing, and the brick pillars on which the sills rested. The house itself, we had been informed, had fallen victim to the fortunes of war.

We alighted from the buggy, walked about the yard for a while, and then wandered off into the adjoining vineyard. Upon Annie's complaining of weariness I led the way back to the yard, where a pine log, lying under a spreading elm, afforded a shady though somewhat hard seat. One end of the log was already occupied by a venerable-looking colored man. He held on his knees a hat full of grapes, over which he was smacking his lips with great gusto, and a pile of grapeskins near him indicated that the performance was no new thing. We approached him at an angle from the rear, and were close to him before he perceived us. He respectfully rose as we drew near, and was moving away, when I begged him to keep his seat.

"Don't let us disturb you," I said. "There is plenty of room for us all."

He resumed his seat with somewhat of embarrassment. While he had been standing, I had observed that he was a tall man, and, though slightly bowed by the weight of years, apparently quite vigorous. He was not entirely black, and this fact, together with the quality of his hair, which was about six inches long and very bushy, except on the top of his head, where he was quite bald, suggested a slight strain of other than negro blood. There was a shrewdness in his eyes, too, which was not altogether African, and which, as we afterwards learned from experience, was indicative of a corresponding shrewdness in his character. He went on eating the grapes, but did not seem to enjoy himself quite so well as he had apparently done before he became aware of our presence.

"Do you live around here?" I asked, anxious to put him at ease.

"Yas, suh. I lives des ober yander, behine de nex' san'-hill, on de Lumberton plank-road."

"Do you know anything about the time when this vineyard was cultivated?"

"Lawd bless you, suh, I knows all about it. Dey ain' na'er a man in dis settlement w'at won' tell you ole Julius AcAdoo 'us bawn en raise' on dis yer same plantation. Is you de Norv'n gemman w'at's gwine ter buy de ole vimya'd?"

"I am looking at it," I replied; "but I don't know that I shall care to buy unless I can be reasonably sure of making something out of it."

"Well, suh, you is a stranger ter me, en I is a stranger ter you, en we is bofe strangers ter one anudder, but 'f I 'uz in yo' place, I would n' buy dis vimya'd."

"Why not?" I asked.

"Well, I dunno whe'r you b'lieves in cunj'in' er not—some er de w'ite folks don't, er says dey don't,—but de truf er de matter is dat dis yer ole vimya'd is goophered."

"Is what?" I asked, not grasping the meaning of this unfamiliar word.

"Is goophered,—cunju'd, bewitch'."

He imparted this information with such solemn earnestness, and with such an air of confidential mystery, that I felt somewhat interested, while Annie was evidently much impressed, and drew closer to me.

"How do you know it is bewitched?" I asked.

"I would n' spec' fer you ter b'lieve me 'less you know all 'bout de fac's. But ef you en young miss dere doan' min' lis'nin' ter a ole nigger run on a minute er two w'ile you er restin', I kin 'splain to you how it all happen'."

We assured him that we would be glad to hear how it all happened, and he began to tell us. At first the current of his memory—or imagination—seemed somewhat sluggish; but as his embarrassment wore off, his language flowed more freely, and the story acquired perspective and coherence. As he became more and more absorbed in the narrative, his eyes assumed a dreamy expression, and he seemed to lose sight of his auditors, and to be living over again in monologue his life on the old plantation.

"Ole Mars Dugal' McAdoo," he began, "bought dis place long many years befo' de wah, en I 'member well w'en he sot out all dis yer part er de plantation in scuppernon's. De vimes growed monst'us fas', en Mars Dugal' made a thousan' gallon er scuppernon' wine eve'y year.

"Now, ef dey's an'thing a nigger lub, nex' ter 'possum, en chick'n, en watermillyums, it's scuppernon's. Dey ain' nuffin dat kin stan' up side'n de scuppernon' fer sweetness; sugar ain't a suckumstance ter scuppernon'. W'en de season is nigh 'bout ober, en de grapes begin ter swivel up des a little wid de wrinkles er ole age,—w'en de skin git sof' en brown,—den de scuppernon' make you smack yo' lip en roll yo' eye en wush fer mo'; so I reckon it ain' very 'stonishin' dat niggers lub scuppernon'.

"Dey wuz a sight er niggers in de naberhood er de vimya'd. Dere wuz ole Mars Henry Brayboy's niggers, en ole Mars Jeems McLean's niggers, en Mars Dugal's own niggers; den dey wuz a settlement er free niggers en po' buckrahs down by de Wim'l'-ton Road, en Mars Dugal' had de only vimya'd in de naberhood. I reckon it ain' so much so nowadays, but befo' de wah, in slab'ry times, a nigger did n' mine goin' fi' er ten mile in a night, w'en dey wuz sump'n good ter eat at de yuther een'.

"So after a w'ile Mars Dugal' begin ter miss his scuppernon's. Co'se he 'cuse' de niggers er it, but dey all 'nied it ter de las', Mars Dugal' sot spring guns en steel traps, en he en de oberseah sot up nights once't er twice't, tel one night Mars Dugal'—he 'uz a monst'us keerless man—got his leg shot full er cow-peas. But somehow er nudder dey could n' nebber ketch none er de niggers. I dunner how it happen, but it happen des like I tell you, en de grapes kep' on agoin' des de same.

"But bimeby old Mars Dugal' fix' up a plan ter stop it. Dey wuz a cunjuh 'oman livin' down 'mongs' de free niggers on de Wim'l'ton Road, en all de darkies fum Rockfish ter Beaver Crick wuz feared er her. She could wuk de mos' powerfulles' kin' er goopher,—could make people hab fits, er rheumatiz, er make 'em des dwinel away en die; en dey say she went out ridin' de niggers at night, fer she wuz a witch 'sides bein' a cunjuh 'oman. Mars Dugal' hearn 'bout Aun' Peggy's doin's, en begun ter 'flect whe'r er no he could n' git her ter he'p him keep de niggers off'n de grapevimes. One day in de spring er de year, ole miss pack' up a basket er chick'n en poun'-cake, en a bottle er scuppernon' wine, en Mars Dugal' tuk it in his buggy en driv ober ter Aun' Peggy's cabin. He tuk de basket in, en had a long talk wid Aun' Peggy.

"De nex' day Aun' Peggy come up ter de vimya'd. De niggers seed her slippin' 'round', en dey soon foun' out what she 'uz doin' dere. Mars Dugal' had hi'ed her ter goopher de grape-vimes. She sa'ntered 'roun' 'mongs' de vimes, en tuk a leaf fum dis one, en a grape-hull fum dat one, en a grape-seed fum anud-der one; en den a little twig fum here, en a little pinch er dirt fum dere,—en put it all in a big black bottle, wid a snake's toof en a speckle hen's gall en some ha'rs fum a black cat's tail, en den fill' de bottle wid scuppernon' wine. W'en she got de goo-pher all ready en fix', she tuk 'n went out in de woods en buried it under de root uv a red oak tree, en den come back en tole one er de niggers she done goopher de grapevimes, en a'er a nigger w'at eat dem grapes 'ud be sho ter die inside'n twel' mont's.

"Atter dat de niggers let de scuppernon's 'lone, en Mars Du-gal' did n' hab no 'casion ter fine no mo' fault; en de season wuz mos' gone, w'en a strange gemman stop at de plantation one night ter see Mars Dugal' on some business; en his coach-man, seein' de scuppernon's growin' so nice en sweet, slip 'roun' behine de smoke-house, en et all de scuppernon's he could hole. Nobody did n' notice it at de time, but dat night, on de way home, de gemman's hoss runned away en kill' de coach-man. W'en we hearn de noos, Aun' Lucy, de cook, she up'n say she seed de strange nigger eat'n' er de scuppernon's behine de smoke-house; en den we knowed de goopher had b'en er wuk-kin'. Den one er de nigger chilluns runned away fum de quar-ters one day, en got in de scuppernon's, en died de nex' week. W'ite folks say he die' er de fevuh, but de niggers knowed it wuz de goopher. So you k'n be sho de darkies did n' hab much ter do wid dem scuppernon' vimes.

"We'en de scuppernon' season 'uz ober fer dat year, Mars Dugal' foun' he had made fifteen hund'ed gallon er wine; en one er de niggers hearn him laffin' wid de oberseah fit ter kill, en sayin' dem fifteen hund'ed gallon er wine wuz monst'us good intrus' on de ten dollars he laid out on de vimya'd. So I 'low ez he paid Aun' Peggy ten dollars fer to goopher de grapevimes.

"De goopher did n' wuk no mo' tel de nex' summer, w'en 'long to'ds de middle er de season one er de fiel' han's died; en ez dat lef' Mars Dugal' sho't er han's, he went off ter town fer ter buy anudder. He fotch de noo nigger home wid 'im. He wuz er ole nigger, er de color er a gingy-cake, en ball ez a hoss-apple on de top er his head. He wuz a peart ole nigger, do', en could do a big day's wuk.

"Now it happen dat one er de niggers on de nex' plantation, one er ole Mars Henry Brayboy's niggers, had runned away de day befo', en tuk ter de swamp, en old Mars Dugal' en some er de yuther nabor w'ite folks had gone out wid dere guns en dere dogs fer ter he'p 'em hunt fer de nigger; en de han's on our own plantation wuz all so flusterated dat we fuhgot ter tell de noo han' 'bout the goopher on de scuppernon' vimes. Co'se he smell de grapes en see de vimes, an atter dahk de fus' thing he done wuz ter slip off ter de grapevimes 'dout sayin' nuffin ter nobody. Nex' mawnin' he tole some er de niggers 'bout de fine bait er scuppernon' he et de night befo'.

"W'en dey tole 'im 'bout de goopher on de grapevimes, he 'uz dat tarrified dat he turn pale, en look des like he gwine ter die right in his tracks. De oberseah come up en axed w'at 'uz de matter; en w'en dey tole 'im Henry be'n eatin' er de scuppernon's, en got de goopher on 'im, he gin Henry a big drink er w'iskey, en 'low dat de nex' rainy day he take 'im ober ter Aun' Peggy's, en see ef she would n' take de goopher off'n him, seein' ez he did n' know nuffin erbout it tel he done et de grapes.

"Sho nuff, it rain de nex' day, en de oberseah went ober ter Aun' Peggy's wid Henry. En Aun' Peggy say dat bein' ez Henry did n' know 'bout de goopher, en et de grapes in ign'ance er de conseq'ences, she reckon she mought be able fer ter take de goopher off'n him. So she fotch out er bottle wid some cunjuh medicine in it, en po'd some out in a go'd fer Henry ter drink. He manage ter git it down; he say it tas'e like whiskey wid sump'n bitter in it. She 'lowed dat 'ud keep de goopher off'n him tel de spring; but w'en de sap begin ter rise in de grapevimes he ha' ter come en see her ag'in, en she tell him w'at e's ter do.

"Nex' spring, w'en de sap commence' ter rise in de scuppernon' vime, Henry tuk a ham one night. Whar'd he git de ham?

I doan know; dey wa'n't no hams on de plantation 'cep'n' w'at 'uz in de smoke-house, but *I* never see Henry 'bout de smoke-house. But ez I wuz a-sayin', he tuk de ham ober ter Aun' Peggy's; en Aun' Peggy tole 'im dat w'en Mars Dugal' begin ter prune de grapevimes, he mus' go en take 'n scrape off de sap whar it ooze out'n de cut een's er de vimes, en 'n'int his ball head wid it; en ef he do dat once't a year de goopher would n' wuk agin 'im long ez he done it. En bein' ez he fotch her de ham, she fix' it so he kin eat all de scuppernon' he want.

"So Henry 'n'int his head wid de sap out'n de big grapevimes des ha'f way 'twix' de quarters en de big house, en de goopher nebber wuk agin him dat summer. But de beatenes' thing you eber see happen ter Henry. Up ter dat time he wuz ez ball ez a sweeten' 'tater, but des ez soon ez de young leaves begun ter come out on de grapevimes, de ha'r begun ter grow out on Henry's head, en by de middle er de summer he had de bigges' head er ha'r on de plantation. Befo' dat, Henry had tol'able good ha'r 'roun' de aidges, but soon ez de young grapes begun ter come, Henry's ha'r begun to quirl all up in little balls, des like dis yer reg'lar grapy ha'r, en by de time de grapes got ripe his head look des like a bunch er grapes. Combin' it did n' do no good; he wuk at it ha'f de night wid er Jim Crow,* en think he git it straighten' out, but in de mawnin' de grapes 'ud be dere des de same. So he gin it up, en tried ter keep de grapes down by havin' his ha'r cut sho't.

"But dat wa'n't de quares' thing 'bout de goopher. When Henry come ter de plantation, he wuz gittin' a little ole an stiff in de j'ints. But dat summer he got des ez spry en libely ez any young nigger on de plantation; fac', he got so biggity dat Mars Jackson, de oberseah, ha' ter th'eaten ter whip 'im, ef he did n' stop cuttin' up his didos en behave hisse'f. But de mos' cur'ouses' thing happen' in de fall, when de sap begin ter go down in de grapevimes. Fus', when de grapes 'uz gethered, de knots begun ter straighten out'n Henry's ha'r; en w'en de leaves begin ter fall, Henry's ha'r 'mence' ter drap out; en when de

---

*A small card, resembling a currycomb in construction, and used by negroes in the rural districts instead of a comb.—Au.

vimes 'uz bar', Henry's head wuz baller 'n it wuz in de spring, en he begin ter git ole en stiff in de j'ints ag'in, en paid no mo' 'tention ter de gals dyoin' er de whole winter. En nex' spring, w'en he rub de sap on ag'in, he got young ag'in, en so soopl en libely dat none er de young niggers on de plantation could n' jump, ner dance, ner hoe ez much cotton ez Henry. But in de fall er de year his grapes 'mence' ter straighten out, en his j'ints ter git stiff, en his ha'r drap off, en de rheumatiz begin ter wrastle wid 'im.

"Now, ef you'd 'a' knowed ole Mars Dugal' McAdoo, you'd 'a' knowed dat it ha' ter be a mighty rainy day when he could n' fine sump'n fer his niggers ter do, en it ha' ter be a mighty little hole he could n' crawl thoo, en ha' ter be a monst'us cloudy night when a dollar git by him in de dahkness; en w'en he see how Henry git young in de spring en ole in de fall, he 'lowed ter hisse'f ez how he could make mo' money out'n Henry dan by wukkin' him in de cotton-fiel'. 'Long de nex' spring, atter de sap 'mence' ter rise, en Henry 'n'int 'is head en sta'ted fer ter git young en soopl, Mars Dugal' up 'n tuk Henry ter town, en sole 'im fer fifteen hunder' dollars. Co'se de man w'at bought Henry did n' know nuffin 'bout de goopher, en Mars Dugal' did n' see no 'casion fer ter tell 'im. Long to'ds de fall, w'en de sap went down, Henry begin ter git ole ag'in same ez yuzhal, en his noo marster begin ter git skeered les'n he gwine ter lose his fifteen-hunder'-dollar nigger. He sent fer a mighty fine doctor, but de med'cine did n' 'pear ter do no good; de goopher had a good holt. Henry tole de doctor 'bout de goopher, but de doctor des laff at 'im.

"One day in de winter Mars Dugal' went ter town, en wuz santerin' 'long de Main Street, when who should he meet but Henry's noo marster. Dey said 'Hoddy,' en Mars Dugal' ax 'im ter hab a seegyar; en atter dey run on awhile 'bout de craps en de weather, Mars Dugal' ax 'im, sorter keerless, like ez ef he des thought of it,—

"'How you like de nigger I sole you las' spring?'

"Henry's marster shuck his head en knock de ashes off'n his seegyar.

"'Spec' I made a bad bahgin when I bought dat nigger.

Henry done good wuk all de summer, but sence de fall set in he 'pears ter be sorter pinin' away. Dey ain' nuffin pertickler de matter wid 'im—leastways de doctor say so—'cep'n' a tech er de rheumatiz; but his ha'r is all fell out, en ef he don't pick up his strenk mighty soon, I spec' I'm gwine ter lose 'im.'

"Dey smoked on awhile, en bimeby ole mars say, 'Well, a bahgin's a bahgin, but you en me is good fren's, en I doan wan' ter see you lose all de money you paid fer dat nigger; en ef w'at you say is so, en I ain't 'sputin' it, he ain't wuf much now. I 'spec's you wukked him too ha'd dis summer, er e'se de swamps down here don't agree wid de san'-hill nigger. So you des lemme know, en ef he gits any wusser I'll be willin' ter gib yer five hund'ed dollars fer 'im, en take my chances on his livin'.'

"Sho 'nuff, when Henry begun ter draw up wid de rheumatiz en it look like he gwine ter die fer sho, his noo marster sen' fer Mars Dugal', en Mars Dugal' gin him what he promus, en brung Henry home ag'in. He tuk good keer uv 'im dyoin' er de winter,—give 'im w'iskey to rub his rheumatiz, en terbacker ter smoke, en all he want ter eat,—'caze a nigger w'at he could make a thousan' dollars a year off'n did n' grow on eve'y huckleberry bush.

"Nex' spring, w'en de sap ris en Henry's ha'r commence' ter sprout, Mars Dugal' sole 'im ag'in, down in Robeson County dis time; en he kep' dat sellin' business up fer five year er mo'. Henry nebber say nuffin 'bout de goopher ter his noo marsters, 'caze he know he gwine ter be tuk good keer uv de nex' winter, w'en Mars Dugal' buy him back. En Mars Dugal' made 'nuff money off'n Henry ter buy anudder plantation ober on Beaver Crick.

"But 'long 'bout de een' er dat five year dey come a stranger ter stop at de plantation. De fus' day he 'uz dere he went out wid Mars Dugal' en spent all de mawnin' lookin' ober de vimya'd, en atter dinner dey spent all de evenin' playin' kya'ds. De niggers soon 'skiver' dat he wuz a Yankee, en dat he come down ter Norf C'lina fer ter l'arn de w'ite folks how to raise grapes en make wine. He promus Mars Dugal' he c'd make de grapevimes b'ar twice't ez many grapes, en dat de noo wine-press he wuz a-sellin' would make mo' d'n twice't ez many gallons er wine. En ole Mars Dugal' des drunk it all in, des 'peared ter be bewitch' wid dat Yankee. W'en de darkies see dat Yankee runnin' 'roun' de vimya'd en diggin' under de grape-vimes, dey shuk dere heads, en 'lowed dat dey feared Mars Dugal' losin' his min'. Mars Dugal' had all de dirt dug away fum under de roots er all de scuppernon' vimes, an' let 'em stan' dat away fer a week er mo'. Den dat Yankee made de niggers fix up a mixtry er lime en ashes en manyo, en po' it 'roun' de roots er de grapevimes. Den he 'vise Mars Dugal' fer ter trim de vimes close't, en Mars Dugal' tuck 'n done eve'ything de Yankee tole him ter do. Dyoin' all er dis time, mind yer, dis yer Yankee wuz libbin' off'n de fat er de lan', at de big house, en playin' kya'ds wid Mars Dugal' eve'y night; en dey say Mars Dugal' los' mo'n a thousan' dollars dyoin' er de week dat Yankee wuz a-ruinin' de grapevimes.

"W'en de sap ris nex' spring, ole Henry 'n'inted his head ez yuzhal, en his ha'r, 'mence' ter grow des de same ez it done eve'y year. De scuppernon' vimes growed monst'us fas', en de leaves wuz greener en thicker dan dey eber be'n dyoin' my re-memb'ance; en Henry's ha'r growed out thicker dan eber, en he 'peared ter git younger 'n younger, en soopler 'n soopler; en seein' ez he wuz sho't er han's dat spring, havin' tuk in consid-'able noo groun', Mars Dugal' 'cluded he would n' sell Henry 'tel he git de crap in en de cotton chop'. So he kep' Henry on de plantation.

"But 'long 'bout time fer de grapes ter come on de scupper-non' vimes, dey 'peared ter come a change ober 'em; de leaves withered en swivel' up, en de young grapes turn' yaller, en bimeby eve'ybody on de plantation could see dat de whole vimya'd wuz dyin'. Mars Dugal' tuk 'n water de vimes en done all he could, but 't wa'n' no use; dat Yankee had done bus' de watermillyum. One time de vimes picked up a bit, en Mars Du-gal' 'lowed dey wuz gwine ter come out ag'in; but dat Yankee done dug too close under de roots, en prune de branches too close ter de vime, en all dat lime en ashes done burn' de life out'n de vimes, en dey des kep' a-with'in en a-swivelin'.

"All dis time de goopher wuz a-wukkin'. When de vimes sta'ted ter wither, Henry 'mence' ter complain er his rheumatiz; en when de leaves begn ter dry up, his ha'r 'mence' ter drap out. When de vimes fresh' up a bit, Henry 'd git peart ag'in, en when de vimes wither' ag'in, Henry 'd get ole ag'in, en des kep' gittin' mo' en mo' fitten fer nuffin; he des pined away, en pined away, en fine'ly tuk ter his cabin; en when de big vime whar he got de sap ter 'n'int his head withered en turned yaller en died, Henry died too,—des went out sorter like a cannel. Dey did n't 'pear ter be nuffin de matter wid'im, 'cep'n' de rheumatiz, but his strenk des dwinel' away 'tel he did n' hab ernuff lef' ter draw his bref. De goopher had got de under holt, en th'owed Henry dat time fer good en all.

"Mars Dugal' tuk on might'ly 'bout losin' his vimes en his nigger in de same year; en he swo' dat ef he could git holt er dat Yankee he'd wear 'im ter a frazzle, en den chaw up de frazzle; en he'd done it, too, for Mars Dugal' 'uz a monst'us brash man w'en he once git started. He sot de vimya'd out ober ag'in, but it wuz th'ee er fo' year befo' de vimes got ter b'arin' any scuppernon's.

"W'en de wah broke out, Mars Dugal' raise' a comp'ny, en went off ter fight de Yankees. He say he wuz mighty glad dat wah come, en he des want ter kill a Yankee fer eve'y dollar he los' 'long er dat grape-raisin' Yankee. En I 'spec' he would 'a' done it, too, ef de Yankees had n' s'picioned sump'n, en killed him fus'. Atter de s'render ole miss move' ter town, de niggers all scattered 'way fum de plantation, en de vimya'd ain' be'n cultervated sence."

"Is that story true?" asked Annie doubtfully, but seriously, as the old man concluded his narrative.

"It's des ez true ez I'm a-settin' here, miss. Dey's a easy way ter prove it: I kin lead de way right ter Henry's grave ober yander in de plantation buryin-groun'. En I tell yer w'at, marster, I would n' 'vise you to buy dis yer ole vimya'd, 'caze de goopher's on it yit, en dey ain' no tellin' w'en it's gwine ter crap out."

"But I thought you said all the old vines died."

"Dey did 'pear ter die, but a few un 'em come out ag'in, en is mixed in 'mongs' de yuthers. I ain' skeered ter eat de grapes, 'caze I knows de old vimes fum de noo ones; but wid strangers dey ain' no tellin' w'at mought happen. I would n' 'vise yer ter buy dis vimya'd."

I bought the vineyard, nevertheless, and it has been for a long time in a thriving condition, and is often referred to by the local press as a striking illustration of the opportunities open to Northern capital in the development of Southern industries. The luscious scuppernong holds first rank among our grapes, though we cultivate a great many other varieties, and our income from grapes packed and shipped to the Northern markets is quite considerable. I have not noticed any developments of the goopher in the vineyard, although I have a mild suspicion that our colored assistants do not suffer from want of grapes during the season.

I found, when I bought the vineyard, that Uncle Julius had occupied a cabin on the place for many years, and derived a respectable revenue from the product of the neglected grape-vines. This, doubtless, accounted for his advice to me not to buy the vineyard, though whether it inspired the goopher story I am unable to state. I believe, however, that the wages I paid him for his services as coach-man, for I gave him employment in that capacity, were more than an equivalent for anything he lost by the sale of the vineyard.

PO' SANDY

On the northeast corner of my vineyard in central North Carolina, and fronting on the Lumberton plank-road, there stood a small frame house, of the simplest construction. It was built of pine lumber, and contained but one room, to which one window gave light and one door admission. Its weather-beaten sides revealed a virgin innocence of paint. Against one end of the house, and occupying half its width, there stood a huge brick chimney; the crumbling mortar had left large cracks between the bricks; the bricks themselves had begun to scale off in large flakes, leaving the chimney sprinkled with unsightly blotches. These evidences of decay were but partially concealed by a creeping vine, which extended its slender branches hither and thither in an ambitious but futile attempt to cover the whole chimney. The wooden shutter, which had once protected the unglazed window, had fallen from its hinges, and lay rotting in the rank grass and jimson-weeds beneath. This building, I learned when I bought the place, had been used as a schoolhouse for several years prior to the breaking out of the war, since which time it had remained unoccupied, save when some stray cow or vagrant hog had sought shelter within its walls from the chill rains and nipping winds of winter.

One day my wife requested me to build her a new kitchen. The house erected by us, when we first came to live upon the vineyard, contained a very conveniently arranged kitchen; but for some occult reason my wife wanted a kitchen in the back yard, apart from the dwelling-house, after the usual Southern fashion. Of course I had to build it.

To save expense, I decided to tear down the old school-house, and use the lumber, which was in a good state of preservation, in the construction of the new kitchen. Before demolishing the old house, however, I made an estimate of the amount of material contained in it, and found that I would have to buy several hundred feet of lumber additional, in order to build the new kitchen according to my wife's plan.

One morning old Julius McAdoo, our colored coachman, harnessed the gray mare to the rockaway, and drove my wife and me over to the sawmill from which I meant to order the new lumber. We drove down the long lane which led from our house to the plank-road; following the plank-road for about a mile, we turned into a road running through the forest and across the swamp to the sawmill beyond. Our carriage jolted over the half-rotted corduroy road which traversed the swamp, and then climbed the long hill leading to the sawmill. When we reached the mill, the foreman had gone over to a neighboring farmhouse, probably to smoke or gossip, and we were compelled to await his return before we could transact our business. We remained seated in the carriage, a few rods from the mill, and watched the leisurely movements of the mill-hands. We had not waited long before a huge pine log was placed in position, the machinery of the mill was set in motion, and the circular saw began to eat its way through the log, with a loud whir which resounded throughout the vicinity of the mill. The sound rose and fell in a sort of rhythmic cadence, which, heard from where we sat, was not unpleasing, and not loud enough to prevent conversation. When the saw started on its second journey through the log, Julius observed, in a lugubrious tone, and with a perceptible shudder:—

"Ugh! but dat des do cuddle my blood!"

"What's the matter, Uncle Julius?" inquired my wife, who is of a very sympathetic turn of mind. "Does the noise affect your nerves?"

"No, Mis' Annie," replied the old man, with emotion, "I ain' narvous; but dat saw, a-cuttin' en grindin' thoo dat stick er timber, en moanin', en groanin', en sweekin', kyars my 'memb'ance back ter ole times, en 'min's me er po' Sandy." The pathetic intonation with which he lengthened out the "po' Sandy" touched a responsive chord in our own hearts.

"And who was poor Sandy?" asked my wife, who takes a deep interest in the stories of plantation life which she hears from the lips of the older colored people. Some of these stories are quaintly humorous; others wildly extravagant, revealing the Oriental cast of the negro's imagination; while others, poured freely into the sympathetic ear of a Northern-bred woman, disclose many a tragic incident of the darker side of slavery.

"Sandy," said Julius, in reply to my wife's question, "was a nigger w'at useter b'long ter ole Mars Marrabo McSwayne. Mars Marrabo's place wuz on de yuther side'n de swamp, right nex' ter yo' place. Sandy wuz a monst'us good nigger, en could do so many things erbout a plantation, en alluz 'ten' ter his wuk so well, dat w'en Mars Marrabo's chilluns growed up en married off, dey all un 'em wanted dey daddy fer ter gin 'em Sandy fer a weddin' present. Bur Mars Marrabo knowed de res' would n' be satisfied ef he gin Sandy ter a'er one un 'em; so w'en dey wuz all done married, he fix it by 'lowin' one er his chilluns ter take Sandy fer a mont' er so, en den ernudder fer a mont' er so, en so on dat erway tel dey had all had 'im de same lenk er time; en den dey would all take him roun' ag'in, 'cep'n' oncet in a w'ile w'en Mars Marrabo would len' 'im ter some er his yuther kinfolks 'roun' de country, w'en dey wuz short er han's; tel bimeby it got so Sandy did n' hardly knowed what he wuz gwine ter stay fum one week's een' ter de yuther.

"One time w'en Sandy wuz lent out ez yushal, a spekilater come erlong wid a lot er niggers, en Mars Marrabo swap' Sandy's wife off fer a noo 'oman. W'en Sandy come back, Mars Marrabo gin 'im a dollar, en 'lowed he wuz monst'us sorry fer ter break up de fambly, but de spekilater had gin 'im big boot, en times wuz hard en money skase, en so he wuz bleedst ter make de trade. Sandy tuk on some 'bout losin' his wife, but he soon seed dey want no use cryin' ober split merlasses; en bein' ez he lacked de looks er do noo 'oman, he tuk up wid her atter she'd be'n on de plantation a mont' er so.

"Sandy en his noo wife got on mighty well tergedder, en de

niggers all 'mence' ter talk about how lovin' dey wuz. W'en Tenie wuz tuk sick oncet, Sandy useter set up all night wid 'er, en den go ter wuk in de mawnin' des lack he had his reg'lar sleep; en Tenie would 'a' done anythin' in de worl' for her Sandy.

"Sandy en Tenie had n' be'n libbin' tergedder fer mo' d'n two mont's befo' Mars Marrabo's old uncle, w'at libbed down in Robeson County, sent up ter fin' out ef Mars Marrabo could n' len' 'im er hire 'im a good han' fer a mont' er so. Sandy's marster wuz one er dese yer easy-gwine folks w'at wanter please eve'ybody, en he says yas, he could len' 'im Sandy. En Mars Marrabo tol' Sandy fer ter git ready ter go down ter Robeson nex' day, fer ter stay a mont' er so.

"It wuz monst'us hard on Sandy fer ter take 'im 'way fum Tenie. It wuz so fur down ter Robeson dat he did n' hab no chance er comin' back ter see her tel de time wuz up; he would n' 'a' mine comin' ten er fifteen mile at night ter see Tenie, but Mars Marrabo's uncle's plantation wuz mo' d'n forty mile off. Sandy wuz mighty sad en cas' down atter w'at Mars Marrabo tol' 'im, en he says ter Tenie, sezee:—

"'I'm gittin' monst'us ti'ed er dish yer gwine roun' so much. Here I is lent ter Mars Jeems dis mont', en I got ter do so-en-so; en ter Mars Archie de nex' mont', en I got ter do so-en-so; den I got ter go ter Miss Jinnie's: en hit's Sandy dis en Sandy dat, en Sandy yer en Sandy dere, tel it 'pears ter me I ain' got no home, ner no marster, ner no mistiss, ner no nuffin. I can't eben keep a wife: my yuther ole 'oman wuz sol' away without my gittin' a chance fer ter tell her good-by; en now I got ter go off en leab you, Tenie, en I dunno whe'r I'm eber gwine ter see you ag'in er no. I wisht I wuz a tree, er a stump, er a rock, er sump'n w'at could stay on de plantation fer a w'ile.'

"Atter Sandy got thoo talkin', Tenie did n' say naer word, but des sot dere by de fier, studyin' en studyin'. Bimeby she up'n' says:—

"'Sandy, is I eber tol' you I wuz a cunjuh 'oman?'

"Co'se Sandy had n' nebber dremp' er nuffin lack dat, en he made a great 'miration w'en he hear w'at Tenie say. Bimeby Tenie went on:—

"'I ain' goophered nobody, ner done no cunjuh wuk, fer fif-

teen year er mo'; en w'en I got religion I made up my mine I
would n' wuk no mo' goopher. But dey is some things I doan
b'lieve it's no sin fer ter do; en ef you doan wanter be sent roun'
fum pillar ter pos', en ef you doan wanter go down ter Robeson, I kin fix things so you won't haf ter. Ef you'll des say de
word, I kin turn you ter w'ateber you wanter be, en you kin
stay right whar you wanter, ez long ez you mineter.'

"Sandy say he doan keer; he's willin' fer ter do anythin' fer
ter stay close ter Tenie. Den Tenie ax 'im ef he doan wanter be
turnt inter a rabbit.

"Sandy say, 'No, de dogs mought git atter me.'

"'Shill I turn you ter a wolf?' sez Tenie.

"'No, eve'ybody skeered er a wolf, en I doan want nobody
ter be skeered er me.'

"'Shill I turn you ter a mawkin'-bird?'

"'No, a hawk mought ketch me. I wanter be turnt inter
sump'n w'at 'll stay in one place.'

"'I kin turn you ter a tree,' sez Tenie. 'You won't hab no
mouf ner years, but I kin turn you back oncet in a w'ile, so you
kin git sump'n ter eat, en hear w'at's gwine on.'

"Well, Sandy say dat 'll do. En so Tenie tuk 'im down by de
aidge er de swamp, not fur fum de quarters, en turnt 'im inter
a big pine-tree, en sot 'im out 'mongs' some yuther trees. En de
nex' mawnin', ez some er de fiel' han's wuz gwine long dere,
dey seed a tree w'at dey did n' 'member er habbin' seed befo';
it wuz monst'us quare, en dey wuz bleedst ter 'low dat dey had
n' 'membered right, er e'se one er de saplin's had be'n growin'
monst'us fas'.

"W'en Mars Marrabo 'skiver' dat Sandy wuz gone, he
'lowed Sandy had runned away. He got de dogs out, but de las'
place dey could track Sandy ter wuz de foot er dat pine-tree. En
dere de dogs stood en barked, en bayed, en pawed at de tree, en
tried ter climb up on it; en w'en dey wuz tuk roun' thoo de
swamp ter look fer de scent, dey broke loose en made fer dat
tree ag'in. It wuz de beatenis' thing de w'ite folks eber hearn of,
en Mars Marrabo 'lowed dat Sandy must 'a' clim' up on de tree
en jump' off on a mule er sump'n, en rid fur ernuff fer ter spile
de scent. Mars Marrabo wanted ter 'cuse some er de yuther

niggers er heppin' Sandy off, but dey all 'nied it ter de las'; en eve'ybody knowed Tenie sot too much sto' by Sandy fer ter he'p 'im run away whar she could n' nebber see 'im no mo'.

"W'en Sandy had be'n gone long ernuff fer folks ter think he done got clean away, Tenie useter go down ter de woods at night en turn 'im back, en den dey 'd slip up ter de cabin en set by de fire en talk. But dey ha' ter be monst'us keerful, er e'se somebody would 'a' seed 'em, en dat would 'a' spile' de whole thing; so Tenie alluz turnt Sandy back in de mawnin' early, befo' anybody wuz a-stirrin'.

"But Sandy did n' git erlong widout his trials en tribberlations. One day a woodpecker come erlong en 'mence' ter peck at de tree; en de nex' time Sandy wuz turnt back he had a little roun' hole in his arm, des lack a sharp stick be'n stuck in it. Atter dat Tenie sot a sparrer-hawk fer ter watch de tree; en w'en de woodpecker come erlong nex' mawnin' fer ter finish his nes', he got gobble' up mos'fo' he stuck his bill in de bark.

"Nudder time, Mars Marrabo sent a nigger out in de woods fer ter chop tuppentime boxes. De man chop a box in dish yer tree, en hack' de bark up two er th'ee feet, fer ter let de tuppentime run. De nex' time Sandy wuz turnt back he had a big skyar on his lef' leg, des lack it be'n skunt; en it tuk Tenie nigh 'bout all night fer ter fix a mixtry fer ter kyo it up. Atter dat, Tenie sot a hawnet fer ter watch de tree; en w'en de nigger come back ag'in fer ter cut ernudder box on de yuther side'n de tree, de hawnet stung 'im so hard dat de ax slip en cut his foot nigh 'bout off.

"W'en Tenie see so many things happenin' ter de tree, she 'cluded she'd ha' ter turn Sandy ter sump'n e'se; en atter studyin' de matter ober, en talkin' wid Sandy one ebenin', she made up her mine fer ter fix up a goopher mixtry w'at would turn herse'f en Sandy ter foxes, er sump'n, so dey could run away en go some'rs what dey could be free en lib lack w'ite folks.

"But dey ain' no tellin' w'at 's gwine ter happen in dis worl'. Tenie had got de night sot fer her en Sandy ter run away, w'en dat ve'y day one er Mars Marrobo's sons rid up ter de big house in his buggy, en say his wife wuz monst'us sick, en he

want his mammy ter len' 'im a 'oman fer ter nuss his wife. Tenie's mistiss say sen' Tenie; she wuz a good nuss. Young mars
wuz in a tarrible hurry fer ter git back home. Tenie wuz washin'
at de big house dat day, en her mistiss say she should go right
'long wid her young marster. Tenie tried ter make some 'scuse
fer ter git away en hide 'tel night, w'en she would have eve'y-
thing fix' up fer her en Sandy; she say she wanter go ter her
cabin fer ter git her bonnet. Her mistiss say it doan matter
'bout de bonnet; her head-hankcher wuz good ernuff. Den Tenie say she wanter git her bes' frock; her mistiss say no, she
doan need no mo' frock, en w'en dat one got dirty she could git
a clean one whar she wuz gwine. So Tenie had ter git in de
buggy en go 'long wid young Mars Dunkin ter his plantation,
w'ich wuz mo' d'n twenty mile away; en dey wa'n't no chance
er her seein' Sandy no mo' 'tel she come back home. De po' gal
felt monst'us bad 'bout de way things wuz gwine on, en she
knowed Sandy mus' be a wond'rin' why she did n' come en
turn 'im back no mo'.

"W'iles Tenie wuz away nussin' young Mars Dunkin's wife,
Mars Marrabo tuk a notion fer ter buil' 'im a noo kitchen; en
bein' ez he had lots er timber on his place, he begun ter look
'roun' fer a tree ter hab de lumber sawed out'n. En I dunno
how it come to be so, but he happen fer ter hit on de ve'y tree
w'at Sandy wuz turnt inter. Tenie wuz gone, en dey wa'n't nobody ner nuffin fer ter watch de tree.

"De two men w'at cut de tree down say dey nebber had sech
a time wid a tree befo': dey axes would glansh off, en did n'
'pear ter make no pro gress thoo de wood; en of all de creakin',
en shakin', en wobblin' you eber see, dat tree done it w'en it
commence' ter fall. It wuz de beatenis' thing!

"W'en dey got de tree all trim' up, dey chain it up ter a timber waggin, en start fer de sawmill. But dey had a hard time gittin' de log dere: fus' dey got stuck in de mud w'en dey wuz
gwine crosst de swamp, en it wuz two er th'ee hours befo' dey
could git out. W'en dey start' on ag'in, de chain kep' a-comin'
loose; en dey had ter keep a-stoppin' en a-stoppin' fer ter hitch
de log up ag'in. W'en dey commence' ter climb de hill ter de
sawmill, de log broke loose, en roll down de hill en in 'mongs'

de trees, en hit tuk nigh 'bout half a day mo' ter git it haul' up ter de sawmill.

"De nex' mawnin' atter de day de tree wuz haul' ter de sawmill, Tenie come home. W'en she got back ter her cabin, de fus' thing she done wuz ter run down ter de woods en see how Sandy wuz gittin' on. W'en she seed de stump standin' dere, wid de sap runnin' out'n it, en de limbs layin' scattered roun', she nigh 'bout went out'n her min'. She run ter her cabin, en got her goopher mixtry, en den follered de track er de timber waggin ter de sawmill. She knowed Sandy could 'n' lib mo' d'n a minute er so ef she turnt him back, fer he wuz all chop' up so he 'd 'a' be'n bleedst ter die. But she wanted ter turn 'im back long ernuff fer ter 'splain ter 'im dat she had n' went off a-purpose, en lef' 'im ter be chop' down en sawed up. She did n' want Sandy ter die wid no hard feelin's to'ds her.

"De han's at de sawmill had des got de big log on de ker-ridge, en wuz startin' up de saw, w'en dey seed a 'oman runnin' up de hill, all out er bref, cryin' en gwine on des lack she wuz plumb 'stracted. It wuz Tenie; she come right inter de mill, en th'owed herse'f on de log, right in front er de saw, a-hollerin' en cryin' ter her Sandy ter fergib her, en not ter think hard er her, fer it wa'n't no fault er hern. Den Tenie 'membered de tree did n' hab no years, en she wuz gittin' ready fer ter wuk her goopher mixtry se ez ter turn Sandy back, w'en de mill-hands kotch holt er her en tied her arms wid a rope, en fasten' her to one er de posts in de sawmill; en den dey started de saw up ag'in, en cut de log up inter bo'ds en scantlin's right befo' her eyes. But it wuz mighty hard wuk; fer of all de sweekin', en moanin', en groanin', dat log done it w'iles de saw wuz a-cuttin' thoo it. De saw wuz one er dese yer ole-timey, up-en-down saws, en hit tuk longer dem days ter saw a log 'en it do now. Dey greased de saw, but dat did n' stop de fuss; hit kep' right on, tel fin'ly dey got de log all sawed up.

"W'en de oberseah w'at run de sawmill come fum breakfas', de han's up en tell him 'bout de crazy 'oman—ez dey s'posed she wuz—w'at had come runnin' in de sawmill, a-hollerin' en gwine on, en tried ter th'ow herse'f befo' de saw. En de ober-

seah sent two er th'ee er de han's fer ter take Tenie back ter her
marster's plantation.

"Tenie 'peared ter be out'n her min' fer a long time, en her
marster ha' ter lock her up in de smoke-'ouse 'tel she got ober
her spells. Mars Marrabo wuz monst'us mad, en hit would 'a'
made yo' flesh crawl fer ter hear him cuss, 'caze he say de spekilater w'at he got Tenie fum had fooled 'im by wukkin' a crazy
'oman off on him. W'iles Tenie wuz lock up in de smoke-'ouse,
Mars Marrabo tuk 'n' haul de lumber fum de sawmill, en put
up his noo kitchen.

"W'en Tenie got quiet' down, so she could be 'lowed ter go
'roun' de plantation, she up'n' tole her marster all erbout
Sandy en de pine-tree; en w'en Mars Marrabo hearn it, he
'lowed she wuz de wuss 'stracted nigger he eber hearn of. He
did n' know w'at ter do wid Tenie: fus' he thought he'd put her
in de po'-house; but fin'ly, seein' ez she did n' do no harm ter
nobody ner nuffin, but des went 'roun' moanin', en groanin',
en shakin' her head, he 'cluded ter let her stay on de plantation
en nuss de little nigger chilluns w'en dey mammies wuz ter wuk
in de cotton-fiel'.

"De noo kitchen Mars Marrabo buil' wuz n' much use, fer it
had n' be'n put up long befo' de niggers 'mence' ter notice
quare things erbout it. Dey could hear sump'n moanin' en
groanin' 'bout de kitchen in de nighttime, en we'n de win'
would blow dey could hear sump'n a-hollerin' en sweekin' lack
it wuz in great pain en sufferin'. En it got so atter a w'ile dat it
wuz all Mars Marrabo's wife could do ter git a 'oman ter stay
in de kitchen in de daytime long ernuff ter do de cookin'; en
dey wa'n't naer nigger on de plantation w'at would n' rudder
take forty dan ter go 'bout dat kitchen atter dark,—dat is,
'cep'n' Tenie; she did n' 'pear ter min' de ha'nts. She useter slip
'roun' at night, en set on de kitchen steps, en lean up agin de
do'-jamb, en run on ter herse 'f wid some kine er foolishness
w'at nobody could n' make out; fer Mars Marrabo had
th'eaten' ter sen' her off'n de plantation ef she say anything ter
any er de yuther niggers 'bout de pine-tree. But somehow er
'nudder de niggers foun' out all erbout it, en dey all knowed de

kitchen wuz ha'nted by Sandy's sperrit. En bimeby hit got so Mars Marrabo's wife herse'f wuz skeered ter go out in de yard atter dark.

"W'en it come ter dat, Mars Marrabo tuk en to' de kitchen down, en use' de lumber fer ter buil' dat ole school'ouse w'at you er talkin' 'bout pullin' down. De school'ouse wuz n' use' 'cep'n' in de daytime, en on dark nights folks gwine 'long de road would hear quare soun's en see quare things. Po' ole Tenie useter go down dere at night, en wander 'roun' de school'ouse; en de niggers all 'lowed she went fer ter talk wid Sandy's sperrit. En one winter mawnin', w'en one er de boys went ter school early fer ter start de fire, w'at should he fin' but po' ole Tenie, layin' on de flo', stiff, en col', en dead. Dere did n' 'pear ter be nuffin pertickler de matter wid her,—she had des grieve' herse'f ter def fer her Sandy. Mars Marrabo did n' shed no tears. He though Tenie wuz crazy, en dey wa'n't no tellin' w'at she mought do nex'; en dey ain' much room in dis worl' fer crazy w'ite folks, let 'lone a crazy nigger.

"Hit wa'n't long atter dat befo' Mars Marrabo sol' a piece er his track er lan' ter Mars Dugal' McAdoo,—*my* ole marster,— en dat's how de ole school'ouse happen to be on yo' place. W'en de wah broke out, de school stop', en de old school'ouse be'n stannin' empty ever sence,—dat is 'cep'n' fer de ha'nts. En folks sez dat de ole school'ouse, er any yuther house w'at got any er dat lumber in it w'at wuz sawed out'n de tree w'at Sandy wuz turnt inter, is gwine ter be ha'nted tel de las' piece er plank is rotted en crumble' inter dus'."

Annie had listened to this gruesome narrative with strained attention.

"What a system it was," she exclaimed, when Julius had finished, "under which such things were possible!"

"What things?" I asked, in amazement. "Are you seriously considering the possibility of a man's being turned into a tree?"

"Oh, no," she replied quickly, "not that;" and then she murmured absently, and with a dim look in her fine eyes, "Poor Tenie!"

We ordered the lumber, and returned home. That night, after we had gone to bed, and my wife had to all appearances been sound asleep for half an hour, she startled me out of an incipient doze by exclaiming suddenly,—

"John, I don't believe I want my new kitchen built out of the lumber in that old schoolhouse."

"You would n't for a moment allow yourself," I replied, with some asperity, "to be influenced by that absurdly impossible yarn which Julius was spinning to-day?"

"I know the story is absurd," she replied dreamily, "and I am not so silly as to believe it. But I don't think I should ever be able to take any pleasure in that kitchen if it were built out of that lumber. Besides, I think the kitchen would look better and last longer if the lumber were all new."

Of course she had her way. I bought the new lumber, though not without grumbling. A week or two later I was called away from home on business. On my return, after an absence of several days, my wife remarked to me,—

"John, there has been a split in the Sandy Run Colored Baptist Church, on the temperance question. About half the members have come out from the main body, and set up for themselves. Uncle Julius is one of the seceders, and he came to me yesterday and asked if they might not hold their meetings in the old schoolhouse for the present."

"I hope you did n't just let the old rascal have it," I returned, with some warmth. I had just received a bill for the new lumber I had bought.

"Well," she replied, "I could n't refuse him the use of the house for so good a purpose."

"And I'll venture to say," I continued, "that you subscribed something toward the support of the new church?"

She did not attempt to deny it.

"What are they going to do about the ghost?" I asked, somewhat curious to know how Julius would get around this obstacle.

"Oh," replied Annie. "Uncle Julius says that ghosts never disturb religious worship, but that if Sandy's spirit *should* happen to stray into meeting by mistake, no doubt the preaching would do it good."

MARS JEEMS'S
NIGHTMARE

We found old Julius very useful when we moved to our new residence. He had a thorough knowledge of the neighborhood, was familiar with the roads and the watercourses, knew the qualities of the various soils and what they would produce, and where the best hunting and fishing were to be had. He was a marvelous hand in the management of horses and dogs, with whose mental processes he manifested a greater familiarity than mere use would seem to account for, though it was doubtless due to the simplicity of a life that had kept him close to nature. Toward my tract of land and the things that were on it—the creeks, the swamps, the hills, the meadows, the stones, the trees—he maintained a peculiar personal attitude, that might be called predial rather than proprietary. He had been accustomed, until long after middle life, to look upon himself as the property of another. When this relation was no longer possible, owing to the war, and to his master's death and the dispersion of the family, he had been unable to break off entirely the mental habits of a lifetime, but had attached himself to the old plantation, of which he seemd to consider himself an appurtenance. We found him useful in many ways and entertaining in others, and my wife and I took quite a fancy to him.

Shortly after we became established in our home on the sand-hills, Julius brought up to the house one day a colored boy of about seventeen, whom he introduced as his grandson, and for whom he solicited employment. I was not favorably impressed by the youth's appearance,—quite the contrary, in fact; but mainly to please the old man I hired Tom—his name was Tom—to help about the stables, weed the garden, cut wood and bring water, and in general to make himself useful about the outdoor work of the household.

My first impression of Tom proved to be correct. He turned out to be very trifling, and I was much annoyed by his laziness, his carelessness, and his apparent lack of any sense of responsibility. I kept him longer than I should, on Julius's account, hoping that he might improve; but he seemed to grow worse instead of better, and when I finally reached the limit of my patience, I discharged him.

"I am sorry, Julius," I said to the old man; "I should have liked to oblige you by keeping him; but I can't stand Tom any longer. He is absolutely untrustworthy."

"Yas, suh," replied Julius, with a deep sigh and a long shake of the head, "I knows he ain' much account, en dey ain' much 'pen'ence ter be put on 'im. But I wuz hopin' dat you mought make some 'lowance fuh a' ign'ant young nigger, suh, en gib 'im one mo' chance."

But I had hardened my heart. I had always been too easily imposed upon, and had suffered too much from this weakness. I determined to be firm as a rock in this instance.

"No, Julius," I rejoined decidedly, "it is impossible. I gave him more than a fair trial, and he simply won't do."

When my wife and I set out for our drive in the cool of the evening,—afternoon is "evening" in Southern parlance,—one of the servants put into the rockaway two large earthenware jugs. Our drive was to be down through the swamp to the mineral spring at the foot of the sand-hills beyond. The water of this spring was strongly impregnated with sulphur and iron, and, while not particularly agreeable of smell or taste, was used by us, in moderation, for sanitary reasons.

When we reached the spring, we found a man engaged in cleaning it out. In answer to an inquiry he said that if we would wait five or ten minutes, his task would be finished and the spring in such condition that we could fill our jugs. We might have driven on, and come back by way of the spring, but there was a bad stretch of road beyond, and we concluded to remain where we were until the spring should be ready. We were in a cool and shady place. It was often necessary to wait awhile in

North Carolina; and our Northern energy had not been entirely proof against the influences of climate and local custom.

While we sat there, a man came suddenly around a turn of
the road ahead of us. I recognized in him a neighbor with
whom I had exchanged formal calls. He was driving a horse,
apparently a high-spirited creature, possessing, so far as I could
see at a glance, the marks of good temper and good breeding;
the gentleman, I had heard it suggested, was slightly deficient in
both. The horse was rearing and plunging, and the man was
beating him furiously with a buggywhip. When he saw us, he
flushed a fiery red, and, as he passed, held the reins with one
hand, at some risk to his safety, lifted his hat, and bowed somewhat constrainedly as the horse darted by us, still panting and
snorting with fear.

"He looks as though he were ashamed of himself," I observed.

"I'm sure he ought to be," exclaimed my wife indignantly. "I
think there is no worse sin and no more disgraceful thing than
cruelty."

"I quite agree with you," I assented.

"A man w'at 'buses his hoss is gwine ter be ha'd on de folks
w'at wuks fer 'im," remarked Julius. "Ef young Mistah McLean
doan min', he'll hab a bad dream one er dese days, des lack 'is
grandaddy had way back yander, long yeahs befo' de wah."

"What was it about Mr. McLean's dream, Julius?" I asked.
The man had not yet finished cleaning the spring, and we might
as well put in time listening to Julius as in any other way. We
had found some of his plantation tales quite interesting.

"Mars Jeems McLean," said Julius, "wuz de grandaddy er
dis yer gent'eman w'at is des gone by us beatin' his hoss. He
had a big plantation en a heap er niggers. Mars Jeems wuz a
ha'd man, en monst'us stric' wid his han's. Eber sence he
growed up he nebber 'peared ter hab no feelin' fer no body.
W'en his daddy, ole Mars John McLean, died, de plantation en
all de niggers fell ter young Mars Jeems. He had be'n bad 'nuff
befo', but it wa'n't long atterwa'ds 'tel he got so dey wuz no
use in libbin' at all ef you ha' ter lib roun' Mars Jeems. His niggers wuz bleedzd ter slabe fum daylight ter da'k, w'iles yuther

folks's did n' hafter wuk 'cep'n' fum sun ter sun; en dey did n' git no mo' ter eat dan dey oughter, en dat de coa'ses' kin'. Dey wa'n't 'lowed ter sing, ner dance, ner play de banjo w'en Mars Jeems wuz roun' de place; fer Mars Jeems say he would n' hab no sech gwines-on,—said he bought his han's ter wuk, en not ter play, en w'en night com dey mus' sleep en res', so dey'd be ready ter git up soon in de mawnin' en go ter dey wuk fresh en strong.

"Mars Jeems did n' 'low no co'tin' er juneseyin' roun' his plantation,—said he wanted his niggers ter put dey min's on dey wuk, en not to be wastin' dey time wid no sech foolis'ness. En he would n' let his han's git married,—said he wuz n' raisin' niggers, but wuz raisin' cotton. En w'eneber any er de boys en gals 'ud 'mence ter git sweet on one ernudder, he'd sell one er de yuther un 'em, er sen' 'em way down in Robeson County ter his yuther plantation, whar dey could n' nebber see one ernudder.

"Ef any er de niggers eber complained, dey got fo'ty; so co'se dey did n' many un 'em complain. But dey did n' lack it, des de same, en nobody could n' blame 'em, fer dey had a ha'd time. Mars Jeems did n' make no 'lowance fer nachul bawn laz'ness, ner sickness, ner trouble in de min', ner nuffin; he wuz des gwine ter git so much wuk outer eve'y han', er know de reason w'y.

"Dey wuz one time de niggers 'lowed, fer a spell, dat Mars Jeems mought git bettah. He tuk a lackin' ter Mars Marrabo McSwayne's oldes' gal, Miss Libbie, en useter go ober dere eve'y day er eve'y ebenin', en folks said dey wuz gwine ter git married sho'. But it 'pears dat Miss Libbie heared 'bout de gwines-on on Mars Jeems's plantation, en she des 'lowed she could n' trus' herse'f wid no sech a man; dat he mought git so useter 'busin' his niggers dat he'd 'mence ter 'buse his wife at-ter he got useter habbin' her roun' de house. So she 'clared she wuz n' gwine ter hab nuffin mo' ter do wid young Mars Jeems.

"De niggers wuz all monst'us sorry w'en de match wuz bust' up, fer now Mars Jeems got wusser'n he wuz befo' he sta'ted sweethea'tin'. De time he useter spen' co'tin' Miss Libbie he put in findin' fault wid de niggers, en all his bad feelin's 'ca'se Miss

Libbie th'owed 'im ober he 'peared ter try ter wuk off on de po' niggers.

"W'iles Mars Jeems wuz co'tin' Miss Libbie, two er de han's on de plantation had got ter settin' a heap er sto' by one er-nudder. One un 'em wuz name' Solomon, en de yuther wuz a 'oman w'at wukked in de fiel' long er 'im—I fe'git dat 'oman's name, but it doan 'mount ter much in de tale nohow. Now, whuther 'ca'se Mars Jeems wuz so tuk up wid his own junesey* dat he did n' paid no 'tention fer a w'ile ter w'at wuz gwine on 'twix' Solomon en his junesey, er whuther his own co'tin' made 'im kin' er easy on de co'tin' in de qua'ters, dey ain' no tellin'. But dey's one thing sho', dat w'en Miss Libbie th'owed 'im ober, he foun' out 'bout Solomon en de gal monst'us quick, en gun Solomon fo'ty, en sont de gal down ter de Robeson County plantation, en tol' all de niggers ef he ketch 'em at any mo' sech foolishness, he wuz gwine ter skin 'em alibe en tan dey hides befo' dey ve'y eyes. Co'se he would n' 'a' done it, but he mought 'a' made things wusser 'n dey wuz. So you kin 'magine dey wa'n't much lub-makin' in de qua'ters fer a long time.

"Mars Jeems useter go down ter de yuther plantation some-times fer a week or mo', en so he had ter hab a oberseah ter look atter his wuk w'iles he 'uz gone. Mars Jeems's oberseah wuz a po' w'ite man name' Nick Johnson,—de niggers called 'im Mars Johnson ter his face, but behin' his back dey useter call 'im Ole Nick, en de name suited 'im ter a T. He wuz wusser 'n Mars Jeems ever da'ed ter be. Co'se de darkies did n' lack de way Mars Jeems used 'em, but he wuz de marster, en had a right to do ez he please'; but dis yer Ole Nick wa'n't nuffin but a po' buckrah, en all de niggers 'spised 'im ez much ez dey hated 'im, fer he did n' own nobody, en wa'n't no bettah 'n a nigger, fer in dem days any 'spectable pusson would ruther be a nigger den a po' w'ite man.

"Now, atter Solomon's gal had be'n sont away, he kep' feelin' mo' en mo' bad erbout it, 'tel fin'lly he 'lowed he wuz gwine ter see ef dey could n' be sump'n done fer ter git 'er back, en ter make Mars Jeems treat de darkies bettah. So he tuk a

*Sweetheart.—Au.

peck er co'n out'n de ba'n one night, en went ober ter see old
Aun' Peggy, de free-nigger cunjuh 'oman down by de Wim'l'ton
Road.

"Aun' Peggy listen' ter 'is tale, en ax' him some queshtuns,
en den tol' 'im she'd wuk her roots, en see w'at dey'd say 'bout
it, en ter-morrer night he sh'd come back ag'in en fetch ernudder peck er co'n, en den she'd hab sump'n fer ter tel 'im.

"So Solomon went back de nex' night, en sho' 'nuff, Aun'
Peggy tol' 'im w'at ter do. She gun 'im some stuff w'at look'
lack it be'n made by poundin' up some roots en yarbs wid a
pestle in a mo'tar.

"'Dis yer stuff,' sez she, 'is monst'us pow'ful kin' er goopher.
You take dis home, en gin it ter de cook, ef you kin trus' her, en
tell her fer ter put it in yo' marster's soup de fus' cloudy day he
hab okra soup fer dinnah. Min' you follers de d'rections.'

"'It ain' gwineter p'isen 'im, is it?' ax' Solomon, gittin' kin'
er skeered; fer Solomon wuz a good man, en did n' want er do
nobody no rale ha'm.

"'Oh, no,' sez old Aun' Peggy, 'it's gwine ter do 'im good,
but he'll hab a monst'us bad dream fus.' A mont' fum now you
come down heah en lemme know how de goopher is wukkin'.
Fer I ain' done much er dis kin' er cunj'in' er late yeahs, en I has
ter kinder keep track un it ter see dat it doan 'complish no mo'
d'n I 'lows fer it ter do. En I has ter be kinder keerful 'bout cun-
j'in' w'ite folks; so be sho' en lemme know, w'ateber you do, des
w'at is gwine on roun' de plantation.'

"So Solomon say all right, en tuk de goopher mixtry up ter
de big house en gun it ter de cook, en tol' her fer ter put it in
Mars Jeems's soup de fus' cloudy day she hab okra soup fer
dinnah. It happen' dat de ve'y nex' day wuz a cloudy day, en so
de cook made okra soup fer Mars Jeems's dinnah, en put de
powder Solomon gun her inter de soup, en made de soup rale
good, so Mars Jeems eat a whole lot of it en 'peared ter enjoy it.

"De nex' mawnin' Mars Jeems tol' de oberseah he wuz
gwine 'way on some bizness, en den he wuz gwine ter his
yuther plantation, down in Robeson County, en he did n' 'spec'
he'd be back fer a mont' er so.

"'But,' sezee, 'I wants you ter run dis yer plantation fer all it's wuth. Dese yer niggers is gittin' monst'us triflin' en lazy en keerless, en dey ain' no 'pen'ence ter be put in 'em. I wants dat stop', en w'iles I'm gone erway I wants de 'spenses cut 'way down en a heap mo' wuk done. Fac', I wants dis yer plantation ter make a reco'd dat 'll show w'at kinder oberseah you is.'

"Ole Nick did n' said nuffin' but 'Yas, suh,' but de way he kinder grin' ter hisse'f en show' his big yaller teef, en snap' de rawhide he useter kyar roun' wid 'im, made col' chills run up and down de backbone er dem niggers w'at heared Mars Jeems a-talkin'. En dat night dey wuz mo'nin' en groanin' down in de qua'ters, fer de niggers all knowed w'at wuz comin'.

"So, sho' 'nuff, Mars Jeems went erway nex' mawnin', en de trouble begun. Mars Johnson sta'ted off de ve'y fus' day fer ter see w'at he could hab ter show Mars Jeems w'en he come back. He made de tasks bigger en de rashuns littler, en w'en de niggers had wukked all day, he'd fin' sump'n fer 'em ter do roun' de ba'n er som'ers atter da'k, fer ter keep 'em busy a' hour er so befo' dey went ter sleep.

"About th'ee er fo' days atter Mars Jeems went erway, young Mars Dunkin McSwayne rode up ter de big house one day wid a nigger settin' behin' 'im in de buggy, tied ter de seat, en ax' ef Mars Jeems wuz home. Mars Johnson wuz at de house, and he say no.

"'Well,' sez Mars Dunkin, sezee, 'I fotch dis nigger ober ter Mistah McLean fer ter pay a bet I made wid 'im las' week w'en we wuz playin' kya'ds te'gedder. I bet 'im a nigger man, en heah 's one I reckon 'll fill de bill. He wuz tuk up de yuther day fer a stray nigger, en he could n' gib no 'count er hisse'f, en so he wuz sol' at oction, en I bought 'im. He 's kinder brash, but I knows yo' powers, Mistah Johnson, en I reckon ef anybody kin make 'im toe de ma'k, you is de man.'

"Mars Johnson grin' one er dem grins w'at show' all his snaggle teef, en make de niggers 'low he look lack de ole debbil, en sezee ter Mars Dunkin:—

"'I reckon you kin trus' me, Mistah Dunkin, fer ter tame any nigger wuz eber bawn. De nigger doan lib w'at I can't take down in 'bout fo' days.'

"Well, Ole Nick had 'is han's full long er dat noo nigger; en w'iles de res' er de darkies wuz sorry fer de po' man, dey 'lowed he kep' Mars Johnson so busy dat dey got along better 'n dey'd 'a' done ef de noo nigger had nebber come.

"De fus' thing dat happen', Mars Johnson sez ter dis yer noo man:—

"'W'at 's yo' name, Sambo?'

"'My name ain' Sambo,' 'spon' de noo nigger.

"'Did I ax you w'at yo' name wa'n't?' sez Mars Johnson. 'You wants ter be pa'tic'lar how you talks ter me. Now, w'at is yo' name, en whar did you come fum?'

"'I dunno my name,' sez de nigger, 'en I doan 'member whar I come fum. My head is all kin' er mix' up.'

"'Yas,' sez Mars Johnson, 'I reckon I'll ha' ter gib you sump'n fer ter cl'ar yo' head. At de same time, it'll l'arn you some manners, en atter dis mebbe you'll say "suh" w'en you speaks ter me.'

"Well, Mars Johnson haul' off wid his rawhide en hit de noo nigger once. De noo man look' at Mars Johnson fer a minute ez ef he did n' know w'at ter make er dis yer kin' er l'arnin'. But w'en de oberseah raise' his w'ip ter hit him ag'in, de noo nigger des haul' off en made fer Mars Johnson, en ef some er de yuther niggers had n' stop' 'im, it 'peared ez ef he mought 'a' made it wa'm fer Ole Nick dere for a w'ile. But de oberseah made de yuther niggers he'p tie de noo nigger up, en den gun 'im fo'ty, wid a dozen er so th'owed in fer good measure, fer Ole Nick wuz nebber stingy wid dem kin' er rashuns. De nigger went on at a tarrable rate, des lack a wil' man, but co'se he wuz bleedzd ter take his med'cine, fer he wuz tied up en could n' he'p hisse'f.

"Mars Johnson lock' de noo nigger up in de ba'n, en did n' gib 'im nuffin ter eat fer a day er so, 'tel he got 'im kin'er quiet' down, en den he tu'nt 'im loose en put 'im ter wuk. De nigger 'lowed he wa'n't useter wukkin', en would n' wuk, en Mars Johnson gun 'im anudder fo'ty fer laziness en impidence, en let 'im fas' a day er so mo', en den put 'im ter wuk ag'in. De nigger went ter wuk, but did n' 'pear ter know how ter han'le a hoe. It tuk des 'bout half de oberseah's time lookin' atter 'im, en dat po' nigger got mo' lashin's en cussin's en cuffin's dan any fo' yuthers on de plantation. He did n' mix wid ner talk much

ter de res' er de niggers, en could n' 'pear ter git it th'oo his min'
dat he wuz a slabe en had ter wuk en min' de w'ite folks, spite
er de fac' dat Ole Nick gun 'im a lesson eve'y day. En fin'lly
Mars Johnson 'lowed dat he could n' do nuffin wid 'im; dat ef
he wuz his nigger, he'd break his sperrit er break 'is neck, one
er de yuther. But co'se he wuz only sont ober on trial, en ez he
did n' gib sat'sfaction, en he had n' heared fum Mars Jeems
'bout w'en he wuz comin' back; en ez he wuz feared he'd git
mad some time er 'nuther en kill de nigger befo' he knowed it,
he 'lowed he'd better sen' 'im back whar he come fum. So he
tied 'im up en sont 'im back ter Mars Dunkin.

"Now, Mars Dunkin McSwayne wuz one er dese yer easy-
gwine gent'eman w'at did n' lack ter hab no trouble wid
niggers er nobody e'se, en he knowed ef Mars Ole Nick could
n' git 'long wid dis nigger, nobody could. So he tuk de nigger ter town dat same day, en sol' 'im ter a trader w'at wuz
gittin' up a gang er lackly niggers fer ter ship off on de steamboat ter go down de ribber ter Wim'l'ton en fum dere ter Noo
Orleens.

"De nex' day atter de noo man had be'n sont away, Solomon
wuz wukkin' in de cotton-fiel', en w'en he got ter de fence nex'
ter de woods, at de een' er de row, who sh'd he see on de yuther
side but ole Aun' Peggy. She beckon' ter 'im—de oberseah wuz
down on de yuther side er de fiel',—en sez she:—

"'W'y ain' you done come en 'po'ted ter me lack I tol' you?'

"'W'y, law! Aun' Peggy,' sez Solomon, 'dey ain' nuffin ter
'po't. Mars Jeems went away de day atter we gun 'im de goopher mixtry, en we ain' seed hide ner hair un 'im sence, en co'se
we doan know nuffin 'bout w'at 'fec' it had on 'im.'

"'I doan keer nuffin 'bout yo' Mars Jeems now; w'at I wants
ter know is w'at is be'n gwine on 'mongs' de niggers. Has you
be'n gittin' 'long any better on de plantation?'

"'No, Aun' Peggy, we be'n gittin' 'long wusser. Mars Johnson is stric'er 'n he eber wuz befo', en de po' niggers doan
ha'dly git time ter draw dey bref, en dey 'lows dey mought des
ez well be dead ez alibe.'

"'Uh huh!' sez Aun' Peggy, sez she, 'I tol' you dat 'uz
monst'us pow'ful goopher, en its wuk doan 'pear all at once.'

" 'Long ez we had dat noo nigger heah,' Solomon went on, 'he kep' Mars Johnson busy pa't er de time; but now he's gone erway, I s'pose de res' un us 'll ketch it wusser 'n eber.'

" 'W'at 's gone wid de noo nigger?' sez Aun' Peggy, rale quick, battin' her eyes en straight'nin' up.

" 'Ole Nick done sont 'im back ter Mars Dunkin, who had fotch 'im heah fer ter pay a gamblin' debt ter Mars Jeems,' sez Solomon, 'en I heahs Mars Dunkin has sol' 'im ter a nigger-trader up in Patesville, w'at's gwine ter ship 'im off wid a gang ter-morrer.'

"Ole Aun' Peggy 'peared ter git rale stirred up w'en Solomon tol' 'er dat, en sez she, shakin' her stick at 'im:—

" 'W'y did n' you come en tell me 'bout dis noo nigger bein' sol' erway? Did n' you promus me, ef I'd gib you dat goopher, you'd come en 'po't ter me 'bout all w'at wuz gwine on on dis plantation? Co'se I could 'a' foun' out fer myse'f, but I 'pended on yo' tellin' me, en now by not doin' it I's feared you gwine spile my cunj'in'. You come down ter my house ter-night en do w'at I tells you, er I'll put a spell on you dat'll make yo' ha'r fall out so you'll be bal', en yo' eyes drap out so you can't see, en yo' teef fall out so you can't eat, en yo' years grow up so you can't heah. W'en you is foolin' wid a cunjuh 'oman lack me, you got ter min' yo' P's en Q's er dey 'll be trouble sho' 'nuff.'

"So co'se Solomon went down ter Aun' Peggy's dat night, en she gun 'im a roasted sweet'n' 'tater.

" 'You take dis yer sweet'n' 'tater,' sez she,—'I done goophered it 'speshly fer dat noo nigger, so you better not eat it yo'se'f er you'll wush you had n',—en slip off ter town, en fin' dat strange man, en gib 'im dis yer sweet'n' 'tater. He mus' eat it befo' mawnin', sho', ef he doan wanter be sol' erway ter Noo Orleens.'

" 'But s'posen de patteroles ketch me, Aun' Peggy, w'at I gwine ter do?' sez Solomon.

" 'De patteroles ain' gwine tech you, but ef you doan fin' dat nigger, *I'm* gwine git you, en you 'll fin' me wusser 'n de pat-teroles. Des hol' on a minute, en I'll sprinkle you wid some er dis mixtry out'n dis yer bottle, so de patteroles can't see you, en you kin rub yo' feet wid some er dis yer grease out'n dis go'd, so you kin run fas', en rub some un it on yo' eyes so you kin see in de da'k; en den you mus' fin' dat noo nigger en gib 'im dis yer 'tater, er you gwine ter hab mo' trouble on yo' han's 'n you eber had befo' in yo' life er eber will hab sence.'

"So Solomon tuk de sweet'n' 'tater en sta'ted up de road fas' ez he could go, en befo' long he retch' town. He went right 'long by de patteroles, en dey did n' 'pear ter notice 'im, en bimeby he foun' whar de strange nigger was kep', en he walked right pas' de gyard at de do' en foun' 'im. De nigger could n' see 'im, ob co'se, en he could n' 'a' seed de nigger in de da'k, ef it had n' be'n fer de stuff Aun' Peggy gun 'im ter rub on 'is eyes. De nigger wuz layin' in a co'nder, 'sleep, en Solomon des slip' up ter 'im, en hilt dat sweet'n' 'tater 'fo' de nigger's nose, en he des nach'ly retch' up wid his han', en tuck de 'tater en eat it in his sleep, widout knowin' it. W'en Solomon seed he'd done eat de 'tater, he went back en tol' Aun' Peggy, en den went home ter his cabin ter sleep, 'way 'long 'bout two o'clock in de mawnin'.

"De nex' day wuz Sunday, en so de niggers had a little time ter deyse'ves. Solomon wuz kinder 'sturb' in his min' thinkin' 'bout his junesey w'at 'uz gone away, en wond'rin' w'at Aun' Peggy had ter do wid dat noo nigger; en he had sa'ntered up in de woods so 's ter be by hisse'f a little, en at de same time ter look atter a rabbit-trap he'd sot down in de aidge er de swamp, w'en who sh'd he see stan'in' unner a tree but a w'ite man.

"Solomon did n' knowed de w'ite man at fus', 'tel de w'ite man spoke up ter 'im.

"'Is dat you, Solomon?' sezee.

"Den Solomon reco'nized de voice.

"'Fer de Lawd's sake, Mars Jeems! is dat you?'

"'Yas, Solomon,' sez his marster, 'dis is me, er w'at 's lef' er me.'

"It wa'n't no wonder Solomon had n' knowed Mars Jeems at fus', fer he wuz dress' lack a po' w'ite man, en wuz barefooted, en look' monst'us pale en peaked, ez ef he'd des come th'oo a ha'd spell er sickness.

"'You er lookin' kinder po'ly, Mars Jeems', sez Solomon. 'Is you be'n sick, suh?'

"'No, Solomon,' sez Mars Jeems, shakin' his head, en

speakin' sorter slow en sad, 'I ain' be'n sick, but I's had a mon-st'us bad dream,—fac', a reg'lar, nach'ul nightmare. But tell me how things has be'n gwine on up ter de plantation since I be'n gone, Solomon.'

"So Solomon up en tol' 'im 'bout de craps, en 'bout de hosses en de mules, en 'bout de cows en de hawgs. En w'en he 'mence' ter tell 'bout de noo nigger, Mars Jeems prick' up 'is yeahs en listen', en eve'y now en den he'd say, 'Uh huh! uh huh!' en nod 'is head. En bimeby, w'en he'd ax' Solomon some mo' quesh-tuns, he sez, sezee:—

" 'Now, Solomon, I doan want you ter say a wo'd ter nobody 'bout meetin' me heah, but I wants you ter slip up ter de house, en fetch me some clo's en some shoes,—I fergot ter tell you dat a man rob' me back yander on de road en swap' clo's wid me widout axin' me whuther er no,—but you neenter say nuf-fin 'bout dat, nuther. You go en fetch me some clo's heah, so nobody won't see you, en keep yo' mouf shet, en I'll gib you a dollah.'

"Solomon wuz so 'stonish' he lack ter fell ober in his tracks, w'en Mars Jeems promus' ter gib 'im a dollah. Dey su't'nly wuz a change come ober Mars Jeems, w'en he offer' one er his nig-gers dat much money. Solomon 'mence' ter 'spec' dat Aun' Peggy's cunj'ation had be'n wukkin' monst'us strong.

"Solomon fotch Mars Jeems some clo's en shoes, en dat same eb'nin' Mars Jeems 'peared at de house, en let on lack he des dat minute got home fum Robeson County. Mars Johnson was all ready ter talk ter 'im, but Mars Jeems sont 'im wo'd he wa'n't feelin' ve'y well dat night, en he'd see 'im ter-morrer.

"So nex' mawnin' atter breakfus' Mars Jeems sont fer de oberseah, en ax' 'im fer ter gib 'count er his styoa'dship. Ole Nick tol' Mars Jeems how much wuk be'n done, en got de books en showed 'im how much money be'n save'. Den Mars Jeems ax' 'im how de darkies be'n behabin', en Mars Johnson say dey be'n behabin' good, most un 'em, en dem w'at did n' behabe good at fus' change dey conduc' atter he got holt un 'em a time er two.

" 'All,' sezee, ' 'cep'n' de noo nigger Mistah Dunkin fotch ober heah en lef' on trial, w'iles you wuz gone.'

"'Oh, yas,' 'lows Mars Jeems, 'tell me all 'bout dat noo nigger. I heared a little 'bout dat quare noo nigger las' night, en it wuz des too redik'lus. Tell me all 'bout dat noo nigger.'

"So seein' Mars Jeems so good-natchu'd 'bout it, Mars Johnson up en tol' 'im how he tied up de noo han' de fus' day en gun 'im fo'ty 'ca'se he would n' tell 'im 'is name.

"'Ha, ha, ha!' sez Mars Jeems, laffin' fit ter kill, 'but dat is too funny fer any use. Tell me some mo' 'bout dat noo nigger.'

"So Mars Johnson went on en tol' 'im how he had ter starbe de noo nigger 'fo' he could make 'im take holt er a hoe.

"'Dat wuz de beatinis' notion fer a nigger,' sez Mars Jeems, 'puttin' on airs, des lack he wuz a w'ite man! En I reckon you did n' do nuffin ter 'im?'

"'Oh, no, suh,' sez de oberseah, grinnin' lack a chessy-cat, 'I did n' do nuffin but take de hide off'n 'im.'

"Mars Jeems lafft en lafft, 'te it 'peared lack he wuz des gwine ter bu'st. 'Tell me some mo' 'bout dat noo nigger, oh, tell me some mo'. Dat noo nigger int'rusts me, he do, en dat is a fac'.'

"Mars Johnson did n' quite un'erstan' w'y Mars Jeems sh'd make sich a great 'miration 'bout de noo nigger, but co'se he want' ter please de gent'eman w'at hi'ed 'im, en so he 'splain' all 'bout how many times he had ter cowhide de noo nigger, en how he made 'im do tasks twicet ez big ez some er de yuther han's, en how he'd chain 'im up in de ba'n at night en feed 'im on co'n-bread en water.

"'Oh! but you is a monst'us good oberseah; you is de bes' oberseah in dis county, Mistah Johnson,' sez Mars Jeems, w'en de oberseah got th'oo wid his tale; 'en dey ain' nebber be'n no nigger-breaker lack you roun' heah befo'. En you desarbes great credit fer sendin' dat nigger 'way befo' you sp'ilt 'im fer de market. Fac', you is sech a monst'us good oberseah, en you is got dis yer plantation in sech fine shape, dat I reckon I doan need you no mo'. You is got dese yer darkies so well train' dat I 'spec' I kin run 'em myse'f fum dis time on. But I does wush you had 'a' hilt on ter dat noo nigger 'tel I got home, fer I'd 'a' lack ter 'a' seed 'im, I su't'nly should.'

"De oberseah wuz so 'stonish' he did n' ha'dly know w'at ter say, but fin'lly he ax' Mars Jeems ef he would n' gib 'im a ric-commen' fer ter git ernudder place.

"'No, suh,' sez Mars Jeems, 'somehow er'nuther I doan lack yo' looks sence I come back dis time, en I'd much ruther you would n' stay roun' heah. Fac', I's feared ef I'd meet you alone in de woods some time, I mought wanter ha'm you. But layin' dat aside, I be'n lookin' ober dese yer books er yo'n w'at you kep' w'iles I wuz 'way, en fer a yeah er so back, en dere's some figgers w'at ain' des cl'ar ter me. I ain' got no time fer ter talk 'bout 'em now, but I 'spec' befo' I settles wid you fer dis las' mount', you better come up heah ter-morrer, atter I's look' de books en 'counts ober some mo', en den we'll straighten ou' business all up.'

"Mars Jeems 'lowed atterwa'ds dat he wuz des shootin' in de da'k w'en he said dat 'bout de books, but howsomeber, Mars Nick Johnson lef' dat naberhood 'twix' de nex' two suns, en nobody roun' dere nebber seed hide ner hair un 'im sence. En all de darkies t'ank de Lawd, en 'lowed it wuz a good riddance er bad rubbage.

"But all dem things I done tol' you ain' nuffin 'side'n de change w'at come ober Mars Jeems fum dat time on. Aun' Peggy's goopher had made a noo man un 'im enti'ely. De nex' day atter he come back, he tol' de han's dey neenter wuk on'y fum sun ter sun, en he cut dey tasks down so dey did n' nobody hab ter stan' ober 'em wid a rawhide er a hick'ry. En he 'lowed ef de niggers want ter hab a dance in de big ba'n any Sad'day night, dey mought hab it. En bimeby w'en Solomon seed how good Mars Jeems wuz, he ax' 'im ef he would n' please sen' down ter de yuther plantation fer his junesey. Mars Jeems say su't'nly, en gun Solomon a pass en a note ter de oberseah on de yuther plantation, en sont Solomon down ter Robeson County wid a hoss en buggy fer ter fetch his junesey back. W'en de nig-gers see how fine Mars Jeems gwine treat 'em, dey all tuk ter sweethea'tin' en juneseyin' en singin' en dancin', en eight er ten couples got married, en bimeby eve'body 'mence' ter say Mars Jeems McLean got a finer plantation, en slicker-lookin' nig-gers, en dat he 'uz makin' mo' cotton en co'n, dan any yuther gent'eman in de county. En Mars Jeems's own junesey, Miss

Libbie, heared 'bout do noo gwines-on on Mars Jeems's plantation, en she change' her min' 'bout Mars Jeems en tuk 'im back ag'in, en 'fo' long dey had a fine weddin', en all de darkies had a feas', en dey wuz fiddlin' en dancin' en funnin' en frolic'in' fum sundown 'tel mawnin."

"And they all lived happy ever after," I said, as the old man reached a full stop.

"Yas, suh," he said interpreting my remarks as a question, "dey did. Solomon useter say," he added, "dat Aun' Peggy's goopher had turnt Mars Jeems ter a nigger, en dat dat noo han' wuz Mars Jeems hisse'f. But co'se Solomon did n' das' ter let on 'bout w'at he spicioned, en ole Aun' Peggy would 'a' 'nied it ef she had be'n ax', fer she 'd 'a' got in trouble sho', ef it 'uz knowed she'd be'n cunj'in' de w'ite folks.

"Dis yer tale goes ter show," concluded Julius sententiously, as the man came up and announced that the spring was ready for us to get water, "dat w'ite folks w'at is so ha'd en stric', en doan make no 'lowance fer po' ign'ant niggers w'at ain' had no chanst ter l'arn, is li'ble ter hab bad dreams, ter say de leas', en dat dem w'at is kin' en good ter po' people is sho' ter prosper en git 'long in de worl'."

"That is a very strange story, Uncle Julius," observed my wife, smiling, "and Solomon's explanation is quite improbable."

"Yes, Julius," said I, "that was powerful goopher. I am glad, too, that you told us the moral of the story; it might have escaped us otherwise. By the way, did you make that up all by yourself?"

The old man's face assumed an injured look, expressive more of sorrow than of anger, and shaking his head he replied:—

"No, suh, I heared dat tale befo' you er Mis' Annie dere wuz bawn, suh. My mammy tol' me dat tale w'en I wa'n't mo' d'n knee-high ter a hopper-grass."

I drove to town next morning, on some business, and did not return until noon; and after dinner I had to visit a neighbor, and did not get back until supper-time. I was smoking a cigar on the back piazza in the early evening, when I saw a familiar figure carrying a bucket of water to the barn. I called my wife.

"My dear," I said severely, "what is that rascal doing here? I thought I discharged him yesterday for good and all."

"Oh, yes," she answered, "I forgot to tell you. He was hanging round the place all morning, and looking so down in the mouth, that I told him that if he would try to do better, we would give him one more chance. He seems so grateful, and so really in earnest in his promises of amendment, that I'm sure you'll not regret taking him back."

I was seriously enough annoyed to let my cigar go out. I did not share my wife's rose-colored hopes in regard to Tom; but as I did not wish the servants to think there was any conflict of authority in the household, I let the boy stay.

SIS' BECKY'S
PICKANINNY

We had not lived in North Carolina very long before I was able to note a marked improvement in my wife's health. The ozone-laden air of the surrounding piney woods, the mild and equable climate, the peaceful leisure of country life, had brought about in hopeful measure the cure we had anticipated. Toward the end of our second year, however, her ailment took an unexpected turn for the worse. She became the victim of a settled melancholy attended with vague forebodings of impending misfortune.

"You must keep up her spirits," said our physician, the best in the neighboring town. "This melancholy lowers her tone too much, tends to lessen her strength, and, if it continues too long, may be fraught with grave consequences."

I tried various expedients to cheer her up. I read novels to her. I had the hands on the place come up in the evening and serenade her with plantation songs. Friends came in sometimes and talked, and frequent letters from the North kept her in touch with her former home. But nothing seemed to rouse her from the depression into which she had fallen.

One pleasant afternoon in spring, I placed an armchair in a shaded portion of the front piazza, and filling it with pillows led my wife out of the house and seated her where she would have the pleasantest view of a somewhat monotonous scenery. She was scarcely placed when old Julius came through the yard, and, taking off his tattered straw hat, inquired, somewhat anxiously:—

"How is you feelin' dis afternoon, ma'm?"

"She is not very cheerful, Julius," I said. My wife was apparently without energy enough to speak for herself.

The old man did not seem inclined to go away, so I asked him to sit down. I had noticed, as he came up, that he held some small object in his hand. When he had taken his seat on the top step, he kept fingering this object,—what it was I could not quite make out.

"What is that you have there, Julius?" I asked, with mild curiosity.

"Dis is my rabbit foot, suh."

This was at a time before this curious superstition had attained its present jocular popularity among white people, and while I had heard of it before, it had not yet outgrown the charm of novelty.

"What do you do with it?"

"I kyars it wid me fer luck, suh."

"Julius," I observed, half to him and half to my wife, "your people will never rise in the world until they throw off these childish superstitions and learn to live by the light of reason and common sense. How absurd to imagine that the fore-foot of a poor dead rabbit, with which he timorously felt his way along through a life surrounded by snares and pitfalls, beset by enemies on every hand, can promote happiness or success, or ward off failure or misfortune!"

"It is ridiculous," assented my wife, with faint interest.

"Dat's w'at I tells dese niggers roun' heah," said Julius. "De fo'-foot ain' got no power. It has ter be de hin'-foot, suh,—de lef' hin'-foot er a grabe-ya'd rabbit, killt by a cross-eyed nigger on a da'k night in de full er de moon."

"They must be very rare and valuable," I said.

"Dey is kinder ska'ce, suh, en dey ain' no 'mount er money could buy mine, suh. I mought len' it ter anybody I sot sto' by, but I would n' sell it, no indeed, suh, I would n'."

"How do you know it brings good luck?" I asked.

"'Ca'se I ain' had no bad luck sence I had it, suh, en I 's had dis rabbit foot fer fo'ty yeahs. I had a good marster befo' de wah, en I wa'n't sol' erway, en I wuz sot free; en dat 'uz all good luck."

"But that does n't prove anything," I rejoined. "Many other people have gone through a similar experience, and probably more than one of them had no rabbit's foot."

"Law, suh! you doan hafter prove 'bout de rabbit foot! Eve'ybody knows dat; leas'ways eve'ybody roun' heah knows it. But ef it has ter be prove' ter folks w'at wa'n't bawn en raise' in dis naberhood, dey is a' easy way ter prove it. Is I eber tol' you de tale er Sis' Becky en her pickaninny?"

"No," I said, "let us hear it." I thought perhaps the story might interest my wife as much or more than the novel I had meant to read from.

"Dis yer Becky," Julius began, "useter b'long ter ole Kunnel Pen'leton, who owned a plantation down on de Wim'l'ton Road, 'bout ten miles fum heah, des befo' you gits ter Black Swamp. Dis yer Becky wuz a fiel-han', en a monst'us good 'un. She had a husban' oncet, a nigger w'at b'longed on de nex' plantation, but de man w'at owned her husban' died, en his lan' en his niggers had ter be sol' fer ter pay his debts. Kunnel Pen'leton 'lowed he 'd 'a' bought dis nigger, but he had be'n bettin' on hoss races, en did n' hab no money, en so Becky's husban' wuz sol' erway ter Fuhginny.

"Co'se Becky went on some 'bout losin' her man, but she could n' he'p herse'f; en 'sides dat, she had her pickaninny fer ter comfo't her. Dis yer little Mose wuz de cutes', blackes', shiny-eyedes' little nigger you eber laid eyes on, en he wuz ez fon' er his mammy ez his mammy wuz er him. Co'se Becky had ter wuk en did n' hab much time ter was'e wid her baby. Ole Aun' Nancy, de plantation nuss down at de qua'ters, useter take keer er little Mose in de daytime, en atter de niggers come in fum de cotton-fiel' Becky 'ud git her chile en kiss 'im en nuss 'im, en keep 'im 'tel mawnin'; en on Sundays she 'd hab 'im in her cabin wid her all day long.

"Sis' Becky had got sorter useter gittin' 'long widout her husban', w'en one day Kunnel Pen'leton went ter de races. Co'se w'en he went ter de races, he tuk his hosses, en co'se he bet on 'is own hosses, en co'se he los' his money; fer Kunnel Pen'leton did n' nebber hab no luck wid his hosses, ef he did keep hisse'f po' projeckin' wid 'em. But dis time dey wuz a hoss

name' Lightnin' Bug, w'at b'longed ter ernudder man, en dis
hoss won de sweep-stakes; en Kunnel Pen'leton tuk a lackin' ter
dat hoss, en ax' his owner w'at he wuz willin' ter take fer 'im.

"'I'll take a thousan' dollahs fer dat hoss,' sez dis yer man,
who had a big plantation down to'ds Wim'l'ton, whar he raise'
hosses fer ter race en ter sell.

"Well, Kunnel Pen'leton scratch' 'is head, en wonder whar
he wuz gwine ter raise a thousan' dollahs; en he did n' see des
how he could do it, fer he owed ez much ez he could borry
a'ready on de skyo'ity he could gib. But he wuz des boun' ter
hab dat hoss, so sezee:—

"'I'll gib you my note fer 'leven hun'ed dollahs fer dat hoss.'

"De yuther man shuck 'is head, en sezee:—

"'Yo' note, suh, is better'n gol', I doan doubt; but I is
made it a rule in my bizness not ter take no notes fum nobody.
Howsomeber, suh, ef you is kinder sho't er fun's, mos' lackly
we kin make some kin' er bahg'in. En w'iles we is talkin',
I mought is well say dat I needs ernudder good nigger down
on my place. Ef you is got a good one ter spar', I mought trade
wid you.'

"Now, Kunnel Pen'leton did n' r'ally hab no niggers fer ter
spar', but he 'lowed ter hisse'f he wuz des bleedzd ter hab dat
hoss, en so he sez, sezee:—

"'Well, I doan lack ter, but I reckon I'll haf ter. You come out
ter my plantation ter-morrer en look ober my niggers, en pick
out de one you wants.'

"So sho' 'nuff nex' day dis yer man come out ter Kunnel
Pen'leton's place en rid roun' de plantation en glanshed at de
niggers, en who sh'd he pick out fum 'em all but Sis' Becky.

"'I needs a noo nigger 'oman down ter my place,' sezee, 'fer
ter cook en wash, en so on; en dat young 'oman 'll des fill de
bill. You gimme her, en you kin hab Lightnin' Bug.'"

"Now, Kunnel Pen'leton did n' lack ter trade Sis' Becky,
'ca'se she wuz nigh 'bout de bes' fiel'-han' he had; en 'sides, Mars
Kunnel did n' keer ter take de mammies 'way fum dey chillun
w'iles de chillun wuz little. But dis man say he want Becky, er
e'se Kunnel Pen'leton could n' hab de race hoss.

"'Well,' sez de kunnel, 'you kin hab de 'oman. But I doan

lack ter sen' her 'way fum her baby. W'at 'll you gimme fer dat nigger baby?'

"'I doan want de baby,' sez de yuther man. 'I ain' got no use fer de baby.'

"'I tell yer w'at I 'll do,' 'lows Kunnel Pen'leton, 'I 'll th'ow dat pickaninny in fer good measure.'

"But de yuther man shuck his head. 'No,' sezee, 'I 's much erbleedzd, but I doan raise niggers; I raises hosses, en I doan wanter be both'rin' wid no nigger babies. Nemmine de baby. I'll keep dat 'oman so busy she'll fergit de baby; fer niggers is made ter wuk, en dey ain' got no time fer no sich foolis'ness ez babies.'

"Kunnel Pen'leton did n' wanter hu't Becky's feelin's,— fer Kunnel Pen'leton wuz a kin'-hea'ted man, en nebber lack' ter make no trouble fer nobody,—en so he tol' Becky he wuz gwine sen' her down ter Robeson County fer a day er so, ter he'p out his son-in-law in his wuk; en bein' ez dis yuther man wuz gwine dat way, he had ax' 'im ter take her 'long in his buggy.

"'Kin I kyar little Mose wid me, marster?' ax' Sis' Becky.

"'N-o,' sez de kunnel, ez ef he wuz studyin' whuther ter let her take 'im er no; 'I reckon you better let Aun' Nancy look at-ter yo' baby fer de day er two you 'll be gone, en she 'll see dat he gits ernuff ter eat 'tel you gits back.'

"So Sis' Becky hug' en kiss' little Mose, en tol' 'im ter be a good little pickaninny, en take keer er hisse'f, en not fergit his mammy w'iles she wuz gone. En little Mose put his arms roun' his mammy en lafft en crowed des lack it wuz monst'us fine fun fer his mammy ter go 'way en leabe 'im.

"Well, dis yer hoss trader sta'ted out wid Becky, en bimeby, atter dey 'd gone down de Lumbe'ton Road fer a few miles er so, dis man tu'nt roun' in a diffe'nt d'rection, en kep' goin' dat erway, 'tel bimeby Sis' Becky up 'n ax' 'im ef he wuz gwine ter Robeson County by a noo road.

"'No, nigger,' sezee, 'I ain' gwine ter Robeson County at all. I 's gwine ter Bladen County, whar my plantation is, en whar I raises all my hosses.'

" 'But how is I gwine ter git ter Mis' Laura's plantation down in Robeson County?' sez Becky, wid her hea't in her mouf, fer she 'mence' ter git skeered all er a sudden.

" 'You ain' gwine ter git dere at all,' sez de man. 'You b'longs ter me now, fer I done traded my bes' race hoss fer you, wid yo' ole marster. Ef you is a good gal, I'll treat you right, en ef you doan behabe yo'se'f,—w'y, w'at e'se happens 'll be yo' own fault.'

"Co'se Sis' Becky cried en went on 'bout her pickaninny, but co'se it did n' do no good, en bimeby dey got down ter dis yer man's place, en he put Sis' Becky ter wuk, en fergot all 'bout her habin' a pickaninny.

"Meanw'iles, w'en ebenin' come, de day Sis' Becky wuz tuk 'way, little Mose 'mence' ter git res'less, en bimeby, w'en his mammy did n' come, he sta'ted ter cry fer 'er. Aun' Nancy fed 'im en rocked 'im en rocked 'im, en fin'lly he des cried en cried 'tel he cried hisse'f ter sleep.

"De nex' day he did n' 'pear ter be as peart ez yushal, en w'en night come he fretted en went on wuss'n he did de night befo'. De nex' day his little eyes 'mence' ter lose dey shine, en he would n' eat nuffin, en he 'mence' ter look so peaked dat Aun' Nancy tuk 'n kyared 'im up ter de big house, en showed 'im ter her ole missis, en her ole missis gun her some med'cine fer 'im, en 'lowed ef he did n' git no better she sh'd fetch 'im up ter de big house ag'in, en dey 'd hab a doctor, en nuss little Mose up dere. Fer Aun' Nancy's ole missis 'lowed he wuz a lackly little nigger en wu'th raisin'.

"But Aun' Nancy had l'arn' ter lack little Mose, en she did n' wanter hab 'im tuk up ter de big house. En so w'en he did n' git no better, she gethered a mess er green peas, and tuk de peas en de baby, en went ter see ole Aun' Peggy, de cunjuh 'oman down by de Wim'l'ton Road. She gun Aun' Peggy de mess er peas, en tol' her all 'bout Sis' Becky en little Mose.

" 'Dat is a monst'us small mess er peas you is fotch' me,' sez Aun' Peggy, sez she.

" 'Yas, I knows,' 'lowed Aun' Nancy, 'but dis yere is a monst'us small pickaninny.'

" 'You'll hafter fetch me sump'n mo',' sez Aun' Peggy, 'fer you can't 'spec' me ter was'e my time diggin roots en wukkin' cunj'ation fer nuffin.'

" 'All right,' sez Aun' Nancy, 'I'll fetch you sump'n mo' nex' time.'

" 'You bettah,' sez Aun' Peggy, 'er e'se dey 'll be trouble. W'at dis yer little pickaninny needs is ter see his mammy. You leabe 'im heah 'tel ebenin' en I 'll show 'im his mammy.'

"So w'en Aun' Nancy had gone 'way, Aun' Peggy tuk 'n wukked her roots, en tu'nt little Mose ter a hummin'-bird, en sont 'im off fer ter fin' his mammy.

So little Mose flewed, en flewed, en flewed away, 'tel bimeby he got ter de place whar Sis' Becky b'longed. He seed his mammy wukkin' roun' de ya'd, en he could tell fum lookin' at her dat she wuz trouble' in her min' 'bout sump'n, en feelin' kin' er po'ly. Sis' Becky heared sump'in hummin' roun' en roun' her, sweet en low. Fus' she 'lowed it wuz a hummin'-bird; den she thought it sounded lack her little Mose croonin' on her breas' way back yander on de ole plantation. En she des 'mag-ine' it wuz her little Mose, en it made her feel bettah, en she went on 'bout her wuk pearter 'n she 'd done since she 'd be'n down dere. Little Mose stayed roun' 'tel late in de ebenin', en den flewed back ez hard ez he could ter Aun' Peggy. Ez fer Sis' Becky, she dremp all dat night dat she wuz holdin' her pick-aninny in her arms, en kissin' him, en nussin' him, des lack she useter do back on de ole plantation whar he wuz bawn. En fer th'ee er fo' days Sis' Becky went 'bout her wuk wid mo' sperrit dan she'd showed since she 'd be'n down dere ter dis man's plantation.

"De nex' day atter he comes back, little Mose wuz mo' pearter en better 'n he had be'n fer a long time. But to'ds de een' er de week he 'mence' ter git res'less ag'in, en stop' eatin', en Aun' Nancy kyared 'im down ter Aun' Peggy once mo', en she tu'nt 'im ter a mawkin'-bird dis time, en sont 'im off ter see his mammy ag'in.

"It did n' take him long fer ter git dere, en w'en he did, he seed his mammy standin' in de kitchen, lookin' back in de d'rection little Mose wuz comin' fum. End dey wuz tears in her

eyes, en she look' mo' po'ly en peaked 'n she had w'en he
wuz down dere befo'. So little Mose sot on a tree in de ya'd en
sung, en sung, en sung, des fittin' ter split his th'oat. Fus' Sis'
Becky did n' notice 'im much, but dis mawkin'-bird kep' stayin'
roun' de house all day, en bimeby Sis' Becky des 'magine' dat
mawkin'-bird wuz her little Mose crowin' en crowin', des lack
he useter do w'en his mammy would come home at night fum
de cotton-fiel'. De mawkin'-bird stayed roun' dere 'mos' all
day, en w'en Sis' Becky went out in de ya'd one time, dis yer
mawkin'-bird lit on her shoulder en peck' at de piece er bread
she wuz eatin', en fluttered his wings so dey rub' up agin de side
er her head. En w'en he flewed away 'long late in de ebenin',
des 'fo' sundown, Sis' Becky felt mo' better 'n she had sence she
had heared dat hummin'-bird a week er so pas'. En dat night
she dremp 'bout ole times ag'in, des lack she did befo'.

"But dis yer totin' little Mose down ter ole Aun' Peggy, en dis
yer gittin' things fer ter pay de cunjuh 'oman, use' up a lot er
Aun' Nancy's time, en she begun ter git kinder ti'ed. 'Sides dat,
w'en Sis' Becky had be'n on de plantation, she had useter he'p
Aun' Nancy wid de young uns ebenin's en Sundays; en Aun'
Nancy 'mence' ter miss 'er monst'us, 'speshly sence she got a
tech er de rheumatiz herse'f, en so she 'lows ter ole Aun' Peggy
one day:—

"'Aun' Peggy, ain' dey no way you kin fetch Sis' Becky back
home?'

"'Huh!' sez Aun' Peggy, 'I dunno 'bout dat. I 'll hafter wuk
my roots en fin' out whuther I kin er no. But it 'll take a monst'us heap er wuk, en I can't was'e my time fer nuffin. Ef you
'll fetch me sump'n ter pay me fer my trouble, I reckon we kin
fix it.'

"So nex' day Aun' Nancy went down ter see Aun' Peggy
ag'in.

"'Aun' Peggy,' sez she, 'I is fotch' you my bes' Sunday head-
hankercher. Will dat do?'

"Aun' Peggy look' at de head-hankercher, en run her han'
ober it, en sez she:—

"'Yas, dat 'll do fus'-rate. I's be'n wukkin' my roots sence
you be'n gone, en I 'lows mos' lackly I kin git Sis' Becky back,

but it 's gwine take fig'rin' en studyin' ez well ez cunj'in'. De fus' thing ter do 'll be ter stop fetchin' dat pickaninny down heah, en not sen' 'im ter see his mammy no mo.' Ef he gits too po'ly, you lemme know, en I'll gib you some kin' er mixtry fer ter make 'im fergit Sis' Becky fer a week er so. So 'less'n you comes fer dat, you neenter come back ter see me no mo' 'tel I sen's fer you.'

"So Aun' Peggy sont Aun' Nancy erway, en de fus' thing she done wuz ter call a hawnet fum a nes' unner her eaves.

"'You go up ter Kunnel Pen'leton's stable, hawnet,' sez she, 'en sting de knees er de race hoss name' Lightnin' Bug. Be sho' en git de right one.'

"So de hawnet flewed up ter Kunnel Pen'leton's stable en stung Lightnin' Bug roun' de laigs, en de nex' mawnin' Lightnin' Bug's knees wuz all swoll' up, twice't ez big ez dey oughter be. W'en Kunnel Pen'leton went out ter de stable en see de hoss's laigs, hit would 'a' des made you trimble lack a leaf fer ter heah him cuss dat hoss trader. Howsomeber, he cool' off bimeby en tol' de stable boy fer ter rub Lightnin' Bug's laigs wid some linimum. De boy done ez his marster tol' 'im, en by de nex' day de swellin' had gone down consid'able. Aun' Peggy had sont a sparrer, w'at had a nes' in one er de trees close ter her cabin, fer ter watch w'at wuz gwine on 'roun' de big house, en w'en dis yer sparrer tol' 'er de hoss wuz gittin' ober de swellin', she sont de hawnet back fer ter sting 'is knees some mo', en de nex' mawnin' Lightnin' Bug's laigs wuz swoll' up wuss 'n befo'.

"Well, dis time Kunnel Pen'leton wuz mad th'oo en th'oo, en all de way 'roun', en he cusst dat hoss trader up en down, fum A ter *Izzard*. He cusst so ha'd dat de stable boy got mos' skeered ter def, en went off en hid hisse'f in de hay.

"Ez fer Kunnel Pen'leton, he went right up ter de house en got out his pen en ink, en tuk off his coat en roll' up his sleeves, en writ a letter ter dis yer hoss trader, en sezee:—

"'You is sol' me a hoss w'at is got a ringbone er a spavin er sump'n, en w'at I paid you fer wuz a soun' hoss. I wants you ter sen' my nigger 'oman back en take yo' ole hoss, er e'se I 'll sue you, sho 's you bawn.'

"But dis yer man wa'n't skeered a bit, en he writ back ter

Kunnel Pen'leton dat a bahg'in wuz a bahg'in; dat Lightnin'
Bug wuz soun' w'en he sol' 'im, en ef Kunnel Pen'leton did n'
knowed ernuff 'bout hosses ter take keer er a fine racer, dat
wuz his own fune'al. En he say Kunnel Pen'leton kin sue en be
cusst fer all he keer, but he ain' gwine ter gib up de nigger he
bought en paid fer.

"W'en Kunnel Pen'leton got dis letter he wuz madder 'n he
wuz befo', 'speshly 'ca'se dis man 'lowed he did n' know how
ter take keer er fine hosses. But he could n' do nuffin but fetch
a lawsuit, en he knowed, by his own 'spe'ience, dat lawsuits
wuz slow ez de seben-yeah eetch en cos' mo' d'n dey come ter,
en he 'lowed he better go slow en wait awhile.

"Aun' Peggy knowed w'at wuz gwine on all dis time, en she
fix' up a little bag wid some roots en one thing en ernudder in
it, en gun it ter dis sparrer er her'n, en tol' 'im ter take it 'way
down yander whar Sis' Becky wuz, en drap it right befo' de do'
er her cabin, so she 'd be sho' en fin' it de fus' time she come
out'n de do'.

"One night Sis' Becky dremp' her pickaninny wuz dead, en
de nex' day she wuz mo'nin' en groanin' all day. She dremp' de
same dream th'ee nights runnin', en den, de nex' mawnin' atter
de las' night, she foun' dis yer little bag de sparrer had drap' in
front her do'; en she 'lowed she'd be'n cunju'd, en wuz gwine
ter die, en ez long ez her pickaninny wuz dead dey wa'n't no
use tryin' ter do nuffin nowhow. En so she tuk 'n went ter bed,
en tol' her marster she 'd be'n conju'd en wuz gwine ter die.

"Her marster lafft at her, en argyed wid her, en tried ter
'suade her out'n dis yer fool notion, ez he called it,—fer he wuz
one er dese yer w'ite folks w'at purten' dey doan b'liebe in cun-
j'in',—but hit wa'n't no use. Sis' Becky kep' gittin' wusser en
wusser, 'tel fin'lly dis yer man 'lowed Sis' Becky wuz gwine ter
die, sho' 'nuff. En ez he knowed dey had n' be'n nuffin de matter wid Lightnin' Bug w'en he traded 'im, he 'lowed mebbe he
could kyo' 'im en fetch 'im roun' all right, leas'ways good 'nuff
ter sell ag'in. En anyhow, a lame hoss wuz better 'n a dead nigger. So he sot down en writ Kunnel Pen'leton a letter.

"'My conscience,' sezee, 'has be'n troublin' me 'bout dat
ringbone' hoss I sol' you. Some folks 'lows a hoss trader ain'

got no conscience, but dey doan know me, fer dat is my weak spot en de reason I ain' made no mo' money hoss tradin'. Fac' is,' sezee, 'I is got so I can't sleep nights fum studyin' 'bout dat spavin' hoss; en I is made up my min' dat, w'iles a bahg'in is a bahg'in, en you seed Lightnin' Bug befo' you traded fer 'im, principle is wuth mo' d'n money er hosses er niggers. So ef you 'll sen' Lightnin' Bug down heah, I'll sen' yo' nigger 'oman back, en we 'll call de trade off, en be ez good frien's ez we eber wuz, en no ha'd feelin's.'

"So sho' 'nuff, Kunnel Pen'leton sont de hoss back. En w'en de man w'at come ter bring Lightnin' Bug tol' Sis' Becky her pickaninny wa'n't dead, Sis' Becky wuz so glad dat she 'lowed she wuz gwine ter try ter lib 'tel she got back whar she could see little Mose once mo'. En w'en she retch' de ole plantation en seed her baby kickin' en crowin' en holdin' out his little arms to'ds her, she wush' she was n' cunju'd en did n' hafter die. En w'en Aun' Nancy tol' 'er all 'bout Aun' Peggy, Sis' Becky went down ter see de cunjuh 'oman, en Aun' Peggy tol' her she had cunju'd her. En den Aun' Peggy tuk de goopher off'n her, en she got well, en stayed on de plantation, en raise' her pickaninny. En w'en little Mose growed up, he could sing en whistle des lack a mawkin'bird, so dat de w'ite folks useter hab 'im come up ter de big house at night, en whistle en sing fer 'em, en dey useter gib 'im money en vittles en one thing er ernudder, w'ich he alluz tuk home ter his mammy; fer he knowed all 'bout w'at she had gone th'oo. He tu'nt out ter be a sma't man, en l'arnt de blacksmif trade; en Kunnel Pen'leton let 'im hire his time. En bimeby he bought his mammy en sot her free, en den he bought hisse'f, en tuk keer er Sis' Becky ez long ez dey bofe libbed."

My wife had listened to this story with greater interest than she had manifested in any subject for several days. I had watched her furtively from time to time during the recital, and had observed the play of her countenance. It had expressed in turn sympathy, indignation, pity, and at the end lively satisfaction.

"That is a very ingenious fairy tale, Julius," I said, "and we are much obliged to you."

"Why, John!" said my wife severely, "the story bears the stamp of truth, if ever a story did."

"Yes," I replied, "especially the humming-bird episode, and the mocking-bird digression, to say nothing of the doings of the hornet and the sparrow."

"Oh, well, I don't care," she rejoined, with delightful animation; "those are mere ornamental details and not at all essential. The story is true to nature, and might have happened half a hundred times, and no doubt did happen, in those horrid days before the war."

"By the way, Julius," I remarked, "your story does n't establish what you started out to prove,—that a rabbit's foot brings good luck."

"Hit's plain 'nuff ter me, suh," replied Julius. "I bet young missis dere kin 'splain it herse'f."

"I rather suspect," replied my wife promptly, "that Sis' Becky had no rabbit's foot."

"You is hit de bull's-eye de fus' fire, ma'm," assented Julius. "Ef Sis' Becky had had a rabbit foot, she nebber would 'a' went th'oo all dis trouble."

I went into the house for some purpose, and left Julius talking to my wife. When I came back a moment later, he was gone.

My wife's condition took a turn for the better from this very day, and she was soon on the way to ultimate recovery. Several weeks later, after she had resumed her afternoon drives, which had been interrupted by her illness, Julius brought the rockaway round to the front door one day, and I assisted my wife into the carriage.

"John," she said, before I had taken my seat, "I wish you would look in my room, and bring me my handkerchief. You will find it in the pocket of my blue dress."

I went to execute the commission. When I pulled the handkerchief out of her pocket, something else came with it and fell on the floor. I picked up the object and looked at it. It was Julius's rabbit's foot.

THE WIFE OF HIS YOUTH

I

Mr. Ryder was going to give a ball. There were several reasons why this was an opportune time for such an event.

Mr. Ryder might aptly be called the dean of the Blue Veins. The original Blue Veins were a little society of colored persons organized in a certain Northern city shortly after the war. Its purpose was to establish and maintain correct social standards among a people whose social condition presented almost un-limited room for improvement. By accident, combined perhaps with some natural affinity, the society consisted of individuals who were, generally speaking, more white than black. Some envious outsider made the suggestion that no one was eligible for membership who was not white enough to show blue veins. The suggestion was readily adopted by those who were not of the favored few, and since that time the society, though pos-sessing a longer and more pretentious name, had been known far and wide as the "Blue Vein Society," and its members as the "Blue Veins."

The Blue Veins did not allow that any such requirement ex-isted for admission to their circle, but, on the contrary, declared that character and culture were the only things considered; and that if most of their members were light-colored, it was because such persons, as a rule, had had better opportunities to qual-ify themselves for membership. Opinions differed, too, as to the usefulness of the society. There were those who had been known to assail it violently as a glaring example of the very prejudice from which the colored race had suffered most; and later, when such critics had succeeded in getting on the inside, they had been heard to maintain with zeal and earnestness that the society was a lifeboat, an anchor, a bulwark and a shield,— a pillar of cloud by day and of fire by night, to guide their people through the social wilderness. Another alleged prerequisite for Blue Vein membership was that of free birth; and while there was really no such requirement, it is doubtless true that very few of the members would have been unable to meet it if there had been. If there were one or two of the older members who had come up from the South and from slavery, their history presented enough romantic circumstances to rob their servile origin of its grosser aspects.

While there were no such tests of eligibility, it is true that the Blue Veins had their notions on these subjects, and that not all of them were equally liberal in regard to the things they collectively disclaimed. Mr. Ryder was one of the most conservative. Though he had not been among the founders of the society, but had come in some years later, his genius for social leadership was such that he had speedily become its recognized adviser and head, the custodian of its standards, and the preserver of its traditions. He shaped its social policy, was active in providing for its entertainment, and when the interest fell off, as it sometimes did, he fanned the embers until they burst again into a cheerful flame.

There were still other reasons for his popularity. While he was not as white as some of the Blue Veins, his appearance was such as to confer distinction upon them. His features were of a refined type, his hair was almost straight; he was always neatly dressed; his manners were irreproachable, and his morals above suspicion. He had come to Groveland a young man, and obtaining employment in the office of a railroad company as messenger had in time worked himself up to the position of stationery clerk, having charge of the distribution of the office supplies for the whole company. Although the lack of early training had hindered the orderly development of a naturally fine mind, it had not prevented him from doing a great deal of reading or from forming decidedly literary tastes. Poetry was his passion. He could repeat whole pages of the great English poets; and if his pronunciation was sometimes faulty, his eye, his voice, his gestures, would respond to the changing sentiment with a precision that revealed a poetic soul and disarmed criticism. He was economical, and had saved money; he owned and occupied a very comfortable house on a respectable street. His residence was handsomely furnished, containing among other things a good library, especially rich in poetry, a piano, and some choice engravings. He generally shared his house with some young couple, who looked after his wants and were company for him; for Mr. Ryder was a single man. In the early days of his connection with the Blue Veins he had been regarded as quite a catch, and young ladies and their mothers had manœuvred with much ingenuity to capture him. Not, however, until Mrs. Molly Dixon visited Groveland had any woman ever made him wish to change his condition to that of a married man.

Mrs. Dixon had come to Groveland from Washington in the spring, and before the summer was over she had won Mr. Ryder's heart. She possessed many attractive qualities. She was much younger than he; in fact, he was old enough to have been her father, though no one knew exactly how old he was. She was whiter than he, and better educated. She had moved in the best colored society of the country, at Washington, and had taught in the schools of that city. Such a superior person had been eagerly welcomed to the Blue Vein Society, and had taken a leading part in its activities. Mr. Ryder had at first been attracted by her charms of person, for she was very good looking and not over twenty-five; then by her refined manners and the vivacity of her wit. Her husband had been a government clerk, and at his death had left a considerable life insurance. She was visiting friends in Groveland, and, finding the town and the people to her liking, had prolonged her stay indefinitely. She had not seemed displeased at Mr. Ryder's attentions, but on the contrary had given him every proper encouragement; indeed, a younger and less cautious man would long since have spoken. But he had made up his mind, and had only to determine the time when he would ask her to be his wife. He decided to give a ball in her honor, and at some time during the evening of the ball to offer her his heart and hand. He had no special fears about the outcome, but, with a little touch of romance, he wanted the surroundings to be in harmony with his own feelings when he should have received the answer he expected.

Mr. Ryder resolved that this ball should mark an epoch in the social history of Groveland. He knew, of course,—no one could know better,—the entertainments that had taken place in past years, and what must be done to surpass them. His ball must be worthy of the lady in whose honor it was to be given, and must, by the quality of its guests, set an example for the future. He had observed of late a growing liberality, almost a laxity, in social matters, even among members of his own set, and had several times been forced to meet in a social way persons whose complexions and callings in life were hardly up to the standard which he considered proper for the society to maintain. He had a theory of his own.

"I have no race prejudice," he would say, "but we people of mixed blood are ground between the upper and the nether millstone. Our fate lies between absorption by the white race and extinction in the black. The one does n't want us, but may take us in time. The other would welcome us, but it would be for us a backward step. 'With malice towards none, with charity for all,' we must do the best we can for ourselves and those who are to follow us. Self-preservation is the first law of nature."

His ball would serve by its exclusiveness to counteract leveling tendencies, and his marriage with Mrs. Dixon would help to further the upward process of absorption he had been wishing and waiting for.

II

The ball was to take place on Friday night. The house had been put in order, the carpets covered with canvas, the halls and stairs decorated with palms and potted plants; and in the afternoon Mr. Ryder sat on his front porch, which the shade of a vine running up over a wire netting made a cool and pleasant lounging place. He expected to respond to the toast "The

Ladies" at the supper, and from a volume of Tennyson—his favorite poet—was fortifying himself with apt quotations. The volume was open at "A Dream of Fair Women." His eyes fell on these lines, and he read them aloud to judge better of their effect:—

> "At length I saw a lady within call,
>   Stiller than chisell'd marble, standing there;
> A daughter of the gods, divinely tall
> And most divinely fair."

He marked the verse, and turning the page read the stanza beginning,—

> "O sweet pale Margaret,
>   O rare pale Margaret."

He weighed the passage a moment, and decided that it would not do. Mrs. Dixon was the palest lady he expected at the ball, and she was of a rather ruddy complexion, and of lively disposition and buxom build. So he ran over the leaves until his eyes rested on the description of Queen Guinevere:—

> "She seem'd a part of joyous Spring:
>   A gown of grass-green silk she wore,
>   Buckled with golden clasps before;
> A light-green tuft of plumes she bore
>   Closed in a golden ring.

> "She look'd so lovely, as she sway'd
>   The rein with dainty finger-tips,
> A man had given all other bliss,
> And all his worldly worth for this,
> To waste his whole heart in one kiss
>   Upon her perfect lips."

As Mr. Ryder murmured these words audibly, with an appreciative thrill, he heard the latch of his gate click, and a light footfall sounding on the steps. He turned his head, and saw a woman standing before his door.

She was a little woman, not five feet tall, and proportioned to her height. Although she stood erect, and looked around her with very bright and restless eyes, she seemed quite old; for her face was crossed and re-crossed with a hundred wrinkles, and around the edges of her bonnet could be seen protruding here and there a tuft of short gray wool. She wore a blue calico gown of ancient cut, a little red shawl fastened around her shoulders with an old-fashioned brass brooch, and a large bonnet profusely ornamented with faded red and yellow artificial flowers. And she was very black,—so black that her toothless gums, revealed when she opened her mouth to speak, were not red, but blue. She looked like a bit of the old plantation life, summoned up from the past by the wave of a magician's wand, as the poet's fancy had called into being the gracious shapes of which Mr. Ryder had just been reading.

He rose from his chair and came over to where she stood.

"Good-afternoon, madam," he said.

"Good-evenin', suh," she answered, ducking suddenly with a quaint curtsy. Her voice was shrill and piping, but softened somewhat by age. "Is dis yere whar Mistuh Ryduh lib, suh?" she asked, looking around her doubtfully, and glancing into the open windows, through which some of the preparations for the evening were visible.

"Yes," he replied, with an air of kindly patronage, unconsciously flattered by her manner, "I am Mr. Ryder. Did you want to see me?"

"Yas, suh, ef I ain't 'sturbin' of you too much."

"Not at all. Have a seat over here behind the vine, where it is cool. What can I do for you?"

"'Scuse me, suh," she continued, when she had sat down on the edge of a chair, "'scuse me, suh, I's lookin' for my husban'. I heerd you wuz a big man an' had libbed heah a long time, an' I 'lowed you would n't min' ef I'd come roun' an' ax you ef you'd ever heerd of a merlatter man by de name er Sam Taylor 'quirin' roun' in de chu'ches ermongs' de people fer his wife 'Liza Jane?"

Mr. Ryder seemed to think for a moment.

"There used to be many such cases right after the war," he said, "but it has been so long that I have forgotten them. There are very few now. But tell me your story, and it may refresh my memory."

She sat back farther in her chair so as to be more comfortable, and folded her withered hands in her lap.

"My name's 'Liza," she began, "'Liza Jane. W'en I wuz young I us'ter b'long ter Marse Bob Smif, down in ole Missoura. I wuz bawn down dere. W'en I wuz a gal I wuz married ter a man named Jim. But Jim died, an' after dat I married a merlatter man named Sam Taylor. Sam wuz free-bawn, but his mammy and daddy died, an' de w'ite folks 'prenticed him ter my marster fer ter work fer 'im 'tel he wuz growed up. Sam worked in de fiel', an' I wuz de cook. One day Ma'y Ann, old miss's maid, came rushin' out ter de kitchen, an' says she, "'Liza Jane, old marse gwine sell yo' Sam down de ribber.'

"'Go way f'm yere,' says I; 'my husban's free!'

"'Don' make no diff'ence. I heerd ole marse tell ole miss he wuz gwine take yo' Sam 'way wid 'im ter-morrow, fer he needed money, an' he knowed whar he could get a t'ousan' dollars for Sam an' no questions axed.'

"W'en Sam come home f'm de fiel' dat night, I tole him 'bout ole marse gwine steal 'im, an' Sam run erway. His time wuz mo's up, an' he swo' dat w'en he wuz twenty-one he would come back an' he'p me run erway, er else save up de money ter buy my freedom. An' I know he'd 'a' done it, fer he thought a heap er me, Sam did. But w'en he come back he did n' fin' me, fer I wuz n' dere. Ole marse had heerd dat I warned Sam, so he had me whip' an' sol' down de ribber.

"Den de wah broke out, an' w'en it wuz ober de cullud folks wuz scattered. I went back ter de ole home; but Sam wuz n' dere, an' I could n' l'arn nuffin' 'bout 'im. But I knowed he 'd be'n dere to look fer me an' had n' foun' me, an' had gone erway ter hunt fer me.

"I's be'n lookin' fer 'im eber sence," she added simply, as though twenty-five years were but a couple of weeks, "an' I knows he's be'n lookin' fer me. Fer he sot a heap er sto' by me, Sam did, an' I know he's be'n huntin' fer me all dese years,—

'less'n he's be'n sick er sump'n, so he could n' work, er out'n his head, so he could n' 'member his promise. I went back down de ribber, fer I 'lowed he'd gone down dere lookin' fer me. I's be'n ter Noo Orleens, an' Atlanty, an' Charleston, an' Richmon'; an' w'en I'd be'n all ober de Souf I come ter de Norf. Fer I knows I'll fin' 'im some er dese days," she added softly, "er he 'll fin' me, an' den we 'll bofe be as happy in freedom as we wuz in de ole days befo' de wah." A smile stole over her withered countenance as she paused a moment, and her bright eyes softened into a faraway look.

This was the substance of the old woman's story. She had wandered a little here and there. Mr. Ryder was looking at her curiously when she finished.

"How have you lived all these years?" he asked.

"Cookin', suh. I's a good cook. Does you know anybody w'at needs a good cook, suh? I's stoppin' wid a cullud fam'ly roun' de corner yonder 'tel I kin git a place."

"Do you really expect to find your husband? He may be dead long ago."

She shook her head emphatically. "Oh no, he ain' dead. De signs an' de tokens tells me. I dremp three nights runnin' on'y dis las' week dat I foun' him."

"He may have married another woman. Your slave marriage would not have prevented him, for you never lived with him after the war, and without that your marriage does n't count."

"Would n' make no diff'ence wid Sam. He would n' marry no yuther 'oman 'tel he foun' out 'bout me. I knows it," she added. "Sump'n 's be'n tellin' me all dese years dat I's gwine fin' Sam 'fo' I dies."

"Perhaps he's outgrown you, and climbed up in the world where he would n't care to have you find him."

"No, indeed, suh," she replied, "Sam ain' dat kin' er man. He wuz good ter me, Sam wuz, but he wuz n' much good ter nobody e'se, fer he wuz one er de triflin'es' han's on de plantation. I 'spec's ter haf ter suppo't 'im w'en I fin' 'im, fer he nebber would work 'less'n he had ter. But den he wuz free, an' he did n' git no pay fer his work, an' I don' blame 'im much. Mebbe he's done better sence he run erway, but I ain' 'spectin' much."

"You may have passed him on the street a hundred times during the twenty-five years, and not have known him; time works great changes."

She smiled incredulously. "I'd know 'im 'mongs' a hund'ed men. Fer dey wuz n' no yuther merlatter man like my man Sam, an' I could n' be mistook. I 's toted his picture roun' wid me twenty-five years."

"May I see it?" asked Mr. Ryder. "It might help me to remember whether I have seen the original."

As she drew a small parcel from her bosom he saw that it was fastened to a string that went around her neck. Removing several wrappers, she brought to light an old-fashioned daguerreotype in a black case. He looked long and intently at the portrait. It was faded with time, but the features were still distinct, and it was easy to see what manner of man it had represented.

He closed the case, and with a slow movement handed it back to her.

"I don't know of any man in town who goes by that name," he said, "nor have I heard of any one making such inquiries. But if you will leave me your address, I will give the matter some attention, and if I find out anything I will let you know."

She gave him the number of a house in the neighborhood, and went away, after thanking him warmly.

He wrote the address on the fly-leaf of the volume of Tennyson, and, when she had gone, rose to his feet and stood looking after her curiously. As she walked down the street with mincing step, he saw several persons whom she passed turn and look back at her with a smile of kindly amusement. When she had turned the corner, he went upstairs to his bedroom, and stood for a long time before the mirror of his dressing-case, gazing thoughtfully at the reflection of his own face.

III

At eight o'clock the ballroom was a blaze of light and the guests had begun to assemble; for there was a literary programme and some routine business of the society to be gone through with before the dancing. A black servant in evening dress waited at the door and directed the guests to the dressing-rooms.

The occasion was long and memorable among the colored people of the city; not alone for the dress and display, but for the high average of intelligence and culture that distinguished the gathering as a whole. There were a number of school-teachers, several young doctors, three or four lawyers, some professional singers, an editor, a lieutenant in the United States army spending his furlough in the city, and others in various polite callings; these were colored, though most of them would not have attracted even a casual glance because of any marked difference from white people. Most of the ladies were in evening costume, and dress coats and dancing pumps were the rule among the men. A band of string music, stationed in an alcove behind a row of palms, played popular airs while the guests were gathering.

The dancing began at half past nine. At eleven o'clock supper was served. Mr. Ryder had left the ballroom some little time before the intermission, but reappeared at the supper-table. The spread was worthy of the occasion, and the guests did full justice to it. When the coffee had been served, the toast-master, Mr. Solomon Sadler, rapped for order. He made a brief introductory speech, complimenting host and guests, and then presented in their order the toasts of the evening. They were responded to with a very fair display of after-dinner wit.

"The last toast," said the toast-master, when he reached the end of the list, "is one which must appeal to us all. There is no one of us of the sterner sex who is not at some time dependent upon woman,—in infancy for protection, in manhood for companionship, in old age for care and comforting. Our good host has been trying to live alone, but the fair faces I see around me to-night prove that he too is largely dependent upon the gentler sex for most that makes life worth living,—the society and love of friends,—and rumor is at fault if he does not soon yield entire subjection to one of them. Mr. Ryder will now respond to the toast,—The Ladies."

There was a pensive look in Mr. Ryder's eyes as he took the floor and adjusted his eyeglasses. He began by speaking of woman as the gift of Heaven to man, and after some general observations on the relations of the sexes he said: "But perhaps the quality which most distinguishes woman is her fidelity and devotion to those she loves. History is full of examples, but has recorded none more striking than one which only to-day came under my notice."

He then related, simply but effectively, the story told by his visitor of the afternoon. He gave it in the same soft dialect, which came readily to his lips, while the company listened attentively and sympathetically. For the story had awakened a responsive thrill in many hearts. There were some present who had seen, and others who had heard their fathers and grandfathers tell, the wrongs and sufferings of this past generation, and all of them still felt, in their darker moments, the shadow hanging over them. Mr. Ryder went on:—

"Such devotion and confidence are rare even among women. There are many who would have searched a year, some who would have waited five years, a few who might have hoped ten years; but for twenty-five years this woman has retained her affection for and her faith in a man she has not seen or heard of in all that time.

"She came to me to-day in the hope that I might be able to help her find this long-lost husband. And when she was gone I gave my fancy rein, and imagined a case I will put to you.

"Suppose that this husband, soon after his escape, had learned that his wife had been sold away, and that such inquiries as he could make brought no information of her whereabouts. Suppose that he was young, and she much older than he; that he was light, and she was black; that their marriage was a slave marriage, and legally binding only if they chose to make it so after the war. Suppose, too, that he made his way to the North, as some of us have done, and there, where he had larger opportunities, had improved them, and had in the course of all these years grown to be as different from the ignorant boy who ran away from fear of slavery as the day is from the night. Suppose, even, that he had qualified himself, by industry,

by thrift, and by study, to win the friendship and be considered
worthy of the society of such people as these I see around me
to-night, gracing my board and filling my heart with gladness;
for I am old enough to remember the day when such a gathering would not have been possible in this land. Suppose, too,
that, as the years went by, this man's memory of the past grew
more and more indistinct, until at last it was rarely, except
in his dreams, that any image of his bygone period rose before
his mind. And then suppose that accident should bring to his
knowledge the fact that the wife of his youth, the wife he had
left behind him,—not one who had walked by his side and kept
pace with him in his upward struggle, but one upon whom advancing years and a laborious life had set their mark,—was
alive and seeking him, but that he was absolutely safe from
recognition or discovery, unless he chose to reveal himself. My
friends, what would the man do? I will presume that he was
one who loved honor, and tried to deal justly with all men. I
will even carry the case further, and suppose that perhaps he
had set his heart upon another, whom he had hoped to call his
own. What would he do, or rather what ought he to do, in such
a crisis of a lifetime?

"It seemed to me that he might hesitate, and I imagined that
I was an old friend, a near friend, and that he had come to me
for advice; and I argued the case with him. I tried to discuss it
impartially. After we had looked upon the matter from every
point of view, I said to him, in words that we all know:—

> 'This above all: to thine own self be true
> And it must follow, as the night the day,
> Thou canst not then be false to any man.'

"Then, finally, I put the question to him, 'Shall you acknowledge her?'

"And now, ladies and gentlemen, friends and companions, I
ask you, what should he have done?"

There was something in Mr. Ryder's voice that stirred the
hearts of those who sat around him. It suggested more than
mere sympathy with an imaginary situation; it seemed rather in

the nature of a personal appeal. It was observed, too, that his look rested more especially upon Mrs. Dixon, with a mingled expression of renunciation and inquiry.

She had listened, with parted lips and streaming eyes. She was the first to speak: "He should have acknowledged her."

"Yes," they all echoed, "he should have acknowledged her."

"My friends and companions," responded Mr. Ryder, "I thank you, one and all. It is the answer I expected, for I knew your hearts."

He turned and walked toward the closed door of an adjoining room, while every eye followed him in wondering curiosity. He came back in a moment, leading by the hand his visitor of the afternoon, who stood startled and trembling at the sudden plunge into this scene of brilliant gayety. She was neatly dressed in gray, and wore the white cap of an elderly woman.

"Ladies and gentlemen," he said, "this is the woman, and I am the man, whose story I have just told you. Permit me to introduce to you the wife of my youth."

THE SHERIFF'S CHILDREN

mulatto: sympathetic/tragic protagonist

Branson County, North Carolina, is in a sequestered district of one of the staidest and most conservative States of the Union. Society in Branson County is almost primitive in its simplicity. Most of the white people own the farms they till, and even before the war there were no very wealthy families to force their neighbors, by comparison, into the category of "poor whites."

To Branson County, as to most rural communities in the South, the war is the one historical event that overshadows all others. It is the era from which all local chronicles are dated,—births, deaths, marriages, storms, freshets. No description of the life of any Southern community would be perfect that failed to emphasize the all-pervading influence of the great conflict.

Yet the fierce tide of war that had rushed through the cities and along the great highways of the country had comparatively speaking but slightly disturbed the sluggish current of life in this region, remote from railroads and navigable streams. To the north in Virginia, to the west in Tennessee, and all along the seaboard the war had raged; but the thunder of its cannon had not disturbed the echoes of Branson County, where the loudest sounds heard were the crack of some hunter's rifle, the baying of some deep-mouthed hound, or the yodel of some tuneful negro on his way through the pine forest. To the east, Sherman's army had passed on its march to the sea; but no straggling band of "bummers" had penetrated the confines of Branson County. The war, it is true, had robbed the county of the flower of its young manhood; but the burden of taxation, the doubt and uncertainty of the conflict, and the sting of ultimate defeat,

the war was "over there" seems to be the same town its always been

war didn't really change anything

had been borne by the people with an apathy that robbed misfortune of half its sharpness.

The nearest approach to town life afforded by Branson County is found in the little village of Troy, the county seat, a hamlet with a population of four or five hundred.

Ten years make little difference in the appearance of these remote Southern towns. If a railroad is built through one of them, it infuses some enterprise; the social corpse is galvanized by the fresh blood of civilization that pulses along the farthest ramifications of our great system of commercial highways. At the period of which I write, no railroad had come to Troy. If a traveler, accustomed to the bustling life of cities, could have ridden through Troy on a summer day, he might easily have fancied himself in a deserted village. Around him he would have seen weather-beaten houses, innocent of paint, the shingled roofs in many instances covered with a rich growth of moss. Here and there he would have met a razor-backed hog lazily rooting his way along the principal thoroughfare; and more than once he would probably have had to disturb the slumbers of some yellow dog, dozing away the hours in ardent sunshine and reluctantly yielding up his place in the middle of the dusty road.

On Saturdays the village presented a somewhat livelier appearance, and the shade trees around the court-house square and along Front Street served as hitching-posts for a goodly number of horses and mules and stunted oxen, belonging to the farmer-folk who had come in to trade at the two or three local stores.

A murder was a rare event in Branson County. Every well-informed citizen could tell the number of homicides committed in the county for fifty years back, and whether the slayer, in any given instance, had escaped, either by flight or acquittal, or had suffered the penalty of the law. So, when it became known in Troy early one Friday morning in summer, about ten years after the war, that old Captain Walker, who had served in Mexico under Scott, and had left an arm on the field of Gettysburg, had been foully murdered during the night, there was intense excitement in the village. Business was practically suspended, and the citizens gathered in little groups to discuss the murder, and speculate upon the identity of the murderer. It transpired from testimony at the coroner's inquest, held during the morning, that a strange mulatto had been seen going in the direction of Captain Walker's house the night before, and had been met going away from Troy early Friday morning, by a farmer on his way to town. Other circumstances seemed to connect the stranger with the crime. The sheriff organized a posse to search for him, and early in the evening, when most of the citizens of Troy were at supper, the suspected man was brought in and lodged in the county jail.

By the following morning the news of the capture had spread to the farthest limits of the county. A much larger number of people than usual came to town that Saturday—bearded men in straw hats and blue homespun shirts, and butternut trousers of great amplitude of material and vagueness of outline; women in homespun frocks and slat-bonnets, with faces as expressionless as the dreary sand-hills which gave them a meagre sustenance.

The murder was almost the sole topic of conversation. A steady stream of curious observers visited the house of mourning, and gazed upon the rugged face of the old veteran, now stiff and cold in death; and more than one eye dropped a tear at the remembrance of the cheery smile, and the joke—sometimes superannuated, generally feeble, but always good-natured—with which the captain had been wont to greet his acquaintances. There was a growing sentiment of anger among these stern men, toward the murderer who had thus cut down their friend, and a strong feeling that ordinary justice was too slight a punishment for such a crime.

Toward noon there was an informal gathering of citizens in Dan Tyson's store.

"I hear it 'lowed that Square Kyahtah's too sick ter hol' co'te this evenin'," said one, "an' that the purlim'nary hearin' 'll haf ter go over 'tel nex' week."

A look of disappointment went round the crowd.

"Hit 's the durndes', meanes' murder ever committed in this caounty," said another, with moody emphasis.

"I s'pose the nigger 'lowed the Cap'n had some green-backs," observed a third speaker.

"The Cap'n," said another, with an air of superior information, "has left two bairls of Confedrit money, which he 'spected 'ud be good some day er nuther."

This statement gave rise to a discussion of the speculative value of Confederate money; but in a little while the conversation returned to the murder.

"Hangin' air too good fer the murderer," said one; "he oughter be burnt, stidier bein' hung."

There was an impressive pause at this point, during which a jug of moonlight whiskey went the round of the crowd.

"Well," said a round-shouldered farmer, who, in spite of his peaceable expression and faded gray eye, was known to have been one of the most daring followers of a rebel guerrilla chieftain, "what air yer gwine ter do about it? Ef you fellers air gwine ter set down an' let a wuthless nigger kill the bes' white man in Branson, an' not say nuthin' ner do nuthin', I'll move outen the caounty."

This speech gave tone and direction to the rest of the conversation. Whether the fear of losing the round-shouldered farmer operated to bring about the result or not is immaterial to this narrative; but, at all events, the crowd decided to lynch the negro. They agreed that this was the least that could be done to avenge the death of their murdered friend, and that it was a becoming way in which to honor his memory. They had some vague notions of the majesty of the law and the rights of the citizen, but in the passion of the moment these sunk into oblivion; a white man had been killed by a negro.

"The Cap'n was an ole sodger," said one of his friends solemnly. "He 'll sleep better when he knows that a co'te-martial has be'n hilt an' jestice done."

By agreement the lynchers were to meet at Tyson's store at five o'clock in the afternoon, and proceed thence to the jail, which was situated down the Lumberton Dirt Road (as the old turnpike antedating the plank-road was called), about half a mile south of the court-house. When the preliminaries of the lynching had been arranged, and a committee appointed to manage the affair, the crowd dispersed, some to go to their dinners, and some to secure recruits for the lynching party.

It was twenty minutes to five o'clock, when an excited negro, panting and perspiring, rushed up to the back door of Sheriff Campbell's dwelling, which stood at a little distance from the jail and somewhat farther than the latter building from the courthouse. A turbaned colored woman came to the door in response to the negro's knock.

"Hoddy, Sis' Nance."

"Hoddy, Brer Sam."

"Is de shurff in," inquired the negro.

"Yas, Brer Sam, he's eatin' his dinner," was the answer.

"Will yer ax 'im ter step ter de do' a minute, Sis' Nance?"

The woman went into the dining-room, and a moment later the sheriff came to the door. He was a tall, muscular man, of a ruddier complexion than is usual among Southerners. A pair of keen, deep-set gray eyes looked out from under bushy eyebrows, and about his mouth was a masterful expression, which a full beard, once sandy in color, but now profusely sprinkled with gray, could not entirely conceal. The day was hot; the sheriff had discarded his coat and vest, and had his white shirt open at the throat.

"What do you want, Sam?" he inquired of the negro, who stood hat in hand, wiping the moisture from his face with a ragged shirtsleeve.

"Shurff, dey gwine ter hang de pris'ner w'at's lock' up in de jail. Dey're comin' dis a-way now. I wuz layin' down on a sack er corn down at de sto', behine a pile er flour-bairls, w'en I hearn Doc' Cain en Kunnel Wright talkin' erbout it. I slip' outen de back do', en run here as fas' as I could. I hearn you say down ter de sto' once't dat you would n't let nobody take a pris'ner 'way fum you widout walking' over yo' dead body, en I thought I'd let you know 'fo' dey come, so yer could pertec' de pris'ner."

The sheriff listened calmly, but his face grew firmer, and a determined gleam lit up his gray eyes. His frame grew more erect, and he unconsciously assumed the attitude of a soldier who momentarily expects to meet the enemy face to face.

"Much obliged, Sam," he answered. "I'll protect the prisoner. Who's coming?"

"I dunno who-all *is* comin'," replied the negro. "Dere's Mistah McSwayne, en Doc' Cain, en Maje' McDonal', en Kunnel Wright, en a heap er yuthers. I wuz so skeered I done furgot mo' d'n half un em. I spec' dey mus' be mos' here by dis time, so I'll git outen de way, fer I don' want nobody fer ter think I wuz mix' up in dis business." The negro glanced nervously down the road toward the town, and made a movement as if to go away.

"Won't you have some dinner first?" asked the sheriff.

The negro looked longingly in at the open door, and sniffed the appetizing odor of boiled pork and collards.

"I ain't got no time fer ter tarry, Shurff," he said, "but Sis' Nance mought gin me sump'n I could kyar in my han' en eat on de way."

A moment later Nancy brought him a huge sandwich of split corn-pone, with a thick slice of fat bacon inserted between the halves, and a couple of baked yams. The negro hastily replaced his ragged hat on his head, dropped the yams in the pocket of his capacious trousers, and, taking the sandwich in his hand, hurried across the road and disappeared in the woods beyond.

The sheriff re-entered the house, and put on his coat and hat. He then took down a double-barreled shotgun and loaded it with buckshot. Filling the chambers of a revolver with fresh cartridges, he slipped it into the pocket of the sack-coat which he wore.

A comely young woman in a calico dress watched these proceedings with anxious surprise.

"Where are you going, father?" she asked. She had not heard the conversation with the negro.

"I am goin' over to the jail," responded the sheriff. "There's a mob comin' this way to lynch the nigger we've got locked up. But they won't do it," he added, with emphasis.

"Oh, father! don't go!" pleaded the girl, clinging to his arm; "they'll shoot you if you don't give him up."

"You never mind me, Polly," said her father reassuringly, as he gently unclasped her hands from his arm. "I'll take care of

myself and the prisoner, too. There ain't a man in Branson
County that would shoot me. Besides, I have faced fire too often to be scared away from my duty. You keep close in the
house," he continued, "and if any one disturbs you just use the
old horse-pistol in the top bureau drawer. It's a little old-
fashioned, but it did good work a few years ago."

The young girl shuddered at this sanguinary allusion, but
made no further objection to her father's departure.

The sheriff of Branson was a man far above the average of
the community in wealth, education, and social position. His
had been one of the few families in the county that before the
war had owned large estates and numerous slaves. He had
graduated at the State University at Chapel Hill, and had kept
up some acquaintance with current literature and advanced
thought. He had traveled, some in his youth, and was looked
up to in the county as an authority on all subjects connected
with the outer world. At first an ardent supporter of the Union,
he had opposed the secession movement in his native State as
long as opposition availed to stem the tide of public opinion.
Yielding at last to the force of circumstances, he had entered
the Confederate service rather late in the war, and served with
distinction through several campaigns, rising in time to the
rank of colonel. After the war he had taken the oath of allegiance, and had been chosen by the people as the most available candidate for the office of sheriff, to which he had been
elected without opposition. He had filled the office for several
terms, and was universally popular with his constituents.

Colonel or Sheriff Campbell, as he was indifferently called,
as the military or civil title happened to be most important in
the opinion of the person addressing him, had a high sense of
the responsibility attaching to his office. He had sworn to do
his duty faithfully, and he knew what his duty was, as sheriff,
perhaps more clearly than he had apprehended it in other passages of his life. It was, therefore, with no uncertainty in regard
to his course that he prepared his weapons and went over to
the jail. He had no fears for Polly's safety.

The sheriff had just locked the heavy front door of the jail
behind him when a half dozen horsemen, followed by a crowd

of men on foot, came round the bend in the road and drew near the jail. They halted in front of the picket fence that surrounded the building, while several of the committee of arrangements rode on a few rods farther to the sheriff's house. One of them dismounted and rapped on the door with his riding-whip.

"Is the sheriff at home?" he inquired.

"No, he has just gone out," replied Polly, who had come to the door.

"We want the jail keys," he continued.

"They are not here," said Polly. "The sheriff has them himself." Then she added, with assumed indifference, "He is at the jail now."

The man turned away, and Polly went into the front room, from which she peered anxiously between the slats of the green blinds of a window that looked toward the jail. Meanwhile the messenger returned to his companions and announced his discovery. It looked as though the sheriff had learned of their design and was preparing to resist it.

One of them stepped forward and rapped on the jail door.

"Well, what is it?" said the sheriff, from within.

"We want to talk to you, Sheriff," replied the spokesman.

There was a little wicket in the door; this the sheriff opened, and answered through it.

"All right, boys, talk away. You are all strangers to me, and I don't know what business you can have." The sheriff did not think it necessary to recognize anybody in particular on such an occasion; the question of identity sometimes comes up in the investigation of these extra-judicial executions.

"We're a committee of citizens and we want to get into the jail."

"What for? It ain't much trouble to get into jail. Most people want to keep out."

The mob was in no humor to appreciate a joke, and the sheriff's witticism fell dead upon an unresponsive audience.

"We want to have a talk with the nigger that killed Cap'n Walker."

"You can talk to that nigger in the court-house, when he's brought out for trial. Court will be in session here next week. I know what you fellows want, but you can't get my prisoner to-day. Do you want to take the bread out of a poor man's mouth? I get seventy-five cents a day for keeping this prisoner, and he's the only one in jail. I can't have my family suffer just to please you fellows."

One or two young men in the crowd laughed at the idea of Sheriff Campbell's suffering for want of seventy-five cents a day; but they were frowned into silence by those who stood near them.

"Ef yer don't let us in," cried a voice, "we'll bus' the do' open."

"Bust away," answered the sheriff, raising his voice so that all could hear. "But I give you fair warning. The first man that tries it will be filled with buckshot. I'm sheriff of this county; I know my duty, and I mean to do it."

"What's the use of kicking, Sheriff?" argued one of the leaders of the mob. "The nigger is sure to hang anyhow; he richly deserves it; and we've got to do something to teach the niggers their places, or white people won't be able to live in the county."

"There's no use talking, boys," responded the sheriff. "I'm a white man outside, but in this jail I'm sheriff; and if this nigger's to be hung in this county, I propose to do the hanging. So you fellows might as well right-about-face, and march back to Troy. You've had a pleasant trip, and the exercise will be good for you. You know *me*. I've got powder and ball, and I've faced fire before now, with nothing between me and the enemy, and I don't mean to surrender this jail while I'm able to shoot." Having thus announced his determination, the sheriff closed and fastened the wicket, and looked around for the best position from which to defend the building.

The crowd drew off a little, and the leaders conversed together in low tones.

The Branson County jail was a small, two-story brick building, strongly constructed, with no attempt at architectural ornamentation. Each story was divided into two large cells by a passage running from front to rear. A grated iron door gave entrance from the passage to each of the four cells. The jail

seldom had many prisoners' in it, and the lower windows had
been boarded up. When the sheriff had closed the wicket, he
ascended the steep wooden stairs to the upper floor. There was
no window at the front of the upper passage, and the most
available position from which to watch the movements of the
crowd below was the front window of the cell occupied by the
solitary prisoner.

The sheriff unlocked the door and entered the cell. The prisoner was crouched in a corner, his yellow face, blanched with
terror, looking ghastly in the semi-darkness of the room. A cold
perspiration had gathered on his forehead, and his teeth were
chattering with affright.

"For God's sake, Sheriff," he murmured hoarsely, "don't let
'em lynch me; I did n't kill the old man."

The sheriff glanced at the cowering wretch with a look of
mingled contempt and loathing.

"Get up," he said sharply. "You will probably be hung
sooner or later, but it shall not be to-day, if I can help it. I'll unlock your fetters, and if I can't hold the jail, you'll have to make
the best fight you can. If I'm shot, I'll consider my responsibility at an end."

There were iron fetters on the prisoner's ankles, and hand-
cuffs on his wrists. These the sheriff unlocked, and they fell
clanking to the floor.

"Keep back from the window," said the sheriff. "They might
shoot if they saw you."

The sheriff drew toward the window a pine bench which
formed a part of the scanty furniture of the cell, and laid his revolver upon it. Then he took his gun in hand, and took his
stand at the side of the window where he could with least exposure of himself watch the movements of the crowd below.

The lynchers had not anticipated any determined resistance.
Of course they had looked for a formal protest, and perhaps a
sufficient show of opposition to excuse the sheriff in the eye of
any stickler for legal formalities. They had not, however, come
prepared to fight a battle, and no one of them seemed willing to
lead an attack upon the jail. The leaders of the party conferred
together with a good deal of animated gesticulation, which was

visible to the sheriff from his outlook, though the distance was too great for him to hear what was said. At length one of them broke away from the group, and rode back to the main body of the lynchers, who were restlessly awaiting orders.

"Well, boys," said the messenger, "we'll have to let it go for the present. The sheriff says he'll shoot, and he's got the drop on us this time. There ain't any of us that want to follow Cap'n Walker jest yet. Besides, the sheriff is a good fellow, and we don't want to hurt 'im. But," he added, as if to reassure the crowd, which began to show signs of disappointment, "the nigger might as well say his prayers, for he ain't got long to live."

There was a murmur of dissent from the mob, and several voices insisted that an attack be made on the jail. But pacific counsels finally prevailed, and the mob sullenly withdrew.

The sheriff stood at the window until they had disappeared around the bend in the road. He did not relax his watchfulness when the last one was out of sight. Their withdrawal might be a mere feint, to be followed by a further attempt. So closely, indeed, was his attention drawn to the outside, that he neither saw nor heard the prisoner creep stealthily across the floor, reach out his hand and secure the revolver which lay on the bench behind the sheriff, and creep as noiselessly back to his place in the corner of the room.

A moment after the last of the lynching party had disappeared there was a shot fired from the woods across the road; a bullet whistled by the window and buried itself in the wooden casing a few inches from where the sheriff was standing. Quick as thought, with the instinct borne of a semi-guerrilla army experience, he raised his gun and fired twice at the point from which a faint puff of smoke showed the hostile bullet to have been sent. He stood a moment watching, and then rested his gun against the window, and reached behind him mechanically for the other weapon. It was not on the bench. As the sheriff realized this fact, he turned his head and looked into the muzzle of the revolver.

"Stay where you are, Sheriff," said the prisoner, his eyes glistening, his face almost ruddy with excitement.

The sheriff mentally cursed his own carelessness for allowing him to be caught in such a predicament. He had not expected anything of the kind. He had relied on the negro's cowardice and subordination in the presence of an armed white man as a matter of course. The sheriff was a brave man, but realized that the prisoner had him at an immense disadvantage. The two men stood thus for a moment, fighting a harmless duel with their eyes.

"Well, what do you mean to do?" asked the sheriff with apparent calmness.

"To get away, of course," said the prisoner, in a tone which caused the sheriff to look at him more closely, and with an involuntary feeling of apprehension; if the man was not mad, he was in a state of mind akin to madness, and quite as dangerous. The sheriff felt that he must speak to the prisoner fair, and watch for a chance to turn the tables on him. The keen-eyed, desperate man before him was a different being altogether from the groveling wretch who had begged so piteously for life a few minutes before.

At length the sheriff spoke:—

"Is this your gratitude to me for saving your life at the risk of my own? If I had not done so, you would now be swinging from the limb of some neighboring tree."

"True," said the prisoner, "you saved my life, but for how long? When you came in, you said Court would sit next week. When the crowd went away they said I had not long to live. It is merely a choice of two ropes."

"While there's life there's hope," replied the sheriff. He uttered this commonplace mechanically, while his brain was busy in trying to think out some way of escape. "If you are innocent you can prove it."

The mulatto kept his eye on the sheriff. "I did n't kill the old man," he replied; "but I shall never be able to clear myself. I was at his house at nine o'clock. I stole from it the coat that was on my back when I was taken. I would be convicted, even with a fair trial, unless the real murderer were discovered beforehand."

The sheriff knew this only too well. While he was thinking what argument next to use, the prisoner continued:—

"Throw me the keys—no, unlock the door."

The sheriff stood a moment irresolute. The mulatto's eye glittered ominously. The sheriff crossed the room and unlocked the door leading into the passage.

"Now go down and unlock the outside door."

The heart of the sheriff leaped within him. Perhaps he might make a dash for liberty, and gain the outside. He descended the narrow stairs, the prisoner keeping close behind him.

The sheriff inserted the huge iron key into the lock. The rusty bolt yielded slowly. It still remained for him to pull the door open.

"Stop!" thundered the mulatto, who seemed to divine the sheriff's purpose. "Move a muscle, and I'll blow your brains out."

The sheriff obeyed; he realized that his chance had not yet come.

"Now keep on that side of the passage, and go back upstairs."

Keeping the sheriff under cover of the revolver, the mulatto followed him up the stairs. The sheriff expected the prisoner to lock him into the cell and make his own escape. He had about come to the conclusion that the best thing he could do under the circumstances was to submit quietly, and take his chances of recapturing the prisoner after the alarm had been given. The sheriff had faced death more than once upon the battlefield. A few minutes before, well armed, and with a brick wall between him and them, he had dared a hundred men to fight; but he felt instinctively that the desperate man confronting him was not to be trifled with, and he was too prudent a man to risk his life against such heavy odds. He had Polly to look after, and there was a limit beyond which devotion to duty would be quixotic and even foolish.

"I want to get away," said the prisoner, "and I don't want to be captured; for if I am I know I will be hung on the spot. I am afraid," he added somewhat reflectively, "that in order to save myself I shall have to kill you."

"Good God!" exclaimed the sheriff in involuntary terror; "you would not kill the man to whom you owe your own life."

"You speak more truly than you know," replied the mulatto. "I indeed owe my life to you."

The sheriff started. He was capable of surprise, even in

that moment of extreme peril. "Who are you?" he asked in amazement.

"Tom, Cicely's son," returned the other. He had closed the door and stood talking to the sheriff through the grated opening. "Don't you remember Cicely—Cicely whom you sold, with her child, to the speculator on his way to Alabama?"

The sheriff did remember. He had been sorry for it many a time since. It had been the old story of debts, mortgages, and bad crops. He had quarreled with the mother. The price offered for her and her child had been unusually large, and he had yielded to the combination of anger and pecuniary stress.

"Good God!" he gasped, "you would not murder your own father?"

"My father?" replied the mulatto. "It were well enough for me to claim the relationship, but it comes with poor grace from you to ask anything by reason of it. What father's duty have you ever performed for me? Did you give me your name, or even your protection? Other white men gave their colored sons freedom and money, and sent them to the free States. *You* sold *me* to the rice swamps."

"I at least gave you the life you cling to," murmured the sheriff.

"Life?" said the prisoner, with a sarcastic laugh. "What kind of a life? You gave me your own blood, your own features,— no man need look at us together twice to see that,—and you gave me a black mother. Poor wretch! She died under the lash, because she had enough womanhood to call her soul her own. You gave me a white man's spirit, and you made me a slave, and crushed it out."

"But you are free now," said the sheriff. He had not doubted, could not doubt, the mulatto's word. He knew whose passions coursed beneath the swarthy skin and burned in the black eyes opposite his own. He saw in this mulatto what he himself might have become had not the safeguards of parental restraint and public opinion been thrown around him.

"Free to do what?" replied the mulatto. "Free in name, but despised and scorned and set aside by the people to whose race I belong far more than to my mother's."

"There are schools," said the sheriff. "You have been to school." He had noticed that the mulatto spoke more eloquently and used better language than most Branson County people.

"I have been to school, and dreamed when I went that it would work some marvelous change in my condition. But what did I learn? I learned to feel that no degree of learning or wisdom will change the color of my skin and that I shall always wear what in my own country is a badge of degradation. When I think about it seriously I do not care particularly for such a life. It is the animal in me, not the man, that flees the gallows. I owe you nothing," he went on, "and expect nothing of you; and it would be no more than justice if I should avenge upon you my mother's wrongs and my own. But still I hate to shoot you; I have never yet taken human life—for I did *not* kill the old captain. Will you promise to give no alarm and make no attempt to capture me until morning, if I do not shoot?"

So absorbed were the two men in their colloquy and their own tumultuous thoughts that neither of them had heard the door below move upon its hinges. Neither of them had heard a light step come stealthily up the stairs, nor seen a slender form creep along the darkening passage toward the mulatto.

The sheriff hesitated. The struggle between his love of life and his sense of duty was a terrific one. It may seem strange that a man who could sell his own child into slavery should hesitate at such a moment, when his life was trembling in the balance. But the baleful influence of human slavery poisoned the very fountains of life, and created new standards of right. The sheriff was conscientious; his conscience had merely been warped by his environment. Let no one ask what his answer would have been; he was spared the necessity of a decision.

"Stop," said the mulatto, "you need not promise, I could not trust you if you did. It is your life for mine; there is but one safe way for me; you must die."

He raised his arm to fire, when there was a flash—a report from the passage behind him. His arm fell heavily at his side, and the pistol dropped at his feet.

The sheriff recovered first from his surprise, and throwing open the door secured the fallen weapon. Then seizing the prisoner he thrust him into the cell and locked the door upon him; after which he turned to Polly, who leaned half-fainting against the wall, her hands clasped over her heart.

"Oh, father, I was just in time!" she cried hysterically, and, wildly sobbing, threw herself into her father's arms.

"I watched until they all went away," she said. "I heard the shot from the woods and I saw you shoot. Then when you did not come out I feared something had happened, that perhaps you had been wounded. I got out the other pistol and ran over here. When I found the door open, I knew something was wrong, and when I heard voices I crept upstairs, and reached the top just in time to hear him say he would kill you. Oh, it was a narrow escape!"

When she had grown somewhat calmer, the sheriff left her standing there and went back into the cell. The prisoner's arm was bleeding from a flesh wound. His bravado had given place to a stony apathy. There was no sign in his face of fear or disappointment or feeling of any kind. The sheriff sent Polly to the house for cloth, and bound up the prisoner's wound with a rude skill acquired during his army life.

"I'll have a doctor come and dress the wound in the morning," he said to the prisoner. "It will do well until then, if you will keep quiet. If the doctor asks you how the wound was caused, you can say that you were struck by the bullet fired from the woods. It would do you no good to have it known that you were shot while attempting to escape."

The prisoner uttered no word of thanks or apology, but sat in sullen silence. When the wounded arm had been bandaged, Polly and her father returned to the house.

The sheriff was in an unusually thoughtful mood that evening. He put salt in his coffee at supper, and poured vinegar over his pancakes. To many of Polly's questions he returned random answers. When he had gone to bed he lay awake for several hours.

In the silent watches of the night, when he was alone with God, there came into his mind a flood of unaccustomed thoughts. An hour or two before, standing face to face with death, he had experienced a sensation similar to that which

drowning men are said to feel—a kind of clarifying of the
moral faculty, in which the veil of the flesh, with its obscuring
passions and prejudices, is pushed aside for a moment, and all
the acts of one's life stand out, in the clear light of truth, in their
correct proportions and relations,—a state of mind in which
one sees himself as God may be supposed to see him. In the reaction following his rescue, this feeling had given place for
a time to far different emotions. But now, in the silence of
midnight, something of this clearness of spirit returned to the
sheriff. He saw that he had owed some duty to this son of
his,—that neither law nor custom could destroy a responsibility inherent in the nature of mankind. He could not thus, in the
eyes of God at least, shake off the consequences of his sin. Had
he never sinned, this wayward spirit would never have come
back from the vanished past to haunt him. As these thoughts
came, his anger against the mulatto died away, and in its place
there sprang up a great pity. The hand of parental authority
might have restrained the passions he had seen burning in the
prisoner's eyes when the desperate man spoke the words which
had seemed to doom his father to death. The sheriff felt that he
might have saved this fiery spirit from the slough of slavery;
that he might have sent him to the free North, and given him
there, or in some other land, an opportunity to turn to usefulness and honorable pursuits the talents that had run to
crime, perhaps to madness; he might, still less, have given this
son of his the poor simulacrum of liberty which men of his
caste could possess in a slave-holding community; or least of
all, but still something, he might have kept the boy on the plantation, where the burdens of slavery would have fallen lightly
upon him.

The sheriff recalled his own youth. He had inherited an honored name to keep untarnished; he had had a future to make;
the picture of a fair young bride had beckoned him on to happiness. The poor wretch now stretched upon a pallet of straw
between the brick walls of the jail had had none of these
things,—no name, no father, no mother—in the true meaning
of motherhood,—and until the past few years no possible
future, and then one vague and shadowy in its outline, and

dependent for form and substance upon the slow solution of a problem in which there were many unknown quantities.

From what he might have done to what he might yet do was an easy transition for the awakened conscience of the sheriff. It occurred to him, purely as a hypothesis, that he might permit his prisoner to escape; but his oath of office, his duty as sheriff, stood in the way of such a course, and the sheriff dismissed the idea from his mind. He could, however, investigate the circumstances of the murder, and move Heaven and earth to discover the real criminal, for he no longer doubted the prisoner's innocence; he could employ counsel for the accused, and perhaps influence public opinion in his favor. An acquittal once secured, some plan could be devised by which the sheriff might in some degree atone for his crime against this son of his—against society—against God.

When the sheriff had reached this conclusion he fell into an unquiet slumber, from which he awoke late the next morning.

He went over to the jail before breakfast and found the prisoner lying on his pallet, his face turned to the wall; he did not move when the sheriff rattled the door.

"Good-morning," said the latter, in a tone intended to waken the prisoner.

There was no response. The sheriff looked more keenly at the recumbent figure; there was an unnatural rigidity about its attitude.

He hastily unlocked the door and, entering the cell, bent over the prostrate form. There was no sound of breathing; he turned the body over—it was cold and stiff. The prisoner had torn the bandage from his wound and bled to death during the night. He had evidently been dead several hours.

- the two worlds cannot mix
- even after the war, longstanding deep hypocrisy
- 2 children are mirrored
  - same blood
  - very different social spheres
  - NO MIXING

Tom can't fit in W/B world and only can

A MATTER OF PRINCIPLE

I

"What our country needs in its treatment of the race problem," observed Mr. Cicero Clayton at one of the monthly meetings of the Blue Vein Society, of which he was a prominent member, "is a clearer conception of the brotherhood of man."

The same sentiment in much the same words had often fallen from Mr. Clayton's lips,—so often, in fact, that the younger members of the society sometimes spoke of him—among themselves of course—as "Brotherhood Clayton." The sobriquet derived its point from the application he made of the principle involved in this oft-repeated proposition.

The fundamental article of Mr. Clayton's social creed was that he himself was not a negro.

"I know," he would say, "that the white people lump us all together as negroes, and condemn us all to the same social ostracism. But I don't accept this classification, for my part, and I imagine that, as the chief party in interest, I have a right to my opinion. People who belong by half or more of their blood to the most virile and progressive race of modern times have as much right to call themselves white as others have to call them negroes."

Mr. Clayton spoke warmly, for he was well informed, and had thought much upon the subject; too much, indeed, for he had not been able to escape entirely the tendency of too much concentration upon one subject to make even the clearest minds morbid.

"Of course we can't enforce our claims, or protect ourselves from being robbed of our birthright; but we can at least have principles, and try to live up to them the best we can. If we are not accepted as white, we can at any rate make it clear that we object to being called black. Our protest cannot fail in time to impress itself upon the better class of white people; for the Anglo-Saxon race loves justice, and will eventually do it, where it does not conflict with their own interests."

Whether or not the fact that Mr. Clayton meant no sarcasm, and was conscious of no inconsistency in this eulogy, tended to establish the racial identity he claimed may safely be left to the discerning reader.

In living up to his creed Mr. Clayton declined to associate to any considerable extent with black people. This was sometimes a little inconvenient, and occasionally involved a sacrifice of some pleasure for himself and his family, because they would not attend entertainments where many black people were likely to be present. But they had a social refuge in a little society of people like themselves; they attended, too, a church, of which nearly all the members were white, and they were connected with a number of the religious and benevolent associations open to all good citizens, where they came into contact with the better class of white people, and were treated, in their capacity of members, with a courtesy and consideration scarcely different from that accorded to other citizens.

Mr. Clayton's racial theory was not only logical enough, but was in his own case backed up by substantial arguments. He had begun life with a small patrimony, and had invested his money in a restaurant, which by careful and judicious attention had grown from a cheap eating-house into the most popular and successful confectionery and catering establishment in Groveland. His business occupied a double store on Oakwood Avenue. He owned houses and lots, and stocks and bonds, had good credit at the banks, and lived in a style befitting his income and business standing. In person he was of olive complexion, with slightly curly hair. His features approached the Cuban or Latin-American type rather than the familiar broad characteristic of the mulatto, this suggestion of something foreign being heightened by a Vandyke beard and a carefully waxed and pointed mustache. When he walked to church on Sunday mornings with his daughter Alice, they were a couple of such striking appearance as surely to attract attention.

Miss Alice Clayton was queen of her social set. She was young, she was handsome. She was nearly white; she frankly confessed her sorrow that she was not entirely so. She was accomplished and amiable, dressed in good taste, and had for her father by all odds the richest colored man—the term is used with apologies to Mr. Clayton, explaining that it does not necessarily mean a negro—in Groveland. So pronounced was her superiority that really she had but one social rival worthy of the name,—Miss Lura Watkins, whose father kept a prosperous livery stable and lived in almost as good style as the Claytons. Miss Watkins, while good-looking enough, was not so young nor quite so white as Miss Clayton. She was popular, however, among their mutual acquaintances, and there was a good-natured race between the two as to which should make the first and best marriage.

Marriages among Miss Clayton's set were serious affairs. Of course marriage is always a serious matter, whether it be a success or a failure, and there are those who believe that any marriage is better than no marriage. But among Miss Clayton's friends and associates matrimony took on an added seriousness because of the very narrow limits within which it could take place. Miss Clayton and her friends, by reason of their assumed superiority to black people, or perhaps as much by reason of a somewhat morbid shrinking from the curiosity manifested toward married people of strongly contrasting colors, would not marry black men, and except in rare instances white men would not marry them. They were therefore restricted for a choice to the young men of their own complexion. But these, unfortunately for the girls, had a wider choice. In any State where the laws permit freedom of the marriage contract, a man, by virtue of his sex, can find a wife of whatever complexion he prefers; of course he must not always ask too much in other respects, for most women like to better their social position when they marry. To the number thus lost by "going on the other side," as the phrase went, add the worthless contingent whom no self-respecting woman would marry, and the choice was still further restricted; so that it had become fashionable, when the supply of eligible men ran short, for those of Miss Clayton's set who could afford it to go traveling; ostensibly for pleasure, but with the serious hope that they might meet their fate away from home.

Miss Clayton had perhaps a larger option than any of her associates. Among such men as there were she could have taken her choice. Her beauty, her position, her accomplishments, her father's wealth, all made her eminently desirable. But, on the other hand, the same things rendered her more difficult to reach, and harder to please. To get access to her heart, too, it was necessary to run the gauntlet of her parents, which, until she had reached the age of twenty-three, no one had succeeded in doing safely. Many had called, but none had been chosen.

There was, however, one spot left unguarded, and through it Cupid, a veteran sharpshooter, sent a dart. Mr. Clayton had taken into his service and into his household a poor relation, a sort of cousin several times removed. This boy—his name was Jack—had gone into Mr. Clayton's service at a very youthful age,—twelve or thirteen. He had helped about the housework, washed the dishes, swept the floors, taken care of the lawn and the stable for three or four years, while he attended school. His cousin had then taken him into the store, where he had swept the floor, washed the windows, and done a class of work that kept fully impressed upon him the fact that he was a poor dependent. Nevertheless he was a cheerful lad, who took what he could get and was properly grateful, but always meant to get more. By sheer force of industry and affability and shrewdness, he forced his employer to promote him in time to a position of recognized authority in the establishment. Any one outside of the family would have perceived in him a very suitable husband for Miss Clayton; he was of about the same age, or a year or two older, was as fair of complexion as she, when she was not powdered, and was passably good-looking, with a bearing of which the natural manliness had been no more warped than his training and racial status had rendered inevitable; for he had early learned the law of growth, that to bend is better than to break. He was sometimes sent to accompany Miss Clayton to places in the evening, when she had no other escort, and it is quite likely that she discovered his good points before her parents did. That they should in time perceive them was inevitable. But even then, so accustomed were they to looking down upon the object of their former bounty, that they only spoke of the matter jocularly.

"Well, Alice," her father would say in his bluff way, "you'll not be absolutely obliged to die an old maid. If we can't find anything better for you, there's always Jack. As long as he does n't take to some other girl, you can fall back on him as a last chance. He'd be glad to take you to get into the business."

Miss Alice had considered the joke a very poor one when first made, but by occasional repetition she became somewhat familiar with it. In time it got around to Jack himself, to whom it seemed no joke at all. He had long considered it a consummation devoutly to be wished, and when he became aware that the possibility of such a match had occurred to the other parties in interest, he made up his mind that the idea should in due course of time become an accomplished fact. He had even suggested as much to Alice, in a casual way, to feel his ground; and while she had treated the matter lightly, he was not without hope that she had been impressed by the suggestion. Before he had had time, however, to follow up this lead, Miss Clayton, in the spring of 187–, went away on a visit to Washington.

The occasion of her visit was a presidential inauguration. The new President owed his nomination mainly to the votes of the Southern delegates in the convention, and was believed to be correspondingly well disposed to the race from which the Southern delegates were for the most part recruited. Friends of rival and unsuccessful candidates for the nomination had more than hinted that the Southern delegates were very substantially rewarded for their support at the time when it was given; whether this was true or not the parties concerned know best. At any rate the colored politicians did not see it in that light, for they were gathered from near and far to press their claims for recognition and patronage. On the evening following the White House inaugural ball, the colored people of Washington gave an "inaugural" ball at a large public hall. It was under the management of their leading citizens, among them several high officials holding over from the last administration, and a number of professional and business men. This ball was the most noteworthy social event that colored circles up to that time had ever known. There were many visitors from various parts of the country. Miss Clayton attended the ball, the honors of which she carried away easily. She danced with several partners, and was introduced to innumerable people whom she had never seen before, and whom she hardly expected ever to meet again. She went away from the ball, at four o'clock in the morning, in a glow of triumph, and with a confused impression of senators and representatives and lawyers and doctors of all shades, who had sought an introduction, led her through the dance, and overwhelmed her with compliments. She returned home the next day but one, after the most delightful week of her life.

II

One afternoon, about three weeks after her return from Washington, Alice received a letter through the mail. The envelope bore the words "House of Representatives" printed in one corner, and in the opposite corner, in a bold running hand, a Congressman's frank, "Hamilton M. Brown, M. C." The letter read as follows:—

> House of Representatives,
> Washington, D. C., March 30, 187-.
>
> Miss Alice Clayton, Groveland.
>
> Dear Friend (if I may be permitted to call you so after so brief an acquaintance),—I remember with sincerest pleasure our recent meeting at the inaugural ball, and the sensation created by your beauty, your amiable manners, and your graceful dancing. Time has so strengthened the impression I then received, that I should have felt inconsolable had I thought it impossible ever to again behold the charms which had brightened the occasion of

our meeting and eclipsed by their brilliancy the leading belles of
the capital. I had hoped, however, to have the pleasure of meeting you again, and circumstances have fortunately placed it in
my power to do so at an early date. You have doubtless learned
that the contest over the election in the Sixth Congressional District of South Carolina has been decided in my favor, and that I
now have the honor of representing my native State at the national capital. I have just been appointed a member of a special
committee to visit and inspect the Sault River and the Straits of
Mackinac, with reference to the needs of lake navigation. I have
made arrangements to start a week ahead of the other members
of the committee, whom I am to meet in Detroit on the 20th. I
shall leave here on the 2d, and will arrive in Groveland on the
3d, by the 7.30 evening express. I shall remain in Groveland several days, in the course of which I shall be pleased to call, and re-
new the acquaintance so auspiciously begun in Washington,
which it is my fondest hope may ripen into a warmer friendship.

If you do not regard my visit as presumptuous, and do not
write me in the mean while forbidding it, I shall do myself the
pleasure of waiting on you the morning after my arrival in
Groveland.

With renewed expressions of my sincere admiration and profound esteem, I remain,

SINCERELY YOURS,
HAMILTON M. BROWN, M. C.

To Alice, and especially to her mother, this bold and flowery
letter had very nearly the force of a formal declaration. They
read it over again and again, and spent most of the afternoon
discussing it. There were few young men in Groveland eligible
as husbands for so superior a person as Alice Clayton, and an
addition to the number would be very acceptable. But the mere
fact of his being a Congressman was not sufficient to qualify
him; there were other considerations.

"I've never heard of this Honorable Hamilton M. Brown,"
said Mr. Clayton. The letter had been laid before him at the
supper-table. "It's strange, Alice, that you have n't said anything

about him before. You must have met lots of swell folks not to recollect a Congressman."

"But he was n't a Congressman then," answered Alice; "he was only a claimant. I remember Senator Bruce, and Mr. Douglass; but there were so many doctors and lawyers and politicians that I could n't keep track of them all. Still I have a faint impression of a Mr. Brown who danced with me."

She went into the parlor and brought out the dancing programme she had used at the Washington ball. She had decorated it with a bow of blue ribbon and preserved it as a souvenir of her visit.

"Yes," she said, after examining it, "I must have danced with him. Here are the initials—'H. M. B.'"

"What color is he?" asked Mr. Clayton, as he plied his knife and fork.

"I have a notion that he was rather dark—darker than any one I had ever danced with before."

"Why did you dance with him?" asked her father. "You were n't obliged to go back on your principles because you were away from home."

"Well, father, 'when you're in Rome'—you know the rest. Mrs. Clearweather introduced me to several dark men, to him among others. They were her friends, and common decency required me to be courteous."

"If this man is black, we don't want to encourage him. If he's the right sort, we'll invite him to the house."

"And make him feel at home," added Mrs. Clayton, on hospitable thoughts intent.

"We must ask Sadler about him to-morrow," said Mr. Clayton, when he had drunk his coffee and lighted his cigar. "If he's the right man he shall have cause to remember his visit to Groveland. We'll show him that Washington is not the only town on earth."

The uncertainty of the family with regard to Mr. Brown was soon removed. Mr. Solomon Sadler, who was supposed to know everything worth knowing concerning the colored race, and everybody of importance connected with it, dropped in after supper to make an evening call. Sadler was familiar with the history of every man of negro ancestry who had distinguished himself in any walk of life. He could give the pedigree of Alexander Pushkin, the titles of scores of Dumas's novels (even Sadler had not time to learn them all), and could recite the whole of Wendell Phillips's lecture on Toussaint l'Ouverture. He claimed a personal acquaintance with Mr. Frederick Douglass, and had been often in Washington, where he was well known and well received in good colored society.

"Let me see," he said reflectively, when asked for information about the Honorable Hamilton M. Brown. "Yes, I think I know him. He studied at Oberlin just after the war. He was about leaving there when I entered. There were two H. M. Browns there—a Hamilton M. Brown and a Henry M. Brown. One was stout and dark and the other was slim and quite light; you could scarcely tell him from a dark white man. They used to call them 'light Brown' and 'dark Brown.' I did n't know either of them except by sight, for they were there only a few weeks after I went in. As I remember them, Hamilton was the fair one—a very good-looking, gentlemanly fellow, and, as a I heard, a good student and a fine speaker."

"Do you remember what kind of hair he had?" asked Mr. Clayton.

"Very good indeed; straight, as I remember it. He looked something like a Spaniard or a Portuguese."

"Now that you describe him," said Alice, "I remember quite well dancing with such a gentleman; and I'm wrong about my 'H. M. B.' The dark man must have been some one else; there are two others on my card that I can't remember distinctly, and he was probably one of those."

"I guess he's all right, Alice," said her father when Sadler had gone away. "He evidently means business, and we must treat him white. Of course he must stay with us; there are no hotels in Groveland while he is here. Let's see—he'll be here in three days. That is n't very long, but I guess we can get ready. I'll write a letter this afternoon—or you write it, and invite him to the house, and say I'll meet him at the depot. And you may have *carte blanche* for making the preparations."

"We must have some people to meet him."

"Certainly; a reception is the proper thing. Sit down immediately and write the letter and I'll mail it first thing in the morning, so he'll get it before he has time to make other arrangements. And you and your mother put your heads together and make out a list of guests, and I'll have the invitations printed to-morrow. We will show the darkeys of Groveland how to entertain a Congressman."

It will be noted that in moments of abstraction or excitement Mr. Clayton sometimes relapsed into forms of speech not entirely consistent with his principles. But some allowance must be made for his atmosphere; he could no more escape from it than the leopard can change his spots, or the——. In deference to Mr. Clayton's feelings the quotation will be left incomplete.

Alice wrote the letter on the spot and it was duly mailed, and sped on its winged way to Washington.

The preparations for the reception were made as thoroughly and elaborately as possible on so short a notice. The invitations were issued; the house was cleaned from attic to cellar; an orchestra was engaged for the evening; elaborate floral decorations were planned and the flowers ordered. Even the refreshments, which ordinarily, in the household of a caterer, would be mere matter of familiar detail, became a subject of serious consultation and study.

The approaching event was a matter of very much interest to the fortunate ones who were honored with invitations, and this for several reasons. They were anxious to meet this sole representative of their race in the ——th Congress, and as he was not one of the old-line colored leaders, but a new star risen on the political horizon, there was a special curiosity to see who he was and what he looked like. Moreover, the Claytons did not often entertain a large company, but when they did, it was on a scale commensurate with their means and position, and to be present on such an occasion was a thing to remember and to talk about. And, most important consideration of all, some remarks dropped by members of the Clayton family had given rise to the rumor that the Congressman was seeking a wife. This invested his visit with a romantic interest, and gave the reception a practical value; for there were other marriageable girls besides Miss Clayton, and if one was left another might be taken.

III

On the evening of April 3d, at fifteen minutes of six o'clock, Mr. Clayton, accompanied by Jack, entered the livery carriage waiting at his gate and ordered the coachman to drive to the Union Depot. He had taken Jack along, partly for company, and partly that Jack might relieve the Congressman of any trouble about his baggage, and make himself useful in case of emergency. Jack was willing enough to go, for he had foreseen in the visitor a rival for Alice's hand,—indeed he had heard more or less of the subject for several days,—and was glad to make a reconnaissance before the enemy arrived upon the field of battle. He had made—at least he had thought so—considerable progress with Alice during the three weeks since her return from Washington, and once or twice Alice had been perilously near the tender stage. This visit had disturbed the situation and threatened to ruin his chances; but he did not mean to give up without a struggle.

Arrived at the main entrance, Mr. Clayton directed the carriage to wait, and entered the station with Jack. The Union Depot at Groveland was an immense oblong structure, covering a dozen parallel tracks and furnishing terminal passenger facilities for half a dozen railroads. The tracks ran east and west, and the depot was entered from the south, at about the middle of the building. On either side of the entrance, the waiting-rooms, refreshment rooms, baggage and express departments, and other administrative offices, extended in a row for the entire length of the building; and beyond them and parallel with them stretched a long open space, separated from the tracks by an iron fence or *grille*. There were two entrance gates in the fence, at which tickets must be shown before access could be had to trains, and two other gates, by which arriving passengers came out.

Mr. Clayton looked at the blackboard on the wall underneath the station clock, and observed that the 7.30 train from

Washington was five minutes late. Accompanied by Jack he walked up and down the platform until the train, with the usual accompaniment of panting steam and clanging bell and rumbling trucks, pulled into the station, and drew up on the third or fourth track from the iron railing. Mr. Clayton stationed himself at the gate nearest the rear end of the train, reasoning that the Congressman would ride in a parlor car, and would naturally come out by the gate nearest the point at which he left the train.

"You'd better go and stand by the other gate, Jack," he said to his companion, "and stop him if he goes out that way."

The train was well filled and a stream of passengers poured through. Mr. Clayton scanned the crowd carefully as they approached the gate, and scrutinized each passenger as he came through, without seeing any one that met the description of Congressman Brown, as given by Sadler, or any one that could in his opinion be the gentleman for whom he was looking. When the last one had passed through he was left to the conclusion that his expected guest had gone out by the other gate. Mr. Clayton hastened thither.

"Did n't he come out this way, Jack?" he asked.

"No, sir," replied the young man, "I have n't seen him."

"That's strange," mused Mr. Clayton, somewhat anxiously. "He would hardly fail to come without giving us notice. Surely we must have missed him. We'd better look around a little. You go that way and I'll go this."

Mr. Clayton turned and walked several rods along the platform to the men's waiting-room, and standing near the door glanced around to see if he could find the object of his search. The only colored person in the room was a stout and very black man, wearing a broadcloth suit and a silk hat, and seated a short distance from the door. On the seat by his side stood a couple of valises. On one of them, the one nearest him, on which his arm rested, was written, in white letters, plainly legible,—

H. M. Brown, M. C.
Washington, D. C.

Mr. Clayton's feelings at this discovery can better be imagined than described. He hastily left the waiting-room, before the black gentleman, who was looking the other way, was even aware of his presence, and, walking rapidly up and down the platform, communed with himself upon what course of action the situation demanded. He had invited to his house, had come down to meet, had made elaborate preparations to entertain on the following evening, a light-colored man,—a white man by his theory, an acceptable guest, a possible husband for his daughter, an avowed suitor for her hand. If the Congressman had turned out to be brown, even dark brown, with fairly good hair, though he might not have desired him as a son-in-law, yet he could have welcomed him as a guest. But even this softening of the blow was denied him, for the man in the waiting-room was palpably, aggressively black, with pronounced African features and woolly hair, without apparently a single drop of redeeming white blood. Could he, in the face of his well-known principles, his lifelong rule of conduct, take this negro into his home and introduce him to his friends? Could he subject his wife and daughter to the rude shock of such a disappointment? It would be bad enough for them to learn of the ghastly mistake, but to have him in the house would be twisting the arrow in the wound.

Mr. Clayton had the instincts of a gentleman, and realized the delicacy of the situation. But to get out of his difficulty without wounding the feelings of the Congressman required not only diplomacy but dispatch. Whatever he did must be done promptly; for if he waited many minutes the Congressman would probably take a carriage and be driven to Mr. Clayton's residence.

A ray of hope came for a moment to illumine the gloom of the situation. Perhaps the black man was merely sitting there, and not the owner of the valise! For there were two valises, one on each side of the supposed Congressman. For obvious reasons he did not care to make the inquiry himself, so he looked around for his companion, who came up a moment later.

"Jack," he exclaimed excitedly, "I'm afraid we're in the worst kind of a hole, unless there's some mistake! Run down to the men's waiting-room and you'll see a man and a valise, and you'll understand what I mean. Ask that darkey if he is the Honorable Mr. Brown, Congressman from South Carolina. If he says yes, come back right away and let me know, without giving him time to ask any questions, and put your wits to work to help me out of the scrape."

"I wonder what's the matter?" said Jack to himself, but did as he was told. In a moment he came running back.

"Yes, sir," he announced; "he says he's the man."

"Jack," said Mr. Clayton desperately, "if you want to show your appreciation of what I've done for you, you must suggest some way out of this. I'd never dare to take that negro to my house, and yet I'm obliged to treat him like a gentleman."

Jack's eyes had worn a somewhat reflective look since he had gone to make the inquiry. Suddenly his face brightened with intelligence, and then, as a newsboy ran into the station calling his wares, hardened into determination.

"*Clarion,* special extry 'dition! All about de epidemic er dipt'eria!" clamored the newsboy with shrill childish treble, as he made his way toward the waiting-room. Jack darted after him, and saw the man to whom he had spoken buy a paper. He ran back to his employer, and dragged him over toward the ticket-seller's window.

"I have it, sir!" he exclaimed, seizing a telegraph blank and writing rapidly, and reading aloud as he wrote, "How's this for a way out?"—

DEAR SIR,—I write you this note here in the depot to inform you of an unfortunate event which has interfered with my plans and those of my family for your entertainment while in Groveland. Yesterday my daughter Alice complained of a sore throat, which by this afternoon had developed into a case of malignant diphtheria. In consequence our house has been quarantined; and while I have felt myself obliged to come down to the depot, I do not feel that I ought to expose you to the possibility of infection, and I therefore send you this by another hand. The bearer will conduct you to a carriage which I have ordered placed at your service, and unless you should prefer some other hotel, you will be driven to the Forest Hill House, where I beg you will consider yourself my guest during your stay in the city, and make the fullest use of every convenience it may offer. From present indications I fear no one of our family will be able to see you, which we shall regret beyond expression, as we have made elaborate arrangements for your entertainment. I still hope, however, that you may enjoy your visit, as there are many places of interest in the city, and many friends will doubtless be glad to make your acquaintance.

With assurances of my profound regret, I am

SINCERELY YOURS,
CICERO CLAYTON.

"Splendid!" cried Mr. Clayton. "You've helped me out of a horrible scrape. Now, go and take him to the hotel and see him comfortably located, and tell them to charge the bill to me."

"I suspect, sir," suggested Jack, "that I'd better not go up to the house, and you'll have to stay in yourself for a day or two, to keep up appearances. I'll sleep on the lounge at the store, and we can talk business over the telephone."

"All right, Jack, we'll arrange the details later. But for Heaven's sake get him started, or he'll be calling a hack to drive up to the house. I'll go home on a street car."

"So far, so good," sighed Mr. Clayton to himself as he escaped from the station. "Jack is a deuced clever fellow, and I'll have to do something more for him. But the tug-of-war is yet to come. I've got to bribe a doctor, shut up the house for a day or two, and have all the ill-humor of two disappointed women to endure until this negro leaves town. Well, I'm sure my wife and Alice will back me up at any cost. No sacrifice is too great to escape having to entertain him; of course I have no prejudice against his color,—he can't help that,—but it is the *principle* of the thing. If we received him it would be a concession fatal to all my views and theories. And I am really doing him a kindness, for I'm sure that all the world could not make Alice and her mother treat him with anything but cold politeness. It'll be a great mortification to Alice, but I don't see how else I could have got out of it."

He boarded the first car that left the depot, and soon reached home. The house was lighted up, and through the lace curtains of the parlor windows he could see his wife and daughter, elegantly dressed, waiting to receive their distinguished visitor. He rang the bell impatiently, and a servant opened the door.

"The gentleman did n't come?" asked the maid.

"No," he said as he hung up his hat. This brought the ladies to the door.

"He did n't come?" they exclaimed. "What's the matter?"

"I'll tell you," he said, "Mary," this to the servant, a white girl, who stood in open-eyed curiosity, "we shan't need you any more to-night."

Then he went into the parlor, and, closing the door, told his story. When he reached the point where he had discovered the color of the honorable Mr. Brown, Miss Clayton caught her breath, and was on the verge of collapse.

"That nigger," said Mrs. Clayton indignantly, "can never set foot in this house. But what did you do with him?"

Mr. Clayton quickly unfolded his plan, and described the disposition he had made of the Congressman.

"It's an awful shame," said Mrs. Clayton. "Just think of the trouble and expense we have gone to! And poor Alice'll never get over it, for everybody knows he came to see her and that he's smitten with her. But you've done just right; we never would have been able to hold up our heads again if we had introduced a black man, even a Congressman, to the people that are invited here to-morrow night, as a sweetheart of Alice. Why, she wouldn't marry him if he was President of the United States and plated with gold an inch thick. The very idea!"

"Well," said Mr. Clayton, "then we've got to act quick. Alice must wrap up her throat—by the way, Alice, how *is* your throat?"

"It's sore," sobbed Alice, who had been in tears almost from her father's return, "and I don't care if I do have diphtheria and die, no, I don't!" and she wept on.

"Wrap up your throat and go to bed, and I'll go over to Doctor Pillsbury's and get a diphtheria card to nail up on the house. In the morning, first thing, we'll have to write notes recalling the invitations for to-morrow evening, and have them delivered by messenger boys. We were fools for not finding out all about this man from some one who knew, before we invited him here. Sadler don't know more than half he thinks he does, anyway. And we'll have to do this thing thoroughly, or our motives will be misconstrued, and people will say we are prejudiced and all that, when it is only a matter of principle with us."

The programme outlined above was carried out to the letter. The invitations were recalled, to the great disappointment of the invited guests. The family physician called several times during the day. Alice remained in bed, and the maid left without notice, in such a hurry that she forgot to take her best clothes.

Mr. Clayton himself remained at home. He had a telephone in the house, and was therefore in easy communication with his office, so that the business did not suffer materially by reason of his absence from the store. About ten o'clock in the morning a note came up from the hotel, expressing Mr. Brown's regrets and sympathy. Toward noon Mr. Clayton picked up the morning paper, which he had not theretofore had time to read, and was glancing over it casually, when his eye fell upon a column headed "A Colored Congressman." He read the article with astonishment that rapidly turned to chagrin and dismay. It was an interview describing the Congressman as a tall and shapely man, about thirty-five years old, with an olive complexion not noticeably darker than many a white man's, straight hair, and eyes as black as sloes.

"The bearing of this son of South Carolina reveals the polished manners of the Southern gentleman, and neither from his appearance nor his conversation would one suspect that the white blood which flows in his veins in such preponderating measure had ever been crossed by that of a darker race," wrote the reporter, who had received instructions at the office that for urgent business considerations the lake shipping interest wanted Representative Brown treated with marked consideration.

There was more of the article, but the introductory portion left Mr. Clayton in such a state of bewilderment that the paper fell from his hand. What was the meaning of it? Had he been mistaken? Obviously so, or else the reporter was wrong, which was manifestly improbable. When he had recovered himself somewhat, he picked up the newspaper and began reading where he had left off.

"Representative Brown traveled to Groveland in company with Bishop Jones of the African Methodist Jerusalem Church, who is *en route* to attend the general conference of his denomination at Detroit next week. The bishop, who came in while the writer was interviewing Mr. Brown, is a splendid type of the pure negro. He is said to be a man of great power among his people, which may easily be believed after one has looked upon his expressive countenance and heard him discuss the questions which affect the welfare of his church and his race."

Mr. Clayton stared at the paper. "'The bishop,'" he repeated, "'is a splendid type of the pure negro.' I must have mistaken the bishop for the Congressman! But how in the world did Jack get the thing balled up? I'll call up the store and demand an explanation of him.

"Jack," he asked, "what kind of a looking man was the fellow you gave the note to at the depot?"

"He was a very wicked-looking fellow, sir," came back the answer. "He had a bad eye, looked like a gambler, sir. I am not surprised that you did n't want to entertain him, even if he was a Congressman."

"What color was he—that's what I want to know—and what kind of hair did he have?"

"Why, he was about my complexion, sir, and had straight black hair."

The rules of the telephone company did not permit swearing over the line. Mr. Clayton broke the rules.

"Was there any one else with him?" he asked when he had relieved his mind.

"Yes, sir, Bishop Jones of the African Methodist Jerusalem Church was sitting there with him; they had traveled from Washington together. I drove the bishop to his stopping-place after I had left Mr. Brown at the hotel. I did n't suppose you'd mind."

Mr. Clayton fell into a chair, and indulged in thoughts unutterable.

He folded up the paper and slipped it under the family Bible, where it was least likely to be soon discovered.

"I'll hide the paper, anyway," he groaned. "I'll never hear the last of this till my dying day, so I may as well have a few hours' respite. It's too late to go back, and we've got to play the farce out. Alice is really sick with disappointment, and to let her know this now would only make her worse. Maybe he'll leave town in a day or two, and then she'll be in condition to stand it. Such luck is enough to disgust a man with trying to do right and live up to his principles."

Time hung a little heavy on Mr. Clayton's hands during the day. His wife was busy with the housework. He answered several telephone calls about Alice's health, and called up the store occasionally to ask how the business was getting on. After lunch he lay down on a sofa and took a nap, from which he was aroused by the sound of the door-bell. He went to the door. The evening paper was lying on the porch, and the newsboy, who had not observed the diphtheria sign until after he had rung, was hurrying away as fast as his legs would carry him.

Mr. Clayton opened the paper and looked it through to see if there was any reference to the visiting Congressman. He found what he sought and more. An article on the local page contained a résumé of the information given in the morning paper, with the following additional paragraph:—

"A reporter, who called at the Forest Hill this morning to interview Representative Brown, was informed that the Congressman had been invited to spend the remainder of his time in Groveland as the guest of Mr. William Watkins, the proprietor of the popular livery establishment on Main Street. Mr. Brown will remain in the city several days, and a reception will be tendered him at Mr. Watkins' on Wednesday evening."

"That ends it," sighed Mr. Clayton. "The dove of peace will never again rest on my roof-tree."

But why dwell longer on the sufferings of Mr. Clayton, or attempt to describe the feelings or chronicle the remarks of his wife and daughter when they learned the facts in the case?

As to Representative Brown, he was made welcome in the hospitable home of Mr. William Watkins. There was a large and brilliant assemblage at the party on Wednesday evening, at which were displayed the costumes prepared for the Clayton reception. Mr. Brown took a fancy to Miss Lura Watkins, to whom, before the week was over, he became engaged to be married. Meantime poor Alice, the innocent victim of circumstances and principles, lay sick abed with a supposititious case of malignant diphtheria, and a real case of acute disappointment and chagrin.

"Oh, Jack!" exclaimed Alice, a few weeks later, on the way home from evening church in company with the young man, "what a dreadful thing it all was! And to think of that hateful Lura Watkins marrying the Congressman!"

The street was shaded by trees at the point where they were passing, and there was no one in sight. Jack put his arm around her waist, and, leaning over, kissed her.

"Never mind, dear," he said soothingly, "you still have your 'last chance' left, and I'll prove myself a better man than the Congressman."

———

Occasionally, at social meetings, when the vexed question of the future of the colored race comes up, as it often does, for discussion, Mr. Clayton may still be heard to remark sententiously:—

"What the white people of the United States need most, in dealing with this problem, is a higher conception of the brotherhood of man. For of one blood God made all the nations of the earth."

THE PASSING OF
GRANDISON

I

When it is said that it was done to please a woman, there ought perhaps to be enough said to explain anything; for what a man will not do to please a woman is yet to be discovered. Nevertheless, it might be well to state a few preliminary facts to make it clear why young Dick Owens tried to run one of his father's negro men off to Canada.

In the early fifties, when the growth of anti-slavery sentiment and the constant drain of fugitive slaves into the North had so alarmed the slaveholders of the border States as to lead to the passage of the Fugitive Slave Law, a young white man from Ohio, moved by compassion for the sufferings of a certain bondman who happened to have a "hard master," essayed to help the slave to freedom. The attempt was discovered and frustrated; the abductor was tried and convicted for slave-stealing, and sentenced to a term of imprisonment in the penitentiary. His death, after the expiration of only a small part of the sentence, from cholera contracted while nursing stricken fellow prisoners, lent to the case a melancholy interest that made it famous in anti-slavery annals.

Dick Owens had attended the trial. He was a youth of about twenty-two, intelligent, handsome, and amiable, but extremely indolent, in a graceful and gentlemanly way; or, as old Judge Fenderson put it more than once, he was lazy as the Devil,— a mere figure of speech, of course, and not one that did justice to the Enemy of Mankind. When asked why he never did anything serious, Dick would good-naturedly reply, with a well-modulated drawl, that he did n't have to. His father was rich; there was but one other child, an unmarried daughter, who because of poor health would probably never marry, and Dick was therefore heir presumptive to a large estate. Wealth or social position he did not need to seek, for he was born to both. Charity Lomax had shamed him into studying law, but notwithstanding an hour or so a day spent at old Judge Fenderson's office, he did not make remarkable headway in his legal studies.

"What Dick needs," said the judge, who was fond of tropes, as became a scholar, and of horses, as was befitting a Kentuckian, "is the whip of necessity, or the spur of ambition. If he had either, he would soon need the snaffle to hold him back."

But all Dick required, in fact, to prompt him to the most remarkable thing he accomplished before he was twenty-five, was a mere suggestion from Charity Lomax. The story was never really known to but two persons until after the war, when it came out because it was a good story and there was no particular reason for its concealment.

Young Owens had attended the trial of this slave-stealer, or martyr,—either or both,—and, when it was over, had gone to call on Charity Lomax, and, while they sat on the veranda after sundown, had told her all about the trial. He was a good talker, as his career in later years disclosed, and described the proceedings very graphically.

"I confess," he admitted, "that while my principles were against the prisoner, my sympathies were on his side. It appeared that he was of good family, and that he had an old father and mother, respectable people, dependent upon him for support and comfort in their declining years. He had been led into the matter by pity for a negro whose master ought to have been run out of the county long ago for abusing his slaves. If it had been merely a question of old Sam Briggs's negro, nobody would have cared anything about it. But father and the rest of them stood on the principle of the thing, and told the judge so, and the fellow was sentenced to three years in the penitentiary."

Miss Lomax had listened with lively interest.

"I've always hated old Sam Briggs," she said emphatically, "ever since the time he broke a negro's leg with a piece of cordwood. When I hear of a cruel deed it makes the Quaker blood that came from my grandmother assert itself. Personally I wish that all Sam Briggs's negroes would run away. As for the young man, I regard him as a hero. He dared something for humanity. I could love a man who would take such chances for the sake of others."

"Could you love me, Charity, if I did something heroic?"

"You never will, Dick. You're too lazy for any use. You'll never do anything harder than playing cards or fox-hunting."

"Oh, come now, sweetheart! I've been courting you for a year, and it's the hardest work imaginable. Are you never going to love me?" he pleaded.

His hand sought hers, but she drew it back beyond his reach.

"I'll never love you, Dick Owens, until you have done something. When that time comes, I'll think about it."

"But it takes so long to do anything worth mentioning, and I don't want to wait. One must read two years to become a lawyer, and work five more to make a reputation. We shall both be gray by then."

"Oh, I don't know," she rejoined. "It does n't require a lifetime for a man to prove that he is a man. This one did something, or at least tried to."

"Well, I'm willing to attempt as much as any other man. What do you want me to do, sweetheart? Give me a test."

"Oh, dear me!" said Charity, "I don't care what you *do,* so you do *something*. Really, come to think of it, why should I care whether you do anything or not?"

"I'm sure I don't know why you should, Charity," rejoined Dick humbly, "for I'm aware that I'm not worthy of it."

"Except that I do hate," she added, relenting slightly, "to see a really clever man so utterly lazy and good for nothing."

"Thank you, my dear; a word of praise from you has sharpened my wits already. I have an idea! Will you love me if *I* run a negro off to Canada?"

"What nonsense!" said Charity scornfully. "You must be

losing your wits. Steal another man's slave, indeed, while your father owns a hundred!"

"Oh, there'll be no trouble about that," responded Dick lightly; "I'll run off one of the old man's; we've got too many anyway. It may not be quite as difficult as the other man found it, but it will be just as unlawful, and will demonstrate what I am capable of."

"Seeing's believing," replied Charity. "Of course, what you are talking about now is merely absurd. I'm going away for three weeks, to visit my aunt in Tennessee. If you're able to tell me, when I return, that you've done something to prove your quality, I'll—well, you may come and tell me about it."

II

Young Owens got up about nine o'clock next morning, and while making his toilet put some questions to his personal attendant, a rather bright looking young mulatto of about his own age.

"Tom," said Dick.

"Yas, Mars Dick," responded the servant.

"I'm going on a trip North. Would you like to go with me?"

Now, if there was anything that Tom would have liked to make, it was a trip North. It was something he had long contemplated in the abstract, but had never been able to muster up sufficient courage to attempt in the concrete. He was prudent enough, however, to dissemble his feelings.

"I would n't min' it, Mars Dick, ez long ez you'd take keer er me an' fetch me home all right."

Tom's eyes belied his words, however, and his young master felt well assured that Tom needed only a good opportunity to make him run away. Having a comfortable home, and a dismal prospect in case of failure, Tom was not likely to take any desperate chances; but young Owens was satisfied that in a free State but little persuasion would be required to lead Tom astray. With a very logical and characteristic desire to gain his end with the least necessary expenditure of effort, he decided to take Tom with him, if his father did not object.

Colonel Owens had left the house when Dick went to breakfast, so Dick did not see his father till luncheon.

"Father," he remarked casually to the colonel, over the fried chicken, "I'm feeling a trifle run down. I imagine my health would be improved somewhat by a little travel and change of scene."

"Why don't you take a trip North?" suggested his father. The colonel added to paternal affection a considerable respect for his son as the heir of a large estate. He himself had been "raised" in comparative poverty, and had laid the foundations of his fortune by hard work; and while he despised the ladder by which he had climbed, he could not entirely forget it, and unconsciously manifested, in his intercourse with his son, some of the poor man's deference toward the wealthy and well-born.

"I think I'll adopt your suggestion, sir," replied the son, "and run up to New York; and after I've been there awhile I may go on to Boston for a week or so. I've never been there, you know."

"There are some matters you can talk over with my factor in New York," rejoined the colonel, "and while you are up there among the Yankees, I hope you'll keep your eyes and ears open to find out what the rascally abolitionists are saying and doing. They're becoming altogether too active for our comfort, and entirely too many ungrateful niggers are running away. I hope the conviction of that fellow yesterday may discourage the rest of the breed. I'd just like to catch any one trying to run off one of my darkeys. He'd get short shrift; I don't think any Court would have a chance to try him."

"They are a pestiferous lot," assented Dick, "and dangerous to our institutions. But say, father, if I go North I shall want to take Tom with me."

Now, the colonel, while a very indulgent father, had pronounced views on the subject of negroes, having studied them, as he often said, for a great many years, and, as he asserted oftener still, understanding them perfectly. It is scarcely worth while to say, either, that he valued more highly than if he had inherited them the slaves he had toiled and schemed for.

"I don't think it safe to take Tom up North," he declared, with promptness and decision. "He's a good enough boy, but too smart to trust among those low-down abolitionists. I strongly suspect him of having learned to read, though I can't imagine how. I saw him with a newspaper the other day, and while he pretended to be looking at a woodcut, I'm almost sure he was reading the paper. I think it by no means safe to take him."

Dick did not insist, because he knew it was useless. The colonel would have obliged his son in any other matter, but his negroes were the outward and visible sign of his wealth and station, and therefore sacred to him.

"Whom do you think it safe to take?" asked Dick. "I suppose I'll have to have a body-servant."

"What's the matter with Grandison?" suggested the colonel. "He's handy enough, and I reckon we can trust him. He's too fond of good eating to risk losing his regular meals; besides, he's sweet on your mother's maid, Betty, and I've promised to let 'em get married before long. I'll have Grandison up, and we'll talk to him. Here, you boy Jack," called the colonel to a yellow youth in the next room who was catching flies and pulling their wings off to pass the time, "go down to the barn and tell Grandison to come here."

"Grandison," said the colonel, when the negro stood before him, hat in hand.

"Yas, marster."

"Have n't I always treated you right?"

"Yas, marster."

"Have n't you always got all you wanted to eat?"

"Yas, marster."

"And as much whiskey and tobacco as was good for you, Grandison?"

"Y-a-s, marster."

"I should just like to know, Grandison, whether you don't think yourself a great deal better off than those poor free negroes down by the plank road, with no kind master to look after them and no mistress to give them medicine when they're sick and—and"—

"Well, I sh'd jes' reckon I is better off, suh, dan dem low-down free niggers, suh! Ef anybody ax 'em who dey b'long ter, dey has ter say nobody, er e'se lie erbout it. Anybody ax me who I b'longs ter, I ain' got no 'casion ter be shame' ter tell 'em, no, suh,'deed I ain', suh!"

The colonel was beaming. This was true gratitude, and his feudal heart thrilled at such appreciative homage. What cold-blooded, heartless monsters they were who would break up this blissful relationship of kindly protection on the one hand, of wise subordination and loyal dependence on the other! The colonel always became indignant at the mere thought of such wickedness.

"Grandison," the colonel continued, "your young master Dick is going North for a few weeks, and I am thinking of letting him take you along. I shall send you on this trip, Grandison, in order that you may take care of your young master. He will need some one to wait on him, and no one can ever do it so well as one of the boys brought up with him on the old plantation. I am going to trust him in your hands, and I'm sure you'll do your duty faithfully, and bring him back home safe and sound—to old Kentucky."

Grandison grinned. "Oh yas, marster, I'll take keer er young Mars Dick."

"I want to warn you, though, Grandison," continued the colonel impressively, "against these cussed abolitionists, who try to entice servants from their comfortable homes and their indulgent masters, from the blue skies, the green fields, and the warm sunlight of their Southern home, and send them away off yonder to Canada, a dreary country, where the woods are full of wildcats and wolves and bears, where the snow lies up to the eaves of the houses for six months of the year, and the cold is so severe that it freezes your breath and curdles your blood; and where, when runaway niggers get sick and can't work, they are turned out to starve and die, unloved and uncared for. I reckon, Grandison, that you have too much sense to permit yourself to be led astray by any such foolish and wicked people."

"'Deed, suh, I would n' 'low none er dem cussed, low-down abolitioners ter come nigh me, suh. I'd—I'd—would I be 'lowed ter hit 'em, suh?"

"Certainly, Grandison," replied the colonel, chuckling, "hit 'em as hard as you can. I reckon they'd rather like it. Begad, I believe they would! It would serve 'em right to be hit by a nigger!"

"Er ef I did n't hit 'em, suh," continued Grandison reflectively, "I'd tell Mars Dick, en *he 'd* fix 'em. He 'd smash de face off'n 'em suh, I jes' knows he would."

"Oh yes, Grandison, your young master will protect you. You need fear no harm while he is near."

"Dey won't try ter steal me, will dey, marster?" asked the negro, with sudden alarm.

"I don't know, Grandison," replied the colonel, lighting a fresh cigar. "They're a desperate set of lunatics, and there's no telling what they may resort to. But if you stick close to your young master, and remember always that he is your best friend, and understands your real needs, and has your true interests at heart, and if you will be careful to avoid strangers who try to talk to you, you'll stand a fair chance of getting back to your home and your friends. And if you please your master Dick, he'll buy you a present, and a string of beads for Betty to wear when you and she get married in the fall."

"Thanky, marster, thanky, suh," replied Grandison, oozing gratitude at every pore; "you is a good marster, to be sho', suh; yas, 'deed you is. You kin jes' bet me and Mars Dick gwine git 'long jes' lack I wuz own boy ter Mars Dick. En it won't be my fault ef he don' want me fer his boy all de time, w'en we come back home ag'in."

"All right, Grandison, you may go now. You need n't work any more to-day, and here's a piece of tobacco for you off my own plug."

"Thanky, marster, thanky, marster! You is de bes' marster any nigger ever had in dis worl'." And Grandison bowed and scraped and disappeared round the corner, his jaws closing around a large section of the colonel's best tobacco.

"You may take Grandison," said the colonel to his son. "I allow he's abolitionist-proof."

III

Richard Owens, Esq., and servant, from Kentucky, registered
at the fashionable New York hostelry for Southerners in those
days, a hotel where an atmosphere congenial to Southern institutions was sedulously maintained. But there were negro waiters in the dining-room, and mulatto bell-boys, and Dick had no
doubt that Grandison, with the native gregariousness and gar-
rulousness of his race, would foregather and palaver with them
sooner or later, and Dick hoped that they would speedily inoc-
ulate him with the virus of freedom. For it was not Dick's intention to say anything to his servant about his plan to free
him, for obvious reasons. To mention one of them, if Grandison should go away, and by legal process be recaptured, his
young master's part in the matter would doubtless become
known, which would be embarrassing to Dick, to say the least.
If, on the other hand, he should merely give Grandison sufficient latitude, he had no doubt he would eventually lose him.
For while not exactly skeptical about Grandison's perfervid
loyalty, Dick had been a somewhat keen observer of human nature, in his own indolent way, and based his expectations upon
the force of the example and argument that his servant could
scarcely fail to encounter. Grandison should have a fair chance
to become free by his own initiative; if it should become necessary to adopt other measures to get rid of him, it would be time
enough to act when the necessity arose; and Dick Owens was
not the youth to take needless trouble.

The young master renewed some acquaintances and made
others, and spent a week or two very pleasantly in the best society of the metropolis, easily accessible to a wealthy, well-bred
young Southerner, with proper introductions. Young women
smiled on him, and young men of convivial habits pressed their
hospitalities; but the memory of Charity's sweet, strong face
and clear blue eyes made him proof against the blandishments
of the one sex and the persuasions of the other. Meanwhile
he kept Grandison supplied with pocket-money, and left him
mainly to his own devices. Every night when Dick came in he

hoped he might have to wait upon himself, and every morning he looked forward with pleasure to the prospect of making his toilet unaided. His hopes, however, were doomed to disappointment, for every night when he came in Grandison was on hand with a bootjack, and a nightcap mixed for his young master as the colonel had taught him to mix it, and every morning Grandison appeared with his master's boots blacked and his clothes brushed, and laid his linen out for the day.

"Grandison," said Dick one morning, after finishing his toilet, "this is the chance of your life to go around among your own people and see how they live. Have you met any of them?"

"Yas, suh, I's seen some of 'em. But I don' keer nuffin fer 'em, suh. Dey're diffe'nt f'm de niggers down ou' way. Dey 'lows dey 're free, but dey ain' got sense 'nuff ter know dey ain' half as well off as dey would be down Souf, whar dey'd be 'preciated."

When two weeks had passed without any apparent effect of evil example upon Grandison, Dick resolved to go on to Boston, where he thought the atmosphere might prove more favorable to his ends. After he had been at the Revere House for a day or two without losing Grandison, he decided upon slightly different tactics.

Having ascertained from a city directory the addresses of several well-known abolitionists, he wrote them each a letter something like this:—

DEAR FRIEND AND BROTHER:

A wicked slaveholder from Kentucky, stopping at the Revere House, has dared to insult the liberty-loving people of Boston by bringing his slave into their midst. Shall this be tolerated? Or shall steps be taken in the name of liberty to rescue a fellow-man from bondage? For obvious reasons I can only sign myself,

A FRIEND OF HUMANITY.

That his letter might have an opportunity to prove effective, Dick made it a point to send Grandison away from the hotel on various errands. On one of these occasions Dick watched him for quite a distance down the street. Grandison had scarcely left the hotel when a long-haired, sharp-featured man came out behind him, followed him, soon overtook him, and kept along beside him until they turned the next corner. Dick's hopes were roused by this spectacle, but sank correspondingly when Grandison returned to the hotel. As Grandison said nothing about the encounter, Dick hoped there might be some self-consciousness behind this unexpected reticence the results of which might develop later on.

But Grandison was on hand again when his master came back to the hotel at night, and was in attendance again in the morning, with hot water, to assist at his master's toilet. Dick sent him on further errands from day to day, and upon one occasion came squarely up to him—inadvertently of course—while Grandison was engaged in conversation with a young white man in clerical garb. When Grandison saw Dick approaching, he edged away from the preacher and hastened toward his master, with a very evident expression of relief upon his countenance.

"Mars Dick," he said, "dese yer abolitioners is jes' pesterin' de life out er me tryin' ter git me ter run away. I don' pay no 'tention ter 'em, but dey riles me so sometimes dat I'm feared I'll hit some of 'em some er dese days, an' dat mought git me inter trouble. I ain' said nuffin' ter you 'bout it, Mars Dick, fer I did n' wanter 'sturb yo' min'; but I don' like it, suh; no, suh, I don'! Is we gwine back home 'fo' long, Mars Dick?"

"We'll be going back soon enough," replied Dick somewhat shortly, while he inwardly cursed the stupidity of a slave who could be free and would not, and registered a secret vow that if he were unable to get rid of Grandison without assassinating him, and were therefore compelled to take him back to Kentucky, he would see that Grandison got a taste of an article of slavery that would make him regret his wasted opportunities. Meanwhile he determined to tempt his servant yet more strongly.

"Grandison," he said next morning, "I'm going away for a day or two, but I shall leave you here. I shall lock up a hundred dollars in this drawer and give you the key. If you need any of it, use it and enjoy yourself,—spend it all if you like,—for this is probably the last chance you'll have for some time to be in a free State, and you'd better enjoy your liberty while you may."

When he came back a couple of days later and found the faithful Grandison at his post, and the hundred dollars intact, Dick felt seriously annoyed. His vexation was increased by the fact that he could not express his feelings adequately. He did not even scold Grandison; how could he, indeed, find fault with one who so sensibly recognized his true place in the economy of civilization, and kept it with such touching fidelity?

"I can't say a thing to him," groaned Dick. "He deserves a leather medal, made out of his own hide tanned. I reckon I'll write to father and let him know what a model servant he has given me."

He wrote his father a letter which made the colonel swell with pride and pleasure. "I really think," the colonel observed to one of his friends, "that Dick ought to have the nigger interviewed by the Boston papers, so that they may see how contented and happy our darkeys really are."

Dick also wrote a long letter to Charity Lomax, in which he said, among many other things, that if she knew how hard he was working, and under what difficulties, to accomplish something serious for her sake, she would no longer keep him in suspense, but overwhelm him with love and admiration.

Having thus exhausted without result the more obvious methods of getting rid of Grandison, and diplomacy having also proved a failure, Dick was forced to consider more radical measures. Of course he might run away himself, and abandon Grandison, but this would be merely to leave him in the United States, where he was still a slave, and where, with his notions of loyalty, he would speedily be reclaimed. It was necessary, in order to accomplish the purpose of his trip to the North, to leave Grandison permanently in Canada, where he would be legally free.

"I might extend my trip to Canada," he reflected, "but that would be too palpable. I have it! I'll visit Niagara Falls on the way home, and lose him on the Canada side. When he once realizes that he is actually free, I'll warrant that he'll stay."

So the next day saw them westward bound, and in due course of time, by the somewhat slow conveyances of the period, they found themselves at Niagara. Dick walked and drove about the Falls for several days, taking Grandison along with him on most occasions. One morning they stood on the Canadian side, watching the wild whirl of the waters below them.

"Grandison," said Dick, raising his voice above the roar of the cataract, "do you know where you are now?"

"I's wid you, Mars Dick; dats all I keers."

"You are now in Canada, Grandison, where your people go when they run away from their masters. If you wished, Grandison, you might walk away from me this very minute, and I could not lay my hand upon you to take you back."

Grandison looked around uneasily.

"Let's go back ober de ribber, Mars Dick. I's feared I'll lose you ovuh heah, an' den I won' hab no marster, an' won't nebber be able to git back home no mo'."

Discouraged, but not yet hopeless, Dick said, a few minutes later,—

"Grandison, I'm going up the road a bit, to the inn over yonder. You stay here until I return. I'll not be gone a great while."

Grandison's eyes opened wide and he looked somewhat fearful.

"Is dey any er dem dadblasted abolitioners roun' heah, Mars Dick?"

"I don't imagine that there are," replied his master, hoping there might be. "But I'm not afraid of *your* running away, Grandison. I only wish I were," he added to himself.

Dick walked leisurely down the road to where the whitewashed inn, built of stone, with true British solidity, loomed up through the trees by the roadside. Arrived there he ordered a glass of ale and a sandwich, and took a seat at a table by a window, from which he could see Grandison in the distance. For a while he hoped that the seed he had sown might have fallen on fertile ground, and that Grandison, relieved from the restraining power of a master's eye, and finding himself in a free country, might get up and walk away; but the hope was vain, for

Grandison remained faithfully at his post, awaiting his master's return. He had seated himself on a broad flat stone, and, turning his eyes away from the grand and awe-inspiring spectacle that lay close at hand, was looking anxiously toward the inn where his master sat cursing his ill-timed fidelity.

By and by a girl came into the room to serve his order, and Dick very naturally glanced at her; and as she was young and pretty and remained in attendance, it was some minutes before he looked for Grandison. When he did so his faithful servant had disappeared.

To pay his reckoning and go away without the change was a matter quickly accomplished. Retracing his footsteps toward the Falls, he saw, to his great disgust, as he approached the spot where he had left Grandison, the familiar form of his servant stretched out on the ground, his face to the sun, his mouth open, sleeping the time away, oblivious alike to the grandeur of the scenery, the thunderous roar of the cataract, or the insidious voice of sentiment.

"Grandison," soliloquized his master, as he stood gazing down at his ebony encumbrance, "I do not deserve to be an American citizen; I ought not to have the advantages I possess over you; and I certainly am not worthy of Charity Lomax, if I am not smart enough to get rid of you. I have an idea! You shall yet be free, and I will be the instrument of your deliverance. Sleep on, faithful and affectionate servitor, and dream of the blue grass and the bright skies of old Kentucky, for it is only in your dreams that you will ever see them again!"

Dick retraced his footsteps towards the inn. The young woman chanced to look out of the window and saw the handsome young gentleman she had waited on a few minutes before, standing in the road a short distance away, apparently engaged in earnest conversation with a colored man employed as hostler for the inn. She thought she saw something pass from the white man to the other, but at that moment her duties called her away from the window, and when she looked out again the young gentleman had disappeared, and the hostler, with two other young men of the neighborhood, one white and one colored, were walking rapidly towards the Falls.

IV

Dick made the journey homeward alone, and as rapidly as the conveyances of the day would permit. As he drew near home his conduct in going back without Grandison took on a more serious aspect than it had borne at any previous time, and although he had prepared the colonel by a letter sent several days ahead, there was still the prospect of a bad quarter of an hour with him; not, indeed, that his father would upbraid him, but he was likely to make searching inquiries. And notwithstanding the vein of quiet recklessness that had carried Dick through his preposterous scheme, he was a very poor liar, having rarely had occasion or inclination to tell anything but the truth. Any reluctance to meet his father was more than offset, however, by a stronger force drawing him homeward, for Charity Lomax must long since have returned from her visit to her aunt in Tennessee.

Dick got off easier than he had expected. He told a straight story, and a truthful one, so far as it went.

The colonel raged at first, but rage soon subsided into anger, and anger moderated into annoyance, and annoyance into a sort of garrulous sense of injury. The colonel thought he had been hardly used; he had trusted this negro, and he had broken faith. Yet, after all, he did not blame Grandison so much as he did the abolitionists, who were undoubtedly at the bottom of it.

As for Charity Lomax, Dick told her, privately of course, that he had run his father's man, Grandison, off to Canada, and left him there.

"Oh, Dick," she had said with shuddering alarm, "what have you done? If they knew it they'd send you to the penitentiary, like they did that Yankee."

"But they don't know it," he had replied seriously; adding, with an injured tone, "you don't seem to appreciate my heroism like you did that of the Yankee; perhaps it's because I wasn't caught and sent to the penitentiary. I thought you wanted me to do it."

"Why, Dick Owens!" she exclaimed. "You know I never dreamed of any such outrageous proceeding.

"But I presume I'll have to marry you," she concluded, after some insistence on Dick's part, "if only to take care of you. You are too reckless for anything; and a man who goes chasing all over the North, being entertained by New York and Boston society and having negroes to throw away, needs some one to look after him."

"It's a most remarkable thing," replied Dick fervently, "that your views correspond exactly with my profoundest convictions. It proves beyond question that we were made for one another."

They were married three weeks later. As each of them had just returned from a journey, they spent their honeymoon at home.

A week after the wedding they were seated, one afternoon, on the piazza of the colonel's house, where Dick had taken his bride, when a negro from the yard ran down the lane and threw open the big gate for the colonel's buggy to enter. The colonel was not alone. Beside him, ragged and travel-stained, bowed with weariness and upon his face a haggard look that told of hardship and privation, sat the lost Grandison.

The colonel alighted at the steps.

"Take the lines, Tom," he said to the man who had opened the gate, "and drive round to the barn. Help Grandison down,—poor devil, he's so stiff he can hardly move!—and get a tub of water and wash him and rub him down, and feed him, and give him a big drink of whiskey, and then let him come round and see his young master and his new mistress."

The colonel's face wore an expression compounded of joy and indignation,—joy at the restoration of a valuable piece of property; indignation for reasons he proceeded to state.

"It's astounding, the depths of depravity the human heart is capable of! I was coming along the road three miles away, when I heard some one call me from the roadside. I pulled up the mare, and who should come out of the woods but Grandison. The poor nigger could hardly crawl along, with the help

THE PASSING OF GRANDISON

of a broken limb. I was never more astonished in my life. You could have knocked me down with a feather. He seemed pretty far gone,—he could hardly talk above a whisper,—and I had to give him a mouthful of whiskey to brave him up so he could tell his story. It's just as I thought from the beginning, Dick; Grandison had no notion of running away; he knew when he was well off, and where his friends were. All the persuasions of abolition liars and runaway niggers did not move him. But the desperation of those fanatics knew no bounds; their guilty consciences gave them no rest. They got the notion somehow that Grandison belonged to a nigger-catcher, and had been brought North as a spy to help capture ungrateful runaway servants. They actually kidnapped him—just think of it!—and gagged him and bound him and threw him rudely into a wagon, and carried him into the gloomy depths of a Canadian forest, and locked him in a lonely hut, and fed him on bread and water for three weeks. One of the scoundrels wanted to kill him, and persuaded the others that it ought to be done; but they got to quarreling about how they should do it, and before they had their minds made up Grandison escaped, and, keeping his back steadily to the North Star, made his way, after suffering incredible hardships, back to the old plantation, back to his master, his friends, and his home. Why, it's as good as one of Scott's novels! Mr. Simms or some other one of our Southern authors ought to write it up."

"Don't you think, sir," suggested Dick, who had calmly smoked his cigar throughout the colonel's animated recital, "that that kidnapping yarn sounds a little improbable? Is n't there some more likely explanation?"

"Nonsense, Dick; it's the gospel truth! Those infernal abolitionists are capable of anything—everything! Just think of their locking the poor, faithful nigger up, beating him, kicking him, depriving him of his liberty, keeping him on bread and water for three long, lonesome weeks, and he all the time pining for the old plantation!"

There were almost tears in the colonel's eyes at the picture of Grandison's sufferings that he conjured up. Dick still professed to be slightly skeptical, and met Charity's severely questioning eye with bland unconsciousness.

The colonel killed the fatted calf for Grandison, and for two or three weeks the returned wanderer's life was a slave's dream of pleasure. His fame spread throughout the county, and the colonel gave him a permanent place among the house servants, where he could always have him conveniently at hand to relate his adventures to admiring visitors.

About three weeks after Grandison's return the colonel's faith in sable humanity was rudely shaken, and its foundations almost broken up. He came near losing his belief in the fidelity of the negro to his master,—the servile virtue most highly prized and most sedulously cultivated by the colonel and his kind. One Monday morning Grandison was missing. And not only Grandison, but his wife, Betty the maid; his mother, aunt Eunice; his father, uncle Ike; his brothers, Tom and John, and his little sister, Elsie, were likewise absent from the plantation; and a hurried search and inquiry in the neighborhood resulted in no information as to their whereabouts. So much valuable property could not be lost without an effort to recover it, and the wholesale nature of the transaction carried consternation to the hearts of those whose ledgers were chiefly bound in black. Extremely energetic measures were taken by the colonel and his friends. The fugitives were traced, and followed from point to point, on their northward run through Ohio. Several times the hunters were close upon their heels, but the magnitude of the escaping party begot unusual vigilance on the part of those who sympathized with the fugitives, and strangely enough, the underground railroad seemed to have had its tracks cleared and signals set for this particular train. Once, twice, the colonel thought he had them, but they slipped through his fingers.

One last glimpse he caught of his vanishing property, as he stood, accompanied by a United States marshal, on a wharf at a port on the south shore of Lake Erie. On the stern of a small steamboat which was receding rapidly from the wharf, with her nose pointing toward Canada, there stood a group of familiar dark faces, and the look they cast backward was not one of longing for the fleshpots of Egypt. The colonel saw Grandison point him out to one of the crew of the vessel, who waved his hand derisively toward the colonel. The latter shook his fist impotently—and the incident was closed.

UNCLE WELLINGTON'S
WIVES

I

Uncle Wellington Braboy was so deeply absorbed in thought as he walked slowly homeward from the weekly meeting of the Union League, that he let his pipe go out, a fact of which he remained oblivious until he had reached the little frame house in the suburbs of Patesville, where he lived with aunt Milly, his wife. On this particular occasion the club had been addressed by a visiting brother from the North, Professor Patterson, a tall, well-formed mulatto, who wore a perfectly fitting suit of broad-cloth, a shiny silk hat, and linen of dazzling whiteness,— in short, a gentleman of such distinguished appearance that the doors and windows of the offices and stores on Front Street were filled with curious observers as he passed through that thoroughfare in the early part of the day. This polished stranger was a traveling organizer of Masonic lodges, but he also claimed to be a high officer in the Union League, and had been invited to lecture before the local chapter of that organization at Patesville.

The lecture had been largely attended, and uncle Wellington Braboy had occupied a seat just in front of the platform. The subject of the lecture was "The Mental, Moral, Physical, Political, Social, and Financial Improvement of the Negro Race in America," a theme much dwelt upon, with slight variations, by colored orators. For to this struggling people, then as now, the problem of their uncertain present and their doubtful future was the chief concern of life. The period was the hopeful one. The Federal Government retained some vestige of authority in

the South, and the newly emancipated race cherished the delusion that under the Constitution, that enduring rock on which
our liberties are founded, and under the equal laws it pur-
ported to guarantee, they would enter upon the era of freedom
and opportunity which their Northern friends had inaugurated
with such solemn sanctions. The speaker pictured in eloquent
language the state of ideal equality and happiness enjoyed by
colored people at the North: how they sent their children to
school with the white children; how they sat by white people in
the churches and theatres, ate with them in the public restau-
rants, and buried their dead in the same cemeteries. The professor waxed eloquent with the development of his theme, and,
as a finishing touch to an alluring picture, assured the excited
audience that the intermarriage of the races was common, and
that he himself had espoused a white woman.

Uncle Wellington Braboy was a deeply interested listener. He
had heard something of these facts before, but his information
had always come in such vague and questionable shape that he
had paid little attention to it. He knew that the Yankees had
freed the slaves, and that runaway negroes had always gone to
the North to seek liberty; any such equality, however, as the visiting brother had depicted, was more than uncle Wellington
had ever conceived as actually existing anywhere in the world.
At first he felt inclined to doubt the truth of the speaker's statements; but the cut of his clothes, the eloquence of his language,
and the flowing length of his whiskers, were so far superior
to anything uncle Wellington had ever met among the colored
people of his native State, that he felt irresistibly impelled to the
conviction that nothing less than the advantages claimed for
the North by the visiting brother could have produced such
an exquisite flower of civilization. Any lingering doubts uncle
Wellington may have felt were entirely dispelled by the courtly
bow and cordial grasp of the hand with which the visiting
brother acknowledged the congratulations showered upon him
by the audience at the close of his address.

The more uncle Wellington's mind dwelt upon the professor's speech, the more attractive seemed the picture of Northern life presented. Uncle Wellington possessed in large measure

the imaginative faculty so freely bestowed by nature upon the race from which the darker half of his blood was drawn. He had indulged in occasional day-dreams of an ideal state of social equality, but his wildest flights of fancy had never located it nearer than heaven, and he had felt some misgivings about its practical working even there. Its desirability he had never doubted, and the speech of the evening before had given a local habitation and a name to the forms his imagination had bodied forth. Giving full rein to his fancy, he saw in the North a land flowing with milk and honey,—a land peopled by noble men and beautiful women, among whom colored men and women moved with the ease and grace of acknowledged right. Then he placed himself in the foreground of the picture. What a fine figure he would have made in the world if he had been born at the free North! He imagined himself dressed like the professor, and passing the contribution-box in a white church; and most pleasant of his dreams, and the hardest to realize as possible, was that of the gracious white lady he might have called wife. Uncle Wellington was a mulatto, and his features were those of his white father, though tinged with the hue of his mother's race; and as he lifted the kerosene lamp at evening, and took a long look at his image in the little mirror over the mantelpiece, he said to himself that he was a very good-looking man, and could have adorned a much higher sphere in life than that in which the accident of birth had placed him. He fell asleep and dreamed that he lived in a two-story brick house, with a spacious flower garden in front, the whole inclosed by a high iron fence; that he kept a carriage and servants, and never did a stroke of work. This was the highest style of living in Patesville, and he could conceive of nothing finer.

Uncle Wellington slept later than usual the next morning, and the sunlight was pouring in at the open window of the bedroom, when his dreams were interrupted by the voice of his wife, in tones meant to be harsh, but which no ordinary degree of passion could rob of their native unctuousness.

"Git up f'm dere, you lazy, good-fuh-nuffin' nigger! Is you gwine ter sleep all de mawnin'? I's ti'ed er dis yer runnin' 'roun'

all night an' den sleepin' all day. You won't git dat tater patch
hoed ovuh ter-day 'less'n you git up f'm dere an' git at it."

Uncle Wellington rolled over, yawned cavernously, stretched
himself, and with a muttered protest got out of bed and put on
his clothes. Aunt Milly had prepared a smoking breakfast of
hominy and fried bacon, the odor of which was very grateful to
his nostrils.

"Is breakfus' done ready?" he inquired, tentatively, as he
came into the kitchen and glanced at the table.

"No, it ain't ready, an' 't ain't gwine ter be ready 'tel you tote
dat wood an' water in," replied aunt Milly severely, as she
poured two teacups of boiling water on two tablespoonfuls of
ground coffee.

Uncle Wellington went down to the spring and got a pail of
water, after which he brought in some oak logs for the fireplace
and some lightwood for kindling. Then he drew a chair towards
the table and started to sit down.

"Wonduh what's de matter wid you dis mawnin' anyhow,"
remarked aunt Milly. "You must 'a' be'n up ter some devilment
las' night, fer yo' recommemb'ance is so po' dat you fus' fergit
ter git up, an' den fergit ter wash yo' face an' hands fo' you set
down ter de table. I don' 'low nobody ter eat at my table dat
a-way."

"I don' see no use'n washin' 'em so much," replied Wellington wearily. "Dey gits dirty ag'in right off, an' den you got ter
wash 'em ovuh ag'in; it's jes' pilin' up wuk what don' fetch in
nuffin'. De dirt don' show nohow, 'n' I don' see no advantage
in bein' black, ef you got to keep on washin' yo' face 'n' han's
jes' lack w'ite folks." He nevertheless performed his ablutions
in a perfunctory way, and resumed his seat at the breakfast-
table.

"Ole 'oman," he asked, after the edge of his appetite had
been taken off, "how would you lack ter live at de Norf?"

"I dunno nuffin' 'bout de Norf," replied aunt Milly. "It's
hard 'nuff ter git erlong heah, whar we knows all erbout it."

"De brother what 'dressed de meetin' las' night say dat de
wages at de Norf is twicet ez big ez dey is heah."

"You could make a sight mo' wages heah ef you'd 'ten' ter yo' wuk better," replied aunt Milly.

Uncle Wellington ignored this personality, and continued, "An' he say de cullud folks got all de privileges er de w'ite folks,—dat dey chillen goes ter school tergedder, dat dey sets on same seats in chu'ch, an' sarves on jury, 'n' rides on de kyars an' steamboats wid de w'ite folks, an' eats at de fus' table."

"Dat 'u'd suit you," chuckled aunt Milly, "an' you'd stay dere fer de secon' table, too. How dis man know 'bout all dis yer foolis'ness?" she asked incredulously.

"He come f'm de Norf," said uncle Wellington, "an' he 'spe-unced it all hisse'f."

"Well, he can't make me b'lieve it," she rejoined, with a shake of her head.

"An' you would n' lack ter go up dere an' 'joy all dese privileges?" asked uncle Wellington, with some degree of earnestness.

The old woman laughed until her sides shook. "Who gwine ter take me up dere?" she inquired.

"You got de money yo'se'f."

"I ain't got no money fer ter was'e," she replied shortly, becoming serious at once; and with that the subject was dropped.

Uncle Wellington pulled a hoe from under the house, and took his way wearily to the potato patch. He did not feel like working, but aunt Milly was the undisputed head of the establishment, and he did not dare to openly neglect his work. In fact, he regarded work at any time as a disagreeable necessity to be avoided as much as possible.

His wife was cast in a different mould. Externally she would have impressed the casual observer as a neat, well-preserved, and good-looking black woman, of middle age, every curve of whose ample figure—and her figure was all curves—was suggestive of repose. So far from being indolent, or even deliberate in her movements, she was the most active and energetic woman in the town. She went through the physical exercises of a prayer-meeting with astonishing vigor. It was exhilarating to see her wash a shirt, and a study to watch her do it up. A quick jerk shook out the dampened garment; one pass of her ample palm spread it over the ironing-board, and a few well-directed strokes with the iron accomplished what would have occupied the ordinary laundress for half an hour.

To this uncommon, and in uncle Wellington's opinion, unnecessary and unnatural, activity, his own habits were a steady protest. If aunt Milly had been willing to support him in idleness, he would have acquiesced without a murmur in her habits of industry. This she would not do, and, moreover, insisted on his working at least half the time. If she had invested the proceeds of her labor in rich food and fine clothing, he might have endured it better; but to her passion for work was added a most detestable thrift. She absolutely refused to pay for Wellington's clothes, and required him to furnish a certain proportion of the family supplies. Her savings were carefully put by, and with them she had bought and paid for the modest cottage which she and her husband occupied. Under her careful hand it was always neat and clean; in summer the little yard was gay with bright-colored flowers, and woe to the heedless pickaninny who should stray into her yard and pluck a rose or a verbena! In a stout oaken chest under her bed she kept a capacious stocking, into which flowed a steady stream of fractional currency. She carried the key to this chest in her pocket, a proceeding regarded by uncle Wellington with no little disfavor. He was of the opinion—an opinion he would not have dared to assert in her presence—that his wife's earnings were his own property; and he looked upon this stocking as a drunkard's wife might regard the saloon which absorbed her husband's wages.

Uncle Wellington hurried over the potato patch on the morning of the conversation above recorded, and as soon as he saw aunt Milly go away with a basket of clothes on her head, returned to the house, put on his coat, and went uptown.

He directed his steps to a small frame building fronting on the main street of the village, at a point where the street was intersected by one of the several creeks meandering through the town, cooling the air, providing numerous swimming-holes for the amphibious small boy, and furnishing water-power for grist-mills and sawmills. The rear of the building rested on long brick pillars, built up from the bottom of the steep bank of the creek, while the front was level with the street. This was the office of Mr. Matthew Wright, the sole representative of the colored race at the bar of Chinquapin County. Mr. Wright came of an "old issue" free colored family, in which, though the negro blood was present in an attenuated strain, a line of free ancestry could be traced beyond the Revolutionary War. He had enjoyed exceptional opportunities, and enjoyed the distinction of being the first, and for a long time the only colored lawyer in North Carolina. His services were frequently called into requisition by impecunious people of his own race; when they had money they went to white lawyers, who, they shrewdly conjectured, would have more influence with judge or jury than a colored lawyer, however able.

Uncle Wellington found Mr. Wright in his office. Having inquired after the health of the lawyer's family and all his relations in detail, uncle Wellington asked for a professional opinion.

"Mistah Wright, ef a man's wife got money, whose money is dat befo' de law—his'n er her'n?"

The lawyer put on his professional air, and replied:—

"Under the common law, which in default of special legislative enactment is the law of North Carolina, the personal property of the wife belongs to her husband."

"But dat don' jes' tech de p'int, suh. I wuz axin' 'bout money."

"You see, uncle Wellington, your education has not rendered you familiar with legal phraseology. The term 'personal property' or 'estate' embraces, according to Blackstone, all property other than land, and therefore includes money. Any money a man's wife has is his, constructively, and will be recognized as his actually, as soon as he can secure possession of it."

"Dat is ter say, suh—my eddication don' quite 'low me ter understan' dat—dat is ter say"—

"That is to say, it's yours when you get it. It is n't yours so that the law will help you get it; but on the other hand, when you once lay your hands on it, it is yours so that the law won't take it away from you."

Uncle Wellington nodded to express his full comprehension of the law as expounded by Mr. Wright, but scratched his head in a way that expressed some disappointment. The law seemed to wobble. Instead of enabling him to stand up fearlessly and demand his own, it threw him back upon his own efforts; and the prospect of his being able to overpower or outwit aunt Milly by any ordinary means was very poor.

He did not leave the office, but hung around awhile as though there were something further he wished to speak about. Finally, after some discursive remarks about the crops and politics, he asked, in an offhand, disinterested manner, as though the thought had just occurred to him:—

"Mistah Wright, w'ile's we 're talkin' 'bout law matters, what do it cos' ter git a defoce?"

"That depends upon circumstances. It is n't altogether a matter of expense. Have you and aunt Milly been having trouble?"

"Oh no, suh; I was jes' a-wond'rin'."

"You see," continued the lawyer, who was fond of talking, and had nothing else to do for the moment, "a divorce is not an easy thing to get in this State under any circumstances. It used to be the law that divorce could be granted only by special act of the legislature; and it is but recently that the subject has been relegated to the jurisdiction of the courts."

Uncle Wellington understood a part of this, but the answer had not been exactly to the point in his mind.

"S'pos'n', den, jes' fer de argument, me an' my ole 'oman sh'd fall out en wanter separate, how could I git a defoce?"

"That would depend on what you quarreled about. It's pretty hard work to answer general questions in a particular way. If you merely wished to separate, it would n't be necessary to get a divorce; but if you should want to marry again, you would have to be divorced, or else you would be guilty of bigamy, and could be sent up to the penitentiary. But, by the way, uncle Wellington, when were you married?"

"I got married 'fo' de wah, when I was livin' down on Rockfish Creek."

"When you were in slavery?"

"Yas, suh."

"Did you have your marriage registered after the surrender?"

"No, suh; never knowed nuffin' 'bout dat."

After the war, in North Carolina and other States, the freed people who had sustained to each other the relation of husband and wife as it existed among slaves were required by law to register their consent to continue in the marriage relation. By this simple expedient their former marriages of convenience received the sanction of law, and their children the seal of legitimacy. In many cases, however, where the parties lived in districts remote from the larger towns, the ceremony was neglected, or never heard of by the freedmen.

"Well," said the lawyer, "if that is the case, and you and aunt Milly should disagree, it would n't be necessary for you to get a divorce, even if you should want to marry again. You were never legally married."

"So Milly ain't my lawful wife, den?"

"She may be your wife in one sense of the word, but not in such a sense as to render you liable to punishment for bigamy if you should marry another woman. But I hope you will never want to do anything of the kind for you have a very good wife now."

Uncle Wellington went away thoughtfully, but with a feeling of unaccustomed lightness and freedom. He had not felt so free since the memorable day when he had first heard of the Emancipation Proclamation. On leaving the lawyer's office, he called at the workshop of one of his friends, Peter Williams, a shoemaker by trade, who had a brother living in Ohio.

"Is you hearn f'm Sam lately?" uncle Wellington inquired, after the conversation had drifted through the usual generalities.

"His mammy got er letter f'm 'im last week; he's livin' in de town er Groveland now."

"How's he gittin' on?"

"He says he gittin' on monst'us well. He 'low ez how he make five dollars a day w'itewashin', an' have all he kin do."

The shoemaker related various details of his brother's prosperity, and uncle Wellington returned home in a very thoughtful mood, revolving in his mind a plan of future action. This plan had been vaguely assuming form ever since the professor's lecture, and the events of the morning had brought out the detail in bold relief.

Two days after the conversation with the shoemaker, aunt Milly went, in the afternoon, to visit a sister of hers who lived several miles out in the country. During her absence, which lasted until nightfall, uncle Wellington went uptown and purchased a cheap oilcloth valise from a shrewd son of Israel, who had penetrated to this locality with a stock of notions and cheap clothing. Uncle Wellington had his purchase done up in brown paper, and took the parcel under his arm. Arrived at home he unwrapped the valise, and thrust into its capacious jaws his best suit of clothes, some underwear, and a few other small articles for personal use and adornment. Then he carried the valise out into the yard, and, first looking cautiously around to see if there was any one in sight, concealed it in a clump of bushes in a corner of the yard.

It may be inferred from this proceeding that uncle Wellington was preparing for a step of some consequence. In fact, he had fully made up his mind to go to the North; but he still lacked the most important requisite for traveling with comfort, namely, the money to pay his expenses. The idea of tramping the distance which separated him from the promised land of liberty and equality had never occurred to him. When a slave, he had several times been importuned by fellow servants to join them in the attempt to escape from bondage, but he had never wanted his freedom badly enough to walk a thousand miles for it; if he could have gone to Canada by stage-coach, or by rail, or on horseback, with stops for regular meals, he would probably have undertaken the trip. The funds he now needed for his journey were in aunt Milly's chest. He had thought a great deal about his right to this money. It was his wife's savings, and he had never dared to dispute, openly, her right to exercise exclusive control over what she earned; but the lawyer had assured him of his right to the money, of which he was already constructively in possession, and he had therefore determined to possess himself actually of the coveted stocking. It was impracticable for him to get the key of the chest. Aunt Milly kept it in her pocket by day and under her pillow at night. She was a light sleeper, and, if not awakened by the abstraction of the key, would certainly have been disturbed by the unlocking of the chest. But one alternative remained, and that was to break open the chest in her absence.

There was a revival in progress at the colored Methodist church. Aunt Milly was as energetic in her religion as in other respects, and had not missed a single one of the meetings. She returned at nightfall from her visit to the country and prepared a frugal supper. Uncle Wellington did not eat as heartily as usual. Aunt Milly perceived his want of appetite, and spoke of it. He explained it by saying that he did not feel very well.

"Is you gwine ter chu'ch ter-night?" inquired his wife.

"I reckon I'll stay home an' go ter bed," he replied. "I ain't be'n feelin' well dis evenin', an' I 'spec' I better git a good night's res'."

"Well, you kin stay ef you mineter. Good preachin' 'u'd make you feel better, but ef you ain't gwine, don' forgit ter tote in some wood an' lighterd 'fo' you go ter bed. De moon is shinin' bright, an' you can't have no 'scuse 'bout not bein' able ter see."

Uncle Wellington followed her out to the gate, and watched her receding form until it disappeared in the distance. Then he re-entered the house with a quick step, and taking a hatchet from a corner of the room, drew the chest from under the bed. As he applied the hatchet to the fastenings, a thought struck him, and by the flickering light of the pine-knot blazing on the hearth, a look of hesitation might have been seen to take the place of the determined expression his face had worn up to that time. He had argued himself into the belief that his present action was lawful and justifiable. Though this conviction had not prevented him from trembling in every limb, as though he were committing a mere vulgar theft, it had still nerved him to the deed. Now even his moral courage began to weaken. The lawyer had told him that his wife's property was his own; in taking it he was therefore only exercising his lawful right. But at the point of breaking open the chest, it occurred to him that he was taking this money in order to get away from aunt Milly, and

that he justified his desertion of her by the lawyer's opinion
that she was not his lawful wife. If she was not his wife, then he
had no right to take the money; if she was his wife, he had no
right to desert her, and would certainly have no right to marry
another woman. His scheme was about to go to shipwreck on
this rock, when another idea occurred to him.

"De lawyer say dat in one sense er de word de ole 'oman is
my wife, an' in anudder sense er de word she ain't my wife. Ef
I goes ter de Norf an' marry a w'ite 'oman, I ain't commit no
brigamy, 'caze in dat sense er de word she ain't my wife; but ef
I takes dis money, I ain't stealn' it, 'caze in dat sense er de word
she is my wife. Dat 'splains all de trouble away."

Having reached this ingenious conclusion, uncle Wellington
applied the hatchet vigorously, soon loosened the fastenings of
the chest, and with trembling hands extracted from its depths
a capacious blue cotton stocking. He emptied the stocking on
the table. His first impulse was to take the whole, but again
there arose in his mind a doubt—a very obtrusive, unreason-
able doubt, but a doubt, nevertheless—of the absolute rectitude
of his conduct; and after a moment's hesitation he hurriedly
counted the money—it was in bills of small denominations—
and found it to be about two hundred and fifty dollars. He then
divided it into two piles of one hundred and twenty-five dollars
each. He put one pile into his pocket, returned the remainder to
the stocking, and replaced it where he had found it. He then
closed the chest and shoved it under the bed. After having
arranged the fire so that it could safely be left burning, he took
a last look around the room, and went out into the moonlight,
locking the door behind him, and hanging the key on a nail in
the wall, where his wife would be likely to look for it. He then
secured his valise from behind the bushes, and left the yard. As
he passed by the wood-pile, he said to himself:—

"Well, I declar' ef I ain't done fergot ter tote in dat lighterd;
I reckon de ole 'oman 'll ha' ter fetch it in herse'f dis time."

He hastened through the quiet streets, avoiding the few
people who were abroad at that hour, and soon reached the
railroad station, from which a North-bound train left at nine
o'clock. He went around to the dark side of the train, and

climbed into a second-class car, where he shrank into the darkest corner and turned his face away from the dim light of the single dirty lamp. There were no passengers in the car except one or two sleepy negroes, who had got on at some other station, and a white man who had gone into the car to smoke, accompanied by a gigantic bloodhound.

Finally the train crept out of the station. From the window uncle Wellington looked out upon the familiar cabins and turpentine stills, the new barrel factory, the brickyard where he had once worked for some time; and as the train rattled through the outskirts of the town, he saw gleaming in the moonlight the white headstones of the colored cemetery where his only daughter had been buried several years before.

Presently the conductor came around. Uncle Wellington had not bought a ticket, and the conductor collected a cash fare. He was not acquainted with uncle Wellington, but had just had a drink at the saloon near the depot, and felt at peace with all mankind.

"Where are you going, uncle?" he inquired carelessly.

Uncle Wellington's face assumed the ashen hue which does duty for pallor in dusty countenances, and his knees began to tremble. Controlling his voice as well as he could, he replied that he was going up to Jonesboro, the terminus of the railroad, to work for a gentleman at that place. He felt immensely relieved when the conductor pocketed the fare, picked up his lantern, and moved away. It was very unphilosophical and very absurd that a man who was only doing right should feel like a thief, shrink from the sight of other people, and lie instinctively. Fine distinctions were not in uncle Wellington's line, but he was struck by the unreasonableness of his feelings, and still more by the discomfort they caused him. By and by, however, the motion of the train made him drowsy; his thoughts all ran together in confusion; and he fell asleep with his head on his valise, and one hand in his pocket, clasped tightly around the roll of money.

II

The train from Pittsburg drew into the Union Depot at Groveland, Ohio, one morning in the spring of 187–, with bell ring-
ing and engine puffing; and from a smoking-car emerged the
form of uncle Wellington Braboy, a little dusty and travel-
stained, and with a sleepy look about his eyes. He mingled in
the crowd, and, valise in hand, moved toward the main exit
from the depot. There were several tracks to be crossed, and
more than once a watchman snatched him out of the way of a
baggage-truck, or a train backing into the depot. He at length
reached the door, beyond which, and as near as the regulations
would permit, stood a number of hackmen, vociferously soliciting patronage. One of them, a colored man, soon secured several passengers. As he closed the door after the last one he
turned to uncle Wellington, who stood near him on the sidewalk, looking about irresolutely.

"Is you goin' uptown?" asked the hackman, as he prepared
to mount the box.

"Yas, suh."

"I'll take you up fo' a quahtah, ef you want ter git up here
an' ride on de box wid me."

Uncle Wellington accepted the offer and mounted the box.
The hackman whipped up his horses, the carriage climbed the
steep hill leading up to the town, and the passengers inside
were soon deposited at their hotels.

"Whereabouts do you want to go?" asked the hackman of
uncle Wellington, when the carriage was emptied of its last passengers.

"I want ter go ter Brer Sam Williams's," said Wellington.

"What's his street an' number?"

Uncle Wellington did not know the street and number, and
the hackman had to explain to him the mystery of numbered
houses, to which he was a total stranger.

"Where is he from?" asked the hackman, "and what is his
business?"

"He is f'm Norf Ca'lina," replied uncle Wellington, "an' makes his livin' w'itewashin'."

"I reckon I knows de man," said the hackman. "I 'spec' he's changed his name. De man I knows is name' Johnson. He b'longs ter my chu'ch. I'm gwine out dat way ter git a passenger fer de ten o'clock train, an' I'll take you by dere."

They followed one of the least handsome streets of the city for more than a mile, turned into a cross street, and drew up before a small frame house, from the front of which a sign, painted in white upon a black background, announced to the reading public, in letters inclined to each other at various angles, that whitewashing and kalsomining were "dun" there. A knock at the door brought out a slatternly looking colored woman. She had evidently been disturbed at her toilet, for she held a comb in one hand, and the hair on one side of her head stood out loosely, while on the other side it was braided close to her head. She called her husband, who proved to be the Patesville shoemaker's brother. The hackman introduced the traveler, whose name he had learned on the way out, collected his quarter, and drove away.

Mr. Johnson, the shoemaker's brother, welcomed uncle Wellington to Groveland, and listened with eager delight to the news of the old town, from which he himself had run away many years before, and followed the North Star to Groveland. He had changed his name from "Williams" to "Johnson," on account of the Fugitive Slave Law, which, at the time of his escape from bondage, had rendered it advisable for runaway slaves to court obscurity. After the war he had retained the adopted name. Mrs. Johnson prepared breakfast for her guest, who ate it with an appetite sharpened by his journey. After breakfast he went to bed, and slept until late in the afternoon.

After supper Mr. Johnson took uncle Wellington to visit some of the neighbors who had come from North Carolina before the war. They all expressed much pleasure at meeting "Mr. Braboy," a title which at first sounded a little odd to uncle Wellington. At home he had been "Wellin'ton," "Brer Wellin'-ton," or "uncle Wellin'ton"; it was a novel experience to be called "Mister," and he set it down, with secret satisfaction, as one of the first fruits of Northern liberty.

"Would you lack ter look 'roun' de town a little?" asked Mr. Johnson at breakfast next morning. "I ain' got no job dis mawnin' an' I kin show you some er de sights."

Uncle Wellington acquiesced in this arrangement, and they walked up to the corner to the street-car line. In a few moments a car passed. Mr. Johnson jumped on the moving car, and uncle Wellington followed his example, at the risk of life or limb, as it was his first experience of street cars.

There was only one vacant seat in the car and that was between two white women in the forward end. Mr. Johnson motioned to the seat, but Wellington shrank from walking between those two rows of white people, to say nothing of sitting between the two women, so he remained standing in the rear part of the car. A moment later, as the car rounded a short curve, he was pitched sidewise into the lap of a stout woman magnificently attired in a ruffled blue calico gown. The lady colored up, and uncle Wellington, as he struggled to his feet amid the laughter of the passengers, was absolutely helpless with embarrassment, until the conductor came up behind him and pushed him toward the vacant place.

"Sit down, will you," he said; and before uncle Wellington could collect himself, he was seated between the two white women. Everybody in the car seemed to be looking at him. But he came to the conclusion, after he had pulled himself together and reflected a few moments, that he would find this method of locomotion pleasanter when he got used to it, and then he could score one more glorious privilege gained by his change of residence.

They got off at the public square, in the heart of the city, where there were flowers and statues, and fountains playing. Mr. Johnson pointed out the court-house, the post-office, the jail, and other public buildings fronting on the square. They visited the market near by, and from an elevated point, looked down upon the extensive lumber yards and factories that were the chief sources of the city's prosperity. Beyond these they could see the fleet of ships that lined the coal and iron ore docks of the harbor. Mr. Johnson, who was quite a fluent talker, enlarged upon the wealth and prosperity of the city; and Wellington, who had never before been in a town of more than three thousand inhabitants, manifested sufficient interest and wonder to satisfy the most exacting *cicerone*. They called at the office of a colored lawyer and member of the legislature, formerly from North Carolina, who, scenting a new constituent and a possible client, greeted the stranger warmly, and in flowing speech pointed out the superior advantages of life at the North, citing himself as an illustration of the possibilities of life in a country really free. As they wended their way homeward to dinner uncle Wellington, with quickened pulse and rising hopes, felt that this was indeed the promised land, and that it must be flowing with milk and honey.

Uncle Wellington remained at the residence of Mr. Johnson for several weeks before making any effort to find employment. He spent this period in looking about the city. The most commonplace things possessed for him the charm of novelty, and he had come prepared to admire. Shortly after his arrival, he had offered to pay for his board, intimating at the same time that he had plenty of money. Mr. Johnson declined to accept anything from him for board, and expressed himself as being only too proud to have Mr. Braboy remain in the house on the footing of an honored guest, until he had settled himself. He lightened in some degree, however, the burden of obligation under which a prolonged stay on these terms would have placed his guest, by soliciting from the latter occasional small loans, until uncle Wellington's roll of money began to lose its plumpness, and with an empty pocket staring him in the face, he felt the necessity of finding something to do.

During his residence in the city he had met several times his first acquaintance, Mr. Peterson, the hackman, who from time to time inquired how he was getting along. On one of these occasions Wellington mentioned his willingness to accept employment. As good luck would have it, Mr. Peterson knew of a vacant situation. He had formerly been coachman for a wealthy gentleman residing on Oakwood Avenue, but had resigned the situation to go into business for himself. His place had been filled by an Irishman, who had just been discharged for drunkenness, and the gentleman that very day had sent word to Mr. Peterson, asking him if he could recommend a competent and trustworthy coachman.

"Does you know anything erbout hosses?" asked Mr. Peterson.

"Yas, indeed, I does," said Wellington. "I wuz raise' 'mongs' hosses."

"I tol' my ole boss I'd look out fer a man, an' ef you reckon you kin fill de 'quirements er de situation, I'll take yo' roun' dere ter-morrer mornin'. You wants ter put on yo' bes' clothes an' slick up, fer dey're partic'lar people. Ef you git de place I'll expec' you ter pay me for de time I lose in 'tendin' ter yo' business, fer time is money in dis country, an' folks don't do much fer nuthin'."

Next morning Wellington blacked his shoes carefully, put on a clean collar, and with the aid of Mrs. Johnson tied his cravat in a jaunty bow which gave him quite a sprightly air and a much younger look than his years warranted. Mr. Peterson called for him at eight o'clock. After traversing several cross streets they turned into Oakwood Avenue and walked along the finest part of it for about half a mile. The handsome houses of this famous avenue, the stately trees, the wide-spreading lawns, dotted with flower beds, fountains, and statuary, made up a picture so far surpassing anything in Wellington's experience as to fill him with an almost oppressive sense of its beauty.

"Hit looks lack hebben," he said softly.

"It's a pootty fine street," rejoined his companion, with a judicial air, "but I don't like dem big lawns. It's too much trouble ter keep de grass down. One er dem lawns is big enough to pasture a couple er cows."

They went down a street running at right angles to the avenue, and turned into the rear of the corner lot. A large building of pressed brick, trimmed with stone, loomed up before them.

"Do de gemman lib in dis house?" asked Wellington, gazing with awe at the front of the building.

"No, dat's de barn," said Mr. Peterson with good-natured

contempt; and leading the way past a clump of shrubbery to the dwelling-house, he went up the back steps and rang the door-bell.

The ring was answered by a buxom Irishwoman, of a natural freshness of complexion deepened to a fiery red by the heat of a kitchen range. Wellington thought he had seen her before, but his mind had received so many new impressions lately that it was a minute or two before he recognized in her the lady whose lap he had involuntarily occupied for a moment on his first day in Groveland.

"Faith," she exclaimed as she admitted them, "an' it's mighty glad I am to see ye ag'in, Misther Payterson! An' how hev ye be'n, Misther Payterson, since I see ye lahst?"

"Middlin' well, Mis' Flannigan, middlin' well, 'ceptin' a tech er de rheumatiz. S'pose you be'n doin' well as usual?"

"Oh yis, as well as a dacent woman could do wid a drunken baste about the place like the lahst coachman. O Misther Payterson, it would make yer heart bleed to see the way the spalpeen cut up a-Saturday! But Misther Todd discharged 'im the same avenin', widout a character, bad 'cess to 'im, an' we've had no coachman sence at all, at all. An' it's sorry I am"—

The lady's flow of eloquence was interrupted at this point by the appearance of Mr. Todd himself, who had been informed of the men's arrival. He asked some questions in regard to Wellington's qualifications and former experience, and in view of his recent arrival in the city was willing to accept Mr. Peterson's recommendation instead of a reference. He said a few words about the nature of the work, and stated his willingness to pay Wellington the wages formerly allowed Mr. Peterson, thirty dollars a month and board and lodging.

This handsome offer was eagerly accepted, and it was agreed that Wellington's term of service should begin immediately. Mr. Peterson, being familiar with the work, and financially interested, conducted the new coachman through the stables and showed him what he would have to do. The silver-mounted harness, the variety of carriages, the names of which he learned for the first time, the arrangements for feeding and watering the horses,—these appointments of a rich man's stable impressed Wellington very much, and he wondered that so much luxury should be wasted on mere horses. The room assigned to him, in the second story of the barn, was a finer apartment than he had ever slept in; and the salary attached to the situation was greater than the combined monthly earnings of himself and aunt Milly in their Southern home. Surely, he thought, his lines had fallen in pleasant places.

Under the stimulus of new surroundings Wellington applied himself diligently to work, and, with the occasional advice of Mr. Peterson, soon mastered the details of his employment. He found the female servants, with whom he took his meals, very amiable ladies. The cook, Mrs. Katie Flannigan, was a widow. Her husband, a sailor, had been lost at sea. She was a woman of many words, and when she was not lamenting the late Flannigan's loss,—according to her story he had been a model of all the virtues,—she would turn the batteries of her tongue against the former coachman. This gentleman, as Wellington gathered from frequent remarks dropped by Mrs. Flannigan, had paid her attentions clearly susceptible of a serious construction. These attentions had not borne their legitimate fruit, and she was still a widow unconsoled,—hence Mrs. Flannigan's tears. The housemaid was a plump, good-natured German girl, with a pronounced German accent. The presence on washdays of a Bohemian laundress, of recent importation, added another to the variety of ways in which the English tongue was mutilated in Mr. Todd's kitchen. Association with the white women drew out all the native gallantry of the mulatto, and Wellington developed quite a helpful turn. His politeness, his willingness to lend a hand in kitchen or laundry, and the fact that he was the only male servant on the place, combined to make him a prime favorite in the servants' quarters.

It was the general opinion among Wellington's acquaintances that he was a single man. He had come to the city alone, had never been heard to speak of a wife, and to personal questions bearing upon the subject of matrimony had always returned evasive answers. Though he had never questioned the correctness of the lawyer's opinion in regard to his slave marriage, his conscience had never been entirely at ease since his departure from the South, and any positive denial of his married condition would have stuck in his throat. The inference naturally drawn from his reticence in regard to the past, coupled with his expressed intention of settling permanently in Groveland, was that he belonged in the ranks of the unmarried, and was therefore legitimate game for any widow or old maid who could bring him down. As such game is bagged easiest at short range, he received numerous invitations to tea-parties, where he feasted on unlimited chicken and pound cake. He used to compare these viands with the plain fare often served by aunt Milly, and the result of the comparison was another item to the credit of the North upon his mental ledger. Several of the colored ladies who smiled upon him were blessed with good looks, and uncle Wellington, naturally of a susceptible temperament, as people of lively imagination are apt to be, would probably have fallen a victim to the charms of some woman of his own race, had it not been for a strong counter-attraction in the person of Mrs. Flannigan. The attentions of the lately discharged coachman had lighted anew the smouldering fires of her widowed heart, and awakened longings which still remained unsatisfied. She was thirty-five years old, and felt the need of some one else to love. She was not a woman of lofty ideals; with her a man was a man—

For a' that an' a' that;

and, aside from the accident of color, uncle Wellington was as personable a man as any of her acquaintance. Some people might have objected to his complexion; but then, Mrs. Flannigan argued, he was at least half white; and, this being the case, there was no good reason why he should be regarded as black.

Uncle Wellington was not slow to perceive Mrs. Flannigan's charms of person, and appreciated to the full the skill that prepared the choice tidbits reserved for his plate at dinner. The prospect of securing a white wife had been one of the principal inducements offered by a life at the North; but the awe of white people in which he had been reared was still too strong to per-

mit his taking any active steps toward the object of his secret
desire, had not the lady herself come to his assistance with a little of the native coquetry of her race.

"Ah, Misther Braboy," she said one evening when they sat at
the supper table alone,—it was the second girl's afternoon off,
and she had not come home to supper,—"it must be an awful
lonesome life ye 've been afther l'adin', as a single man, wid no
one to cook fer ye, or look afther ye."

"It are a kind er lonesome life, Mis' Flannigan, an' dat's a
fac'. But sence I had de privilege er eatin' yo' cookin' an' 'joyin'
yo' society, I ain' felt a bit lonesome."

"Yer flatthrin' me, Misther Braboy. An' even if ye mane it"—

"I means eve'y word of it, Mis' Flannigan."

"An' even if ye mane it, Misther Braboy, the time is liable to
come when things 'll be different; for service is uncertain, Misther Braboy. An' then you 'll wish you had some nice, clean
woman, 'at knowed how to cook an' wash an' iron, ter look afther ye, an' make yer life comfortable."

Uncle Wellington sighed, and looked at her languishingly.

"It 'u'd all be well ernuff, Mis' Flannigan, ef I had n' met
you; but I don' know whar I's ter fin' a colored lady w'at 'll begin ter suit me after habbin' libbed in de same house wid you."

"Colored lady, indade! Why, Misther Braboy, ye don't nade
ter demane yerself by marryin' a colored lady—not but they're
as good as anybody else, so long as they behave themselves.
There's many a white woman 'u'd be glad ter git as fine a
lookin' man as ye are."

"Now *you 're* flattrin' *me,* Mis' Flannigan," said Wellington.
But he felt a sudden and substantial increase in courage when
she had spoken, and it was with astonishing ease that he found
himself saying:—

"Dey ain' but one lady, Mis' Flannigan, dat could injuce me
ter want ter change de lonesomeness er my singleness fer de
'sponsibilities er matermony, an' I'm feared she'd say no ef I 'd
ax her."

"Ye 'd better ax her, Misther Braboy, an' not be wastin' time
a-wond'rin'. Do I know the lady?"

"You knows 'er better 'n anybody else, Mis' Flannigan. *You* is de only lady I'd be satisfied ter marry after knowin' you. Ef you casts me off I 'll spen' de rest er my days in lonesomeness an' mis'ry."

Mrs. Flannigan affected much surprise and embarrassment at this bold declaration.

"Oh, Misther Braboy," she said, covering him with a coy glance, "an' it's rale 'shamed I am to hev b'en talkin' ter ye ez I hev. It looks as though I'd b'en doin' the coortin'. I did n't drame that I 'd b'en able ter draw yer affections to mesilf."

"I's loved you ever sence I fell in yo' lap on de street car de fus' day I wuz in Groveland," he said, as he moved his chair up closer to hers.

One evening in the following week they went out after supper to the residence of Rev. Cæsar Williams, pastor of the colored Baptist church, and, after the usual preliminaries, were pronounced man and wife.

III

According to all his preconceived notions, this marriage ought to have been the acme of uncle Wellington's felicity. But he soon found that it was not without its drawbacks. On the following morning Mr. Todd was informed of the marriage. He had no special objection to it, or interest in it, except that he was opposed on principle to having husband and wife in his employment at the same time. As a consequence, Mrs. Braboy, whose place could be more easily filled than that of her husband, received notice that her services would not be required after the end of the month. Her husband was retained in his place as coachman.

Upon the loss of her situation, Mrs. Braboy decided to exercise the married woman's prerogative of letting her husband support her. She rented the upper floor of a small house in an Irish neighborhood. The newly wedded pair furnished their rooms on the installment plan and began housekeeping.

There was one little circumstance, however, that interfered slightly with their enjoyment of that perfect freedom from care which ought to characterize a honeymoon. The people who owned the house and occupied the lower floor had rented the upper part to Mrs. Braboy in person, it never occurring to them that her husband could be other than a white man. When it became known that he was colored, the landlord, Mr. Dennis O'Flaherty, felt that he had been imposed upon, and, at the end of the first month, served notice upon his tenants to leave the premises. When Mrs. Braboy, with characteristic impetuosity, inquired the meaning of this proceeding, she was informed by Mr. O'Flaherty that he did not care to live in the same house "wid naygurs." Mrs. Braboy resented the epithet with more warmth than dignity, and for a brief space of time the air was green with choice specimens of brogue, the altercation barely ceasing before it had reached the point of blows.

It was quite clear that the Braboys could not longer live comfortably in Mr. O'Flaherty's house, and they soon vacated the premises, first letting the rent get a couple of weeks in arrears as a punishment to the too fastidious landlord. They moved to a small house on Hackman Street, a favorite locality with colored people.

For a while, affairs ran smoothly in the new home. The colored people seemed, at first, well enough disposed toward Mrs. Braboy, and she made quite a large acquaintance among them. It was difficult, however, for Mrs. Braboy to divest herself of the consciousness that she was white, and therefore superior to her neighbors. Occasional words and acts by which she manifested this feeling were noticed and resented by her keen-eyed and sensitive colored neighbors. The result was a slight coolness between them. That her few white neighbors did not visit her, she naturally and no doubt correctly imputed to disapproval of her matrimonial relations.

Under these circumstances, Mrs. Braboy was left a good deal to her own company. Owing to lack of opportunity in early life, she was not a woman of many resources, either mental or moral. It is therefore not strange that, in order to relieve her loneliness, she should occasionally have recourse to a glass of beer, and, as the habit grew upon her, to still stronger stimulants. Uncle Wellington himself was no teetotaler, and did not interpose any objection so long as she kept her potations within reasonable limits, and was apparently none the worse for them; indeed, he sometimes joined her in a glass. On one of these occasions he drank a little too much, and, while driving the ladies of Mr. Todd's family to the opera, ran against a lamppost and overturned the carriage, to the serious discomposure of the ladies' nerves, and at the cost of his situation.

A coachman discharged under such circumstances is not in the best position for procuring employment at his calling, and uncle Wellington, under the pressure of need, was obliged to seek some other means of livelihood. At the suggestion of his friend Mr. Johnson, he bought a whitewash brush, a peck of lime, a couple of pails, and a handcart, and began work as a whitewasher. His first efforts were very crude, and for a while he lost a customer in every person he worked for. He nevertheless managed to pick up a living during the spring and summer months, and to support his wife and himself in comparative comfort.

The approach of winter put an end to the whitewashing season, and left uncle Wellington dependent for support upon occasional jobs of unskilled labor. The income derived from these was very uncertain, and Mrs. Braboy was at length driven, by stress of circumstances, to the washtub, that last refuge of honest, able-bodied poverty, in all countries where the use of clothing is conventional.

The last state of uncle Wellington was now worse than the first. Under the soft firmness of aunt Milly's rule, he had not been required to do a great deal of work, prompt and cheerful obedience being chiefly what was expected of him. But matters were very different here. He had not only to bring in the coal and water, but to rub the clothes and turn the wringer, and to humiliate himself before the public by emptying the tubs and hanging out the wash in full view of the neighbors; and he had to deliver the clothes when laundered.

At times Wellington found himself wondering if his second marriage had been a wise one. Other circumstances combined to change in some degree his once rose-colored conception of life at the North. He had believed that all men were equal in this favored locality, but he discovered more degrees of inequality than he had ever perceived at the South. A colored man might be as good as a white man in theory, but neither of them was of any special consequence without money, or talent, or position. Uncle Wellington found a great many privileges open to him at the North, but he had not been educated to the point where he could appreciate them or take advantage of them; and the enjoyment of many of them was expensive, and, for that reason alone, as far beyond his reach as they had ever been. When he once began to admit even the possibility of a mistake on his part, these considerations presented themselves to his mind with increasing force. On occasions when Mrs. Braboy would require of him some unusual physical exertion, or when too frequent applications to the bottle had loosened her tongue, uncle Wellington's mind would revert, with a remorseful twinge of conscience, to the *dolce far niente* of his Southern home; a film would come over his eyes and brain, and, instead of the red-faced Irishwoman opposite him, he could see the black but comely disk of aunt Milly's countenance bending over the washtub; the elegant brogue of Mrs. Braboy would deliquesce into the soft dialect of North Carolina; and he would only be aroused from this blissful reverie by a wet shirt or a handful of suds thrown into his face, with which gentle reminder his wife would recall his attention to the duties of the moment.

There came a time, one day in spring, when there was no longer any question about it: uncle Wellington was desperately homesick.

Liberty, equality, privileges—all were but as dust in the balance when weighed against his longing for old scenes and faces. It was the natural reaction in the mind of a middle-aged man who had tried to force the current of a sluggish existence into a new and radically different channel. An active, industrious man, making the change in early life, while there was time to spare for the waste of adaptation, might have found in the new place more favorable conditions than in the old. In Wellington age and temperament combined to prevent the success of the experiment; the spirit of enterprise and ambition into which he had been temporarily galvanized could no longer prevail against the inertia of old habits of life and thought.

One day when he had been sent to deliver clothes he performed his errand quickly, and boarding a passing street car, paid one of his very few five-cent pieces to ride down to the office of the Hon. Mr. Brown, the colored lawyer whom he had visited when he first came to the city, and who was well known to him by sight and reputation.

"Mr. Brown," he said, "I ain' gitt'n' 'long very well wid my ole 'oman."

"What's the trouble?" asked the lawyer, with business-like curtness, for he did not scent much of a fee.

"Well, de main trouble is she doan treat me right. An' den she gits drunk, an' wuss'n dat, she lays vi'lent han's on me. I kyars de marks er dat 'oman on my face now."

He showed the lawyer a long scratch on the neck.

"Why don't you defend yourself?"

"You don' know Mis' Braboy, suh; you don' know dat 'oman," he replied, with a shake of the head. "Some er dese yer w'ite women is monst'us strong in de wris'."

"Well, Mr. Braboy, it's what you might have expected when you turned your back on your own people and married a white woman. You were n't content with being a slave to the white folks once, but you must try it again. Some people never know when they've got enough. I don't see that there's any help for you; unless," he added suggestively, "you had a good deal of money."

"'Pears ter me I heared somebody say sence I be'n up heah, dat it wuz 'gin de law for w'ite folks an' colored folks ter marry."

"That was once the law, though it has always been a dead letter in Groveland. In fact, it was the law when you got married, and until I introduced a bill in the legislature last fall to repeal it. But even that law did n't hit cases like yours. It was unlawful to make such a marriage, but it was a good marriage when once made."

"I don' jes' git dat th'oo my head,"said Wellington, scratching that member as though to make a hole for the idea to enter.

"It's quite plain, Mr. Braboy. It's unlawful to kill a man, but when he's killed he's just as dead as though the law permitted it. I'm afraid you have n't much of a case, but if you'll go to work and get twenty-five dollars together, I'll see what I can do for you. We may be able to pull a case through on the ground of extreme cruelty. I might even start the case if you brought in ten dollars."

Wellington went away sorrowfully. The laws of Ohio were very little more satisfactory than those of North Carolina. And as for the ten dollars—the lawyer might as well have told him to bring in the moon, or a deed for the Public Square. He felt very, very low as he hurried back home to supper, which he would have to go without if he were not on hand at the usual supper-time.

But just when his spirits were lowest, and his outlook for the future most hopeless, a measure of relief was at hand. He noticed, when he reached home, that Mrs. Braboy was a little preoccupied, and did not abuse him as vigorously as he expected after so long an absence. He also perceived the smell of strange tobacco in the house, of a better grade than he could afford to use. He thought perhaps some one had come in to see about the washing; but he was too glad of a respite from Mrs. Braboy's rhetoric to imperil it by indiscreet questions.

Next morning she gave him fifty cents.

"Braboy," she said, "ye've be'n helpin' me nicely wid the washin', an' I'm going ter give ye a holiday. Ye can take yer hook an' line an' go fishin' on the breakwater. I'll fix ye a lunch, an' ye needn't come back till night. An' there's half a dollar; ye can buy yerself a pipe er terbacky. But be careful an' don't waste it," she added, for fear she was overdoing the thing.

Uncle Wellington was overjoyed at this change of front on the part of Mrs. Braboy; if she would make it permanent he did not see why they might not live together very comfortably.

The day passed pleasantly down on the breakwater. The weather was agreeable, and the fish bit freely. Towards evening

Wellington started home with a bunch of fish that no angler need have been ashamed of. He looked forward to a good warm supper; for even if something should have happened during the day to alter his wife's mood for the worse, any ordinary variation would be more than balanced by the substantial addition of food to their larder. His mouth watered at the thought of the finny beauties sputtering in the frying-pan.

He noted, as he approached the house, that there was no smoke coming from the chimney. This only disturbed him in connection with the matter of supper. When he entered the gate he observed further that the window-shades had been taken down.

"'Spec' de ole 'oman's been house-cleanin'," he said to himself. "I wonder she did n' make me stay an' he'p 'er."

He went round to the rear of the house and tried the kitchen door. It was locked. This was somewhat of a surprise, and disturbed still further his expectations in regard to supper. When he had found the key and opened the door, the gravity of his next discovery drove away for the time being all thoughts of eating.

The kitchen was empty. Stove, table, chairs, washtubs, pots and pans, had vanished as if into thin air.

"Fo' de Lawd's sake!" he murmured in open-mouthed astonishment.

He passed into the other room,—they had only two,—which had served as bedroom and sitting-room. It was as bare as the first, except that in the middle of the floor were piled uncle Wellington's clothes. It was not a large pile, and on the top of it lay a folded piece of yellow wrapping-paper.

Wellington stood for a moment as if petrified. Then he rubbed his eyes and looked around him.

"W'at do dis mean?" he said. "Is I er-dreamin', er does I see w'at I 'pears ter see?" He glanced down at the bunch of fish which he still held. "Heah 's de fish; heah 's de house; heah I is; but whar 's de ole 'oman, an' whar 's de fu'niture? I can't figure out w'at dis yer all means."

He picked up the piece of paper and unfolded it. It was written on one side. Here was the obvious solution of the mystery,—that is, it would have been obvious if he could have read it; but he could not, and so his fancy continued to play upon the subject. Perhaps the house had been robbed, or the furniture taken back by the seller, for it had not been entirely paid for.

Finally he went across the street and called to a boy in a neighbor's yard.

"Does you read writin', Johnnie?"

"Yes, sir, I'm in the seventh grade."

"Read dis yer paper fuh me."

The youngster took the note, and with much labor read the following:—

MR. BRABOY:

In lavin' ye so suddint I have ter say that my first husban' has turned up unixpected, having been saved onbeknownst ter me from a warthry grave an' all the money wasted I spint fer masses fer ter rist his sole an' I wish I had it back I feel it my dooty ter go an' live wid 'im again. I take the furnacher because I bought it yer close is yors I leave them and wishin' yer the best of luck I remane oncet yer wife but now agin

MRS. KATIE FLANNIGAN.

N.B. I'm lavin' town terday so it won't be no use lookin' fer me.

On inquiry uncle Wellington learned from the boy that shortly after his departure in the morning a white man had appeared on the scene, followed a little later by a moving-van, into which the furniture had been loaded and carried away. Mrs. Braboy, clad in her best clothes, had locked the door, and gone away with the strange white man.

The news was soon noised about the street. Wellington swapped his fish for supper and a bed at a neighbor's, and during the evening learned from several sources that the strange white man had been at his house the afternoon of the day before. His neighbors intimated that they thought Mrs. Braboy's departure a good riddance of bad rubbish, and Wellington did not dispute the proposition.

Thus ended the second chapter of Wellington's matrimonial experiences. His wife's departure had been the one thing needful to convince him, beyond a doubt, that he had been a great fool. Remorse and homesickness forced him to the further conclusion that he had been knave as well as fool, and had treated aunt Milly shamefully. He was not altogether a bad old man, though very weak and erring, and his better nature now gained the ascendancy. Of course his disappointment had a great deal to do with his remorse; most people do not perceive the hideousness of sin until they begin to reap its consequences. Instead of the beautiful Northern life he had dreamed of, he found himself stranded, penniless, in a strange land, among people whose sympathy he had forfeited, with no one to lean upon, and no refuge from the storms of life. His outlook was very dark, and there sprang up within him a wild longing to get back to North Carolina,—back to the little whitewashed cabin, shaded with china and mulberry trees; back to the wood-pile and the garden; back to the old cronies with whom he had swapped lies and tobacco for so many years. He longed to kiss the rod of aunt Milly's domination. He had purchased his liberty at too great a price.

The next day he disappeared from Groveland. He had announced his departure only to Mr. Johnson, who sent his love to his relations in Patesville.

It would be painful to record in detail the return journey of uncle Wellington—Mr. Braboy no longer—to his native town; how many weary miles he walked; how many times he risked his life on railroad trucks and between freight cars; how he depended for sustenance on the grudging hand of back-door charity. Nor would it be profitable or delicate to mention any slight deviations from the path of rectitude, as judged by conventional standards, to which he may occasionally have been driven by a too insistent hunger; or to refer in the remotest degree to a compulsory sojourn of thirty days in a city where he had no references, and could show no visible means of support. True charity will let these purely personal matters remain locked in the bosom of him who suffered them.

IV

Just fifteen months after the date when uncle Wellington had left North Carolina, a weather-beaten figure entered the town of Patesville after nightfall, following the railroad track from the north. Few would have recognized in the hungry-looking old brown tramp, clad in dusty rags and limping along with bare feet, the trim-looking middle-aged mulatto who so few months before had taken the train from Patesville for the distant North; so, if he had but known it, there was no necessity for him to avoid the main streets and sneak around by unfrequented paths to reach the old place on the other side of the town. He encountered nobody that he knew, and soon the familiar shape of the little cabin rose before him. It stood distinctly outlined against the sky, and the light streaming from the half-opened shutters showed it to be occupied. As he drew nearer, every familiar detail of the place appealed to his memory and to his affections, and his heart went out to the old home and the old wife. As he came nearer still, the odor of fried chicken floated out upon the air and set his mouth to watering, and awakened unspeakable longings in his half-starved stomach.

At this moment, however, a fearful thought struck him; suppose the old woman had taken legal advice and married again during his absence? Turn about would have been only fair play. He opened the gate softly, and with his heart in his mouth approached the window on tiptoe and looked in.

A cheerful fire was blazing on the hearth, in front of which sat the familiar form of aunt Milly—and another, at the sight of whom uncle Wellington's heart sank within him. He knew the other person very well; he had sat there more than once before uncle Wellington went away. It was the minister of the church to which his wife belonged. The preacher's former visits, however, had signified nothing more than pastoral courtesy, or appreciation of good eating. His presence now was of serious portent; for Wellington recalled, with acute alarm, that the

elder's wife had died only a few weeks before his own departure for the North. What was the occasion of his presence this
evening? Was it merely a pastoral call? or was he courting? or
had aunt Milly taken legal advice and married the elder?

Wellington remembered a crack in the wall, at the back of
the house, through which he could see and hear, and quietly
stationed himself there.

"Dat chicken smells mighty good, Sis' Milly," the elder was
saying; "I can't fer de life er me see why dat low-down husban'
er yo'n could ever run away f'm a cook like you. It 's one er de
beatenis' things I ever heared. How he could lib wid you an'
not 'preciate you I can't understan', no indeed I can't."

Aunt Milly sighed. "De trouble wid Wellin'ton wuz," she
replied, "dat he did n' know when he wuz well off. He wuz alluz wishin' fer change, er studyin' 'bout somethin' new."

"Ez fer me," responded the elder earnestly, "I likes things
what has be'n prove' an' tried an' has stood de tes', an' I can't
'magine how anybody could spec' ter fin' a better housekeeper
er cook dan you is, Sis' Milly. I'm a gittin' mighty lonesome
sence my wife died. De Good Book say it is not good fer man
ter lib alone, en it 'pears ter me dat you an' me mought get erlong tergether monst'us well."

Wellington's heart stood still, while he listened with strained
attention. Aunt Milly sighed.

"I ain't denyin', elder, but what I 've be'n kinder lonesome
myse'f fer quite a w'ile, an' I doan doubt dat w'at de Good
Book say 'plies ter women as well as ter men."

"You kin be sho' it do," averred the elder, with professional
authoritativeness; "yas'm, you kin be cert'n sho'."

"But, of co'se," aunt Milly went on, "havin' los' my ole man
de way I did, it has tuk me some time fer ter git my feelin's
straighten' out like dey oughter be."

"I kin 'magine yo' feelin's, Sis' Milly," chimed in the elder
sympathetically, "w'en you come home dat night an' foun' yo'
chist broke open, an' yo' money gone dat you had wukked an'
slaved fuh f'm mawnin' 'tel night, year in an' year out, an' w'en
you foun' dat no-'count nigger gone wid his clo's an' you lef' all
alone in de worl' ter scuffle 'long by yo'self."

"Yas, elder," responded aunt Milly, "I wa'n't used right. An' den w'en I heared 'bout his goin' ter de lawyer ter fin' out 'bout a defoce, an' w'en I heared w'at de lawyer said 'bout my not bein' his wife 'less he wanted me, it made me so mad, I made up my min' dat ef he ever put his foot on my do'-sill ag'in, I'd shet de do' in his face an' tell 'im ter go back whar he come f'm."

To Wellington, on the outside, the cabin had never seemed so comfortable, aunt Milly never so desirable, chicken never so appetizing, as at this moment when they seemed slipping away from his grasp forever.

"Yo' feelin's does you credit, Sis' Milly," said the elder, taking her hand, which for a moment she did not withdraw. "An' de way fer you ter close yo' do' tightes' ag'inst 'im is ter take me in his place. He ain' got no claim on you no mo'. He tuk his ch'ice 'cordin' ter w'at de lawyer tol' 'im, an' 'termine' dat he wa'n't yo' husban'. Ef he wa'n't yo' husban', he had no right ter take yo' money, an' ef he comes back here ag'in you kin hab 'im tuck up an' sent ter de penitenchy fer stealin' it."

Uncle Wellington's knees, already weak from fasting, trembled violently beneath him. The worst that he had feared was now likely to happen. His only hope of safety lay in flight, and yet the scene within so fascinated him that he could not move a step.

"It 'u'd serve him right," exclaimed aunt Milly indignantly, "ef he wuz sent ter de penitenchy fer life! Dey ain't nuthin' too mean ter be done ter 'im. What did I ever do dat he should use me like he did?"

The recital of her wrongs had wrought upon aunt Milly's feelings so that her voice broke, and she wiped her eyes with her apron.

The elder looked serenely confident, and moved his chair nearer hers in order the better to play the rôle of comforter. Wellington, on the outside, felt so mean that the darkness of the night was scarcely sufficient to hide him; it would be no more than right if the earth were to open and swallow him up.

"An' yet aftuh all, elder," said Milly with a sob, "though I knows you is a better man, an' would treat me right, I wuz so use' ter dat ole nigger, an' libbed wid 'im so long, dat ef he'd open dat do' dis minute an' walk in, I'm feard I'd be foolish er-nuff an' weak ernuff to forgive 'im an' take 'im back ag'in."

With a bound, uncle Wellington was away from the crack in the wall. As he ran round the house he passed the wood-pile and snatched up an armful of pieces. A moment later he threw open the door.

"Ole 'oman," he exclaimed, "here's dat wood you tol' me ter fetch in! Why, elder," he said to the preacher, who had started from his seat with surprise, "w'at's yo' hurry? Won't you stay an' hab some supper wid us?"

THE WEB OF
CIRCUMSTANCE

I

Within a low clapboarded hut, with an open front, a forge was glowing. In front a blacksmith was shoeing a horse, a sleek, well-kept animal with the signs of good blood and breeding. A young mulatto stood by and handed the blacksmith such tools as he needed from time to time. A group of negroes were sitting around, some in the shadow of the shop, one in the full glare of the sunlight. A gentleman was seated in a buggy a few yards away, in the shade of a spreading elm. The horse had loosened a shoe, and Colonel Thornton, who was a lover of fine horse-flesh, and careful of it, had stopped at Ben Davis's blacksmith shop, as soon as he discovered the loose shoe, to have it fastened on.

"All right, Kunnel," the blacksmith called out. "Tom," he said, addressing the young man, "he'p me hitch up."

Colonel Thornton alighted from the buggy, looked at the shoe, signified his approval of the job, and stood looking on while the blacksmith and his assistant harnessed the horse to the buggy.

"Dat's a mighty fine whip yer got dere, Kunnel," said Ben, while the young man was tightening the straps of the harness on the opposite side of the horse. "I wush I had one like it. Where kin yer git dem whips?"

"My brother brought me this from New York," said the Colonel. "You can't buy them down here."

The whip in question was a handsome one. The handle was wrapped with interlacing threads of variegated colors, forming an elaborate pattern, the lash being dark green. An octagonal ornament of glass was set in the end of the handle. "It cert'n'y is fine," said Ben; "I wish I had one like it." He looked at the whip longingly as Colonel Thornton drove away.

" 'Pears ter me Ben gittin' mighty blooded," said one of the bystanders, "drivin' a hoss an' buggy, an' wantin' a whip like Colonel Thornton's."

"What's de reason I can't hab a hoss an' buggy an' a whip like Kunnel Tho'nton's, ef I pay fer 'em?" asked Ben. "We colored folks never had no chance ter git nothin' befo' de wah, but ef eve'y nigger in dis town had a tuck keer er his money sence de wah, like I has, an' bought as much lan' as I has, de niggers might 'a' got half de lan' by dis time," he went on, giving a finishing blow to a horseshoe, and throwing it on the ground to cool.

Carried away by his own eloquence, he did not notice the approach of two white men who came up the street from behind him.

"An' ef you niggers," he continued, raking the coals together over a fresh bar of iron, "would stop wastin' yo' money on 'scursions to put money in w'ite folks' pockets, an' stop buildin' fine chu'ches, an' buil' houses fer yo'se'ves, you'd git along much faster."

"You're talkin' sense, Ben," said one of the white men. "Yo'r people will never be respected till they've got property."

The conversation took another turn. The white men transacted their business and went away. The whistle of a neighboring steam sawmill blew a raucous blast for the hour of noon, and the loafers shuffled away in different directions.

"You kin go ter dinner, Tom," said the blacksmith. "An' stop at de gate w'en yer go by my house, and tell Nancy I'll be dere in 'bout twenty minutes. I got ter finish dis yer plough p'int fus'."

The young man walked away. One would have supposed, from the rapidity with which he walked, that he was very hungry. A quarter of an hour later the blacksmith dropped his hammer, pulled off his leather apron, shut the front door of the shop, and went home to dinner. He came into the house out of the fervent heat, and, throwing off his straw hat, wiped his brow vigorously with a red cotton handkerchief.

"Dem collards smells good," he said, sniffing the odor that came in through the kitchen door, as his good-looking yellow wife opened it to enter the room where he was. "I've got a monst'us good appetite ter-day. I feels good, too. I paid Majah Ransom de intrus' on de mortgage dis mawnin' an' a hund'ed dollahs besides, an' I spec's ter hab de balance ready by de fust of nex' Jiniwary; an' den we won't owe nobody a cent. I tell yer dere ain' nothin' like propputy ter make a pusson feel like a man. But w'at's de matter wid yer, Nancy? Is sump'n' skeered yer?"

The woman did seem excited and ill at ease. There was a heaving of the full bust, a quickening breathing, that betokened suppressed excitement.

"I—I—jes' seen a rattlesnake out in de gyahden," she stammered.

The blacksmith ran to the door. "Which way? Whar wuz he?" he cried.

He heard a rustling in the bushes at one side of the garden, and the sound of a breaking twig, and, seizing a hoe which stood by the door, he sprang toward the point from which the sound came.

"No, no," said the woman hurriedly, "it wuz over here," and she directed her husband's attention to the other side of the garden.

The blacksmith, with the uplifted hoe, its sharp blade gleaming in the sunlight, peered cautiously among the collards and tomato plants, listening all the while for the ominous rattle, but found nothing.

"I reckon he's got away," he said, as he set the hoe up again by the door. "Whar's de chillen?" he asked with some anxiety. "Is dey playin' in de woods?"

"No," answered his wife, "dey've gone ter de spring."

The spring was on the opposite side of the garden from that on which the snake was said to have been seen, so the blacksmith sat down and fanned himself with a palm-leaf fan until the dinner was served.

"Yer ain't quite on time ter-day, Nancy," he said, glancing up at the clock on the mantel, after the edge of his appetite had been taken off. "Got ter make time ef yer wanter make money. Didn't Tom tell yer I'd be heah in twenty minutes?"

"No," she said; "I seen him goin' pas'; he didn' say nothin'."

"I dunno w'at's de matter wid dat boy," mused the blacksmith over his apple dumpling. "He's gittin mighty keerless heah lately; mus' hab sump'n' on 'is min',—some gal, I reckon."

The children had come in while he was speaking,—a slender, shapely boy, yellow like his mother, a girl several years younger, dark like her father: both bright-looking children and neatly dressed.

"I seen cousin Tom down by de spring," said the little girl, as she lifted off the pail of water that had been balanced on her head. "He come out er de woods jest ez we wuz fillin' our buckets."

"Yas," insisted the blacksmith, "he's got some gal on his min'."

II

The case of the State of North Carolina *vs.* Ben Davis was called. The accused was led into court, and took his seat in the prisoner's dock.

"Prisoner at the bar, stand up."

The prisoner, pale and anxious, stood up. The clerk read the indictment, in which it was charged that the defendant by force and arms had entered the barn of one G. W. Thornton, and feloniously taken therefrom one whip, of the value of fifteen dollars.

"Are you guilty or not guilty?" asked the judge.

"Not guilty, yo' Honah; not guilty, Jedge. I never tuck de whip."

The State's attorney opened the case. He was young and zealous. Recently elected to the office, this was his first batch of cases, and he was anxious to make as good a record as possible. He had no doubt of the prisoner's guilt. There had been a great deal of petty thieving in the county, and several gentlemen had suggested to him the necessity for greater severity in punishing it. The jury were all white men. The prosecuting attorney stated the case.

"We expect to show, gentlemen of the jury, the facts set out in the indictment,—not altogether by direct proof, but by a chain of circumstantial evidence which is stronger even than the testimony of eyewitnesses. Men might lie, but circumstances cannot. We expect to show that the defendant is a man of dangerous character, a surly, impudent fellow; a man whose views of property are prejudicial to the welfare of society, and who has been heard to assert that half the property which is owned in this county has been stolen, and that, if justice were done, the white people ought to divide up the land with the negroes; in other words, a negro nihilist, a communist, a secret devotee of Tom Paine and Voltaire, a pupil of the anarchist propaganda, which, if not checked by the stern hand of the law, will fasten its insidious fangs on our social system, and drag it down to ruin."

"We object, may it please your Honor," said the defendant's attorney. "The prosecutor should defer his argument until the testimony is in."

"Confine yourself to the facts, Major," said the court mildly.

The prisoner sat with half-open mouth, overwhelmed by this flood of eloquence. He had never heard of Tom Paine or Voltaire. He had no conception of what a nihilist or an anarchist might be, and could not have told the difference between a propaganda and a potato.

"We expect to show, may it please the court, that the prisoner had been employed by Colonel Thornton to shoe a horse; that the horse was taken to the prisoner's blacksmith shop by a servant of Colonel Thornton's; that, this servant expressing a desire to go somewhere on an errand before the horse had been shod, the prisoner volunteered to return the horse to Colonel Thornton's stable; that he did so, and the following morning the whip in question was missing; that, from circumstances, suspicion naturally fell upon the prisoner, and a search was made of his shop, where the whip was found secreted; that the prisoner denied that the whip was there, but when confronted with the evidence of his crime, showed by his confusion that he was guilty beyond a peradventure."

The prisoner looked more anxious; so much eloquence could not but be effective with the jury.

The attorney for the defendant answered briefly, denying the defendant's guilt, dwelling upon his previous good character for honesty, and begging the jury not to prejudge the case, but to remember that the law is merciful, and that the benefit of the doubt should be given to the prisoner.

The prisoner glanced nervously at the jury. There was nothing in their faces to indicate the effect upon them of the opening statements. It seemed to the disinterested listeners as if the defendant's attorney had little confidence in his client's cause.

Colonel Thornton took the stand and testified to his ownership of the whip, the place where it was kept, its value, and the fact that it had disappeared. The whip was produced in court and identified by the witness. He also testified to the conversation at the blacksmith shop in the course of which the prisoner had expressed a desire to possess a similar whip. The cross-examination was brief, and no attempt was made to shake the Colonel's testimony.

The next witness was the constable who had gone with a warrant to search Ben's shop. He testified to the circumstances under which the whip was found.

"He wuz brazen as a mule at fust, an' wanted ter git mad about it. But when we begun ter turn over that pile er truck in the cawner, he kinder begun ter trimble; when the whiphandle stuck out, his eyes commenced ter grow big, an' when we hauled the whip out he turned pale ez ashes, an' begun to swear he did n' take the whip an' did n' know how it got thar."

"You may cross-examine," said the prosecuting attorney triumphantly.

The prisoner felt the weight of the testimony, and glanced furtively at the jury, and then appealingly at his lawyer.

"You say that Ben denied that he had stolen the whip," said the prisoner's attorney, on cross-examination. "Did it not occur to you that what you took for brazen impudence might have been but the evidence of conscious innocence?"

The witness grinned incredulously, revealing thereby a few blackened fragments of teeth.

"I've tuck up more'n a hundred niggers fer stealin', Kurnel, an' I never seed one yit that did n' 'ny it ter the las'."

"Answer my question. Might not the witness's indignation have been a manifestation of conscious innocence? Yes or no?"

"Yes, it mought, an' the moon mought fall—but it don't."

Further cross-examination did not weaken the witness's testimony, which was very damaging, and every one in the court room felt instinctively that a strong defense would be required to break down the State's case.

"The State rests," said the prosecuting attorney, with a ring in his voice which spoke of certain victory.

There was a temporary lull in the proceedings, during which a bailiff passed a pitcher of water and a glass along the line of jurymen. The defense was then begun.

The law in its wisdom did not permit the defendant to testify in his own behalf. There were no witnesses to the facts, but several were called to testify to Ben's good character. The colored witnesses made him out possessed of all the virtues. One or two white men testified that they had never known anything against his reputation for honesty.

The defendant rested his case, and the State called its witnesses in rebuttal. They were entirely on the point of character. One testified that he had heard the prisoner say that, if the negroes had their rights, they would own at least half the property. Another testified that he had heard the defendant say that the negroes spent too much money on churches, and that they cared a good deal more for God than God had ever seemed to care for them.

Ben Davis listened to this testimony with half-open mouth and staring eyes. Now and then he would lean forward and speak perhaps a word, when his attorney would shake a warning finger at him, and he would fall back helplessly, as if abandoning himself to fate; but for a moment only, when he would resume his puzzled look.

The arguments followed. The prosecuting attorney briefly summed up the evidence, and characterized it as almost a mathematical proof of the prisoner's guilt. He reserved his eloquence for the closing argument.

The defendant's attorney had a headache, and secretly believed his client guilty. His address sounded more like an appeal for mercy than a demand for justice. Then the State's attorney delivered the maiden argument of his office, the speech that made his reputation as an orator, and opened up to him a successful political career.

The judge's charge to the jury was a plain, simple statement of the law as applied to circumstantial evidence, and the mere statement of the law foreshadowed the verdict.

The eyes of the prisoner were glued to the jury-box, and he looked more and more like a hunted animal. In the rear of the crowd of blacks who filled the back part of the room, partly concealed by the projecting angle of the fireplace, stood Tom, the blacksmith's assistant. If the face is the mirror of the soul, then this man's soul, taken off its guard in this moment of excitement, was full of lust and envy and all evil passions.

The jury filed out of their box, and into the jury room behind the judge's stand. There was a moment of relaxation in the court room. The lawyers fell into conversation across the table. The judge beckoned to Colonel Thornton, who stepped forward, and they conversed together a few moments. The prisoner was all eyes and ears in this moment of waiting, and from an involuntary gesture on the part of the judge he divined that they were speaking of him. It is a pity he could not hear what was said.

"How do you feel about the case, Colonel?" asked the judge.

"Let him off easy," replied Colonel Thornton. "He's the best blacksmith in the county."

The business of the court seemed to have halted by tacit consent, in anticipation of a quick verdict. The suspense did not last long. Scarcely ten minutes had elapsed when there was a rap on the door, the officer opened it, and the jury came out.

The prisoner, his soul in his eyes, sought their faces, but met no reassuring glance; they were all looking away from him.

"Gentlemen of the jury, have you agreed upon a verdict?"

"We have," responded the foreman. The clerk of the court stepped forward and took the fateful slip from the foreman's hand.

The clerk read the verdict: "We, the jury impaneled and sworn to try the issues in this cause, do find the prisoner guilty as charged in the indictment."

There was a moment of breathless silence. Then a wild burst of grief from the prisoner's wife, to which his two children, not understanding it all, but vaguely conscious of some calamity, added their voices in two long, discordant wails, which would have been ludicrous had they not been heart-rending.

The face of the young man in the back of the room expressed relief and badly concealed satisfaction. The prisoner fell back upon the seat from which he had half risen in his anxiety, and his dark face assumed an ashen hue. What he thought could only be surmised. Perhaps, knowing his innocence, he had not believed conviction possible; perhaps, conscious of guilt, he dreaded the punishment, the extent of which was optional with the judge, within very wide limits. Only one other person present knew whether or not he was guilty, and that other had slunk furtively from the court room.

Some of the spectators wondered why there should be so much ado about convicting a negro of stealing a buggy-whip. They had forgotten their own interest of the moment before. They did not realize out of what trifles grow the tragedies of life.

It was four o'clock in the afternoon, the hour for adjournment, when the verdict was returned. The judge nodded to the bailiff.

"Oyez, oyez! this court is now adjourned until ten o'clock to-morrow morning," cried the bailiff in a singsong voice. The judge left the bench, the jury filed out of the box, and a buzz of conversation filled the court room.

"Brace up, Ben, brace up, my boy," said the defendant's lawyer, half apologetically. "I did what I could for you, but you can never tell what a jury will do. You won't be sentenced till to-morrow morning. In the meantime I'll speak to the judge and try to get him to be easy with you. He may let you off with a light fine."

The negro pulled himself together, and by an effort listened.

"Thanky, Majah," was all he said. He seemed to be thinking of something far away.

He barely spoke to his wife when she frantically threw herself on him, and clung to his neck, as he passed through the side room on his way to jail. He kissed his children mechanically, and did not reply to the soothing remarks made by the jailer.

III

There was a good deal of excitement in town the next morning. Two white men stood by the post office talking.

"Did yer hear the news?"

"No, what wuz it?"

"Ben Davis tried ter break jail las' night."

"You don't say so! What a fool! He ain't be'n sentenced yit."

"Well, now," said the other, "I've knowed Ben a long time, an' he wuz a right good nigger. I kinder found it hard ter b'lieve he did steal that whip. But what's a man's feelin's ag'in the proof?"

They spoke on awhile, using the past tense as if they were speaking of a dead man.

"Ef I know Jedge Hart, Ben'll wish he had slep' las' night, 'stidder tryin' ter break out'n jail."

At ten o'clock the prisoner was brought into court. He walked with shambling gait, bent at the shoulders, hopelessly, with downcast eyes, and took his seat with several other prisoners who had been brought in for sentence. His wife, accompanied by the children, waited behind him, and a number of his friends were gathered in the court room.

The first prisoner sentenced was a young white man, convicted several days before of manslaughter. The deed was done in the heat of passion, under circumstances of great provocation, during a quarrel about a woman. The prisoner was admonished of the sanctity of human life, and sentenced to one year in the penitentiary.

The next case was that of a young clerk, eighteen or nineteen years of age, who had committed a forgery in order to procure the means to buy lottery tickets. He was well connected, and the case would not have been prosecuted if the judge had not refused to allow it to be nolled, and, once brought to trial, a conviction could not have been avoided.

"You are a young man," said the judge gravely, yet not un-kindly, "and your life is yet before you. I regret that you should have been led into evil courses by the lust for speculation, so dangerous in its tendencies, so fruitful of crime and misery. I am led to believe that you are sincerely penitent, and that, after such punishment as the law cannot remit without bringing itself into contempt, you will see the error of your ways and follow the strict path of rectitude. Your fault has entailed distress not only upon yourself, but upon your relatives, people of good name and good family, who suffer as keenly from your disgrace as you yourself. Partly out of consideration for their feelings, and partly because I feel that, under the circumstances, the law will be satisfied by the penalty I shall inflict, I sentence you to imprisonment in the county jail for six months, and a fine of one hundred dollars and the costs of this action."

"The jedge talks well, don't he?" whispered one spectator to another.

"Yes, and kinder likes ter hear hisse'f talk," answered the other.

"Ben Davis, stand up," ordered the judge.

He might have said "Ben Davis, wake up," for the jailer had to touch the prisoner on the shoulder to rouse him from his stupor. He stood up, and something of the hunted look came again into his eyes, which shifted under the stern glance of the judge.

"Ben Davis, you have been convicted of larceny, after a fair trial before twelve good men of this county. Under the testimony, there can be no doubt of your guilt. The case is an aggravated one. You are not an ignorant, shiftless fellow, but a man of more than ordinary intelligence among your people, and one who ought to know better. You have not even the poor excuse of having stolen to satisfy hunger or a physical appetite. Your conduct is wholly without excuse, and I can only regard your crime as the result of a tendency to offenses of this nature, a tendency which is only too common among your people; a tendency which is a menace to civilization, a menace to society itself, for society rests upon the sacred right of property. Your opinions, too, have been given a wrong turn; you have been heard to utter sentiments which, if disseminated among an ignorant people, would breed discontent, and give rise to strained relations between them and their best friends, their old masters, who understand their real nature and their real needs, and to whose justice and enlightened guidance they can safely trust. Have you anything to say why sentence should not be passed upon you?"

"Nothin', suh, cep'n dat I did n' take de whip."

"The law, largely, I think, in view of the peculiar circumstances of your unfortunate race, has vested a large discretion in courts as to the extent of the punishment for offenses of this kind. Taking your case as a whole, I am convinced that it is one which, for the sake of the example, deserves a severe punishment. Nevertheless, I do not feel disposed to give you the full extent of the law, which would be twenty years in the penitentiary,* but, considering the fact that you have a family, and have heretofore borne a good reputation in the community, I will impose upon you the light sentence of imprisonment for five years in the penitentiary at hard labor. And I hope that this will be a warning to you and others who may be similarly disposed, and that after your sentence has expired you may lead the life of a law-abiding citizen."

"O Ben! O my husband! O God!" moaned the poor wife, and tried to press forward to her husband's side.

"Keep back, Nancy, keep back," said the jailer. "You can see him in jail."

Several people were looking at Ben's face. There was one

---

*There are no degrees of larceny in North Carolina, and the penalty for any offense lies in the discretion of the judge, to the limit of twenty years.—Au.

flash of despair, and then nothing but a stony blank, behind which he masked his real feelings, whatever they were.

Human character is a compound of tendencies inherited and habits acquired. In the anxiety, the fear of disgrace, spoke the nineteenth-century civilization with which Ben Davis had been more or less closely in touch during twenty years of slavery and fifteen years of freedom. In the stolidity with which he received this sentence for a crime which he had not committed, spoke who knows what trait of inherited savagery? For stoicism is a savage virtue.

IV

One morning in June, five years later, a black man limped slowly along the old Lumberton plank road; a tall man, whose bowed shoulders made him seem shorter than he was, and a face from which it was difficult to guess his years, for in it the wrinkles and flabbiness of age were found side by side with firm white teeth, and eyes not sunken,—eyes bloodshot, and burning with something, either fever or passion. Though he limped painfully with one foot, the other hit the ground impatiently, like the good horse in a poorly matched team. As he walked along, he was talking to himself:—

"I wonder what dey 'll do w'en I git back? I wonder how Nancy 's s'ported the fambly all dese years? Tuck in washin', I s'ppose,—she was a monst'us good washer an' ironer. I wonder ef de chillun 'll be too proud ter reco'nize deir daddy come back f'um de penetenchy? I 'spec' Billy must be a big boy by dis time. He won' b'lieve his daddy ever stole anything. I'm gwine ter slip roun' an' s'prise 'em."

Five minutes later a face peered cautiously into the window of what had once been Ben Davis's cabin,—at first an eager face, its coarseness lit up with the fire of hope; a moment later a puzzled face; then an anxious, fearful face as the man stepped away from the window and rapped at the door.

"Is Mis' Davis home?" he asked of the woman who opened the door.

"Mis' Davis don' live here. You er mistook in de house."

"Whose house is dis?"

"It b'longs ter my husban', Mr. Smith,—Primus Smith."

"'Scuse me, but I knowed de house some years ago w'en I wuz here oncet on a visit, an' it b'longed ter a man name' Ben Davis."

"Ben Davis—Ben Davis?—oh yes, I 'member now. Dat wuz de gen'man w'at wuz sent ter de penitenchy fer sump'n er nuther,—sheep-stealin', I b'lieve. Primus," she called, "w'at wuz Ben Davis, w'at useter own dis yer house, sent ter de penitenchy fer?"

"Hoss-stealin'," came back the reply in sleepy accents, from the man seated by the fireplace.

The traveler went on to the next house. A neat-looking yellow woman came to the door when he rattled the gate, and stood looking suspiciously at him.

"W'at you want?" she asked.

"Please, ma'am, will you tell me whether a man name' Ben Davis useter live in dis neighborhood?"

"Useter live in de nex' house; wuz sent ter de penitenchy fer killin' a man."

"Kin yer tell me w'at went wid Mis' Davis?"

"Umph! I's a 'spectable 'oman, I is, en don' mix wid dem kind er people. She wuz 'n' better'n her husban'. She tuk up wid a man dat useter wuk fer Ben, an' dey 're livin' down by de ole wagonya'd, where no 'spectable 'oman ever puts her foot."

"An' de chillen?"

"De gal's dead. Wuz'n' no better 'n she oughter be'n. She fell in de crick an' got drown'; some folks say she wuz 'n' sober w'en it happen'. De boy tuck atter his pappy. He wuz 'rested las' week fer shootin' a w'ite man, an' wuz lynch' de same night. Dey wa'n't none of 'em no 'count after deir pappy went ter de penitenchy."

"What went wid de proputty?"

"Hit wuz sol' fer de mortgage, er de taxes, er de lawyer, er sump'n,—I don' know w'at. A w'ite man got it."

The man with the bundle went on until he came to a creek

that crossed the road. He descended the sloping bank, and, sitting on a stone in the shade of a water-oak, took off his coarse brogans, unwound the rags that served him in lieu of stockings, and laved in the cool water the feet that were chafed with many a weary mile of travel.

After five years of unrequited toil, and unspeakable hardship in convict camps,—five years of slaving by the side of human brutes, and of nightly herding with them in vermin-haunted huts—Ben Davis had become like them. For a while he had received occasional letters from home, but in the shifting life of the convict camp they had long since ceased to reach him, if indeed they had been written. For a year or two, the consciousness of his innocence had helped to make him resist the debasing influences that surrounded him. The hope of shortening his sentence by good behavior, too, had worked a similar end. But the transfer from one contractor to another, each interested in keeping as long as possible a good worker, had speedily dissipated any such hope. When hope took flight, its place was not long vacant. Despair followed, and black hatred of all mankind, hatred especially of the man to whom he attributed all his misfortunes. One who is suffering unjustly is not apt to indulge in fine abstractions, nor to balance probabilities. By long brooding over his wrongs, his mind became, if not unsettled, at least warped, and he imagined that Colonel Thornton had deliberately set a trap into which he had fallen. The Colonel, he convinced himself, had disapproved of his prosperity, and had schemed to destroy it. He reasoned himself into the belief that he represented in his person the accumulated wrongs of a whole race, and Colonel Thornton the race who had oppressed them. A burning desire for revenge sprang up in him, and he nursed it until his sentence expired and he was set at liberty. What he had learned since reaching home had changed his desire into a deadly purpose.

When he had again bandaged his feet and slipped them into his shoes, he looked around him, and selected a stout sapling from among the undergrowth that covered the bank of the stream. Taking from his pocket a huge clasp-knife, he cut off the length of an ordinary walking stick and trimmed it. The result was an ugly-looking bludgeon, a dangerous weapon when in the grasp of a strong man.

With the stick in his hand, he went on down the road until he approached a large white house standing some distance back from the street. The grounds were filled with a profusion of shrubbery. The negro entered the gate and secreted himself in the bushes, at a point where he could hear any one that might approach.

It was near midday, and he had not eaten. He had walked all night, and had not slept. The hope of meeting his loved ones had been meat and drink and rest for him. But as he sat waiting, outraged nature asserted itself, and he fell asleep, with his head on the rising root of a tree, and his face upturned.

And as he slept, he dreamed of his childhood; of an old black mammy taking care of him in the daytime, and of a younger face, with soft eyes, which bent over him sometimes at night, and a pair of arms which clasped him closely. He dreamed of his past,—of his young wife, of his bright children. Somehow his dreams all ran to pleasant themes for a while.

Then they changed again. He dreamed that he was in the convict camp, and, by an easy transition, that he was in hell, consumed with hunger, burning with thirst. Suddenly the grinning devil who stood over him with a barbed whip faded away, and a little white angel came and handed him a drink of water. As he raised it to his lips the glass slipped, and he struggled back to consciousness.

"Poo' man! Poo' man sick, an' sleepy. Dolly b'ing f'owers to cover poo' man up. Poo' man mus' be hungry. W'en Dolly get him covered up, she go b'ing poo' man some cake."

A sweet little child, as beautiful as a cherub escaped from Paradise, was standing over him. At first he scarcely comprehended the words the baby babbled out. But as they became clear to him, a novel feeling crept slowly over his heart. It had been so long since he had heard anything but curses and stern words of command, or the ribald songs of obscene merriment, that the clear tones of this voice from heaven cooled his calloused heart as the water of the brook had soothed his blistered feet. It was so strange, so unwonted a thing, that he lay there with half-closed eyes while the child brought leaves and flowers and laid them on his face and on his breast, and arranged them with little caressing taps.

She moved away, and plucked a flower. And then she spied another farther on, and then another, and, as she gathered them, kept increasing the distance between herself and the man lying there, until she was several rods away.

Ben Davis watched her through eyes over which had come an unfamiliar softness. Under the lingering spell of his dream, her golden hair, which fell in rippling curls, seemed like a halo of purity and innocence and peace, irradiating the atmosphere around her. It is true the thought occurred to Ben, vaguely, that through harm to her he might inflict the greatest punishment upon her father; but the idea came like a dark shape that faded away and vanished into nothingness as soon as it came within the nimbus that surrounded the child's person.

The child was moving on to pluck still another flower, when there came a sound of hoof-beats, and Ben was aware that a horseman, visible through the shrubbery, was coming along the curved path that led from the gate to the house. It must be the man he was waiting for, and now was the time to wreak his vengeance. He sprang to his feet, grasped his club, and stood for a moment irresolute. But either the instinct of the convict, beaten, driven, and debased, or the influence of the child, which was still strong upon him, impelled him, after the first momentary pause, to flee as though seeking safety.

His flight led him toward the little girl, whom he must pass in order to make his escape, and as Colonel Thornton turned the corner of the path he saw a desperate-looking negro, clad in filthy rags, and carrying in his hand a murderous bludgeon, running toward the child, who, startled by the sound of footsteps, had turned and was looking toward the approaching man with wondering eyes. A sickening fear came over the father's heart, and drawing the ever-ready revolver, which according to the Southern custom he carried always upon his person, he fired with unerring aim. Ben Davis ran a few yards farther, faltered, threw out his hands, and fell dead at the child's feet.

———

Some time, we are told, when the cycle of years has rolled around, there is to be another golden age, when all men will dwell together in love and harmony, and when peace and righteousness shall prevail for a thousand years. God speed the day, and let not the shining thread of hope become so enmeshed in the web of circumstance that we lose sight of it; but give us here and there, and now and then, some little foretaste of this golden age, that we may the more patiently and hopefully await its coming!

DAVE'S NECKLISS

"Have some dinner, Uncle Julius?" said my wife.

It was a Sunday afternoon in early autumn. Our two women-servants had gone to a camp-meeting some miles away, and would not return until evening. My wife had served the dinner, and we were just rising from the table when Julius came up the lane, and, taking off his hat, seated himself on the piazza.

The old man glanced through the open door at the dinner-table, and his eyes rested lovingly upon a large sugar-cured ham, from which several slices had been cut, exposing a rich pink expanse that would have appealed strongly to the appetite of any hungry Christian.

"Thanky, Miss Annie," he said, after a momentary hesitation. "I dunno ez I keers ef I does tas'e a piece er dat ham, ef yer 'll cut me off a slice un it."

"No," said Annie, "I won't. Just sit down to the table and help yourself; eat all you want, and don't be bashful."

Julius drew a chair up to the table, while my wife and I went out on the piazza. Julius was in my employment; he took his meals with his own family, but when he happened to be about our house at mealtimes, my wife never let him go away hungry.

I threw myself into a hammock, from which I could see Julius through an open window. He ate with evident relish, devoting his attention chiefly to the ham, slice after slice of which disappeared in the spacious cavity of his mouth. At first the old man ate rapidly, but after the edge of his appetite had been taken off he proceeded in a more leisurely manner. When he had cut the sixth piece of ham (I kept count of them from a lazy curiosity to see how much he *could* eat) I saw him lay it on his plate; as he adjusted the knife and fork to cut it into smaller pieces, he paused, as if struck by a sudden thought, and a tear rolled down his rugged cheek and fell upon the slice of ham before him. But the emotion, whatever the thought that caused it, was transitory, and in a moment he continued his dinner. When he was through eating, he came out on the porch, and resumed his seat with the satisfied expression of countenance that usually follows a good dinner.

"Julius," I said, "you seemed to be affected by something a moment ago. Was the mustard so strong that it moved you to tears?"

"No, suh, it wa'n't de mustard; I wuz studyin' 'bout Dave."

"Who was Dave, and what about him?" I asked.

The conditions were all favorable to storytelling. There was an autumnal languor in the air, and a dreamy haze softened the dark green of the distant pines and the deep blue of the Southern sky. The generous meal he had made had put the old man in a very good humor. He was not always so, for his curiously undeveloped nature was subject to moods which were almost childish in their variableness. It was only now and then that we were able to study, through the medium of his recollection, the simple but intensely human inner life of slavery. His way of looking at the past seemed very strange to us; his view of certain sides of life was essentially different from ours. He never indulged in any regrets for the Arcadian joyousness and irresponsibility which was a somewhat popular conception of slavery; his had not been the lot of the petted house-servant, but that of the toiling fieldhand. While he mentioned with a warm appreciation the acts of kindness which those in authority had shown to him and his people, he would speak of a cruel deed, not with the indignation of one accustomed to quick feeling and spontaneous expression, but with a furtive disapproval which suggested to us a doubt in his own mind as to whether he had a right to think or to feel, and presented to us the curious psychological spectacle of a mind enslaved long after the shackles had been struck off from the limbs of its possessor. Whether the sacred name of liberty ever set his soul aglow with a generous fire; whether he had more than the most elementary ideas of love, friendship, patriotism, religion—things which are half, and the better half, of life to us; whether he even realized, except in a vague, uncertain way, his own degradation, I do not know. I fear not; and if not, then centuries of repression had borne their legitimate fruit. But in the simple human feeling, and still more in the undertone of sadness which pervaded his stories, I thought I could see a spark which, fanned by favoring breezes and fed by the memories of the past, might become in his children's children a glowing flame of sensibility, alive to every thrill of human happiness or human woe.

"Dave use' ter b'long ter my old marster," said Julius; "he wuz raise' on dis yer plantation, en I kin 'member all erbout 'im, fer I wuz old 'nuff ter chop cotton w'en it all happen'. Dave wuz a tall man, en monst'us strong: he could do mo' wuk in a day dan any yuther two niggers on de plantation. He wuz one er dese yer solemn kine er men, en nebber run on wid much foolishness, like de yuther darkies. He use' ter go out in de woods en pray; en w'en he hear de han's on de plantation cussin' en gwine on wid dere dancin' en foolishness, he use' ter tell 'em 'bout religion en jedgmen'-day, w'en dey would half ter gin account fer eve'y idle word en all dey yuther sinful kyarin's-on.

"Dave had l'arn' how ter read de Bible. Dey wuz a free nigger boy in de settlement w'at wuz monst'us smart, en could write en cipher, en wuz alluz readin' books er papers. En Dave had hi'ed dis free boy fer ter l'arn 'im how ter read. Hit wuz 'g'in' de law, but co'se none er de niggers did n' say nuffin ter de w'ite folks 'bout it. Howsomedever, one day Mars Walker—he wuz de obserseah—foun' out Dave could read. Mars Walker wa'n't nuffin but a po' bockrah, en folks said he could n' read ner write hisse'f, en co'se he did n' lack ter see a nigger w'at knowed mo' d'n he did; so he went en tole Mars Dugal'. Mars Dugal' sont fer Dave, en ax' 'im 'bout it.

"Dave did n't hardly knowed w'at ter do; but he could n' tell no lie, so he 'fessed he could read de Bible a little by spellin' out de words. Mars Dugal' look' mighty solemn.

"'Dis yer is a se'ious matter,' sezee; 'it 's 'g'in de law ter l'arn niggers how ter read, er 'low 'em ter hab books. But w'at yer l'arn out'n dat Bible, Dave?'

"Dave wa'n't no fool, ef he wuz a nigger, en sezee:

"'Marster, I l'arns dat it's a sin fer ter steal, er ter lie, er fer ter want w'at doan b'long ter yer; en I l'arns fer ter love de Lawd en ter 'bey my marster.'

"Mars Dugal' sorter smile' en laf' ter hisse'f, like he 'uz might'ly tickle' 'bout sump'n, en sezee:

"'Doan 'pear ter me lack readin' de Bible done yer much harm, Dave. Dat's w'at I wants all my niggers fer ter know. Yer keep right on readin', en tell de yuther han's w'at yer be'n tellin' me. How would yer lack fer ter preach ter de niggers on Sunday?'

"Dave say he'd be glad fer ter do w'at he could. So Mars Dugal' tole de obserseah fer ter let Dave preach ter de niggers, en tell 'em w'at wuz in de Bible, en it would he'p ter keep 'em fum stealin' er runnin' erway.

"So Dave 'mence' ter preach, en done de han's on de plantation a heap er good, en most un 'em lef' off dey wicked ways, en 'mence' ter love ter hear 'bout God, en religion, en de Bible; en dey done dey wuk better, en did n' gib de obserseah but mighty little trouble fer ter manage 'em.

"Dave wuz one er dese yer men w'at did n' keer much fer de gals—leastways he did n' 'tel Dilsey come ter de plantation. Dilsey wuz a monst'us peart, good-lookin', gingybread-colored gal—one er dese yer high-steppin' gals w'at hol's dey heads up, en won' stan' no foolishness fum no man. She had b'long' ter a gemman over on Rockfish, w'at died, en whose 'state ha' ter be sol' fer ter pay his debts. En Mars Dugal' had be'n ter de oc-tion, en w'en he seed dis gal a-cryin' en gwine on 'bout bein' sol' erway fum her ole mammy, Aun' Mahaly, Mars Dugal' bid 'em bofe in, en fotch 'em ober ter our plantation.

"De young nigger men on de plantation wuz des wil' atter Dilsey, but it did n' do no good, en none un 'em could n' git Dilsey fer dey junesey,* 'tel Dave 'mence' fer ter go roun' Aun' Mahaly's cabin. Dey wuz a fine-lookin' couple, Dave en Dilsey wuz, bofe tall, en well-shape', en soopl'. En dey sot a heap by one ernudder, Mars Dugal' seed 'em tergedder one Sunday, en de nex' time he seed Dave atter dat, sezee:

*Sweetheart.—Au.

"'Dave, w'en yer en Dilsey gits ready fer ter git married, I ain' got no rejections. Dey 's a poun' er so er chawin'ter-backer up at de house, en I reckon yo' mist'iss kin fine a frock en a rib-bin er two fer Dilsey. Youer bofe good niggers, en yer neenter be feared er bein' sol' 'way fum one ernudder long ez I owns dis plantation; en I 'spec's ter own it fer a long time yit.'

"But dere wuz one man on de plantation w'at did n' lack ter see Dave en Dilsey tergedder ez much ez ole marster did. W'en Mars Dugal' went ter de sale what he got Dilsey en Mahaly, he bought ernudder han', by de name er Wiley. Wiley wuz one er dese yer shiny-eyed, double-headed little niggers, sha'p ez a steel trap, en sly ez de fox w'at keep out'n it. Dis yer Wiley had be'n pesterin' Dilsey 'fo' she come ter our plantation, en had nigh 'bout worried de life out'n her. She did n' keer nuffin fer 'im, but he pestered her so she ha' ter th'eaten ter tell her marster fer ter make Wiley let her 'lone. W'en he come ober to our place it wuz des ez bad, 'tel bimeby Wiley seed dat Dilsey had got ter thinkin' a heap 'bout Dave, en den he sorter hilt off aw'ile, en purten' lack he gin Dilsey up. But he wuz one er dese yer 'ceitful niggers, en w'ile he wuz laffin' en jokin' wid de yuther han's 'bout Dave en Dilsey, he wuz settin' a trap fer ter ketch Dave en git Dilsey back fer hisse'f.

"Dave en Dilsey made up dere min's fer ter git married long 'bout Christmas time, w'en dey 'd hab mo' time fer a weddin'. But 'long 'bout two weeks befo' dat time ole mars 'mence' ter lose a heap er bacon. Eve'y night er so somebody 'ud steal a side er bacon, er a ham, er a shoulder, er sump'n, fum one er de smoke'ouses. De smoke'ouses wuz lock', but somebody had a key, en manage' ter git in some way er 'nudder. Dey 's mo' ways 'n one ter skin a cat, en dey 's mo' d'n one way ter git in a smoke'ouse—leastways dat 's w'at I hearn say. Folks w'at had bacon fer ter sell did n' hab no trouble 'bout gittin' rid un it. Hit wuz 'g'in de law fer ter buy things fum slaves; but Lawd! Dat law did n' 'mount ter a hill er peas. Eve'y week er so one er dese yer big covered waggins would come 'long de road, ped-dlin' terbacker en w'iskey. Dey wuz a sight er room in one er dem big waggins, en it wuz monst'us easy fer ter swop off ba-con fer sump'n ter chaw er ter wa'm yer up in de wintertime.

I s'pose de peddlers did n' knowed dey wuz breakin' de law, caze de niggers alluz went at night, en stayed on de dark side er de waggin; en it wuz mighty hard fer ter tell *w'at* kine er folks dey wuz.

"Atter two er th'ee hund'ed er meat had be'n stole', Mars Walker call all de niggers up one ebenin', en tol' 'em dat de fus' nigger he cot stealin' bacon on dat plantation would git sump'n fer ter 'member it by long ez he lib'. En he say he'd gin fi' dollars ter de nigger w'at 'skiver' de rogue. Mars Walker say he s'picion' one er two er de niggers, but he could n' tell fer sho, en co'se dey all 'nied it w'en he 'cuse em un it.

"Dey wa'n't no bacon stole' fer a week er so, 'tel one dark night w'en somebody tuk a ham fum one er de smoke'ouses. Mars Walker des cusst awful w'en he foun' out de ham wuz gone, en say he gwine ter sarch all de niggers' cabins; w'en dis yer Wiley I wuz tellin' yer 'bout up'n say he s'picion' who tuk de ham, fer he seed Dave comin' 'cross de plantation fum to'ds de smoke'ouse de night befo'. W'en Mars Walker hearn dis fum Wiley, he went en sarch' Dave's cabin, en foun' de ham hid under de flo'.

"Eve'ybody wuz 'stonish'; but dere wuz de ham. Co'se Dave 'nied it ter de las', but dere wuz de ham. Mars Walker says it wuz des ez he 'spected: he did n' b'lieve in dese yer readin' en prayin' niggers; it wuz all 'pocrisy, en sarve' Mars Dugal' right fer 'lowin' Dave ter be readin' books w'en it wuz 'g'in' de law.

"W'en Mars Dugal' hearn 'bout de ham, he say he wuz might'ly 'ceived en dissapp'inted in Dave. He say he would n' nebber hab no mo' conference in no nigger, en Mars Walker could do des ez he wuz a mineter wid Dave er any er de res' er de niggers. So Mars Walker tuk'n tied Dave up en gin 'im forty; en den he got some er dis yer wire clof w'at dey uses fer ter make sifters out'n, en tuk'n wrap' it roun' de ham en fasten it tergedder at de little een'. Den he tuk Dave down ter de blacksmif shop, en had Unker Silas, de plantation blacksmif, fasten a chain ter de ham, en den fasten de yuther een' er de chain roun' Dave's neck. En den he says ter Dave, sezee:

"'Now, suh, yer 'll wear dat neckliss fer de nex' six mont's;

en I 'spec's yer ner none er de yuther niggers on dis plantation won' steal no mo' bacon dyoin' er dat time."

"Well, it des 'peared ez if fum dat time Dave did n' hab nuffin but trouble. De niggers all turnt ag'in' 'im, caze he be'n de 'casion er Mars Dugal' turnin' 'em all ober ter Mars Walker. Mars Dugal' wa'n't a bad marster hisse'f, but Mars Walker wuz hard ez a rock. Dave kep' on sayin' he did n' take de ham, but none un 'em did n' b'lieve 'im.

"Dilsey wa'n't on de plantation w'en Dave wuz 'cused er stealin' de bacon. Ole mist'iss had sont her ter town fer a week er so fer ter wait on one er her darters w'at had a young baby, en she did n' fine out nuffin 'bout Dave's trouble 'tel she got back ter de plantation. Dave had patien'ly endyoed de finger er scawn, en all de hard words w'at de niggers pile' on 'im, caze he wuz sho' Dilsey would stan' by 'em, en would n' b'lieve he wuz a rogue, ner none er de yuther tales de darkies wuz tellin' 'bout 'im.

"W'en Dilsey come back fum town, en got down fum behine de buggy whar she b'en ridin' wid ole mars, de fus' nigger 'ooman she met says ter her—

"'Is yer seed Dave, Dilsey?'

"'No, I ain' seed Dave,' says Dilsey.

"'Yes des oughter look at dat nigger; reckon yer would n' want 'im fer yo' junesey no mo'. Mars Walker cotch 'im stealin' bacon, en gone en fasten' a ham roun' his neck, so he can't git it off'n hisse'f. He sut'nly do look quare.' En den de 'ooman bus' out laffin; fit ter kill herse'f. W'en she got thoo laffin' she up'n tole Dilsey all 'bout de ham, en all de yuther lies w'at de niggers be'n tellin' on Dave.

"W'en Dilsey started down ter de quarters, who should she meet but Dave, comin' in fum de cotton-fiel'. She turnt her head ter one side, en purten' lack she did n' seed Dave.

"'Dilsey!' sezee.

"Dilsey walk' right on, en did n' notice 'im.

"'*Oh*, Dilsey!'

"Dilsey did n' paid no 'tention ter 'im, en den Dave knowed some er de niggers be'n tellin' her 'bout de ham. He felt monst'us bad, but he 'lowed ef he could des git Dilsey fer ter listen ter 'im for a minute er so, he could make her b'lieve he did n' stole de bacon. It wuz a week er two befo' he could git a chance ter speak ter her ag'in; but fine'ly he cotch her down by de spring one day, en sezee:

"'Dilsey, w'at fer yer won' speak ter me, en purten' lack yer doan see me? Dilsey, yer knows me too well fer ter b'lieve I'd steal, er do dis yuther wick'ness de niggers is all layin' ter me— yer *knows* I would n' do dat, Dilsey. Yer ain' gwine back on yo' Dave, is yer?'

"But w'at Dave say did n' hab no 'fec' on Dilsey. Dem lies folks b'en tellin' her had p'isen' her min' 'g'in' Dave.

"'I doan wanter talk ter no nigger,' says she, 'w'at be'n whip' fer stealin', en w'at gwine roun' wid sich a lookin' thing ez dat hung roun' his neck. I's a 'spectable gal, *I* is. W'at yer call dat, Dave? Is dat a cha'm fer to keep off witches, er is it a noo kine er neckliss yer got?'

"Po' Dave did n' knowed w'at ter do. De las' one he had 'pended on fer ter stan' by 'im had gone back on 'im, en dey did n' 'pear ter be nuffin mo' wuf libbin' fer. He could n' hol' no mo' pra'r-meetin's, fer Mars Walker would n' 'low 'im ter preach, en de darkies would n' 'a' listen' ter 'im ef he had preach'. He did n' eben hab his Bible fer ter comfort hisse'f wid, fer Mars Walker had tuk it erway fum 'im en burnt it up, en say ef he ketch any mo' niggers wid Bibles on de plantation he 'd do 'em wuss'n he done Dave.

"En ter make it still harder fer Dave, Dilsey tuk up wid Wiley. Dave could see him gwine up ter Aun' Mahaly's cabin, en settin' out on de bench in de moonlight wid Dilsey, en singin' sinful songs en playin' de banjer. Dave use' ter scrouch down behine de bushes, en wonder w'at de Lawd sen' 'im all dem tribberlations fer.

"But all er Dave's yuther troubles wa'n't nuffin side er dat ham. He had wrap' de chain roun' wid a rag, so it did n' hurt his neck; but w'eneber he went ter wuk, dat ham would be in his way; he had ter do his task, howsomedever, des de same ez ef he did n' hab de ham. W'eneber he went ter lay down, dat ham would be in de way. Ef he turn ober in his sleep, dat ham would be tuggin' at his neck. It wuz de las' thing he seed at

night, en de fus' thing he seed in de mawnin'. W'eneber he met
a stranger, de ham would be de fus' thing de stranger would
see. Most un 'em would 'mence' ter laf, en whareber Dave went
he could see folks p'intin' at him, en year 'em sayin':

" 'W'at kine er collar dat nigger got roun' his neck?' er, ef dey
knowed 'im, 'Is yer stole any mo' hams lately?' er 'W'at yer take
fer yo' neckliss, Dave?' er some joke er 'nuther 'bout dat ham.

"Fus' Dave did n' mine it so much, caze he knowed he had n'
done nuffin. But bimeby he got so he could n' stan' it no longer,
en he'd hide hisse'f in de bushes w'eneber he seed anybody
comin', en alluz kep' hisse'f shet up in his cabin atter he come
in fum wuk.

"It wuz monst'us hard on Dave, en bimeby, w'at wid dat
ham eberlastin' en etarnally draggin' roun' his neck, he 'mence'
fer ter do en say quare things, en make de niggers wonder ef he
wa'n't gittin' out'n his mine. He got ter gwine roun' talkin' ter
hisse'f, en singin' cornshuckin' songs, en laffin' fit ter kill 'bout
nuffin. En one day he tole one er de niggers he had 'skivered a
noo way fer ter raise hams—gwine ter pick 'em off'n trees, en
save de expense er smoke'ouses by kyoin' 'em in de sun. En one
day he up'n tole Mars Walker he got sump'n pertickler fer ter
say ter 'im; en he tuk Mars Walker off ter one side, en tole 'im
he wuz gwine ter show 'im a place in de swamp whar dey wuz
a whole trac' er lan' covered wid ham trees.

"W'en Mars Walker hearn Dave talkin' dis kine er fool-talk,
en w'en he seed how Dave wuz 'mencin' ter git behine in his
wuk, en w'en he ax' de niggers en dey tole 'im how Dave be'n
gwine on, he 'lowed he reckon' he 'd punish' Dave ernuff, en it
mou't do mo' harm dan good fer ter keep de ham on his neck
any longer. So he sont Dave down ter de blacksmif shop en had
de ham tuk off. Dey wa'n't much er de ham lef' by dat time, fer
de sun had melt all de fat, en de lean had all swivel' up, so dey
wa'n't but th'ee er fo' poun's lef'.

"W'en de ham had be'n tuk off'n Dave, folks kinder stopped
talkin' 'bout 'im so much. But de ham had be'n on his neck so
long dat Dave had sorter got use' ter it. He look des lack he 'd
los' sump'n fer a day er so atter de ham wuz tuk off, en did n'
'pear ter know w'at ter do wid hisse'f; en fine'ly he up'n tuk'n

tied a lighterd-knot ter a string, en hid it under de flo' er his cabin, en w'en nobody wuz n' lookin' he'd take it out en hang it roun' his neck, en go off in de woods en holler en sing; en he allus tied it roun' his neck w'en he went ter sleep. Fac', it 'peared lack Dave done gone clean out'n his mine. En atter a w'ile he got one er de quarest notions you eber hearn tell un. It wuz 'bout dat time dat I come back ter de plantation fer ter wuk—I had be'n out ter Mars Dugal's yuther place on Beaver Crick for a mont' er so. I had hearn 'bout Dave en de bacon, en 'bout w'at wuz gwine on on de plantation; but I did n' b'lieve w'at dey all say 'bout Dave, fer I knowed Dave w'n't dat kine er man. One day atter I come back, me'n Dave wuz choppin' cotton tergedder, w'en Dave lean' on his hoe, en motion fer me ter come ober close ter 'im; en den he retch ober en w'ispered ter me.

"'Julius,' sezee, 'did yer knowed yer wuz wukkin' long yer wid a ham?'

"I could n' 'magine w'at he meant. 'G'way fum yer, Dave,' says I. 'Yer ain' wearin' no ham no mo; try en fergit 'bout dat; 't ain' gwine ter do yer no good fer ter 'member it.'

"'Look a-yer, Julius,' sezee, 'kin yer keep a secret?'

"'Co'se I kin, Dave,' says I. 'I doan go roun' tellin' people w'at yuther folks says ter me.'

"'Kin I trus' yer, Julius? Will yer cross yo' heart?'

"I cross' my heart. 'Wush I may die ef I tells a soul,' says I.

"Dave look' at me des lack he wuz lookin' thoo me en 'way on de yuther side er me, en sezee:

"'Did yer knowed I wuz turnin' ter a ham, Julius?'

"I tried ter 'suade Dave dat dat wuz all foolishness, en dat he ought n't ter be talkin' dat-a-way—hit wa'n't right. En I tole 'im ef he'd des be patien', de time would sho'ly come w'en eve'ything would be straighten' out, en folks would fine out who de rale rogue wuz w'at stole de bacon. Dave 'peared ter listen ter w'at I say, en promise' ter do better, en stop gwine on dat-a-way; en it seem lack he pick' up a bit w'en he seed dey wuz one pusson did n' b'lieve dem tales 'bout 'im.

"Hit wa'n't long atter dat befo' Mars Archie McIntyre, ober on de Wimbleton road, 'mence' ter complain 'bout somebody stealin' chickens fum his hen'ouse. De chickens kep' on gwine, en at las' Mars Archie tole de han's on his plantation dat he gwine ter shoot de fus' man he ketch in his hen'ouse. In less'n a week atter he gin dis warnin', he cotch a nigger in de hen'ouse, en fill' 'em full er squir'l-shot. W'en he got a light, he 'skivered it wuz a strange nigger; en w'en he call' one er his own sarven's, de nigger tole 'im it wuz our Wiley. W'en Mars Archie foun' dat out, he sont ober ter our plantation fer ter tell Mars Dugal' he had shot one er his niggers, en dat he could sen' ober dere en git w'at wuz lef' un 'im.

"Mars Dugal' wuz mad at fus'; but w'en he got ober dere en hearn how it all happen', he did n' hab much ter say. Wiley wuz shot so bad he wuz sho' he wuz gwine ter die, so he up'n says ter ole marster:

"'Mars Dugal,' sezee, 'I knows I's be'n a monst'us bad nigger, but befo' I go I wanter git sump'n off'n my mine. Dave did n' steal dat bacon w'at wuz tuk out'n de smoke'ouse. *I* stole it all, en I hid de ham under Dave's cabin fer ter th'ow de blame on him—en may de good Lawd fergib me fer it.'

"Mars Dugal' had Wiley tuk back ter de plantation, en sont fer a doctor fer ter pick de shot out'n 'im. En de ve'y next' mawnin' Mars Dugal' sont fer Dave ter come up ter de big house; he felt kinder sorry fer de way Dave had be'n treated. Co'se it wa'n't no fault er Mars Dugal's, but he wuz gwine ter do w'at he could fer ter make up fer it. So he sont word down ter de quarters fer Dave en all de yuther han's ter 'semble up in de yard befo' de big house at sun up nex' mawnin'.

"Yearly in de mawnin' de niggers all swarm' up in de yard. Mars Dugal' wuz feelin' so kine dat he had brung up a bairl er cider, en tole de niggers all fer ter he'p deyselves.

"All de han's on de plantation come but Dave; en bimeby, w'en it seem lack he wa'n't comin', Mars Dugal' sont a nigger down ter de quarters ter look fer 'im. De sun wuz gittin' up, en dey wuz a heap er wuk ter be done, en Mars Dugal' sorter got ti'ed waitin'; so he up'n says:

"'Well, boys en gals, I sont fer yer all up yer fer ter tell yer dat all dat 'bout Dave's stealin' er de bacon wuz a mistake, ez I s'pose yer all done hearn befo' now, en I's mighty sorry it happen'. I wants ter treat all my niggers right, en I wants yer all ter know dat I sets a heap by all er my han's w'at is hones' en smart. En I want yer all ter treat Dave des lack yer did befo' dis thing happen', en mine w'at he preach ter yer; fer Dave is a good nigger, en has had a hard row ter hoe. En de fus' one I ketch sayin' anythin' 'g'in' Dave, I'll tell Mister Walker ter gin 'im forty. Now take ernudder drink er cider all roun', en den git at dat cotton, fer I wanter git dat Persimmon Hill trac' all pick' ober terday.'

"W'en de niggers wuz gwine 'way, Mars Dugal' tole me fer ter go en hunt up Dave, en bring 'im up ter de house. I went down ter Dave's cabin, but could n' fine 'im dere. Den I look' roun' de plantation, en in de aidge er de woods, en 'long de road; but I could n' fine no sign er Dave. I wuz 'bout ter gin up de sarch, w'en I happen' fer ter run 'cross a foot-track w'at look' lack Dave's. I had wukked 'long wid Dave so much dat I knowed his tracks: he had a monst'us long foot, wid a holler instep, w'ich wuz sump'n skase 'mongs' black folks. So I follered dat track 'cross de fiel' fum de quarters 'tel I get ter de smoke'ouse. De fus' thing I notice' wuz smoke comin' out'n de cracks: it wuz cu'ous, caze dey had n' be'n no hogs kill on de plantation fer six mont' er so, en all de bacon in de smoke'ouse wuz done kyoed. I could n' 'magine fer ter sabe my life w'at Dave wuz doin' in dat smoke'ouse. I went up ter de do' en hollered:

"'Dave!'

"Dey did n' nobody answer. I did n' wanter open de do', fer w'ite folks is monst'us pertickler 'bout dey smoke'ouses; en ef de oberseah had a-come up en cotch me in dere, he mou't not wanter b'lieve I wuz des lookin' fer Dave. So I sorter knock at de do' en call' out ag'in:

"'O Dave, hit's me—Julius! Doan be skeered. Mars Dugal' wants yer ter come up ter de big house—he done 'skivered who stole de ham.'

"But Dave did n' answer. En w'en I look' roun' ag'in en did n' seed none er his tracks gwine way fum de smoke'ouse, I knowed he wuz in dere yit, en I wuz 'termine' fer ter fetch 'im out; so I push de do' open en look in.

"Dey wuz a pile er bark burnin' in de middle er de flo', en right ober de fier, hangin' fum one er de rafters, wuz Dave; dey wuz a rope roun' his neck, en I did n' haf ter look at his face mo' d'n once fer ter see he wuz dead.

"Den I knowed how it all happen'. Dave had kep' on gittin' wusser en wusser in his mine, 'tel he des got ter b'lievin' he wuz all done turnt ter a ham; en den he had gone en built a fier, en tied a rope roun' his neck, des lack de hams wuz tied, en had hung hisse'f up in de smoke'ouse fer ter kyo.

"Dave wuz buried down by the swamp, in de plantation buryin' groun'. Wiley did n' died fum de woun' he got in Mars McIntyre's hen'ouse; he got well atter a w'ile, but Dilsey would n' hab nuffin mo' ter do wid 'im, en 't wa'n't long 'fo' Mars Dugal' sol' 'im ter a spekilater on his way souf—he say he did n' want no sich a nigger on de plantation, ner in de county, ef he could he'p it. En w'en de een' er de year come, Mars Dugal' turnt Mars Walker off, en run de plantation hisse'f atter dat.

"Eber sence den," said Julius in conclusion, "w'eneber I eats ham it min's me er Dave. I lacks ham, but I nebber kin eat mo' d'n two er th'ee poun's befo' I gits ter studyin' 'bout Dave, en den I has ter stop en leab de res' fer ernudder time."

There was a short silence after the old man had finished his story, and then my wife began to talk to him about the weather, on which subject he was an authority. I went into the house. When I came out, half an hour later, I saw Julius disappearing down the lane, with a basket on his arm.

At breakfast, next morning, it occurred to me that I should like a slice of ham. I said as much to my wife.

"Oh, no, John," she responded, "you shouldn't eat anything so heavy for breakfast."

I insisted.

"The fact is," she said, pensively, "I couldn't have eaten any more of that ham, so I gave it to Julius."

BAXTER'S
PROCRUSTES

Baxter's *Procrustes* is one of the publications of the Bodleian Club. The Bodleian Club is composed of gentlemen of culture, who are interested in books and book collecting. It was named, very obviously, after the famous library of the same name, and not only became in our city a sort of shrine for local worshipers of fine bindings and rare editions, but was visited occasionally by pilgrims from afar. The Bodleian has entertained Mark Twain, Joseph Jefferson, and other literary and histrionic celebrities. It possesses quite a collection of personal mementos of distinguished authors, among them a paperweight which once belonged to Goethe, a lead pencil used by Emerson, an autograph letter of Matthew Arnold, and a chip from a tree felled by Mr. Gladstone. Its library contains a number of rare books, including a fine collection on chess, of which game several of the members are enthusiastic devotees.

The activities of the club are not, however, confined entirely to books. We have a very handsome clubhouse, and much taste and discrimination have been exercised in its adornment. There are many good paintings, including the portraits of the various presidents of the club, which adorn the entrance hall. After books, perhaps the most distinctive feature of the club is our collection of pipes. In a large rack in the smoking-room—really a superfluity, since smoking is permitted all over the house—is as complete an assortment of pipes as perhaps exists in the civilized world. Indeed, it is an unwritten rule of the club that no one is eligible for membership who cannot produce a new variety of pipe, which is filed with his application for membership, and, if he passes, deposited with the club collection, he, how-

ever, retaining the title in himself. Once a year, upon the an-
niversary of the death of Sir Walter Raleigh, who, it will be
remembered, first introduced tobacco into England, the full
membership of the club, as a rule, turns out. A large supply of
the very best smoking mixture is laid in. At nine o'clock sharp
each member takes his pipe from the rack, fills it with tobacco,
and then the whole club, with the president at the head, all
smoking furiously, march in solemn procession from room to
room, upstairs and downstairs, making the tour of the clubhouse
and returning to the smoking-room. The president then deliv-
ers an address, and each member is called upon to say something, either by way of a quotation or an original sentiment,
in praise of the virtues of nicotine. This ceremony—facetiously
known as "hitting the pipe"—being thus concluded, the membership pipes are carefully cleaned out and replaced in the club
rack.

As I have said, however, the *raison d'être* of the club, and
the feature upon which its fame chiefly rests, is its collection of
rare books, and of these by far the most interesting are its own
publications. Even its catalogues are works of art, published in
numbered editions, and sought by libraries and book collectors. Early in its history it began the occasional publication of
books which emphasis should be laid upon the qualities that
make a book valuable in the eyes of collectors. Of these, age
could not, of course, be imparted, but in the matter of fine and
curious bindings, of hand-made linen papers, of uncut or
deckle edges, of wide margins and limited editions, the club
could control its own publications. The matter of contents was,
it must be confessed, a less important consideration. At first
it was felt by the publishing committee that nothing but the
finest products of the human mind should be selected for
enshrinement in the beautiful volumes which the club should
issue. The length of the work was an important consideration—
long things were not compatible with wide margins and graceful slenderness. For instance, we brought out Coleridge's *Ancient
Mariner*, an essay by Emerson, and another by Thoreau. Our
Rubáyát of Omar Khayyám was Heron-Allen's translation of
the original manuscript in the Bodleian Library at Oxford, which

though less poetical than Fitz-Gerald's was not so common. Several years ago we began to publish the works of our own members. Bascom's *Essay on Pipes* was a very creditable performance. It was published in a limited edition of one hundred copies, and since it had not previously appeared elsewhere and was copyrighted by the club, it was sufficiently rare to be valuable for that reason. The second publication of local origin was Baxter's *Procrustes*.

I have omitted to say that once or twice a year, at a meeting of which notice has been given, an auction is held at the Bodleian. The members of the club send in their duplicate copies, or books they for any reason wish to dispose of, which are auctioned off to the highest bidder. At these sales, which are well attended, the club's publications have of recent years formed the leading feature. Three years ago, number three of Bascom's *Essay on Pipes* sold for fifteen dollars—the original cost of publication was one dollar and seventy-five cents. Later in the evening an uncut copy of the same brought thirty dollars. At the next auction the price of the cut copy was run up to twenty-five dollars, while the uncut copy was knocked down at seventy-five dollars. The club had always appreciated the value of uncut copies, but this financial endorsement enhanced their desirability immensely. This rise in the *Essay on Pipes* was not without a sympathetic effect upon all the club publications. The Emerson essay rose from three dollars to seventeen, and the Thoreau, being by an author less widely read, and by his own confession commercially unsuccessful, brought a somewhat higher figure. The prices, thus inflated, were not permitted to come down appreciably. Since every member of the club possessed one or more of these valuable editions, they were all manifestly interested in keeping up the price. The publication, however, which brought the highest prices, and, but for the sober second thought, might have wrecked the whole system, was Baxter's *Procrustes*.

Baxter was, perhaps, the most scholarly member of the club. A graduate of Harvard, he had traveled extensively, had read widely, and while not so enthusiastic a collector as some of us, possessed as fine a private library as any man of his age in the city. He was about thirty-five when he joined the club, and apparently some bitter experience—some disappointment in love or ambition—had left its mark upon his character. With light, curly hair, fair complexion and gray eyes, one would have expected Baxter to be genial of temper, with a tendency toward wordiness of speech. But though he had occasional flashes of humor, his ordinary demeanor was characterized by a mild cynicism, which, with his gloomy, pessimistic philosophy, so foreign to the temperament that should accompany his physical type, could only be accounted for upon the hypothesis of some secret sorrow such as I have suggested. What it might be no one knew. He had means and social position, and was an uncommonly handsome man. The fact that he remained unmarried at thirty-five furnished some support for the theory of a disappointment in love, though this the several intimates of Baxter who belonged to the club were not able to verify.

It had occurred to me, in a vague way, that perhaps Baxter might be an unsuccessful author. That he was a poet we knew very well, and typewritten copies of his verses had occasionally circulated among us. But Baxter had always expressed such a profound contempt for modern literature, had always spoken in terms of such unmeasured pity for the slaves of the pen, who were dependent upon the whim of an undiscriminating public for recognition and a livelihood, that no one of us had ever suspected him of aspirations toward publication, until, as I have said, it occurred to me one day that Baxter's attitude with regard to publication might be viewed in the light of effect as well as of cause—that his scorn of publicity might as easily arise from failure to achieve it, as his never having published might be due to his preconceived disdain of the vulgar popularity which one must share with the pugilist or balloonist of the hour.

The notion of publishing Baxter's *Procrustes* did not emanate from Baxter—I must do him the justice to say this. But he had spoken to several of the fellows about the theme of his poem, until the notion that Baxter was at work upon something fine had become pretty well disseminated throughout our membership. He would occasionally read brief passages to a small coterie of friends in the sitting room or library—never more than ten lines at once, or to more than five people at a time—and these excerpts gave at least a few of us a pretty fair idea of the motive and scope of the poem. As I, for one, gathered it, it was quite along the line of Baxter's philosophy. Society was the Procrustes which, like the Greek bandit of old, caught every man born into the world, and endeavored to fit him to some preconceived standard, generally to the one for which he was least adapted. The world was full of men and women who were merely square pegs in round holes, and vice versa. Most marriages were unhappy because the contracting parties were not properly mated. Religion was mostly superstition, science for the most part sciolism, popular education merely a means of forcing the stupid and repressing the bright, so that all the youth of the rising generation might conform to the same dull, dead level of democratic mediocrity. Life would soon become so monotonously uniform and so uniformly monotonous as to be scarce worth the living.

It was Smith, I think, who first proposed that the club publish Baxter's *Procrustes*. The poet himself did not seem enthusiastic when the subject was broached; he demurred for some little time, protesting that the poem was not worthy of publication. But when it was proposed that the edition be limited to fifty copies, he agreed to consider the proposition. When I suggested, having in mind my secret theory of Baxter's failure in authorship, that the edition would at least be in the hands of friends, that it would be difficult for a hostile critic to secure a copy, and that if it should not achieve success from a literary point of view, the extent of the failure would be limited to the size of the edition, Baxter was visibly impressed. When the literary committee at length decided to request formally of Baxter the privilege of publishing his *Procrustes,* he consented, with evident reluctance, upon condition that he should supervise the printing, binding, and delivery of the books, merely submitting to the committee, in advance, the manuscript, and taking their views in regard to the bookmaking.

The manuscript was duly presented to the literary committee. Baxter having expressed the desire that the poem not be read aloud at a meeting of the club, as was the custom, since he wished it to be given to the world clad in suitable garb, the committee went even farther. Having entire confidence in Baxter's taste and scholarship, they, with great delicacy, refrained from even reading the manuscript, contenting themselves with Baxter's statement of the general theme and the topics grouped under it. The details of the bookmaking, however, were gone into thoroughly. The paper was to be of handmade linen, from the Kelmscott Mills; the type black-letter, with rubricated initials. The cover, which was Baxter's own selection, was to be of dark green morocco, with a cap-and-bells border in red inlays, and doublures of maroon morocco with a blind-tooled design. Baxter was authorized to contract with the printer and superintend the publication. The whole edition of fifty numbered copies was to be disposed of at auction, in advance, to the highest bidder, only one copy to each, the proceeds to be devoted to paying for the printing and binding, the remainder, if any, to go into the club treasury, and Baxter himself to receive one copy by way of remuneration. Baxter was inclined to protest at this, on the ground that his copy would probably be worth more than the royalties on the edition, at the usual ten percent, would amount to, but was finally prevailed upon to accept an author's copy.

While the *Procrustes* was under consideration, someone read, at one of our meetings, a note from some magazine which stated that a sealed copy of a new translation of Campanella's *Sonnets,* published by the Grolier Club, had been sold for three hundred dollars. This impressed the members greatly. It was a novel idea. A new work might thus be enshrined in a sort of holy of holies, which, if the collector so desired, could be forever sacred from the profanation of any vulgar or unappreciative eye. The possessor of such a treasure could enjoy it by the eye of imagination, having at the same time the exaltation of grasping what was for others the unattainable. The literary committee were so impressed with this idea that they presented it to Baxter in regard to the *Procrustes*. Baxter making no objection, the subscribers who might wish their copies delivered sealed were directed to notify the author. I sent in my name. A fine book, after all, was an investment, and if there was any way of enhancing its rarity, and therefore its value, I was quite willing to enjoy such an advantage.

When the *Procrustes* was ready for distribution, each subscriber received his copy by mail, in a neat pasteboard box. Each number was wrapped in a thin and transparent but very strong paper, through which the cover design and toolings were clearly visible. The number of the copy was endorsed upon the wrapper, the folds of which were securely fastened at each end with sealing-wax, upon which was impressed, as a guarantee of its inviolateness, the monogram of the club.

At the next meeting of the Bodleian a great deal was said about the *Procrustes,* and it was unanimously agreed that no finer specimen of bookmaking had ever been published by the club. By a curious coincidence, no one had brought his copy with him, and the two club copies had not yet been received from the binder, who, Baxter had reported, was retaining them for some extra fine work. Upon resolution, offered by a member who had not subscribed for the volume, a committee of three was appointed to review the *Procrustes* at the next literary meeting of the club. Of this committee it was my doubtful fortune to constitute one.

In pursuance of my duty in the premises, it of course became necessary for me to read the *Procrustes*. In all probability I should have cut my own copy for this purpose, had not one of the club auctions intervened between my appointment and the date set for the discussion of the *Procrustes*. At this meeting a copy of the book, still sealed, was offered for sale and bought by a non-subscriber for the unprecedented price of one hundred and fifty dollars. After this a proper regard for my own interests would not permit me to spoil my copy by opening it, and I was therefore compelled to procure my information concerning the poem from some other source. As I had no desire to appear mercenary, I said nothing about my own copy, and made no attempt to borrow. I did, however, casually remark to Baxter that I should like to look at his copy of the proof sheets, since I wished to make some extended quotations for my review, and would rather not trust my copy to a typist for that purpose. Baxter assured me, with every evidence of regret, that he had considered them of so little importance that he had thrown them into the fire. This indifference of Baxter to literary values struck me as just a little overdone. The proof sheets of "Hamlet," corrected in Shakespeare's own hand, would be well-nigh priceless.

At the next meeting of the club I observed that Thompson and Davis, who were with me on the reviewing committee, very soon brought up the question of the *Procrustes* in conversation in the smoking-room, and seemed anxious to get from the members their views concerning Baxter's production, I supposed upon the theory that the appreciation of any book review would depend more or less upon the degree to which it reflected the opinion of those to whom the review should be presented. I presumed, of course, that Thompson and Davis had each read the book—they were among the subscribers—and I was desirous of getting their point of view.

"What do you think," I inquired, "of the passage on Social Systems?" I have forgotten to say that the poem was in blank verse, and divided into parts, each with an appropriate title.

"Well," replied Davis, it seemed to me a little cautiously, "it is not exactly Spencerian, although it squints at the Spencerian view, with a slight deflection toward Hegelianism. I should consider it an harmonious fusion of the best views of all the modern philosophers, with a strong Baxterian flavor."

"Yes," said Thompson, "the charm of the chapter lies in this very quality. The style is an emanation from Baxter's own intellect—he has written himself into the poem. By knowing Baxter we are able to appreciate the book, and after having read the book we feel that we are so much the more intimately acquainted with Baxter—the real Baxter."

Baxter had come in during this colloquy and was standing by the fireplace smoking a pipe. I was not exactly sure whether the faint smile which marked his face was a token of pleasure or cynicism; it was Baxterian, however, and I had already learned that Baxter's opinions upon any subject were not to be gathered always from his facial expression. For instance, when the club porter's crippled child died, Baxter remarked, it seemed to me unfeelingly, that the poor little devil was doubtless better off, and that the porter himself had certainly been relieved of a burden; and only a week later the porter told me in confidence that Baxter had paid for an expensive operation, undertaken in the hope of prolonging the child's life. I therefore drew no conclusions from Baxter's somewhat enigmatical smile. He left the room at this point in the conversation, somewhat to my relief.

"By the way, Jones," said Davis, addressing me, "are you impressed by Baxter's views on Degeneration?"

Having often heard Baxter express himself upon the general downward tendency of modern civilization, I felt safe in discussing his views in a broad and general manner.

"I think," I replied, "that they are in harmony with those of Schopenhauer, without his bitterness; with those of Nordau, without his flippancy. His materialism is Haeckel's, presented with something of the charm of Omar Khayyám."

"Yes," chimed in Davis, "it answers the strenuous demand of our day—dissatisfaction with an unjustified optimism—and voices for us the courage of human philosophy facing the unknown."

I had a vague recollection of having read something like this somewhere, but so much has been written that one can scarcely discuss any subject of importance without unconsciously borrowing, now and then, the thoughts or the language of others. Quotation, like imitation, is a superior grade of flattery.

"The *Procrustes*," said Thompson, to whom the metrical review had been apportioned, "is couched in sonorous lines, of haunting melody and charm; and yet so closely interrelated as to be scarcely quotable with justice to the author. To be appreciated the poem should be read as a whole—I shall say as much in my review. What shall you say of the letter-press?" he concluded, addressing me. I was supposed to discuss the technical excellence of the volume from the connoisseur's viewpoint.

"The setting," I replied judicially, "is worthy of the gem. The dark green cover, elaborately tooled, the old English lettering, the heavy linen paper, mark this as one of our very choicest publications. The letter-press is of course De Vinne's best—there is nothing better on this side of the Atlantic. The text is a beautiful, slender stream, meandering gracefully through a wide meadow of margin."

For some reason I left the room for a minute. As I stepped into the hall, I almost ran into Baxter, who was standing near the door, facing a hunting print, of a somewhat humorous character, hung upon the wall, and smiling with an immensely pleased expression.

"What a ridiculous scene!" he remarked. "Look at that fat old squire on that tall hunter! I'll wager dollars to doughnuts that he won't get over the first fence!"

It was a very good bluff, but did not deceive me. Under his mask of unconcern, Baxter was anxious to learn what we thought of his poem and had stationed himself in the hall that he might overhear our discussion without embarrassing us by his presence. He had covered up his delight at our appreciation by this simulated interest in the hunting print.

When the night came for the review of the *Procrustes* there was a large attendance of members, and several visitors, among them a young English cousin of one of the members, on his first visit to the United States; some of us had met him at other clubs, and in society, and found him a very jolly boy, with a youthful exuberance of spirits and naïve ignorance of things American that made his views refreshing and, at times, amusing.

The critical essays were well considered, if a trifle vague. Baxter received credit for poetic skill of a high order.

"Our brother Baxter," said Thompson, "should no longer bury his talent in a napkin. This gem, of course, belongs to the club, but the same brain from which issues this exquisite emanation can produce others to inspire and charm an appreciative world."

"The author's view of life," said Davis, "as expressed in these beautiful lines, will help us to fit our shoulders for the heavy burden of life, by bringing to our realization those profound truths of philosophy which find hope in despair and pleasure in pain. When he shall see fit to give to the wider world, in fuller form, the thoughts of which we have been vouchsafed this foretaste, let us hope that some little ray of his fame may rest upon the Bodleian, from which can never be taken away the proud privilege of saying that he was one of its members."

I then pointed out the beauties of the volume as a piece of bookmaking. I knew, from conversation with the publication committee, the style of type and rubrication, and could see the cover through the wrapper of my sealed copy. The dark green morocco, I said, in summing up, typified the author's serious view of life, as a thing to be endured as patiently as might be. The cap-and-bells border was significant of the shams by which the optimist sought to delude himself into the view that life was a desirable thing. The intricate blind-tooling of the doublure shadowed forth the blind fate which left us in ignorance of our future and our past, or of even what the day itself might bring forth. The black-letter type, with rubricated initials, signified a philosophic pessimism enlightened by the conviction that in duty one might find, after all, an excuse for life and a hope for humanity. Applying this test to the club, this work, which might be said to represent all that the Bodleian stood for, was in itself sufficient to justify the club's existence. If the Bodleian had done nothing else, if it should do nothing more, it had produced a masterpiece.

There was a sealed copy of the *Procrustes*, belonging, I believe, to one of the committee, lying on the table by which I stood, and I had picked it up and held it in my hand for a moment, to emphasize one of my periods, but had laid it down immediately. I noted, as I sat down, that young Hankin, our English visitor, who sat on the other side of the table, had picked up the volume and was examining it with interest. When the last review was read, and the generous applause had subsided, there were cries for Baxter.

"Baxter! Baxter! Author! Author!"

Baxter had been sitting over in a corner during the reading of the reviews, and had succeeded remarkably well, it seemed to me, in concealing, under his mask of cynical indifference, the exultation which I was sure he must feel. But this outburst of enthusiasm was too much even for Baxter, and it was clear that he was struggling with strong emotion when he rose to speak.

"Gentlemen, and fellow members of the Bodleian, it gives me unaffected pleasure—sincere pleasure—someday you may know how much pleasure—I cannot trust myself to say it now—to see the evident care with which your committee have read my poor verses, and the responsive sympathy with which my friends have entered into my views of life and conduct. I thank you again, and again, and when I say that I am too full for utterance—I'm sure you will excuse me from saying more."

Baxter took his seat, and the applause had begun again when it was broken by a sudden exclamation.

"By Jove!" exclaimed our English visitor, who still sat behind the table, "what an extraordinary book!"

Everyone gathered around him.

"You see," he exclaimed, holding up the volume, "you fellows said so much about the bally book that I wanted to see what it was like, so I untied the ribbon and cut the leaves with the paper knife lying here and found—and found that there wasn't a single line in it, don't you know!"

Blank consternation followed this announcement, which proved only too true. Everyone knew instinctively, without further investigation, that the club had been badly sold. In the resulting confusion Baxter escaped, but later was waited upon by a committee, to whom he made the rather lame excuse that he had always regarded uncut and sealed books as tommy-rot, and that he had merely been curious to see how far the thing could go; and that the result had justified his belief that a book with nothing in it was just as useful to a book-collector as one embodying a work of genius. He offered to pay all the bills for the sham *Procrustes,* or to replace the blank copies with the real thing, as we might choose. Of course, after such an insult, the club did not care for the poem. He was permitted to pay the expense, however, and it was more than hinted to him that his resignation from the club would be favorably acted upon. He never sent it in, and, as he went to Europe shortly afterwards, the affair had time to blow over.

In our first disgust at Baxter's duplicity, most of us cut our copies of the *Procrustes*, some of us mailed them to Baxter with cutting notes, and others threw them into the fire. A few wiser spirits held on to theirs, and this fact leaking out, it began to dawn upon the minds of the real collectors among us that the volume was something unique in the way of a publication.

"Baxter," said our president one evening to a select few of us who sat around the fireplace, "was wiser than we knew, or than he perhaps appreciated. His *Procrustes*, from the collector's point of view, is entirely logical, and might be considered as the acme of bookmaking. To the true collector, a book is a work of art, of which the contents are no more important than the words of an opera. Fine binding is a desideratum, and, for its cost, that of the *Procrustes* could not be improved upon. The paper is above criticism. The true collector loves wide margins, and the *Procrustes*, being all margin, merely touches the vanishing point of the perspective. The smaller the edition, the greater the collector's eagerness to acquire a copy. There are but six uncut copies left, I am told, of the *Procrustes*, and three sealed copies, of one of which I am the fortunate possessor."

After this deliverance, it is not surprising that, at our next auction, a sealed copy of Baxter's *Procrustes* was knocked down, after spirited bidding, for two hundred and fifty dollars, the highest price ever brought by a single volume published by the club.

II

NOVEL

THE MARROW OF
TRADITION

I

AT BREAK OF DAY

"Stay here beside her, major. I shall not be needed for an hour yet. Meanwhile I'll go downstairs and snatch a bit of sleep, or talk to old Jane."

The night was hot and sultry. Though the windows of the chamber were wide open, and the muslin curtains looped back, not a breath of air was stirring. Only the shrill chirp of the cicada and the muffled croaking of the frogs in some distant marsh broke the night silence. The heavy scent of magnolias, overpowering even the strong smell of drugs in the sickroom, suggested death and funeral wreaths, sorrow and tears, the long home, the last sleep. The major shivered with apprehension as the slender hand which he held in his own contracted nervously and in a spasm of pain clutched his fingers with a viselike grip.

Major Carteret, though dressed in brown linen, had thrown off his coat for greater comfort. The stifling heat, in spite of the palm-leaf fan which he plied mechanically, was scarcely less oppressive than his own thoughts. Long ago, while yet a mere boy in years, he had come back from Appomattox to find his family, one of the oldest and proudest in the state, hopelessly impoverished by the war,—even their ancestral home swallowed up in the common ruin. His elder brother had sacrificed his life on the bloody altar of the lost cause, and his father, broken and chagrined, died not many years later, leaving the major the last of his line. He had tried in various pursuits to gain a foothold in the new life, but with indifferent success until he won the hand of Olivia Merkell, whom he had seen grow from a small girl to glorious womanhood. With her money he had founded the Morning Chronicle, which he had made the leading organ of his party and the most influential paper in the State. The fine old house in which they lived was hers. In this very room she had first drawn the breath of life; it had been their nuptial chamber; and here, too, within a few hours, she might die, for it seemed impossible that one could long endure such frightful agony and live.

One cloud alone had marred the otherwise perfect serenity of their happiness. Olivia was childless. To have children to perpetuate the name of which he was so proud, to write it still higher on the roll of honor, had been his dearest hope. His disappointment had been proportionately keen. A few months ago this dead hope had revived, and altered the whole aspect of their lives. But as time went on, his wife's age had begun to tell upon her, until even Dr. Price, the most cheerful and optimistic of physicians, had warned him, while hoping for the best, to be prepared for the worst. To add to the danger, Mrs. Carteret had only this day suffered from a nervous shock, which, it was feared, had hastened by several weeks the expected event.

Dr. Price went downstairs to the library, where a dim light was burning. An old black woman, dressed in a gingham frock, with a red bandana handkerchief coiled around her head by way of turban, was seated by an open window. She rose and curtsied as the doctor entered and dropped into a willow rocking-chair near her own.

"How did this happen, Jane?" he asked in a subdued voice, adding, with assumed severity, "You ought to have taken better care of your mistress."

"Now look a-hyuh, Doctuh Price," returned the old woman in an unctuous whisper, "you don' wanter come talkin' none er yo' foolishness 'bout my not takin' keer er Mis' 'Livy. *She* never would 'a' said sech a thing! Seven er eight mont's ago, w'en she sent fer me, I says ter her, says I:—

"'Lawd, Lawd, honey! You don' tell me dat after all dese long w'ary years er waitin' de good Lawd is done heared yo' prayer an' is gwine ter sen' you de chile you be'n wantin' so long an' so bad? Bless his holy name! Will I come an' nuss yo' baby? Why, honey, I nussed you, an' nussed yo' mammy thoo her las' sickness, an' laid her out w'en she died. I would n' *let* nobody e'se nuss yo' baby; an mo'over, I'm gwine ter come an' nuss you too. You 're young side er me, Mis' 'Livy, but you 're ove'ly ole ter be havin' yo' fus' baby, an' you 'll need somebody roun', honey, w'at knows all 'bout de fam'ly, an' deir ways an' deir weaknesses, an' I don' know who dat'd be ef it wa'n't me.'

"''Deed, Mammy Jane,' says she, 'dere ain' nobody e'se I'd have but you. You kin come ez soon ez you wanter an' stay ez long ez you mineter.'

"An hyuh I is, an' hyuh I'm gwine ter stay. Fer Mis' 'Livy is my ole mist'ess's daughter, an' my ole mist'ess wuz good ter me, an' dey ain' none er her folks gwine ter suffer ef ole Jane kin he'p it."

"Your loyalty does you credit, Jane," observed the doctor; "but you have n't told me yet what happened to Mrs. Carteret to-day. Did the horse run away, or did she see something that frightened her?"

"No, suh, de hoss did n' git skeered at nothin', but Mis' 'Livy did see somethin', er somebody; an' it wa'n't no fault er mine ner her'n neither,—it goes fu'ther back, suh, fu'ther dan dis day er dis year. Does you 'member de time w'en my ole mist'ess, Mis' 'Livy upstairs's mammy, died? No? Well, you wuz prob'ly 'way ter school den, studyin' ter be a doctuh. But I'll tell you all erbout it.

"W'en my old mist'ess, Mis' 'Liz'beth Merkell,—an' a good mist'ess she wuz,—tuck sick fer de las' time, her sister Polly— ole Mis' Polly Ochiltree w'at is now—come ter de house ter he'p nuss her. Mis' 'Livy upstairs yander wuz erbout six years ole den, de sweetes' little angel you ever laid eyes on; an' on her dyin' bed Mis' 'Liz'beth ax' Mis' Polly fer ter stay hyuh an' take keer er her chile, an' Mis' Polly she promise'. She wuz a widder fer de secon' time, an' did n' have no child'en, an' could jes' as well come as not.

"But dere wuz trouble after de fune'al, an' it happen' right hyuh in dis lib'ary. Mars Sam wuz settin' by de table, w'en Mis' Polly come downstairs, slow an' solemn, an' stood dere in de middle er de flo', all in black, till Mars Sam sot a cheer fer her.

" 'Well, Samuel,' says she, 'now dat we've done all we can fer po' 'Liz'beth, it only 'mains fer us ter consider Olivia's future.'

"Mars Sam nodded his head, but did n' say nothin'.

" 'I don' need ter tell you,' says she, 'dat I am willin' ter carry out de wishes er my dead sister, an' sac'ifice my own comfo't, an' make myse'f yo' housekeeper an' yo' child's nuss, fer my dear sister's sake. It wuz her dyin' wish, an' on it I will ac', ef it is also yo'n.'

"Mars Sam did n' want Mis' Polly ter come, suh; fur he did n' like Mis' Polly. He wuz skeered er Miss Polly."

"I don't wonder," yawned the doctor, "if she was anything like she is now."

"Wuss, suh, fer she wuz younger, an' stronger. She always would have her say, no matter 'bout what, an' her own way, no matter who 'posed her. She had already be'n in de house fer a week, an' Mars Sam knowed ef she once come ter stay, she 'd be de mist'ess of eve'ybody in it an' him too. But w'at could he do but say yas?

" 'Den it is unde'stood, is it,' says Mis' Polly, w'en he had spoke, 'dat I am ter take cha'ge er de house?'

" 'All right, Polly,' says Mars Sam, wid a deep sigh.

"Mis' Polly 'lowed he wuz sighin' fer my po' dead mist'ess, fer she did n' have no idee er his feelin's to'ds her,—she alluz did 'low dat all de gent'emen wuz in love wid 'er.

" 'You won' fin' much ter do,' Mars Sam went on, 'fer Julia is a good housekeeper, an' kin ten' ter mos' eve'ything, under yo' d'rections.'

"Mis' Polly stiffen' up like a ramrod. 'It mus' be unde'stood, Samuel,' says she, 'dat w'en I 'sumes cha'ge er yo' house, dere ain' gwine ter be no 'vided 'sponsibility; an' as fer dis Julia, me an' her could n' git 'long tergether nohow. Ef I stays, Julia goes.'

"W'en Mars Sam heared dat, he felt better, an' 'mence' ter pick up his courage. Mis' Polly had showed her han' too plain.

My mist'ess had n' got col' yit, an' Mis' Polly, who 'd be'n a widder fer two years dis las' time, wuz already fig'rin' on takin' her place fer good, an' she did n' want no other woman roun' de house dat Mars Sam might take a' intrus' in.

"'My dear Polly,' says Mars Sam, quite determine', 'I could n' possibly sen' Julia 'way. Fac' is, I could n' git 'long widout Julia. She 'd be'n runnin' dis house like clockwo'k befo' you come, an' I likes her ways. My dear, dead 'Liz'beth sot a heap er sto' by Julia, an' I'm gwine ter keep her here for 'Liz'beth's sake.'

"Mis' Polly's eyes flash' fire.

"'Ah,' says she, 'I see—I see! You perfers her housekeepin' ter mine, indeed! Dat is a fine way ter talk ter a lady! An' a heap er rispec' you is got fer de mem'ry er my po' dead sister!'

"Mars Sam knowed w'at she 'lowed she seed wa'n't so; but he did n' let on, fer it only made him de safer. He wuz willin' fer her ter 'magine w'at she please', jes' so long ez she kep' out er his house an' let him alone.

"'No, Polly,' says he, gittin' bolder ez she got madder, 'dere ain' no use talkin'. Nothin' in de worl' would make me part wid Julia.'

"Mis' Polly she r'ared an' she pitch', but Mars Sam helt on like grim death. Mis' Polly would n' give in neither, an' so she fin'lly went away. Dey made some kind er 'rangement afterwa'ds, an' Miss Polly tuck Mis' 'Livy ter her own house. Mars Sam paid her bo'd an' 'lowed Mis' Polly somethin' fer takin' keer er her."

"And Julia stayed?"

"Julia stayed, suh, an' a couple er years later her chile wuz bawn, right here in dis house."

"But you said," observed the doctor, "that Mrs. Ochiltree was in error about Julia."

"Yas, suh, so she wuz, w'en my ole mist'ess died. But dis wuz two years after,—an' w'at has ter be has ter be. Julia had a easy time; she had a black gal ter wait on her, a buggy to ride in, an' eve'ything she wanted. Eve'ybody s'posed Mars Sam would give her a house an' lot, er leave her somethin' in his will. But he died suddenly, and did n' leave no will, an' Mis' Polly got herse'f 'pinted gyardeen ter young Mis' 'Livy, an' driv Julia an' her young un out er de house, an' lived here in dis house wid Mis' 'Livy till Mis' 'Livy ma'ied Majah Carteret."

"And what became of Julia?" asked Dr. Price.

Such relations, the doctor knew very well, had been all too common in the old slavery days, and not a few of them had been projected into the new era. Sins, like snakes, die hard. The habits and customs of a people were not to be changed in a day, nor by the stroke of a pen. As family physician, and father confessor by brevet, Dr. Price had looked upon more than one hidden skeleton; and no one in town had had better opportunities than old Jane for learning the undercurrents in the lives of the old families.

"Well," resumed Jane, "eve'ybody s'posed, after w'at had happen', dat Julia 'd keep on livin' easy, fer she wuz young an' good-lookin'. But she did n'. She tried ter make a livin' sewin', but Mis' Polly would n' let de bes' w'ite folks hire her. Den she tuck up washin', but did n' do no better at dat; an' bimeby she got so discourage' dat she ma'ied a shif'less yaller man, an' died er consumption soon after,—an' wuz 'bout ez well off, fer dis man could n' hardly feed her nohow."

"And the child?"

"One er de No'the'n w'ite lady teachers at de mission school tuck a likin' ter little Janet, an' put her thoo school, an' den sent her off ter de No'th fer ter study ter be a school teacher. W'en she come back, 'stead er teachin' she ma'ied ole Adam Miller's son."

"The rich stevedore's son, Dr. Miller?"

"Yas, suh, dat's de man,—you knows 'im. Dis yer boy wuz jes' gwine 'way fer ter study ter be a doctuh, an' he ma'ied dis Janet, an' tuck her 'way wid 'im. Dey went off ter Europe, er Irope, er Orope, er somewhere er 'nother, 'way off yander, an' come back here las' year an' sta'ted dis yer horspital an' school fer ter train de black gals fer nusses."

"He's a very good doctor, Jane, and is doing a useful work. Your chapter of family history is quite interesting,—I knew part of it before, in a general way; but you have n't yet told me what brought on Mrs. Carteret's trouble."

"I 'm jes' comin' ter dat dis minute, suh,—w'at I be'n tellin' you is all a part of it. Dis yer Janet, w'at 's Mis' 'Livy's half-sister, is ez much like her ez ef dey wuz twins. Folks sometimes takes 'em fer one ernudder,—I s'pose it tickles Janet mos' ter death, but it do make Mis' 'Livy rippin'. An' den 'way back yander jes' after de wah, w'en de ole Carteret mansion had ter be sol', Adam Miller bought it, an' dis yer Janet an' her husban' is be'n livin' in it ever sence ole Adam died, 'bout a year ago; an' dat makes de majah mad, 'ca'se he don' wanter see cullud folks livin' in de ole fam'ly mansion w'at he wuz bawn in. An' mo'over, an' dat 's de wust of all, w'iles Mis' 'Livy ain' had no child'en befo', dis yer sister er her'n is got a fine-lookin' little yaller boy, w'at favors de fam'ly so dat ef Mis' 'Livy 'd see de chile anywhere, it 'd mos' break her heart fer ter think 'bout her not havin' no child'en herse'f. So ter-day, w'en Mis' 'Livy wuz out ridin' an' met dis yer Janet wid her boy, an' w'en Mis' 'Livy got ter studyin' 'bout her own chances, an' how she mought not come thoo safe, she jes' had a fit er hysterics right dere in de buggy. She wuz mos' home, an' William got her here, an' you knows de res'."

Major Carteret, from the head of the stairs, called the doctor anxiously.

"You had better come along up now, Jane," said the doctor.

For two long hours they fought back the grim spectre that stood by the bedside. The child was born at dawn. Both mother and child, the doctor said, would live.

"Bless its 'ittle hea't!" exclaimed Mammy Jane, as she held up the tiny mite, which bore as much resemblance to mature humanity as might be expected of an infant which had for only a few minutes drawn the breath of life. "Bless its 'ittle hea't! it 's de ve'y spit an' image er its pappy!"

The doctor smiled. The major laughed aloud. Jane's unconscious witticism, or conscious flattery, whichever it might be, was a welcome diversion from the tense strain of the last few hours.

"Be that as it may," said Dr. Price cheerfully, "and I 'll not dispute it, the child is a very fine boy,—a very fine boy, indeed! Take care of it, major," he added with a touch of solemnity, "for your wife can never bear another."

With the child's first cry a refreshing breeze from the distant ocean cooled the hot air of the chamber; the heavy odor of the magnolias, with its mortuary suggestiveness gave place to the scent of rose and lilac and honeysuckle. The birds in the garden were singing lustily.

All these sweet and pleasant things found an echo in the major's heart. He stood by the window, and looking toward the rising sun, breathed a silent prayer of thanksgiving. All nature seemed to rejoice in sympathy with his happiness at the fruition of this long-deferred hope, and to predict for this wonderful child a bright and glorious future.

Old Mammy Jane, however, was not entirely at ease concerning the child. She had discovered, under its left ear, a small mole, which led her to fear that the child was born for bad luck. Had the baby been black, or yellow, or poor-white, Jane would unhesitatingly have named, as his ultimate fate, a not uncommon form of taking off, usually resultant upon the infraction of certain laws, or, in these swift modern days, upon too violent a departure from established social customs. It was manifestly impossible that a child of such high quality as the grandson of her old mistress should die by judicial strangulation; but nevertheless the warning was a serious thing, and not to be lightly disregarded.

Not wishing to be considered as a prophet of evil omen, Jane kept her own counsel in regard to this significant discovery. But later, after the child was several days old, she filled a small vial with water in which the infant had been washed, and took it to a certain wise old black woman, who lived on the farther edge of the town and was well known to be versed in witchcraft and conjuration. The conjure woman added to the contents of the bottle a bit of calamus root, and one of the cervical vertebræ from the skeleton of a black cat, with several other mysterious ingredients, the nature of which she did not disclose. Following instructions given her, Aunt Jane buried the bottle in Carteret's back yard, one night during the full moon, as a good-luck charm to ward off evil from the little grandson of her dear mistress, so long since dead and gone to heaven.

II

THE CHRISTENING PARTY

They named the Carteret baby Theodore Felix. Theodore was a family name, and had been borne by the eldest son for several generations, the major himself being a second son. Having thus given the child two beautiful names, replete with religious and sentimental significance, they called him—"Dodie."

The baby was christened some six weeks after its birth, by which time Mrs. Carteret was able to be out. Old Mammy Jane, who had been brought up in the church, but who, like some better informed people in all ages, found religion not inconsistent with a strong vein of superstition, felt her fears for the baby's future much relieved when the rector had made the sign of the cross and sprinkled little Dodie with the water from the carved marble font, which had come from England in the reign of King Charles the Martyr, as the ill-fated son of James I. was known to St. Andrew's. Upon this special occasion Mammy Jane had been provided with a seat downstairs among the white people, to her own intense satisfaction, and to the secret envy of a small colored attendance in the gallery, to whom she was ostentatiously pointed out by her grandson Jerry, porter at the Morning Chronicle office, who sat among them in the front row.

On the following Monday evening the major gave a christening party in honor of this important event. Owing to Mrs. Carteret's still delicate health, only a small number of intimate friends and family connections were invited to attend. These were the rector of St. Andrew's; old Mrs. Polly Ochiltree, the godmother; old Mr. Delamere, a distant relative and also one of the sponsors; and his grandson, Tom Delamere. The major had also invited Lee Ellis, his young city editor, for whom he had a great liking apart from his business value, and who was a frequent visitor at the house. These, with the family itself, which consisted of the major, his wife, and his half-sister, Clara Pemberton, a young woman of about eighteen, made up the eight persons for whom covers were laid.

Ellis was the first to arrive, a tall, loose-limbed young man, with a slightly freckled face, hair verging on auburn, a firm chin, and honest gray eyes. He had come half an hour early, and was left alone for a few minutes in the parlor, a spacious, high-ceilinged room, with large windows, and fitted up in excellent taste, with stately reminiscences of a past generation. The walls were hung with figured paper. The ceiling was white-washed, and decorated in the middle with a plaster centre-piece, from which hung a massive chandelier sparkling with prismatic rays from a hundred crystal pendants. There was a handsome mantel, set with terra-cotta tiles, on which fauns and satyrs, nymphs and dryads, disported themselves in idyllic abandon. The furniture was old, and in keeping with the room.

At seven o'clock a carriage drove up, from which alighted an elderly gentleman, with white hair and mustache, and bowed somewhat with years. Short of breath and painfully weak in the legs, he was assisted from the carriage by a colored man, apparently about forty years old, to whom short side-whiskers and spectacles imparted an air of sobriety. This attendant gave his arm respectfully to the old gentleman, who leaned upon it heavily, but with as little appearance of dependence as possible. The servant, assuming a similar unconsciousness of the weight resting upon his arm, assisted the old gentleman carefully up the steps.

"I 'm all right now, Sandy," whispered the gentleman as soon as his feet were planted firmly on the piazza. "You may come back for me at nine o'clock."

Having taken his hand from his servant's arm, he advanced to meet a lady who stood in the door awaiting him, a tall, elderly woman, gaunt and angular of frame, with a mottled face, and high cheekbones partially covered by bands of hair entirely too black and abundant for a person of her age, if one might judge from the lines of her mouth, which are rarely deceptive in such matters.

"Perhaps you'd better not send your man away, Mr. Delamere," observed the lady, in a high shrill voice, which grated upon the old gentleman's ears. He was slightly hard of hearing, but, like most deaf people, resented being screamed at. "You might need him before nine o'clock. One never knows what may happen after one has had the second stroke. And moreover, our butler has fallen down the back steps—negroes are so careless!—and sprained his ankle so that he can't stand. I'd like to have Sandy stay and wait on the table in Peter's place, if you don't mind."

"I thank you, Mrs. Ochiltree, for your solicitude," replied Mr. Delamere, with a shade of annoyance in his voice, "but my health is very good just at present, and I do not anticipate any catastrophe which will require my servant's presence before I am ready to go home. But I have no doubt, madam," he continued, with a courteous inclination, "that Sandy will be pleased to serve you, if you desire it, to the best of his poor knowledge."

"I shill be honored, ma'am," assented Sandy, with a bow even deeper than his master's, "only I'm 'feared I ain't rightly dressed fer ter wait on table. I wuz only goin' ter pra'r-meetin', an' so I did n' put on my bes' clo's. Ef Mis' Ochiltree ain' gwine ter need me fer de nex' fifteen minutes, I kin ride back home in de ca'ige an' dress myse'f suitable fer de occasion, suh."

"If you think you'll wait on the table any better," said Mrs. Ochiltree, "you may go along and change your clothes; but hurry back, for it is seven now, and dinner will soon be served."

Sandy retired with a bow. While descending the steps to the carriage, which had waited for him, he came face to face with a young man just entering the house.

"Am I in time for dinner, Sandy?" asked the newcomer.

"Yas, Mistuh Tom, you 're in plenty er time. Dinner won't be ready till *I* git back, which won' be fer fifteen minutes er so yit."

Throwing away the cigarette which he held between his fingers, the young man crossed the piazza with a light step, and after a preliminary knock, for an answer to which he did not wait, entered the house with the air of one thoroughly at home. The lights in the parlor had been lit, and Ellis, who sat talking to Major Carteret when the newcomer entered, covered him with a jealous glance.

Slender and of medium height, with a small head of almost perfect contour, a symmetrical face, dark almost to swarthiness, black eyes, which moved somewhat restlessly, curly hair of raven tint, a slight mustache, small hands and feet, and fashionable attire, Tom Delamere, the grandson of the old gentleman who had already arrived, was easily the handsomest young man in Wellington. But no discriminating observer would have characterized his beauty as manly. It conveyed no impression of strength, but did possess a certain element, feline rather than feminine, which subtly negatived the idea of manliness.

He gave his hand to the major, nodded curtly to Ellis, saluted his grandfather respectfully, and inquired for the ladies.

"Olivia is dressing for dinner," replied the major; "Mrs. Ochiltree is in the kitchen, struggling with the servants. Clara— Ah, here she comes now!"

Ellis, whose senses were preternaturally acute where Clara was concerned, was already looking toward the hall and was the first to see her. Clad in an evening gown of simple white, to the close-fitting corsage of which she had fastened a bunch of pink roses, she was to Ellis a dazzling apparition. To him her erect and well-moulded form was the embodiment of symmetry, her voice sweet music, her movements the perfection of grace; and it scarcely needed a lover's imagination to read in her fair countenance a pure heart and a high spirit,—the truthfulness that scorns a lie, the pride which is not haughtiness. There were suggestive depths of tenderness, too, in the curl of her lip, the droop of her long lashes, the glance of her blue eyes,—depths that Ellis had long since divined, though he had never yet explored them. She gave Ellis a friendly nod as she came in, but for the smile with which she greeted Delamere, Ellis would have given all that he possessed,—not a great deal, it is true, but what could a man do more?

"You are the last one, Tom," she said reproachfully. "Mr. Ellis has been here half an hour."

Delamere threw a glance at Ellis which was not exactly friendly. Why should this fellow always be on hand to emphasize his own shortcomings?

"The rector is not here," answered Tom triumphantly. "You see I am not the last."

"The rector," replied Clara, "was called out of town at six o'clock this evening, to visit a dying man, and so cannot be here. You are the last, Tom, and Mr. Ellis was the first."

Ellis was ruefully aware that this comparison in his favor was the only visible advantage that he had gained from his early arrival. He had not seen Miss Pemberton a moment sooner by reason of it. There had been a certain satisfaction in being in the same house with her, but Delamere had arrived in time to share or, more correctly, to monopolize, the sunshine of her presence.

Delamere gave a plausible excuse which won Clara's pardon and another enchanting smile, which pierced Ellis like a dagger. He knew very well that Delamere's excuse was a lie. Ellis himself had been ready as early as six o'clock, but judging this to be too early, had stopped in at the Clarendon Club for half an hour, to look over the magazines. While coming out he had glanced into the card-room, where he had seen his rival deep in a game of cards, from which Delamere had evidently not been able to tear himself until the last moment. He had accounted for his lateness by a story quite inconsistent with these facts.

The two young people walked over to a window on the opposite side of the large room, where they stood talking to one another in low tones. The major had left the room for a moment. Old Mr. Delamere, who was watching his grandson and Clara with an indulgent smile, proceeded to rub salt into Ellis's wounds.

"They make a handsome couple," he observed. "I remember well when her mother, in her youth an ideally beautiful woman, of an excellent family, married Daniel Pemberton, who was not of so good a family, but had made money. The major, who was only a very young man then, disapproved of the match; he considered that his mother, although a widow and nearly forty, was marrying beneath her. But he has been a good brother to Clara, and a careful guardian of her estate. Ah, young gentleman, you cannot appreciate, except in imagination, what it means, to one standing on the brink of eternity, to feel sure that he will live on in his children and his children's children!"

Ellis was appreciating at that moment what it meant, in cold blood, with no effort of the imagination, to see the girl whom he loved absorbed completely in another man. She had looked at him only once since Tom Delamere had entered the room, and then merely to use him as a spur with which to prick his favored rival.

"Yes, sir," he returned mechanically, "Miss Clara is a beautiful young lady."

"And Tom is a good boy—a fine boy," returned the old gentleman. "I am very well pleased with Tom, and shall be entirely happy when I see them married."

Ellis could not echo this sentiment. The very thought of this marriage made him miserable. He had always understood that the engagement was merely tentative, a sort of family understanding, subject to confirmation after Delamere should have attained his majority, which was still a year off, and when the major should think Clara old enough to marry. Ellis saw Delamere with the eye of a jealous rival, and judged him mercilessly,—whether correctly or not the sequel will show. He did not at all believe that Tom Delamere would make a fit husband for Clara Pemberton; but his opinion would have had no weight,—he could hardly have expressed it without showing his own interest. Moreover, there was no element of the sneak in Lee Ellis's make-up. The very fact that he might profit by the other's discomfiture left Delamere secure, so far as he could be affected by anything that Ellis might say. But Ellis did not shrink from a fair fight, and though in this one the odds were heavily against him, yet so long as this engagement remained indefinite, so long, indeed, as the object of his love was still unwed, he would not cease to hope. Such a sacrifice as this marriage clearly belonged in the catalogue of impossibilities. Ellis had not lived long enough to learn that impossibilities are merely things of which we have not learned, or which we do not wish to happen.

Sandy returned at the end of a quarter of an hour, and dinner was announced. Mr. Delamere led the way to the dining-room with Mrs. Ochiltree. Tom followed with Clara. The major went to the head of the stairs and came down with Mrs. Carteret upon his arm, her beauty rendered more delicate by the pallor of her countenance and more complete by the happiness with which it glowed. Ellis went in alone. In the rector's absence it was practically a family party which sat down, with the exception of Ellis, who, as we have seen, would willingly have placed himself in the same category.

The table was tastefully decorated with flowers, which grew about the house in lavish profusion. In warm climates nature adorns herself with true feminine vanity.

"What a beautiful table!" exclaimed Tom, before they were seated.

"The decorations are mine," said Clara proudly. "I cut the flowers and arranged them all myself."

"Which accounts for the admirable effect," rejoined Tom with a bow, before Ellis, to whom the same thought had occurred, was able to express himself. He had always counted himself the least envious of men, but for this occasion he coveted Tom Delamere's readiness.

"The beauty of the flowers," observed old Mr. Delamere, with sententious gallantry, "is reflected upon all around them. It is a handsome company."

Mrs. Ochiltree beamed upon the table with a dry smile.

"I don't perceive any effect that it has upon you or me," she said. "And as for the young people, 'Handsome is as handsome does.' If Tom here, for instance, were as good as he looks"—

"You flatter me, Aunt Polly," Tom broke in hastily, anticipating the crack of the whip; he was familiar with his aunt's conversational idiosyncrasies.

"If you are as good as you look," continued the old lady, with a cunning but indulgent smile, "some one has been slandering you."

"Thanks, Aunt Polly! Now you don't flatter me."

"There is Mr. Ellis," Mrs. Ochiltree went on, "who is not half so good-looking, but is steady as a clock, I dare say."

"Now, Aunt Polly," interposed Mrs. Carteret, "let the gentlemen alone."

"She does n't mean half what she says," continued Mrs. Carteret apologetically, "and only talks that way to people whom she likes."

Tom threw Mrs. Carteret a grateful glance. He had been apprehensive, with the sensitiveness of youth, lest his old great-aunt should make a fool of him before Clara's family. Nor had he relished the comparison with Ellis, who was out of place, anyway, in this family party. He had never liked the fellow, who was too much of a plodder and a prig to make a suitable associate for a whole-souled, generous-hearted young gentleman. He tolerated him as a visitor at Carteret's and as a member of the Clarendon Club, but that was all.

"Mrs. Ochiltree has a characteristic way of disguising her feelings," observed old Mr. Delamere, with a touch of sarcasm.

Ellis had merely flushed and felt uncomfortable at the reference to himself. The compliment to his character hardly offset the reflection upon his looks. He knew he was not exactly handsome, but it was not pleasant to have the fact emphasized in the presence of the girl he loved; he would like at least fair play, and judgment upon the subject left to the young lady.

Mrs. Ochiltree was quietly enjoying herself. In early life she had been accustomed to impale fools on epigrams, like flies on pins, to see them wiggle. But with advancing years she had lost in some measure the faculty of nice discrimination,—it was pleasant to see her victims squirm, whether they were fools or friends. Even one's friends, she argued, were not always wise, and were sometimes the better for being told the truth. At her niece's table she felt at liberty to speak her mind, which she invariably did, with a frankness that sometimes bordered on brutality. She had long ago outgrown the period where ambition or passion, or its partners, envy and hatred, were springs of action in her life, and simply retained a mild enjoyment in the exercise of an old habit, with no active malice whatever. The ruling passion merely grew stronger as the restraining faculties decreased in vigor.

A diversion was created at this point by the appearance of old Mammy Jane, dressed in a calico frock, with clean white neckerchief and apron, carrying the wonderful baby in honor of whose naming this feast had been given. Though only six weeks old, the little Theodore had grown rapidly, and Mammy Jane declared was already quite large for his age, and displayed signs of an unusually precocious intelligence. He was passed around the table and duly admired. Clara thought his hair was fine. Ellis inquired about his teeth. Tom put his finger in the baby's fist to test his grip. Old Mr. Delamere was unable to decide as yet whether he favored most his father or his mother. The object of these attentions endured them patiently for several minutes, and then protested with a vocal vigor which led to his being taken promptly back upstairs. Whatever fate might be in store for him, he manifested no sign of weak lungs.

"Sandy," said Mrs. Carteret when the baby had retired, "pass that tray standing upon the side table, so that we may all see the presents."

Mr. Delamere had brought a silver spoon, and Tom a napkin ring. Ellis had sent a silver watch; it was a little premature, he admitted, but the boy would grow to it, and could use it to play with in the mean time. It had a glass back, so that he might see the wheels go round. Mrs. Ochiltree's present was an old and yellow ivory rattle, with a handle which the child could bite while teething, and a knob screwed on at the end to prevent the handle from slipping through the baby's hand.

"I saw that in your cedar chest, Aunt Polly," said Clara, "when I was a little girl, and you used to pull the chest out from under your bed to get me a dime."

"You kept the rattle in the right-hand corner of the chest," said Tom, "in the box with the red silk purse, from which you took the gold piece you gave me every Christmas."

A smile shone on Mrs. Ochiltree's severe features at this appreciation, like a ray of sunlight on a snowbank.

"Aunt Polly's chest is like the widow's cruse," said Mrs. Carteret, "which was never empty."

"Or Fortunatus's purse, which was always full," added old Mr. Delamere, who read the Latin poets, and whose allusions were apt to be classical rather than scriptual.

"It will last me while I live," said Mrs. Ochiltree, adding

cautiously, "but there 'll not be a great deal left. It won't take much to support an old woman for twenty years."

Mr. Delamere's man Sandy had been waiting upon the table with the decorum of a trained butler, and a gravity all his own. He had changed his suit of plain gray for a long blue coat with brass buttons, which dated back to the fashion of a former generation, with which he wore a pair of plaid trousers of strikingly modern cut and pattern. With his whiskers, his spectacles, and his solemn air of responsibility, he would have presented, to one unfamiliar with the negro type, an amusingly impressive appearance. But there was nothing incongruous about Sandy to this company, except perhaps to Tom Delamere, who possessed a keen eye for contrasts and always regarded Sandy, in that particular rig, as a very comical darkey.

"Is it quite prudent, Mrs. Ochiltree," suggested the major at a moment when Sandy, having set down the tray, had left the room for a little while, "to mention, in the presence of the servants, that you keep money in the house?"

"I beg your pardon, major," observed old Mr. Delamere, with a touch of stiffness. "The only servant in hearing of the conversation has been my own; and Sandy is as honest as any man in Wellington."

"You mean, sir," replied Carteret, with a smile, "as honest as any *negro* in Wellington."

"I make no exceptions, major," returned the old gentleman, with emphasis. "I would trust Sandy with my life,—he saved it once at the risk of his own."

"No doubt," mused the major, "the negro is capable of a certain doglike fidelity,—I make the comparison in a kindly sense,—a certain personal devotion which is admirable in itself, and fits him eminently for a servile career. I should imagine, however, that one could more safely trust his life with a negro than his portable property."

"Very clever, major! I read your paper, and know that your feeling is hostile toward the negro, but"—

The major made a gesture of dissent, but remained courteously silent until Mr. Delamere had finished.

"For my part," the old gentleman went on, "I think they

have done very well, considering what they started from, and their limited opportunities. There was Adam Miller, for instance, who left a comfortable estate. His son George carries on the business, and the younger boy, William, is a good doctor and stands well with his profession. His hospital is a good thing, and if my estate were clear, I should like to do something for it."

"You are mistaken, sir, in imagining me hostile to the negro," explained Carteret. "On the contrary, I am friendly to his best interests. I give him employment; I pay taxes for schools to educate him, and for court-houses and jails to keep him in order. I merely object to being governed by an inferior and servile race."

Mrs. Carteret's face wore a tired expression. This question was her husband's hobby, and therefore her own nightmare. Moreover, she had her personal grievance against the negro race, and the names mentioned by old Mr. Delamere had brought it vividly before her mind. She had no desire to mar the harmony of the occasion by the discussion of a distasteful subject.

Mr. Delamere, glancing at his hostess, read something of this thought, and refused the challenge to further argument.

"I do not believe, major," he said, "that Olivia relishes the topic. I merely wish to say that Sandy is an exception to any rule which you may formulate in derogation of the negro. Sandy is a gentleman in ebony!"

Tom could scarcely preserve his gravity at this characterization of old Sandy, with his ridiculous air of importance, his long blue coat, and his loud plaid trousers. That suit would make a great costume for a masquerade. He would borrow it some time,—there was nothing in the world like it.

"Well, Mr. Delamere," returned the major good-humoredly, "no doubt Sandy is an exceptionally good negro,—he might well be, for he has had the benefit of your example all his life,—and we know that he is a faithful servant. But nevertheless, if I were Mrs. Ochiltree, I should put my money in the bank. Not all negroes are as honest as Sandy, and an elderly lady might not prove a match for a burly black burglar."

"Thank you, major," retorted Mrs. Ochiltree, with spirit, "I'm not yet too old to take care of myself. That cedar chest has been my bank for forty years, and I shall not change my habits at my age."

At this moment Sandy reëntered the room. Carteret made a warning gesture, which Mrs. Ochiltree chose not to notice.

"I've proved a match for two husbands, and am not afraid of any man that walks the earth, black or white, by day or night. I have a revolver, and know how to use it. Whoever attempts to rob me will do so at his peril."

After dinner Clara played the piano and sang duets with Tom Delamere. At nine o'clock Mr. Delamere's carriage came for him, and he went away accompanied by Sandy. Under cover of the darkness the old gentleman leaned on his servant's arm with frank dependence, and Sandy lifted him into the carriage with every mark of devotion.

Ellis had already excused himself to go to the office and look over the late proofs for the morning paper. Tom remained a few minutes longer than his grandfather, and upon taking his leave went round to the Clarendon Club, where he spent an hour or two in the card-room with a couple of congenial friends. Luck seemed to favor him, and he went home at midnight with a comfortable balance of winnings. He was fond of excitement, and found a great deal of it in cards. To lose was only less exciting than to win. Of late he had developed into a very successful player,—so successful, indeed, that several members of the club generally found excuses to avoid participating in a game where he made one.

III

THE EDITOR AT WORK

To go back a little, for several days after his child's birth Major Carteret's chief interest in life had been confined to the four walls of the chamber where his pale wife lay upon her bed of pain, and those of the adjoining room where an old black woman crooned lovingly over a little white infant. A new ele-

ment had been added to the major's consciousness, broadening
the scope and deepening the strength of his affections. He did
not love Olivia the less, for maternity had crowned her wifehood with an added glory; but side by side with this old and
tried attachment was a new passion, stirring up dormant hopes
and kindling new desires. His regret had been more than personal at the thought that with himself an old name should be
lost to the State; and now all the old pride of race, class, and
family welled up anew, and swelled and quickened the current
of his life.

Upon the major's first appearance at the office, which took
place the second day after the child's birth, he opened a box of
cigars in honor of the event. The word had been passed around
by Ellis, and the whole office force, including reporters, com-
positors, and pressmen, came in to congratulate the major and
smoke at his expense. Even Jerry, the colored porter,—Mammy
Jane's grandson and therefore a protégé of the family,—
presented himself among the rest, or rather, after the rest. The
major shook hands with them all except Jerry, though he
acknowledged the porter's congratulations with a kind nod
and put a good cigar into his outstretched palm, for which
Jerry thanked him without manifesting any consciousness of
the omission. He was quite aware that under ordinary circumstances the major would not have shaken hands with white
workingmen, to say nothing of negroes; and he had merely
hoped that in the pleasurable distraction of the moment the
major might also overlook the distinction of color. Jerry's hope
had been shattered, though not rudely; for the major had spoken pleasantly and the cigar was a good one. Mr. Ellis had once
shaken hands with Jerry,—but Mr. Ellis was a young man,
whose Quaker father had never owned any slaves, and he
could not be expected to have as much pride as one of the best
"quality," whose families had possessed land and negroes for
time out of mind. On the whole, Jerry preferred the careless
nod of the editor-in-chief to the more familiar greeting of the
subaltern.

Having finished this pleasant ceremony, which left him
with a comfortable sense of his new dignity, the major turned

to his desk. It had been much neglected during the week, and more than one matter claimed his attention; but as typical of the new trend of his thoughts, the first subject he took up was one bearing upon the future of his son. Quite obviously the career of a Carteret must not be left to chance,—it must be planned and worked out with a due sense of the value of good blood.

There lay upon his desk a letter from a well-known promoter, offering the major an investment which promised large returns, though several years must elapse before the enterprise could be put upon a paying basis. The element of time, however, was not immediately important. The Morning Chronicle provided him an ample income. The money available for this investment was part of his wife's patrimony. It was invested in a local cotton mill, which was paying ten per cent., but this was a beggarly return compared with the immense profits promised by the offered investment,—profits which would enable his son, upon reaching manhood, to take a place in the world commensurate with the dignity of his ancestors, one of whom, only a few generations removed, had owned an estate of ninety thousand acres of land and six thousand slaves.

This letter having been disposed of by an answer accepting the offer, the major took up his pen to write an editorial. Public affairs in the state were not going to his satisfaction. At the last state election his own party, after an almost unbroken rule of twenty years, had been defeated by the so-called "Fusion" ticket, a combination of Republicans and Populists. A clean sweep had been made of the offices in the state, which were now filled by new men. Many of the smaller places had gone to colored men, their people having voted almost solidly for the Fusion ticket. In spite of the fact that the population of Wellington was two thirds colored, this state of things was gall and wormwood to the defeated party, of which the Morning Chronicle was the acknowledged organ. Major Carteret shared this feeling. Only this very morning, while passing the city hall, on his way to the office, he had seen the steps of that noble building disfigured by a fringe of job-hunting negroes, for all the world—to use a local simile—like a string of buzzards sitting on a rail, awaiting their opportunity to batten upon the helpless corpse of a moribund city.

Taking for his theme the unfitness of the negro to participate in government,—an unfitness due to his limited education, his lack of experience, his criminal tendencies, and more especially to his hopeless mental and physical inferiority to the white race,—the major had demonstrated, it seemed to him clearly enough, that the ballot in the hands of the negro was a menace to the commonwealth. He had argued, with entire conviction, that the white and black races could never attain social and political harmony by commingling their blood; he had proved by several historical parallels that no two unassimilable races could ever live together except in the relation of superior and inferior; and he was just dipping his gold pen into the ink to indite his conclusions from the premises thus established, when Jerry, the porter, announced two visitors.

"Gin'l Belmont an' Cap'n McBane would like ter see you, suh."

"Show them in, Jerry."

The man who entered first upon his invitation was a dapper little gentleman with light-blue eyes and a Vandyke beard. He wore a frock coat, patent leather shoes, and a Panama hat. There were crow's-feet about his eyes, which twinkled with a hard and, at times, humorous shrewdness. He had sloping shoulders, small hands and feet, and walked with the leisurely step characteristic of those who have been reared under hot suns.

Carteret gave his hand cordially to the gentleman thus described.

"How do you do, Captain McBane," he said, turning to the second visitor.

The individual thus addressed was strikingly different in appearance from his companion. His broad shoulders, burly form, square jaw, and heavy chin betokened strength, energy, and unscrupulousness. With the exception of a small, bristling mustache, his face was clean shaven, with here and there a speck of dried blood due to a carelessly or unskillfully handled razor. A single deep-set gray eye was shadowed by a beetling brow, over which a crop of coarse black hair, slightly streaked with gray, fell almost low enough to mingle with his black, bushy eyebrows. His coat had not been brushed for several days, if one might judge from the accumulation of dandruff upon the collar, and his shirt-front, in the middle of which blazed a showy diamond, was plentifully stained with tobacco juice. He wore a large slouch hat, which, upon entering the office, he removed and held in his hand.

Having greeted this person with an unconscious but quite perceptible diminution of the warmth with which he had welcomed the other, the major looked around the room for seats for his visitors, and perceiving only one chair, piled with exchanges, and a broken stool propped against the wall, pushed a button, which rang a bell in the hall, summoning the colored porter to his presence.

"Jerry," said the editor when his servant appeared, "bring a couple of chairs for these gentlemen."

While they stood waiting, the visitors congratulated the major on the birth of his child, which had been announced in the Morning Chronicle, and which the prominence of the family made in some degree a matter of public interest.

"And now that you have a son, major," remarked the gentleman first described, as he lit one of the major's cigars, "you 'll be all the more interested in doing something to make this town fit to live in, which is what we came up to talk about. Things are in an awful condition! A negro justice of the peace has opened an office on Market Street, and only yesterday summoned a white man to appear before him. Negro lawyers get most of the business in the criminal court. Last evening a group of young white ladies, going quietly along the street arm-in-arm, were forced off the sidewalk by a crowd of negro girls. Coming down the street just now, I saw a spectacle of social equality and negro domination that made my blood boil with indignation,—a white and a black convict, chained together, crossing the city in charge of a negro officer! We cannot stand that sort of thing, Carteret,—it is the last straw! Something must be done, and that quickly!"

The major thrilled with responsive emotion. There was something prophetic in this opportune visit. The matter was not only in his own thoughts, but in the air; it was the spontaneous revulsion of white men against the rule of an inferior race. These were the very men, above all others in the town, to join him in a movement to change these degrading conditions.

General Belmont, the smaller of the two, was a man of good family, a lawyer by profession, and took an active part in state and local politics. Aristocratic by birth and instinct, and a former owner of slaves, his conception of the obligations and rights of his caste was nevertheless somewhat lower than that of the narrower but more sincere Carteret. In serious affairs Carteret desired the approval of his conscience, even if he had to trick that docile organ into acquiescence. This was not difficult to do in politics, for he believed in the divine right of white men and gentlemen, as his ancestors had believed in and died for the divine right of kings. General Belmont was not without a gentleman's distaste for meanness, but he permitted no fine scruples to stand in the way of success. He had once been minister, under a Democratic administration, to a small Central American state. Political rivals had characterized him as a tricky demagogue, which may of course have been a libel. He had an amiable disposition, possessed the gift of eloquence, and was a prime social favorite.

Captain George McBane had sprung from the poor-white class, to which, even more than to the slaves, the abolition of slavery had opened the door of opportunity. No longer overshadowed by a slaveholding caste, some of this class had rapidly pushed themselves forward. Some had made honorable records. Others, foremost in negro-baiting and election frauds, had done the dirty work of politics, as their fathers had done that of slavery, seeking their reward at first in minor offices,—for which men of gentler breeding did not care,—until their ambition began to reach out for higher honors.

Of this class McBane—whose captaincy, by the way, was merely a polite fiction—had been one of the most successful. He had held, until recently, as the reward of questionable political services, a contract with the State for its convict labor, from which in a few years he had realized a fortune. But the methods which made his contract profitable had not commended themselves to humane people, and charges of cruelty and worse had been preferred against him. He was rich enough to escape serious consequences from the investigation which followed, but when the Fusion ticket carried the state he lost his contract, and the system of convict labor was abolished. Since then McBane had devoted himself to politics: he was ambitious for greater wealth, for office, and for social recognition. A man of few words and self-engrossed, he seldom spoke of his aspirations except where speech might favor them, preferring to seek his ends by secret "deals" and combinations rather than to challenge criticism and provoke rivalry by more open methods.

At sight, therefore, of these two men, with whose careers and characters he was entirely familiar, Carteret felt sweep over his mind the conviction that now was the time and these the instruments with which to undertake the redemption of the state from the evil fate which had befallen it.

Jerry, the porter, who had gone downstairs to the counting-room to find two whole chairs, now entered with one in each hand. He set a chair for the general, who gave him an amiable nod, to which Jerry responded with a bow and a scrape. Captain McBane made no acknowledgment, but fixed Jerry so fiercely with his single eye that upon placing the chair Jerry made his escape from the room as rapidly as possible.

"I don' like dat Cap'n McBane," he muttered, upon reaching the hall. "Dey says he got dat eye knock' out tryin' ter whip a cullud 'oman, when he wuz a boy, an' dat he ain' never had no use fer niggers sence,—'cep'n fer what he could make outen 'em wid convic' labor contrac's. His daddy wuz a' overseer befo' 'im, an' it come nachul fer him ter be a nigger-driver. I don' want dat one eye er his'n restin' on me no longer 'n I kin he'p, an' I don' know how I'm gwine ter like dis job ef he's gwine ter be comin' roun' here. He ain' nothin' but po' w'ite trash nohow; but Lawd! Lawd! look at de money he 's got,—

livin' at de hotel, werin' di'mon's, an' colloquin' wid de bes' quality er dis town! 'Pears ter me de bottom rail is gittin' mighty
close ter de top. Well, I s'pose it all comes f'm bein' w'ite. I
wush ter Gawd I wuz w'ite!"

After this fervent aspiration, having nothing else to do for
the time being, except to remain within call, and having caught
a few words of the conversation as he went in with the chairs,
Jerry, who possessed a certain amount of curiosity, placed close
to the wall the broken stool upon which he sat while waiting in
the hall, and applied his ear to a hole in the plastering of the
hallway. There was a similar defect in the inner wall, between
the same two pieces of studding, and while this inner opening
was not exactly opposite the outer, Jerry was enabled, through
the two, to catch in a more or less fragmentary way what was
going on within.

He could hear the major, now and then, use the word "negro," and McBane's deep voice was quite audible when he referred, it seemed to Jerry with alarming frequency, to "the
damned niggers," while the general's suave tones now and then
pronounced the word "niggro,"—a sort of compromise between ethnology and the vernacular. That the gentlemen were
talking politics seemed quite likely, for gentlemen generally
talked politics when they met at the Chronicle office. Jerry
could hear the words "vote," "franchise," "eliminate," "constitution," and other expressions which marked the general
tenor of the talk, though he could not follow it all,—partly because he could not hear everything distinctly, and partly because of certain limitations which nature had placed in the way
of Jerry's understanding anything very difficult or abstruse.

He had gathered enough, however, to realize, in a vague
way, that something serious was on foot, involving his own
race, when a bell sounded over his head, at which he sprang
up hastily and entered the room where the gentlemen were
talking.

"Jerry," said the major, "wait on Captain McBane."

"Yas, suh," responded Jerry, turning toward the captain,
whose eye he carefully avoided meeting directly.

"Take that half a dollar, boy," ordered McBane, "an' go 'cross the street to Mr. Sykes's, and tell him to send me three whiskies. Bring back the change, and make has'e."

The captain tossed the half dollar at Jerry, who, looking to one side, of course missed it. He picked the money up, however, and backed out of the room. Jerry did not like Captain McBane, to begin with, and it was clear that the captain was no gentleman, or he would not have thrown the money at him. Considering the source, Jerry might have overlooked this discourtesy had it not been coupled with the remark about the change, which seemed to him in very poor taste.

Returning in a few minutes with three glasses on a tray, he passed them round, handed Captain McBane his change, and retired to the hall.

"Gentlemen," exclaimed the captain, lifting his glass, "I propose a toast: 'No nigger domination.'"

"Amen!" said the others, and three glasses were solemnly drained.

"Major," observed the general, smacking his lips, "*I* should like to use Jerry for a moment, if you will permit me."

Jerry appeared promptly at the sound of the bell. He had remained conveniently near,—calls of this sort were apt to come in sequence.

"Jerry," said the general, handing Jerry half a dollar, "go over to Mr. Brown's,—I get my liquor there,—and tell them to send me three glasses of my special mixture. And, Jerry,—you may keep the change!"

"Thank y', gin'l, thank y', marster," replied Jerry, with unctuous gratitude, bending almost double as he backed out of the room.

"Dat 's a gent'eman, a rale ole-time gent'eman," he said to himself when he had closed the door. "But dere 's somethin' gwine on in dere,—dere sho' is! 'No nigger damnation!' Dat soun's all right,—I'm sho' dere ain' no nigger I knows w'at wants damnation, do' dere 's lots of 'em w'at deserves it; but ef dat one-eyed Cap'n McBane got anything ter do wid it, w'atever it is, it don' mean no good fer de niggers,—damnation 'd be better fer 'em dan dat Cap'n McBane! He looks at a nigger lack he could jes' eat 'im alive."

"This mixture, gentlemen," observed the general when Jerry had returned with the glasses, "was originally compounded by no less a person than the great John C. Calhoun himself, who confided the recipe to my father over the convivial board. In this nectar of the gods, gentlemen, I drink with you to 'White Supremacy!'"

"White Supremacy everywhere!" added McBane with fervor.

"Now and forever!" concluded Carteret solemnly.

When the visitors, half an hour later, had taken their departure, Carteret, inspired by the theme, and in less degree by the famous mixture of the immortal Calhoun, turned to his desk and finished, at a white heat, his famous editorial in which he sounded the tocsin of a new crusade.

At noon, when the editor, having laid down his pen, was leaving the office, he passed Jerry in the hall without a word or a nod. The major wore a rapt look, which Jerry observed with a vague uneasiness.

"He looks jes' lack he wuz walkin' in his sleep," muttered Jerry uneasily. "Dere's somethin' up, sho's you bawn! 'No nigger damnation!' Anybody 'd 'low dey wuz all gwine ter heaven; but I knows better! W'en a passel er w'ite folks gits ter talkin' 'bout de niggers lack dem in yander, it 's mo' lackly dey 're gwine ter ketch somethin' e'se dan heaven! I got ter keep my eyes open an' keep up wid w'at 's happenin'. Ef dere's gwine ter be anudder flood 'roun' here, I wants ter git in de ark wid de w'ite folks,—I may haf ter be anudder Ham, an' sta't de cullud race all over ag'in."

IV

THEODORE FELIX

The young heir of the Carterets had thriven apace, and at six months old was, according to Mammy Jane, whose experience qualified her to speak with authority, the largest, finest, smartest, and altogether most remarkable baby that had ever lived in Wellington. Mammy Jane had recently suffered from an attack of inflammatory rheumatism, as the result of which she had returned to her own home. She nevertheless came now and then to see Mrs. Carteret. A younger nurse had been procured to take her place, but it was understood that Jane would come whenever she might be needed.

"You really mean that about Dodie, do you, Mammy Jane?" asked the delighted mother, who never tired of hearing her own opinion confirmed concerning this wonderful child, which had come to her like an angel from heaven.

"Does I mean it!" exclaimed Mammy Jane, with a tone and an expression which spoke volumes of reproach. "Now, Mis' 'Livy, what is I ever uttered er said er spoke er done dat would make you s'pose I coud tell you a lie 'bout yo' own chile?"

"No, Mammy Jane, I 'm sure you would n't."

"'Deed, ma'am, I 'm tellin' you de Lawd's truf. I don' haf ter tell no lies ner strain no p'ints 'bout my ole mist'ess's gran'chile. Dis yer boy is de ve'y spit an' image er yo' brother, young Mars Alick, w'at died w'en he wuz 'bout eight mont's ole, w'iles I wuz laid off havin' a baby er my own, an' could n' be roun' ter look after 'im. An' dis chile is a rale quality chile, he is,— I never seed a baby wid sech fine hair fer his age, ner sech blue eyes, ner sech a grip, ner sech a heft. W'y, dat chile mus' weigh 'bout twenty-fo' poun's, an' he not but six mont's ole. Does dat gal w'at does de nussin' w'iles I'm gone ten' ter dis chile right, Mis' 'Livy?"

"She does fairly well, Mammy Jane, but I could hardly expect her to love the baby as you do. There's no one like you, Mammy Jane."

"'Deed dere ain't, honey; you is talkin' de gospel truf now! None er dese yer young folks ain' got de trainin' my ole mist'ess give me. Dese yer newfangle' schools don' l'arn 'em nothin' ter compare wid it. I'm jes' gwine ter give dat gal a piece er my min', befo' I go, so she'll ten' ter dis chile right."

The nurse came in shortly afterwards, a neat-looking brown girl, dressed in a clean calico gown, with a nurse's cap and apron.

"Look a-here, gal," said Mammy Jane sternly, "I wants you ter understan' dat you got ter take good keer er dis chile; fer I nussed his mammy dere, an' his gran'mammy befo' 'im, an' you is got a priv'lege dat mos' lackly you don' 'preciate. I wants you to 'member, in yo' incomin's an' outgoin's, dat I got my eye on you, an' am gwine ter see dat you does yo' wo'k right."

"Do you need me for anything, ma'am?" asked the young nurse, who had stood before Mrs. Carteret, giving Mammy Jane a mere passing glance, and listening impassively to her harangue. The nurse belonged to the younger generation of colored people. She had graduated from the mission school, and had received some instruction in Dr. Miller's class for nurses. Standing, like most young people of her race, on the border line between two irreconcilable states of life, she had neither the picturesqueness of the slave, nor the unconscious dignity of those of whom freedom has been the immemorial birthright; she was in what might be called the chip-on-the-shoulder stage, through which races as well as individuals must pass in climbing the ladder of life,—not an interesting, at least not an agreeable stage, but an inevitable one, and for that reason entitled to a paragraph in a story of Southern life, which, with its as yet imperfect blending of old with new, of race with race, of slavery with freedom, is like no other life under the sun.

Had this old woman, who had no authority over her, been a little more polite, or a little less offensive, the nurse might have returned her a pleasant answer. These old-time negroes, she said to herself, made her sick with their slavering over the white folks, who, she supposed, favored them and made much of them because they had once belonged to them,—much the same reason why they fondled their cats and dogs. For her own part, they gave her nothing but her wages, and small wages at that, and she owed them nothing more than equivalent service. It was purely a matter of business; she sold her time for their money. There was no question of love between them.

Receiving a negative answer from Mrs. Carteret, she left the room without a word, ignoring Mammy Jane completely, and leaving that venerable relic of ante-bellum times gasping in helpless astonishment.

"Well, I nevuh!" she ejaculated, as soon as she could get her breath, "ef dat ain' de beatinis' pe'fo'mance I ever seed er heared of! Dese yer young niggers ain' got de manners dey wuz bawned wid! I don' know w'at dey 're comin' to, w'en dey ain' got no mo' rispec' fer ole age—I don' know—I don' know!"

"Now what are you croaking about, Jane?" asked Major Carteret, who came into the room and took the child into his arms.

Mammy Jane hobbled to her feet and bobbed a curtsy. She was never lacking in respect to white people of proper quality; but Major Carteret, the quintessence of artistocracy, called out all her reserves of deference. The major was always kind and considerate to these old family retainers, brought up in the feudal atmosphere now so rapidly passing away. Mammy Jane loved Mrs. Carteret; toward the major she entertained a feeling bordering upon awe.

"Well, Jane," returned the major sadly, when the old nurse had related her grievance, "the old times have vanished, the old ties have been ruptured. The old relations of dependence and loyal obedience on the part of the colored people, the responsibility of protection and kindness upon that of the whites, have passed away forever. The young negroes are too self-assertive. Education is spoiling them, Jane; they have been badly taught. They are not content with their station in life. Some time they will overstep the mark. The white people are patient, but there is a limit to their endurance."

"Dat 's w'at I tells dese young niggers," groaned Mammy Jane, with a portentous shake of her turbaned head, "w'en I hears 'em gwine on wid deir foolishniss; but dey don' min' me. Dey 'lows dey knows mo' d'n I does, 'ca'se dey be'n l'arnt ter look in a book. But, pshuh! my ole mist'ess showed me mo' d'n dem niggers 'll l'arn in a thousan' years! I 's fetch' my gran'son' Jerry up ter be 'umble, an' keep in 'is place. An' I tells dese other niggers dat ef dey 'd do de same, an' not crowd de w'ite folks, dey 'd git ernuff ter eat, an' live out deir days in peace an' comfo't. But dey don' min' me—dey don' min' me!"

"If all the colored people were like you and Jerry, Jane," rejoined the major kindly, "there would never be any trouble.

You have friends upon whom, in time of need, you can rely implicitly for protection and succor. You served your mistress faithfully before the war; you remained by her when the other negroes were running hither and thither like sheep without a shepherd; and you have transferred your allegiance to my wife and her child. We think a great deal of you, Jane."

"Yes, indeed, Mammy Jane," assented Mrs. Carteret, with sincere affection, glancing with moist eyes from the child in her husband's arms to the old nurse, whose dark face was glowing with happiness at these expressions of appreciation, "you shall never want so long as we have anything. We would share our last crust with you."

"Thank y', Mis' 'Livy," said Jane with reciprocal emotion, "I knows who my frien's is, an' I ain' gwine ter let nothin' worry me. But fer de Lawd's sake, Mars Philip, gimme dat chile, an' lemme pat 'im on de back, er he'll choke hisse'f ter death!"

The old nurse had been the first to observe that little Dodie, for some reason, was gasping for breath. Catching the child from the major's arms, she patted it on the back, and shook it gently. After a moment of this treatment, the child ceased to gasp, but still breathed heavily, with a strange, whistling noise.

"Oh, my child!" exclaimed the mother, in great alarm, taking the baby in her own arms, "what can be the matter with him, Mammy Jane?"

"Fer de Lawd's sake, ma'am, I don' know, 'less he 's swallered somethin'; an' he ain' had nothin' in his han's but de rattle Mis' Polly give 'im."

Mrs. Carteret caught up the ivory rattle, which hung suspended by a ribbon from the baby's neck.

"He has swallowed the little piece off the end of the handle," she cried, turning pale with fear, "and it has lodged in his throat. Telephone Dr. Price to come immediately, Philip, before my baby chokes to death! Oh, my baby, my precious baby!"

An anxious half hour passed, during which the child lay quiet, except for its labored breathing. The suspense was relieved by the arrival of Dr. Price, who examined the child carefully.

"It 's a curious accident," he announced at the close of his inspection. "So far as I can discover, the piece of ivory has been drawn into the trachea, or windpipe, and has lodged in the mouth of the right bronchus. I 'll try to get it out without an operation, but I can't guarantee the result."

At the end of another half hour Dr. Price announced his inability to remove the obstruction without resorting to more serious measures.

"I do not see," he declared, "how an operation can be avoided."

"Will it be dangerous?" inquired the major anxiously, while Mrs. Carteret shivered at the thought.

"It will be necessary to cut into his throat from the outside. All such operations are more or less dangerous, especially on small children. If this were some other child, I might undertake the operation unassisted; but I know how you value this one, major, and I should prefer to share the responsibility with a specialist."

"Is there one in town?" asked the major.

"No, but we can get one from out of town."

"Send for the best one in the country," said the major, "who can be got here in time. Spare no expense, Dr. Price. We value this child above any earthly thing."

"The best is the safest," replied Dr. Price. "I will send for Dr. Burns, of Philadelphia, the best surgeon in that line in America. If he can start at once, he can reach here in sixteen or eighteen hours, and the case can wait even longer, if inflammation does not set in."

The message was dispatched forthwith. By rare good fortune the eminent specialist was able to start within an hour or two after the receipt of Dr. Price's telegram. Meanwhile the baby remained restless and uneasy, the doctor spending most of his time by its side. Mrs. Carteret, who had never been quite strong since the child's birth, was a prey to the most agonizing apprehensions.

Mammy Jane, while not presuming to question the opinion of Dr. Price, and not wishing to add to her mistress's distress, was secretly oppressed by forebodings which she was unable to shake off. The child was born for bad luck. The mole under its ear, just at the point where the hangman's knot would strike, had foreshadowed dire misfortune. She had already observed several little things which had rendered her vaguely anxious.

For instance, upon one occasion, on entering the room where the baby had been left alone, asleep in his crib, she had met a strange cat hurrying from the nursery, and, upon examining closely the pillow upon which the child lay, had found a depression which had undoubtedly been due to the weight of the cat's body. The child was restless and uneasy, and Jane had ever since believed that the cat had been sucking little Dodie's breath, with what might have been fatal results had she not appeared just in the nick of time.

This untimely accident of the rattle, a fatality for which no one coud be held responsible, had confirmed the unlucky omen. Jane's duties in the nursery did not permit her to visit her friend the conjure woman; but she did find time to go out in the back yard at dusk, and to dig up the charm which she had planted there. It had protected the child so far; but perhaps its potency had become exhausted. She picked up the bottle, shook it vigorously, and then laid it back, with the other side up. Refilling the hole, she made a cross over the top with the thumb of her left hand, and walked three times around it.

What this strange symbolism meant, or whence it derived its origin, Aunt Jane did not know. The cross was there, and the Trinity, though Jane was scarcely conscious of these, at this moment, as religious emblems. But she hoped, on general principles, that this performance would strengthen the charm and restore little Dodie's luck. It certainly had its moral effect upon Jane's own mind, for she was able to sleep better, and contrived to impress Mrs. Carteret with her own hopefulness.

V

A JOURNEY SOUTHWARD

As the south-bound train was leaving the station at Philadelphia, a gentleman took his seat in the single sleeping-car attached to the train, and proceeded to make himself comfortable. He hung up his hat and opened his newspaper, in which he remained absorbed for a quarter of an hour. When the train had left the city behind, he threw the paper aside, and looked around at the other occupants of the car. One of these, who had been on the car since it had left New York, rose from his seat upon perceiving the other's glance, and came down the aisle.

"How do you do, Dr. Burns?" he said, stopping beside the seat of the Philadelphia passenger.

The gentleman looked up at the speaker with an air of surprise, which, after the first keen, incisive glance, gave place to an expression of cordial recognition.

"Why, it 's Miller!" he exclaimed, rising and giving the other his hand, "William Miller—Dr. Miller, of course. Sit down, Miller, and tell me all about yourself,—what you 're doing, where you 've been, and where you 're going. I'm delighted to meet you, and to see you looking so well—and so prosperous."

"I deserve no credit for either, sir," returned the other, as he took the proffered seat, "for I inherited both health and prosperity. It is a fortunate chance that permits me to meet you."

The two acquaintances, thus opportunely thrown together so that they might while away in conversation the tedium of their journey, represented very different and yet very similar types of manhood. A celebrated traveler, after many years spent in barbarous or savage lands, has said that among all varieties of mankind the similarities are vastly more important and fundamental than the differences. Looking at these two men with the American eye, the differences would perhaps be the more striking, or at least the more immediately apparent, for the first was white and the second black, or, more correctly speaking, brown; it was even a light brown, but both his swarthy complexion and his curly hair revealed what has been described in the laws of some of our states as a "visible admixture" of African blood.

Having disposed of this difference, and having observed that the white man was perhaps fifty years of age and the other not more than thirty, it may be said that they were both tall and sturdy, both well dressed, the white man with perhaps a little more distinction; both seemed from their faces and their manners to be men of culture and accustomed to the society of cultivated people. They were both handsome men, the elder representing a fine type of Anglo-Saxon, as the term is used in speaking of our composite white population; while the mulatto's erect form, broad shoulders, clear eyes, fine teeth, and pleasingly moulded features showed nowhere any sign of that degeneration which the pessimist so sadly maintains is the inevitable heritage of mixed races.

As to their personal relations, it has already appeared that they were members of the same profession. In past years they had been teacher and pupil. Dr. Alvin Burns was professor in the famous medical college where Miller had attended lectures. The professor had taken an interest in his only colored pupil, to whom he had been attracted by his earnestness of purpose, his evident talent, and his excellent manners and fine physique. It was in part due to Dr. Burns's friendship that Miller had won a scholarship which had enabled him, without drawing too heavily upon his father's resources, to spend in Europe, studying in the hospitals of Paris and Vienna, the two most delightful years of his life. The same influence had strengthened his natural inclination toward operative surgery, in which Dr. Burns was a distinguished specialist of national reputation.

Miller's father, Adam Miller, had been a thrifty colored man, the son of a slave, who, in the olden time, had bought himself with money which he had earned and saved, over and above what he had paid his master for his time. Adam Miller had inherited his father's thrift, as well as his trade, which was that of a stevedore, or contractor for the loading and unloading of vessels at the port of Wellington. In the flush turpentine days following a few years after the civil war, he had made money. His savings, shrewdly invested, had by constant accessions become a competence. He had brought up his eldest son to the trade; the other he had given a professional education, in the proud hope that his children or his grandchildren might be gentlemen in the town where their ancestors had once been slaves.

Upon his father's death, shortly after Dr. Miller's return from Europe, and a year or two before the date at which this story opens, he had promptly spent part of his inheritance in founding a hospital, to which was to be added a training school for nurses, and in time perhaps a medical college and a school of pharmacy. He had been strongly tempted to leave the South, and seek a home for his family and a career for himself in the freer North, where race antagonism was less keen, or at least less oppressive, or in Europe, where he had never found his color work to his disadvantage. But his people had needed him, and he had wished to help them, and had sought by means of this institution to contribute to their uplifting. As he now informed Dr. Burns, he was returning from New York, where he had been in order to purchase equipment for his new hospital, which would soon be ready for the reception of patients.

"How much I can accomplish I do not know," said Miller, "but I 'll do what I can. There are eight or nine million of us, and it will take a great deal of learning of all kinds to leaven that lump."

"It is a great problem, Miller, the future of your race," returned the other, "a tremendously interesting problem. It is a serial story which we are all reading, and which grows in vital interest with each successive installment. It is not only your problem, but ours. Your race must come up or drag ours down."

"We shall come up," declared Miller; "slowly and painfully, perhaps, but we shall win our way. If our race had made as much progress everywhere as they have made in Wellington, the problem would be well on the way toward solution."

"Wellington?" exclaimed Dr. Burns. "That 's where I 'm going. A Dr. Price, of Wellington, has sent for me to perform an operation on a child's throat. Do you know Dr. Price?"

"Quite well," replied Miller, "he is a friend of mine."

"So much the better. I shall want you to assist me. I read in the Medical Gazette, the other day, an account of a very interesting operation of yours. I felt proud to number you among my pupils. It was a remarkable case—a rare case. I must certainly have you with me in this one."

"I shall be delighted, sir," returned Miller, "if it is agreeable to all concerned."

Several hours were passed in pleasant conversation while the train sped rapidly southward. They were already far down in

Virginia, and had stopped at a station beyond Richmond, when the conductor entered the car.

"All passengers," he announced, "will please transfer to the day coaches ahead. The sleeper has a hot box, and must be switched off here."

Dr. Burns and Miller obeyed the order, the former leading the way into the coach immediately in front of the sleeping-car.

"Let 's sit here, Miller," he said, having selected a seat near the rear of the car and deposited his suitcase in a rack. "It 's on the shady side."

Miller stood a moment hesitatingly, but finally took the seat indicated, and a few minutes later the journey was again resumed.

When the train conductor made his round after leaving the station, he paused at the seat occupied by the two doctors, glanced interrogatively at Miller, and then spoke to Dr. Burns, who sat in the end of the seat nearest the aisle.

"This man is with you?" he asked, indicating Miller with a slight side movement of his head, and a keen glance in his direction.

"Certainly," replied Dr. Burns curtly, and with some surprise. "Don't you see that he is?"

The conductor passed on. Miller paid no apparent attention to this little interlude, though no syllable had escaped him. He resumed the conversation where it had been broken off, but nevertheless followed with his eyes the conductor, who stopped at a seat near the forward end of the car, and engaged in conversation with a man whom Miller had not hitherto noticed.

As this passenger turned his head and looked back toward Miller, the latter saw a broad-shouldered, burly white man, and recognized in his square-cut jaw, his coarse, firm mouth, and the single gray eye with which he swept Miller for an instant with a scornful glance, a well-known character of Wellington, with whom the reader has already made acquaintance in these pages. Captain McBane wore a frock coat and a slouch hat; several buttons of his vest were unbuttoned, and his solitaire diamond blazed in his soiled shirt-front like the headlight of a locomotive.

The conductor in his turn looked back at Miller, and retraced his steps. Miller braced himself for what he feared was coming, though he had hoped, on account of his friend's presence, that it might be avoided.

"Excuse me, sir," said the conductor, addressing Dr. Burns, "but did I understand you to say that this man was your servant?"

"No, indeed!" replied Dr. Burns indignantly. "The gentleman is not my servant, nor anybody's servant, but is my friend. But, by the way, since we are on the subject, may I ask what affair it is of yours?"

"It 's very much my affair," returned the conductor, somewhat nettled at this questioning of his authority. "I 'm sorry to part *friends,* but the law of Virginia does not permit colored passengers to ride in the white cars. You 'll have to go forward to the next coach," he added, addressing Miller this time.

"I have paid my fare on the sleeping-car, where the separate-car law does not apply," remonstrated Miller.

"I can't help that. You can doubtless get your money back from the sleeping-car company. But this is a day coach, and is distinctly marked 'White,' as you must have seen before you sat down here. The sign is put there for that purpose."

He indicated a large card neatly framed and hung at the end of the car, containing the legend, "White," in letters about a foot long, painted in white upon a dark background, typical, one might suppose, of the distinction thereby indicated.

"You shall not stir a step, Miller," exclaimed Dr. Burns wrathfully. "This is an outrage upon a citizen of a free country. You shall stay right here."

"I 'm sorry to discommode you," returned the conductor, "but there 's no use kicking. It 's the law of Virginia, and I am bound by it as well as you. I have already come near losing my place because of not enforcing it, and I can take no more such chances, since I have a family to support."

"And my friend has his rights to maintain," returned Dr. Burns with determination. "There is a vital principle at stake in the matter."

"Really, sir," argued the conductor, who was a man of peace and not fond of controversy, "there 's no use talking—he absolutely cannot ride in this car."

"How can you prevent it?" asked Dr. Burns, lapsing into the argumentative stage.

"The law gives me the right to remove him by force. I can call on the train crew to assist me, or on the other passengers. If I should choose to put him off the train entirely, in the middle of a swamp, he would have no redress—the law so provides. If I did not wish to use force, I could simply switch this car off at the next siding, transfer the white passengers to another, and leave you and your friend in possession until you were arrested and fined or imprisoned."

"What he says is absolutely true, doctor," interposed Miller at this point. "It is the law, and we are powerless to resist it. If we made any trouble, it would merely delay your journey and imperil a life at the other end. I 'll go into the other car."

"You shall not go alone," said Dr. Burns stoutly, rising in his turn. "A place that is too good for you is not good enough for me. I will sit wherever you do."

"I 'm sorry again," said the conductor, who had quite recovered his equanimity, and calmly conscious of his power, could scarcely restrain an amused smile; "I dislike to interfere, but white passengers are not permitted to ride in the colored car."

"This is an outrage," declared Dr. Burns, "a d——d outrage! You are curtailing the rights, not only of colored people, but of white men as well. I shall sit where I please!"

"I warn you, sir," rejoined the conductor, hardening again, "that the law will be enforced. The beauty of the system lies in its strict impartiality—it applies to both races alike."

"And is equally infamous in both cases," declared Dr. Burns. "I shall immediately take steps"—

"Never mind, doctor," interrupted Miller, soothingly, "it 's only for a little while. I 'll reach my destination just as surely in the other car, and we can't help it anyway. I'll see you again at Wellington."

Dr. Burns, finding resistance futile, at length acquiesced and made way for Miller to pass him.

The colored doctor took up his valise and crossed the platform to the car ahead. It was an old car, with faded upholstery, from which the stuffing projected here and there through torn places. Apparently the floor had not been swept for several days. The dust lay thick upon the window sills, and the water-cooler, from which he essayed to get a drink, was filled with stale water which had made no recent acquaintance with ice. There was no other passenger in the car, and Miller occupied himself in making a rough calculation of what it would cost the Southern railroads to haul a whole car for every colored passenger. It was expensive, to say the least; it would be cheaper, and quite as considerate of their feelings, to make the negroes walk.

The car was conspicuously labeled at either end with large cards, similar to those in the other car, except that they bore the word "Colored" in black letters upon a white background. The author of this piece of legislation had contrived, with an ingenuity worthy of a better cause, that not merely should the passengers be separated by the color line, but that the reason for this division should be kept constantly in mind. Lest a white man should forget that he was white,—not a very likely contingency,—these cards would keep him constantly admonished of the fact; should a colored person endeavor, for a moment, to lose sight of his disability, these staring signs would remind him continually that between him and the rest of mankind not of his own color, there was by law a great gulf fixed.

Having composed himself, Miller had opened a newspaper, and was deep in an editorial which set forth in glowing language the inestimable advantages which would follow to certain recently acquired islands by the introduction of American liberty, when the rear door of the car opened to give entrance to Captain George McBane, who took a seat near the door and lit a cigar. Miller knew him quite well by sight and by reputation, and detested him as heartily. He represented the aggressive, offensive element among the white people of the New South, who made it hard for a negro to maintain his self-respect or to enjoy even the rights conceded to colored men by Southern laws. McBane had undoubtedly identified him to the conductor in the other car. Miller had no desire to thrust himself upon the society of white people, which, indeed, to one who had traveled so much and so far, was no novelty; but he very naturally resented being at this late day—the law had been in operation only a few months—branded and tagged and set apart from the rest of mankind upon the public highways, like an unclean thing. Nevertheless, he preferred even this to the exclusive society of Captain George McBane.

"Porter," he demanded of the colored train attaché who passed through the car a moment later, "is this a smoking car for white men?"

"No, suh," replied the porter, "but they comes in here sometimes, when they ain' no cullud ladies on the kyar."

"Well, I have paid first-class fare, and I object to that man's smoking in here. You tell him to go out."

"I 'll tell the conductor, suh," returned the porter in a low tone. "I 'd jus' as soon talk ter the devil as ter that man."

The white man had spread himself over two seats, and was smoking vigorously, from time to time spitting carelessly in the aisle, when the conductor entered the compartment.

"Captain," said Miller, "this car is plainly marked 'Colored.' I have paid first-class fare, and I object to riding in a smoking car."

"All right," returned the conductor, frowning irritably. "I 'll speak to him."

He walked over to the white passenger, with whom he was evidently acquainted, since he addressed him by name.

"Captain McBane," he said, "it 's against the law for you to ride in the nigger car."

"Who are you talkin' to?" returned the other. "I 'll ride where I damn please."

"Yes, sir, but the colored passenger objects. I 'm afraid I 'll have to ask you to go into the smoking-car."

"The hell you say!" rejoined McBane. "I 'll leave this car when I get good and ready, and that won't be till I 've finished this cigar. See?"

He was as good as his word. The conductor escaped from the car before Miller had time for further expostulation. Finally McBane, having thrown the stump of his cigar into the aisle and added to the floor a finishing touch in the way of expectoration, rose and went back into the white car.

Left alone in his questionable glory, Miller buried himself again in his newspaper, from which he did not look up until the engine stopped at a tank station to take water.

As the train came to a standstill, a huge negro, covered thickly with dust, crawled off one of the rear trucks unobserved, and ran round the rear end of the car to a watering-trough by a neighboring well. Moved either by extreme thirst or by the fear that his time might be too short to permit him to draw a bucket of water, he threw himself down by the trough, drank long and deep, and plunging his head into the water, shook himself like a wet dog, and crept furtively back to his dangerous perch.

Miller, who had seen this man from the car window, had noticed a very singular thing. As the dusty tramp passed the rear coach, he cast toward it a glance of intense ferocity. Up to that moment the man's face, which Miller had recognized under its grimy coating, had been that of an ordinarily good-natured, somewhat reckless, pleasure-loving negro, at present rather the worse for wear. The change that now came over it suggested a concentrated hatred almost uncanny in its murderousness. With awakened curiosity Miller followed the direction of the negro's glance, and saw that it rested upon a window where Captain McBane sat looking out. When Miller looked back, the negro had disappeared.

At the next station a Chinaman, of the ordinary laundry type, boarded the train, and took his seat in the white car without objection. At another point a colored nurse found a place with her mistress.

"White people," said Miller to himself, who had seen these passengers from the window, "do not object to the negro as a servant. As the traditional negro,—the servant,—he is welcomed; as an equal, he is repudiated."

Miller was something of a philosopher. He had long ago had

the conclusion forced upon him that an educated man of his race, in order to live comfortably in the United States, must be either a philosopher or a fool; and since he wished to be happy, and was not exactly a fool, he had cultivated philosophy. By and by he saw a white man, with a dog, enter the rear coach. Miller wondered whether the dog would be allowed to ride with his master, and if not, what disposition would be made of him. He was a handsome dog, and Miller, who was fond of animals, would not have objected to the company of a dog, as a dog. He was nevertheless conscious of a queer sensation when he saw the porter take the dog by the collar and start in his own direction, and felt consciously relieved when the canine passenger was taken on past him into the baggage-car ahead. Miller's hand was hanging over the arm of his seat, and the dog, an intelligent shepherd, licked it as he passed. Miller was not entirely sure that he would not have liked the porter to leave the dog there; he was a friendly dog, and seemed inclined to be sociable.

Toward evening the train drew up at a station where quite a party of farm laborers, fresh from their daily toil, swarmed out from the conspicuously labeled colored waiting-room, and into the car with Miller. They were a jolly, good-natured crowd, and, free from the embarrassing presence of white people, proceeded to enjoy themselves after their own fashion. Here an amorous fellow sat with his arm around a buxom girl's waist. A musically inclined individual—his talents did not go far beyond inclination—produced a mouth-organ and struck up a tune, to which a limber-legged boy danced in the aisle. They were noisy, loquacious, happy, dirty, and malodorous. For a while Miller was amused and pleased. They were his people, and he felt a certain expansive warmth toward them in spite of their obvious shortcomings. By and by, however, the air became too close, and he went out upon the platform. For the sake of the democratic ideal, which meant so much to his race, he might have endured the affliction. He could easily imagine that people of refinement, with the power in their hands, might be tempted to strain the democratic ideal in order to avoid such contact; but personally, and apart from the mere matter of racial sympathy, these people were just as offensive to him as to the whites in the other end of the train. Surely, if a classification of passengers on trains was at all desirable, it might be made upon some more logical and considerate basis than a mere arbitrary, tactless, and, by the very nature of things, brutal drawing of a color line. It was a veritable bed of Procrustes, this standard which the whites had set for the negroes. Those who grew above it must have their heads cut off, figuratively speaking,—must be forced back to the level assigned to their race; those who fell beneath the standard set had their necks stretched, literally enough, as the ghastly record in the daily papers gave conclusive evidence.

Miller breathed more freely when the lively crowd got off at the next station, after a short ride. Moreover, he had a light heart, a conscience void of offense, and was only thirty years old. His philosophy had become somewhat jaded on this journey, but he pulled it together for a final effort. Was it not, after all, a wise provision of nature that had given to a race, destined to a long servitude and a slow emergence therefrom, a cheerfulness of spirit which enabled them to catch pleasure on the wing, and endure with equanimity the ills that seemed inevitable? The ability to live and thrive under adverse circumstances is the surest guaranty of the future. The race which at the last shall inherit the earth—the residuary legatee of civilization— will be the race which remains longest upon it. The negro was here before the Anglo-Saxon was evolved, and his thick lips and heavy-lidded eyes looked out from the inscrutable face of the Sphinx across the sands of Egypt while yet the ancestors of those who now oppress him were living in caves, practicing human sacrifice, and painting themselves with woad—and the negro is here yet.

"'Blessed are the meek,'" quoted Miller at the end of these consoling reflections, "'for they shall inherit the earth.' If this be true, the negro may yet come into his estate, for meekness seems to be set apart as his portion."

The journey came to an end just as the sun had sunk into the west.

Simultaneously with Miller's exit from the train, a great black figure crawled off the trucks of the rear car, on the side opposite the station platform. Stretching and shaking himself with a free gesture, the black man, seeing himself unobserved, moved somewhat stiffly round the end of the car to the station platform.

"'Fo de Lawd!" he muttered, "ef I had n' had a cha'm' life, I 'd 'a' never got here on dat ticket, an' dat's a fac'—it sho' am! I kind er 'lowed I wuz gone a dozen times, ez it wuz. But I got my job ter do in dis worl', an' I knows I ain' gwine ter die 'tel I 've 'complished it. I jes' want one mo' look at dat man, an' den I 'll haf ter git somethin' ter eat; fer two raw turnips in twelve hours is slim pickin's fer a man er my size!"

VI
JANET

As the train drew up at the station platform, Dr. Price came forward from the white waiting-room, and stood expectantly by the door of the white coach. Miller, having left his car, came down the platform in time to intercept Burns as he left the train, and to introduce him to Dr. Price.

"My carriage is in waiting," said Dr. Price. "I should have liked to have you at my own house, but my wife is out of town. We have a good hotel, however, and you will doubtless find it more convenient."

"You are very kind, Dr. Price. Miller, won't you come up and dine with me?"

"Thank you, no," said Miller, "I am expected at home. My wife and child are waiting for me in the buggy yonder by the platform."

"Oh, very well; of course you must go; but don't forget our appointment. Let 's see, Dr. Price, I can eat and get ready in half an hour—that will make it"—

"I have asked several of the local physicians to be present at eight o'clock," said Dr. Price. "The case can safely wait until then."

"Very well, Miller, be on hand at eight. I shall expect you without fail. Where shall he come, Dr. Price?"

"To the residence of Major Philip Carteret, on Vine Street."

"I have invited Dr. Miller to be present and assist in the operation," Dr. Burns continued, as they drove toward the hotel. "He was a favorite pupil of mine, and is a credit to the profession. I presume you saw his article in the Medical Gazette?"

"Yes, and I assisted him in the case," returned Dr. Price. "It was a colored lad, one of his patients, and he called me in to help him. He is a capable man, and very much liked by the white physicians."

Miller's wife and child were waiting for him in fluttering anticipation. He kissed them both as he climbed into the buggy.

"We came at four o'clock," said Mrs. Miller, a handsome young woman, who might be anywhere between twenty-five and thirty, and whose complexion, in the twilight, was not distinguishable from that of a white person, "but the train was late two hours, they said. We came back at six, and have been waiting ever since."

"Yes, papa," piped the child, a little boy of six or seven, who sat between them, "and I am very hungry."

Miller felt very much elated as he drove homeward through the twilight. By his side sat the two persons whom he loved best in all the world. His affairs were prosperous. Upon opening his office in the city, he had been received by the members of his own profession with a cordiality generally frank, and in no case much reserved. The colored population of the city was large, but in the main poor, and the white physicians were not unwilling to share this unprofitable practice with a colored doctor worthy of confidence. In the intervals of the work upon his hospital, he had built up a considerable practice among his own people; but except in the case of some poor unfortunate whose pride had been lost in poverty or sin, no white patient had ever called upon him for treatment. He knew very well the measure of his powers,—a liberal education had given him opportunity to compare himself with other men,—and was secretly conscious that in point of skill and knowledge he did not suffer by comparison with any other physician in the town. He liked to believe that the race antagonism which hampered his progress and that of his people was a mere temporary thing, the outcome of former conditions, and bound to disappear in time, and that when a colored man should demonstrate to the community in which he lived that he possessed character and power, that community would find a way in which to enlist his services for the public good.

He had already made himself useful, and had received many kind words and other marks of appreciation. He was now offered a further confirmation of his theory: having recognized his skill, the white people were now ready to take advantage of it. Any lurking doubt he may have felt when first invited by Dr. Burns to participate in the operation, had been dispelled by Dr. Price's prompt acquiescence.

On the way homeward Miller told his wife of this appointment. She was greatly interested; she was herself a mother, with an only child. Moreover, there was a stronger impulse than mere humanity to draw her toward the stricken mother. Janet had a tender heart, and could have loved this white sister, her sole living relative of whom she knew. All her life long she had yearned for a kind word, a nod, a smile, the least thing that imagination might have twisted into a recognition of the tie between them. But it had never come.

And yet Janet was not angry. She was of a forgiving temper; she could never bear malice. She was educated, had read many books, and appreciated to the full the social forces arrayed against any such recognition as she had dreamed of. Of the two barriers between them a man might have forgiven the one; a woman would not be likely to overlook either the bar sinister or the difference of race, even to the slight extent of a silent recognition. Blood is thicker than water, but, if it flow too far from conventional channels, may turn to gall and wormwood. Nevertheless, when the heart speaks, reason falls into the background, and Janet would have worshiped this sister, even afar off, had she received even the slightest encouragement. So strong was this weakness that she had been angry with herself for her lack of pride, or even of a decent self-respect. It was, she sometimes thought, the heritage of her mother's race, and she was ashamed of it as part of the taint of slavery. She had never acknowledged, even to her husband, from whom she concealed nothing else, her secret thoughts upon this lifelong sorrow. This silent grief was nature's penalty, or society's revenge, for whatever heritage of beauty or intellect or personal charm had come to her with her father's blood. For she had received no other inheritance. Her sister was rich by right of her birth; if Janet had been fortunate, her good fortune had not been due to any provision made for her by her white father.

She knew quite well how passionately, for many years, her proud sister had longed and prayed in vain for the child which had at length brought joy into her household, and she could feel, by sympathy, all the sickening suspense with which the child's parents must await the result of this dangerous operation.

"O Will," she adjured her husband anxiously, when he had told her of the engagement, "you must be very careful. Think of the child's poor mother! Think of our own dear child, and what it would mean to lose him!"

VII

THE OPERATION

Dr. Price was not entirely at ease in his mind as the two doctors drove rapidly from the hotel to Major Carteret's. Himself a liberal man, from his point of view, he saw no reason why a colored doctor might not operate upon a white male child,—there are fine distinctions in the application of the color line,—but several other physicians had been invited, some of whom were men of old-fashioned notions, who might not relish such an innovation.

This, however, was but a small difficulty compared with what might be feared from Major Carteret himself. For he knew Carteret's unrelenting hostility to anything that savored of recognition of the negro as the equal of white men. It was traditional in Wellington that no colored person had ever entered the front door of the Carteret residence, and that the luckless individual who once presented himself there upon alleged business and resented being ordered to the back door had been unceremoniously thrown over the piazza railing into a rather thorny clump of rosebushes below. If Miller were going as a servant, to hold a basin or a sponge, there would be no difficulty; but as a surgeon—well, he would n't borrow trouble. Under the circumstances the major might yield a point.

But as they neared the house the major's unyielding disposition loomed up formidably. Perhaps if the matter were properly presented to Dr. Burns, he might consent to withdraw the invitation. It was not yet too late to send Miller a note.

"By the way, Dr. Burns," he said, "I'm very friendly to Dr. Miller, and should personally like to have him with us to-night. But—I ought to have told you this before, but I could n't very well do so, on such short notice, in Miller's presence—we are a conservative people, and our local customs are not very flexible. We jog along in much the same old way our fathers did. I'm not at all sure that Major Carteret or the other gentlemen would consent to the presence of a negro doctor."

"I think you misjudge your own people," returned Dr. Burns, "they are broader than you think. We have our prejudices against the negro at the North, but we do not let them stand in the way of anything that *we* want. At any rate, it is too late now, and I will accept the responsibility. If the question is raised, I will attend to it. When I am performing an operation I must be *aut Cæsar, aut nullus.*"

Dr. Price was not reassured, but he had done his duty and felt the reward of virtue. If there should be trouble, he would not be responsible. Moreover, there was a large fee at stake, and Dr. Burns was not likely to prove too obdurate.

They were soon at Carteret's, where they found assembled the several physicians invited by Dr. Price. These were successively introduced as Drs. Dudley, Hooper, and Ashe, all of whom were gentlemen of good standing, socially and in their profession, and considered it a high privilege to witness so delicate an operation at the hands of so eminent a member of their profession.

Major Carteret entered the room and was duly presented to the famous specialist. Carteret's anxious look lightened somewhat at sight of the array of talent present. It suggested, of course, the gravity of the impending event, but gave assurance of all the skill and care which science could afford.

Dr. Burns was shown to the nursery, from which he returned in five minutes.

"The case is ready," he announced. "Are the gentlemen all present?"

"I believe so," answered Dr. Price quickly.

Miller had not yet arrived. Perhaps, thought Dr. Price, a happy accident, or some imperative call, had detained him. This would be fortunate indeed. Dr. Burns's square jaw had a very determined look. It would be a pity if any acrimonious discussion should arise on the eve of a delicate operation. If the clock on the mantel would only move faster, the question might never come up.

"I don't see Dr. Miller," observed Dr. Burns, looking around the room. "I asked him to come at eight. There are ten minutes yet."

Major Carteret looked up with a sudden frown.

"May I ask to whom you refer?" he inquired, in an ominous tone.

The other gentlemen showed signs of interest, not to say emotion. Dr. Price smiled quizzically.

"Dr. Miller, of your city. He was one of my favorite pupils. He is also a graduate of the Vienna hospitals, and a surgeon of unusual skill. I have asked him to assist in the operation."

Every eye was turned toward Carteret, whose crimsoned face had set in a look of grim determination.

"The person to whom you refer is a negro, I believe?" he said.

"He is a colored man, certainly," returned Dr. Burns, "though one would never think of his color after knowing him well."

"I do not know, sir," returned Carteret, with an effort at self-control, "what the customs of Philadelphia or Vienna may be; but in the South we do not call negro doctors to attend white patients. I could not permit a negro to enter my house upon such an errand."

"I am here, sir," replied Dr. Burns with spirit, "to perform a certain operation. Since I assume the responsibility, the case must be under my entire control. Otherwise I cannot operate."

"Gentlemen," interposed Dr. Price, smoothly, "I beg of you both—this is a matter for calm discussion, and any asperity is to be deplored. The life at stake here should not be imperiled by any consideration of minor importance."

"Your humanity does you credit, sir," retorted Dr. Burns. "But other matters, too, are important. I have invited this gentleman here. My professional honor is involved, and I merely invoke my rights to maintain it. It is a matter of principle, which ought not to give way to a mere prejudice."

"That also states the case for Major Carteret," rejoined Dr. Price, suavely. "He has certain principles,—call them prejudices, if you like,—certain inflexible rules of conduct by which he regulates his life. One of these, which he shares with us all in some degree, forbids the recognition of the negro as a social equal."

"I do not know what Miller's social value may be," replied Dr. Burns, stoutly, "or whether you gain or lose by your attitude toward him. I have invited him here in a strictly professional capacity, with which his color is not at all concerned."

"Dr. Burns does not quite appreciate Major Carteret's point of view," said Dr. Price. "This is not with him an unimportant matter, or a mere question of prejudice, or even of personal taste. It is a sacred principle, lying at the very root of our social order, involving the purity and prestige of our race. You Northern gentlemen do not quite appreciate our situation; if you lived here a year or two you would act as we do. Of course," he added, diplomatically, "if there were no alternative—if Dr. Burns were willing to put Dr. Miller's presence on the ground of imperative necessity"—

"I do nothing of the kind, sir," retorted Dr. Burns with some heat. "I have not come all the way from Philadelphia to undertake an operation which I cannot perform without the aid of some particular physician. I merely stand upon my professional rights."

Carteret was deeply agitated. The operation must not be deferred; his child's life might be endangered by delay. If the negro's presence were indispensable he would even submit to it, though in order to avoid so painful a necessity, he would rather humble himself to the Northern doctor. The latter course involved merely a personal sacrifice—the former a vital principle. Perhaps there was another way of escape. Miller's presence could not but be distasteful to Mrs. Carteret for other reasons. Miller's wife was the living evidence of a painful episode in Mrs. Carteret's family, which the doctor's presence would inevitably recall. Once before, Mrs. Carteret's life had been endangered by encountering, at a time of great nervous strain, this ill-born sister and her child. She was even now upon the verge of collapse at the prospect of her child's suffering, and should be protected from the intrusion of any idea which might add to her distress.

"Dr. Burns," he said, with the suave courtesy which was part of his inheritance, "I beg your pardon for my heat, and throw myself upon your magnanimity, as between white men"—

"I am a gentleman, sir, before I am a white man," interposed Dr. Burns, slightly mollified, however, by Carteret's change of manner.

"The terms should be synonymous," Carteret could not refrain from saying. "As between white men, and gentlemen, I say to you, frankly, that there are vital, personal reasons, apart from Dr. Miller's color, why his presence in this house would be distasteful. With this statement, sir, I throw myself upon your mercy. My child's life is worth more to me than any earthly thing, and I must be governed by your decision."

Dr. Burns was plainly wavering. The clock moved with provoking slowness. Miller would be there in five minutes.

"May I speak with you privately a moment, doctor?" asked Dr. Price.

They withdrew from the room and were engaged in conversation for a few moments. Dr. Burns finally yielded.

"I shall nevertheless feel humiliated when I meet Miller again," he said, "but of course if there is a personal question involved, that alters the situation. Had it been merely a matter of color, I should have maintained my position. As things stand, I wash my hands of the whole affair, so far as Miller is concerned, like Pontius Pilate—yes, indeed, sir, I feel very much like that individual."

"I 'll explain the matter to Miller," returned Dr. Price, amiably, "and make it all right with him. We Southern people understand the negroes better than you do, sir. Why should we not? They have been constantly under our interested observation for several hundred years. You feel this vastly more than Miller will. He knows the feeling of the white people, and is accustomed to it. He wishes to live and do business here, and is quite too shrewd to antagonize his neighbors or come where he is not wanted. He is in fact too much of a gentleman to do so."

"I shall leave the explanation to you entirely," rejoined Dr. Burns, as they reëntered the other room.

Carteret led the way to the nursery, where the operation was to take place. Dr. Price lingered for a moment. Miller was not likely to be behind the hour, if he came at all, and it would be well to head him off before the operation began.

Scarcely had the rest left the room when the doorbell sounded, and a servant announced Dr. Miller.

Dr. Price stepped into the hall and met Miller face to face.

He had meant to state the situation to Miller frankly, but now that the moment had come he wavered. He was a fine physician, but he shrank from strenuous responsibilities. It had been easy to theorize about the negro; it was more difficult to look this man in the eyes—whom at this moment he felt to be as essentially a gentleman as himself—and tell him the humiliating truth.

As a physician his method was to ease pain—he would rather take the risk of losing a patient from the use of an anæsthetic than from the shock of an operation. He liked Miller, wished him well, and would not wittingly wound his feelings. He really thought him too much of a gentleman for the town, in view of the restrictions with which he must inevitably be hampered. There was something melancholy, to a cultivated mind, about a sensitive, educated man who happened to be off color. Such a person was a sort of social misfit, an odd quantity, educated out of his own class, with no possible hope of entrance into that above it. He felt quite sure that if he had been in Miller's place, he would never have settled in the South—he would have moved to Europe, or to the West Indies, or some

Central or South American state where questions of color were not regarded as vitally important.

Dr. Price did not like to lie, even to a negro. To a man of his own caste, his word was his bond. If it were painful to lie, it would be humiliating to be found out. The principle of *noblesse oblige* was also involved in the matter. His claim of superiority to the colored doctor rested fundamentally upon the fact that he was white and Miller was not; and yet this superiority, for which he could claim no credit, since he had not made himself, was the very breath of his nostrils,—he would not have changed places with the other for wealth untold; and as a gentleman, he would not care to have another gentleman, even a colored man, catch him in a lie. Of this, however, there was scarcely any danger. A word to the other surgeons would insure their corroboration of whatever he might tell Miller. No one of them would willingly wound Dr. Miller or embarrass Dr. Price; indeed, they need not know that Miller had come in time for the operation.

"I 'm sorry, Miller," he said with apparent regret, "but we were here ahead of time, and the case took a turn which would admit of no delay, so the gentlemen went in. Dr. Burns is with the patient now, and asked me to explain why we did not wait for you."

"I 'm sorry too," returned Miller, regretfully, but nothing doubting. He was well aware that in such cases danger might attend upon delay. He had lost his chance, through no fault of his own or of any one else.

"I hope that all is well?" he said, hesitatingly, not sure whether he would be asked to remain.

"All is well, so far. Step round to my office in the morning, Miller, or come in when you 're passing, and I 'll tell you the details."

This was tantamount to a dismissal, so Miller took his leave. Descending the doorsteps, he stood for a moment, undecided whether to return home or to go to the hotel and await the return of Dr. Burns, when he heard his name called from the house in a low tone.

"Oh, doctuh!"

He stepped back toward the door, outside of which stood the colored servant who had just let him out.

"Dat's all a lie, doctuh," he whispered, "'bout de operation bein' already pe'fo'med. Dey-all had jes' gone in de minute befo' you come—Doctuh Price had n' even got out 'n de room. Dey be'n quollin' 'bout you fer de las' ha'f hour. Majah Ca'te'et say he would n' have you, an' de No'then doctuh say he would n't do nothin' widout you, an' Doctuh Price he j'ined in on bofe sides, an' dey had it hot an' heavy, nip an' tuck, till bimeby Major Ca'te'et up an' say it wa'n't altogether yo' color he objected to, an' wid dat de No'then doctuh give in. He's a fine man, suh, but dey wuz too much fer 'im!"

"Thank you, Sam, I'm much obliged," returned Miller mechanically. "One likes to know the truth."

Truth, it has been said, is mighty, and must prevail; but it sometimes leaves a bad taste in the mouth. In the ordinary course of events Miller would not have anticipated such an invitation, and for that reason had appreciated it all the more. The rebuff came with a corresponding shock. He had the heart of a man, the sensibilities of a cultivated gentleman; the one was sore, the other deeply wounded. He was not altogether sure, upon reflection, whether he blamed Dr. Price very much for the amiable lie, which had been meant to spare his feelings, or thanked Sam a great deal for the unpalatable truth.

Janet met him at the door. "How is the baby?" she asked excitedly.

"Dr. Price says he is doing well."

"What is the matter, Will, and why are you back so soon?"

He would have spared her the story, but she was a woman, and would have it. He was wounded, too, and wanted sympathy, of which Janet was an exhaustless fountain. So he told her what had happened. She comforted him after the manner of a loving woman, and felt righteously indignant toward her sister's husband, who had thus been instrumental in the humiliation of her own. Her anger did not embrace her sister, and yet she felt obscurely that their unacknowledged relationship had been the malignant force which had given her husband pain, and defeated his honorable ambition.

When Dr. Price entered the nursery, Dr. Burns was leaning attentively over the operating table. The implements needed for the operation were all in readiness—the knives, the basin, the sponge, the materials for dressing the wound—all the ghastly paraphernalia of vivisection.

Mrs. Carteret had been banished to another room, where Clara vainly attempted to soothe her. Old Mammy Jane, still burdened by her fears, fervently prayed the good Lord to spare the life of the sweet little grandson of her dear old mistress.

Dr. Burns had placed his ear to the child's chest, which had been bared for the incision. Dr. Price stood ready to administer the anæsthetic. Little Dodie looked up with a faint expression of wonder, as if dimly conscious of some unusual event. The major shivered at the thought of what the child must undergo.

"There's a change in his breathing," said Dr. Burns, lifting his head. "The whistling noise is less pronounced, and he breathes easier. The obstruction seems to have shifted."

Applying his ear again to the child's throat, he listened for a moment intently, and then picking the baby up from the table, gave it a couple of sharp claps between the shoulders. Simultaneously a small object shot out from the child's mouth, struck Dr. Price in the neighborhood of his waistband, and then rattled lightly against the floor. Whereupon the baby, as though conscious of his narrow escape, smiled and gurgled, and reaching upward clutched the doctor's whiskers with his little hand, which, according to old Jane, had a stronger grip than any other infant's in Wellington.

VIII

THE CAMPAIGN DRAGS

The campaign for white supremacy was dragging. Carteret had set out, in the columns of the Morning Chronicle, all the reasons why this movement, inaugurated by the three men who had met, six months before, at the office of the Chronicle, should be supported by the white public. Negro citizenship was a grotesque farce—Sambo and Dinah raised from the kitchen to the cabinet were a spectacle to make the gods laugh. The laws by which it had been sought to put the negroes on a level with the whites must be swept away in theory, as they had failed in fact. If it were impossible, without a further education of public opinion, to secure the repeal of the fifteenth amendment, it was at least the solemn duty of the state to endeavor, through its own constitution, to escape from the domination of a weak and incompetent electorate and confine the negro to that inferior condition for which nature had evidently designed him.

In spite of the force and intelligence with which Carteret had expressed these and similar views, they had not met the immediate response anticipated. There were thoughtful men, willing to let well enough alone, who saw no necessity for such a movement. They believed that peace, prosperity, and popular education offered a surer remedy for social ills than the reopening of issues supposed to have been settled. There were timid men who shrank from civic strife. There were busy men, who had something else to do. There were a few fair men, prepared to admit, privately, that a class constituting half to two thirds of the population were fairly entitled to some representation in the law-making bodies. Perhaps there might have been found, somewhere in the state, a single white man ready to concede that all men were entitled to equal rights before the law.

That there were some white men who had learned little and forgotten nothing goes without saying, for knowledge and wisdom are not impartially distributed among even the most favored race. There were ignorant and vicious negroes, and they had a monopoly of neither ignorance nor crime, for there were prosperous negroes and poverty-striken whites. Until Carteret and his committee began their baleful campaign the people of the state were living in peace and harmony. The anti-negro legislation in more Southern states, with large negro majorities, had awakened scarcely an echo in this state, with a population two thirds white. Even the triumph of the Fusion party had not been regarded as a race issue. It remained for Carteret and his friends to discover, with inspiration from whatever supernatural source the discriminating reader may elect, that the darker race, docile by instinct, humble by training, patiently waiting upon its as yet uncertain destiny, was an incubus, a corpse chained to the body politic, and that the negro vote was a source of danger to the state, no matter how cast or by whom directed.

To discuss means for counteracting this apathy, a meeting of the "Big Three," as they had begun to designate themselves jocularly, was held at the office of the Morning Chronicle, on the next day but one after little Dodie's fortunate escape from the knife.

"It seems," said General Belmont, opening the discussion, "as though we had undertaken more than we can carry through. It is clear that we must reckon on opposition, both at home and abroad. If we are to hope for success, we must extend the lines of our campaign. The North, as well as our own people, must be convinced that we have right upon our side. We are conscious of the purity of our motives, but we should avoid even the appearance of evil."

McBane was tapping the floor impatiently with his foot during this harangue.

"I don't see the use," he interrupted, "of so much beating about the bush. We may as well be honest about this thing. We are going to put the niggers down because we want to, and think we can; so why waste our time in mere pretense? I 'm no hypocrite myself,—if I want a thing I take it, provided I'm strong enough."

"My dear captain," resumed the general, with biting suavity, "your frankness does you credit,—'an honest man's the noblest work of God,'—but we cannot carry on politics in these degenerate times without a certain amount of diplomacy. In the good old days when your father was alive, and perhaps nowadays in the discipline of convicts, direct and simple methods might be safely resorted to; but this is a modern age, and in dealing with so fundamental a right as the suffrage we must profess a decent regard for the opinions of even that misguided portion of mankind which may not agree with us. This is the age of crowds, and we must have the crowd with us."

The captain flushed at the allusion to his father's calling, at which he took more offense than at the mention of his own. He knew perfectly well that these old aristocrats, while reaping the profits of slavery, had despised the instruments by which they were attained—the poor-white overseer only less than the black slave. McBane was rich; he lived in Wellington, but he had never been invited to the home of either General Belmont or Major Carteret, nor asked to join the club of which they were members. His face, therefore, wore a distinct scowl, and his single eye glowed ominously. He would help these fellows carry the state for white supremacy, and then he would have his innings,—he would have more to say than they dreamed, as to who should fill the offices under the new deal. Men of no better birth or breeding than he had represented Southern states in Congress since the war. Why should he not run for governor, representative, whatever he chose? He had money enough to buy out half a dozen of these broken-down aristocrats, and money was all-powerful.

"You see, captain," the general went on, looking McBane smilingly and unflinchingly in the eye, "we need white immigration—we need Northern capital. 'A good name is better than great riches,' and we must prove our cause a righteous one."

"We must be armed at all points," added Carteret, "and prepared for defense as well as for attack,—we must make our campaign a national one."

"For instance," resumed the general, "you, Carteret, represent the Associated Press. Through your hands passes all the news of the state. What more powerful medium for the propagation of an idea? The man who would govern a nation by writing its songs was a blethering idiot beside the fellow who can edit its news dispatches. The negroes are playing into our hands,—every crime that one of them commits is reported by us. With the latitude they have had in this state they are growing more impudent and self-assertive every day. A yellow demagogue in New York made a speech only a few days ago, in which he deliberately, and in cold blood, advised negroes to defend themselves to the death when attacked by white people! I remember well the time when it was death for a negro to strike a white man."

"It 's death now, if he strikes the right one," interjected McBane, restored to better humor by this mention of a congenial subject.

The general smiled a fine smile. He had heard the story of how McBane had lost his other eye.

"The local negro paper is quite outspoken, too," continued the general, "if not impudent. We must keep track of that; it may furnish us some good campaign material."

"Yes," returned Carteret, "we must see to that. I threw a copy into the waste-basket this morning, without looking at it. Here it is now!"

IX

A WHITE MAN'S "NIGGER"

Carteret fished from the depths of the waste-basket and handed to the general an eighteen by twenty-four sheet, poorly printed on cheap paper, with a "patent" inside, a number of advertisements of proprietary medicines, quack doctors, and fortune-tellers, and two or three columns of editorial and local news. Candor compels the admission that it was not an impressive sheet in any respect, except when regarded as the first local effort of a struggling people to make public expression of their life and aspirations. From this point of view it did not speak at all badly for a class to whom, a generation before, newspapers, books, and learning had been forbidden fruit.

"It 's an elegant specimen of journalism, is n't it?" laughed the general, airily. "Listen to this 'ad':—

"'Kinky, curly hair made straight by one application of our specific. Our face bleach will turn the skin of a black or brown person four or five shades lighter, and of a mulatto perfectly white. When you get the color you wish, stop using the preparation.'

"Just look at those heads!—'Before using' and 'After using.' We'd better hurry, or there'll be no negroes to disfranchise! If they don't stop till they get the color they desire, and the stuff works according to contract, they 'll all be white. Ah! what have we here? This looks as though it might be serious."

Opening the sheet the general read aloud an editorial article to which Carteret listened intently, his indignation increasing in strength from the first word to the last, while McBane's face grew darkly purple with anger.

The article was a frank and somewhat bold discussion of lynching and its causes. It denied that most lynchings were for the offense most generally charged as their justification, and declared that, even of those seemingly traced to this cause, many were not for crimes at all, but for voluntary acts which might naturally be expected to follow from the miscegenation laws by which it was sought, in all the Southern States, to destroy liberty of contract, and, for the purpose of maintaining a fanciful purity of race, to make crimes of marriages to which neither nature nor religion nor the laws of other states interposed any insurmountable barrier. Such an article in a Northern newspaper would have attracted no special attention, and might merely have furnished food to an occasional reader for serious thought upon a subject not exactly agreeable; but coming from a colored man, in a Southern city, it was an indictment of the laws and social system of the South that could not fail of creating a profound sensation.

"Infamous—infamous!" exclaimed Carteret, his voice trembling with emotion. "The paper should be suppressed immediately."

"The impudent nigger ought to be horsewhipped and run out of town," growled McBane.

"Gentlemen," said the general soothingly, after the first burst of indignation had subsided, "I believe we can find a more effective use for this article, which, by the way, will not bear too close analysis,—there's some truth in it, at least there's an argument."

"That is not the point," interrupted Carteret.

"No," interjected McBane with an oath, "that ain't at all the point. Truth or not, no damn nigger has any right to say it."

"This article," said Carteret, violates an unwritten law of the South. If we are to tolerate this race of weaklings among us, until they are eliminated by the stress of competition, it must be upon terms which we lay down. One of our conditions is violated by this article, in which our wisdom is assailed, and our women made the subject of offensive comment. We must make known our disapproval."

"I say lynch the nigger, break up the press, and burn down the newspaper office," McBane responded promptly.

"Gentlemen," interposed the general, "would you mind suspending the discussion for a moment, while I send Jerry across the street? I think I can then suggest a better plan."

Carteret rang the bell for Jerry, who answered promptly. He had been expecting such a call ever since the gentlemen had gone in.

"Jerry," said the general, "step across to Brown's and tell him to send me three Calhoun cocktails. Wait for them,—here's the money."

"Yas, suh," replied Jerry, taking the proffered coin.

"And make has'e, charcoal," added McBane, "for we're gettin' damn dry."

A momentary cloud of annoyance darkened Carteret's brow. McBane had always grated upon his aristocratic susceptibilities. The captain was an upstart, a product of the democratic idea operating upon the poor white man, the descendant of the indentured bondservant and the socially unfit. He had wealth and energy, however, and it was necessary to make use of him; but the example of such men was a strong incentive to Carteret in his campaign against the negro. It was distasteful enough to rub elbows with an illiterate and vulgar white man of no ancestry,—the risk of similar contact with negroes was to be avoided at any cost. He could hardly expect McBane to be a gentleman, but when among men of that class he might at least try to imitate their manners. A gentleman did not order his own servants around offensively, to say nothing of another's.

The general ·had observed Carteret's annoyance, and re-marked pleasantly while they waited for the servant's return:—

"Jerry, now, is a very good negro. He 's not one of your new negroes, who think themselves as good as white men, and want to run the government. Jerry knows his place,—he is respectful, humble, obedient, and content with the face and place assigned to him by nature."

"Yes, he's one of the best of 'em," sneered McBane. "He 'll call any man 'master' for a quarter, or 'God' for half a dollar; for a dollar he'll grovel at your feet, and for a cast-off coat you can buy an option on his immortal soul,—if he has one! I 've handled niggers for ten years, and I know 'em from the ground up. They 're all alike,—they 're a scrub race, an affliction to the country, and the quicker we 're rid of 'em all the better."

Carteret had nothing to say by way of dissent. McBane's sentiments, in their last analysis, were much the same as his, though he would have expressed them less brutally.

"The negro," observed the general, daintily flicking the ash from his cigar, "is all right in his place and very useful to the community. We lived on his labor for quite a long time, and lived very well. Nevertheless we are better off without slavery, for we can get more out of the free negro, and with less responsibility. I really do not see how we could get along without the negroes. If they were all like Jerry, we 'd have no trouble with them."

Having procured the drinks, Jerry, the momentary subject of the race discussion which goes on eternally in the South, was making his way back across the street, somewhat disturbed in mind.

"O Lawd!" he groaned, "I never troubles trouble till trouble troubles me; but w'en I got dem drinks befo', Gin'l Belmont gimme half a dollar an' tol' me ter keep de change. Dis time he did n' say nothin' 'bout de change. I s'pose he jes' fergot erbout it, but w'at is a po' nigger gwine ter do w'en he has ter conten' wid w'ite folks's fergitfulniss? I don' see no way but ter do some fergittin' myse'f. I'll jes' stan' outside de do' here till dey gits so wrop' up in deir talk dat dey won' 'member nothin' e'se, an' den at de right minute I'll han' de glasses 'roun, an' mos' lackly de gin'l 'll fergit all 'bout de change."

While Jerry stood outside, the conversation within was plainly audible, and some inkling of its purport filtered through his mind.

"Now, gentlemen," the general was saying, "here's my plan. That editorial in the negro newspaper is good campaign matter, but we should reserve it until it will be most effective. Suppose we just stick it in a pigeon-hole, and let the editor,—what's his name?"

"The nigger's name is Barber," replied McBane. "I'd like to have him under me for a month or two; he'd write no more editorials."

"Let Barber have all the rope he wants," resumed the general, "and he'll be sure to hang himself. In the mean time we will continue to work up public opinion,—we can use this letter privately for that purpose,—and when the state campaign opens we'll print the editorial, with suitable comment, scatter it broadcast throughout the state, fire the Southern heart, organize the white people on the color line, have a little demonstration with red shirts and shotguns, scare the negroes into fits, win the state for white supremacy, and teach our colored fellow citizens that we are tired of negro domination and have put an end to it forever. The Afro-American Banner will doubtless die about the same time."

"And so will the editor!" exclaimed McBane ferociously; "I'll see to that. But I wonder where that nigger is with them cocktails? I'm so thirsty I could swallow blue blazes."

"Here's yo' drinks, gin'l," announced Jerry, entering with the glasses on a tray.

The gentlemen exchanged compliments and imbibed— McBane at a gulp, Carteret with more deliberation, leaving about half the contents of his glass.

The general drank slowly, with every sign of appreciation. "If the illustrious statesman," he observed, "whose name this mixture bears, had done nothing more than invent it, his fame would still deserve to go thundering down the endless ages."

"It ain't bad liquor," assented McBane, smacking his lips.

Jerry received the empty glasses on the tray and left the

room. He had scarcely gained the hall when the general called him back.

"O Lawd!" groaned Jerry, "he's gwine ter ax me fer de change. Yas, suh, yas, suh; comin', gin'l, comin', suh!"

"You may keep the change, Jerry," said the general.

Jerry's face grew radiant at this announcement. "Yas, suh, gin'l; thank y', suh; much obleedzed, suh. I wuz jus' gwine ter fetch it in, suh, w'en I had put de tray down. Thank y', suh, truly, suh!"

Jerry backed and bowed himself out into the hall.

"Dat wuz a close shave," he muttered, as he swallowed the remaining contents of Major Carteret's glass. "I 'lowed dem twenty cents wuz gone dat time,—an' whar I wuz gwine ter git de money ter take my gal ter de chu'ch festibal ter-night, de Lawd only knows!—'less'n I borried it off'n Mr. Ellis, an' I owes him sixty cents a'ready. But I wonduh w'at dem w'ite folks in dere is up ter? Dere 's one thing sho',—dey 're gwine ter git after de niggers some way er 'nuther, an' w'en dey does, whar is Jerry gwine ter be? Dat 's de mos' impo'tantes' question. I 'm gwine ter look at dat newspaper dey be'n talkin' 'bout, an' less'n my min' changes might'ly, I'm gwine ter keep my mouf shet an' stan' in wid de Angry-Saxon race,—ez dey calls deyse'ves nowadays,—an' keep on de right side er my bread an' meat. W'at nigger ever give me twenty cents in all my bawn days?"

"By the way, major," said the general, who lingered behind McBane as they were leaving, "is Miss Clara's marriage definitely settled upon?"

"Well, general, not exactly; but it 's the understanding that they will marry when they are old enough."

"I was merely thinking," the general went on, "that if I were you I 'd speak to Tom about cards and liquor. He gives more time to both than a young man can afford. I 'm speaking in his interest and in Miss Clara's,—we of the old families ought to stand together."

"Thank you, general, for the hint. I 'll act upon it."

This political conference was fruitful in results. Acting upon the plans there laid out, McBane traveled extensively through the state, working up sentiment in favor of the new movement. He possessed a certain forceful eloquence; and white supremacy was so obviously the divine intention that he had merely to affirm the doctrine in order to secure adherents.

General Belmont, whose business required him to spend much of the winter in Washington and New York, lost no opportunity to get the ear of lawmakers, editors, and other leaders of national opinion, and to impress upon them, with persuasive eloquence, the impossibility of maintaining existing conditions, and the tremendous blunder which had been made in conferring the franchise upon the emancipated race.

Carteret conducted the press campaign, and held out to the Republicans of the North the glittering hope that, with the elimination of the negro vote, and a proper deference to Southern feeling, a strong white Republican party might be built up in the New South. How well the bait took is a matter of history,—but the promised result is still in the future. The disfranchisement of the negro has merely changed the form of the same old problem. The negro had no vote before the rebellion, and few other rights, and yet the negro question was, for a centry, the pivot of American politics. It plunged the nation into a bloody war, and it will trouble the American government and the American conscience until a sustained attempt is made to settle it upon principles of justice and equity.

The personal ambitions entertained by the leaders of this movement are but slightly involved in this story. McBane's aims have been touched upon elsewhere. The general would have accepted the nomination for governor of the state, with a vision of a senatorship in the future. Carteret hoped to vindicate the supremacy of his race, and make the state fit for his son to live in, and, incidentally, he would not refuse any office, worthy of his dignity, which a grateful people might thrust upon him.

So powerful a combination of bigot, self-seeking demagogue, and astute politician was fraught with grave menace to the peace of the state and the liberties of the people,—by which is meant the whole people, and not any one class, sought to be built up at the expense of another.

X

DELAMERE PLAYS A TRUMP

Carteret did not forget what General Belmont had said in regard to Tom. The major himself had been young, not so very long ago, and was inclined toward indulgence for the foibles of youth. A young gentleman should have a certain knowledge of life,—but there were limits. Clara's future happiness must not be imperiled.

The opportunity to carry out this purpose was not long delayed. Old Mr. Delamere wished to sell some timber which had been cut at Belleview, and sent Tom down to the Chronicle office to leave an advertisement. The major saw him at the desk, invited him into his sanctum, and delivered him a mild lecture. The major was kind, and talked in a fatherly way about the danger of extremes, the beauty of moderation, and the value of discretion as a rule of conduct. He mentioned collaterally the unblemished honor of a fine old family, its contemplated alliance with his own, and dwelt upon the sweet simplicity of Clara's character. The major was a man of feeling and of tact, and could not have put the subject in a way less calculated to wound the *amour propre* of a very young man.

Delamere had turned red with anger while the major was speaking. He was impulsive, and an effort was required to keep back the retort that sprang once or twice to his lips; but his conscience was not clear, and he could not afford hard words with Clara's guardian and his grandfather's friend. Clara was rich, and the most beautiful girl in town; they were engaged; he loved her as well as he could love anything of which he seemed sure; and he did not mean that any one else should have her. The major's mild censure disturbed slightly his sense of security; and while the major's manner did not indicate that he knew anything definite against him, it would be best to let well enough alone.

"Thank you, major," he said, with well-simulated frankness. "I realize that I may have been a little careless, more from thoughtlessness than anything else; but my heart is all right, sir,

and I am glad that my conduct has been brought to your attention, for what you have said enables me to see it in a different
light. I will be more careful of my company hereafter; for I love
Clara, and mean to try to be worthy of her. Do you know
whether she will be at home this evening?"

"I have heard nothing to the contrary," replied the major
warmly. "Call her up by telephone and ask—or come up and
see. You 're always welcome, my boy."

Upon leaving the office, which was on the second floor, Tom
met Ellis coming up the stairs. It had several times of late occurred to Tom that Ellis had a sneaking fondness for Clara.
Panoplied in his own engagement, Tom had heretofore rather
enjoyed the idea of a hopeless rival. Ellis was such a solemn
prig, and took life so seriously, that it was a pleasure to see him
sit around sighing for the unattainable. That he should be giving pain to Ellis added a certain zest to his own enjoyment.

But this interview with the major had so disquieted him that
upon meeting Ellis upon the stairs he was struck by a sudden
suspicion. He knew that Major Carteret seldom went to the
Clarendon Club, and that he must have got his information
from some one else. Ellis was a member of the club, and a frequent visitor. Who more likely than he to try to poison Clara's
mind, or the minds of her friends, against her accepted lover?
Tom did not think that the world was using him well of late;
bad luck had pursued him, in cards and other things, and despite his assumption of humility, Carteret's lecture had left him
in an ugly mood. He nodded curtly to Ellis without relaxing the
scowl that disfigured his handsome features.

"That 's the damned sneak who 's been giving me away," he
muttered. "I 'll get even with him yet for this."

Delamere's suspicions with regard to Ellis's feelings were
not, as we have seen, entirely without foundation. Indeed, he
had underestimated the strength of this rivalry and its chances
of success. Ellis had been watching Delamere for a year. There
had been nothing surreptitious about it, but his interest in
Clara had led him to note things about his favored rival which
might have escaped the attention of others less concerned.

Ellis was an excellent judge of character, and had formed a

very decided opinion of Tom Delamere. To Ellis, unbiased by
ancestral traditions, biased perhaps by jealousy, Tom Delamere
was a type of the degenerate aristocrat. If, as he had often
heard, it took three or four generations to make a gentleman,
and as many more to complete the curve and return to the base
from which it started, Tom Delamere belonged somewhere on
the downward slant, with large possibilities of further decline.
Old Mr. Delamere, who might be taken as the apex of an ideal
aristocratic development, had been distinguished, during his
active life, as Ellis had learned, for courage and strength of will,
courtliness of bearing, deference to his superiors, of whom
there had been few, courtesy to his equals, kindness and consideration for those less highly favored, and above all, a
scrupulous sense of honor; his grandson Tom was merely the
shadow without the substance, the empty husk without the
grain. Of grace he had plenty. In manners he could be perfect,
when he so chose. Courage and strength he had none. Ellis had
seen this fellow, who boasted of his descent from a line of cav-
aliers, turn pale with fright and spring from a buggy to which
was harnessed a fractious horse, which a negro stable-boy
drove fearlessly. A valiant carpet-knight, skilled in all parlor
exercises, great at whist or euchre, a dream of a dancer, unex-
celled in cakewalk or "coon" impersonations, for which he
was in large social demand, Ellis had seen him kick an inoffensive negro out of his path and treat a poor-white man with
scant courtesy. He suspected Delamere of cheating at cards,
and knew that others entertained the same suspicion. For while
regular in his own habits,—his poverty would not have permitted him any considerable extravagance,—Ellis's position as a
newspaper man kept him in touch with what was going on
about town. He was a member, proposed by Carteret, of the
Clarendon Club, where cards were indulged in within reasonable limits, and a certain set were known to bet dollars in terms
of dimes.

Delamere was careless, too, about money matters. He had a
habit of borrowing, right and left, small sums which might be
conveniently forgotten by the borrower, and for which the
lender would dislike to ask. Ellis had a strain of thrift, derived

from a Scotch ancestry, and a tenacious memory for financial details. Indeed, he had never had so much money that he could lose track of it. He never saw Delamere without being distinctly conscious that Delamere owed him four dollars, which he had lent at a time when he could ill afford to spare it. It was a prerogative of aristocracy, Ellis reflected, to live upon others, and the last privilege which aristocracy in decay would willingly relinquish. Neither did the aristocratic memory seem able to retain the sordid details of a small pecuniary transaction.

No doubt the knowledge that Delamere was the favored lover of Miss Pemberton lent a touch of bitterness to Ellis's reflections upon his rival. Ellis had no grievance against the "aristocracy" of Wellington. The "best people" had received him cordially, though his father had not been of their caste; but Ellis hated a hypocrite, and despised a coward, and he felt sure that Delamere was both. Otherwise he would have struggled against his love for Clara Pemberton. His passion for her had grown with his appreciation of Delamere's unworthiness. As a friend of the family, he knew the nature and terms of the engagement, and that if the marriage took place at all, it would not be for at least a year. This was a long time,—many things might happen in a year, especially to a man like Tom Delamere. If for any reason Delamere lost his chance, Ellis meant to be next in the field. He had not made love to Clara, but he had missed no opportunity of meeting her and making himself quietly and unobtrusively agreeable.

On the day after this encounter with Delamere on the stairs of the Chronicle office, Ellis, while walking down Vine Street, met old Mrs. Ochiltree. She was seated in her own buggy, which was of ancient build and pattern, driven by her colored coachman and man of all work.

"Mr. Ellis," she called in a shrill voice, having directed her coachman to draw up at the curb as she saw the young man approaching, "come here. I want to speak to you."

Ellis came up to the buggy and stood uncovered beside it.

"People are saying," said Mrs. Ochiltree, "that Tom Delamere is drinking hard, and has to be carried home intoxicated, two or three times a week, by old Mr. Delamere's man Sandy. Is there any truth in the story?"

"My dear Mrs. Ochiltree, I am not Tom Delamere's keeper. Sandy could tell you better than I."

"You are dodging my question, Mr. Ellis. Sandy would n't tell me the truth, and I know that you would n't lie,—you don't look like a liar. They say Tom is gambling scandalously. What do you know about that?"

"You must excuse me, Mrs. Ochiltree. A great deal of what we hear is mere idle gossip, and the truth is often grossly exaggerated. I 'm a member of the same club with Delamere, and gentlemen who belong to the same club are not in the habit of talking about one another. As long as a man retains his club membership, he 's presumed to be a gentleman. I would n't say anything against Delamere if I could."

"You don't need to," replied the old lady, shaking her finger at him with a cunning smile. "You are a very open young man, Mr. Ellis, and I can read you like a book. You are much smarter than you look, but you can't fool me. Good-morning."

Mrs. Ochiltree drove immediately to her niece's, where she found Mrs. Carteret and Clara at home. Clara was very fond of the baby, and was holding him in her arms. He was a fine baby, and bade fair to realize the bright hopes built upon him.

"You hold a baby very naturally, Clara," chuckled the old lady. "I suppose you are in training. But you ought to talk to Tom. I have just learned from Mr. Ellis that Tom is carried home drunk two or three times a week, and that he is gambling in the most reckless manner imaginable."

Clara's eyes flashed indignantly. Ere she could speak, Mrs. Carteret exclaimed:—

"Why, Aunt Polly! did Mr. Ellis say that?"

"I got it from Dinah," she replied, "who heard it from her husband, who learned it from a waiter at the club. And"—

"Pshaw!" said Mrs. Carteret, "mere servants' gossip."

"No, it is n't, Olivia. I met Mr. Ellis on the street, and asked him point blank, and he did n't deny it. He's a member of the club, and ought to know."

"Well, Aunt Polly, it can't be true. Tom is here every other night, and how could he carry on so without showing the signs of it? and where would he get the money? You know he has only a moderate allowance."

"He may win it at cards,—it 's better to be born lucky than rich," returned Mrs. Ochiltree. "Then he has expectations, and can get credit. There 's no doubt that Tom is going on shamefully."

Clara's indignation had not yet found vent in speech; Olivia had said all that was necessary, but she had been thinking rapidly. Even if all this had been true, why should Mr. Ellis have said it? Or, if he had not stated it directly, he had left the inference to be drawn. It seemed a most unfair and ungentlemanly thing. What motive could Ellis have for such an act?

She was not long in reaching a conclusion which was not flattering to Ellis. Mr. Ellis came often to the house, and she had enjoyed his society in a friendly way. That he had found her pleasant company had been very evident. She had never taken his attentions seriously, however, or regarded his visits as made especially to her, nor had the rest of the family treated them from that point of view. Her engagement to Tom Delamere, though not yet formally ratified, was so well understood by the world of Wellington that Mr. Ellis would scarcely have presumed to think of her as anything more than a friend.

This revelation of her aunt's, however, put a different face upon his conduct. Certain looks and sighs and enigmatical remarks of Ellis, to which she had paid but casual attention and attached no particular significance, now recurred to her memory with a new meaning. He had now evidently tried, in a roundabout way, to besmirch Tom's character and undermine him in her regard. While loving Tom, she had liked Ellis well enough, as a friend; but he had abused the privilege of friendship, and she would teach him a needed lesson.

Nevertheless, Mrs. Ochiltree's story had given Clara food for thought. She was uneasily conscious, after all, that there might be a grain of truth in what had been said, enough, at least, to justify her in warning Tom to be careful, lest his enemies should distort some amiable weakness into a serious crime.

She put this view of the case to Tom at their next meeting, assuring him, at the same time, of her unbounded faith and confidence. She did not mention Ellis's name, lest Tom, in righteous indignation, might do something rash, which he might thereafter regret. If any subtler or more obscure motive kept her silent as to Ellis, she was not aware of it; for Clara's views of life were still in the objective stage, and she had not yet fathomed the deepest recesses of her own consciousness.

Delamere had the cunning of weakness. He knew, too, better than any one else could know, how much truth there was in the rumors concerning him, and whether or not they could be verified too easily for him to make an indignant denial. After a little rapid reflection, he decided upon a different course.

"Clara," he said with a sigh, taking the hand which she generously yielded to soften any suggestion of reproach which he may have read into her solicitude, "you are my guardian angel. I do not know, of course, who told you this pack of lies,—for I can see that you have heard more than you have told me,— but I think I could guess the man they came from. I am not perfect, Clara, though I have done nothing of which a gentleman should be ashamed. There is one sure way to stop the tongue of calumny. My home life is not ideal,—grandfather is an old, weak man, and the house needs the refining and softening influence of a lady's presence. I do not love club life; its ideals are not elevating. With you by my side, dearest, I should be preserved from every influence except the purest and the best. Don't you think, dearest, that the major might be induced to shorten our weary term of waiting?"

"Oh, Tom," she demurred blushingly, "I shall be young enough at eighteen; and you are barely twenty-one."

But Tom proved an eloquent pleader, and love a still more persuasive advocate. Clara spoke to the major the same evening, who looked grave at the suggestion, and said he would think about it. They were both very young; but where both parties were of good family, in good health and good circumstances, an early marriage might not be undesirable. Tom was perhaps a little unsettled, but blood would tell in the long run, and marriage always exercised a steadying influence.

The only return, therefore, which Ellis received for his well-meant effort to ward off Mrs. Ochiltree's embarrassing inquiries was that he did not see Clara upon his next visit, which was made one afternoon while he was on night duty at the office. In conversation with Mrs. Carteret he learned that Clara's marriage had been definitely agreed upon, and the date fixed,—it was to take place in about six months. Meeting Miss Pemberton on the street the following day, he received the slightest of nods. When he called again at the house, after a week of misery, she treated him with a sarcastic coolness which chilled his heart.

"How have I offended you, Miss Clara?" he demanded desperately, when they were left alone for a moment.

"Offended me?" she replied, lifting her eyebrows with an air of puzzled surprise. "Why, Mr. Ellis! What could have put such a notion into your head? Oh dear, I think I hear Dodie,—I know you 'll excuse me, Mr. Ellis, won't you? Sister Olivia will be back in a moment; and we 're expecting Aunt Polly this afternoon,—if you 'll stay awhile she 'll be glad to talk to you! You can tell her all the interesting news about your friends!"

XI

THE BABY AND THE BIRD

When Ellis, after this rebuff, had disconsolately taken his leave, Clara, much elated at the righteous punishment she had inflicted upon the slanderer, ran upstairs to the nursery, and, snatching Dodie from Mammy Jane's arms, began dancing gayly with him round the room.

"Look a-hyuh, honey," said Mammy Jane, "you better be keerful wid dat chile, an' don' drap 'im on de flo'. You might let him fall on his head an' break his neck. My, my! but you two does make a pretty pictur'! You 'll be wantin' ole Jane ter come an' nuss yo' child'en some er dese days," she chuckled unctuously.

Mammy Jane had been very much disturbed by the recent dangers through which little Dodie had passed; and his escape from strangulation, in the first place, and then from the knife had impressed her as little less than miraculous. She was not certain whether this result had been brought about by her manipulation of the buried charm, or by the prayers which had been offered for the child, but was inclined to believe that both had coöperated to avert the threatened calamity. The favorable outcome of this particular incident had not, however, altered the general situation. Prayers and charms, after all, were merely temporary things, which must be constantly renewed, and might be forgotten or overlooked; while the mole, on the contrary, neither faded nor went away. If its malign influence might for a time seem to disappear, it was merely lying dormant, like the germs of some deadly disease, awaiting its opportunity to strike at an unguarded spot.

Clara and the baby were laughing in great glee, when a mockingbird, perched on the topmost bough of a small tree opposite the nursery window, burst suddenly into song, with many a trill and quaver. Clara, with the child in her arms, sprang to the open window.

"Sister Olivia," she cried, turning her face toward Mrs. Carteret, who at that moment entered the room, "come and look at Dodie."

The baby was listening intently to the music, meanwhile gurgling with delight, and reaching his chubby hands toward the source of this pleasing sound. It seemed as though the mockingbird were aware of his appreciative audience, for he ran through the songs of a dozen different birds, selecting, with the discrimination of a connoisseur and entire confidence in his own powers, those which were most difficult and most alluring.

Mrs. Carteret approached the window, followed by Mammy Jane, who waddled over to join the admiring party. So absorbed were the three women in the baby and the bird that neither one of them observed a neat top buggy, drawn by a sleek sorrel pony, passing slowly along the street before the house. In the buggy was seated a lady, and beside her a little boy, dressed in a child's sailor suit and a straw hat. The lady, with a wistful expression, was looking toward the party grouped in the open window.

Mrs. Carteret, chancing to lower her eyes for an instant, caught the other woman's look directed toward her and her child. With a glance of cold aversion she turned away from the window.

Old Mammy Jane had observed this movement, and had divined the reason for it. She stood beside Clara, watching the retreating buggy.

"Uhhuh!" she said to herself, "it 's huh sister Janet! She ma'ied a doctuh, an' all dat, an' she lives in a big house, an' she 's be'n roun' de worl' an de Lawd knows where e'se: but Mis' 'Livy don' like de sight er her, an' never will, ez long ez de sun rises an' sets. Dey ce't'nly does favor one anudder,—anybody mought 'low dey wuz twins, ef dey did n' know better. Well, well! Fo'ty yeahs ago who 'd 'a' ever expected ter see a nigger gal ridin' in her own buggy? My, my! but I don' know,—I don' know! It don' look right, an' it ain' gwine ter las'!—you can't make me b'lieve!"

Meantime Janet, stung by Mrs. Carteret's look,—the nearest approach she had ever made to a recognition of her sister's existence,—had turned away with hardening face. She had struck her pony sharply with the whip, much to the gentle creature's surprise, when the little boy, who was still looking back, caught his mother's sleeve and exclaimed excitedly:—

"Look, look, mamma! The baby,—the baby!"

Janet turned instantly, and with a mother's instinct gave an involuntary cry of alarm.

At the moment when Mrs. Carteret had turned away from the window, and while Mammy Jane was watching Janet, Clara had taken a step forward, and was leaning against the window sill. The baby, convulsed with delight, had given a spasmodic spring and slipped from Clara's arms. Instinctively the young woman gripped the long skirt as it slipped through her hands, and held it tenaciously, though too frightened for an instant to do more. Mammy Jane, ashen with sudden dread, uttered an inarticulate scream, but retained self-possession enough to reach down and draw up the child, which hung dangerously suspended, head downward, over the brick pavement below.

"Oh, Clara, Clara, how could you!" exclaimed Mrs. Carteret reproachfully; "you might have killed my child!"

She had snatched the child from Jane's arms, and was holding him closely to her own breast. Struck by a sudden thought, she drew near the window and looked out. Twice within a few weeks her child had been in serious danger, and upon each occasion a member of the Miller family had been involved, for she had heard of Dr. Miller's presumption in trying to force himself where he must have known he would be unwelcome.

Janet was just turning her head away as the buggy moved slowly off. Olivia felt a violent wave of antipathy sweep over her toward this baseborn sister who had thus thrust herself beneath her eyes. If she had not cast her brazen glance toward the window, she herself would not have turned away and lost sight of her child. To this shameless intrusion, linked with Clara's carelessness, had been due the catastrophe, so narrowly averted, which might have darkened her own life forever. She took to her bed for several days, and for a long time was cold toward Clara, and did not permit her to touch the child.

Mammy Jane entertained a theory of her own about the accident, by which the blame was placed, in another way, exactly where Mrs. Carteret had laid it. Julia's daughter, Janet, had been looking intently toward the window just before little Dodie had sprung from Clara's arms. Might she not have cast the evil eye upon the baby, and sought thereby to draw him out of the window? One would not ordinarily expect so young a woman to possess such a power, but she might have acquired it, for this very purpose, from some more experienced person. By the same reasoning, the mockingbird might have been a familiar of the witch, and the two might have conspired to lure the infant to destruction. Whether this were so or not, the transaction at least wore a peculiar look. There was no use telling Mis' 'Livy about it, for she did n't believe, or pretended not to believe, in witchcraft and conjuration. But one could not be too careful. The child was certainly born to be exposed to great dangers,—the mole behind the left ear was an unfailing sign,—and no precaution should be omitted to counteract its baleful influence.

While adjusting the baby's crib, a few days later, Mrs. Carteret found fastened under one of the slats a small bag of cotton cloth, about half an inch long and tied with a black thread, upon opening which she found a few small roots or fibres and a pinch of dried and crumpled herbs. It was a good-luck charm which Mammy Jane had placed there to ward off the threatened evil from the grandchild of her dear old mistress. Mrs. Carteret's first impulse was to throw the bag into the fire, but on second thoughts she let it remain. To remove it would give unnecessary pain to the old nurse. Of course these old negro superstitions were absurd,—but if the charm did no good, it at least would do no harm.

XII
ANOTHER SOUTHERN PRODUCT

One morning shortly after the opening of the hospital, while Dr. Miller was making his early rounds, a new patient walked in with a smile on his face and a broken arm hanging limply by his side. Miller recognized in him a black giant by the name of Josh Green, who for many years had worked on the docks for Miller's father,—and simultaneously identified him as the dust-begrimed negro who had stolen a ride to Wellington on the trucks of a passenger car.

"Well, Josh," asked the doctor, as he examined the fracture, "how did you get this? Been fighting again?"

"No, suh, I don' s'pose you could ha'dly call it a fight. One er dem dagoes off'n a Souf American boat gimme some er his jaw, an' I give 'im a back answer, an' here I is wid a broken arm. He got holt er a belayin'-pin befo' I could hit 'im."

"What became of the other man?" demanded Miller suspiciously. He perceived, from the indifference with which Josh bore the manipulation of the fractured limb, that such an accident need not have interfered seriously with the use of the remaining arm, and he knew that Josh had a reputation for absolute fearlessness.

"Lemme see," said Josh reflectively, "ef I kin 'member w'at *did* become er him! Oh, yes, I 'member now! Dey tuck him ter de Marine Horspittle in de amberlance, 'cause his leg wuz broke, an' I reckon somethin' must 'a' accident'ly hit 'im in de jaw, fer he wuz scatt'rin' teeth all de way 'long de street. I did n' wan' ter kill de man, fer he might have somebody dependin' on 'im, an' I knows how dat 'd be ter dem. But no man kin call me a damn' low-down nigger and keep on enjoyin' good health right along."

"It was considerate of you to spare his life," said Miller dryly, "but you 'll hit the wrong man some day. These are bad times for bad negroes. You 'll get into a quarrel with a white man, and at the end of it there 'll be a lynching, or a funeral. You 'd better be peaceable and endure a little injustice, rather than run the risk of a sudden and violent death."

"I expec's ter die a vi'lent death in a quarrel wid a w'ite man," replied Josh, in a matter-of-fact tone, "an' fu'thermo', he 's gwine ter die at the same time, er a little befo'. I be'n takin' my own time 'bout killin' 'im; I ain' be'n crowdin' de man, but I 'll be ready after a w'ile, an' den he kin look out!"

"And I suppose you 're merely keeping in practice on these other fellows who come your way. When I get your arm dressed, you 'd better leave town till that fellow's boat sails; it may save you the expense of a trial and three months in the chain-gang. But this talk about killing a man is all nonsense. What has any man in this town done to you, that you should thirst for his blood?"

"No, suh, it ain' nonsense,—it 's straight, solem' fac'. I 'm gwine ter kill dat man as sho' as I 'm settin' in dis cheer; an' dey ain' nobody kin say I ain' got a right ter kill 'im. Does you 'member de Ku-Klux?"

"Yes, but I was a child at the time, and recollect very little about them. It is a page of history which most people are glad to forget."

"Yas, suh; I was a chile, too, but I wuz right in it, an' so I 'member mo' erbout it 'n you does. My mammy an' daddy lived 'bout ten miles f'm here, up de river. One night a crowd er w'ite men come ter ou' house an' tuck my daddy out an' shot 'im ter death, an' skeered my mammy so she ain' be'n herse'f f'm dat day ter dis. I wa'n't mo' 'n ten years ole at de time, an' w'en my mammy seed de w'ite men comin', she tol' me ter run. I hid in de bushes an' seen de whole thing, an' it wuz branded on my mem'ry, suh, like a red-hot iron bran's de skin. De w'ite folks had masks on, but one of 'em fell off,—he wuz de boss, he wuz de head man, an' tol' de res' w'at ter do,—an' I seen his face. It wuz a easy face ter 'member; an' I swo' den, 'way down deep in my hea't, little ez I wuz, dat some day er 'nother I'd kill dat man. I ain't never had no doubt erbout it; it 's jus w'at I 'm livin' fer, an' I know I ain' gwine ter die till I 've done it. Some lives fer one thing an' some fer another, but dat 's my job. I ain' be'n in no has'e, fer I 'm not ole yit, an' dat man is in good health. I 'd like ter see a little er de worl' befo' I takes chances on leavin' it sudden; an', mo'over, somebody's got ter take keer er de ole 'oman. But her time 'll come some er dese days, an den *his* time 'll be come—an' prob'ly mine. But I ain' keerin' 'bout myse'f: w'en I git thoo wid him, it won' make no diff'ence 'bout me."

Josh was evidently in dead earnest. Miller recalled, very vividly, the expression he had seen twice on his patient's face, during the journey to Wellington. He had often seen Josh's mother, old Aunt Milly,—"Silly Milly," the children called her,—wandering aimlessly about the street, muttering to herself incoherently. He had felt a certain childish awe at the sight of one of God's creatures who had lost the light of reason, and he had always vaguely understood that she was the victim of human cruelty, though he had dated it farther back into the past. This was his first knowledge of the real facts of the case.

He realized, too, for a moment, the continuity of life, how inseparably the present is woven with the past, how certainly the future will be but the outcome of the present. He had supposed this old wound healed. The negroes were not a vindictive people. If, swayed by passion or emotion, they sometimes gave way to gusts of rage, these were of brief duration. Absorbed in the contemplation of their doubtful present and their uncertain future, they gave little thought to the past,—it was a dark story, which they would willingly forget. He knew the timeworn explanation that the Ku-Klux movement, in the main, was merely an ebullition of boyish spirits, begun to amuse young white

men by playing upon the fears and superstitions of ignorant negroes. Here, however, was its tragic side,—the old wound still
bleeding, the fruit of one tragedy, the seed of another. He could
not approve of Josh's application of the Mosaic law of revenge,
and yet the incident was not without significance. Here was a
negro who could remember an injury, who could shape his life
to a definite purpose, if not a high or holy one. When his race
reached the point where they would resent a wrong, there was
hope that they might soon attain the stage where they would
try, and, if need be, die, to defend a right. This man, too, had a
purpose in life, and was willing to die that he might accomplish
it. Miller was willing to give up his life to a cause. Would he be
equally willing, he asked himself, to die for it? Miller had no
prophetic instinct to tell him how soon he would have the opportunity to answer his own question. But he could not encourage Josh to carry out this dark and revengeful purpose.
Every worthy consideration required him to dissuade his patient from such a desperate course.

"You had better put away these murderous fancies, Josh,"
he said seriously. "The Bible says that we should 'forgive our
enemies, bless them that curse us, and do good to them that de-
spitefully use us.'"

"Yas, suh, I 've l'arnt all dat in Sunday-school, an' I 've
heared de preachers say it time an' time ag'in. But it 'pears ter
me dat dis fergitfulniss an' fergivniss is mighty one-sided. De
w'ite folks don' fergive nothin' de niggers does. Dey got up de
Ku-Klux, dey said, on 'count er de kyarpit-baggers. Dey be'n
talkin' 'bout de kyarpit-baggers ever sence, an' dey 'pears ter
fergot all 'bout de Ku-Klux. But I ain' fergot. De niggers is be'n
train' ter fergiveniss; an' fer fear dey might fergit how ter fergive, de w'ite folks gives 'em somethin' new ev'y now an' den,
ter practice on. A w'ite man kin do w'at he wants ter a nigger,
but de minute de nigger gits back at 'im, up goes de nigger, an'
don' come down tell somebody cuts 'im down. If a nigger gits
a' office, er de race 'pears ter be prosperin' too much, de w'ite
folks up an' kills a few, so dat de res' kin keep on fergivin' an'
bein' thankful dat dey 're lef' alive. Don' talk ter me 'bout dese
w'ite folks,—I knows 'em, I does! Ef a nigger wants ter git

down on his marrow-bones, an' eat dirt, an' call 'em 'marster,' *he 's* a good nigger, dere 's room fer *him*. But I ain' no w'ite folks' nigger, I ain'. I don' call no man 'marster.' I don' wan' nothin' but w'at I wo'k fer, but I wants all er dat. I never moles's no w'ite man, 'less 'n he moles's me fus'. But w'en de ole 'oman dies, doctuh, an' I gits a good chance at dat w'ite man,—dere ain' no use talkin', suh!—dere 's gwine ter be a mix-up, an' a fune'al, er two fune'als—er may be mo', ef anybody is keerliss enough to git in de way."

"Josh," said the doctor, laying a cool hand on the other's brow, "you 're feverish, and don't know what you 're talking about. I should n't let my mind dwell on such things, and you must keep quiet until this arm is well, or you may never be able to hit any one with it again."

Miller determined that when Josh got better he would talk to him seriously and dissuade him from this dangerous design. He had not asked the name of Josh's enemy, but the look of murderous hate which the dust-begrimed tramp of the railway journey had cast at Captain George McBane rendered any such question superfluous. McBane was probably deserving of any evil fate which might befall him; but such a revenge would do no good, would right no wrong; while every such crime, committed by a colored man, would be imputed to the race, which was already staggering under a load of obloquy because, in the eyes of a prejudiced and undiscriminating public, it must answer as a whole for the offenses of each separate individual. To die in defense of the right was heroic. To kill another for revenge was pitifully human and weak: "Vengeance is mine, I will repay," saith the Lord.

XIII

THE CAKEWALK

Old Mr. Delamere's servant, Sandy Campbell, was in deep trouble.

A party of Northern visitors had been staying for several days at the St. James Hotel. The gentlemen of the party were concerned in a projected cotton mill, while the ladies were much interested in the study of social conditions, and especially in the negro problem. As soon as their desire for information became known, they were taken courteously under the wing of prominent citizens and their wives, who gave them, at elaborate luncheons, the Southern white man's views of the negro, sighing sentimentally over the disappearance of the good old negro of before the war, and gravely deploring the degeneracy of his descendants. They enlarged upon the amount of money the Southern whites had spent for the education of the negro, and shook their heads over the inadequate results accruing from this unexampled generosity. It was sad, they said, to witness this spectacle of a dying race, unable to withstand the competition of a superior type. The severe reprisals taken by white people for certain crimes committed by negroes were of course not the acts of the best people, who deplored them; but still a certain charity should be extended towards those who in the intense and righteous anger of the moment should take the law into their own hands and deal out rough but still substantial justice; for no negro was ever lynched without incontestable proof of his guilt. In order to be perfectly fair, and give their visitors an opportunity to see both sides of the question, they accompanied the Northern visitors to a colored church where they might hear a colored preacher, who had won a jocular popularity throughout the whole country by an oft-repeated sermon intended to demonstrate that the earth was flat like a pancake. This celebrated divine could always draw a white audience, except on the days when his no less distinguished white rival in the field of sensationalism preached his equally famous sermon to prove that hell was exactly one half mile, linear measure, from the city limits of Wellington. Whether accidentally or not, the Northern visitors had no opportunity to meet or talk alone with any colored person in the city except the servants at the hotel. When one of the party suggested a visit to the colored mission school, a Southern friend kindly volunteered to accompany them.

The visitors were naturally much impressed by what they learned from their courteous hosts, and felt inclined to sympathize with the Southern people, for the negro is not counted as a Southerner, except to fix the basis of congressional representation. There might of course be things to criticise here and there, certain customs for which they did not exactly see the necessity, and which seemed in conflict with the highest ideals of liberty but surely these courteous, soft-spoken ladies and gentlemen, entirely familiar with local conditions, who descanted so earnestly and at times pathetically upon the grave problems confronting them, must know more about it than people in the distant North, without their means of information. The negroes who waited on them at the hotel seemed happy enough, and the teachers whom they had met at the mission school had been well-dressed, well-mannered, and apparently content with their position in life. Surely a people who made no complaints could not be very much oppressed.

In order to give the visitors, ere they left Wellington, a pleasing impression of Southern customs, and particularly of the joyous, happy-go-lucky disposition of the Southern darky and his entire contentment with existing conditions, it was decided by the hotel management to treat them, on the last night of their visit, to a little diversion, in the shape of a genuine negro cakewalk.

On the afternoon of this same day Tom Delamere strolled into the hotel, and soon gravitated to the bar, where he was a frequent visitor. Young men of leisure spent much of their time around the hotel, and no small part of it in the bar. Delamere had been to the club, but had avoided the card-room. Time hanging heavy on his hands, he had sought the hotel in the hope that some form of distraction might present itself.

"Have you heard the latest, Mr. Delamere?" asked the bartender, as he mixed a cocktail for his customer.

"No, Billy; what is it?"

"There 's to be a big cakewalk upstairs to-night. The No'the'n gentlemen an' ladies who are down here to see about the new cotton fact'ry want to study the nigger some more, and the boss has got up a cakewalk for 'em, 'mongst the waiters and chambermaids, with a little outside talent."

"Is it to be public?" asked Delamere.

"Oh, no, not generally, but friends of the house won't be barred out. The clerk 'll fix it for you. Ransom, the head waiter, will be floor manager."

Delamere was struck with a brilliant idea. The more he considered it, the brighter it seemed. Another cocktail imparted additional brilliancy to the conception. He had been trying, after a feeble fashion, to keep his promise to Clara, and was really suffering from lack of excitement.

He left the bar-room, found the head waiter, held with him a short conversation, and left in his intelligent and itching palm a piece of money.

The cakewalk was a great success. The most brilliant performer was a late arrival, who made his appearance just as the performance was about to commence. The newcomer was dressed strikingly, the conspicuous features of his attire being a long blue coat with brass buttons and a pair of plaid trousers. He was older, too, than the other participants, which made his agility the more remarkable. His partner was a new chambermaid, who had just come to town, and whom the head waiter introduced to the newcomer upon his arrival. The cake was awarded to this couple by a unanimous vote. The man presented it to his partner with a grandiloquent flourish, and returned thanks in a speech which sent the Northern visitors into spasms of delight at the quaintness of the darky dialect and the darky wit. To cap the climax, the winner danced a buck dance with a skill and agility that brought a shower of complimentary silver, which he gathered up and passed to the head waiter.

Ellis was off duty for the evening. Not having ventured to put in an appearance at Carteret's since his last rebuff, he found himself burdened with a superfluity of leisure, from which he essayed to find relief by dropping into the hotel office at about nine o'clock. He was invited up to see the cakewalk, which he rather enjoyed, for there was some graceful dancing and posturing. But the grotesque contortions of one participant had struck him as somewhat overdone, even for the comical type of negro. He recognized the fellow, after a few minutes' scrutiny, as the body-servant of old Mr. Delamere. The man's present occupation, or choice of diversion, seemed out of keeping with his employment as attendant upon an invalid old gentleman, and strangely inconsistent with the gravity and decorum which had been so noticeable when this agile cakewalker had served as butler at Major Carteret's table, upon the occasion of the christening dinner. There was a vague suggestion of unreality about this performance, too, which Ellis did not attempt to analyze, but which recurred vividly to his memory upon a subsequent occasion.

Ellis had never pretended to that intimate knowledge of negro thought and character by which some of his acquaintances claimed the ability to fathom every motive of a negro's conduct, and predict in advance what any one of the darker race would do under a given set of circumstances. He would not have believed that a white man could possess two so widely varying phases of character; but as to negroes, they were as yet a crude and undeveloped race, and it was not safe to make predictions concerning them. No one could tell at what moment the thin veneer of civilization might peel off and reveal the underlying savage.

The champion cakewalker, much to the surprise of his sable companions, who were about equally swayed by admiration and jealousy, disappeared immediately after the close of the performance. Any one watching him on his way home through the quiet streets to old Mr. Delamere's would have seen him now and then shaking with laughter. It had been excellent fun. Nevertheless, as he neared home, a certain aspect of the affair, hitherto unconsidered, occurred to him, and it was in a rather serious frame of mind that he cautiously entered the house and sought his own room.

The cakewalk had results which to Sandy were very serious. The following week he was summoned before the disciplinary committee of his church and charged with unchristian conduct, in the following particulars, to wit: dancing, and participating in a sinful diversion called a cakewalk, which was calculated to bring the church into disrepute and make it the mockery of sinners.

Sandy protested his innocence vehemently, but in vain. The

proof was overwhelming. He was positively identified by Sister 'Manda Patterson, the hotel cook, who had watched the whole performance from the hotel corridor for the sole, single, solitary, and only purpose, she averred, of seeing how far human wickedness could be carried by a professing Christian. The whole thing had been shocking and offensive to her, and only a stern sense of duty had sustained her in looking on, that she might be qualified to bear witness against the offender. She had recognized his face, his clothes, his voice, his walk—there could be no shadow of doubt that it was Brother Sandy. This testimony was confirmed by one of the deacons, whose son, a waiter at the hotel, had also seen Sandy at the cakewalk.

Sandy stoutly insisted that he was at home the whole evening; that he had not been near the hotel for three months; that he had never in his life taken part in a cakewalk, and that he did not know how to dance. It was replied that wickedness, like everything else, must have a beginning; that dancing was an art that could be acquired in secret, and came natural to some people. In the face of positive proof, Sandy's protestations were of no avail; he was found guilty, and suspended from church fellowship until he should have repented and made full confession.

Sturdily refusing to confess a fault of which he claimed to be innocent, Sandy remained in contumacy, thereby falling somewhat into disrepute among the members of his church, the largest in the city. The effect of a bad reputation being subjective as well as objective, and poor human nature arguing that one may as well have the game as the name, Sandy insensibly glided into habits of which the church would not have approved, though he took care that they should not interfere with his duties to Mr. Delamere. The consolation thus afforded, however, followed as it was by remorse of conscience, did not compensate him for the loss of standing in the church, which to him was a social club as well as a religious temple. At times, in conversation with young Delamere, he would lament his hard fate.

Tom laughed until he cried at the comical idea which Sandy's plaint always brought up, of half-a-dozen negro preachers sitting in solemn judgment upon that cakewalk,—it had certainly been a good cakewalk!—and sending poor Sandy to spiritual Coventry.

"Cheer up, Sandy, cheer up!" he would say when Sandy seemed most depressed. "Go into my room and get yourself a good drink of liquor. The devil's church has a bigger congregation than theirs, and we have the consolation of knowing that when we die, we 'll meet all our friends on the other side. Brace up, Sandy, and be a man, or, if you can't be a man, be as near a man as you can!"

Hoping to revive his drooping spirits, Sandy too often accepted the proffered remedy.

XIV

THE MAUNDERINGS OF OLD
MRS. OCHILTREE

When Mrs. Carteret had fully recovered from the shock attendant upon the accident at the window, where little Dodie had so narrowly escaped death or serious injury, she ordered her carriage one afternoon and directed the coachman to drive her to Mrs. Ochiltree's.

Mrs. Carteret had discharged her young nurse only the day before, and had sent for Mammy Jane, who was now recovered from her rheumatism, to stay until she could find another girl. The nurse had been ordered not to take the child to negroes' houses. Yesterday, in driving past the old homestead of her husband's family, now occupied by Dr. Miller and his family, Mrs. Carteret had seen her own baby's carriage standing in the yard.

When the nurse returned home, she was immediately discharged. She offered some sort of explanation, to the effect that her sister worked for Mrs. Miller, and that some family matter had rendered it necessary for her to see her sister. The explanation only aggravated the offense: if Mrs. Carteret could have overlooked the disobedience, she would by no means have retained in her employment a servant whose sister worked for the Miller woman.

Old Mrs. Ochiltree had within a few months begun to show signs of breaking up. She was over seventy years old, and had been of late, by various afflictions, confined to the house much of the time. More than once within the year, Mrs. Carteret had asked her aunt to come and live with her; but Mrs. Ochiltree, who would have regarded such a step as an acknowledgment of weakness, preferred her lonely independence. She resided in a small, old-fashioned house, standing back in the middle of a garden on a quiet street. Two old servants made up her modest household.

This refusal to live with her niece had been lightly borne, for Mrs. Ochiltree was a woman of strong individuality, whose comments upon her acquaintance, present or absent, were marked by a frankness at times no less than startling. This characteristic caused her to be more or less avoided. Mrs. Ochiltree was aware of this sentiment on the part of her acquaintance, and rather exulted in it. She hated fools. Only fools ran away from her, and that because they were afraid she would expose their folly. If most people were fools, it was no fault of hers, and she was not obliged to indulge them by pretending to believe that they knew anything. She had once owned considerable property, but was reticent about her affairs, and told no one how much she was worth, though it was supposed that she had considerable ready money, besides her house and some other real estate. Mrs. Carteret was her nearest living relative, though her grand-nephew Tom Delamere had been a great favorite with her. If she did not spare him her tongue-lashings, it was nevertheless expected in the family that she would leave him something handsome in her will.

Mrs. Ochiltree had shared in the general rejoicing upon the advent of the Carteret baby. She had been one of his godmothers, and had hinted at certain intentions held by her concerning him. During Mammy Jane's administration she had tried the old nurse's patience more or less by her dictatorial interference. Since her partial confinement to the house, she had gone, when her health and the weather would permit, to see the child, and at other times had insisted that it be sent to her in charge of the nurse at least every other day.

Mrs. Ochiltree's faculties had shared insensibly in the decline of her health. This weakness manifested itself by fits of absent-mindedness, in which she would seemingly lose connection with the present, and live over again, in imagination, the earlier years of her life. She had buried two husbands, had tried in vain to secure a third, and had never borne any children. Long ago she had petrified into a character which nothing under heaven could change, and which, if death is to take us as it finds us, and the future life to keep us as it takes us, promised anything but eternal felicity to those with whom she might associate after this life. Tom Delamere had been heard to say, profanely, that if his Aunt Polly went to heaven, he would let his mansion in the skies on a long lease, at a low figure.

When the carriage drove up with Mrs. Carteret, her aunt was seated on the little front piazza, with her wrinkled hands folded in her lap, dozing the afternoon away in fitful slumber.

"Tie the horse, William," said Mrs. Carteret, "and then go in and wake Aunt Polly, and tell her I want her to come and drive with me."

Mrs. Ochiltree had not observed her niece's approach, nor did she look up when William drew near. Her eyes were closed, and she would let her head sink slowly forward, recovering it now and then with a spasmodic jerk.

"Colonel Ochiltree," she muttered, "was shot at the battle of Culpepper Court House, and left me a widow for the second time. But I would not have married any man on earth after him."

"Mis' Ochiltree!" cried William, raising his voice, "oh, Mis' Ochiltree!"

"If I had found a man,—a real man,—I might have married again. I did not care for weaklings. I could have married John Delamere if I had wanted him. But pshaw! I could have wound him round"—

"Go round to the kitchen, William," interrupted Mrs. Carteret impatiently, "and tell Aunt Dinah to come and wake her up."

William returned in a few moments with a fat, comfortable looking black woman, who curtsied to Mrs. Carteret at the gate, and then going up to her mistress seized her by the shoulder and shook her vigorously.

"Wake up dere, Mis' Polly," she screamed, as harshly as her mellow voice would permit. "Mis' 'Livy wants you ter go drivin' wid 'er!"

"Dinah," exclaimed the old lady, sitting suddenly upright with a defiant assumption of wakefulness, "why do you take so long to come when I call? Bring me my bonnet and shawl. Don't you see my niece waiting for me at the gate?"

"Hyuh dey is, hyuh dey is!" returned Dinah, producing the bonnet and shawl, and assisting Mrs. Ochiltree to put them on.

Leaning on William's arm, the old lady went slowly down the walk, and was handed to the rear seat with Mrs. Carteret.

"How 's the baby to-day, Olivia, and why did n't you bring him?"

"He has a cold to-day, and is a little hoarse," replied Mrs. Carteret, "so I thought it best not to bring him out. Drive out the Weldon road, William, and back by Pine Street."

The drive led past an eminence crowned by a handsome brick building of modern construction, evidently an institution of some kind, surrounded on three sides by a grove of venerable oaks.

"Hugh Poindexter," Mrs. Ochiltree exclaimed explosively, after a considerable silence, "has been building a new house, in place of the old family mansion burned during the war."

"It is n't Mr. Poindexter's house, Aunt Polly. That is the new colored hospital built by the colored doctor."

"The new colored hospital, indeed, and the colored doctor! Before the war the negroes were all healthy, and when they got sick we took care of them ourselves! Hugh Poindexter has sold the graves of his ancestors to a negro,—I should have starved first!"

"He had his grandfather's grave opened, and there was nothing to remove, except a few bits of heart-pine from the coffin. All the rest had crumbled into dust."

"And he sold the dust to a negro! The world is upside down."

"He had the tombstone transferred to the white cemetery, Aunt Polly, and he has moved away."

"Esau sold his birthright for a mess of pottage. When I die, if you outlive me, Olivia, which is not likely, I shall leave my house and land to this child! He is a Carteret,—he would never sell them to a negro. I can't trust Tom Delamere, I'm afraid."

The carriage had skirted the hill, passing to the rear of the new building.

"Turn to the right, William," ordered Mrs. Carteret, addressing the coachman, "and come back past the other side of the hospital."

A turn to the right into another road soon brought them to the front of the building, which stood slightly back from the street, with no intervening fence or inclosure. A sorrel pony in a light buggy was fastened to a hitching-post near the entrance. As they drove past, a lady came out of the front door and descended the steps, holding by the hand a very pretty child about six years old.

"Who is that woman, Olivia?" asked Mrs. Ochiltree abruptly, with signs of agitation.

The lady coming down the steps darted at the approaching carriage a look which lingered involuntarily.

Mrs. Carteret, perceiving this glance, turned away coldly.

With a sudden hardening of her own features the other woman lifted the little boy into the buggy and drove sharply away in the direction opposite to that taken by Mrs. Carteret's carriage.

"Who is that woman, Olivia?" repeated Mrs. Ochiltree, with marked emotion.

"I have not the honor of her acquaintance," returned Mrs. Carteret sharply. "Drive faster, William."

"I want to know who that woman is," persisted Mrs. Ochiltree querulously. "William," she cried shrilly, poking the coachman in the back with the end of her cane, "who is that woman?"

"Dat 's Mis' Miller, ma'am," returned the coachman, touching his hat; "Doctuh Miller's wife."

"What was her mother's name?"

"Her mother's name wuz Julia Brown. She 's be'n dead dese twenty years er mo'. Why, you knowed Julia, Mis' Polly!—she used ter b'long ter yo' own father befo' de wah; an' after de wah she kep' house fer"—

"Look to your horses, William!" exclaimed Mrs. Carteret sharply.

"It 's that hussy's child," said Mrs. Ochiltree, turning to her niece with great excitement. "When your father died, I turned the mother and the child out into the street. The mother died and went to—the place provided for such as she. If I had n't been just in time, Olivia, they would have turned you out. I saved the property for you and your son! You can thank me for it all!"

"Hush, Aunt Polly, for goodness' sake! William will hear you. Tell me about it when you get home."

Mrs. Ochiltree was silent, except for a few incoherent mumblings. What she might say, what distressing family secret she might repeat in William's hearing, should she take another talkative turn, was beyond conjecture.

Olivia looked anxiously around for something to distract her aunt's attention, and caught sight of a colored man, dressed in sober gray, who was coming toward the carriage.

"There 's Mr. Delamere's Sandy!" exclaimed Mrs. Carteret, touching her aunt on the arm. "I wonder how his master is? Sandy, oh, Sandy!"

Sandy approached the carriage, lifting his hat with a slight exaggeration of Chesterfieldian elegance. Sandy, no less than his master, was a survival of an interesting type. He had inherited the feudal deference for his superiors in position, joined to a certain self-respect which saved him from sycophancy. His manners had been formed upon those of old Mr. Delamere, and were not a bad imitation; for in the man, as in the master, they were the harmonious reflection of a mental state.

"How is Mr. Delamere, Sandy?" asked Mrs. Carteret, acknowledging Sandy's salutation with a nod and a smile.

"He ain't ez peart ez he has be'n, ma'am," replied Sandy, "but he 's doin tol'able well. De doctuh say he 's good fer a dozen years yit, ef he 'll jes' take good keer of hisse'f an' keep f'm gittin' excited; fer sence dat secon' stroke, excitement is dange'ous fer 'im."

"I 'm sure you take the best care of him," returned Mrs. Carteret kindly.

"You can't do anything for him, Sandy," interposed old Mrs. Ochiltree, shaking her head slowly to emphasize her dissent. "All the doctors in creation could n't keep him alive another year. I shall outlive him by twenty years, though we are not far from the same age."

"Lawd, ma'am!" exclaimed Sandy, lifting his hands in affected amazement,—his study of gentle manners had been more than superficial,—"whoever would 'a' s'picion' dat you an' Mars John wuz nigh de same age? I 'd 'a' 'lowed you wuz ten years younger 'n him, easy, ef you wuz a day!"

"Give my compliments to the poor old gentleman," returned Mrs. Ochiltree, with a simper of senile vanity, though her back was weakening under the strain of the effort to sit erect that she might maintain this illusion of comparative youthfulness. "Bring him to see me some day when he is able to walk."

"Yas 'm, I will," rejoined Sandy. "He 's gwine out ter Belleview nex' week, fer ter stay a mont' er so, but I 'll fetch him 'roun' w'en he comes back. I 'll tell 'im dat you ladies 'quired fer 'im."

Sandy made another deep bow, and held his hat in his hand until the carriage had moved away. He had not condescended to notice the coachman at all, who was one of the young negroes of the new generation; while Sandy regarded himself as belonging to the quality, and seldom stooped to notice those beneath him. It would not have been becoming in him, either, while conversing with white ladies, to have noticed a colored servant. Moreover, the coachman was a Baptist, while Sandy was a Methodist, though under a cloud, and considered a Methodist in poor standing as better than a Baptist of any degree of sanctity.

"Lawd, Lawd!" chuckled Sandy, after the carriage had departed, "I never seed nothin' lack de way dat ole lady do keep up her temper! Wid one foot in de grave, an' de other hov'rin' on de edge, she talks 'bout my ole marster lack he wuz in his secon' chil'hood. But I 'm jes' willin' ter bet dat he 'll outlas' her! She ain't half de woman she wuz dat night I waited on de table at de christenin' pa'ty, w'en she 'lowed she wuz n' feared er no man livin'.' "

XV

MRS. CARTERET SEEKS
AN EXPLANATION

As a stone dropped into a pool of water sets in motion a series of concentric circles which disturb the whole mass in varying degree, so Mrs. Ochiltree's enigmatical remark had started in her niece's mind a disturbing train of thought. Had her words, Mrs. Carteret asked herself, any serious meaning, or were they the mere empty babblings of a clouded intellect?

"William," she said to the coachman when they reached Mrs. Ochiltree's house, "you may tie the horse and help us out. I shall be here a little while."

William helped the ladies down, assisted Mrs. Ochiltree into the house, and then went round to the kitchen. Dinah was an excellent hand at potato-pone and other culinary delicacies dear to the Southern heart, and William was a welcome visitor in her domain.

"Now, Aunt Polly," said Mrs. Carteret resolutely, as soon as they were alone, "I want to know what you meant by what you said about my father and Julia, and this—this child of hers?"

The old woman smiled cunningly, but her expression soon changed to one more grave.

"Why do you want to know?" she asked suspiciously. "You 've got the land, the houses, and the money. You've nothing to complain of. Enjoy yourself, and be thankful!"

"I 'm thankful to God," returned Olivia, "for all his good gifts,—and He has blessed me abundantly,—but why should I be thankful to *you* for the property my father left me?"

"Why should you be thankful to me?" rejoined Mrs. Ochiltree with querulous indignation. "You 'd better ask why *should n't* you be thankful to me. What have I not done for you?"

"Yes, Aunt Polly, I know you 've done a great deal. You reared me in your own house when I had been cast out of my father's; you have been a second mother to me, and I am very grateful,—you can never say that I have not shown my gratitude. But if you have done anything else for me, I wish to know it. Why should I thank you for my inheritance?"

"Why should you thank me? Well, because I drove that woman and her brat away."

"But she had no right to stay, Aunt Polly, after father died. Of course she had no moral right before, but it was his house, and he could keep her there if he chose. But after his death she surely had no right."

"Perhaps not so surely as you think,—if she had not been a negro. Had she been white, there might have been a difference. When I told her to go, she said"—

"What did she say, Aunt Polly," demanded Olivia eagerly.

It seemed for a moment as though Mrs. Ochiltree would speak no further: but her once strong will, now weakened by her bodily infirmities, yielded to the influence of her niece's imperious demand.

"I 'll tell you the whole story," she said, "and then you 'll know what I did for you and yours."

Mrs. Ochiltree's eyes assumed an introspective expression, and her story, as it advanced, became as keenly dramatic as though memory had thrown aside the veil of intervening years and carried her back directly to the events which she now described.

"Your father," she said, "while living with that woman, left home one morning the picture of health. Five minutes later he tottered into the house groaning with pain, stricken unto death by the hand of a just God, as a punishment for his sins."

Olivia gave a start of indignation, but restrained herself.

"I was at once informed of what had happened, for I had means of knowing all that took place in the household. Old

Jane—she was younger then—had come with you to my house; but her daughter remained, and through her I learned all that went on.

"I hastened immediately to the house, entered without knocking, and approached Mr. Merkell's bedroom, which was on the lower floor and opened into the hall. The door was ajar, and as I stood there for a moment I heard your father's voice.

"'Listen, Julia,' he was saying. 'I shall not live until the doctor comes. But I wish you to know, *dear* Julia!'—he called her 'dear Julia!'—'before I die, that I have kept my promise. You did me one great service, Julia,—you saved me from Polly Ochiltree!' Yes, Olivia, that is what he said! 'You have served me faithfully and well, and I owe you a great deal, which I have tried to pay.'

"'Oh, Mr. Merkell, dear Mr. Merkell,' cried the hypocritical hussy, falling to her knees by his bedside, and shedding her crocodile tears, 'you owe me nothing. You have done more for me than I could ever repay. You will not die and leave me,—no, no, it cannot be!'

"'Yes, I am going to die,—I am dying now, Julia. But listen,—compose yourself and listen, for this is a more important matter. Take the keys from under my pillow, open the desk in the next room, look in the second drawer on the right, and you will find an envelope containing three papers: one of them is yours, one is the paper I promised to make, and the third is a letter which I wrote last night. As soon as the breath has left my body, deliver the envelope to the address indorsed upon it. Do not delay one moment, or you may live to regret it. Say nothing until you have delivered the package, and then be guided by the advice which you receive,—it will come from a friend of mine who will not see you wronged.'

"I slipped away from the door without making my presence known and entered, by a door from the hall, the room adjoining the one where Mr. Merkell lay. A moment later there was a loud scream. Returning quickly to the hall, I entered Mr. Merkell's room as though just arrived.

"'How is Mr. Merkell?' I demanded, as I crossed the threshold.

" 'He is dead,' sobbed the woman, without lifting her head,—she had fallen on her knees by the bedside. She had good cause to weep, for my time had come.

" 'Get up,' I said. 'You have no right here. You pollute Mr. Merkell's dead body by your touch. Leave the house immediately,—your day is over!'

" 'I will not!' she cried, rising to her feet and facing me with brazen-faced impudence. 'I have a right to stay,—he has given me the right!'

" 'Ha, ha!' I laughed. 'Mr. Merkell is dead, and I am mistress here henceforth. Go, and go at once,—do you hear?'

" 'I hear, but I shall not heed. I can prove my rights! I shall not leave!'

" 'Very well,' I replied, 'we shall see. The law will decide.'

"I left the room, but did not leave the house. On the contrary, I concealed myself where I could see what took place in the room adjoining the death-chamber.

"She entered the room a moment later, with her child on one arm and the keys in the other hand. Placing the child on the floor, she put the key in the lock, and seemed surprised to find the desk already unfastened. She opened the desk, picked up a roll of money and a ladies' watch, which first caught her eye, and was reaching toward the drawer upon the right, when I interrupted her:—

" 'Well, thief, are you trying to strip the house before you leave it?'

"She gave an involuntary cry, clasped one hand to her bosom and with the other caught up her child, and stood like a wild beast at bay.

" 'I am not a thief,' she panted. 'The things are mine!'

" 'You lie,' I replied. 'You have no right to them,—no more right than you have to remain in this house!'

" 'I have a right,' she persisted, 'and I can prove it!'

"She turned toward the desk, seized the drawer, and drew it open. Never shall I forget her look,—never shall I forget that moment; it was the happiest of my life. The drawer was empty!

"Pale as death she turned and faced me.

"'The papers!' she shrieked, 'the papers! You have stolen them!'

"'Papers?" I laughed, 'what papers? Do you take me for a thief, like yourself?'

"'There were papers here,' she cried, 'only a minute since. They are mine,—give them back to me!'

"'Listen, woman,' I said sternly, 'you are lying—or dreaming. My brother-in-law's papers are doubtless in his safe at his office, where they ought to be. As for the rest,—you are a thief.'

"'I am not,' she screamed; 'I am his wife. He married me, and the papers that were in the desk will prove it.'

"'Listen,' I exclaimed, when she had finished,—'listen carefully, and take heed to what I say. You are a liar. You have no proofs,—there never were any proofs of what you say, because it never happened,—it is absurd upon the face of it. Not one person in Wellington would believe it. Why should he marry you? He did not need to! You are merely lying,—you are not even self-deceived. If he had really married you, you would have made it known long ago. That you did not is proof that your story is false.'

"She was hit so hard that she trembled and sank into a chair. But I had no mercy—she had saved your father from me—'dear Julia,' indeed!

"'Stand up,' I ordered. 'Do not dare to sit down in my presence. I have you on the hip, my lady, and will teach you your place.'

"She struggled to her feet, and stood supporting herself with one hand on the chair. I could have killed her, Olivia! She had been my father's slave; if it had been before the war, I would have had her whipped to death.

"'You are a thief,' I said, 'and of that there are proofs. I have caught you in the act. The watch in your bosom is my own, the money belongs to Mr. Merkell's estate, which belongs to my niece, his daughter Olivia. I saw you steal them. My word is worth yours a hundred times over, for I am a lady, and you are—what? And now hear me: if ever you breathe to a living soul one word of this preposterous story, I will charge you with the theft, and have you sent to the penitentiary. Your child will be taken from you, and you shall never see it again. I will give you now just ten minutes to take your brat and your rags out of this house forever. But before you go, put down your plunder there upon the desk!'

"She laid down the money and the watch, and a few minutes later left the house with the child in her arms.

"And now, Olivia, you know how I saved your estate, and why you should be grateful to me."

Olivia had listened to her aunt's story with intense interest. Having perceived the old woman's mood, and fearful lest any interruption might break the flow of her narrative, she had with an effort kept back the one question which had been hovering upon her lips, but which could now no longer be withheld.

"What became of the papers, Aunt Polly?"

"Ha, ha!" chuckled Mrs. Ochiltree with a cunning look, "did I not tell you that she found no papers?"

A change had come over Mrs. Ochiltree's face, marking the reaction from her burst of energy. Her eyes were half closed, and she was muttering incoherently. Olivia made some slight effort to arouse her, but in vain, and realizing the futility of any further attempt to extract information from her aunt at this time, she called William and drove homeward.

XVI

ELLIS TAKES A TRICK

Late one afternoon a handsome trap, drawn by two spirited bays, drove up to Carteret's gate. Three places were taken by Mrs. Carteret, Clara, and the major, leaving the fourth seat vacant.

"I 've asked Ellis to drive out with us," said the major, as he took the lines from the colored man who had the trap in charge. "We 'll go by the office and pick him up."

Clara frowned, but perceiving Mrs. Carteret's eye fixed upon her, restrained any further expression of annoyance.

The major's liking for Ellis had increased within the year.

The young man was not only a good journalist, but possessed sufficient cleverness and tact to make him excellent company. The major was fond of argument, but extremely tenacious of his own opinions. Ellis handled the foils of discussion with just the requisite skill to draw out the major, permitting himself to be vanquished, not too easily, but, as it were, inevitably, by the major's incontrovertible arguments.

Olivia had long suspected Ellis of feeling a more than friendly interest in Clara. Herself partial to Tom, she had more than once thought it hardly fair to Delamere, or even to Clara, who was young and impressionable, to have another young man constantly about the house. True, there had seemed to be no great danger, for Ellis had neither the family nor the means to make him a suitable match for the major's sister; nor had Clara made any secret of her dislike for Ellis, or of her resentment for his supposed depreciation of Delamere. Mrs. Carteret was inclined to a more just and reasonable view of Ellis's conduct in this matter, but nevertheless did not deem it wise to undeceive Clara. Dislike was a stout barrier, which remorse might have broken down. The major, absorbed in schemes of empire and dreams of his child's future, had not become cognizant of the affair. His wife, out of friendship for Tom, had refrained from mentioning it; while the major, with a delicate regard for Clara's feelings, had said nothing at home in regard to his interview with her lover.

At the Chronicle office Ellis took the front seat beside the major. After leaving the city pavements, they bowled along merrily over an excellent toll-road, built of oyster shells from the neighboring sound, stopping at intervals to pay toll to the gate-keepers, most of whom were white women with tallow complexions and snuff-stained lips,—the traditional "poor-white." For part of the way the road was bordered with a growth of scrub oak and pine, interspersed with stretches of cleared land, white with the opening cotton or yellow with ripening corn. To the right, along the distant river-bank, were visible here and there groups of turpentine pines, though most of this growth had for some years been exhausted. Twenty years before, Wellington had been the world's greatest shipping port for naval stores. But as the turpentine industry had moved southward, leaving a trail of devastated forests in its rear, the city had fallen to a poor fifth or sixth place in this trade, relying now almost entirely upon cotton for its export business.

Occasionally our party passed a person, or a group of persons,—mostly negroes approximating the pure type, for those of lighter color grew noticeably scarcer as the town was left behind. Now and then one of these would salute the party respectfully, while others glanced at them indifferently or turned away. There would have seemed, to a stranger, a lack of spontaneous friendliness between the people of these two races, as though each felt that it had no part or lot in the other's life. At one point the carriage drew near a party of colored folks who were laughing and jesting among themselves with great glee. Paying no attention to the white people, they continued to laugh and shout boisterously as the carriage swept by.

Major Carteret's countenance wore an angry look.

"The negroes around this town are becoming absolutely insufferable," he averred. "They are sadly in need of a lesson in manners."

Half an hour later they neared another group, who were also making merry. As the carriage approached, they became mute and silent as the grave until the major's party had passed.

"The negroes are a sullen race," remarked the major thoughtfully. "They will learn their lesson in a rude school, and perhaps much sooner than they dream. By the way," he added, turning to the ladies, "what was the arrangement with Tom? Was he to come out this evening?"

"He came out early in the afternoon," replied Clara, "to go a-fishing. He is to join us at the hotel."

After an hour's drive they reached the hotel, in front of which stretched the beach, white and inviting, along the shallow sound. Mrs. Carteret and Clara found seats on the veranda. Having turned the trap over to a hostler, the major joined a group of gentlemen, among whom was General Belmont, and was soon deep in the discussion of the standing problem of how best to keep the negroes down.

Ellis remained by the ladies. Clara seemed restless and ill at ease. Half an hour elapsed and Delamere had not appeared.

"I wonder where Tom is," said Mrs. Carteret.

"I guess he has n't come in yet from fishing," said Clara. "I wish he would come. It 's lonesome here. Mr. Ellis, would you mind looking about the hotel and seeing if there 's any one here that we know?"

For Ellis the party was already one too large. He had accepted this invitation eagerly, hoping to make friends with Clara during the evening. He had never been able to learn definitely the reason of her coldness, but had dated it from his meeting with old Mrs. Ochiltree, with which he felt it was obscurely connected. He had noticed Delamere's scowling look, too, at their last meeting. Clara's injustice, whatever its cause, he felt keenly. To Delamere's scowl he had paid little attention,— he despised Tom so much that, but for his engagement to Clara, he would have held his opinions in utter contempt.

He had even wished that Clara might make some charge against him,—he would have preferred that to her attitude of studied indifference, the only redeeming feature about which was that it *was* studied, showing that she, at least, had him in mind. The next best thing, he reasoned, to having a woman love you, is to have her dislike you violently,—the main point is that you should be kept in mind, and made the subject of strong emotions. He thought of the story of Hall Caine's, where the woman, after years of persecution at the hands of an unwelcome suitor, is on the point of yielding, out of sheer irresistible admiration for the man's strength and persistency, when the lover, unaware of his victory and despairing of success, seizes her in his arms and, springing into the sea, finds a watery grave for both. The analogy of this case with his own was, of course, not strong. He did not anticipate any tragedy in their relations; but he was glad to be thought of upon almost any terms. He would not have done a mean thing to make her think of him; but if she did so because of a misconception, which he was given no opportunity to clear up, while at the same time his conscience absolved him from evil and gave him the compensating glow of martyrdom, it was at least better than nothing.

He would, of course, have preferred to be upon a different footing. It had been a pleasure to have her speak to him during the drive,—they had exchanged a few trivial remarks in the general conversation. It was a greater pleasure to have her ask a favor of him,—a pleasure which, in this instance, was partly offset when he interpreted her request to mean that he was to look for Tom Delamere. He accepted the situation gracefully, however, and left the ladies alone.

Knowing Delamere's habits, he first went directly to the bar-room,—the atmosphere would be congenial, even if he were not drinking. Delamere was not there. Stepping next into the office, he asked the clerk if young Mr. Delamere had been at the hotel.

"Yes, sir," returned the man at the desk, "he was here at luncheon, and then went out fishing in a boat with several other gentlemen. I think they came back about three o'clock. I 'll find out for you."

He rang the bell, to which a colored boy responded.

"Front," said the clerk, "see if young Mr. Delamere 's upstairs. Look in 255 or 256, and let me know at once."

The bell-boy returned in a moment.

"Yas, suh," he reported, with a suppressed grin, "he 's in 256, suh. De do' was open, an' I seed 'im from de hall, suh."

"I wish you 'd go up and tell him," said Ellis, "that—What are you grinning about?" he asked suddenly, noticing the waiter's expression.

"Nothin', suh, nothin' at all, suh," responded the negro, lapsing into the stolidity of a wooden Indian. "What shall I tell Mistah Delamere, suh?"

"Tell him," resumed Ellis, still watching the boy suspiciously,—"no, I 'll tell him myself."

He ascended the broad stair to the second floor. There was an upper balcony and a parlor, with a piano for the musically inclined. To reach these one had to pass along the hall upon which the room mentioned by the bell-boy opened. Ellis was quite familiar with the hotel. He could imagine circumstances under which he would not care to speak to Delamere; he would merely pass through the hall and glance into the room casually, as any one else might do, and see what the darky downstairs might have meant by his impudence.

It required but a moment to reach the room. The door was not wide open, but far enough ajar for him to see what was going on within.

Two young men, members of the fast set at the Clarendon Club, were playing cards at a small table, near which stood another, decorated with an array of empty bottles and glasses. Sprawling on a lounge, with flushed face and disheveled hair, his collar unfastened, his vest buttoned awry, lay Tom Delamere, breathing stertorously, in what seemed a drunken sleep. Lest there should be any doubt of the cause of his condition, the fingers of his right hand had remained clasped mechanically around the neck of a bottle which lay across his bosom.

Ellis turned away in disgust, and went slowly back to the ladies.

"There seems to be no one here yet," he reported. "We came a little early for the evening crowd. The clerk says Tom Delamere was here to luncheon, but he has n't seen him for several hours."

"He 's not a very gallant cavalier," said Mrs. Carteret severely. "He ought to have been waiting for us."

Clara was clearly disappointed, and made no effort to conceal her displeasure, leaving Ellis in doubt as to whether or not he were its object. Perhaps she suspected him of not having made a very thorough search. Her next remark might have borne such a construction.

"Sister Olivia," she said pettishly, "let 's go up to the parlor. I can play the piano anyway, if there 's no one to talk to."

"I find it very comfortable here, Clara," replied her sister placidly. "Mr. Ellis will go with you. You 'll probably find some one in the parlor, or they 'll come when you begin to play."

Clara's expression was not cordial, but she rose as if to go. Ellis was in a quandary. If she went through the hall, the chances were at least even that she would see Delamere. He did not care a rap for Delamere,—if he chose to make a public exhibition of himself, it was his own affair; but to see him would surely spoil Miss Pemberton's evening, and, in her frame of mind, might lead to the suspicion that Ellis had prearranged the exposure. Even if she should not harbor this unjust thought, she would not love the witness of her discomfiture. We had rather not meet the persons who have seen, even though they never mention, the skeletons in our closets. Delamere had disposed of himself for the evening. Ellis would have a fairer field with Delamere out of sight and unaccounted for, than with Delamere in evidence in his present condition.

"Would n't you rather take a stroll on the beach, Miss Clara?" he asked, in the hope of creating a diversion.

"No, I 'm going to the parlor. *You* need n't come, Mr. Ellis, if you 'd rather go down to the beach. I can quite as well go alone."

"I 'd rather go with you," he said meekly.

They were moving toward the door opening into the hall, from which the broad staircase ascended. Ellis, whose thoughts did not always respond quickly to a sudden emergency, was puzzling his brain as to how he should save her from any risk of seeing Delamere. Through the side door leading from the hall into the office, he saw the bell-boy to whom he had spoken seated on the bench provided for the servants.

"Won't you wait for me just a moment, Miss Clara, while I step into the office? I'll be with you in an instant."

Clara hesitated.

"Oh, certainly," she replied nonchalantly.

Ellis went direct to the bell-boy. "Sit right where you are," he said, "and don't move a hair. What is the lady in the hall doing?"

"She 's got her back tu'ned this way, suh. I 'spec' she's lookin' at the picture on the opposite wall, suh."

"All right," whispered Ellis, pressing a coin into the servant's hand. "I 'm going up to the parlor with the lady. You go up ahead of us, and keep in front of us along the hall. Don't dare to look back. I shall keep on talking to the lady, so that you can tell by my voice where we are. When you get to room 256, go in and shut the door behind you: pretend that you were called,— ask the gentlemen what they want,—tell any kind of a lie you like,—but keep the door shut until you 're sure we 've got by. Do you hear?"

"Yes, suh," replied the negro intelligently.

The plan worked without a hitch. Ellis talked steadily, about the hotel, the furnishings, all sorts of irrelevant subjects, to which Miss Pemberton paid little attention. She was angry with Delamere, and took no pains to conceal her feelings. The bell-boy entered room 256 just before they reached the door. Ellis had heard loud talking as they approached, and as they were passing there was a crash of broken glass, as though some object had been thrown at the door.

"What is the matter there?" exclaimed Clara, quickening her footsteps and instinctively drawing closer to Ellis.

"Some one dropped a glass, I presume," replied Ellis calmly.

Miss Pemberton glanced at him suspiciously. She was in a decidedly perverse mood. Seating herself at the piano, she played brilliantly for a quarter of an hour. Quite a number of couples strolled up to the parlor, but Delamere was not among them.

"Oh dear!" exclaimed Miss Pemberton, as she let her fingers fall upon the keys with a discordant crash, after the last note, "I don't see why we came out here to-night. Let 's go back downstairs."

Ellis felt despondent. He had done his utmost to serve and to please Miss Pemberton, but was not likely, he foresaw, to derive much benefit from his opportunity. Delamere was evidently as much or more in her thoughts by reason of his absence than if he had been present. If the door should have been opened, and she should see him from the hall upon their return, Ellis could not help it. He took the side next to the door, however, meaning to hurry past the room so that she might not recognize Delamere.

Fortunately the door was closed and all quiet within the room. On the stairway they met the bell-boy, rubbing his head with one hand and holding a bottle of seltzer upon a tray in the other. The boy was well enough trained to give no sign of recognition, though Ellis guessed the destination of the bottle.

Ellis hardly knew whether to feel pleased or disappointed at the success of his manœuvres. He had spared Miss Pemberton some mortification, but he had saved Tom Delamere from merited exposure. Clara ought to know the truth, for her own sake.

On the beach, a few rods away, fires were burning, around which several merry groups had gathered. The smoke went mostly to one side, but a slight whiff came now and then to where Mrs. Carteret sat awaiting them.

"They 're roasting oysters," said Mrs. Carteret. "I wish you 'd bring me some, Mr. Ellis."

Ellis strolled down to the beach. A large iron plate, with a turned-up rim like a great baking-pan, supported by legs which held it off the ground, was set over a fire built upon the sand. This primitive oven was heaped with small oysters in the shell, taken from the neighboring sound, and hauled up to the hotel by a negro whose pony cart stood near by. A wet coffee-sack of burlaps was spread over the oysters, which, when steamed sufficiently, were opened by a colored man and served gratis to all who cared for them.

Ellis secured a couple of plates of oysters, which he brought to Mrs. Carteret and Clara; they were small, but finely flavored.

Meanwhile Delamere, who possessed a remarkable faculty of recuperation from the effects of drink, had waked from his sleep, and remembering his engagement, had exerted himself to overcome the ravages of the afternoon's debauch. A dash of cold water braced him up somewhat. A bottle of seltzer and a big cup of strong coffee still further strengthened his nerves.

When Ellis returned to the veranda, after having taken away the plates, Delamere had joined the ladies and was explaining the cause of his absence.

He had been overcome by the heat, he said, while out fishing, and had been lying down ever since. Perhaps he ought to have sent for a doctor, but the fellows had looked after him. He had n't sent word to his friends because he had n't wished to spoil their evening.

"That was very considerate of you, Tom," said Mrs. Carteret dryly, "but you ought to have let us know. We have been worrying about you very much. Clara has found the evening dreadfully dull."

"Indeed, no, sister Olivia," said the young lady cheerfully,

"I've been having a lovely time. Mr. Ellis and I have been up in the parlor; I played the piano; and we've been eating oysters and having a most delightful time. Won't you take me down there to the beach, Mr. Ellis? I want to see the fires. Come on."

"Can't I go?" asked Tom jealously.

"No, indeed, you must n't stir a foot! You must not overtax yourself so soon; it might do you serious injury. Stay here with sister Olivia."

She took Ellis's arm with exaggerated cordiality. Delamere glared after them angrily. Ellis did not stop to question her motives, but took the goods the gods provided. With no very great apparent effort, Miss Pemberton became quite friendly, and they strolled along the beach, in sight of the hotel, for nearly half an hour. As they were coming up she asked him abruptly,—

"Mr. Ellis, did you know Tom was in the hotel?"

Ellis was looking across the sound, at the lights of a distant steamer which was making her way toward the harbor.

"I wonder," he said musingly, as though he had not heard her question, "if that is the Ocean Belle?"

"And was he really sick?" she demanded.

"She's later than usual this trip," continued Ellis, pursuing his thought. "She was due about five o'clock."

Miss Pemberton, under cover of the darkness, smiled a fine smile, which foreboded ill for some one. When they joined the party on the piazza, the major had come up and was saying that it was time to go. He had been engaged in conversation, for most of the evening, with General Belmont and several other gentlemen.

"Here comes the general now. Let me see. There are five of us. The general has offered me a seat in his buggy, and Tom can go with you-all."

The general came up and spoke to the ladies. Tom murmured his thanks; it would enable him to make up a part of the delightful evening he had missed.

When Mrs. Carteret had taken the rear seat, Clara promptly took the place beside her. Ellis and Delamere sat in front. When Delamere, who had offered to drive, took the reins, Ellis saw that his hands were shaking.

"Give me the lines," he whispered. "Your nerves are unsteady and the road is not well lighted."

Delamere prudently yielded the reins. He did not like Ellis's tone, which seemed sneering rather than expressive of sympathy with one who had been suffering. He wondered if the beggar knew anything about his illness. Clara had been acting strangely. It would have been just like Ellis to have slandered him. The upstart had no business with Clara anyway. He would cheerfully have strangled Ellis, if he could have done so with safety to himself and no chance of discovery.

The drive homeward through the night was almost a silent journey. Mrs. Carteret was anxious about her baby. Clara did not speak, except now and then to Ellis with reference to some object in or near the road. Occasionally they passed a vehicle in the darkness, sometimes barely avoiding a collision. Far to the north the sky was lit up with the glow of a forest fire. The breeze from the Sound was deliciously cool. Soon the last tollgate was passed and the lights of the town appeared.

Ellis threw the lines to William, who was waiting, and hastened to help the ladies out.

"Good-night, Mr. Ellis," said Clara sweetly, as she gave Ellis her hand. "Thank you for a very pleasant evening. Come up and see us soon."

She ran into the house without a word to Tom.

XVII

THE SOCIAL ASPIRATIONS
OF CAPTAIN MCBANE

It was only eleven o'clock, and Delamere, not being at all sleepy, and feeling somewhat out of sorts as the combined results of his afternoon's debauch and the snubbing he had received at Clara's hands, directed the major's coachman, who had taken charge of the trap upon its arrival, to drive him to the St. James Hotel before returning the horses to the stable. First, however, the coachman left Ellis at his boarding-house, which was near by. The two young men parted with as scant courtesy as was possible without an open rupture.

Delamere hoped to find at the hotel some form of distraction to fill in an hour or two before going home. Ill fortune favored him by placing in his way the burly form of Captain George McBane, who was sitting in an armchair alone, smoking a midnight cigar, under the hotel balcony. Upon Delamere's making known his desire for amusement, the captain proposed a small game of poker in his own room.

McBane had been waiting for some such convenient opportunity. We have already seen that the captain was desirous of social recognition, which he had not yet obtained beyond the superficial acquaintance acquired by association with men about town. He had determined to assault society in its citadel by seeking membership in the Clarendon Club, of which most gentlemen of the best families of the city were members.

The Clarendon Club was a historic institution, and its membership a social cult, the temple of which was located just off the main street of the city, in a dignified old colonial mansion which had housed it for the nearly one hundred years during which it had maintained its existence unbroken. There had grown up around it many traditions and special usages. Membership in the Clarendon was the *sine qua non* of high social standing, and was conditional upon two of three things,—birth, wealth, and breeding. Breeding was the prime essential, but, with rare exceptions, must be backed by either birth or money.

Having decided, therefore, to seek admission into this social arcanum, the captain, who had either not quite appreciated the standard of the Clarendon's membership, or had failed to see that he fell beneath it, looked about for an intermediary through whom to approach the object of his desire. He had already thought of Tom Delamere in this connection, having with him such an acquaintance as one forms around a hotel, and having long ago discovered that Delamere was a young man of superficially amiable disposition, vicious instincts, lax principles, and a weak will, and, which was quite as much to the purpose, a member of the Clarendon Club. Possessing mental characteristics almost entirely opposite, Delamere and the captain had certain tastes in common, and had smoked, drunk, and played cards together more than once.

Still more to his purpose, McBane had detected Delamere trying to cheat him at cards. He had said nothing about this discovery, but had merely noted it as something which at some future time might prove useful. The captain had not suffered by Delamere's deviation from the straight line of honor, for while Tom was as clever with the cards as might be expected of a young man who had devoted most of his leisure for several years to handling them, McBane was past master in their manipulation. During a stormy career he had touched more or less pitch, and had escaped few sorts of defilement.

The appearance of Delamere at a late hour, unaccompanied, and wearing upon his countenance an expression in which the captain read aright the craving for mental and physical excitement, gave him the opportunity for which he had been looking. McBane was not the man to lose an opportunity, nor did Delamere require a second invitation. Neither was it necessary, during the progress of the game, for the captain to press upon his guest the contents of the decanter which stood upon the table within convenient reach.

The captain permitted Delamere to win from him several small amounts, after which he gradually increased the stakes and turned the tables.

Delamere, with every instinct of a gamester, was no more a match for McBane in self-control than in skill. When the young man had lost all his money, the captain expressed his entire willingness to accept notes of hand, for which he happened to have convenient blanks in his apartment.

When Delamere, flushed with excitement and wine, rose from the gaming table at two o'clock, he was vaguely conscious that he owed McBane a considerable sum, but could not have stated how much. His opponent, who was entirely cool and collected, ran his eye carelessly over the bits of paper to which Delamere had attached his signature.

"Just one thousand dollars even," he remarked.

The announcement of this total had as sobering an effect upon Delamere as though he had been suddenly deluged with a shower of cold water. For a moment he caught his breath. He had not a dollar in the world with which to pay this sum. His only source of income was an allowance from his grandfather, the monthly installment of which, drawn that very day, he had just lost to McBane, before starting in upon the notes of hand.

"I 'll give you your revenge another time," said McBane, as they rose. "Luck is against you to-night, and I 'm unwilling to take advantage of a clever young fellow like you. Meantime," he added, tossing the notes of hand carelessly on a bureau, "don't worry about these bits of paper. Such small matters should n't cut any figure between friends; but if you are around the hotel to-morrow, I should like to speak to you upon another subject."

"Very well, captain," returned Tom somewhat ungraciously.

Delamere had been completely beaten with his own weapons. He had tried desperately to cheat McBane. He knew perfectly well that McBane had discovered his efforts and had cheated him in turn, for the captain's play had clearly been gauged to meet his own. The biter had been bit, and could not complain of the outcome.

The following afternoon McBane met Delamere at the hotel, and bluntly requested the latter to propose him for membership in the Clarendon Club.

Delamere was annoyed at this request. His aristocratic gorge rose at the presumption of this son of an overseer and ex-driver of convicts. McBane was good enough to win money from, or even to lose money to, but not good enough to be recognized as a social equal. He would instinctively have blackballed McBane had he been proposed by some one else; with what grace could he put himself forward as the sponsor for this impossible social aspirant? Moreover, it was clearly a vulgar, cold-blooded attempt on McBane's part to use his power over him for a personal advantage.

"Well, now, Captain McBane," returned Delamere diplomatically, "I 've never put any one up yet, and it 's not regarded as good form for so young a member as myself to propose candidates. I 'd much rather you'd ask some older man."

"Oh, well," replied McBane, "just as you say, only I thought you had cut your eye teeth."

Delamere was not pleased with McBane's tone. His remark was not acquiescent, though couched in terms of assent. There was a sneering savagery about it, too, that left Delamere uneasy. He was, in a measure, in McBane's power. He could not pay the thousand dollars, unless it fell from heaven, or he could win it from some one else. He would not dare go to his grandfather for help. Mr. Delamere did not even know that his grandson gambled. He might not have objected, perhaps, to a gentleman's game, with moderate stakes, but he would certainly, Tom knew very well, have looked upon a thousand dollars as a preposterous sum to be lost at cards by a man who had nothing with which to pay it. It was part of Mr. Delamere's creed that a gentleman should not make debts that he was not reasonably able to pay.

There was still another difficulty. If he had lost the money to a gentleman, and it had been his first serious departure from Mr. Delamere's perfectly well understood standard of honor, Tom might have risked a confession and thrown himself on his grandfather's mercy; but he owed other sums here and there, which, to his just now much disturbed imagination, loomed up in alarming number and amount. He had recently observed signs of coldness, too, on the part of certain members of the club. Moreover, like most men with one commanding vice, he was addicted to several subsidiary forms of iniquity, which in case of a scandal were more than likely to come to light. He was clearly and most disagreeably caught in the net of his own hypocrisy. His grandfather believed him a model of integrity, a pattern of honor; he could not afford to have his grandfather undeceived.

He thought of old Mrs. Ochiltree. If she were a liberal soul, she could give him a thousand dollars now, when he needed it, instead of making him wait until she died, which might not be for ten years or more, for a legacy which was steadily growing less and might be entirely exhausted if she lived long enough,—some old people were very tenacious of life! She was a careless old woman, too, he reflected, and very foolishly kept her money in the house. Latterly she had been growing weak and childish. Some day she might be robbed, and then his prospective inheritance from that source would vanish into thin air!

With regard to this debt to McBane, if he could not pay it, he could at least gain a long respite by proposing the captain at the club. True, he would undoubtedly be blackballed, but before this inevitable event his name must remain posted for several weeks, during which interval McBane would be conciliatory. On the other hand, to propose McBane would arouse suspicion of his own motives; it might reach his grandfather's ears, and lead to a demand for an explanation, which it would be difficult to make. Clearly, the better plan would be to temporize with McBane, with the hope that something might intervene to remove this cursed obligation.

"Suppose, captain," he said affably, "we leave the matter open for a few days. This is a thing that can't be rushed. I 'll feel the pulse of my friends and yours, and when we get the lay of the land, the affair can be accomplished much more easily."

"Well, that 's better," returned McBane, somewhat mollified,—"*if* you 'll do that."

"To be sure I will," replied Tom easily, too much relieved to resent, if not too preoccupied to perceive, the implied doubt of his veracity.

McBane ordered and paid for more drinks, and they parted on amicable terms.

"We 'll let these notes stand for the time being, Tom," said McBane, with significant emphasis, when they separated.

Delamere winced at the familiarity. He had reached that degree of moral deterioration where, while principles were of little moment, the externals of social intercourse possessed an exaggerated importance. McBane had never before been so personal. He had addressed the young aristocrat first as "Mr. Delamere," then, as their acquaintance advanced, as "Delamere." He had now reached the abbreviated Christian name stage of familiarity. There was no lower depth to which Tom could sink, unless McBane should invent a nickname by which to address him.

He did not like McBane's manner,—it was characterized by a veiled insolence which was exceedingly offensive. He would go over to the club and try his luck with some honest player,—perhaps something might turn up to relieve him from his embarrassment.

He put his hand in his pocket mechanically,—and found it empty! In the present state of his credit, he could hardly play without money.

A thought struck him. Leaving the hotel, he hastened home, where he found Sandy dusting his famous suit of clothes on the back piazza. Mr. Delamere was not at home, having departed for Belleview about two o'clock, leaving Sandy to follow him in the morning.

"Hello, Sandy," exclaimed Tom, with an assumed jocularity which he was very far from feeling, "what are you doing with those gorgeous garments?"

"I 'm a-dustin' of 'em, Mistuh Tom, dat 's w'at I 'm a-doin'. Dere 's somethin' wrong 'bout dese clo's er mine—I don' never seem ter be able ter keep 'em clean no mo'. Ef I b'lieved in dem ole-timey sayin's, I 'd 'low dere wuz a witch come here eve'y night an' tuk 'em out an' wo' 'em, er tuk me out an' rid me in 'em. Dere wuz somethin' wrong 'bout dat cakewalk business, too, dat I ain' never unde'stood an' don' know how ter 'count fer, 'less dere wuz some kin' er dev'lishness goin' on dat don' show on de su'face."

"Sandy," asked Tom irrelevantly, "have you any money in the house?"

"Yas, suh, I got de money Mars John give me ter git dem things ter take out ter Belleview in de mawnin'."

"I mean money of your own."

"I got a qua'ter ter buy terbacker wid," returned Sandy cautiously.

"Is that all? Have n't you some saved up?"

"Well, yas, Mistuh Tom," returned Sandy, with evident reluctance, "dere 's a few dollahs put away in my bureau drawer fer a rainy day,—not much, suh."

"I 'm a little short this afternoon, Sandy, and need some money right away. Grandfather is n't here, so I can't get any from him. Let me take what you have for a day or two, Sandy, and I 'll return it with good interest."

"Now, Mistuh Tom," said Sandy seriously, "I don' min' let-tin' you take my money, but I hopes you ain' gwine ter use it fer none er dem rakehelly gwines-on er yo'n,—gamblin' an' bettin' an' so fo'th. Yo' grandaddy 'll fin' out 'bout you yit, ef you don' min' yo' P's an' Q's. I does my bes' ter keep yo' misdoin's f'm 'im, an' sense I b'en tu'ned out er de chu'ch—thoo no fault er my own, God knows!—I 've tol' lies 'nuff 'bout you ter sink a ship. But it ain't right, Mistuh Tom, it ain't right! an' I only does it fer de sake er de fam'ly honuh, dat Mars John sets so much sto' by, an' ter save his feelin's; fer de doctuh says he mus' n' git ixcited 'bout nothin', er it mought bring on another stroke."

"That 's right, Sandy," replied Tom approvingly; "but the family honor is as safe in my hands as in grandfather's own, and I 'm going to use the money for an excellent purpose, in fact to relieve a case of genuine distress; and I 'll hand it back to you in a day or two,—perhaps to-morrow. Fetch me the money, Sandy,—that's a good darky!"

"All right, Mistuh Tom, you shill have de money; but I wants ter tell you, suh, dat in all de yeahs I has wo'ked fer yo' gran'-daddy, he has never called me a 'darky' ter my face, suh. Co'se I knows dere 's w'ite folks an' black folks,—but dere 's man-ners, suh, dere 's manners, an' gent'emen oughter be de ones ter use 'em, suh, ef dey ain't ter be fergot enti'ely!"

"There, there, Sandy," returned Tom in a conciliatory tone, "I beg your pardon! I 've been associating with some Northern white folks at the hotel, and picked up the word from them. You 're a high-toned colored gentleman, Sandy,—the finest one on the footstool."

Still muttering to himself, Sandy retired to his own room, which was in the house, so that he might be always near his master. He soon returned with a time-stained leather pocket-book and a coarse-knit cotton sock, from which two recepta-cles he painfully extracted a number of bills and coins.

"You count dat, Mistuh Tom, so I 'll know how much I 'm lettin' you have."

"This is n't worth anything," said Tom, pushing aside one roll of bills. "It 's Confederate money."

"So it is, suh. It ain't wuth nothin' now; but it has be'n money, an' who kin tell but what it mought be money agin? De rest er dem bills is greenbacks,—dey 'll pass all right, I reckon."

The good money amounted to about fifty dollars, which Delamere thrust eagerly into his pocket.

"You won't say anything to grandfather about this, will you, Sandy," he said, as he turned away.

"No, suh, co'se I won't! Does I ever tell 'im 'bout yo' gwines-on? Ef I did," he added to himself, as the young man disappeared down the street, "I would n' have time ter do nothin' e'se ha'dly. I don' know whether I 'll ever see dat money agin er no, do' I 'magine de ole gent'eman would n' lemme lose it ef he knowed. But I ain' gwine ter tell him, whether I git my money back er no, fer he is jes' so wrop' up in dat boy dat I b'lieve it 'd jes' break his hea't ter fin' out how he 's be'n gwine on. Doctuh Price has tol' me not ter let de ole gent'eman git ixcited, er e'se dere 's no tellin' w'at mought happen. He 's be'n good ter me, he has, an' I 'm gwine ter take keer er him,—dat 's w'at I is, ez long ez I has de chance."

Delamere went directly to the club, and soon lounged into the card-room, where several of the members were engaged in play. He sauntered here and there, too much absorbed in his own thoughts to notice that the greetings he received were less cordial than those usually exchanged between the members of a small and select social club. Finally, when Augustus, commonly and more appropriately called "Gus," Davidson came into the room, Tom stepped toward him.

"Will you take a hand in a game, Gus?"

"Don't care if I do," said the other. "Let 's sit over here."

Davidson led the way to a table near the fireplace, near which stood a tall screen, which at times occupied various places in the room. Davidson took the seat opposite the fireplace, leaving Delamere with his back to the screen.

Delamere staked half of Sandy's money, and lost. He staked the rest, and determined to win, because he could not afford to lose. He had just reached out his hand to gather in the stakes, when he was charged with cheating at cards, of which two members, who had quietly entered the room and posted themselves behind the screen, had secured specific proof.

A meeting of the membership committee was hastily summoned, it being an hour at which most of them might be found at the club. To avoid a scandal, and to save the feelings of a prominent family, Delamere was given an opportunity to resign quietly from the club, on condition that he paid all his gambling debts within three days, and took an oath never to play cards again for money. This latter condition was made at the suggestion of an elderly member, who apparently believed that a man who would cheat at cards would stick at perjury.

Delamere acquiesced very promptly. The taking of the oath was easy. The payment of some fifteen hundred dollars of debts was a different matter. He went away from the club thoughtfully, and it may be said, in full justice to a past which was far from immaculate, that in his present thoughts he touched a depth of scoundrelism far beyond anything of which he had as yet deemed himself capable. When a man of good position, of whom much is expected, takes to evil courses, his progress is apt to resemble that of a well-bred woman who has started on the downward path,—the pace is all the swifter because of the distance which must be traversed to reach the bottom. Delamere had made rapid headway; having hitherto played with sin, his servant had now become his master, and held him in an iron grip.

XVIII

SANDY SEES HIS OWN HA'NT

Having finished cleaning his clothes, Sandy went out to the kitchen for supper, after which he found himself with nothing to do. Mr. Delamere's absence relieved him from attendance at the house during the evening. He might have smoked his pipe tranquilly in the kitchen until bedtime, had not the cook intimated, rather pointedly, that she expected other company. To a man of Sandy's tact a word was sufficient, and he resigned himself to seeking companionship elsewhere.

Under normal circumstances, Sandy would have attended prayer-meeting on this particular evening of the week; but being still in contumacy, and cherishing what he considered the just resentment of a man falsely accused, he stifled the inclination which by long habit led him toward the church, and set out for the house of a friend with whom it occurred to him that he might spend the evening pleasantly. Unfortunately, his friend proved to be not at home, so Sandy turned his footsteps toward the lower part of the town, where the streets were well lighted, and on pleasant evenings quite animated. On the way he met Josh Green, whom he had known for many years, though their paths did not often cross. In his loneliness Sandy accepted an invitation to go with Josh and have a drink,—a single drink.

When Sandy was going home about eleven o'clock, three sheets in the wind, such was the potent effect of the single drink and those which had followed it, he was scared almost into soberness by a remarkable apparition. As it seemed to Sandy, he saw himself hurrying along in front of himself toward the house. Possibly the muddled condition of Sandy's intellect had so affected his judgment as to vitiate any conclusion he might draw, but Sandy was quite sober enough to perceive that the figure ahead of him wore his best clothes and looked exactly like him, but seemed to be in something more of a hurry, a discrepancy which Sandy at once corrected by quickening his own pace so as to maintain as nearly as possible an equal distance between himself and his double. The situation was certainly an incomprehensible one, and savored of the supernatural.

"Ef dat 's me gwine 'long in front," mused Sandy, in vinous perplexity, "den who is dis behin' here? Dere ain' but one er me, an' my ha'nt would n' leave my body 'tel I wuz dead. Ef dat's me in front, den I mus' be my own ha'nt; an' whichever one of us is de ha'nt, de yuther must be dead an' don' know it. I don' know what ter make er no sech gwines-on, I don't. Maybe it ain' me after all, but it certainly do look lack me."

When the apparition disappeared in the house by the side door, Sandy stood in the yard for several minutes, under the shade of an elm-tree, before he could make up his mind to enter the house. He took courage, however, upon the reflection that perhaps, after all, it was only the bad liquor he had drunk. Bad liquor often made people see double.

He entered the house. It was dark, except for a light in Tom Delamere's room. Sandy tapped softly at the door.

"Who 's there?" came Delamere's voice, in a somewhat startled tone, after a momentary silence.

"It 's me, suh; Sandy."

They both spoke softly. It was the rule of the house when Mr. Delamere had retired, and though he was not at home, habit held its wonted sway.

"Just a moment, Sandy."

Sandy waited patiently in the hall until the door was opened. If the room showed any signs of haste or disorder, Sandy was too full of his own thoughts—and other things—to notice them.

"What do you want, Sandy," asked Tom.

"Mistuh Tom," asked Sandy solemnly, "ef I wuz in yo' place, an' you wuz in my place, an' we wuz bofe in de same place, whar would I be?"

Tom looked at Sandy keenly, with a touch of apprehension. Did Sandy mean anything in particular by this enigmatical inquiry, and if so, what? But Sandy's face clearly indicated a state of mind in which consecutive thought was improbable; and after a brief glance Delamere breathed more freely.

"I give it up, Sandy," he responded lightly. "That's too deep for me."

"'Scuse me, Mistuh Tom, but is you heared er seed anybody er anything come in de house fer de las' ten minutes?"

"Why, no, Sandy, I have n't heard any one. I came from the club an hour ago. I had forgotten my key, and Sally got up and let me in, and then went back to bed. I 've been sitting here reading ever since. I should have heard any one who came in."

"Mistuh Tom," inquired Sandy anxiously, "would you 'low dat I 'd be'n drinkin' too much?"

"No, Sandy, I should say you were sober enough, though of course you may have had a few drinks. Perhaps you 'd like another? I've got something good here."

"No, suh, Mistuh Tom, no, suh! No mo' liquor fer me, suh, never! When liquor kin make a man see his own ha'nt, it 's 'bout time fer dat man ter quit drinkin', it sho' is! Good-night, Mistuh Tom."

As Sandy turned to go, Delamere was struck by a sudden and daring thought. The creature of impulse, he acted upon it immediately.

"By the way, Sandy," he exclaimed carelessly, "I can pay you back that money you were good enough to lend me this afternoon. I think I 'll sleep better if I have the debt off my mind, and I should n't wonder if you would. You don't mind having it in gold, do you?"

"No, indeed, suh," replied Sandy. "I ain' seen no gol' fer so long dat de sight er it 'd be good fer my eyes."

Tom counted out ten five-dollar gold pieces upon the table at his elbow.

"And here's another, Sandy," he said, adding an eleventh, "as interest for the use of it."

"Thank y', Mistuh Tom. I did n't spec' no intrus', but I don' never 'fuse gol' w'en I kin git it."

"And here," added Delamere, reaching carelessly into a bureau drawer, "is a little old silk purse that I 've had since I was a boy. I'll put the gold in it, Sandy; it will hold it very nicely."

"Thank y', Mistuh Tom. You 're a gentleman, suh, an' wo'thy er de fam'ly name. Good-night, suh, an' I hope yo' dreams 'll be pleasanter 'n' mine. Ef it wa'n't fer dis gol' kinder takin' my min' off'n dat han't, I don' s'pose I 'd be able to do much sleepin' ter-night. Good-night, suh."

"Good-night, Sandy."

Whether or not Delamere slept soundly, or was troubled by dreams, pleasant or unpleasant, it is nevertheless true that he locked his door, and sat up an hour later, looking through the drawers of his bureau, and burning several articles in the little iron stove which constituted part of the bedroom furniture.

It is also true that he rose very early, before the household was stirring. The cook slept in a room off the kitchen, which was in an outhouse in the back yard. She was just stretching herself, preparatory to getting up, when Tom came to her window and said that he was going off fishing, to be gone all day, and that he would not wait for breakfast.

XIX

A MIDNIGHT WALK

Ellis left the office of the Morning Chronicle about eleven o'clock the same evening and set out to walk home. His boarding-house was only a short distance beyond old Mr. Delamere's residence, and while he might have saved time and labor by a slightly shorter route, he generally selected this one because it led also by Major Carteret's house. Sometimes there would be a ray of light from Clara's room, which was on one of the front corners; and at any rate he would have the pleasure of gazing at the outside of the casket that enshrined the jewel of his heart. It was true that this purely sentimental pleasure was sometimes dashed with bitterness at the thought of his rival; but one in love must take the bitter with the sweet, and who would say that a spice of jealousy does not add a certain zest to love? On this particular evening, however, he was in a hopeful mood. At the Clarendon Club, where he had gone, a couple of hours before, to verify a certain news item for the morning paper, he had heard a story about Tom Delamere which, he imagined, would spike that gentleman's guns for all time, so far as Miss Pemberton was concerned. So grave an affair as cheating at cards could never be kept secret,—it was certain to reach her ears; and Ellis was morally certain that Clara would never marry a man who had been proved dishonorable. In all probability there would be no great sensation about the matter. Delamere was too well connected; too many prominent people would be involved,—even Clara, and the editor himself, of whom Delamere was a distant cousin. The reputation of the club was also to be considered. Ellis was not the man to feel a malicious delight in the misfortunes of another, nor was he a pessimist who welcomed scandal and disgrace with open arms, as confirming a gloomy theory of human life. But, with the best intentions in the world, it was no more than human nature that he should

feel a certain elation in the thought that his rival had been practically disposed of, and the field left clear; especially since this
good situation had been brought about merely by the unmasking of a hypocrite, who had held him at an unfair disadvantage
in the race for Clara's favor.

The night was quiet, except for the faint sound of distant
music now and then, or the mellow laughter of some group of
revelers. Ellis met but few pedestrians, but as he neared old Mr.
Delamere's, he saw two men walking in the same direction as
his own, on the opposite side of the street. He had observed
that they kept at about an equal distance apart, and that the
second, from the stealthy manner in which he was making his
way, was anxious to keep the first in sight, without disclosing
his own presence. This aroused Ellis's curiosity, which was satisfied in some degree when the man in advance stopped beneath a lamp-post and stood for a moment looking across the
street, with his face plainly visible in the yellow circle of light.
It was a dark face, and Ellis recognized it instantly as that of
old Mr. Delamere's body servant, whose personal appearance
had been very vividly impressed upon Ellis at the christening
dinner at Major Carteret's. He had seen Sandy once since, too,
at the hotel cakewalk. The negro had a small bundle in his
hand, the nature of which Ellis could not make out.

When Sandy had stopped beneath the lamp-post, the man
who was following him had dodged behind a tree-trunk. When
Sandy moved on, Ellis, who had stopped in turn, saw the man
in hiding come out and follow Sandy. When this second man
came in range of the light, Ellis wondered that there should be
two men so much alike. The first of the two had undoubtedly
been Sandy. Ellis had recognized the peculiar, old-fashioned
coat that Sandy had worn upon the two occasions when he had
noticed him. Barring this difference, and the somewhat unsteady gait of the second man, the two were as much alike as
twin brothers.

When they had entered Mr. Delamere's house, one after the
other,—in the stillness of the night Ellis could perceive that
each of them tried to make as little noise as possible,—Ellis
supposed that they were probably relatives, both employed

as servants, or that some younger negro, taking Sandy for a model, was trying to pattern himself after his superior. Why all this mystery, of course he could not imagine, unless the younger man had been out without permission and was trying to avoid the accusing eye of Sandy. Ellis was vaguely conscious that he had seen the other negro somewhere, but he could not for the moment place him,—there were so many negroes, nearly three negroes to one white man in the city of Wellington!

The subject, however, while curious, was not important as compared with the thoughts of his sweetheart which drove it from his mind. Clara had been kind to him the night before,—whatever her motive, she had been kind, and could not consistently return to her attitude of coldness. With Delamere hopelessly discredited, Ellis hoped to have at least fair play,—with fair play, he would take his chances of the outcome.

XX

A SHOCKING CRIME

On Friday morning, when old Mrs. Ochiltree's cook Dinah went to wake her mistress, she was confronted with a sight that well-nigh blanched her ebony cheek and caused her eyes almost to start from her head with horror. As soon as she could command her trembling limbs sufficiently to make them carry her, she rushed out of the house and down the street, bareheaded, covering in an incredibly short time the few blocks that separated Mrs. Ochiltree's residence from that of her niece.

She hastened around the house, and finding the back door open and the servants stirring, ran into the house and up the stairs with the familiarity of an old servant, not stopping until she reached the door of Mrs. Carteret's chamber, at which she knocked in great agitation.

Entering in response to Mrs. Carteret's invitation, she found the lady, dressed in a simple wrapper, superintending the morning toilet of little Dodie, who was a wakeful child, and insisted upon rising with the birds, for whose music he still showed a great fondness, in spite of his narrow escape while listening to the mockingbird.

"What is it, Dinah?" asked Mrs. Delamere, alarmed at the frightened face of her aunt's old servitor.

"O my Lawd, Mis' 'Livy, my Lawd, my Lawd! My legs is trim'lin' so dat I can't ha'dly hol' my han's stiddy 'nough ter say w'at I got ter say! O Lawd have mussy on us po' sinners! W'atever is gwine ter happen in dis worl' er sin an' sorrer!"

"What in the world is the matter, Dinah?" demanded Mrs. Carteret, whose own excitement had increased with the length of this preamble. "Has anything happened to Aunt Polly?"

"Somebody done broke in de house las' night, Mis' 'Livy, an' kill' Mis' Polly, an' lef' her layin' dead on de flo', in her own blood, wid her cedar chis' broke' open, an' eve'thing scattered roun' de flo'! O my Lawd, my Lawd, my Lawd, my Lawd!"

Mrs. Carteret was shocked beyond expression. Perhaps the spectacle of Dinah's unrestrained terror aided her to retain a greater measure of self-control than she might otherwise have been capable of. Giving the nurse some directions in regard to the child, she hastily descended the stairs, and seizing a hat and jacket from the rack in the hall, ran immediately with Dinah to the scene of the tragedy. Before the thought of this violent death all her aunt's faults faded into insignificance, and only her good qualities were remembered. She had reared Olivia; she had stood up for the memory of Olivia's mother when others had seemed to forget what was due to it. To her niece she had been a second mother, and had never been lacking in affection.

More than one motive, however, lent wings to Mrs. Carteret's feet. Her aunt's incomplete disclosures on the day of the drive past the hospital had been weighing upon Mrs. Carteret's mind, and she had intended to make another effort this very day, to get an answer to her question about the papers which the woman had claimed were in existence. Suppose her aunt had really found such papers,—papers which would seem to prove the preposterous claim made by her father's mulatto mistress? Suppose that, with the fatuity which generally leads human beings to keep compromising documents, her aunt had preserved these papers? If they should be found there in the house, there might be a scandal, if nothing worse, and this was to be avoided at all hazards.

Guided by some fortunate instinct, Dinah had as yet informed no one but Mrs. Carteret of her discovery. If they could reach the house before the murder became known to any third person, she might be the first to secure access to the remaining contents of the cedar chest, which would be likely to be held as evidence in case the officers of the law forestalled her own arrival.

They found the house wrapped in the silence of death. Mrs. Carteret entered the chamber of the dead woman. Upon the floor, where it had fallen, lay the body in a pool of blood, the strongly marked countenance scarcely more grim in the rigidity of death than it had been in life. A gaping wound in the head accounted easily for the death. The cedar chest stood open, its strong fastenings having been broken by a steel bar which still lay beside it. Near it were scattered pieces of old lace, antiquated jewelry, tarnished silverware,—the various mute souvenirs of the joys and sorrows of a long and active life.

Kneeling by the open chest, Mrs. Carteret glanced hurriedly through its contents. There were no papers there except a few old deeds and letters. She had risen with a sigh of relief, when she perceived the end of a paper projecting from beneath the edge of a rug which had been carelessly rumpled, probably by the burglar in his hasty search for plunder. This paper, or sealed envelope as it proved to be, which evidently contained some inclosure, she seized, and at the sound of approaching footsteps thrust hastily into her own bosom.

The sight of two agitated women rushing through the quiet streets at so early an hour in the morning had attracted attention and aroused curiosity, and the story of the murder, having once become known, spread with the customary rapidity of bad news. Very soon a policeman, and a little later a sheriff's officer, arrived at the house and took charge of the remains to await the arrival of the coroner.

By nine o'clock a coroner's jury had been summoned, who, after brief deliberation, returned a verdict of willful murder at the hands of some person or persons unknown, while engaged in the commission of a burglary.

No sooner was the verdict announced than the community, or at least the white third of it, resolved itself spontaneously into a committee of the whole to discover the perpetrator of this dastardly crime, which, at this stage of the affair, seemed merely one of robbery and murder.

Suspicion was at once directed toward the negroes, as it always is when an unexplained crime is committed in a Southern community. The suspicion was not entirely an illogical one. Having been, for generations, trained up to thriftlessness, theft, and immorality, against which only thirty years of very limited opportunity can be offset, during which brief period they have been denied in large measure the healthful social stimulus and sympathy which holds most men in the path of rectitude, colored people might reasonably be expected to commit at least a share of crime proportionate to their numbers. The population of the town was at least two thirds colored. The chances were, therefore, in the absence of evidence, at least two to one that a man of color had committed the crime. The Southern tendency to charge the negroes with all the crime and immorality of that region, unjust and exaggerated as the claim may be, was therefore not without a logical basis to the extent above indicated.

It must not be imagined that any logic was needed, or any reasoning consciously worked out. The mere suggestion that the crime had been committed by a negro was equivalent to proof against any negro that might be suspected and could not prove his innocence. A committee of white men was hastily formed. Acting independently of the police force, which was practically ignored as likely to favor the negroes, this committee set to work to discover the murderer.

The spontaneous activity of the whites was accompanied by a visible shrinkage of the colored population. This could not be taken as any indication of guilt, but was merely a recognition of the palpable fact that the American habit of lynching had so whetted the thirst for black blood that a negro suspected of crime had to face at least the possibility of a short shrift and a long rope, not to mention more gruesome horrors, without the intervention of judge or jury. Since to have a black face at such a time was to challenge suspicion, and since there was neither the martyr's glory nor the saint's renown in being killed for some one else's crime, and very little hope of successful resistance in case of an attempt at lynching, it was obviously the part of prudence for those thus marked to seek immunity in a temporary disappearance from public view.

XXI

THE NECESSITY OF AN EXAMPLE

About ten o'clock on the morning of the discovery of the murder, Captain McBane and General Belmont, as though moved by a common impulse, found themselves at the office of the Morning Chronicle. Carteret was expecting them, though there had been no appointment made. These three resourceful and energetic minds, representing no organized body, and clothed with no legal authority, had so completely arrogated to themselves the leadership of white public sentiment as to come together instinctively when an event happened which concerned the public, and, as this murder presumably did, involved the matter of race.

"Well, gentlemen," demanded McBane impatiently, "what are we going to do with the scoundrel when we catch him?"

"They 've got the murderer," announced a reporter, entering the room.

"Who is he?" they demanded in a breath.

"A nigger by the name of Sandy Campbell, a servant of old Mr. Delamere."

"How did they catch him?"

"Our Jerry saw him last night, going toward Mrs. Ochiltree's house, and a white man saw him coming away, half an hour later."

"Has he confessed?"

"No, but he might as well. When the posse went to arrest him, they found him cleaning the clothes he had worn last night, and discovered in his room a part of the plunder. He denies it strenuously, but it seems a clear case."

"There can be no doubt," said Ellis, who had come into the room behind the reporter. "I saw the negro last night, at twelve o'clock, going into Mr. Delamere's yard, with a bundle in his hand."

"He is the last negro I should have suspected," said Carteret. "Mr. Delamere had implicit confidence in him."

"All niggers are alike," remarked McBane sententiously. "The only way to keep them from stealing is not to give them the chance. A nigger will steal a cent off a dead man's eye. He has assaulted and murdered a white woman,—an example should be made of him."

Carteret recalled very distinctly the presence of this negro at his own residence on the occasion of little Theodore's christening dinner. He remembered having questioned the prudence of letting a servant know that Mrs. Ochiltree kept money in the house. Mr. Delamere had insisted strenuously upon the honesty of this particular negro. The whole race, in the major's opinion, was morally undeveloped, and only held within bounds by the restraining influence of the white people. Under Mr. Delamere's thumb this Sandy had been a model servant,—faithful, docile, respectful, and self-respecting; but Mr. Delamere had grown old, and had probably lost in a measure his moral influence over his servant. Left to his own degraded ancestral instincts, Sandy had begun to deteriorate, and a rapid decline had culminated in this robbery and murder,—and who knew what other horror? The criminal was a negro, the victim a white woman;—it was only reasonable to expect the worst.

"He 'll swing for it," observed the general.

Ellis went into another room, where his duty called him.

"He should burn for it," averred McBane. "I say, burn the nigger."

"This," said Carteret, "is something more than an ordinary crime, to be dealt with by the ordinary processes of law. It is a murderous and fatal assault upon a woman of our race,— upon our race in the person of its womanhood, its crown and flower. If such crimes are not punished with swift and terrible directness, the whole white womanhood of the South is in danger."

"Burn the nigger," repeated McBane automatically.

"Neither is this a mere sporadic crime," Carteret went on. "It is symptomatic; it is the logical and inevitable result of the conditions which have prevailed in this town for the past year. It is the last straw."

"Burn the nigger," reiterated McBane. "We seem to have the right nigger, but whether we have or not, burn *a* nigger. It is an assault upon the white race, in the person of old Mrs. Ochiltree, committed by the black race, in the person of some nigger. It would justify the white people in burning *any* nigger. The example would be all the more powerful if we got the wrong one. It would serve notice on the niggers that we shall hold the whole race responsible for the misdeeds of each individual."

"In ancient Rome," said the general, "when a master was killed by a slave, all his slaves were put to the sword."

"We could n't afford that before the war," said McBane, "but the niggers don't belong to anybody now, and there 's nothing to prevent our doing as we please with them. A dead nigger is no loss to any white man. I say, burn the nigger."

"I do not believe," said Carteret, who had gone to the window and was looking out,—"I do not believe that we need trouble ourselves personally about his punishment. I should judge, from the commotion in the street, that the public will take the matter into its own hands. I, for one, would prefer that any violence, however justifiable, should take place without my active intervention."

"It won't take place without mine, if I know it," exclaimed McBane, starting for the door.

"Hold on a minute, captain," exclaimed Carteret. "There 's more at stake in this matter than the life of a black scoundrel. Wellington is in the hands of negroes and scalawags. What better time to rescue it?"

"It 's a trifle premature," replied the general. "I should have preferred to have this take place, if it was to happen, say three months hence, on the eve of the election,—but discussion always provokes thirst with me; I wonder if I could get Jerry to bring us some drinks?"

Carteret summoned the porter. Jerry's usual manner had taken on an element of self-importance, resulting in what one might describe as a sort of condescending obsequiousness. Though still a porter, he was also a hero, and wore his aureole.

"Jerry," said the general kindly, "the white people are very much pleased with the assistance you have given them in apprehending this scoundrel Campbell. You have rendered a great public service, Jerry, and we wish you to know that it is appreciated."

"Thank y', gin', thank y', suh! I alluz tries ter do my duty, suh, an' stan' by dem dat stan's by me. Dat low-down nigger oughter be lynch', suh, don't you think, er e'se bu'nt? Dere ain' nothin' too bad ter happen ter 'im."

"No doubt he will be punished as he deserves, Jerry," returned the general, "and we will see that you are suitably rewarded. Go across the street and get me three Calhoun cocktails. I seem to have nothing less than a two-dollar bill, but you may keep the change, Jerry,—all the change."

Jerry was very happy. He had distinguished himself in the public view, for to Jerry, as to the white people themselves, the white people were the public. He had won the goodwill of the best people, and had already begun to reap a tangible reward. It is true that several strange white men looked at him with lowering brows as he crossed the street, which was curiously empty of colored people; but he nevertheless went firmly forward, panoplied in the consciousness of his own rectitude, and serenely confident of the protection of the major and the major's friends.

"Jerry is about the only negro I have seen since nine o'clock," observed the general when the porter had gone. "If this were election day, where would the negro vote be?"

"In hiding, where most of the negro population is to-day," answered McBane. "It 's a pity, if old Mrs. Ochiltree had to go this way, that it could n't have been deferred a month or six weeks."

Carteret frowned at this remark, which, coming from McBane, seemed lacking in human feeling, as well as in respect to his wife's dead relative.

"But," resumed the general, "if this negro is lynched, as he well deserves to be, it will not be without its effect. We still have in reserve for the election a weapon which this affair will only render more effective. What became of the piece in the negro paper?"

"I have it here," answered Carteret. "I was just about to use it as the text for an editorial."

"Save it awhile longer," responded the general. "This crime itself will give you text enough for a four-volume work."

When this conference ended, Carteret immediately put into press an extra edition of the Morning Chronicle, which was soon upon the streets, giving details of the crime, which was characterized as an atrocious assault upon a defenseless old lady, whose age and sex would have protected her from harm at the hands of any one but a brute in the lowest human form. This event, the Chronicle suggested, had only confirmed the opinion, which had been of late growing upon the white people, that drastic efforts were necessary to protect the white women of the South against brutal, lascivious, and murderous assaults at the hands of negro men. It was only another significant example of the results which might have been foreseen from the application of a false and pernicious political theory, by which ignorance, clothed in a little brief authority, was sought to be exalted over knowledge, vice over virtue, an inferior and degraded race above the heaven-crowned Anglo-Saxon. If an outraged people, justly infuriated, and impatient of the slow processes of the courts, should assert their inherent sovereignty, which the law after all was merely intended to embody, and should choose, in obedience to the higher law, to set aside, temporarily, the ordinary judicial procedure, it would serve as a warning and an example to the vicious elements of the community, of the swift and terrible punishment which would fall, like the judgment of God, upon any one who laid sacrilegious hands upon white womanhood.

XXII

HOW NOT TO PREVENT A LYNCHING

Dr. Miller, who had sat up late the night before with a difficult case at the hospital, was roused, about eleven o'clock, from a deep and dreamless sleep. Struggling back into consciousness, he was informed by his wife, who stood by his bedside, that Mr. Watson, the colored lawyer, wished to see him upon a matter of great importance.

"Nothing but a matter of life and death would make me get up just now," he said with a portentous yawn.

"This *is* a matter of life and death," replied Janet. "Old Mrs. Polly Ochiltree was robbed and murdered last night, and Sandy Campbell has been arrested for the crime,—and they are going to lynch him!"

"Tell Watson to come right up," exclaimed Miller, springing out of bed. "We can talk while I 'm dressing."

While Miller made a hasty toilet Watson explained the situation. Campbell had been arrested on the charge of murder. He had been seen, during the night, in the neighborhood of the scene of the crime, by two different persons, a negro and a white man, and had been identified later while entering Mr. Delamere's house, where he lived, and where damning proofs of his guilt had been discovered; the most important item of which was an old-fashioned knit silk purse, recognized as Mrs. Ochiltree's, and several gold pieces of early coinage, of which the murdered woman was known to have a number. Watson brought with him one of the first copies procurable of the extra edition of the Chronicle, which contained these facts and further information.

They were still talking when Mrs. Miller, knocking at the door, announced that big Josh Green wished to see the doctor about Sandy Campbell. Miller took his collar and necktie in his hand and went downstairs, where Josh sat waiting.

"Doctuh," said Green, "de w'ite folks is talkin' 'bout lynchin' Sandy Campbell fer killin' ole Mis' Ochiltree. He never done it, an' dey ought n' ter be 'lowed ter lynch 'im."

"They ought not to lynch him, even if he committed the crime," returned Miller, "but still less if he did n't. What do you know about it?"

"I know he was wid me, suh, las' night, at de time when dey say ole Mis' Ochiltree wuz killed. We wuz down ter Sam Taylor's place, havin' a little game of kyards an' a little liquor. Den we lef dere an' went up ez fur ez de corner er Main an' Vine Streets, where we pa'ted, an' Sandy went 'long to'ds home. Mo'over, dey say he had on check' britches an' a blue coat. When Sandy wuz wid me he had on gray clo's, an' when we sep'rated he wa'n't in no shape ter be changin' his clo's, let 'lone robbin' er killin' anybody."

"Your testimony ought to prove an alibi for him," declared Miller.

"Dere ain' gwine ter be no chance ter prove nothin', 'less'n we kin do it mighty quick! Dey say dey 're gwine ter lynch 'im ter-night,—some on 'em is talkin' 'bout burnin' 'im. My idee is ter hunt up de niggers an' git 'em ter stan' tergether an' gyard de jail."

"Why should n't we go to the principal white people of the town and tell them Josh's story, and appeal to them to stop this thing until Campbell can have a hearing?"

"It would n't do any good," said Watson despondently; "their blood is up. It seems that some colored man attacked Mrs. Ochiltree,—and he was a murderous villain, whoever he may be. To quote Josh would destroy the effect of his story,— we know he never harmed any one but himself"—

"An' a few keerliss people w'at got in my way," corrected Josh.

"He has been in court several times for fighting,—and that's against him. To have been at Sam Taylor's place is against Sandy, too, rather than in his favor. No, Josh, the white people would believe that you were trying to shield Sandy, and you would probably be arrested as an accomplice."

"But look a-here, Mistuh Watson,—Doctuh Miller, is we-all jes' got ter set down here, widout openin' ou' mouths, an' let dese w'ite folks hang er bu'n a man w'at we *know* ain' guilty? Dat ain't no law, ner jestice, ner nothin'! Ef you-all won't he'p,

I 'll do somethin' myse'f! Dere's two niggers ter one white man in dis town, an' I'm sho' I kin fin' fifty of 'em w'at 'll fight, ef dey kin fin' anybody ter lead 'em."

"Now hold on, Josh," argued Miller; "what is to be gained by fighting? Suppose you got your crowd together and surrounded the jail,—what then?"

"There 'd be a clash," declared Watson, "and instead of one dead negro there 'd be fifty. The white people are claiming now that Campbell did n't stop with robbery and murder. A special edition of the Morning Chronicle, just out, suggests a further purpose, and has all the old shopworn cant about race purity and supremacy and imperative necessity, which always comes to the front whenever it is sought to justify some outrage on the colored folks. The blood of the whites is up, I tell you!"

"Is there anything to that suggestion?" asked Miller incredulously.

"It does n't matter whether there is or not," returned Watson. "Merely to suggest it proves it. Nothing was said about this feature until the paper came out,—and even its statement is vague and indefinite,—but now the claim is in every mouth. I met only black looks as I came down the street. White men with whom I have long been on friendly terms passed me without a word. A negro has been arrested on suspicion,—the entire race is condemned on general principles."

"The whole thing is profoundly discouraging," said Miller sadly. "Try as we may to build up the race in the essentials of good citizenship and win the good opinion of the best people, some black scoundrel comes along, and by a single criminal act, committed in the twinkling of an eye, neutralizes the effect of a whole year's work."

"It 's mighty easy neut'alize', er whatever you call it," said Josh sullenly. "De w'ite folks don' want too good an opinion er de niggers,—ef dey had a good opinion of 'em, dey would n' have no excuse for 'busin' an' hangin' an' burnin' 'em. But ef dey can't keep from doin' it, let 'em git de right man! Dis way er pickin' up de fus' nigger dey comes across, an' stringin' 'im up rega'dliss, ought ter be stop', an' stop' right now!"

"Yes, that 's the worst of lynch law," said Watson; "but we

are wasting valuable time,—it's hardly worth while for us to discuss a subject we are all agreed upon. One of our race, accused of certain acts, is about to be put to death without judge or jury, ostensibly because he committed a crime,—really because he is a negro, for if he were white he would not be lynched. It is thus made a race issue, on the one side as well as on the other. What can we do to protect him?"

"We kin fight, ef we haf ter," replied Josh resolutely.

"Well, now, let us see. Suppose the colored people armed themselves? Messages would at once be sent to every town and county in the neighborhood. White men from all over the state, armed to the teeth, would at the slightest word pour into town on every railroad train, and extras would be run for their benefit."

"They 're already coming in," said Watson.

"We might go to the sheriff," suggested Miller, "and demand that he telegraph the governor to call out the militia."

"I spoke to the sheriff an hour ago," replied Watson. "He has a white face and a whiter liver. He does not dare call out the militia to protect a negro charged with such a brutal crime;—and if he did, the militia are white men, and who can say that their efforts would not be directed to keeping the negroes out of the way, in order that the white devils might do their worst? The whole machinery of the state is in the hands of white men, elected partly by our votes. When the color line is drawn, if they choose to stand together with the rest of their race against us, or to remain passive and let the others work their will, we are helpless,—our cause is hopeless."

"We might call on the general government," said Miller. "Surely the President would intervene."

"Such a demand would be of no avail," returned Watson. "The government can only intervene under certain conditions, of which it must be informed through designated channels. It never sees anything that is not officially called to its attention. The whole negro population of the South might be slaughtered before the necessary red tape could be spun out to inform the President that a state of anarchy prevailed. There 's no hope there."

"Den w'at we gwine ter do?" demanded Josh indignantly; "jes' set here an' let 'em hang Sandy, er bu'n 'im?"

"God knows!" exclaimed Miller. "The outlook is dark, but we should at least try to do something. There must be *some* white men in the town who would stand for law and order,—there 's no possible chance for Sandy to escape hanging by due process of law, if he is guilty. We might at least try half a dozen gentlemen."

"We 'd better leave Josh here," said Watson. "He 's too truculent. If he went on the street he 'd make trouble, and if he accompanied us he 'd do more harm than good. Wait for us here, Josh, until we 've seen what we can do. We 'll be back in half an hour."

In half an hour they had both returned.

"It 's no use," reported Watson gloomily. "I called at the mayor's office and found it locked. He is doubtless afraid on his own account, and would not dream of asserting his authority. I then looked up Judge Everton, who has always seemed to be fair. My reception was cold. He admitted that lynching was, as a rule, unjustifiable, but maintained that there were exceptions to all rules,—that laws were made, after all, to express the will of the people in regard to the ordinary administration of justice, but that in an emergency the sovereign people might assert itself and take the law into its own hands,—the creature was not greater than the creator. He laughed at my suggestion that Sandy was innocent. 'If he is innocent,' he said, 'then produce the real criminal. You negroes are standing in your own light when you try to protect such dastardly scoundrels as this Campbell, who is an enemy of society and not fit to live. I shall not move in the matter. If a negro wants the protection of the law, let him obey the law.' A wise judge,—a second Daniel come to judgment! If this were the law, there would be no need of judges or juries."

"I called on Dr. Price," said Miller, "my good friend Dr. Price, who would rather lie than hurt my feelings. 'Miller,' he declared, 'this is no affair of mine, or yours. I have too much respect for myself and my profession to interfere in such a matter, and you will accomplish nothing, and only lessen your own influence, by having anything to say.' 'But the man may be innocent,' I replied; 'there is every reason to believe that he is.' He shook his head pityingly. 'You are self-deceived, Miller; your prejudice has warped your judgment. The proof is overwhelming that he robbed this old lady, laid violent hands upon her, and left her dead. If he did no more, he has violated the written and unwritten law of the Southern States. I could not save him if I would, Miller, and frankly, I would not if I could. If he is innocent, his people can console themselves with the reflection that Mrs. Ochiltree was also innocent, and balance one crime against the other, the white against the black. Of course I shall take no part in whatever may be done,—but it is not my affair, nor yours. Take my advice, Miller, and keep out of it.'

"That is the situation," added Miller, summing up. "Their friendship for us, a slender stream at the best, dries up entirely when it strikes their prejudices. There is seemingly not one white man in Wellington who will speak a word for law, order, decency, or humanity. Those who do not participate will stand idly by and see an untried man deliberately and brutally murdered. Race prejudice is the devil unchained."

"Well, den, suh," said Josh, "where does we stan' now? W'at is we gwine ter do? I would n' min' fightin', fer my time ain't come yit,—I feels dat in my bones. W'at we gwine ter do, dat 's w'at I wanter know."

"What does old Mr. Delamere have to say about the matter?" asked Miller suddenly. "Why have n't we thought of him before? Has he been seen?"

"No," replied Watson gloomily, "and for a good reason,— he is not in town. I came by the house just now, and learned that he went out to his country place yesterday afternoon, to remain a week. Sandy was to have followed him out there this morning,—it's a pity he did n't go yesterday. The old gentleman has probably heard nothing about the matter."

"How about young Delamere?"

"He went away early this morning, down the river, to fish. He 'll probably not hear of it before night, and he 's only a boy anyway, and could very likely do nothing," said Watson.

Miller looked at his watch.

"Belleview is ten miles away," he said. "It is now eleven o'clock. I can drive out there in an hour and a half at the farthest. I 'll go and see Mr. Delamere,—he can do more than any living man, if he is able to do anything at all. There 's never been a lynching here, and one good white man, if he choose, may stem the flood long enough to give justice a chance. Keep track of the white people while I 'm gone, Watson; and you, Josh, learn what the colored folks are saying, and do nothing rash until I return. In the meantime, do all that you can to find out who did commit this most atrocious murder."

XXIII

BELLEVIEW

Miller did not reach his destination without interruption. At one point a considerable stretch of the road was under repair, which made it necessary for him to travel slowly. His horse cast a shoe, and threatened to go lame; but in the course of time he arrived at the entrance gate of Belleview, entering which he struck into a private road, bordered by massive oaks, whose multitudinous branches, hung with long streamers of trailing moss, formed for much of the way a thick canopy above his head. It took him only a few minutes to traverse the quarter of a mile that lay between the entrance gate and the house itself.

This old colonial plantation, rich in legendary lore and replete with historic distinction, had been in the Delamere family for nearly two hundred years. Along the bank of the river which skirted its domain the famous pirate Blackbeard had held high carnival, and was reputed to have buried much treasure, vague traditions of which still lingered among the negroes and poor-whites of the country roundabout. The beautiful residence, rising white and stately in a grove of ancient oaks, dated from 1750, and was built of brick which had been brought from England. Enlarged and improved from generation to generation, it stood, like a baronial castle, upon a slight eminence from which could be surveyed the large demesne still belonging to the estate, which had shrunk greatly from its colonial dimensions. While still embracing several thousand acres, part forest and part cleared land, it had not of late years been profitable; in spite of which Mr. Delamere, with the conservatism of his age and caste, had never been able to make up his mind to part with any considerable portion of it. His grandson, he imagined, could make the estate pay and yet preserve it in its integrity. Here, in pleasant weather, surrounded by the scenes which he loved, old Mr. Delamere spent much of the time during his declining years.

Dr. Miller had once passed a day at Belleview, upon Mr. Delamere's invitation. For this old-fashioned gentleman, whose ideals not even slavery had been able to spoil, regarded himself as a trustee for the great public, which ought, in his opinion, to take as much pride as he in the contemplation of this historic landmark. In earlier years Mr. Delamere had been a practicing lawyer, and had numbered Miller's father among his clients. He had always been regarded as friendly to the colored people, and, until age and ill health had driven him from active life, had taken a lively interest in their advancement since the abolition of slavery. Upon the public opening of Miller's new hospital, he had made an effort to be present, and had made a little speech of approval and encouragement which had manifested his kindliness and given Miller much pleasure.

It was with the consciousness, therefore, that he was approaching a friend, as well as Sandy's master, that Miller's mind was chiefly occupied as his tired horse, scenting the end of his efforts, bore him with a final burst of speed along the last few rods of the journey; for the urgency of Miller's errand, involving as it did the issues of life and death, did not permit him to enjoy the charm of mossy oak or forest reaches, or even to appreciate the noble front of Belleview House when it at last loomed up before him.

"Well, William," said Mr. Delamere, as he gave his hand to Miller from the armchair in which he was seated under the broad and stately portico, "I did n't expect to see you out here. You 'll excuse my not rising,—I 'm none too firm on my legs. Did you see anything of my man Sandy back there on the road? He ought to have been here by nine o'clock, and it 's now one.

Sandy is punctuality itself, and I don't know how to account for his delay."

Clearly there need be no time wasted in preliminaries. Mr. Delamere had gone directly to the subject in hand.

"He will not be here to-day, sir," replied Miller. "I have come to you on his account."

In a few words Miller stated the situation.

"Preposterous!" exclaimed the old gentleman, with more vigor than Miller had supposed him to possess. "Sandy is absolutely incapable of such a crime as robbery, to say nothing of murder; and as for the rest, that is absurd upon the face of it! And so the poor old woman is dead! Well, well, well! She could not have lived much longer anyway; but Sandy did not kill her,—it 's simply impossible! Why, *I* raised that boy! He was born on my place. I 'd as soon believe such a thing of my own grandson as of Sandy! No negro raised by a Delamere would ever commit such a crime. I really believe, William, that Sandy has the family honor of the Delameres quite as much at heart as I have. Just tell them I say Sandy is innocent, and it will be all right."

"I 'm afraid, sir," rejoined Miller, who kept his voice up so that the old gentleman could understand without having it suggested that Miller knew he was hard of hearing, "that you don't quite appreciate the situation. *I* believe Sandy innocent; *you* believe him innocent; but there are suspicious circumstances which do not explain themselves, and the white people of the city believe him guilty, and are going to lynch him before he has a chance to clear himself."

"Why does n't he explain the suspicious circumstances?" asked Mr. Delamere. "Sandy is truthful and can be believed. I would take Sandy's word as quickly as another man's oath."

"He has no chance to explain," said Miller. "The case is prejudged. A crime has been committed. Sandy is charged with it. He is black, and therefore he is guilty. No colored lawyer would be allowed in the jail, if one should dare to go there. No white lawyer will intervene. He 'll be lynched to-night, without judge, jury, or preacher, unless we can stave the thing off for a day or two."

"Have you seen my grandson?" asked the old gentleman. "Is he not looking after Sandy?"

"No, sir. It seems he went down the river this morning to fish, before the murder was discovered; no one knows just where he has gone, or at what hour he will return."

"Well, then," said Mr. Delamere, rising from his chair with surprising vigor, "I shall have to go myself. No faithful servant of mine shall be hanged for a crime he did n't commit, so long as I have a voice to speak or a dollar to spend. There 'll be no trouble after I get there, William. The people are naturally wrought up at such a crime. A fine old woman,—she had some detestable traits, and I was always afraid she wanted to marry me, but she was of an excellent family and had many good points,—an old woman of one of the best families, struck down by the hand of a murderer! You must remember, William, that blood is thicker than water, and that the provocation is extreme, and that a few hotheads might easily lose sight of the great principles involved and seek immediate vengeance, without too much discrimination. But they are good people, William, and when I have spoken, and they have an opportunity for the sober second thought, they will do nothing rashly, but will wait for the operation of the law, which will, of course, clear Sandy."

"I 'm sure I hope so," returned Miller. "Shall I try to drive you back, sir, or will you order your own carriage?"

"My horses are fresher, William, and I 'll have them brought around. You can take the reins, if you will,—I 'm rather old to drive,—and my man will come behind with your buggy."

In a few minutes they set out along the sandy road. Having two fresh horses, they made better headway than Miller had made coming out, and reached Wellington easily by three o'clock.

"I think, William," said Mr. Delamere, as they drove into the town, "that I had first better talk with Sandy. He may be able to explain away the things that seem to connect him with this atrocious affair; and that will put me in a better position to talk to other people about it."

Miller drove directly to the county jail. Thirty or forty white men, who seemed to be casually gathered near the door, closed up when the carriage approached. The sheriff, who had seen them from the inside, came to the outer door and spoke to the visitor through a grated wicket.

"Mr. Wemyss," said Mr. Delamere, when he had made his way to the entrance with the aid of his cane, "I wish to see my servant, Sandy Campbell, who is said to be in your custody."

The sheriff hesitated. Meantime there was some parleying in low tones among the crowd outside. No one interfered, however, and in a moment the door opened sufficiently to give entrance to the old gentleman, after which it closed quickly and clangorously behind him.

Feeling no desire to linger in the locality, Miller, having seen his companion enter the jail, drove the carriage round to Mr. Delamere's house, and leaving it in charge of a servant with instructions to return for his master in a quarter of an hour, hastened to his own home to meet Watson and Josh and report the result of his efforts.

XXIV

TWO SOUTHERN GENTLEMEN

The iron bolt rattled in the lock, the door of a cell swung open, and when Mr. Delamere had entered was quickly closed again.

"Well, Sandy!"

"Oh, Mars John! Is you fell from hebben ter he'p me out er here? I prayed de Lawd ter sen' you, an' He answered my prayer, an' here you is, Mars John,—here you is! Oh, Mars John, git me out er dis place!"

"Tut, tut, Sandy!" answered his master; "of course I 'll get you out. That 's what I 've come for. How in the world did such a mistake ever happen? You would no more commit such a crime than I would!"

"No, suh, 'deed I would n', an' you know I would n'! I would n' want ter bring no disgrace on de fam'ly dat rais' me, ner ter make no trouble fer you, suh; but here I is, suh, lock' up in jail, an' folks talkin' 'bout hangin' me fer somethin' dat

never entered my min', suh. I swea' ter God I never thought er
sech a thing!"

"Of course you did n't, Sandy," returned Mr. Delamere soothingly; "and now the next thing, and the simplest thing, is to get
you out of this. I 'll speak to the officers, and at the preliminary hearing to-morrow I 'll tell them all about you, and they
will let you go. You won't mind spending one night in jail for
your sins."

"No, suh, ef I wuz sho' I 'd be 'lowed ter spen' it here. But
dey say dey 're gwine ter lynch me ter-night,—I kin hear 'em
talkin' f'm de winders er de cell, suh."

"Well, I say, Sandy, that they shall do no such thing! Lynch
a man brought up by a Delamere, for a crime of which he is
innocent? Preposterous! I 'll speak to the authorities and see
that you are properly protected until this mystery is unrav-
eled. If Tom had been here, he would have had you out before
now, Sandy. My grandson is a genuine Delamere, is he not,
Sandy?"

"Yas, suh, yas, suh," returned Sandy, with a lack of enthusiasm which he tried to conceal from his master. "An' I s'pose ef
he had n' gone fishin' so soon dis mawnin', he 'd 'a' be'n
lookin' after me, suh."

"It has been my love for him and your care of me, Sandy,"
said the old gentleman tremulously, "that have kept me alive so
long; but now explain to me everything concerning this distressing matter, and I shall then be able to state your case to
better advantage."

"Well, suh," returned Sandy, "I mought 's well tell de whole
tale an' not hol' nothing back. I wuz kind er lonesome las'
night, an' sence I be'n tu'ned outen de chu'ch on account er dat
cakewalk I did n' go ter, so he'p me God! I did n' feel like gwine
ter prayer-meetin', so I went roun' ter see Solomon Williams,
an' he wa'n't home, an' den I walk' down street an' met Josh
Green, an' he ax' me inter Sam Taylor's place, an' I sot roun'
dere wid Josh till 'bout 'leven o'clock, w'en I sta'ted back
home. I went straight ter de house, suh, an' went ter bed an' ter
sleep widout sayin' a wo'd ter a single soul excep' Mistuh Tom,
who wuz settin' up readin' a book w'en I come in. I wish I may

drap dead in my tracks, suh, ef dat ain't de God's truf, suh, eve'y wo'd of it!"

"I believe every word of it, Sandy; now tell me about the clothes that you are said to have found cleaning, and the suspicious articles that were found in your room?"

"Dat 's w'at beats me, Mars John," replied Sandy, shaking his head mournfully. "W'en I lef' home las' night after supper, my clo's wuz all put erway in de closet in my room, folded up on de she'f ter keep de moths out. Dey wuz my good clo's,—de blue coat dat you wo' ter de weddin' fo'ty years ago, an' dem dere plaid pants I gun Mistuh Cohen fo' dollars fer three years ago; an' w'en I looked in my closet dis mawnin', suh, befo' I got ready ter sta't for Belleview, dere wuz my clo's layin' on de flo', all muddy an' crumple' up, des lack somebody had wo' 'em in a fight! Somebody e'se had wo' my clo's,—or e'se dere 'd be'n some witchcraf', er some sort er devilment gwine on dat I can't make out, suh, ter save my soul!"

"There was no witchcraft, Sandy, but that there was some deviltry might well be. Now, what other negro, who might have been mistaken for you, could have taken your clothes? Surely no one about the house?"

"No, suh, no, suh. It could n't 'a' be'n Jeff, fer he wuz at Belleview wid you; an' it could n't 'a' be'n Billy, fer he wuz too little ter wear my clo's; an' it could n't 'a' be'n Sally, fer she's a 'oman. It's a myst'ry ter me, suh!"

"Have you no enemies? Is there any one in Wellington whom you imagine would like to do you an injury?"

"Not a livin' soul dat I knows of, suh. I 've be'n tu'ned out'n de chu'ch, but I don' know who my enemy is dere, er ef it wuz all a mistake, like dis yer jailin' is; but de Debbil is in dis somewhar, Mars John,—an' I got my reasons fer sayin' so."

"What do you mean, Sandy?"

Sandy related his experience of the preceding evening: how he had seen the apparition preceding him to the house, and how he had questioned Tom upon the subject.

"There 's some mystery here, Sandy," said Mr. Delamere reflectively. "Have you told me all, now, upon your honor? I am trying to save your life, Sandy, and I must be able to trust your word implicitly. You must tell me every circumstance: a very little and seemingly unimportant bit of evidence may sometimes determine the issue of a great lawsuit. There is one thing especially, Sandy: where did you get the gold which was found in your trunk?"

Sandy's face lit up with hopefulness.

"Why, Mars John, I kin 'splain dat part easy. Dat wuz money I had lent out, an' I got back f'm—But no, suh, I promise' not ter tell."

"Circumstances absolve you from your promise, Sandy. Your life is of more value to you than any other thing. If you will explain where you got the gold, and the silk purse that contained it, which is said to be Mrs. Ochiltree's, you will be back home before night."

Old Mr. Delamere's faculties, which had been waning somewhat in sympathy with his health, were stirred to unusual acuteness by his servant's danger. He was watching Sandy with all the awakened instincts of the trial lawyer. He could see clearly enough that, in beginning to account for the possession of the gold, Sandy had started off with his explanation in all sincerity. At the mention of the silk purse, however, his face had blanched to an ashen gray, and the words had frozen upon his lips.

A less discerning observer might have taken these things as signs of guilt, but not so Mr. Delamere.

"Well, Sandy," said his master encouragingly, "go on. You got the gold from"—

Sandy remained silent. He had had a great shock, and had taken a great resolution.

"Mars John," he asked dreamily, "you don' b'lieve dat I done dis thing?"

"Certainly not, Sandy, else why should I be here?"

"An' nothin' would n' make you b'lieve it, suh?"

"No, Sandy,—I could not believe it of you. I've known you too long and too well."

"An' you would n' b'lieve it, not even ef I would n' say one wo'd mo' about it?"

"No, Sandy, I believe you no more capable of this crime than

I would be,—or my grandson, Tom. I wish Tom were here, that he might help me overcome your stubbornness; but you 'll not be so foolish, so absurdly foolish, Sandy, as to keep silent and risk your life merely to shield some one else, when by speaking you might clear up this mystery and be restored at once to liberty. Just tell me where you got the gold," added the old gentleman persuasively. "Come, now, Sandy, that 's a good fellow!"

"Mars John," asked Sandy softly, "w'en my daddy, 'way back yander befo' de wah, wuz about ter be sol' away f'm his wife an' child'en, you bought him an' dem, an' kep' us all on yo' place tergether, did n't you, suh?"

"Yes, Sandy, and he was a faithful servant, and proved worthy of all I did for him."

"And w'en he had wo'ked fer you ten years, suh, you sot 'im free?"

"Yes, Sandy, he had earned his freedom."

"An' w'en de wah broke out, an' my folks wuz scattered, an' I did n' have nothin' ter do ner nowhar ter go, you kep' me on yo' place, and tuck me ter wait on you, suh, did n't you?"

"Yes, Sandy, and you have been a good servant and a good friend; but tell me now about this gold, and I 'll go and get you out of this, right away, for I need you, Sandy, and you 'll not be of any use to me shut up here!"

"Jes' hol' on a minute befo' you go, Mars John; fer ef dem people outside should git holt er me befo' you *does* git me out er here, I may never see you no mo', suh, in dis worl'. W'en Mars Billy McLean shot me by mistake, w'ile we wuz out huntin' dat day, who wuz it boun' up my woun's an' kep' me from bleedin' ter def, an' kyar'ed me two miles on his own shoulders ter a doctuh?"

"Yes, Sandy, and when black Sally ran away with your young mistress and Tom, when Tom was a baby, who stopped the runaway, and saved their lives at the risk of his own?"

"Dat wa'n't nothin', suh; anybody could 'a' done dat, w'at wuz strong ernuff an' swif' ernuff. You is be'n good ter me, suh, all dese years, an' I 've tried ter do my duty by you, suh, an' by Mistuh Tom, who wuz yo' own gran'son, an' de las' one er de fam'ly."

"Yes, you have, Sandy, and when I am gone, which will not be very long, Tom will take care of you, and see that you never want. But we are wasting valuable time, Sandy, in these old reminiscences. Let us get back to the present. Tell me about the gold, now, so that I may at once look after your safety. It may not even be necessary for you to remain here all night."

"Jes' one wo'd mo', Mars John, befo' you go! I know you 're gwine ter do de bes' you kin fer me, an' I 'm sorry I can't he'p you no mo' wid it; but ef dere should be any accident, er ef you *can't* git me out er here, don' bother yo' min' 'bout it no mo', suh, an' don' git yo'se'f ixcited, fer you know de doctuh says, suh, dat you can't stan' ixcitement; but jes' leave me in de han's er de Lawd, suh—*He 'll* look after me, here er hereafter. I know I 've fell f'm grace mo' d'n once, but I 've done made my peace wid Him in dis here jail-house, suh, an' I ain't 'feared ter die— ef I haf ter. I ain' got no wife ner child'n ter mo'n fer me, an' I 'll die knowin' dat I 've done my duty ter dem dat hi'ed me, an' trusted me, an' had claims on me. Fer I wuz raise' by a De-lamere, suh, an' all de ole Delameres wuz gent'emen, an' deir principles spread ter de niggers 'round 'em, suh; an' ef I has ter die fer somethin' I did n' do,—I kin die, suh, like a gent'eman! But ez fer dat gol', suh, I ain' gwine ter say one wo'd mo' 'bout it ter nobody in dis worl'!"

Nothing could shake Sandy's determination. Mr. Delamere argued, expostulated, but all in vain. Sandy would not speak.

More and more confident of some mystery, which would come out in time, if properly investigated, Mr. Delamere, strangely beset by a vague sense of discomfort over and beyond that occasioned by his servant's danger, hurried away upon his errand of mercy. He felt less confident of the outcome than when he had entered the jail, but was quite as much resolved that no effort should be spared to secure protection for Sandy until there had been full opportunity for the truth to become known.

"Take good care of your prisoner, sheriff," he said sternly, as he was conducted to the door. "He will not be long in your custody, and I shall see that you are held strictly accountable for his safety."

"I 'll do what I can, sir," replied the sheriff in an even tone and seemingly not greatly impressed by this warning. "If the prisoner is taken from me, it will be because the force that comes for him is too strong for resistance."

"There should be no force too strong for an honest man in your position to resist,—whether successfully or not is beyond the question. The officer who is intimidated by threats, or by his own fears, is recreant to his duty, and no better than the mob which threatens him. But you will have no such test, Mr. Wemyss! I shall see to it myself that there is no violence!"

XXV
THE HONOR OF A FAMILY

Mr. Delamere's coachman, who, in accordance with instructions left by Miller, had brought the carriage around to the jail and was waiting anxiously at the nearest corner, drove up with some trepidation as he saw his master emerge from the prison. The old gentleman entered the carriage and gave the order to be driven to the office of the Morning Chronicle. According to Jerry, the porter, whom he encountered at the door, Carteret was in his office, and Mr. Delamere, with the aid of his servant, climbed the stairs painfully and found the editor at his desk.

"Carteret," exclaimed Mr. Delamere, "what is all this talk about lynching my man for murder and robbery and criminal assault? It 's perfectly absurd! The man was raised by me; he has lived in my house forty years. He has been honest, faithful, and trustworthy. He would no more be capable of this crime than you would, or my grandson Tom. Sandy has too much respect for the family to do anything that would reflect disgrace upon it."

"My dear Mr. Delamere," asked Carteret, with an indulgent smile, "how could a negro possibly reflect discredit upon a white family? I should really like to know."

"How, sir? A white family raised him. Like all the negroes, he has been clay in the hands of the white people. They are what we have made them, or permitted them to become."

"We are not God, Mr. Delamere! We do not claim to have created these—masterpieces."

"No; but we thought to overrule God's laws, and we enslaved these people for our greed, and sought to escape the manstealer's curse by laying to our souls the flattering unction that we were making of barbarous negroes civilized and Christian men. If we did not, if instead of making them Christians we have made some of them brutes, we have only ourselves to blame, and if these prey upon society, it is our just punishment! But my negroes, Carteret, were well raised and well behaved. This man is innocent of this offense, I solemnly affirm, and I want your aid to secure his safety until a fair trial can be had."

"On your bare word, sir?" asked Carteret, not at all moved by this outburst.

Old Mr. Delamere trembled with anger, and his withered cheek flushed darkly, but he restrained his feelings, and answered with an attempt at calmness:—

"Time was, sir, when the word of a Delamere was held as good as his bond, and those who questioned it were forced to maintain their skepticism upon the field of honor. Time was, sir, when the law was enforced in this state in a manner to command the respect of the world! Our lawyers, our judges, our courts, were a credit to humanity and civilization. I fear I have outlasted my epoch,—I have lived to hear of white men, the most favored of races, the heirs of civilization, the conservators of liberty, howling like red Indians around a human being slowly roasting at the stake."

"My dear sir," said Carteret soothingly, "you should undeceive yourself. This man is no longer your property. The negroes are no longer under our control, and with their emancipation ceased our responsibility. Their insolence and disregard for law have reached a point where they must be sternly rebuked."

"The law," retorted Mr. Delamere, "furnishes a sufficient penalty for any crime, however heinous, and our code is by no means lenient. To my old-fashioned notions, death would seem an adequate punishment for any crime, and torture has been abolished in civilized countries for a hundred years. It would be better to let a crime go entirely unpunished, than to use it as a pretext for turning the whole white population into a mob of primitive savages, dancing in hellish glee around the mangled body of a man who has never been tried for a crime. All this, however, is apart from my errand, which is to secure your assistance in heading off this mob until Sandy can have a fair hearing and an opportunity to prove his innocence."

"How can I do that, Mr. Delamere?"

"You are editor of the Morning Chronicle. The Chronicle is the leading newspaper of the city. This morning's issue practically suggested the mob; the same means will stop it. I will pay the expense of an extra edition, calling off the mob, on the ground that newly discovered evidence has shown the prisoner's innocence."

"But where is the evidence?" asked Carteret.

Again Mr. Delamere flushed and trembled. "*My* evidence, sir! I say the negro was morally incapable of the crime. A man of forty-five does not change his nature over-night. He is no more capable of a disgraceful deed than my grandson would be!"

Carteret smiled sadly.

"I am sorry, Mr. Delamere," he said, "that you should permit yourself to be so exercised about a worthless scoundrel who has forfeited his right to live. The proof against him is overwhelming. As to his capability of crime, we will apply your own test. You have been kept in the dark too long, Mr. Delamere,—indeed, we all have,—about others as well as this negro. Listen, sir: last night, at the Clarendon Club, Tom Delamere was caught cheating outrageously at cards. He had been suspected for some time; a trap was laid for him, and he fell into it. Out of regard for you and for my family, he has been permitted to resign quietly, with the understanding that he first pay off his debts, which are considerable."

Mr. Delamere's face, which had taken on some color in the excitement of the interview, had gradually paled to a chalky white while Carteret was speaking. His head sunk forward; already an old man, he seemed to have aged ten years in but little more than as many seconds.

"Can this be true?" he demanded in a hoarse whisper. "Is it—entirely authentic?"

"True as gospel; true as it is that Mrs. Ochiltree has been murdered, and that this negro killed her. Ellis was at the club a few minutes after the affair happened, and learned the facts from one of the participants. Tom made no attempt at denial. We have kept the matter out of the other papers, and I would have spared your feelings,—I surely would not wish to wound them,—but the temptation proved too strong for me, and it seemed the only way to convince you: it was your own test. If a gentleman of a distinguished name and an honorable ancestry, with all the restraining forces of social position surrounding him, to hold him in check, can stoop to dishonor, what is the improbability of an illiterate negro's being at least *capable* of crime?"

"Enough, sir," said the old gentleman. "You have proved enough. My grandson may be a scoundrel,—I can see, in the light of this revelation, how he might be; and he seems not to have denied it. I maintain, nevertheless, that my man Sandy is innocent of the charge against him. He *has* denied it, and it has not been proved. Carteret, I owe that negro my life; he, and his father before him, have served me and mine faithfully and well. I cannot see him killed like a dog, without judge or jury,—no, not even if he were guilty, which I do not believe!"

Carteret felt a twinge of remorse for the pain he had inflicted upon this fine old man, this ideal gentleman of the ideal past,— the past which he himself so much admired and regretted. He would like to spare his old friend any further agitation; he was in a state of health where too great excitement might prove fatal. But how could he? The negro was guilty, and sure to die sooner or later. He had not meant to interfere, and his intervention might be fruitless.

"Mr. Delamere," he said gently, "there is but one way to gain time. You say the negro is innocent. Appearances are against him. The only way to clear him is to produce the real criminal, or prove an alibi. If you, or some other white man of equal standing, could swear that the negro was in your presence last night at any hour when this crime could have taken place, it might be barely possible to prevent the lynching for the present; and when he is tried, which will probably be not later than next week, he will have every opportunity to defend himself, with you to see that he gets no less than justice. I think it can be managed, though there is still a doubt. I will do my best, for your sake, Mr. Delamere,—solely for your sake, be it understood, and not for that of the negro, in whom you are entirely deceived."

"I shall not examine your motives, Carteret," replied the other, "if you can bring about what I desire."

"Whatever is done," added Carteret, "must be done quickly. It is now four o'clock; no one can answer for what may happen after seven. If he can prove an alibi, there may yet be time to save him. White men might lynch a negro on suspicion; they would not kill a man who was proven, by the word of white men, to be entirely innocent."

"I do not know," returned Mr. Delamere, shaking his head sadly. "After what you have told me, it is no longer safe to assume what white men will or will not do;—what I have learned here has shaken my faith in humanity. I am going away, but shall return in a short time. Shall I find you here?"

"I will await your return," said Carteret.

He watched Mr. Delamere pityingly as the old man moved away on the arm of the coachman waiting in the hall. He did not believe that Mr. Delamere could prove an alibi for his servant, and without some positive proof the negro would surely die,—as he well deserved to die.

XXVI

THE DISCOMFORT OF ELLIS

Mr. Ellis was vaguely uncomfortable. In the first excitement following the discovery of the crime, he had given his bit of evidence, and had shared the universal indignation against the murderer. When public feeling took definite shape in the intention to lynch the prisoner, Ellis felt a sudden sense of responsibility growing upon himself. When he learned, an hour later, that it was proposed to burn the negro, his part in the affair assumed a still graver aspect; for his had been the final word to fix the prisoner's guilt.

Ellis did not believe in lynch law. He had argued against it, more than once, in private conversation, and had written several editorials against the practice, while in charge of the Morning Chronicle during Major Carteret's absence. A young man, however, and merely representing another, he had not set up as a reformer, taking rather the view that this summary method of punishing crime, with all its possibilities of error, to say nothing of the resulting disrespect of the law and contempt for the time-honored methods of establishing guilt, was a mere temporary symptom of the unrest caused by the unsettled relations of the two races at the South. There had never before been any special need for any vigorous opposition to lynch law, so far as the community was concerned, for there had not been a lynching in Wellington since Ellis had come there, eight years before, from a smaller town, to seek a place for himself in the world of action. Twenty years before, indeed, there had been wild doings, during the brief Ku-Klux outbreak, but that was before Ellis's time,—or at least when he was but a child. He had come of a Quaker family,—the modified Quakers of the South,—and while sharing in a general way the Southern prejudice against the negro, his prejudices had been tempered by the peaceful tenets of his father's sect. His father had been a Whig, and a non-slaveholder; and while he had gone with the South in the civil war so far as a man of peace could go, he had not done so for love of slavery.

As the day wore on, Ellis's personal responsibility for the intended *auto-da-fé* bore more heavily upon him. Suppose he had been wrong? He had seen the accused negro; he had recognized him by his clothes, his whiskers, his spectacles, and his walk; but he had also seen another man, who resembled Sandy so closely that but for the difference in their clothes, he was forced to acknowledge, he could not have told them apart. Had he not seen the first man, he would have sworn with even greater confidence that the second was Sandy. There had been, he recalled, about one of the men—he had not been then nor was he now able to tell which—something vaguely familiar, and yet seemingly discordant to whichever of the two it was, or, as it seemed to him now, to any man of that race. His mind reverted to the place where he had last seen Sandy, and then a sudden wave of illumination swept over him, and filled him with a thrill of horror. The cakewalk,—the dancing,—the speech,—they were not Sandy's at all, nor any negro's! It was a white man who had stood in the light of the street lamp, so that the casual passerby might see and recognize in him old Mr. Delamere's servant. The scheme was a dastardly one, and worthy of a heart that was something worse than weak and vicious.

Ellis resolved that the negro should not, if he could prevent it, die for another's crime; but what proof had he himself to offer in support of his theory? Then again, if he denounced Tom Delamere as the murderer, it would involve, in all probability, the destruction of his own hopes with regard to Clara. Of course she could not marry Delamere after the disclosure,—the disgraceful episode at the club would have been enough to make that reasonably certain; it had put a nail in Delamere's coffin, but this crime had driven it in to the head and clinched it. On the other hand, would Miss Pemberton ever speak again to the man who had been the instrument of bringing disgrace upon the family? Spies, detectives, police officers, may be useful citizens, but they are rarely pleasant company for other people. We fee the executioner, but we do not touch his bloody hand. We might feel a certain tragic admiration for Brutus condemning his sons to death, but we would scarcely invite Brutus to dinner after the event. It would harrow our feelings too much.

Perhaps, thought Ellis, there might be a way out of the dilemma. It might be possible to save this innocent negro without, for the time being, involving Delamere. He believed that murder will out, but it need not be through his initiative. He determined to go to the jail and interview the prisoner, who might give such an account of himself as would establish his innocence beyond a doubt. If so, Ellis would exert himself to stem the tide of popular fury. If, as a last resort, he could save

Sandy only by denouncing Delamere, he would do his duty, let it cost him what it might.

The gravity of his errand was not lessened by what he saw and heard on the way to the jail. The anger of the people was at a white heat. A white woman had been assaulted and murdered by a brutal negro. Neither advanced age, nor high social standing, had been able to protect her from the ferocity of a black savage. Her sex, which should have been her shield and buckler, had made her an easy mark for the villainy of a black brute. To take the time to try him would be a criminal waste of public money. To hang him would be too slight a punishment for so dastardly a crime. An example must be made.

Already the preparations were under way for the impending execution. A T-rail from the railroad yard had been procured, and men were burying it in the square before the jail. Others were bringing chains, and a load of pine wood was piled in convenient proximity. Some enterprising individual had begun the erection of seats from which, for a pecuniary consideration, the spectacle might be the more easily and comfortably viewed.

Ellis was stopped once or twice by persons of his acquaintance. From one he learned that the railroads would run excursions from the neighboring towns in order to bring spectators to the scene; from another that the burning was to take place early in the evening, so that the children might not be kept up beyond their usual bedtime. In one group that he passed he heard several young men discussing the question of which portions of the negro's body they would prefer for souvenirs. Ellis shuddered and hastened forward. Whatever was to be done must be done quickly, or it would be too late. He saw that already it would require a strong case in favor of the accused to overcome the popular verdict.

Going up the steps of the jail, he met Mr. Delamere, who was just coming out, after a fruitless interview with Sandy.

"Mr. Ellis," said the old gentleman, who seemed greatly agitated, "this is monstrous!"

"It is indeed, sir!" returned the younger man. "I mean to stop it if I can. The negro did not kill Mrs. Ochiltree."

Mr. Delamere looked at Ellis keenly, and, as Ellis recalled afterwards, there was death in his eyes. Unable to draw a syllable from Sandy, he had found his servant's silence more eloquent than words. Ellis felt a presentiment that this affair, however it might terminate, would be fatal to this fine old man, whom the city could ill spare, in spite of his age and infirmities.

"Mr. Ellis," asked Mr. Delamere, in a voice which trembled with ill-suppressed emotion, "do you know who killed her?"

Ellis felt a surging pity for his old friend; but every step that he had taken toward the jail had confirmed and strengthened his own resolution that this contemplated crime, which he dimly felt to be far more atrocious than that of which Sandy was accused, in that it involved a whole community rather than one vicious man, should be stopped at any cost. Deplorable enough had the negro been guilty, it became, in view of his certain innocence, an unspeakable horror, which for all time would cover the city with infamy.

"Mr. Delamere," he replied, looking the elder man squarely in the eyes, "I think I do,—and I am very sorry."

"And who was it, Mr. Ellis?"

He put the question hopelessly, as though the answer were a foregone conclusion.

"I do not wish to say at present," replied Ellis, with a remorseful pang, "unless it becomes absolutely necessary, to save the negro's life. Accusations are dangerous,—as this case proves,—unless the proof be certain."

For a moment it seemed as though Mr. Delamere would collapse upon the spot. Rallying almost instantly, however, he took the arm which Ellis involuntarily offered, and said with an effort:—

"Mr. Ellis, you are a gentleman whom it is an honor to know. If you have time, I wish you would go with me to my house,—I can hardly trust myself alone,—and thence to the Chronicle office. This thing shall be stopped, and you will help me stop it."

It required but a few minutes to cover the half mile that lay between the prison and Mr. Delamere's residence.

XXVII

THE VAGARIES OF THE HIGHER LAW

Mr. Delamere went immediately to his grandson's room, which he entered alone, closing and locking the door behind him. He had requested Ellis to wait in the carriage.

The bed had been made, and the room was apparently in perfect order. There was a bureau in the room, through which Mr. Delamere proceeded to look thoroughly. Finding one of the drawers locked, he tried it with a key of his own, and being unable to unlock it, took a poker from beside the stove and broke it ruthlessly open.

The contents served to confirm what he had heard concerning his grandson's character. Thrown together in disorderly confusion were bottles of wine and whiskey; soiled packs of cards; a dice-box with dice; a box of poker chips, several revolvers, and a number of photographs and paper-covered books at which the old gentleman merely glanced to ascertain their nature.

So far, while his suspicion had been strengthened, he had found nothing to confirm it. He searched the room more carefully, and found, in the wood-box by the small heating-stove which stood in the room, a torn and crumpled bit of paper. Stooping to pick this up, his eye caught a gleam of something yellow beneath the bureau, which lay directly in his line of vision.

First he smoothed out the paper. It was apparently the lower half of a label, or part of the cover of a small box, torn diagonally from corner to corner. From the business card at the bottom, which gave the name of a firm of manufacturers of theatrical supplies in a Northern city, and from the letters remaining upon the upper and narrower half, the bit of paper had plainly formed part of the wrapper of a package of burnt cork.

Closing his fingers spasmodically over this damning piece of evidence, Mr. Delamere knelt painfully, and with the aid of his cane drew out from under the bureau the yellow object which had attracted his attention. It was a five-dollar gold piece of a date back toward the beginning of the century.

To make assurance doubly sure, Mr. Delamere summoned the cook from the kitchen in the back yard. In answer to her master's questions, Sally averred that Mr. Tom had got up very early, had knocked at her window,—she slept in a room off the kitchen in the yard,—and had told her that she need not bother about breakfast for him, as he had had a cold bite from the pantry; that he was going hunting and fishing, and would be gone all day. According to Sally, Mr. Tom had come in about ten o'clock the night before. He had forgotten his night-key, Sandy was out, and she had admitted him with her own key. He had said that he was very tired and was going immediately to bed.

Mr. Delamere seemed perplexed; the crime had been committed later in the evening than ten o'clock. The cook cleared up the mystery.

"I reckon he must 'a' be'n dead ti'ed, suh, fer I went back ter his room fifteen er twenty minutes after he come in fer ter fin' out w'at he wanted fer breakfus'; an' I knock two or three times, rale ha'd, an' Mistuh Tom did n' wake up no mo' d'n de dead. He sho'ly had a good sleep, er he'd never 'a' got up so ea'ly."

"Thank you, Sally," said Mr. Delamere, when the woman had finished, "that will do."

"Will you be home ter suppah, suh?" asked the cook.

"Yes."

It was a matter of the supremest indifference to Mr. Delamere whether he should ever eat again, but he would not betray his feelings to a servant. In a few minutes he was driving rapidly with Ellis toward the office of the Morning Chronicle. Ellis could see that Mr. Delamere had discovered something of tragic import. Neither spoke. Ellis gave all his attention to the horses, and Mr. Delamere remained wrapped in his own sombre reflections.

When they reached the office, they were informed by Jerry that Major Carteret was engaged with General Belmont and

Captain McBane. Mr. Delamere knocked peremptorily at the door of the inner office, which was opened by Carteret in person.

"Oh, it is you, Mr. Delamere."

"Carteret," exclaimed Mr. Delamere, "I must speak to you immediately, and alone."

"Excuse me a moment, gentlemen," said Carteret, turning to those within the room. "I 'll be back in a moment—don't go away."

Ellis had left the room, closing the door behind him. Mr. Delamere and Carteret were quite alone.

"Carteret," declared the old gentleman, "this murder must not take place."

"'Murder' is a hard word," replied the editor, frowning slightly.

"It is the right word," rejoined Mr. Delamere, decidedly. "It would be a foul and most unnatural murder, for Sandy did not kill Mrs. Ochiltree."

Carteret with difficulty restrained a smile of pity. His old friend was very much excited, as the tremor in his voice gave proof. The criminal was his trusted servant, who had proved unworthy of confidence. No one could question Mr. Delamere's motives; but he was old, his judgment was no longer to be relied upon. It was a great pity that he should so excite and overstrain himself about a worthless negro, who had forfeited his life for a dastardly crime. Mr. Delamere had had two paralytic strokes, and a third might prove fatal. He must be dealt with gently.

"Mr. Delamere," he said, with patient tolerance, "I think you are deceived. There is but one sure way to stop this execution. If your servant is innocent, you must produce the real criminal. If the negro, with such overwhelming proofs against him, is not guilty, who is?"

"I will tell you who is," replied Mr. Delamere. "The murderer is,"—the words came with a note of anguish, as though torn from his very heart,—"the murderer is Tom Delamere, my own grandson!"

"Impossible, sir!" exclaimed Carteret, starting back involuntarily. "That could not be! The man was seen leaving the house, and he was black!"

"All cats are gray in the dark, Carteret; and, moreover, nothing is easier than for a white man to black his face. God alone knows how many crimes have been done in this guise! Tom Delamere, to get the money to pay his gambling debts, committed this foul murder, and then tried to fasten it upon as honest and faithful a soul as ever trod the earth."

Carteret, though at first overwhelmed by this announcement, perceived with quick intuition that it might easily be true. It was but a step from fraud to crime, and in Delamere's need of money there lay a palpable motive for robbery,—the murder may have been an afterthought. Delamere knew as much about the cedar chest as the negro could have known, and more.

But a white man must not be condemned without proof positive.

"What foundation is there, sir," he asked, "for this astounding charge?"

Mr. Delamere related all that had taken place since he left Belleview a couple of hours before, and as he proceeded, step by step, every word carried conviction to Carteret. Tom Delamere's skill as a mimic and a negro impersonator was well known; he had himself laughed at more than one of his performances. There had been a powerful motive, and Mr. Delamere's discoveries had made clear the means. Tom's unusual departure, before breakfast, on a fishing expedition was a suspicious circumstance. There was a certain devilish ingenuity about the affair which he would hardly have expected of Tom Delamere, but for which the reason was clear enough. One might have thought that Tom would have been satisfied with merely blacking his face, and leaving to change the identification of the negro who might be apprehended. He would hardly have implicated, out of pure malignity, his grandfather's old servant, who had been his own care-taker for many years. Here, however, Carteret could see where Tom's own desperate position operated to furnish a probable motive for the crime.

The surest way to head off suspicion from himself was to direct it strongly toward some particular person, and this he had been able to do conclusively by his access to Sandy's clothes, his skill in making up to resemble him, and by the episode of the silk purse. By placing himself beyond reach during the next day, he would not be called upon to corroborate or deny any inculpating statements which Sandy might make, and in the very probable case that the crime should be summarily avenged, any such statements on Sandy's part would be regarded as mere desperate subterfuges of the murderer to save his own life. It was a bad affair.

"The case seems clear," said Carteret reluctantly but conclusively. "And now, what shall we do about it?"

"I want you to print a handbill," said Mr. Delamere, "and circulate it through the town, stating that Sandy Campbell is innocent and Tom Delamere guilty of this crime. If this is not done, I will go myself and declare it to all who will listen, and I will publicly disown the villain who is no more grandson of mine. There is no deeper sink of iniquity into which he could fall."

Carteret's thoughts were chasing one another tumultuously. There could be no doubt that the negro was innocent, from the present aspect of affairs, and he must not be lynched; but in what sort of position would the white people be placed, if Mr. Delamere carried out his Spartan purpose of making the true facts known? The white people of the city had raised the issue of their own superior morality, and had themselves made this crime a race question. The success of the impending "revolution," for which he and his *confrères* had labored so long, depended in large measure upon the maintenance of their race prestige, which would be injured in the eyes of the world by such a fiasco. While they might yet win by sheer force, their cause would suffer in the court of morals, where they might stand convicted as pirates, instead of being applauded as patriots. Even the negroes would have the laugh on them,—the people whom they hoped to make approve and justify their own despoilment. To be laughed at by the negroes was a calamity only less terrible than failure or death.

Such an outcome of an event which had already been heralded to the four corners of the earth would throw a cloud of suspicion upon the stories of outrage which had gone up from the South for so many years, and had done so much to win the sympathy of the North for the white South and to alienate it from the colored people. The reputation of the race was threatened. They must not lynch the negro, and yet, for the credit of the town, its aristocracy, and the race, the truth of this ghastly story must not see the light,—at least not yet.

"Mr. Delamere," he exclaimed, "I am shocked and humiliated. The negro must be saved, of course, but—consider the family honor."

"Tom is no longer a member of my family. I disown him. He has covered the family name—my name, sir—with infamy. We have no longer a family honor. I wish never to hear his name spoken again!"

For several minutes Carteret argued with his old friend. Then he went into the other room and consulted with General Belmont.

As a result of these conferences, and of certain urgent messages sent out, within half an hour thirty or forty of the leading citizens of Wellington were gathered in the Morning Chronicle office. Several other curious persons, observing that there was something in the wind, and supposing correctly that it referred to the projected event of the evening, crowded in with those who had been invited.

Carteret was in another room, still arguing with Mr. Delamere. "It's a mere formality, sir," he was saying suavely, "accompanied by a mental reservation. We know the facts; but this must be done to justify us, in the eyes of the mob, in calling them off before they accomplish their purpose."

"Carteret," said the old man, in a voice eloquent of the struggle through which he had passed, "I would not perjure myself to prolong my own miserable existence another day, but God will forgive a sin committed to save another's life. Upon your head be it, Carteret, and not on mine!"

"Gentlemen," said Carteret, entering with Mr. Delamere the room where the men were gathered, and raising his hand for silence, "the people of Wellington were on the point of wreaking vengeance upon a negro who was supposed to have been guilty of a terrible crime. The white men of this city, impelled by the highest and holiest sentiments, were about to take steps to defend their hearthstones and maintain the purity and ascendency of their race. Your purpose sprung from hearts wounded in their tenderest susceptibilities."

"'Rah,'rah!" shouted a tipsy sailor, who had edged in with the crowd.

"But this same sense of justice," continued Carteret oratorically, "which would lead you to visit swift and terrible punishment upon the guilty, would not permit you to slay an innocent man. Even a negro, as long as he behaves himself and keeps in his place, is entitled to the protection of the law. We may be stern and unbending in the punishment of crime, as befits our masterful race, but we hold the scales of justice with even and impartial hand."

"'Rah f' 'mpa'tial han'!" cried the tipsy sailor, who was immediately ejected with slight ceremony.

"We have discovered, beyond a doubt, that the negro Sandy Campbell, now in custody, did not commit this robbery and murder, but that it was perpetrated by some unknown man, who has fled from the city. Our venerable and distinguished fellow townsman, Mr. Delamere, in whose employment this Campbell has been for many years, will vouch for his character, and states, furthermore, that Campbell was with him all last night, covering any hour at which this crime could have been committed."

"If Mr. Delamere will swear to that," said some one in the crowd, "the negro should not be lynched."

There were murmurs of dissent. The preparations had all been made. There would be great disappointment if the lynching did not occur.

"Let Mr. Delamere swear, if he wants to save the nigger," came again from the crowd.

"Certainly," assented Carteret. "Mr. Delamere can have no possible objection to taking the oath. Is there a notary public present, or a justice of the peace?"

A man stepped forward. "I am a justice of the peace," he announced.

"Very well, Mr. Smith," said Carteret, recognizing the speaker. "With your permission, I will formulate the oath, and Mr. Delamere may repeat it after me, if he will. I solemnly swear,"—

"I solemnly swear,"—

Mr. Delamere's voice might have come from the tomb, so hollow and unnatural did it sound.

"So help me God,"—

"So help me God,"—

"That the negro Sandy Campbell, now in jail on the charge of murder, robbery, and assault, was in my presence last night between the hours of eight and two o'clock."

Mr. Delamere repeated this statement in a firm voice; but to Ellis, who was in the secret, his words fell upon the ear like clods dropping upon the coffin in an open grave.

"I wish to add," said General Belmont, stepping forward, "that it is not our intention to interfere, by anything which may be done at this meeting, with the orderly process of the law, or to advise the prisoner's immediate release. The prisoner will remain in custody, Mr. Delamere, Major Carteret, and I guaranteeing that he will be proved entirely innocent at the preliminary hearing to-morrow morning."

Several of those present looked relieved; others were plainly disappointed; but when the meeting ended, the news went out that the lynching had been given up. Carteret immediately wrote and had struck off a handbill giving a brief statement of the proceedings, and sent out a dozen boys to distribute copies among the people in the streets. That no precaution might be omitted, a call was issued to the Wellington Grays, the crack independent military company of the city, who in an incredibly short time were on guard at the jail.

Thus a slight change in the point of view had demonstrated the entire ability of the leading citizens to maintain the dignified and orderly processes of the law whenever they saw fit to do so.

———

The night passed without disorder, beyond the somewhat rough handling of two or three careless negroes that came in the way of small parties of the disappointed who had sought alcoholic consolation.

At ten o'clock the next morning, a preliminary hearing of the charge against Campbell was had before a magistrate. Mr. Delamere, perceptibly older and more wizened than he had seemed the day before, and leaning heavily on the arm of a servant, repeated his statement of the evening before. Only one or two witnesses were called, among whom was Mr. Ellis, who swore positively that in his opinion the prisoner was not the man whom he had seen and at first supposed to be Campbell. The most sensational piece of testimony was that of Dr. Price, who had examined the body, and who swore that the wound in the head was not necessarily fatal, and might have been due to a fall,—that she had more than likely died of shock attendant upon the robbery, she being of advanced age and feeble health. There was no evidence, he said, of any other personal violence.

Sandy was not even bound over to the grand jury, but was discharged upon the ground that there was not sufficient evidence upon which to hold him. Upon his release he received the congratulations of many present, some of whom would cheerfully have done him to death a few hours before. With the childish fickleness of a mob, they now experienced a satisfaction almost as great as, though less exciting than, that attendant upon taking life. We speak of the mysteries of inanimate nature. The workings of the human heart are the profoundest mystery of the universe. One moment they make us despair of our kind, and the next we see in them the reflection of the divine image. Sandy, having thus escaped from the Mr. Hyde of the mob, now received the benediction of its Dr. Jekyll. Being no cynical philosopher, and realizing how nearly the jaws of death had closed upon him, he was profoundly grateful for his escape, and felt not the slightest desire to investigate or criticise any man's motives.

With the testimony of Dr. Price, the worst feature of the affair came to an end. The murder eliminated or rendered doubtful, the crime became a mere vulgar robbery, the extent of which no one could estimate, since no living soul knew how much money Mrs. Ochiltree had had in the cedar chest. The absurdity of the remaining charge became more fully apparent in the light of the reaction from the excitement of the day before.

Nothing further was ever done about the case; but though the crime went unpunished, it carried evil in its train. As we have seen, the charge against Campbell had been made against the whole colored race. All over the United States the Associated Press had flashed the report of another dastardly outrage by a burly black brute,—all black brutes it seems are burly,— and of the impending lynching with its prospective horrors. This news, being highly sensational in its character, had been displayed in large black type on the front pages of the daily papers. The dispatch that followed, to the effect that the accused had been found innocent and the lynching frustrated, received slight attention, if any, in a fine-print paragraph on an inside page. The facts of the case never came out at all. The family honor of the Delameres was preserved, and the prestige of the white race in Wellington was not seriously impaired.

Upon leaving the preliminary hearing, old Mr. Delamere had requested General Belmont to call at his house during the day upon professional business. This the general did in the course of the afternoon.

"Belmont," said Mr. Delamere, "I wish to make my will. I should have drawn it with my own hand; but you know my motives, and can testify to my soundness of mind and memory."

He thereupon dictated a will, by the terms of which he left to his servant, Sandy Campbell, three thousand dollars, as a mark of the testator's appreciation of services rendered and sufferings endured by Sandy on behalf of his master. After some minor dispositions, the whole remainder of the estate was devised to Dr. William Miller, in trust for the uses of his hospital and training-school for nurses, on condition that the institution be incorporated and placed under the management of competent trustees. Tom Delamere was not mentioned in the will.

"There, Belmont," he said, "that load is off my mind. Now,

if you will call in some witnesses,—most of my people can write,—I shall feel entirely at ease."

The will was signed by Mr. Delamere, and witnessed by Jeff and Billy, two servants in the house, neither of whom received any information as to its contents, beyond the statement that they were witnessing their master's will.

"I wish to leave that with you for safe keeping, Belmont," said Mr. Delamere, after the witnesses had retired. "Lock it up in your safe until I die, which will not be very long, since I have no further desire to live."

An hour later Mr. Delamere suffered a third paralytic stroke, from which he died two days afterwards, without having in the meantime recovered the power of speech.

The will was never produced. The servants stated, and General Belmont admitted, that Mr. Delamere had made a will a few days before his death; but since it was not discoverable, it seemed probable that the testator had destroyed it. This was all the more likely, the general was inclined to think, because the will had been of a most unusual character. What the contents of the will were, he of course did not state, it having been made under the seal of professional secrecy.

This suppression was justified by the usual race argument: Miller's hospital was already well established, and, like most negro institutions, could no doubt rely upon Northern philanthropy for any further support it might need. Mr. Delamere's property belonged of right to the white race, and by the higher law should remain in the possession of white people. Loyalty to one's race was a more sacred principle than deference to a weak old man's whims.

Having reached this conclusion, General Belmont's first impulse was to destroy the will; on second thoughts he locked it carefully away in his safe. He would hold it awhile. It might some time be advisable to talk the matter over with young Delamere, who was of a fickle disposition and might wish to change his legal adviser.

XXVIII
IN SEASON AND OUT

Wellington soon resumed its wonted calm, and in a few weeks the intended lynching was only a memory. The robbery and assault, however, still remained a mystery to all but a chosen few. The affair had been dropped as absolutely as though it had never occurred. No colored man ever learned the reason of this sudden change of front, and Sandy Campbell's loyalty to his old employer's memory kept him silent. Tom Delamere did not offer to retain Sandy in his service, though he presented him with most of the old gentleman's wardrobe. It is only justice to Tom to state that up to this time he had not been informed of the contents of his grandfather's latest will. Major Carteret gave Sandy employment as butler, thus making a sort of vicarious atonement, on the part of the white race, of which the major felt himself in a way the embodiment, for the risk to which Sandy had been subjected.

Shortly after these events Sandy was restored to the bosom of the church, and, enfolded by its sheltering arms, was no longer tempted to stray from the path of rectitude, but became even a more rigid Methodist than before his recent troubles.

Tom Delamere did not call upon Clara again in the character of a lover. Of course they could not help meeting, from time to time, but he never dared presume upon their former relations. Indeed, the social atmosphere of Wellington remained so frigid toward Delamere that he left town, and did not return for several months.

Ellis was aware that Delamere had been thrown over, but a certain delicacy restrained him from following up immediately the advantage which the absence of his former rival gave him. It seemed to him, with the quixotry of a clean, pure mind, that Clara would pass through a period of mourning for her lost illusion, and that it would be indelicate, for the time being, to approach her with a lover's attentions. The work of the office had been unusually heavy of late. The major, deeply absorbed in politics, left the detail work of the paper to Ellis. Into the intimate counsels of the revolutionary committee Ellis had not been admitted, nor would he have desired to be. He knew, of course, in a general way, the results that it was sought to achieve; and while he did not see their necessity, he deferred to the views of older men, and was satisfied to remain in ignorance of anything which he might disapprove. Moreover, his own personal affairs occupied his mind to an extent that made politics or any other subject a matter of minor importance.

As for Dr. Miller, he never learned of Mr. Delamere's good intentions toward his institution, but regretted the old gentleman's death as the loss of a sincere friend and well-wisher of his race in their unequal struggle.

Despite the untiring zeal of Carteret and his associates, the campaign for the restriction of the suffrage, which was to form the basis of a permanent white supremacy, had seemed to languish for a while after the Ochiltree affair. The lull, however, was only temporary, and more apparent than real, for the forces adverse to the negro were merely gathering strength for a more vigorous assault. While little was said in Wellington, public sentiment all over the country became every day more favorable to the views of the conspirators. The nation was rushing forward with giant strides toward colossal wealth and world-domination, before the exigencies of which mere abstract ethical theories must not be permitted to stand. The same argument that justified the conquest of an inferior nation could not be denied to those who sought the suppression of an inferior race. In the South, an obscure jealousy of the negro's progress, an obscure fear of the very equality so contemptuously denied, furnished a rich soil for successful agitation. Statistics of crime, ingeniously manipulated, were made to present a fearful showing against the negro. Vital statistics were made to prove that he had degenerated from an imaginary standard of physical excellence which had existed under the benign influence of slavery. Constant lynchings emphasized his impotence, and bred everywhere a growing contempt for his rights.

At the North, a new Pharaoh had risen, who knew not Israel,—a new generation, who knew little of the fierce passions which had played around the negro in a past epoch, and

derived their opinions of him from the "coon song" and the
police reports. Those of his old friends who survived were disappointed that he had not flown with clipped wings; that he
had not in one generation of limited opportunity attained the
level of the whites. The whole race question seemed to have
reached a sort of *impasse,* a blind alley, of which no one could
see the outlet. The negro had become a target at which any one
might try a shot. Schoolboys gravely debated the question as to
whether or not the negro should exercise the franchise. The
pessimist gave him up in despair; while the optimist, smilingly
confident that everything would come out all right in the end,
also turned aside and went his buoyant way to more pleasing
themes.

For a time there were white men in the state who opposed
any reactionary step unless it were of general application. They
were conscientious men, who had learned the ten command-
ments and wished to do right; but this class was a small minor-
ity, and their objections were soon silenced by the all-powerful
race argument. Selfishness is the most constant of human motives. Patriotism, humanity, or the love of God may lead to
sporadic outbursts which sweep away the heaped-up wrongs of
centuries; but they languish at times, while the love of self
works on ceaselessly, unwearyingly, burrowing always at the
very roots of life, and heaping up fresh wrongs for other centuries to sweep away. The state was at the mercy of venal and
self-seeking politicians, bent upon regaining their ascendency
at any cost, stultifying their own minds by vague sophistries
and high-sounding phrases, which deceived none but those
who wished to be deceived, and these but imperfectly; and
dulling the public conscience by a loud clamor in which the
calm voice of truth was for the moment silenced. So the cause
went on.

Carteret, as spokesman of the campaign, and sincerest of all
its leaders, performed prodigies of labor. The Morning Chronicle proclaimed, in season and out, the doctrine of "White Supremacy." Leaving the paper in charge of Ellis, the major made
a tour of the state, rousing the white people of the better class
to an appreciation of the terrible danger which confronted

them in the possibility that a few negroes might hold a few offices or dictate the terms upon which white men should fill them. Difficulties were explained away. The provisions of the Federal Constitution, it was maintained, must yield to the "higher law," and if the Constitution could neither be altered nor bent to this end, means must be found to circumvent it.

The device finally hit upon for disfranchising the colored people in this particular state was the notorious "grandfather clause." After providing various restrictions of the suffrage, based upon education, character, and property, which it was deemed would in effect disfranchise the colored race, an exception was made in favor of all citizens whose fathers or grandfathers had been entitled to vote prior to 1867. Since none but white men could vote prior to 1867, this exception obviously took in the poor and ignorant whites, while the same class of negroes were excluded.

It was ingenious, but it was not fair. In due time a constitutional convention was called, in which the above scheme was adopted and submitted to a vote of the people for ratification. The campaign was fought on the color line. Many white Republicans, deluded with the hope that by the elimination of the negro vote their party might receive accessions from the Democratic ranks, went over to the white party. By fraud in one place, by terrorism in another, and everywhere by the resistless moral force of the united whites, the negroes were reduced to the apathy of despair, their few white allies demoralized, and the amendment adopted by a large majority. The negroes were taught that this is a white man's country, and that the sooner they made up their minds to this fact, the better for all concerned. The white people would be good to them so long as they behaved themselves and kept their place. As theoretical equals,—practical equality being forever out of the question, either by nature or by law,—there could have been nothing but strife between them, in which the weaker party would invariably have suffered most.

Some colored men accepted the situation thus outlined, if not as desirable, at least as inevitable. Most of them, however, had little faith in this condescending friendliness which was to

take the place of constitutional rights. They knew they had
been treated unfairly; that their enemies had prevailed against
them; that their whilom friends had stood passively by and
seen them undone. Many of the most enterprising and progressive left the state, and those who remain still labor under a
sense of wrong and outrage which renders them distinctly less
valuable as citizens.

The great steal was made, but the thieves did not turn
honest,—the scheme still shows the mark of the burglar's tools.
Sins, like chickens, come home to roost. The South paid a fearful price for the wrong of negro slavery; in some form or other
it will doubtless reap the fruits of this later iniquity.

Drastic as were these "reforms," the results of which we have
anticipated somewhat, since the new Constitution was not to
take effect immediately, they moved all too slowly for the little
coterie of Wellington conspirators, whose ambitions and needs
urged them to prompt action. Under the new Constitution it
would be two full years before the "nigger amendment" became effective, and meanwhile the Wellington district would
remain hopelessly Republican. The committee decided, about
two months before the fall election, that an active local campaign must be carried on, with a view to discourage the negroes
from attending the polls on election day.

The question came up for discussion one afternoon in a
meeting at the office of the Morning Chronicle, at which all of
the "Big Three" were present.

"Something must be done," declared McBane, "and that
damn quick. Too many white people are saying that it will
be better to wait until the amendment goes into effect. That
would mean to leave the niggers in charge of this town for two
years after the state has declared for white supremacy! I 'm
opposed to leaving it in their hands one hour,—them 's my sentiments!"

This proved to be the general opinion, and the discussion
turned to the subject of ways and means.

"What became of that editorial in the nigger paper?" inquired the general in his blandest tones, cleverly directing a

smoke ring toward the ceiling. "It lost some of its point back there, when we came near lynching that nigger; but now that that has blown over, why would n't it be a good thing to bring into play at the present juncture? Let 's read it over again."

Carteret extracted the paper from the pigeon-hole where he had placed it some months before. The article was read aloud with emphasis and discussed phrase by phrase. Of its wording there could be little criticism,—it was temperately and even cautiously phrased. As suggested by the general, the Ochiltree affair had proved that it was not devoid of truth. Its great offensiveness lay in its boldness: that a negro should publish in a newspaper what white people would scarcely acknowledge to themselves in secret was much as though a Russian *moujik* or a German peasant should rush into print to question the divine right of the Lord's Anointed. The article was racial *lèse-majesté* in the most aggravated form. A peg was needed upon which to hang a *coup d'état,* and this editorial offered the requisite opportunity. It was unanimously decided to republish the obnoxious article, with comment adapted to fire the inflammable Southern heart and rouse it against any further self-assertion of the negroes in politics or elsewhere.

"The time is ripe!" exclaimed McBane. "In a month we can have the niggers so scared that they won't dare stick their heads out of doors on 'lection day."

"I wonder," observed the general thoughtfully, after this conclusion had been reached, "if we could n't have Jerry fetch us some liquor?"

Jerry appeared in response to the usual summons. The general gave him the money, and ordered three Calhoun cocktails. When Jerry returned with the glasses on a tray, the general observed him with pointed curiosity.

"What in h——ll is the matter with you, Jerry? Your black face is splotched with brown and yellow patches, and your hair shines as though you had fallen head-foremost into a firkin of butter. What's the matter with you?"

Jerry seemed much embarrassed by this inquiry.

"Nothin', suh, nothin'," he stammered. "It 's—it 's jes' somethin' I be'n puttin' on my hair, suh, ter improve de quality, suh."

"Jerry," returned the general, bending a solemn look upon the porter, "you have been playing with edged tools, and your days are numbered. You have been reading the Afro-American Banner."

He shook open the paper, which he had retained in his hand, and read from one of the advertisements:—

"'Kinky, curly hair made straight in two applications. Dark skins lightened two shades; mulattoes turned perfectly white.'

"This stuff is rank poison, Jerry," continued the general with a mock solemnity which did not impose upon Jerry, who nevertheless listened with an air of great alarm. He suspected that the general was making fun of him; but he also knew that the general would like to think that Jerry believed him in earnest; and to please the white folks was Jerry's consistent aim in life. "I can see the signs of decay in your face, and your hair will all fall out in a week or two at the latest,—mark my words!"

McBane had listened to this pleasantry with a sardonic sneer. It was a waste of valuable time. To Carteret it seemed in doubtful taste. These grotesque advertisements had their tragic side. They were proof that the negroes had read the handwriting on the wall. These pitiful attempts to change their physical characteristics were an acknowledgment, on their own part, that the negro was doomed, and that the white man was to inherit the earth and hold all other races under his heel. For, as the months had passed, Carteret's thoughts centring more and more upon the negro, had led him farther and farther, until now he was firmly convinced that there was no permanent place for the negro in the United States, if indeed anywhere in the world, except under the ground. More pathetic even than Jerry's efforts to escape from the universal doom of his race was his ignorance that even if he could, by some strange alchemy, bleach his skin and straighten his hair, there would still remain, underneath it all, only the unbleached darky,—the ass in the lion's skin.

When the general had finished his facetious lecture, Jerry backed out of the room shamefacedly, though affecting a greater confusion than he really felt. Jerry had not reasoned so closely as Carteret, but he had realized that it was a distinct advantage to be white,—an advantage which white people had utilized to secure all the best things in the world; and he had entertained the vague hope that by changing his complexion he might share this prerogative. While he suspected the general's sincerity, he nevertheless felt a little apprehensive lest the general's prediction about the effects of the face-bleach and other preparations might prove true,—the general was a white gentleman and ought to know,—and decided to abandon their use.

This purpose was strengthened by his next interview with the major. When Carteret summoned him, an hour later, after the other gentlemen had taken their leave, Jerry had washed his head thoroughly and there remained no trace of the pomade. An attempt to darken the lighter spots in his cuticle by the application of printer's ink had not proved equally successful,— the retouching left the spots as much too dark as they had formerly been too light.

"Jerry," said Carteret sternly, "when I hired you to work for the Chronicle, you were black. The word 'negro' means 'black.' The best negro is a black negro, of the pure type, as it came from the hand of God. If you wish to get along well with the white people, the blacker you are the better,—white people do not like negroes who want to be white. A man should be content to remain as God made him and where God placed him. So no more of this nonsense. Are you going to vote at the next election?"

"What would you 'vise me ter do, suh?" asked Jerry cautiously.

"I do not advise you. You ought to have sense enough to see where your own interests lie. I put it to you whether you cannot trust yourself more safely in the hands of white gentlemen, who are your true friends, than in the hands of ignorant and purchasable negroes and unscrupulous white scoundrels?"

"Dere 's no doubt about it, suh," assented Jerry, with a vehemence proportioned to his desire to get back into favor. "I ain' gwine ter have nothin' ter do wid de 'lection, suh! Ef I don' vote, I kin keep my job, can't I, suh?"

The major eyed Jerry with an air of supreme disgust. What could be expected of a race so utterly devoid of tact? It seemed as though this negro thought a white gentleman might want to bribe him to remain away from the polls; and the negro's willingness to accept the imaginary bribe demonstrated the venal nature of the colored race,—its entire lack of moral principle!

"You will retain your place, Jerry," he said severely, "so long as you perform your duties to my satisfaction and behave yourself properly."

With this grandiloquent subterfuge Carteret turned to his next article on white supremacy. Jerry did not delude himself with any fine-spun sophistry. He knew perfectly well that he held his job upon the condition that he stayed away from the polls at the approaching election. Jerry was a fool—

> The world of fools hath such a store,
> That he who would not see an ass,
> Must stay at home and shut his door
> And break his looking-glass.

But while no one may be entirely wise, there are degrees of folly, and Jerry was not all kinds of a fool.

XXIX
MUTTERINGS OF THE STORM

Events moved rapidly during the next few days. The reproduction, in the Chronicle, of the article from the Afro-American Banner, with Carteret's inflammatory comment, took immediate effect. It touched the Southern white man in his most sensitive spot. To him such an article was an insult to white womanhood, and must be resented by some active steps,—mere words would be no answer at all. To meet words with words upon such a subject would be to acknowledge the equality of the negro and his right to discuss or criticise the conduct of the white people.

The colored people became alarmed at the murmurings of the whites, which seemed to presage a coming storm. A number of them sought to arm themselves, but ascertained, upon

inquiring at the stores, that no white merchant would sell a negro firearms. Since all the dealers in this sort of merchandise
were white men, the negroes had to be satisfied with oiling up
the old army muskets which some of them possessed, and the
few revolvers with which a small rowdy element generally
managed to keep themselves supplied. Upon an effort being
made to purchase firearms from a Northern city, the express
company, controlled by local men, refused to accept the con-
signment. The white people, on the other hand, procured both
arms and ammunition in large quantities, and the Wellington
Grays drilled with great assiduity at their armory.

All this went on without any public disturbance of the
town's tranquillity. A stranger would have seen nothing to excite his curiosity. The white people did their talking among
themselves, and merely grew more distant in their manner
toward the colored folks, who instinctively closed their ranks
as the whites drew away. With each day that passed the feeling grew more tense. The editor of the Afro-American Banner,
whose office had been quietly garrisoned for several nights by
armed negroes, became frightened, and disappeared from the
town between two suns.

The conspirators were jubilant at the complete success of
their plans. It only remained for them to so direct this aroused
public feeling that it might completely accomplish the desired
end,—to change the political complexion of the city government and assure the ascendency of the whites until the amendment should go into effect. A revolution, and not a riot, was
contemplated.

With this end in view, another meeting was called at Carteret's office.

"We are now ready," announced General Belmont, "for the
final act of this drama. We must decide promptly, or events
may run away from us."

"What do you suggest?" asked Carteret.

"Down in the American tropics," continued the general,
"they have a way of doing things. I was in Nicaragua, ten years
ago, when Paterno's revolution drove out Igorroto's government. It was as easy as falling off a log. Paterno had the arms

and the best men. Igorroto was not looking for trouble, and the guns were at his breast before he knew it. We have the guns. The negroes are not expecting trouble, and are easy to manage compared with the fiery mixture that flourishes in the tropics."

"I should not advocate murder," returned Carteret. "We are animated by high and holy principles. We wish to right a wrong, to remedy an abuse, to save our state from anarchy and our race from humiliation. I don't object to frightening the negroes, but I am opposed to unnecessary bloodshed."

"I 'm not quite so particular," struck in McBane. "They need to be taught a lesson, and a nigger more or less would n't be missed. There 's too many of 'em now."

"Of course," continued Carteret, "if we should decide upon a certain mode of procedure, and the negroes should resist, a different reasoning might apply; but I will have no premeditated murder."

"In Central and South America," observed the general reflectively, "none are hurt except those who get in the way."

"There 'll be no niggers hurt," said McBane contemptuously, "unless they strain themselves running. One white man can chase a hundred of 'em. I 've managed five hundred at a time. I 'll pay for burying all the niggers that are killed."

The conference resulted in a well-defined plan, to be put into operation the following day, by which the city government was to be wrested from the Republicans and their negro allies.

"And now," said General Belmont, "while we are cleansing the Augean stables, we may as well remove the cause as the effect. There are several negroes too many in this town, which will be much the better without them. There 's that yellow lawyer, Watson. He 's altogether too mouthy, and has too much business. Every nigger that gets into trouble sends for Watson, and white lawyers, with families to support and social positions to keep up, are deprived of their legitimate source of income."

"There 's that damn nigger real estate agent," blurted out McBane. "Billy Kitchen used to get most of the nigger business, but this darky has almost driven him to the poorhouse. A white business man is entitled to a living in his own profession and his own home. That nigger don't belong here nohow. He came from the North a year or two ago, and is hand in glove with Barber, the nigger editor, which is enough of itself to damn him. *He 'll* have to go!"

"How about the collector of the port?"

"We 'd better not touch him. It would bring the government down upon us, which we want to avoid. We don't need to worry about the nigger preachers either. They want to stay here, where the loaves and the fishes are. We can make 'em write letters to the newspapers justifying our course, as a condition of their remaining."

"What about Billings?" asked McBane. Billlings was the white Republican mayor. "Is that skunk to be allowed to stay in town?"

"No," returned the general, "every white Republican officeholder ought to be made to go. This town is only big enough for Democrats, and negroes who can be taught to keep their place."

"What about the colored doctor," queried McBane, "with the hospital, and the diamond ring, and the carriage, and the other fallals?"

"I should n't interfere with Miller," replied the general decisively. "He 's a very good sort of a negro, does n't meddle with politics, nor tread on any one else's toes. His father was a good citizen, which counts in his favor. He 's spending money in the community too, and contributes to its prosperity."

"That sort of nigger, though, sets a bad example," retorted McBane. "They make it all the harder to keep the rest of 'em down."

" 'One swallow does not make a summer,' " quoted the general. "When we get things arranged there 'll be no trouble. A stream cannot rise higher than its fountain, and a smart nigger without a constituency will no longer be an object of fear. I say, let the doctor alone."

"He 'll have to keep mighty quiet, though," muttered McBane discontentedly. "I don't like smart niggers. I 've had to shoot several of them, in the course of my life."

"Personally, I dislike the man," interposed Carteret, "and if

I consulted my own inclinations, would say expel him with the rest; but my grievance is a personal one, and to gratify it in that way would be a loss to the community. I wish to be strictly impartial in this matter, and to take no step which cannot be entirely justified by a wise regard for the public welfare."

"What 's the use of all this hypocrisy, gentlemen?" sneered McBane. "Every last one of us has an axe to grind! The major may as well put an edge on his. We 'll never get a better chance to have things our way. If this nigger doctor annoys the major, we 'll run him out with the rest. This is a white man's country, and a white man's city, and no nigger has any business here when a white man wants him gone!"

Carteret frowned darkly at this brutal characterization of their motives. It robbed the enterprise of all its poetry, and put a solemn act of revolution upon the plane of a mere vulgar theft of power. Even the general winced.

"I would not consent," he said irritably, "to Miller's being disturbed."

McBane made no further objection.

There was a discreet knock at the door.

"Come in," said Carteret.

Jerry entered. "Mistuh Ellis wants ter speak ter you a minute, suh," he said.

Carteret excused himself and left the room.

"Jerry," said the general, "you lump of ebony, the sight of you reminds me! If your master does n't want you for a minute, step across to Mr. Brown's and tell him to send me three cocktails."

"Yas, suh," responded Jerry, hesitating. The general had said nothing about paying.

"And tell him, Jerry, to charge them. I'm short of change to-day."

"Yas, suh; yas, suh," replied Jerry, as he backed out of the presence, adding, when he had reached the hall: "Dere ain' no change fer Jerry dis time, sho': I 'll jes' make dat *fo'* cocktails, an' de gin'l won't never know de diffe'nce. I ain' gwine 'cross de road fer nothin', not ef I knows it."

Half an hour later, the conspirators dispersed. They had

fixed the hour of the proposed revolution, the course to be pursued, the results to be obtained; but in stating their equation they had overlooked one factor,—God, or Fate, or whatever one may choose to call the Power that holds the destinies of man in the hollow of his hand.

XXX

THE MISSING PAPERS

Mrs. Carteret was very much disturbed. It was supposed that the shock of her aunt's death had affected her health, for since that event she had fallen into a nervous condition which gave the major grave concern. Much to the general surprise, Mrs. Ochiltree had left no will, and no property of any considerable value except her homestead, which descended to Mrs. Carteret as the natural heir. Whatever she may have had on hand in the way of ready money had undoubtedly been abstracted from the cedar chest by the midnight marauder, to whose visit her death was immediately due. Her niece's grief was held to mark a deep-seated affection for the grim old woman who had reared her.

Mrs. Carteret's present state of mind, of which her nervousness was a sufficiently accurate reflection, did in truth date from her aunt's death, and also in part from the time of the conversation with Mrs. Ochiltree, one afternoon, during and after the drive past Miller's new hospital. Mrs. Ochiltree had grown steadily more and more childish after that time, and her niece had never succeeded in making her pick up the thread of thought where it had been dropped. At any rate, Mrs. Ochiltree had made no further disclosure upon the subject.

An examination, not long after her aunt's death, of the papers found near the cedar chest on the morning after the murder had contributed to Mrs. Carteret's enlightenment, but had not promoted her peace of mind.

When Mrs. Carteret reached home, after her hurried exploration of the cedar chest, she thrust into a bureau drawer the envelope she had found. So fully was her mind occupied, for several days, with the funeral, and with the excitement of attending the arrest of Sandy Campbell, that she deferred the examination of the contents of the envelope until near the end of the week.

One morning, while alone in her chamber, she drew the envelope from the drawer, and was holding it in her hand, hesitating as to whether or not she should open it, when the baby in the next room began to cry.

The child's cry seemed like a warning, and yielding to a vague uneasiness, she put the paper back.

"Phil," she said to her husband at luncheon, "Aunt Polly said some strange things to me one day before she died,—I don't know whether she was quite in her right mind or not; but suppose that my father had left a will by which it was provided that half his property should go to that woman and her child?"

"It would never have gone by such a will," replied the major easily. "Your Aunt Polly was in her dotage, and merely dreaming. Your father would never have been such a fool; but even if he had, no such will could have stood the test of the courts. It would clearly have been due to the improper influence of a designing woman."

"So that legally, as well as morally," said Mrs. Carteret, "the will would have been of no effect?"

"Not the slightest. A jury would soon have broken down the legal claim. As for any moral obligation, there would have been nothing moral about the affair. The only possible consideration for such a gift was an immoral one. I don't wish to speak harshly of your father, my dear, but his conduct was gravely reprehensible. The woman herself had no right or claim whatever; she would have been whipped and expelled from the town, if justice—blind, bleeding justice, then prostrate at the feet of slaves and aliens—could have had her way!"

"But the child"—

"The child was in the same category. Who was she, to have inherited the estate of your ancestors, of which, a few years before, she would herself have formed a part? The child of shame, it was hers to pay the penalty. But the discussion is all in the air,

Olivia. Your father never did and never would have left such a will."

This conversation relieved Mrs. Carteret's uneasiness. Going to her room shortly afterwards, she took the envelope from her bureau drawer and drew out a bulky paper. The haunting fear that it might be such a will as her aunt had suggested was now removed; for such an instrument, in the light of what her husband had said confirming her own intuitions, would be of no valid effect. It might be just as well, she thought, to throw the paper in the fire without looking at it. She wished to think as well as might be of her father, and she felt that her respect for his memory would not be strengthened by the knowledge that he had meant to leave his estate away from her; for her aunt's words had been open to the consideration that she was to have been left destitute. Curiosity strongly prompted her to read the paper. Perhaps the will contained no such provision as she had feared, and it might convey some request or direction which ought properly to be complied with.

She had been standing in front of the bureau while these thoughts passed through her mind, and now, dropping the envelope back into the drawer mechanically, she unfolded the document. It was written on legal paper, in her father's own hand.

Mrs. Carteret was not familiar with legal verbiage, and there were several expressions of which she did not perhaps appreciate the full effect; but a very hasty glance enabled her to ascertain the purport of the paper. It was a will, by which, in one item, her father devised to his daughter Janet, the child of the woman known as Julia Brown, the sum of ten thousand dollars, and a certain plantation or tract of land a short distance from the town of Wellington. The rest and residue of his estate, after deducting all legal charges and expenses, was bequeathed to his beloved daughter, Olivia Merkell.

Mrs. Carteret breathed a sigh of relief. Her father had not preferred another to her, but had left to his lawful daughter the bulk of his estate. She felt at the same time a growing indignation at the thought that that woman should so have wrought upon her father's weakness as to induce him to think of leaving so much valuable property to her bastard—property which by right should go, and now would go, to her own son, to whom by every rule of law and decency it ought to descend.

A fire was burning in the next room, on account of the baby—there had been a light frost the night before, and the air was somewhat chilly. For the moment the room was empty. Mrs. Carteret came out from her chamber and threw the offending paper into the fire, and watched it slowly burn. When it had been consumed, the carbon residue of one sheet still retained its form, and she could read the words on the charred portion. A sentence, which had escaped her eye in her rapid reading, stood out in ghostly black upon the gray background:—

"All the rest and residue of my estate I devise and bequeath to my daughter Olivia Merkell, the child of my beloved first wife."

Mrs. Carteret had not before observed the word "first." Instinctively she stretched toward the fire the poker which she held in her hand, and at its touch the shadowy remnant fell to pieces, and nothing but ashes remained upon the hearth.

Not until the next morning did she think again of the envelope which had contained the paper she had burned. Opening the drawer where it lay, the oblong blue envelope confronted her. The sight of it was distasteful. The indorsed side lay uppermost, and the words seemed like a mute reproach:—

"The Last Will and Testament of Samuel Merkell."

Snatching up the envelope, she glanced into it mechanically as she moved toward the next room, and perceived a thin folded paper which had heretofore escaped her notice. When opened, it proved to be a certificate of marriage, in due form, between Samuel Merkell and Julia Brown. It was dated from a county in South Carolina, about two years before her father's death.

For a moment Mrs. Carteret stood gazing blankly at this faded slip of paper. Her father *had* married this woman—at least he had gone through the form of marriage with her, for to him it had surely been no more than an empty formality. The marriage of white and colored persons was forbidden by law.

Only recently she had read of a case where both the parties to such a crime, a colored man and a white woman, had been sentenced to long terms in the penitentiary. She had recalled the circumstances. The couple had been living together unlawfully— they were very low people, whose private lives were beneath public notice—but influenced by a religious movement pervading the community, had sought, they said at the trial, to secure the blessing of God upon their union. The higher law, which imperiously demanded that the purity and prestige of the white race be preserved at any cost, had intervened at this point.

Mechanically she moved toward the fireplace, so dazed by this discovery as to be scarcely conscious of her own actions. She surely had not formed any definite intention of destroying this piece of paper when her fingers relaxed unconsciously and let go their hold upon it. The draught swept it toward the fireplace. Ere scarcely touching the flames it caught, blazed fiercely, and shot upward with the current of air. A moment later the record of poor Julia's marriage was scattered to the four winds of heaven, as her poor body had long since mingled with the dust of earth.

The letter remained unread. In her agitation at the discovery of the marriage certificate, Olivia had almost forgotten the existence of the letter. It was addressed to "John Delamere, Esq., as Executor of my Last Will and Testament," while the lower left-hand corner bore the direction: "To be delivered only after my death, with seal unbroken."

The seal was broken already; Mr. Delamere was dead; the letter could never be delivered. Mrs. Carteret unfolded it and read:—

MY DEAR DELAMERE,—I have taken the liberty of naming you as executor of my last will, because you are my friend, and the only man of my acquaintance whom I feel that I can trust to carry out my wishes, appreciate my motives, and preserve the silence I desire.

I have, first, a confession to make. Inclosed in this letter you will find a certificate of marriage between my child Janet's mother and myself. While I have never exactly repented of this marriage, I have never had the courage to acknowledge it openly. If I had not married Julia, I fear Polly Ochiltree would have married me by main force,—as she would marry you or any other gentleman unfortunate enough to fall in the way of this twice-widowed man-hunter. When my wife died, three years ago, her sister Polly offered to keep house for me and the child. I would sooner have had the devil in the house, and yet I trembled with alarm—there seemed no way of escape,—it was so clearly and obviously the proper thing.

But she herself gave me my opportunity. I was on the point of consenting, when she demanded, as a condition of her coming, that I discharge Julia, my late wife's maid. She was laboring under a misapprehension in regard to the girl, but I grasped at the straw, and did everything to foster her delusion. I declared solemnly that nothing under heaven would induce me to part with Julia. The controversy resulted in my permitting Polly to take the child, while I retained the maid.

Before Polly put this idea into my head, I had scarcely looked at Julia, but this outbreak turned my attention toward her. She was a handsome girl, and, as I soon found out, a good girl. My wife, who raised her, was a Christian woman, and had taught her modesty and virtue. She was free. The air was full of liberty, and equal rights, and all the abolition claptrap, and she made marriage a condition of her remaining longer in the house. In a moment of weakness I took her away to a place where we were not known, and married her. If she had left me, I should have fallen a victim to Polly Ochiltree—to which any fate was preferable.

And then, old friend, my weakness kept to the fore. I was ashamed of this marriage, and my new wife saw it. Moreover, she loved me,—too well, indeed, to wish to make me unhappy. The ceremony had satisfied her conscience, had set her right, she said, with God; for the opinions of men she did not care, since I loved her,—she only wanted to compensate me, as best she could, for the great honor I had done my handmaiden,—for she had read her Bible, and I was the Abraham to her Hagar, compared with whom she considered herself at a great advantage. It was her own proposition that nothing be said of this marriage. If any shame should fall on her, it would fall lightly, for it would be undeserved. When the child came, she still kept silence. No one, she argued, could blame an innocent child for the accident of birth, and in the sight of God this child had every right to exist; while among her own people illegitimacy would involve but little stigma.

I need not say that I was easily persuaded to accept this sacrifice; but touched by her fidelity, I swore to provide handsomely for them both. This I have tried to do by the will of which I ask you to act as executor. Had I left the child more, it might serve as a ground for attacking the will; my acknowledgment of the tie of blood is sufficient to justify a reasonable bequest.

I have taken this course for the sake of my daughter Olivia, who is dear to me, and whom I would not wish to make ashamed; and in deference to public opinion, which it is not easy to defy. If, after my death, Julia should choose to make our secret known, I shall of course be beyond the reach of hard words; but loyalty to my memory will probably keep her silent. A strong man would long since have acknowledged her before the world and taken the consequences; but, alas! I am only myself, and the atmosphere I live in does not encourage moral heroism. I should like to be different, but it is God who hath made us, and not we ourselves!

Nevertheless, old friend, I will ask of you one favor. If in the future this child of Julia's and of mine should grow to womanhood; if she should prove to have her mother's gentleness and love of virtue; if, in the new era which is opening up for her mother's race, to which, unfortunately, she must belong, she should become, in time, an educated woman; and if the time should ever come when, by virtue of her education or the development of her people, it would be to her a source of shame or unhappiness that she was an illegitimate child,—if you are still alive, old friend, and have the means of knowing or divining this thing, go to her and tell her, for me, that she is my lawful child, and ask her to forgive her father's weakness.

When this letter comes to you, I shall have passed to—the Beyond; but I am confident that you will accept this trust, for
which I thank you now, in advance, most heartily.

The letter was signed with her father's name, the same signature which had been attached to the will.

Having firmly convinced herself of the illegality of the papers, and of her own right to destroy them, Mrs. Carteret
ought to have felt relieved that she had thus removed all traces
of her dead father's folly. True, the other daughter remained,—
she had seen her on the street only the day before. The sight of
this person she had always found offensive, and now, she felt,
in view of what she had just learned, it must be even more so.
Never, while this woman lived in the town, would she be able
to throw the veil of forgetfulness over this blot upon her father's memory.

As the day wore on, Mrs. Carteret grew still less at ease. To
herself, marriage was a serious thing,—to a right-thinking
woman the most serious concern of life. A marriage certificate,
rightfully procured, was scarcely less solemn, so far as it went,
than the Bible itself. Her own she cherished as the apple of her
eye. It was the evidence of her wifehood, the seal of her child's
legitimacy, her patent of nobility,—the token of her own and
her child's claim to social place and consideration. She had
burned this pretended marriage certificate because it meant
nothing. Nevertheless, she could not ignore the knowledge of
another such marriage, of which every one in the town knew,—
a celebrated case, indeed, where a white man, of a family quite
as prominent as her father's, had married a colored woman
during the military occupation of the state just before the civil
war. The legality of the marriage had never been questioned. It
had been fully consummated by twenty years of subsequent co-
habitation. No amount of social persecution had ever shaken
the position of the husband. With an iron will he had stayed on
in the town, a living protest against the established customs of
the South, so rudely interrupted for a few short years; and,
though his children were negroes, though he had never ap-

peared in public with his wife, no one had ever questioned the validity of his marriage or the legitimacy of his offspring.

The marriage certificate which Mrs. Carteret had burned dated from the period of the military occupation. Hence Mrs. Carteret, who was a good woman, and would not have done a dishonest thing, felt decidedly uncomfortable. She had destroyed the marriage certificate, but its ghost still haunted her.

Major Carteret, having just eaten a good dinner, was in a very agreeable humor when, that same evening, his wife brought up again the subject of their previous discussion.

"Phil," she asked, "Aunt Polly told me that once, long before my father died, when she went to remonstrate with him for keeping that woman in the house, he threatened to marry Julia if Aunt Polly ever said another word to him about the matter. Suppose he *had* married her, and had *then* left a will,—would the marriage have made any difference, so far as the will was concerned?"

Major Carteret laughed. "Your Aunt Polly," he said, "was a remarkable woman, with a wonderful imagination, which seems to have grown more vivid as her memory and judgment weakened. Why should your father marry his negro housemaid? Mr. Merkell was never rated as a fool,—he had one of the clearest heads in Wellington. I saw him only a day or two before he died, and I could swear before any court in Christendom that he was of sound mind and memory to the last. These notions of your aunt were mere delusions. Your father was never capable of such folly."

"Of course I am only supposing a case," returned Olivia. "Imagining such a case, just for the argument, would the marriage have been legal?"

"That would depend. If he had married her during the military occupation, or over in South Carolina, the marriage would have been legally valid, though morally and socially outrageous."

"And if he had died afterwards, leaving a will?"

"The will would have controlled the disposition of his estate, in all probability."

"Suppose he had left no will?"

"You are getting the matter down pretty fine, my dear! The woman would have taken one third of the real estate for life, and could have lived in the homestead until she died. She would also have had half the other property,—the money and goods and furniture, everything except the land,—and the negro child would have shared with you the balance of the estate. That, I believe, is according to the law of descent and distribution."

Mrs. Carteret lapsed into a troubled silence. Her father *had* married the woman. In her heart she had no doubt of the validity of the marriage, so far as the law was concerned; if one's marriage of such a kind would stand, another contracted under similar conditions was equally as good. If the marriage had been valid, Julia's child had been legitimate. The will she had burned gave this sister of hers—she shuddered at the word— but a small part of the estate. Under the law, which intervened now that there was no will, the property should have been equally divided. If the woman had been white,—but the woman had *not* been white, and the same rule of moral conduct did not, *could* not, in the very nature of things, apply, as between white people! For, if this were not so, slavery had been, not merely an economic mistake, but a great crime against humanity. If it had been such a crime, as for a moment she dimly perceived it might have been, then through the long centuries there had been piled up a catalogue of wrong and outrage which, if the law of compensation be a law of nature, must some time, somewhere, in some way, be atoned for. She herself had not escaped the penalty, of which, she realized, this burden placed upon her conscience was but another installment.

If she should make known the facts she had learned, it would mean what?—a division of her father's estate, a recognition of the legality of her father's relations with Julia. Such a stain upon her father's memory would be infinitely worse than if he had not married her. To have lived with her without marriage was a social misdemeanor, at which society in the old days had winked, or at most had frowned. To have married her was to have committed the unpardonable social sin. Such a scandal Mrs. Carteret could not have endured. Should she seek to make restitution, it would necessarily involve the disclosure of at least some of the facts. Had she not destroyed the will, she might have compromised with her conscience by producing it and acting upon its terms, which had been so stated as not to disclose the marriage. This was now rendered impossible by her own impulsive act; she could not mention the will at all, without admitting that she had destroyed it.

Mrs. Carteret found herself in what might be called, vulgarly, a moral "pocket." She could, of course, remain silent. Mrs. Carteret was a good woman, according to her lights, with a cultivated conscience, to which she had always looked as her mentor and infallible guide.

Hence Mrs. Carteret, after this painful discovery, remained for a long time ill at ease,—so disturbed, indeed, that her mind reacted upon her nerves, which had never been strong; and her nervousness affected her strength, which had never been great, until Carteret, whose love for her had been deepened and strengthened by the advent of his son, became alarmed for her health, and spoke very seriously to Dr. Price concerning it.

XXXI

THE SHADOW OF A DREAM

Mrs. Carteret awoke, with a start, from a troubled dream. She had been sailing across a sunlit sea, in a beautiful boat, her child lying on a bright-colored cushion at her feet. Overhead the swelling sail served as an awning to keep off the sun's rays, which far ahead were reflected with dazzling brilliancy from the shores of a golden island. Her son, she dreamed, was a fairy prince, and yonder lay his kingdom, to which he was being borne, lying there at her feet, in this beautiful boat, across the sunlit sea.

Suddenly and without warning the sky was overcast. A squall struck the boat and tore away the sail. In the distance a huge billow—a great white wall of water—came sweeping toward their frail craft, threatening it with instant destruction. She clasped her child to her bosom, and a moment later found herself struggling in the sea, holding the child's head above the water. As she floated there, as though sustained by some unseen force, she saw in the distance a small boat approaching over the storm-tossed waves. Straight toward her it came, and she had reached out her hand to grasp its side, when the rower looked back, and she saw that it was her sister. The recognition had been mutual. With a sharp movement of one oar the boat glided by, leaving her clutching at the empty air.

She felt her strength begin to fail. Despairingly she signaled with her disengaged hand; but the rower, after one mute, reproachful glance, rowed on. Mrs. Carteret's strength grew less and less. The child became heavy as lead. Herself floating in the water, as though it were her native element, she could no longer support the child. Lower and lower it sank,—she was powerless to save it or to accompany it,—until, gasping wildly for breath, it threw up its little hands and sank, the cruel water gurgling over its head,—when she awoke with a start and a chill, and lay there trembling for several minutes before she heard little Dodie in his crib, breathing heavily.

She rose softly, went to the crib, and changed the child's position to an easier one. He breathed more freely, and she went back to bed, but not to sleep.

She had tried to put aside the distressing questions raised by the discovery of her father's will and the papers accompanying it. Why should she be burdened with such a responsibility, at this late day, when the touch of time had well-nigh healed these old sores? Surely, God had put his curse not alone upon the slave, but upon the stealer of men! With other good people she had thanked Him that slavery was no more, and that those who once had borne its burden upon their consciences could stand erect and feel that they themselves were free. The weed had been cut down, but its roots remained, deeply imbedded in the soil, to spring up and trouble a new generation. Upon her weak shoulders was placed the burden of her father's weakness, her father's folly. It was left to her to acknowledge or not this shameful marriage and her sister's rights in their father's estate.

Balancing one consideration against another, she had almost decided that she might ignore this tie. To herself, Olivia Merkell,—Olivia Carteret,—the stigma of base birth would have meant social ostracism, social ruin, the averted face, the finger of pity or of scorn. All the traditional weight of public disapproval would have fallen upon her as the unhappy fruit of an unblessed union. To this other woman it could have had no such significance,—it had been the lot of her race. To them, twenty-five years before, sexual sin had never been imputed as more than a fault. She had lost nothing by her supposed illegitimacy; she would gain nothing by the acknowledgment of her mother's marriage.

On the other hand, what would be the effect of this revelation upon Mrs. Carteret herself? To have it known that her father had married a negress would only be less dreadful than to have it appear that he had committed some terrible crime. It was a crime now, by the laws of every Southern State, for white and colored persons to intermarry. She shuddered before the possibility that at some time in the future some person, none too well informed, might learn that her father had married a colored woman, and might assume that she, Olivia Carteret, or her child, had sprung from this shocking *mésalliance,*—a fate to which she would willingly have preferred death. No, this marriage must never be made known; the secret should remain buried forever in her own heart!

But there still remained the question of her father's property and her father's will. This woman was her father's child,—of that there could be no doubt, it was written in her features no less than in her father's will. As his lawful child,—of which, alas! there could also be no question,—she was entitled by law to half his estate. Mrs. Carteret's problem had sunk from the realm of sentiment to that of material things, which, curiously enough, she found much more difficult. For, while the negro, by the traditions of her people, was barred from the world of sentiment, his rights of property were recognized. The question had become, with Mrs. Carteret, a question of *meum* and *tuum*. Had the girl Janet been poor, ignorant, or degraded, as might well have been her fate, Mrs. Carteret might have felt a vicarious remorse for her aunt's suppression of the papers; but fate had compensated Janet for the loss; she had been educated, she had married well; she had not suffered for lack of the money of which she had been defrauded, and did not need it now. She had a child, it is true, but this child's career would be so circumscribed by the accident of color that too much wealth would only be a source of unhappiness; to her own child, on the contrary, it would open every door of life.

It would be too lengthy a task to follow the mind and conscience of this much-tried lady in their intricate workings upon this difficult problem; for she had a mind as logical as any woman's, and a conscience which she wished to keep void of offense. She had to confront a situation involving the element of race, upon which the moral standards of her people were hopelessly confused. Mrs. Carteret reached the conclusion, ere daylight dawned, and she would be silent upon the subject of her father's second marriage. Neither party had wished it known,—neither Julia nor her father,—and she would respect her father's wishes. To act otherwise would be to defeat his will, to make known what he had carefully concealed, and to give Janet a claim of title to one half of her father's estate, while he had only meant her to have the ten thousand dollars named in the will.

By the same reasoning, she must carry out her father's will in respect to this bequest. Here there was another difficulty. The mining investment into which they had entered shortly after the birth of little Dodie had tied up so much of her property that it would have been difficult to procure ten thousand dollars immediately; while a demand for half the property at once would mean bankruptcy and ruin. Moreover, upon what ground could she offer her sister any sum of money whatever? So sudden a change of heart, after so many years of silence, would raise the presumption of some right on the part of Janet in her father's estate. Suspicion once aroused, it might be possible to trace this hidden marriage, and establish it by legal proof. The marriage once verified, the claim for half the estate could not be denied. She could not plead her father's will to the contrary, for this would be to acknowledge the suppression of the will, in itself a criminal act.

There was, however, a way of escape. This hospital which had recently been opened was the personal property of her sister's husband. Some time in the future, when their investments matured, she would present to the hospital a sum of money equal to the amount her father had meant his colored daughter to have. Thus indirectly both her father's will and her own conscience would be satisfied.

Mrs. Carteret had reached this comfortable conclusion, and was falling asleep, when her attention was again drawn by her child's breathing. She took it in her own arms and soon fell asleep.

"By the way, Olivia," said the major, when leaving the house next morning for the office, "if you have any business down town to-day, transact it this forenoon. Under no circumstances must you or Clara or the baby leave the house after midday."

"Why, what 's the matter, Phil?"

"Nothing to alarm you, except that there may be a little political demonstration which may render the streets unsafe. You are not to say anything about it where the servants might hear."

"Will there be any danger for you, Phil?" she demanded with alarm.

"Not the slightest, Olivia dear. No one will be harmed; but it is best for ladies and children to stay indoors."

Mrs. Carteret's nerves were still more or less unstrung from her mental struggles of the night, and the memory of her dream came to her like a dim foreboding of misfortune. As though in sympathy with its mother's feelings, the baby did not seem as well as usual. The new nurse was by no means an ideal nurse,—Mammy Jane understood the child much better. If there should be any trouble with the negroes, toward which her husband's remark seemed to point,—she knew the general political situation, though not informed in regard to her husband's plans,—she would like to have Mammy Jane near her, where the old nurse might be protected from danger or alarm.

With this end in view she dispatched the nurse, shortly after breakfast, to Mammy Jane's house in the negro settlement on the other side of the town, with a message asking the old woman to come immediately to Mrs. Carteret's. Unfortunately, Mammy Jane had gone to visit a sick woman in the country, and was not expected to return for several hours.

XXXII
THE STORM BREAKS

The Wellington riot began at three o'clock in the afternoon of a day as fair as was ever selected for a deed of darkness. The sky was clear, except for a few light clouds that floated, white and feathery, high in air, like distant islands in a sapphire sea. A salt-laden breeze from the ocean a few miles away lent a crisp sparkle to the air.

At three o'clock sharp the streets were filled, as if by magic, with armed white men. The negroes, going about, had noted, with uneasy curiosity, that the stores and places of business, many of which closed at noon, were unduly late in opening for the afternoon, though no one suspected the reason for the delay; but at three o'clock every passing colored man was ordered, by the first white man he met, to throw up his hands. If he complied, he was searched, more or less roughly, for firearms, and then warned to get off the street. When he met another group of white men the scene was repeated. The man thus summarily held up seldom encountered more than two groups before disappearing across lots to his own home or some convenient hiding-place. If he resisted any demand of those who halted him— But the records of the day are historical; they may be found in the newspapers of the following date, but they are more firmly engraved upon the hearts and memories of the people of Wellington. For many months there were negro families in the town whose children screamed with fear and ran to their mothers for protection at the mere sight of a white man.

Dr. Miller had received a call, about one o'clock, to attend a case at the house of a well-to-do colored farmer, who lived some three or four miles from the town, upon the very road, by the way, along which Miller had driven so furiously a few weeks before, in the few hours that intervened before Sandy Campbell would probably have been burned at the stake. The drive to his patient's home, the necessary inquiries, the filling of the prescription from his own medicine-case, which he carried along with him, the little friendly conversation about the weather and the crops, and, the farmer being an intelligent and thinking man, the inevitable subject of the future of their race,—these, added to the return journey, occupied at least two hours of Miller's time.

As he neared the town on his way back, he saw ahead of him half a dozen men and women approaching, with fear written in their faces, in every degree from apprehension to terror. Women were weeping and children crying, and all were going as fast as seemingly lay in their power, looking behind now and then as if pursued by some deadly enemy. At sight of Miller's buggy they made a dash for cover, disappearing, like a covey of frightened partridges, in the underbrush along the road.

Miller pulled up his horse and looked after them in startled wonder.

"What on earth can be the matter?" he muttered, struck with a vague feeling of alarm. A psychologist, seeking to trace the effects of slavery upon the human mind, might find in the South many a curious illustration of this curse, abiding long after the actual physical bondage had terminated. In the olden time the white South labored under the constant fear of negro insurrections. Knowing that they themselves, if in the negroes' place, would have risen in the effort to throw off the yoke, all their reiterated theories of negro subordination and inferiority could not remove that lurking fear, founded upon the obscure consciousness that the slaves ought to have risen. There was never, on the continent of America, a successful slave revolt, nor one which lasted more than a few hours, or resulted in the loss of more than a few white lives; yet never was the planter quite free from the fear that there might be one.

On the other hand, the slave had before his eyes always the fear of the master. There were good men, according to their

lights,—according to their training and environment,—among
the Southern slave-holders, who treated their slaves kindly, as
slaves, from principle, because they recognized the claims of
humanity, even under the dark skin of a human chattel. There
was many a one who protected or pampered his negroes, as
the case might be, just as a man fondles his dog,—because
they were his; they were a part of his estate, an integral part
of the entity of property and person which made up the aristocrat; but with all this kindness, there was always present, in
the consciousness of the lowest slave, the knowledge that he
was in his master's power, and that he could make no effectual
protest against the abuse of that authority. There was also the
knowledge, among those who could think at all, that the best
of masters was himself a slave to a system, which hampered his
movements but scarcely less than those of his bondmen.

When, therefore, Miller saw these men and women scam-
pering into the bushes, he divined, with this slumbering race
consciousness which years of culture had not obliterated, that
there was some race trouble on foot. His intuition did not long
remain unsupported. A black head was cautiously protruded
from the shrubbery, and a black voice—if such a description be
allowable—addressed him:—

"Is dat you, Doctuh Miller?"

"Yes. Who are you, and what 's the trouble?"

"What 's de trouble, suh? Why, all hell 's broke loose in town
yonduh. De w'ite folks is riz 'gins' de niggers, an' say dey 're
gwine ter kill eve'y nigger dey kin lay han's on."

Miller's heart leaped to his throat, as he thought of his wife
and child. The story was preposterous; it could not be true, and
yet there must be something in it. He tried to question his informant, but the man was so overcome with excitement and
fear that Miller saw clearly that he must go farther for information. He had read in the Morning Chronicle, a few days before, the obnoxious editorial quoted from the Afro-American
Banner, and had noted the comment upon it by the white editor. He had felt, as at the time of its first publication, that the
editorial was ill-advised. It could do no good, and was calculated to arouse the animosity of those whose friendship, whose

tolerance, at least, was necessary and almost indispensable to the colored people. They were living, at the best, in a sort of armed neutrality with the whites; such a publication, however serviceable elsewhere, could have no other effect in Wellington than to endanger this truce and defeat the hope of a possible future friendship. The right of free speech entitled Barber to publish it; a large measure of common-sense would have made him withhold it. Whether it was the republication of this article that had stirred up anew the sleeping dogs of race prejudice and whetted their thirst for blood, he could not yet tell; but at any rate, there was mischief on foot.

"Fer God's sake, doctuh, don' go no closeter ter dat town," pleaded his informant, "er you 'll be killt sho'. Come on wid us, suh, an' tek keer er yo'se'f. We 're gwine ter hide in de swamps till dis thing is over!"

"God, man!" exclaimed Miller, urging his horse forward, "my wife and child are in the town!"

Fortunately, he reflected, there were no patients confined in the hospital,—if there should be anything in this preposterous story. To one unfamiliar with Southern life, it might have seemed impossible that these good Christian people, who thronged the churches on Sunday, and wept over the sufferings of the lowly Nazarene, and sent missionaries to the heathen, could be hungering and thirsting for the blood of their fellow men; but Miller cherished no such delusion. He knew the history of his country; he had the threatened lynching of Sandy Campbell vividly in mind; and he was fully persuaded that to race prejudice, once roused, any horror was possible. That women or children would be molested of set purpose he did not believe, but that they might suffer by accident was more than likely.

As he neared the town, dashing forward at the top of his horse's speed, he heard his voice called in a loud and agitated tone, and, glancing around him, saw a familiar form standing by the roadside, gesticulating vehemently.

He drew up the horse with a suddenness that threw the faithful and obedient animal back upon its haunches. The colored lawyer, Watson, came up to the buggy. That he was laboring under great and unusual excitement was quite apparent from his pale face and frightened air.

"What 's the matter, Watson?" demanded Miller, hoping now to obtain some reliable information.

"Matter!" exclaimed the other. "Everything 's the matter! The white people are up in arms. They have disarmed the colored people, killing a half a dozen in the process, and wounding as many more. They have forced the mayor and aldermen to resign, have formed a provisional city government *à la française,* and have ordered me and half a dozen other fellows to leave town in forty-eight hours, under pain of sudden death. As they seem to mean it, I shall not stay so long. Fortunately, my wife and children are away. I knew you were out here, however, and I thought I 'd come out and wait for you, so that we might talk the matter over. I don't imagine they mean you any harm, personally, because you tread on nobody's toes; but you 're too valuable a man for the race to lose, so I thought I 'd give you warning. I shall want to sell you my property, too, at a bargain. For I 'm worth too much to my family to dream of ever attempting to live here again."

"Have you seen anything of my wife and child?" asked Miller, intent upon the danger to which they might be exposed.

"No; I did n't go to the house. I inquired at the drugstore and found out where you had gone. You need n't fear for them,—it is not a war on women and children."

"War of any kind is always hardest on the women and children," returned Miller; "I must hurry on and see that mine are safe."

"They 'll not carry the war so far into Africa as that," returned Watson; "but I never saw anything like it. Yesterday I had a hundred white friends in the town, or thought I had,— men who spoke pleasantly to me on the street, and sometimes gave me their hands to shake. Not one of them said to me to-day: 'Watson, stay home this afternoon.' I might have been killed, like any one of half a dozen others who have bit the dust, for any word that one of my 'friends' had said to warn me. When the race cry is started in this neck of the woods, friendship, religion, humanity, reason, all shrivel up like dry leaves in a raging furnace."

The buggy, into which Watson had climbed, was meanwhile rapidly nearing the town.

"I think I 'll leave you here, Miller," said Watson, as they approached the outskirts, "and make my way home by a roundabout path, as I should like to get there unmolested. Home!—a beautiful word that, is n't it, for an exiled wanderer? It might not be well, either, for us to be seen together. If you put the hood of your buggy down, and sit well back in the shadow, you may be able to reach home without interruption; but avoid the main streets. I 'll see you again this evening, if we 're both alive, and I can reach you; for my time is short. A committee are to call in the morning to escort me to the train. I am to be dismissed from the community with public honors."

Watson was climbing down from the buggy, when a small party of men were seen approaching, and big Josh Green, followed by several other resolute-looking colored men, came up and addressed them.

"Doctuh Miller," cried Green, "Mistuh Watson,—we 're lookin' fer a leader. De w'ite folks are killin' de niggers, an' we ain' gwine ter stan' up an' be shot down like dogs. We 're gwine ter defen' ou' lives, an' we ain' gwine ter run away f'm no place where we 've got a right ter be; an' woe be ter de w'ite man w'at lays han's on us! Dere 's two niggers in dis town ter eve'y w'ite man, an' ef we 've got ter be killt, we 'll take some w'ite folks 'long wid us, ez sho' ez dere 's a God in heaven,—ez I s'pose dere is, dough He mus' be 'sleep, er busy somewhar e'se ter-day. Will you-all come an' lead us?"

"Gentlemen," said Watson, "what is the use? The negroes will not back you up. They have n't the arms, nor the moral courage, nor the leadership."

"We 'll git de arms, an' we 'll git de courage, ef you 'll come an' lead us! We wants leaders,—dat's w'y we come ter you!"

"What 's the use?" returned Watson despairingly. "The odds are too heavy. I 've been ordered out of town; if I stayed, I 'd be shot on sight, unless I had a body-guard around me."

"We 'll be yo' body-guard!" shouted half a dozen voices.

"And when my body-guard was shot, what then? I have a wife and children. It is my duty to live for them. If I died, I should get no glory and no reward, and my family would be reduced to beggary,—to which they 'll soon be near enough as it is. This affair will blow over in a day or two. The white people will be ashamed of themselves to-morrow, and apprehensive of the consequences for some time to come. Keep quiet, boys, and trust in God. You won't gain anything by resistance."

"'God he'ps dem dat he'ps demselves,'" returned Josh stoutly. "Ef Mistuh Watson won't lead us, will you, Doctuh Miller?" said the spokesman, turning to the doctor.

For Miller it was an agonizing moment. He was no coward, morally or physically. Every manly instinct urged him to go forward and take up the cause of these leaderless people, and, if need be, to defend their lives and their rights with his own—but to what end?

"Listen, men," he said. "We would only be throwing our lives away. Suppose we made a determined stand and won a temporary victory. By morning every train, every boat, every road leading into Wellington, would be crowded with white men,—as they probably will be any way,—with arms in their hands, curses on their lips, and vengeance in their hearts. In the minds of those who make and administer the laws, we have no standing in the court of conscience. They would kill us in the fight, or they would hang us afterwards,—one way or another, we should be doomed. I should like to lead you; I should like to arm every colored man in this town, and have them stand firmly in line, nor for attack, but for defense; but if I attempted it, and they should stand by me, which is questionable,—for I have met them fleeing from the town,—my life would pay the forfeit. Alive, I may be of some use to you, and you are welcome to my life in that way,—I am giving it freely. Dead, I should be a mere lump of carrion. Who remembers even the names of those who have been done to death in the Southern States for the past twenty years?"

"I 'members de name er one of 'em," said Josh, "an' I 'members de name er de man dat killt 'im, an' I s'pec' his time is mighty nigh come."

"My advice is not heroic, but I think it is wise. In this riot we are placed as we should be in a war: we have no territory, no base of supplies, no organization, no outside sympathy,— we stand in the position of a race, in a case like this, without money and without friends. Our time will come,—the time when we can command respect for our rights; but it is not yet in sight. Give it up, boys, and wait. Good may come of this, after all."

Several of the men wavered, and looked irresolute.

"I reckon that 's all so, doctuh," returned Josh, "an', de way you put it, I don' blame you ner Mistuh Watson; but all dem reasons ain' got no weight wid me. I 'm gwine in dat town, an' ef any w'ite man 'sturbs me, dere 'll be trouble,—dere 'll be double trouble,—I feels it in my bones!"

"Remember your old mother, Josh," said Miller.

"Yas, suh, I 'll 'member her; dat 's all I kin do now. I don' need ter wait for her no mo', fer she died dis mo'nin'. I 'd lack ter see her buried, suh, but I may not have de chance. Ef I gits killt, will you do me a favor?"

"Yes, Josh; what is it?"

"Ef I should git laid out in dis commotion dat 's gwine on, will you collec' my wages f'm yo' brother, and see dat de old 'oman is put away right?"

"Yes, of course."

"Wid a nice coffin, an' a nice fune'al, an' a head-bo'd an' a foot-bo'd?"

"Yes."

"All right, suh! Ef I don' live ter do it, I 'll know it 'll be 'tended ter right. Now we 're gwine out ter de cotton compress, an' git a lot er colored men tergether, an' ef de w'ite folks 'sturbs me, I should n't be s'prise' ef dere 'd be a mix-up;—an' ef dere is, me an *one* w'ite man 'll stan' befo' de jedgment th'one er God dis day; an' it won't be me w'at 'll be 'feared er de jedgment. Come along, boys! Dese gentlemen may have somethin' ter live fer; but ez fer my pa't, I 'd ruther be a dead nigger any day dan a live dog!"

XXXIII
INTO THE LION'S JAWS

The party under Josh's leadership moved off down the road. Miller, while entirely convinced that he had acted wisely in declining to accompany them, was yet conscious of a distinct feeling of shame and envy that he, too, did not feel impelled to throw away his life in a hopeless struggle.

Watson left the buggy and disappeared by a path at the roadside. Miller drove rapidly forward. After entering the town, he passed several small parties of white men, but escaped scrutiny by sitting well back in his buggy, the presumption being that a well-dressed man with a good horse and buggy was white. Torn with anxiety, he reached home at about four o'clock. Driving the horse into the yard, he sprang down from the buggy and hastened to the house, which he found locked, front and rear.

A repeated rapping brought no response. At length he broke a window, and entered the house like a thief.

"Janet, Janet!" he called in alarm, "where are you? It is only I,—Will!"

There was no reply. He ran from room to room, only to find them all empty. Again he called his wife's name, and was about rushing from the house, when a muffled voice came faintly to his ear,—

"Is dat you, Doctuh Miller?"

"Yes. Who are you, and where are my wife and child?"

He was looking around in perplexity, when the door of a low closet under the kitchen sink was opened from within, and a woolly head was cautiously protruded.

"Are you *sho'* dat's you, doctuh?"

"Yes, Sally; where are"—

"An' not some w'ite man come ter bu'n down de house an' kill all de niggers?"

"No, Sally, it 's me all right. Where is my wife? Where is my child?"

"Dey went over ter see Mis' Butler 'long 'bout two o'clock,

befo' dis fuss broke out, suh. Oh, Lawdy, Lawdy, suh! Is all de cullud folks be'n killt 'cep'n' me an' you, suh? Fer de Lawd's sake, suh, you won' let 'em kill me, will you, suh? I 'll wuk fer you fer nuthin', suh, all my bawn days, ef you 'll save my life, suh!"

"Calm yourself, Sally. You 'll be safe enough if you stay right here, I 've no doubt. They 'll not harm women,—of that I 'm sure enough, although I have n't yet got the bearings of this deplorable affair. Stay here and look after the house. I must find my wife and child!"

The distance across the city to the home of the Mrs. Butler whom his wife had gone to visit was exactly one mile. Though Miller had a good horse in front of him, he was two hours in reaching his destination. Never will the picture of that ride fade from his memory. In his dreams he repeats it night after night, and sees the sights that wounded his eyes, and feels the thoughts—the haunting spirits of the thoughts—that tore his heart as he rode through hell to find those whom he was seeking.

For a short distance he saw nothing, and made rapid progress. As he turned the first corner, his horse shied at the dead body of a negro, lying huddled up in the collapse which marks sudden death. What Miller shuddered at was not so much the thought of death, to the sight of which his profession had accustomed him, as the suggestion of what it signified. He had taken with allowance the wild statement of the fleeing fugitives. Watson, too, had been greatly excited, and Josh Green's group were desperate men, as much liable to be misled by their courage as the others by their fears; but here was proof that murder had been done,—and his wife and children were in the town. Distant shouts, and the sound of firearms, increased his alarm. He struck his horse with the whip, and dashed on toward the heart of the city, which he must traverse in order to reach Janet and the child.

At the next corner lay the body of another man, with the red blood oozing from a ghastly wound in the forehead. The negroes seemed to have been killed, as the band plays in circus parades, at the street intersections, where the example would be most effective. Miller, with a wild leap of the heart, had barely passed this gruesome spectacle, when a sharp voice commanded him to halt, and emphasized the order by covering him with a revolver. Forgetting the prudence he preached to others, he had raised his whip to strike the horse, when several hands seized the bridle.

"Come down, you damn fool," growled an authoritative voice. "Don't you see we 're in earnest? Do you want to get killed?"

"Why should I come down?" asked Miller.

"Because we 've ordered you to come down! This is the white people's day, and when they order, a nigger must obey. We 're going to search you for weapons."

"Search away. You 'll find nothing but a case of surgeon's tools, which I 'm more likely to need before this day is over, from all indications."

"No matter; we 'll make sure of it! That 's what we 're here for. Come down, if you don't want to be pulled down!"

Miller stepped down from his buggy. His interlocutor, who made no effort at disguise, was a clerk in a dry-goods store where Miller bought most of his family and hospital supplies. He made no sign of recognition, however, and Miller claimed no acquaintance. This man, who had for several years emptied Miller's pockets in the course of more or less legitimate trade, now went through them, aided by another man, more rapidly than ever before, the searchers convincing themselves that Miller carried no deadly weapon upon his person. Meanwhile, a third ransacked the buggy with like result. Miller recognized several others of the party, who made not the slightest attempt at disguise, though no names were called by any one.

"Where are you going?" demanded the leader.

"I am looking for my wife and child," replied Miller.

"Well, run along, and keep them out of the streets when you find them; and keep your hands out of this affair, if you wish to live in this town, which from now on will be a white man's town, as you niggers will be pretty firmly convinced before night."

Miller drove on as swiftly as might be.

At the next corner he was stopped again. In the white man who held him up, Miller recognized a neighbor of his own. After a short detention and a perfunctory search, the white man remarked apologetically:—

"Sorry to have to trouble you, doctuh, but them 's the o'ders. It ain't men like you that we 're after, but the vicious and criminal class of niggers."

Miller smiled bitterly as he urged his horse forward. He was quite well aware that the virtuous citizen who had stopped him had only a few weeks before finished a term in the penitentiary, to which he had been sentenced for stealing. Miller knew that he could have bought all the man owned for fifty dollars, and his soul for as much more.

A few rods farther on, he came near running over the body of a wounded man who lay groaning by the wayside. Every professional instinct urged him to stop and offer aid to the sufferer; but the uncertainty concerning his wife and child proved a stronger motive and urged him resistlessly forward. Here and there the ominous sound of firearms was audible. He might have thought this merely a part of the show, like the "powder play" of the Arabs, but for the bloody confirmation of its earnestness which had already assailed his vision. Somewhere in this seething caldron of unrestrained passions were his wife and child, and he must hurry on.

His progress was painfully slow. Three times he was stopped and searched. More than once his way was barred, and he was ordered to turn back, each such occasion requiring a detour which consumed many minutes. The man who last stopped him was a well-known Jewish merchant. A Jew—God of Moses!—had so far forgotten twenty centuries of history as to join in the persecution of another oppressed race! When almost reduced to despair by these innumerable delays, he perceived, coming toward him, Mr. Ellis, the sub-editor of the Morning Chronicle. Miller had just been stopped and questioned again, and Ellis came up as he was starting once more upon his endless ride.

"Dr. Miller," said Ellis kindly, "it is dangerous for you on the streets. Why tempt the danger?"

"I am looking for my wife and child," returned Miller in desperation. "They are somewhere in this town,—I don't know where,—and I must find them."

Ellis had been horror-stricken by the tragedy of the afternoon, the wholly superfluous slaughter of a harmless people, whom a show of force would have been quite sufficient to overawe. Elaborate explanations were afterwards given for these murders, which were said, perhaps truthfully, not to have been premeditated, and many regrets were expressed. The young man had been surprised, quite as much as the negroes themselves, at the ferocity displayed. His own thoughts and feelings were attuned to anything but slaughter. Only that morning he had received a perfumed note, calling his attention to what the writer described as a very noble deed of his, and requesting him to call that evening and receive the writer's thanks. Had he known that Miss Pemberton, several weeks after their visit to the Sound, had driven out again to the hotel and made some inquiries among the servants, he might have understood better the meaning of this missive. When Miller spoke of his wife and child, some subtle thread of suggestion coupled the note with Miller's plight.

"I 'll go with you, Dr. Miller," he said, "if you 'll permit me. In my company you will not be disturbed."

He took a seat in Miller's buggy, after which it was not molested.

Neither of them spoke. Miller was sick at heart; he could have wept with grief, even had the welfare of his own dear ones not been involved in this regrettable affair. With prophetic instinct he foresaw the hatreds to which this day would give birth; the long years of constraint and distrust which would still further widen the breach between two peoples whom fate had thrown together in one community.

There was nothing for Ellis to say. In his heart he could not defend the deeds of this day. The petty annoyances which the whites had felt at the spectacle of a few negroes in office; the not unnatural resentment of a proud people at what had seemed to them a presumptuous freedom of speech and lack of deference on the part of their inferiors,—these things, which he knew were to be made the excuse for overturning the city government, he realized full well were no sort of justification for the wholesale murder or other horrors which might well ensue before the day was done. He could not approve the acts of his own people; neither could he, to a negro, condemn them. Hence he was silent.

"Thank you, Mr. Ellis," exclaimed Miller, when they had reached the house where he expected to find his wife. "This is the place where I was going. I am—under a great obligation to you."

"Not at all, Dr. Miller. I need to tell you how much I regret this deplorable affair."

Ellis went back down the street. Fastening his horse to the fence, Miller sprang forward to find his wife and child. They would certainly be there, for no colored woman would be foolhardy enough to venture on the streets after the riot had broken out.

As he drew nearer, he felt a sudden apprehension. The house seemed strangely silent and deserted. The doors were closed, and the venetian blinds shut tightly. Even a dog which had appeared slunk timidly back under the house, instead of barking vociferously according to the usual habit of his kind.

XXXIV

THE VALLEY OF THE SHADOW

Miller knocked at the door. There was no response. He went round to the rear of the house. The dog had slunk behind the woodpile. Miller knocked again, at the back door, and, receiving no reply, called aloud.

"Mrs. Butler! It is I, Dr. Miller. Is my wife here?"

The slats of a near-by blind opened cautiously.

"Is it really you, Dr. Miller?"

"Yes, Mrs. Butler. I am looking for my wife and child,—are they here?"

"No, sir; she became alarmed about you, soon after the shooting commenced, and I could not keep her. She left for home half an hour ago. It is coming on dusk, and she and the child are so near white that she did not expect to be molested."

"Which way did she go?"

"She meant to go by the main street. She thought it would be less dangerous than the back streets. I tried to get her to stay here, but she was frantic about you, and nothing I could say would keep her. Is the riot almost over, Dr. Miller? Do you think they will murder us all, and burn down our houses?"

"God knows," replied Miller, with a groan. "But I must find her, if I lose my own life in the attempt."

Surely, he thought, Janet would be safe. The white people of Wellington were not savages; or at least their temporary reversion to savagery would not go as far as to include violence to delicate women and children. Then there flashed into his mind Josh Green's story of his "silly" mother, who for twenty years had walked the earth as a child, as the result of one night's terror, and his heart sank within him.

Miller realized that his buggy, by attracting attention, had been a hindrance rather than a help in his progress across the city. In order to follow his wife, he must practically retrace his steps over the very route he had come. Night was falling. It would be easier to cross the town on foot. In the dusk his own color, slight in the daytime, would not attract attention, and by dodging in the shadows he might avoid those who might wish to intercept him. But he must reach Janet and the boy at any risk. He had not been willing to throw his life away hopelessly, but he would cheerfully have sacrificed it for those whom he loved.

He had gone but a short distance, and had not yet reached the centre of mob activity, when he intercepted a band of negro laborers from the cotton compress, with big Josh Green at their head.

"Hello, doctuh!" cried Josh, "does you wan' ter jine us?"

"I 'm looking for my wife and child, Josh. They 're somewhere in this den of murderers. Have any of you seen them?"

No one had seen them.

"You men are running a great risk," said Miller. "You are rushing on to certain death."

"Well, suh, maybe we is; but we 're gwine ter die fightin'. Dey say de w'ite folks is gwine ter bu'n all de cullud schools an' chu'ches, an' kill all de niggers dey kin ketch. Dey're gwine ter bu'n yo' new hospittle, ef somebody don' stop 'em."

"Josh—men—you are throwing your lives away. It is a fever; it will wear off to-morrow, or to-night. They 'll not burn the schoolhouses, nor the hospital—they are not such fools, for they benefit the community; and they 'll only kill the colored people who resist them. Every one of you with a gun or a pistol carries his death warrant in his own hand. I 'd rather see the hospital burn than have one of you lose his life. Resistance only makes the matter worse,—the odds against you are too long."

"Things can't be any wuss, doctuh," replied one of the crowd sturdily. "A gun is mo' dange'ous ter de man in front of it dan ter de man behin' it. Dey 're gwine ter kill us anyhow; an' we 're tired,—we read de newspapers,—an' we 're tired er bein' shot down like dogs, widout jedge er jury. We 'd ruther die fightin' dan be stuck like pigs in a pen!"

"God help you!" said Miller. "As for me, I must find my wife and child."

"Good-by, doctuh," cried Josh, brandishing a huge knife. "'Member 'bout de ole 'oman, ef you lives thoo dis. Don' fergit de head-bo'd an' de foot-bo'd, an' a silver plate on de coffin, ef dere 's money ernuff."

They went their way, and Miller hurried on. They might resist attack; he thought it extremely unlikely that they would begin it; but he knew perfectly well that the mere knowledge that some of the negroes contemplated resistance would only further inflame the infuriated whites. The colored men might win a momentary victory, though it was extremely doubtful; and they would as surely reap the harvest later on. The qualities which in a white man would win the applause of the world would in a negro be taken as the marks of savagery. So thoroughly diseased was public opinion in matters of race that the negro who died for the common rights of humanity might look for no meed of admiration or glory. At such a time, in the white man's eyes, a negro's courage would be mere desperation; his love of liberty, a mere animal dislike of restraint. Every finer human instinct would be interpreted in terms of savagery. Or, if forced to admire, they would none the less repress. They would applaud his courage while they stretched his neck, or carried off the fragments of his mangled body as souvenirs, in much the same way that savages preserve the scalps or eat the hearts of their enemies.

But concern for the fate of Josh and his friends occupied only a secondary place in Miller's mind for the moment. His wife and child were somewhere ahead of him. He pushed on. He had covered about a quarter of a mile more, and far down the street could see the signs of great animation, when he came upon the body of a woman lying on the sidewalk. In the dusk he had almost stumbled over it, and his heart came up in his mouth. A second glance revealed that it could not be his wife. It was a fearful portent, however, of what her fate might be. The "war" had reached the women and children. Yielding to a professional instinct, he stooped, and saw that the prostrate form was that of old Aunt Jane Letlow. She was not yet quite dead, and as Miller, with a tender touch, placed her head in a more comfortable position, her lips moved with a last lingering flicker of consciousness:—

"Comin', missis, comin'!"

Mammy Jane had gone to join the old mistress upon whose memory her heart was fixed; and yet not all her reverence for her old mistress, nor all her deference to the whites, nor all their friendship for her, had been able to save her from this raging devil of race hatred which momentarily possessed the town.

Perceiving that he could do no good, Miller hastened onward, sick at heart. Whenever he saw a party of white men approaching,—these brave reformers never went singly,—he sought concealment in the shadow of a tree or the shrubbery in some yard until they had passed. He had covered about two thirds of the distance homeward, when his eyes fell upon a group beneath a lamp-post, at sight of which he turned pale with horror, and rushed forward with a terrible cry.

XXXV

"MINE ENEMY, O MINE ENEMY!"

The proceedings of the day—planned originally as a "demonstration," dignified subsequently as a "revolution," under any name the culmination of the conspiracy formed by Carteret and his colleagues—had by seven o'clock in the afternoon developed into a murderous riot. Crowds of white men and half-grown boys, drunk with whiskey or with license, raged through the streets, beating, chasing, or killing any negro so unfortunate as to fall into their hands. Why any particular negro was assailed, no one stopped to inquire; it was merely a white mob thirsting for black blood, with no more conscience or discrimination than would be exercised by a wolf in a sheepfold. It was race against race, the whites against the negroes; and it was a one-sided affair, for until Josh Green got together his body of armed men, no effective resistance had been made by any colored person, and the individuals who had been killed had so far left no marks upon the enemy by which they might be remembered.

"Kill the niggers!" rang out now and then through the dusk, and far down the street and along the intersecting thoroughfares distant voices took up the ominous refrain,—"Kill the niggers! Kill the damned niggers!"

Now, not a dark face had been seen on the street for half an hour, until the group of men headed by Josh made their appearance in the negro quarter. Armed with guns and axes, they presented quite a formidable appearance as they made their way toward the new hospital, near which stood a schoolhouse and a large church, both used by the colored people. They did not reach their destination without having met a number of white men, singly or in twos or threes; and the rumor spread with incredible swiftness that the negroes in turn were up in arms, determined to massacre all the whites and burn the town. Some of the whites became alarmed, and recognizing the power of the negroes, if armed and conscious of their strength, were impressed by the immediate necessity of overpowering and overawing them. Others, with appetites already whetted by slaughter, saw a chance, welcome rather than not, of shedding more black blood. Spontaneously the white mob flocked toward the hospital, where rumor had it that a large body of desperate negroes, breathing threats of blood and fire, had taken a determined stand.

It had been Josh's plan merely to remain quietly and peaceably in the neighborhood of the little group of public institutions, molesting no one, unless first attacked, and merely letting the white people see that they meant to protect their own; but so rapidly did the rumor spread, and so promptly did the white people act, that by the time Josh and his supporters had reached the top of the rising ground where the hospital stood, a crowd of white men much more numerous than their own party were following them at a short distance.

Josh, with the eye of a general, perceived that some of his party were becoming a little nervous, and decided that they would feel safer behind shelter.

"I reckon we better go inside de hospittle, boys," he exclaimed. "Den we 'll be behind brick walls, an' dem other fellows 'll be outside, an' ef dere's any fightin', we 'll have des bes' show. We ain' gwine ter do no shootin' till we're pestered, an' dey 'll be less likely ter pester us ef dey can't git at us widout runnin' some resk. Come along in! Be men! De gov'ner er de President is gwine ter sen' soldiers ter stop dese gwines-on, an' meantime we kin keep dem white devils f'm bu'nin' down our hospittles an' chu'ch-houses. W'en dey comes an' fin's out dat we jes' means ter pertect ou' prope'ty, dey 'll go 'long 'bout deir own business. Er, ef dey wants a scrap, dey kin have it! Come erlong, boys!"

Jerry Letlow, who had kept out of sight during the day, had started out, after night had set in, to find Major Carteret. Jerry was very much afraid. The events of the day had filled him with terror. Whatever the limitations of Jerry's mind or character may have been, Jerry had a keen appreciation of the danger to the negroes when they came in conflict with the whites, and he had no desire to imperil his own skin. He valued his life for his own sake, and not for any altruistic theory that it might be of service to others. In other words, Jerry was something of a coward. He had kept in hiding all day, but finding, toward evening, that the riot did not abate, and fearing, from the rumors which came to his ears, that all the negroes would be exterminated, he had set out, somewhat desperately, to try to find his white patron and protector. He had been cautious to avoid meeting any white men, and, anticipating no danger from those of his own race, went toward the party which he saw approaching, whose path would cross his own. When they were only a few yards apart, Josh took a step forward and caught Jerry by the arm.

"Come along, Jerry, we need you! Here 's another man, boys. Come on now, and fight fer yo' race!"

In vain Jerry protested. "I don' wan' ter fight," he howled. "De w'ite folks ain' gwine ter pester me; dey 're my frien's. Tu'n me loose,—tu'n me loose, er we all gwine ter git killed!"

The party paid no attention to Jerry's protestations. Indeed, with the crowd of whites following behind, they were simply considering the question of a position from which they could most effectively defend themselves and the building which they imagined to be threatened. If Josh had released his grip of Jerry, that worthy could easily have escaped from the crowd; but Josh maintained his hold almost mechanically, and, in the confusion, Jerry found himself swept with the rest into the hospital, the doors of which were promptly barricaded with the heavier pieces of furniture, and the windows manned by several men each, Josh, with the instinct of a born commander, posting his forces so that they could cover with their guns all the approaches to the building. Jerry still continuing to make himself troublesome, Josh, in a moment of impatience, gave him a terrific box on the ear, which stretched him out upon the floor unconscious.

"Shet up," he said; "ef you can't stan' up like a man, keep still, and don't interfere wid men w'at will fight!"

The hospital, when Josh and his men took possession, had been found deserted. Fortunately there were no patients for that day, except one or two convalescents, and these, with the attendants, had joined the exodus of the colored people from the town.

A white man advanced from the crowd without toward the main entrance to the hospital. Big Josh, looking out from a window, grasped his gun more firmly, as his eyes fell upon the man who had murdered his father and darkened his mother's life. Mechanically he raised his rifle, but lowered it as the white man lifted up his hand as a sign that he wished to speak.

"You niggers," called Captain McBane loudly,—it was that worthy,—"you niggers are courtin' death, an' you won't have to court her but a minute er two mo' befo' she 'll have you. If you surrender and give up your arms, you 'll be dealt with leniently,—you may get off with the chain-gang or the penitentiary. If you resist, you 'll be shot like dogs."

"Dat 's no news, Mistuh White Man," replied Josh, appearing boldly at the window. "We 're use' ter bein' treated like dogs by men like you. If you w'ite people will go 'long an' ten' ter yo' own business an' let us alone, we 'll ten' ter ou'n. You 've got guns, an' we 've got jest as much right ter carry 'em as you have. Lay down yo'n, an' we 'll lay down ou'n,—we did n' take 'em up fust; but we ain' gwine ter let you bu'n down ou' chu'ches an' school'ouses, er dis hospittle, an' we ain' comin' out er dis house, where we ain' disturbin' nobody, fer you ter shoot us down er sen' us ter jail. You hear me!"

"All right," responded McBane. "You 've had fair warning. Your blood be on your"—

His speech was interrupted by a shot from the crowd, which splintered the window-casing close to Josh's head. This was followed by half a dozen other shots, which were replied to, almost simultaneously, by a volley from within, by which one of the attacking party was killed and another wounded.

This roused the mob to frenzy.

"Vengeance! vengence!" they yelled. "Kill the niggers!"

A negro had killed a white man,—the unpardonable sin, admitting neither excuse, justification, nor extenuation. From time immemorial it had been bred in the Southern white consciousness, and in the negro consciousness also, for that matter, that the person of a white man was sacred from the touch of a negro, no matter what the provocation. A dozen colored men lay dead in the streets of Wellington, inoffensive people, slain in cold blood because they had been bold enough to question the authority of those who had assailed them, or frightened enough to flee when they had been ordered to stand still; but their lives counted nothing against that of a riotous white man, who had courted death by attacking a body of armed men.

The crowd, too, surrounding the hospital, had changed somewhat in character. The men who had acted as leaders in the early afternoon, having accomplished their purpose of over-turning the local administration and establishing a provisional government of their own, had withdrawn from active partici-pation in the rioting, deeming the negroes already sufficiently overawed to render unlikely any further trouble from that source. Several of the ringleaders had indeed begun to exert themselves to prevent further disorder, or any loss of property, the possibility of which had become apparent; but those who set in motion the forces of evil cannot always control them af-terwards. The baser element of the white population, recruited from the wharves and the saloons, was now predominant.

Captain McBane was the only one of the revolutionary com-mittee who had remained with the mob, not with any purpose to restore or preserve order, but because he found the company and the occasion entirely congenial. He had had no opportu-nity, at least no tenable excuse, to kill or maim a negro since the termination of his contract with the state for convicts, and this occasion had awakened a dormant appetite for these diver-sions. We are all puppets in the hands of Fate, and seldom see the strings that move us. McBane had lived a life of violence and cruelty. As a man sows, so shall he reap. In works of fic-tion, such men are sometimes converted. More often, in real life, they do not change their natures until they are converted into dust. One does well to distrust a tamed tiger.

On the outskirts of the crowd a few of the better class, or at least of the better clad, were looking on. The double volley de-scribed had already been fired, when the number of these was augmented by the arrival of Major Carteret and Mr. Ellis, who had just come from the Chronicle office, where the next day's paper had been in hasty preparation. They pushed their way towards the front of the crowd.

"This must be stopped, Ellis," said Carteret. "They are burning houses and killing women and children. Old Jane, good old Mammy Jane, who nursed my wife at her bosom, and has waited on her and my child within a few weeks, was killed only a few rods from my house, to which she was evidently fleeing for protection. It must have been by accident,—I cannot believe that any white man in town would be dastard enough to commit such a deed intentionally! I would have defended her with my own life! We must try to stop this thing!"

"Easier said than done," returned Ellis. "It is in the fever stage, and must burn itself out. We shall be lucky if it does not burn the town out. Suppose the negroes should also take a hand at the burning? We have advised the people to put the negroes down, and they are doing the job thoroughly."

"My God!" replied the other, with a gesture of impatience, as he continued to elbow his way through the crowd; "I meant to keep them in their places,—I did not intend wholesale murder and arson."

Carteret, having reached the front of the mob, made an effort to gain their attention.

"Gentlemen!" he cried in his loudest tones. His voice, unfortunately, was neither loud nor piercing.

"Kill the niggers!" clamored the mob.

"Gentlemen, I implore you"—

The crash of a dozen windows, broken by stones and pistol shots, drowned his voice.

"Gentlemen!" he shouted; "this is murder, it is madness; it is a disgrace to our city, to our state, to our civilization!"

"That 's right!" replied several voices. The mob had recognized the speaker. "It *is* a disgrace, and we 'll not put up with it a moment longer. Burn 'em out! Hurrah for Major Carteret, the champion of 'white supremacy'! Three cheers for the Morning Chronicle and 'no nigger domination'!"

"Hurrah, hurrah, hurrah!" yelled the crowd.

In vain the baffled orator gesticulated and shrieked in the effort to correct the misapprehension. Their oracle had spoken;

not hearing what he said, they assumed it to mean encouragement and coöperation. Their present course was but the logical outcome of the crusade which the Morning Chronicle had preached, in season and out of season, for many months. When Carteret had spoken, and the crowd had cheered him, they felt that they had done all that courtesy required, and he was good-naturedly elbowed aside while they proceeded with the work in hand, which was now to drive out the negroes from the hospital and avenge the killing of their comrade.

Some brought hay, some kerosene, and others wood from a pile which had been thrown into a vacant lot near by. Several safe ways of approach to the building were discovered, and the combustibles placed and fired. The flames, soon gaining a foothold, leaped upward, catching here and there at the exposed woodwork, and licking the walls hungrily with long tongues of flame.

Meanwhile a desultory firing was kept up from the outside, which was replied to scatteringly from within the hospital. Those inside either were not good marksmen, or excitement had spoiled their aim. If a face appeared at a window, a dozen pistol shots from the crowd sought the spot immediately.

Higher and higher leaped the flames. Suddenly from one of the windows sprang a black figure, waving a white handkerchief. It was Jerry Letlow. Regaining consciousness after the effect of Josh's blow had subsided, Jerry had kept quiet and watched his opportunity. From a safe vantage-ground he had scanned the crowd without, in search of some white friend. When he saw Major Carteret moving disconsolately away after his futile effort to stem the torrent, Jerry made a dash for the window. He sprang forth, and, waving his handkerchief as a flag of truce, ran toward Major Carteret, shouting frantically:—

"Majah Carteret—O majah! It's me, suh, Jerry, suh! I did n' go in dere myse'f, suh,—I wuz drag' in dere! I would n' do nothin' 'g'inst de w'ite folks, suh,—no, 'ndeed, I would n', suh!"

Jerry's cries were drowned in a roar of rage and a volley of shots from the mob. Carteret, who had turned away with Ellis, did not even hear his servant's voice. Jerry's poor flag of truce, his explanations, his reliance upon his white friends, all failed him in the moment of supreme need. In that hour, as in any hour when the depths of race hatred are stirred, a negro was no more than a brute beast, set upon by other brute beasts whose only instinct was to kill and destroy.

"Let us leave this inferno, Ellis," said Carteret, sick with anger and disgust. He had just become aware that a negro was being killed, though he did not know whom. "We can do nothing. The negroes have themselves to blame,—they tempted us beyond endurance. I counseled firmness, and firm measures were taken, and our purpose was accomplished. I am not responsible for these subsequent horrors,—I wash my hands of them. Let us go!"

The flames gained headway and gradually enveloped the burning building, until it became evident to those within as well as those without that the position of the defenders was no longer tenable. Would they die in the flames, or would they be driven out? The uncertainty soon came to an end.

The besieged had been willing to fight, so long as there seemed a hope of successfully defending themselves and their property; for their purpose was purely one of defense. When they saw the case was hopeless, inspired by Josh Green's reckless courage, they were still willing to sell their lives dearly. One or two of them had already been killed, and as many more disabled. The fate of Jerry Letlow had struck terror to the hearts of several others, who could scarcely hide their fear. After the building had been fired, Josh's exhortations were no longer able to keep them in the hospital. They preferred to fight and be killed in the open, rather than to be smothered like rats in a hole.

"Boys!" exclaimed Josh,—"men!—fer nobody but men would do w'at you have done,—the day has gone 'g'inst us. We kin see ou' finish; but fer my part, I ain' gwine ter leave dis worl' widout takin' a w'ite man 'long wid me, an' I sees my man right out yonder waitin',—I be'n waitin' fer him twenty years, but he won' have ter wait fer me mo' 'n 'bout twenty seconds. Eve'y one er you pick yo' man! We 'll open de do', an' we 'll give some w'ite men a chance ter be sorry dey ever started dis fuss!"

The door was thrown open suddenly, and through it rushed a dozen or more black figures, armed with knives, pistols, or clubbed muskets. Taken by sudden surprise, the white people stood motionless for a moment, but the approaching negroes had scarcely covered half the distance to which the heat of the flames had driven back the mob, before they were greeted with a volley that laid them all low but two. One of these, dazed by the fate of his companions, turned instinctively to flee, but had scarcely faced around before he fell, pierced in the back by a dozen bullets.

Josh Green, the tallest and biggest of them all, had not apparently been touched. Some of the crowd paused in involuntary admiration of this black giant, famed on the wharves for his strength, sweeping down upon them, a smile upon his face, his eyes lit up with a rapt expression which seemed to take him out of mortal ken. This impression was heightened by his apparent immunity from the shower of lead which less susceptible persons had continued to pour at him.

Armed with a huge bowie-knife, a relic of the civil war, which he had carried on his person for many years for a definite purpose, and which he had kept sharpened to a razor edge, he reached the line of the crowd. All but the bravest shrank back. Like a wedge he dashed through the mob, which parted instinctively before him, and all oblivious of the rain of lead which fell around him, reached the point where Captain McBane, the bravest man in the party, stood waiting to meet him. A pistol-flame flashed in his face, but he went on, and raising his powerful right arm, buried his knife to the hilt in the heart of his enemy. When the crowd dashed forward to wreak vengeance on his dead body, they found him with a smile still upon his face.

One of the two died as the fool dieth. Which was it, or was it both? "Vengeance is mine," saith the Lord, and it had not been left to Him. But they that do violence must expect to suffer violence. McBane's death was merciful, compared with the nameless horrors he had heaped upon the hundreds of helpless mortals who had fallen into his hands during his career as a contractor of convict labor.

Sobered by this culminating tragedy, the mob shortly afterwards dispersed. The flames soon completed their work, and this handsome structure, the fruit of old Adam Miller's industry, the monument of his son's philanthropy, a promise of good things for the future of the city, lay smouldering in ruins, a melancholy witness to the fact that our boasted civilization is but a thin veneer, which cracks and scales off at the first impact of primal passions.

XXXVI

FIAT JUSTITIA

By the light of the burning building, which illuminated the street for several blocks, Major Carteret and Ellis made their way rapidly until they turned into the street where the major lived. Reaching the house, Carteret tried the door and found it locked. A vigorous ring at the bell brought no immediate response. Carteret had begun to pound impatiently upon the door, when it was cautiously opened by Miss Pemberton, who was pale, and trembled with excitement.

"Where is Olivia?" asked the major.

"She is upstairs, with Dodie and Mrs. Albright's hospital nurse. Dodie has the croup. Virgie ran away after the riot broke out. Sister Olivia had sent for Mammy Jane, but she did not come. Mrs. Albright let her white nurse come over."

"I 'll go up at once," said the major anxiously. "Wait for me, Ellis,—I 'll be down in a few minutes."

"Oh, Mr. Ellis," exclaimed Clara, coming toward him with both hands extended, "can nothing be done to stop this terrible affair?"

"I wish I could so something," he murmured fervently, taking both her trembling hands in his own broad palms, where they rested with a surrendering trustfulness which he has never since had occasion to doubt. "It has gone too far, already, and the end, I fear, is not yet; but it cannot grow much worse."

The editor hurried upstairs. Mrs. Carteret, wearing a worried and haggard look, met him at the threshold of the nursery.

"Dodie is ill," she said. "At three o'clock, when the trouble began, I was over at Mrs. Albright's,—I had left Virgie with the baby. When I came back, she and all the other servants had gone. They had heard that the white people were going to kill all the negroes, and fled to seek safety. I found Dodie lying in a draught, before an open window, gasping for breath. I ran back to Mrs. Albright's,—I had found her much better to-day,—and she let her nurse come over. The nurse says that Dodie is threatened with membranous croup."

"Have you sent for Dr. Price?"

"There was no one to send,—the servants were gone, and the nurse was afraid to venture out into the street. I telephoned for Dr. Price, and found that he was out of town; that he had gone up the river this morning to attend a patient, and would not be back until to-morrow. Mrs. Price thought that he had anticipated some kind of trouble in the town to-day, and had preferred to be where he could not be called upon to assume any responsibility."

"I suppose you tried Dr. Ashe?"

"I could not get him, nor any one else, after that first call. The telephone service is disorganized on account of the riot. We need medicine and ice. The drugstores are all closed on account of the riot, and for the same reason we could n't get any ice."

Major Carteret stood beside the brass bedstead upon which his child was lying,—his only child, around whose curly head clustered all his hopes; upon whom all his life for the past year had been centered. He stooped over the bed, beside which the nurse had stationed herself. She was wiping the child's face, which was red and swollen and covered with moisture, the nostrils working rapidly, and the little patient vainly endeavoring at intervals to cough up the obstruction to his breathing.

"Is it serious?" he inquired anxiously. He had always thought of the croup as a childish ailment, that yielded readily to proper treatment; but the child's evident distress impressed him with sudden fear.

"Dangerous," replied the young woman laconically. "You came none too soon. If a doctor is n't got at once, the child will die,—and it must be a good doctor."

"Whom can I call?" he asked. "You know them all, I suppose. Dr. Price, our family physician, is out of town."

"Dr. Ashe has charge of his cases when he is away," replied the nurse. "If you can't find him, try Dr. Hooper. The child is growing worse every minute. On your way back you 'd better get some ice, if possible."

The major hastened downstairs.

"Don't wait for me, Ellis," he said. "I shall be needed here for a while. I 'll get to the office as soon as possible. Make up the paper, and leave another stick out for me to the last minute, but fill it up in case I 'm not on hand by twelve. We must get the paper out early in the morning."

Nothing but a matter of the most vital importance would have kept Major Carteret away from his office this night. Upon the presentation to the outer world of the story of this riot would depend the attitude of the great civilized public toward the events of the last ten hours. The Chronicle was the source from which the first word would be expected; it would give the people of Wellington their cue as to the position which they must take in regard to this distressful affair, which had so far transcended in ferocity the most extreme measures which the conspirators had anticipated. The burden of his own responsibility weighed heavily upon him, and could not be shaken off; but he must do first the duty nearest to him,—he must first attend to his child.

Carteret hastened from the house, and traversed rapidly the short distance to Dr. Ashe's office. Far down the street he could see the glow of the burning hospital, and he had scarcely left his own house when the fusillade of shots, fired when the colored men emerged from the burning building, was audible. Carteret would have hastened back to the scene of the riot, to see what was now going on, and to make another effort to stem the tide of bloodshed; but before the dread of losing his child, all other interests fell into the background. Not all the negroes in Wellington could weigh in the balance for one instant against the life of the feeble child now gasping for breath in the house behind him.

Reaching the house, a vigorous ring brought the doctor's wife to the door.

"Good-evening, Mrs. Ashe. Is the doctor at home?"

"No, Major Carteret. He was called to attend Mrs. Wells, who was taken suddenly ill, as a result of the trouble this afternoon. He will be there all night, no doubt."

"My child is very ill, and I must find some one."

"Try Dr. Yates. His house is only four doors away."

A ring at Dr. Yates's door brought out a young man.

"Is Dr. Yates in?"

"Yes, sir."

"Can I see him?"

"You might see him, sir, but that would be all. His horse was frightened by the shooting on the streets, and ran away and threw the doctor, and broke his right arm. I have just set it; he will not be able to attend any patients for several weeks. He is old and nervous, and the shock was great."

"Are you not a physician?" asked Carteret, looking at the young man keenly. He was a serious, gentlemanly looking young fellow, whose word might probably be trusted.

"Yes, I am Dr. Evans, Dr. Yates's assistant. I 'm really little more than a student, but I 'll do what I can."

"My only child is sick with the croup, and requires immediate attention."

"I ought to be able to handle a case of the croup," answered Dr. Evans, "at least in the first stages. I 'll go with you, and stay by the child, and if the case is beyond me, I may keep it in check until another physician comes."

He stepped back into another room, and returning immediately with his hat, accompanied Carteret homeward. The riot had subsided; even the glow from the smouldering hospital was no longer visible. It seemed that the city, appalled at the tragedy, had suddenly awakened to a sense of its own crime. Here and there a dark face, emerging cautiously from some hiding-place, peered from behind fence or tree, but shrank hastily away at the sight of a white face. The negroes of Wellington, with the exception of Josh Green and his party, had not behaved bravely on this critical day in their history; but those who had fought were dead, to the last man; those who had sought safety in flight or concealment were alive to tell the tale.

"We pass right by Dr. Thompson's," said Dr. Evans. "If you have n't spoken to him, it might be well to call him for consultation, in case the child should be very bad."

"Go on ahead," said Carteret, "and I 'll get him."

Evans hastened on, while Carteret sounded the old-fashioned knocker upon the doctor's door. A gray-haired negro servant, clad in a dress suit and wearing a white tie, came to the door.

"De doctuh, suh," he replied politely to Carteret's question, "has gone ter ampitate de ahm er a gent'eman who got one er his bones smashed wid a pistol bullet in de—fightin' dis afternoon, suh. He's jes' gone, suh, and lef' wo'd dat he 'd be gone a' hour er mo', suh."

Carteret hastened homeward. He could think of no other available physician. Perhaps no other would be needed, but if so, he could find out from Evans whom it was best to call.

When he reached the child's room, the young doctor was bending anxiously over the little frame. The little lips had become livid, the little nails, lying against the white sheet, were blue. The child's efforts to breathe were most distressing, and each gasp cut the father like a knife. Mrs. Carteret was weeping hysterically.

"How is he, doctor?" asked the major.

"He is very low," replied the young man. "Nothing short of tracheotomy—an operation to open the windpipe—will relieve him. Without it, in half or three quarters of an hour he will be unable to breathe. It is a delicate operation, a mistake in which would be as fatal as the disease. I have neither the knowledge nor the experience to attempt it, and your child's life is too valuable for a student to practice upon. Neither have I the instruments here."

"What shall we do?" demanded Carteret. "We have called all the best doctors, and none are available."

The young doctor's brow was wrinkled with thought. He

knew a doctor who could perform the operation. He had heard, also, of a certain event at Carteret's house some months before, when an unwelcome physician had been excluded from a consultation,—but it was the last chance.

"There is but one other doctor in town who has performed the operation, so far as I know," he declared, "and that is Dr. Miller. If you can get him, he can save your child's life."

Carteret hesitated involuntarily. All the incidents, all the arguments, of the occasion when he had refused to admit the colored doctor to his house, came up vividly before his memory. He had acted in accordance with his lifelong beliefs, and had carried his point; but the present situation was different,—this was a case of imperative necessity, and every other interest or consideration must give way before the imminence of his child's peril. That the doctor would refuse the call, he did not imagine: it would be too great an honor for a negro to decline,—unless some bitterness might have grown out of the proceedings of the afternoon. That this doctor was a man of some education he knew; and he had been told that he was a man of fine feeling,— for a negro,—and might easily have taken to heart the day's events. Nevertheless, he could hardly refuse a professional call,— professional ethics would require him to respond. Carteret had no reason to suppose that Miller had ever learned of what had occurred at the house during Dr. Burns's visit to Wellington. The major himself had never mentioned the controversy, and no doubt the other gentlemen had been equally silent.

"I 'll go for him myself," said Dr. Evans, noting Carteret's hesitation and suspecting its cause. "I can do nothing here alone, for a little while, and I may be able to bring the doctor back with me. He likes a difficult operation."

It seemed an age ere the young doctor returned, though it was really only a few minutes. The nurse did what she could to relieve the child's sufferings, which grew visibly more and more acute. The mother, upon the other side of the bed, held one of the baby's hands in her own, and controlled her feelings as best she might. Carteret paced the floor anxiously, going every few seconds to the head of the stairs to listen for Evans's footsteps on the piazza without. At last the welcome sound was audible, and a few strides took him to the door.

"Dr. Miller is at home, sir," reported Evans, as he came in. "He says that he was called to your house once before, by a third person who claimed authority to act, and that he was refused admittance. He declares that he will not consider such a call unless it come from you personally."

"That is true, quite true," replied Carteret. "His position is a just one. I will go at once. Will—will—my child live until I can get Miller here?"

"He can live for half an hour without an operation. Beyond that I could give you little hope."

Seizing his hat, Carteret dashed out of the yard and ran rapidly to Miller's house; ordinarily a walk of six or seven minutes, Carteret covered it in three, and was almost out of breath when he rang the bell of Miller's front door.

The ring was answered by the doctor in person.

"Dr. Miller, I believe?" asked Carteret.

"Yes, sir."

"I am Major Carteret. My child is seriously ill, and you are the only available doctor who can perform the necessary operation."

"Ah! You have tried all the others,—and then you come to me!"

"Yes, I do not deny it," admitted the major, biting his lip. He had not counted on professional jealousy as an obstacle to be met. "But I *have* come to you, as a physician, to engage your professional services for my child,—my only child. I have confidence in your skill, or I should not have come to you. I request—nay, I implore you to lose no more time, but come with me at once! My child's life is hanging by a thread, and you can save it!"

"Ah!" replied the other, "as a father whose only child's life is in danger, you implore *me,* of all men in the world, to come and save it!"

There was a strained intensity in the doctor's low voice that struck Carteret, in spite of his own preoccupation. He thought he heard, too, from the adjoining room, the sound of some one sobbing softly. There was some mystery here which he could not fathom unaided.

Miller turned to the door behind him and threw it open. On the white cover of a low cot lay a childish form in the rigidity of death, and by it knelt, with her back to the door, a woman whose shoulders were shaken by the violence of her sobs. Absorbed in her grief, she did not turn, or give any sign that she had recognized the intrusion.

"There, Major Carteret!" exclaimed Miller, with the tragic eloquence of despair, "there lies a specimen of your handiwork! There lies *my* only child, laid low by a stray bullet in this riot which you and your paper have fomented; struck down as much by your hand as though you had held the weapon with which his life was taken!"

"My God!" exclaimed Carteret, struck with horror. "Is the child dead?"

"There he lies," continued the other, "an innocent child,—there he lies dead, his little life snuffed out like a candle, because you and a handful of your friends thought you must override the laws and run this town at any cost!—and there kneels his mother, overcome by grief. We are alone in the house. It is not safe to leave her unattended. My duty calls me here, by the side of my dead child and my suffering wife! I cannot go with you. There is a just God in heaven!—as you have sown, so may you reap!"

Carteret possessed a narrow, but a logical mind, and except when confused or blinded by his prejudices, had always tried to be a just man. In the agony of his own predicament,—in the horror of the situation at Miller's house,—for a moment the veil of race prejudice was rent in twain, and he saw things as they were, in their correct proportions and relations,—saw clearly and convincingly that he had no standing here, in the presence of death, in the home of this stricken family. Miller's refusal to go with him was pure, elemental justice; he could not blame the doctor for his stand. He was indeed conscious of a certain involuntary admiration for a man who held in his hands the power of life and death, and could use it, with strict justice, to avenge his own wrongs. In Dr. Miller's place he would have done the same thing. Miller had spoken the truth,—as he had sown, so must he reap! He could not expect, could not ask, this father to leave his own household at such a moment.

Pressing his lips together with grim courage, and bowing mechanically, as though to Fate rather than the physician, Carteret turned and left the house. At a rapid pace he soon reached home. There was yet a chance for his child: perhaps some one of the other doctors had come; perhaps, after all, the disease had taken a favorable turn,—Evans was but a young doctor, and might have been mistaken. Surely, with doctors all around him, his child would not be permitted to die for lack of medical attention! He found the mother, the doctor, and the nurse still grouped, as he had left them, around the suffering child.

"How is he now?" he asked, in a voice that sounded like a groan.

"No better," replied the doctor; "steadily growing worse. He can go on probably for twenty minutes longer without an operation."

"Where is the doctor?" demanded Mrs. Carteret, looking eagerly toward the door. "You should have brought him right upstairs. There's not a minute to spare! Phil, Phil, our child will die!"

Carteret's heart swelled almost to bursting with an intense pity. Even his own great sorrow became of secondary importance beside the grief which his wife must soon feel at the inevitable loss of her only child. And it was his fault! Would that he could risk his own life to spare her and to save the child!

Briefly, and as gently as might be, he stated the result of his errand. The doctor had refused to come, for a good reason. He could not ask him again.

Young Evans felt the logic of the situation, which Carteret had explained sufficiently. To the nurse it was even clearer. If she or any other woman had been in the doctor's place, she would have given the same answer.

Mrs. Carteret did not stop to reason. In such a crisis a mother's heart usurps the place of intellect. For her, at that moment, there were but two facts in all the world. Her child lay dying. There was within the town, and within reach, a man who could save him. With an agonized cry she rushed wildly from the room.

Carteret sought to follow her, but she flew down the long stairs like a wild thing. The least misstep might have precipitated her to the bottom; but ere Carteret, with a remonstrance on his lips, had scarcely reached the uppermost step, she had thrown open the front door and fled precipitately out into the night.

XXXVII
THE SISTERS

Miller's doorbell rang loudly, insistently, as though demanding a response. Absorbed in his own grief, into which he had relapsed upon Carteret's departure, the sound was an unwelcome intrusion. Surely the man could not be coming back! If it were some one else—What else might happen to the doomed town concerned him not. His child was dead,—his distracted wife could not be left alone.

The doorbell rang—clamorously—appealingly. Through the long hall and the closed door of the room where he sat, he could hear some one knocking, and a faint voice calling.

"Open, for God's sake, open!"

It was a woman's voice,—the voice of a woman in distress. Slowly Miller rose and went to the door, which he opened mechanically.

A lady stood there, so near the image of his own wife, whom he had just left, that for a moment he was well-nigh startled. A little older, perhaps, a little fairer of complexion, but with the same form, the same features, marked by the same wild grief. She wore a loose wrapper, which clothed her like the drapery of a statue. Her long dark hair, the counterpart of his wife's, had fallen down, and hung disheveled about her shoulders. There was blood upon her knuckles, where she had beaten with them upon the door.

"Dr. Miller," she panted, breathless from her flight and laying her hand upon his arm appealingly,—when he shrank from the contact she still held it there,—"Dr. Miller, you will come and save my child? You know what it is to lose a child! I am so sorry about your little boy! You will come to mine!"

"Your sorrow comes too late, madam," he said harshly. "My child is dead. I charged your husband with his murder, and he could not deny it. Why should I save your husband's child?"

"Ah, Dr. Miller!" she cried, with his wife's voice,—she never knew how much, in that dark hour, she owed to that resemblance—"it is *my* child, and I have never injured you. It is my child, Dr. Miller, my only child. I brought it into the world at the risk of my own life! I have nursed it, I have watched over it, I have prayed for it,—and it now lies dying! Oh, Dr. Miller, dear Dr. Miller, if you have a heart, come and save my child!"

"Madam," he answered more gently, moved in spite of himself, "my heart is broken. My people lie dead upon the streets, at the hands of yours. The work of my life is in ashes,—and, yonder, stretched out in death, lies my own child! God! woman, you ask too much of human nature! Love, duty, sorrow, *justice,* call me here. I cannot go!"

She rose to her full height. "Then you are a murderer," she cried wildly. "His blood be on your head, and a mother's curse beside!"

The next moment, with a sudden revulsion of feeling, she had thrown herself at his feet,—at the feet of a negro, this proud white woman,—and was clasping his knees wildly.

"O God!" she prayed, in tones which quivered with anguish, "pardon my husband's sins, and my own, and move this man's hard heart, by the blood of thy Son, who died to save us all!"

It was the last appeal of poor humanity. When the pride of intellect and caste is broken; when we grovel in the dust of humiliation; when sickness and sorrow come, and the shadow of death falls upon us, and there is no hope elsewhere—we turn to God, who sometimes swallows the insult, and answers the appeal.

Miller raised the lady to her feet. He had been deeply moved,—but he had been more deeply injured. This was his wife's sister,—ah, yes! but a sister who had scorned and slighted and ignored the existence of his wife for all her life.

Only Miller, of all the world, could have guessed what this had meant to Janet, and he had merely divined it through the clairvoyant sympathy of love. This woman could have no claim upon him because of this unacknowledged relationship. Yet after all, she *was* his wife's sister, his child's kinswoman. She was a fellow creature, too, and in distress.

"Rise, madam," he said, with a sudden inspiration, lifting her gently. "I will listen to you on one condition. My child lies dead in the adjoining room, his mother by his side. Go in there, and make your request of her. I will abide by her decision."

The two women stood confronting each other across the body of the dead child, mute witness of this first meeting between two children of the same father. Standing thus face to face, each under the stress of the deepest emotions, the resemblance between them was even more striking than it had seemed to Miller when he had admitted Mrs. Carteret to the house. But Death, the great leveler, striking upon the one hand and threatening upon the other, had wrought a marvelous transformation in the bearing of the two women. The sad-eyed Janet towered erect, with menacing aspect, like an avenging goddess. The other, whose pride had been her life, stood in the attitude of a trembling suppliant.

"*You* have come here," cried Janet, pointing with a tragic gesture to the dead child,—"*you*, to gloat over your husband's work. All my life you have hated and scorned and despised me. Your presence here insults me and my dead. What are you doing here?"

"Mrs. Miller," returned Mrs. Carteret tremulously, dazed for a moment by this outburst, and clasping her hands with an imploring gesture, "my child, my only child, is dying, and your husband alone can save his life. Ah, let me have my child," she moaned, heart-rendingly. "It is my only one—my sweet child—my ewe lamb!"

"This was *my* only child!" replied the other mother; "and yours is no better to die than mine!"

"You are young," said Mrs. Carteret, "and may yet have

many children,—this is my only hope! If you have a human heart, tell your husband to come with me. He leaves it to you; he will do as you command."

"Ah," cried Janet, "I have a human heart, and therefore I will not let him go. *My* child is dead—O God, my child, my child!"

She threw herself down by the bedside, sobbing hysterically. The other woman knelt beside her, and put her arm about her neck. For a moment Janet, absorbed in her grief, did not repulse her.

"Listen," pleaded Mrs. Carteret. "You will not let my baby die? You are my sister;—the child is your own near kin!"

"My child was nearer," returned Janet, rising again to her feet and shaking off the other woman's arm. "He was my son, and I have seen him die. I have been your sister for twenty-five years, and you have only now, for the first time, called me so!"

"Listen—sister," returned Mrs. Carteret. Was there no way to move this woman? Her child lay dying, if he were not dead already. She would tell everything, and leave the rest to God. If it would save her child, she would shrink at no sacrifice. Whether the truth would still further incense Janet, or move her to mercy, she could not tell; she would leave the issue to God.

"Listen, sister!" she said. "I have a confession to make. You *are* my lawful sister. My father was married to your mother. You are entitled to his name, and to half his estate."

Janet's eyes flashed with bitter scorn.

"And you have robbed me all these years, and now tell me that as a reason why I should forgive the murder of my child?"

"No, no!" cried the other wildly, fearing the worst. "I have known of it only a few weeks,—since my Aunt Polly's death. I had not meant to rob you,—I had meant to make restitution. Sister! for our father's sake, who did you no wrong, give me my child's life!"

Janet's eyes slowly filled with tears—bitter tears—burning tears. For a moment even her grief at her child's loss dropped to second place in her thoughts. This, then, was the recognition for which, all her life, she had longed in secret. It had come, after many days, and in larger measure than she had dreamed; but it had come, not with frank kindliness and sisterly love, but in a storm of blood and tears; not freely given, from an open heart, but extorted from a reluctant conscience by the agony of a mother's fears. Janet had obtained her heart's desire, and now that it was at her lips, found it but apples of Sodom, filled with dust and ashes!

"Listen!" she cried, dashing her tears aside. "I have but one word for you,—one last word,—and then I hope never to see your face again! My mother died of want, and I was brought up by the hand of charity. Now, when I have married a man who can supply my needs, you offer me back the money which you and your friends have robbed me of! You imagined that the shame of being a negro swallowed up every other ignominy,—and in your eyes I am a negro, though I am your sister, and you are white, and people have taken me for you on the streets,—and you, therefore, left me nameless all my life! Now, when an honest man has given me a name of which I can be proud, you offer me the one of which you robbed me, and of which I can make no use. For twenty-five years I, poor, despicable fool, would have kissed your feet for a word, a nod, a smile. Now, when this tardy recognition comes, for which I have waited so long, it is tainted with fraud and crime and blood, and I must pay for it with my child's life!"

"And I must forfeit that of mine, it seems, for withholding it so long," sobbed the other, as tottering, she turned to go. "It is but just."

"Stay—do not go yet!" commanded Janet, imperiously, her pride still keeping back her tears. "I have not done. I throw you back your father's name, your father's wealth, your sisterly recognition. I want none of them,—they are bought too dear! ah, God, they are bought too dear! But that you may know that a woman may be foully wronged, and yet may have a heart to feel, even for one who has injured her, you may have your child's life, if my husband can save it! Will," she said, throwing open the door into the next room, "go with her!"

"God will bless you for a noble woman!" exclaimed Mrs. Carteret. "You do not mean all the cruel things you have

said,—ah, no! I will see you again, and make you take them
back; I cannot thank you now! Oh, doctor, let us go! I pray
God we may not be too late!"

Together they went out into the night. Mrs. Carteret tottered
under the stress of her emotions, and would have fallen, had
not Miller caught and sustained her with his arm until they
reached the house, where he turned over her fainting form to
Carteret at the door.

"Is the child still alive?" asked Miller.

"Yes, thank God," answered the father, "but nearly gone."

"Come on up, Dr. Miller," called Evans from the head of the
stairs. "There 's time enough, but none to spare."

III

ESSAYS

WHAT IS A WHITE MAN?

The fiat having gone forth from the wise men of the South that the "all-pervading, all-conquering Anglo-Saxon race" must continue forever to exercise exclusive control and direction of the government of this so-called Republic, it becomes important to every citizen who values his birthright to know who are included in this grandiloquent term. It is of course perfectly obvious that the writer or speaker who used this expression—perhaps Mr. Grady* of Georgia—did not say what he meant. It is not probable that he meant to exclude from full citizenship the Celts and Teutons and Gauls and Slavs who make up so large a proportion of our population; he hardly meant to exclude the Jews, for even the most ardent fireeater would hardly venture to advocate the disfranchisement of the thrifty race whose mortgages cover so large a portion of Southern soil. What the eloquent gentleman really meant by this high-sounding phrase was simply the white race; and the substance of the argument of that school of Southern writers to which he belongs, is simply that for the good of the country the Negro should have no voice in directing the government or public policy of the Southern States or of the nation.

But it is evident that where the intermingling of the races had made such progress as it has in this country, the line which separates the races must in many instances have been practically obliterated. And there has arisen in the United States a very large class of the population who are certainly not Negroes in

*Mr. Grady of Georgia: Henry W. Grady (1850–89), editor of the *Atlanta Constitution*, largely responsible for the perpetuation of the myth of the New South.—Ed.

an ethnological sense, and whose children will be no nearer Negroes than themselves. In view, therefore, of the very positive ground taken by the white leaders of the South, where most of these people reside, it becomes in the highest degree important to them to know what race they belong to. It ought to be also a matter of serious concern to the Southern white people; for if their zeal for good government is so great that they contemplate the practical overthrow of the Constitution and laws of the United States to secure it, they ought at least to be sure that no man entitled to it by their own argument, is robbed of a right so precious as that of free citizenship; the "all-pervading, all conquering Anglo-Saxon" ought to set as high a value on American citizenship as the all-conquering Roman placed upon the franchise of his State two thousand years ago. This discussion would of course be of little interest to the genuine Negro, who is entirely outside of the charmed circle, and must content himself with the acquisition of wealth, the pursuit of learning and such other privileges as his "best friends" may find it consistent with the welfare of the nation to allow him; but to every other good citizen the inquiry ought to be a momentous one. What is a white man?

In spite of the virulence and universality of race prejudice in the United States, the human intellect long ago revolted at the manifest absurdity of classifying men fifteen-sixteenths white as black men; and hence there grew up a number of laws in different states of the Union defining the limit which separated the white and colored races, which was, when these laws took their rise and is now to a large extent, the line which separated freedom and opportunity from slavery or hopeless degradation. Some of these laws are of legislative origin; others are judge-made laws, brought out by the exigencies of special cases which came before the courts for determination. Some day they will, perhaps, become mere curiosities of jurisprudence; the "black laws" will be bracketed with the "blue laws,"* and will be at best but landmarks by which to measure the progress of

---

*Blue laws: laws regulating public and private behavior on Sundays in the Puritan colonies of New England. Although a number of these laws remain on state law books, many states no longer enforce them.—Ed.

the nation. But to-day these laws are in active operation, and they are, therefore, worthy of attention; for every good citizen ought to know the law, and, if possible, to respect it; and if not worthy of respect, it should be changed by the authority which enacted it. Whether any of the laws referred to here have been in any manner changed by very recent legislation the writer cannot say, but they are certainly embodied in the latest editions of the revised statutes of the states referred to.

The colored people were divided, in most of the Southern States, into two classes, designated by law as Negroes and mulattoes respectively. The term Negro was used in its ethnological sense, and needed no definition; but the term "mulatto" was held by legislative enactment to embrace all persons of color not Negroes. The words "quadroon" and "mestizo" are employed in some of the law books, tho not defined; but the term "octoroon," as indicating a person having one-eighth of Negro blood, is not used at all, so far as the writer has been able to observe.

The states vary slightly in regard to what constitutes a mulatto or person of color, and as to what proportion of white blood should be sufficient to remove the disability of color. As a general rule, less than one-fourth of Negro blood left the individual white—in theory; race questions being, however, regulated very differently in practice. In Missouri, by the code of 1855, still in operation, so far as not inconsistent with the Federal Constitution and laws, "any person other than a Negro, any one of whose grandmothers or grandfathers is or shall have been a Negro, tho all of his or her progenitors except those descended from the Negro may have been white persons, shall be deemed a mulatto." Thus the color-line is drawn at one-fourth of Negro blood, and persons with only one-eighth are white.

By the Mississippi code of 1880, the color-line is drawn at one-fourth of Negro blood, all persons having less being theoretically white.

Under the code noir* of Louisiana, the descendant of a white

*Code noir: The Code Noir of Louisiana, made at Versailles in March of 1724, limited the rights of blacks in the New World and declared them the personal property of their white owners.—Ed.

and a quadroon is white, thus drawing the line at one-eighth of Negro blood. The code of 1876 abolished all distinctions of color; as to whether they have been re-enacted since the Republican Party went out of power in that state the writer is not informed.

Jumping to the extreme North, persons are white within the meaning of the Constitution of Michigan who have less than one-fourth of Negro blood.

In Ohio the rule, as established by numerous decisions of the Supreme Court, was that a preponderance of white blood constituted a person a white man in the eye of the law, and entitled him to the exercise of all the civil rights of a white man. By a retrogressive step the color-line was extended in 1861 in the case of marriage, which by statute was forbidden between a person of pure white blood and one having a visible admixture of African blood. But by act of legislature, passed in the spring of 1887, all laws establishing or permitting distinctions of color were repealed. In many parts of the state these laws were always ignored, and they would doubtless have been repealed long ago but for the sentiment of the southern counties, separated only by the width of the Ohio River from a former slave-holding state.* There was a bill introduced in the legislature during the last session to reenact the "black laws," but it was hopelessly defeated; the member who introduced it evidently mistook his latitude; he ought to be a member of the Georgia legislature.

But the state which, for several reasons, one might expect to have the strictest laws in regard to the relations of the races, has really the loosest. Two extracts from decisions of the Supreme Court of South Carolina will make clear the law of that state in regard to the color-line.†

The definition of the term mulatto, as understood in this state, seems to be vague, signifying generally a person of mixed white or European and Negro parentage, in whatever proportions the blood of the two races may be mingled in the individual. But it is

---

*Kentucky.—Ed.
†Definition of the term mulatto from *State v. Davis*, S.C. 2 Bailey 558 (1831).—Ed.

not invariably applicable to every admixture of African blood with the European, nor is one having all the features of a white to be ranked with the degraded class designated by the laws of this state as persons of color, because of some remote taint of the Negro race. The line of distinction, however, is not ascertained by any rule of law. . . . Juries would probably be justified in holding a person to be white in whom the admixture of African blood did not exceed the proportion of one-eighth. But it is in all cases a question for the jury, to be determined by them upon the evidence of features and complexion afforded by inspection, the evidence of reputation as to parentage, and the evidence of the rank and station in society occupied by the party. The only rule which can be laid down by the courts is that where there is a distinct and visible admixture of Negro blood, the individual is to be denominated a mulatto or person of color.

In a later case the court held: "The question whether persons are colored or white, where color or feature are doubtful, is for the jury to decide by reputation, by reception into society, and by their exercise of the privileges of the white man, as well as by admixture of blood."

It is an interesting question why such should have been, and should still be, for that matter, the law of South Carolina, and why there should exist in that state a condition of public opinion which would accept such a law. Perhaps it may be attributed to the fact that the colored population of South Carolina always outnumbered the white population, and the eagerness of the latter to recruit their ranks was sufficient to overcome in some measure their prejudice against the Negro blood. It is certainly true that the color-line is, in practice as in law, more loosely drawn in South Carolina than in any other Southern State, and that no inconsiderable element of the population of that state consists of these legal white persons, who were either born in the state, or attracted thither by this feature of the laws, have come in from surrounding states, and, forsaking home and kindred, have taken their social position as white people. A reasonable degree of reticence in regard to one's antecedents is, however, usual in such cases.

Before the War the color-line, as fixed by law, regulated in theory the civil and political status of persons of color. What the status was, was expressed in the Dred Scott decision.* But since the War, or rather since the enfranchisement of the colored people, these laws have been mainly confined—in theory, be it always remembered—to the regulation of the intercourse of the races in schools and in the marriage relation. The extension of the color-line to places of public entertainment and resort, to inns and public highways, is in most states entirely a matter of custom. A colored man can sue in the courts of any Southern State for the violation of his common-law rights, and recover damages of say fifty cents without costs. A colored minister who sued a Baltimore steamboat company a few weeks ago for refusing him first-class accommodation, he having paid first-class fare, did not even meet with that measure of success; the learned judge, a Federal judge by the way, held that the plaintiff's rights had been invaded, and that he had suffered humiliation at the hands of the defendant company, but that "the humiliation was not sufficient to entitle him to damages." And the learned judge dismissed the action without costs to either party.

Having thus ascertained what constitutes a white man, the good citizen may be curious to know what steps have been taken to preserve the purity of the white race. Nature, by some unaccountable oversight having to some extent neglected a matter so important to the future prosperity and progress of mankind. The marriage laws referred to here are in active operation, and cases under them are by no means infrequent. Indeed, instead of being behind the age, the marriage laws in the Southern States are in advance of public opinion; for very rarely will a Southern community stop to figure on the pedigree of the contracting parties to a marriage where one is white and the other is known to have any strain of Negro blood.

In Virginia, under the title "Offenses against Morality," the law provides that "any white person who shall intermarry with

---

*In *Dred Scott v. Sandford* (1857) the U.S. Supreme Court ruled that Congress could not prohibit slavery in federal Midwest territories and that free blacks were not U.S. citizens.—Ed.

a Negro shall be confined in jail not more than one year and fined not exceeding one hundred dollars." In a marginal note on the statute-book, attention is called to the fact that "a similar penalty is not imposed on the Negro"—a stretch of magnanimity to which the laws of other states are strangers. A person who performs the ceremony of marriage in such a case is fined two hundred dollars, one-half of which goes to the informer.

In Maryland, a minister who performs the ceremony of marriage between a Negro and a white person is liable to a fine of one hundred dollars.

In Mississippi, code of 1880, it is provided that "the marriage of a white person to a Negro or mulatto or person who shall have one-fourth or more of Negro blood, shall be unlawful"; and as this prohibition does not seem sufficiently emphatic, it is further declared to be "incestuous and void," and is punished by the same penalty prescribed for marriage within the forbidden degrees of consanguinity.

But it is Georgia, the *alma genetrix** of the chain-gang, which merits the questionable distinction of having the harshest set of color laws. By the law of Georgia the term "person of color" is defined to mean "all such as have an admixture of Negro blood, and the term 'Negro,' includes mulattoes." This definition is perhaps restricted somewhat by another provision, by which "all Negroes, mestizoes, and their descendants, having one-eighth of Negro or mulatto blood in their veins, shall be known in this State as persons of color." A colored minister is permitted to perform the ceremony of marriage between colored persons only, tho white ministers are not forbidden to join persons of color in wedlock. It is further provided that "the marriage relation between white persons and persons of African descent is forever prohibited, and such marriages shall be null and void." This is a very sweeping provision; it will be noticed that the term "persons of color," previously defined, is not employed, the expression "persons of African descent"

*Alma genetrix: fostering progenitor.—Ed.

being used instead. A court which was so inclined would find no difficulty in extending this provision of the law to the remotest strain of African blood. The marriage relation is forever prohibited. Forever is a long time. There is a colored woman in Georgia said to be worth $300,000—an immense fortune in the poverty stricken South. With a few hundred such women in that state, possessing a fair degree of good looks, the color-line would shrivel up like a scroll in the heat of competition for their hands in marriage. The penalty for the violation of the law against intermarriage is the same sought to be imposed by the defunct Glenn Bill* for violation of its provisions; i.e., a fine not to exceed one thousand dollars, and imprisonment not to exceed six months, or twelve months in the chain-gang.

Whatever the wisdom or justice of these laws, there is one objection to them which is not given sufficient prominence in the consideration of the subject, even where it is discussed at all; they make mixed blood a *prima-facie*† proof of illegitimacy. It is a fact that at present, in the United States, a colored man or woman whose complexion is white or nearly white is presumed, in the absence of any knowledge of his or her antecedents, to be the offspring of a union not sanctified by law. And by a curious but not uncommon process, such persons are not held in the same low estimation as white people in the same position. The sins of their fathers are not visited upon the children, in that regard at least; and their mothers' lapses from virtue are regarded either as misfortunes or as faults excusable under the circumstances.‡ But in spite of all this, illegitimacy is not a desirable distinction, and is likely to become less so, as these people of mixed blood advance in wealth and social standing. This presumption of illegitimacy was once, perhaps, true of the majority of such persons; but the times have changed.

---

*Glenn Bill: Introduced into the lower house of the Georgia State Legislature in 1887, this bill would have mandated school segregation in Georgia, but it never passed the state senate.—Ed.

†*Prima-facie:* a legal presumption of fact, literally "at first sight."—Ed.

‡Exodus 20:5: "Thou shalt not bow down thyself to them, nor serve them: for I the LORD thy God am a jealous God, visiting the iniquity of the fathers upon the children unto the third and fourth generation of them that hate me."—Ed.

More than half of the colored people of the United States are of mixed blood; they marry and are given in marriage, and they beget children of complexions similar to their own.* Whether or not, therefore, laws which stamp these children as illegitimate, and which by indirection establish a lower standard of morality for a large part of the population than the remaining part is judged by, are wise laws; and whether or not the purity of the white race could not be as well preserved by the exercise of virtue, and the operation of those natural laws which are so often quoted by Southern writers as the justification of all sorts of Southern "policies"—are questions which the good citizen may at least turn over in his mind occasionally, pending the settlement of other complications which have grown out of the presence of the Negro on this continent.

---

*Matthew 22:30: "For in the resurrection they neither marry, nor are given in marriage, but are as the angels of God in heaven."—Ed.

THE DISFRANCHISEMENT
OF THE NEGRO

The right of American citizens of African descent, commonly called Negroes, to vote upon the same terms as other citizens of the United States is plainly declared and firmly fixed by the Constitution. No such person is called upon to present reasons why he should possess the right: that question is foreclosed by the Constitution. The object of the elective franchise is to give representation. So long as the Constitution retains its present form, any State Constitution, or statute, which seeks, by juggling the ballot, to deny the colored race fair representation, is a clear violation of the fundamental law of the land, and a corresponding injustice to those thus deprived of this right.

For thirty-five years this has been the law. As long as it was measurably respected, the colored people made rapid strides in education, wealth, character and self-respect. This the census proves, all statements to the contrary notwithstanding. A generation has grown to manhood and womanhood under the great, inspiring freedom conferred by the Constitution and protected by the right of suffrage—protected in large degree by the mere naked right, even when its exercise was hindered or denied by unlawful means. They have developed, in every Southern community, good citizens, who, if sustained and encouraged by just laws and liberal institutions, would greatly augment their number with the passing years, and soon wipe out the reproach of ignorance, unthrift, low morals and social inefficiency, thrown at them indiscriminately and therefore unjustly, and made the excuse for the equally undiscriminating contempt of their persons and their rights. They have reduced their illiteracy nearly 50 per cent. Excluded from the institutions of higher learning in their own States, their young men hold their own, and occasionally carry away honors, in the universities of the North. They have accumulated three hundred million dollars worth of real and personal property. Individuals among them have acquired substantial wealth, and several have attained to something like national distinction in art, letters and educational leadership. They are numerously represented in the learned professions. Heavily handicapped, they have made such rapid progress that the suspicion is justified that their advancement, rather than any stagnation or retrogression, is the true secret of the virulent Southern hostility to their rights, which has so influenced Northern opinion that it stands mute, and leaves the colored people, upon whom the North conferred liberty, to the tender mercies of those who have always denied their fitness for it.

It may be said, in passing, that the word "Negro," where used in this paper, is used solely for convenience. By the census of 1890 there were 1,000,000 colored people in the country who were half, or more than half, white, and logically there must be, as in fact there are so many who share the white blood in some degree, as to justify the assertion that the race problem in the United States concerns the welfare and the status of a mixed race. Their rights are not one whit the more sacred because of this fact; but in an argument where injustice is sought to be excused because of fundamental differences of race, it is well enough to bear in mind that the race whose rights and liberties are endangered all over this country by disfranchisement at the South, are the colored people who live in the United States to-day, and not the low-browed, man-eating savage whom the Southern white likes to set upon a block and contrast with Shakespeare and Newton and Washington and Lincoln.

Despite and in defiance of the Federal Constitution, to-day in the six Southern States of Mississippi, Louisiana, Alabama, North Carolina, South Carolina and Virginia, containing an aggregate colored population of about 6,000,000, these have been, to all intents and purposes, denied, so far as the States can effect it, the right to vote. This disfranchisement is accomplished by various methods, devised with much transparent ingenuity, the effort being in each instance to violate the spirit of the Federal Constitution by disfranchising the Negro, while seeming to respect its letter by avoiding the mention of race or color.

These restrictions fall into three groups. The first comprises a property qualification—the ownership of $300 worth or more of real or personal property (Alabama, Louisiana, Virginia and South Carolina); the payment of a poll tax (Mississippi, North Carolina, Virginia); an educational qualification—the ability to read and write (Alabama, Louisiana, North Carolina). Thus far, those who believe in a restricted suffrage everywhere, could perhaps find no reasonable fault with any one of these qualifications, applied either separately or together.

But the Negro has made such progress that these restrictions alone would perhaps not deprive him of effective representation. Hence the second group. This comprises an "understanding" clause—the applicant must be able "to read, or understand when read to him, any clause in the Constitution" (Mississippi), or to read and explain, or to understand and explain when read to him, any section of the Constitution (Virginia); an employment qualification—the voter must be regularly employed in some lawful occupation (Alabama); a character qualification—the voter must be a person of good character and who "understands the duties and obligations of citizens under a republican (!) form of government" (Alabama). The qualifications under the first group it will be seen, are capable of exact demonstration; those under the second group are left to the discretion and judgment of the registering officer—for in most instances these are all requirements for registration, which must precede voting.

But the first group, by its own force, and the second group, under imaginable conditions, might exclude not only the Negro vote, but a large part of the white vote. Hence, the third group, which comprises: a military service qualification—any man who went to war, willingly or unwillingly, in a good cause or a bad, is entitled to register (Ala., Va.); a prescriptive qualification, under which are included all male persons who were entitled to vote on January 1, 1867, at which date the Negro had not yet been given the right to vote; a hereditary qualification, (the so-called "grandfather" clause), whereby any son (Va.), or descendant (Ala.), of a soldier, and (N.C.) the descendant of any person who had the right to vote on January 1, 1867, inherits that right. If the voter wish to take advantage of these last provisions, which are in the nature of exceptions to a general rule, he must register within a stated time, whereupon he becomes a member of a privileged class of permanently enrolled voters not subject to any of the other restrictions.

It will be seen that these restrictions are variously combined in the different States, and it is apparent that if combined to their declared end, practically every Negro may, under color of law, be denied the right to vote, and practically every white man accorded that right. The effectiveness of these provisions to exclude the Negro vote is proved by the Alabama registration under the new State Constitution. Out of a total, by the census of 1900, of 181,471 Negro "males of voting age," less than 3,000 are registered; in Montgomery county alone, the seat of the State capital, where there are 7,000 Negro males of voting age, only 47 have been allowed to register, while in several counties not one single Negro is permitted to exercise the franchise.

These methods of disfranchisement have stood such tests as the United States Courts, including the Supreme Court, have thus far seen fit to apply, in such cases as have been before them for adjudication. These include a case based upon the "understanding" clause of the Mississippi Constitution, in which the Supreme Court held, in effect, that since there was no ambiguity in the language employed and the Negro was not directly named, the Court would not go behind the wording of the Constitution to find a meaning which discriminated against the colored voter; and the recent case of Jackson vs. Giles, brought by a colored citizen of Montgomery, Alabama, in which the Supreme Court confesses itself impotent to provide a remedy for what, by inference, it acknowledges *may* be a "great political wrong," carefully avoiding, however, to state that it is a wrong, although the vital prayer of the petition was for a decision upon this very point.

Now, what is the effect of this wholesale disfranchisement of colored men, upon their citizenship. The value of food to the human organism is not measured by the pains of an occasional surfeit, but by the effect of its entire deprivation. Whether a class of citizens should vote, even if not always wisely—what class does?—may best be determined by considering their condition when they are without the right to vote.

The colored people are left, in the States where they have been disfranchised, absolutely without representation, direct or indirect, in any law-making body, in any court of justice, in any branch of government—for the feeble remnant of voters left by law is so inconsiderable as to be without a shadow of power. Constituting one-eighth of the population of the whole country, two-fifths of the whole Southern people, and a majority in several States, they are not able, because disfranchised where most numerous, to send one representative to the Congress, which, by the decision in the Alabama case, is held by the Supreme Court to be the only body, outside of the State itself, competent to give relief from a great political wrong. By former decisions of the same tribunal, even Congress is impotent to protect their civil rights, the Fourteenth Amendment having long since, by the consent of the same Court, been in many respects as completely nullified as the Fifteenth Amendment is now sought to be. They have no direct representation in any Southern legislature, and no voice in determining the choice of white men who might be friendly to their rights. Nor are they able to influence the election of judges or other public officials, to whom are entrusted the protection of their lives, their liberties and their property. No judge is rendered careful, no sheriff diligent, for fear that he may offend a black constituency; the contrary is most lamentably true; day after day the catalogue of lynchings and anti-Negro riots upon every imaginable pretext, grows longer and more appalling. The country stands face to face with the revival of slavery; at the moment of this writing a federal grand jury in Alabama is uncovering a system of peonage established under cover of law.

Under the Southern program it is sought to exclude colored men from every grade of the public service; not only from the higher administrative functions, to which few of them would in any event, for a long time aspire, but from the lowest as well. A Negro may not be a constable or a policeman. He is subjected by law to many degrading discriminations. He is required to be separated from white people on railroads and street cars, and, by custom, debarred from inns and places of public entertainment. His equal right to a free public education is constantly threatened and is nowhere equitably recognized. In Georgia, as has been shown by Dr. DuBois, where the law provides for a pro rata distribution of the public school fund between the races, and where the colored school population is 48 per cent of the total, the amount of the fund devoted to their schools is only 20 per cent. In New Orleans, with an immense colored population, many of whom are persons of means and culture, all colored public schools above the fifth grade have been abolished.

The Negro is subjected to taxation without representation, which the forefathers of this Republic made the basis of a bloody revolution. Flushed with their local success, and encouraged by the timidity of the Courts and the indifference of public opinion, the Southern whites have carried their campaign into the national government, with an ominous degree of success. If they shall have their way, no Negro can fill any federal office, or occupy, in the public service, any position that is not menial. This is not an inference, but the openly, passionately avowed sentiment of the white South. The right to employment in the public service is an exceedingly valuable one, for which white men have struggled and fought. A vast army of men are employed in the administration of public affairs. Many avenues of employment are closed to colored men by popular prejudice. If their right to public employment is recognized, and the way to it open through the civil service, or the appointing power, or the suffrages of the people, it will prove, as it has already, a strong incentive to effort and a powerful lever for advancement. Its value to the Negro, like that of the right to vote, may be judged by the eagerness of the whites to deprive him of it.

Not only is the Negro taxed without representation in the States referred to, but he pays, through the tariff and internal revenue, a tax to a National government whose supreme judicial tribunal declares that it cannot, through the executive arm, enforce its own decrees, and, therefore, refuses to pass upon a question squarely before it, involving a basic right of citizenship. For the decision of the Supreme Court in the Giles case, if it foreshadows the attitude which the Court will take upon other cases to the same general end which will soon come before it, is scarcely less than a reaffirmation of the Dred Scott decision; it certainly amounts to this—that in spite of the Fifteenth Amendment, colored men in the United States have no political rights which the States are bound to respect. To say this much is to say that all privileges and immunities which Negroes henceforth enjoy, must be by favor of the whites; they are not *rights*. The whites have so declared; they proclaim that the country is theirs, that the Negro should be thankful that he has so much, when so much more might be withheld from him. He stands upon a lower footing than any alien; he has no government to which he may look for protection.

Moreover, the white South sends to Congress, on a basis including the Negro population, a delegation nearly twice as large as it is justly entitled to, and one which may always safely be relied upon to oppose in Congress every measure which seeks to protect the equality, or to enlarge the rights of colored citizens. The grossness of this injustice is all the more apparent since the Supreme Court, in the Alabama case referred to, has declared the legislative and political department of the government to be the only power which can right a political wrong. Under this decision still further attacks upon the liberties of the citizen may be confidently expected. Armed with the Negro's sole weapon of defense, the white South stands ready to smite down his rights. The ballot was first given to the Negro to defend him against this very thing. He needs it now far more than then, and for even stronger reasons. The 9,000,000 free colored people of to-day have vastly more to defend than the 3,000,000 hapless blacks who had just emerged from slavery. If there be those who maintain that it was a mistake to give the Negro the ballot at the time and in the manner in which it was given, let them take to heart this reflection: that to deprive him of it to-day, or to so restrict it as to leave him utterly defense-less against the present relentless attitude of the South toward his rights, will prove to be a mistake so much greater than the first, as to be no less than a crime, from which not alone the Southern Negro must suffer, but for which the nation will as surely pay the penalty as it paid for the crime of slavery. Contempt for law is death to a republic, and this one has developed alarming symptoms of the disease.

And now, having thus robbed the Negro of every political and civil *right,* the white South, in palliation of its course, makes a great show of magnanimity in leaving him, as the sole remnant of what he acquired through the Civil War, a very inadequate public school education, which, by the present program, is to be directed mainly towards making him a better agricultural laborer. Even this is put forward as a favor, although the Negro's property is taxed to pay for it, and his labor as well. For it is a well settled principle of political economy, that land and machinery of themselves produce nothing, and that labor indirectly pays its fair proportion of the tax upon the public's wealth. The white South seems to stand to the Negro at present as one, who, having been reluctantly compelled to release another from bondage, sees him stumbling forward and upward, neglected by his friends and scarcely yet conscious of his own strength; seizes him, binds him, and having bereft him of speech, of sight and of manhood, "yokes him with the mule" and exclaims, with a show of virtue which ought to deceive no one: "Behold how good a friend I am of yours! Have I not left you a stomach and a pair of arms, and will I not generously permit you to work for me with the one, that you may thereby gain enough to fill the other? A brain you do not need. We will relieve you of any responsibility that might seem to demand such an organ."

The argument of peace-loving Northern white men and Negro opportunists that the political power of the Negro having long ago been suppressed by unlawful means, his right to vote is a mere paper right, of no real value, and therefore to be lightly yielded for the sake of a hypothetical harmony, is fatally shortsighted. It is precisely the attitude and essentially the

argument which would have surrendered to the South in the
sixties, and would have left this country to rot in slavery for
another generation. White men do not thus argue concerning
their own rights. They know too well the value of ideals.
Southern white men see too clearly the latent power of these
unexercised rights. If the political power of the Negro was a
nullity because of his ignorance and lack of leadership, why
were they not content to leave it so, with the pleasing assurance
that if it ever became effective, it would be because the Negroes
had grown fit for its exercise? On the contrary, they have not
rested until the possibility of its revival was apparently headed
off by new State Constitutions. Nor are they satisfied with this.
There is no doubt that an effort will be made to secure the repeal of the Fifteenth Amendment, and thus forestall the development of the wealthy and educated Negro, whom the South
seems to anticipate as a greater menace than the ignorant ex-
slave. However improbable this repeal may seem, it is not a
subject to be lightly dismissed; for it is within the power of the
white people of the nation to do whatever they wish in the
premises—they did it once; they can do it again. The Negro
and his friends should see to it that the white majority shall
never wish to do anything to his hurt. There still stands, before
the Negro-hating whites of the South, the specter of a Supreme
Court which will interpret the Constitution to mean what it
says, and what those who enacted it meant, and what the nation, which ratified it, understood, and which will find power,
in a nation which goes beyond seas to administer the affairs
of distant peoples, to enforce its own fundamental laws; the
specter, too, of an aroused public opinion which will compel
Congress and the Courts to preserve the liberties of the Republic, which are the liberties of the people. To wilfully neglect the
suffrage, to hold it lightly, is to tamper with a sacred right; to
yield it for anything else whatever is simply suicidal. Dropping
the element of race, disfranchisement is no more than to say to
the poor and poorly taught, that they must relinquish the right
to defend themselves against oppression until they shall have
become rich and learned, in competition with those already
thus favored and possessing the ballot in addition. This is not

the philosophy of history. The growth of liberty has been the constant struggle of the poor against the privileged classes; and the goal of that struggle has ever been the equality of all men before the law. The Negro who would yield this right, deserves to be a slave; he has the servile spirit. The rich and the educated can, by virtue of their influence, command many votes; can find other means of protection; the poor man has but one, he should guard it as a sacred treasure. Long ago, by fair treatment, the white leaders of the South might have bound the Negro to themselves with hoops of steel. They have not chosen to take this course, but by assuming from the beginning an attitude hostile to his rights, have never gained his confidence, and now seek by foul means to destroy where they have never sought by fair means to control.

I have spoken of the effect of disfranchisement upon the colored race; it is to the race as a whole, that the argument of the problem is generally directed. But the unit of society in a republic is the individual, and not the race, the failure to recognize this fact being the fundamental error which has beclouded the whole discussion. The effect of disfranchisement upon the individual is scarcely less disastrous. I do not speak of the moral effect of injustice upon those who suffer from it; I refer rather to the practical consequences which may be appreciated by any mind. No country is free in which the way upward is not open for every man to try, and for every properly qualified man to attain whatever of good the community life may offer. Such a condition does not exist, at the South, even in theory, for any man of color. In no career can such a man compete with white men upon equal terms. He must not only meet the prejudice of the individual, not only the united prejudice of the white community; but lest some one should wish to treat him fairly, he is met at every turn with some legal prohibition which says, "Thou shalt not," or "Thus far shalt thou go and no farther." But the Negro race is viable; it adapts itself readily to circumstances; and being thus adaptable, there is always the temptation to

> Crook the pregnant hinges of the knee,
> Where thrift may follow fawning.

He who can most skilfully balance himself upon the advancing or receding wave of white opinion concerning his race, is surest of such measure of prosperity as is permitted to men of dark skins. There are Negro teachers in the South—the privilege of teaching in their own schools is the one respectable branch of the public service still left open to them—who, for a grudging appropriation from a Southern legislature, will decry their own race, approve their own degradation, and laud their oppressors. Deprived of the right to vote, and, therefore, of any power to demand what is their due, they feel impelled to buy the tolerance of the whites at any sacrifice. If to live is the first duty of man, as perhaps it is the first instinct, then those who thus stoop to conquer may be right. But is it needful to stoop so low, and if so, where lies the ultimate responsibility for this abasement?

I shall say nothing about the moral effect of disfranchisement upon the white people, or upon the State itself. What slavery made of the Southern whites is a matter of history. The abolition of slavery gave the South an opportunity to emerge from barbarism. Present conditions indicate that the spirit which dominated slavery still curses the fair section over which that institution spread its blight.

And now, is the situation remediless? If not so, where lies the remedy? First let us take up those remedies suggested by the men who approve of disfranchisement, though they may sometimes deplore the method, or regret the necessity.

Time, we are told, heals all diseases, rights all wrongs, and is the only cure for this one. It is a cowardly argument. These people are entitled to their rights to-day, while they are yet alive to enjoy them; and it is poor statesmanship and worse morals to nurse a present evil and thrust it forward upon a future generation for correction. The nation can no more honestly do this than it could thrust back upon a past generation the responsibility for slavery. It had to meet that responsibility; it ought to meet this one.

Education has been put forward as the great corrective—preferably industrial education. The intellect of the whites is to be educated to the point where they will so appreciate the blessings of liberty and equality, as of their own motion to enlarge and defend the Negro's rights. The Negroes, on the other hand, are to be so trained as to make them, not equal with the whites in any way—God save the mark! this would be unthinkable!—but so useful to the community that the whites will protect them rather than to lose their valuable services. Some few enthusiasts go so far as to maintain that by virtue of education the Negro will, in time, become strong enough to protect himself against any aggression of the whites; this, it may be said, is a strictly Northern view.

It is not quite clearly apparent how education alone, in the ordinary meaning of the word, is to solve, in any appreciable time, the problem of the relations of Southern white and black people. The need of education of all kinds for both races is woefully apparent. But men and nations have been free without being learned, and there have been educated slaves. Liberty has been known to languish where culture had reached a very high development. Nations do not first become rich and learned and then free, but the lesson of history has been that they first become free and then rich and learned, and oftentimes fall back into slavery again because of too great wealth, and the resulting luxury and carelessness of civic virtues. The process of education has been going on rapidly in the Southern States since the Civil War, and yet, if we take superficial indications, the rights of the Negroes are at a lower ebb than at any time during the thirty-five years of their freedom, and the race prejudice more intense and uncompromising. It is not apparent that educated Southerners are less rancorous than others in their speech concerning the Negro, or less hostile in their attitude toward his rights. It is their voice alone that we have heard in this discussion; and if, as they state, they are liberal in their views as compared with the more ignorant whites, then God save the Negro!

I was told, in so many words, two years ago, by the Superintendent of Public Schools of a Southern city that "there was no place in the modern world for the Negro, except under the ground." If gentlemen holding such opinions are to instruct the white youth of the South, would it be at all surprising if these, later on, should devote a portion of their leisure to the improvement of civilization by putting under the ground as many of this superfluous race as possible?

The sole excuse made in the South for the prevalent injustice to the Negro is the difference in race, and the inequalities and antipathies resulting therefrom. It has nowhere been declared as a part of the Southern program that the Negro, when educated, is to be given a fair representation in government or an equal opportunity in life; the contrary has been strenuously asserted; education can never make of him anything but a Negro, and, therefore, essentially inferior, and not to be safely trusted with any degree of power. A system of education which would tend to soften the asperities and lessen the inequalities between the races would be of inestimable value. An education which by a rigid separation of the races from the kindergarten to the university, fosters this racial antipathy, and is directed toward emphasizing the superiority of one class and the inferiority of another, might easily have disastrous, rather than beneficial results. It would render the oppressing class more powerful to injure, the oppressed quicker to perceive and keener to resent the injury, without proportionate power of defense. The same assimilative education which is given at the North to all children alike, whereby native and foreign, black and white, are taught side by side in every grade of instruction, and are compelled by the exigencies of discipline to keep their prejudices in abeyance, and are given the opportunity to learn and appreciate one another's good qualities, and to establish friendly relations which may exist throughout life, is absent from the Southern system of education, both of the past and as proposed for the future. Education is in a broad sense a remedy for all social ills; but the disease we have to deal with now is not only constitutional but acute. A wise physician does not simply give a tonic for a diseased limb, or a high fever; the patient might be dead before the constitutional remedy could become effective. The evils of slavery, its injury to whites and blacks, and to the body politic, was clearly perceived and acknowledged by the educated leaders of the South as far back as the Revolutionary War and the Constitutional Convention, and yet they made no effort to abolish it. Their remedy was the same—time, education, social and economic development;—and yet a bloody war was necessary to destroy slavery and put its spirit temporarily to sleep. When the South and its friends are ready to propose a system of education which will recognize and teach the equality of all men before the law, the potency of education alone to settle the race problem will be more clearly apparent.

At present even good Northern men, who wish to educate the Negroes, feel impelled to buy this privilege from the none too eager white South, by conceding away the civil and political rights of those whom they would benefit. They have, indeed, gone farther than the Southerners themselves in approving the disfranchisement of the colored race. Most Southern men, now that they have carried their point and disfranchised the Negro, are willing to admit, in the language of a recent number of the *Charleston Evening Post,* that "the attitude of the Southern white male toward the Negro is incompatible with the fundamental ideas of the republic." It remained for our Clevelands and Abbotts and Parkhursts to assure them that their unlawful course was right and justifiable, and for the most distinguished Negro leader to declare that "every revised Constitution throughout the Southern States has put a premium upon intelligence, ownership of property, thrift and character." So does every penitentiary sentence put a premium upon good conduct; but it is poor consolation to the one unjustly condemned, to be told that he may shorten his sentence somewhat by good behavior. Dr. Booker T. Washington, whose language is quoted above, has, by his eminent services in the cause of education, won deserved renown. If he has seemed, at times, to those jealous of the best things for their race, to decry the higher education, it can easily be borne in mind that his career is bound up in the success of an industrial school; hence any undue stress which he may put upon that branch of education may safely be ascribed to the natural zeal of the promoter, without detracting in any degree from the essential value of his teachings in favor of manual training, thrift and character-building. But Mr. Washington's prominence as an educational leader, among a race whose prominent leaders are so few, has at times forced him, perhaps reluctantly, to express himself in regard to the political condition of his people, and here his utterances have not always been so wise nor so happy. He has declared himself in favor of a restricted suffrage, which at present means, for his own people, nothing less than complete loss of representation—indeed it is only in that connection that the question has been seriously mooted; and he has advised them to go slow in seeking to enforce their civil and political rights, which, in effect, means silent submission to injustice. Southern white men may applaud this advice as wise, because it fits in with their purposes; but Senator McEnery of Louisiana, in a recent article in the *Independent,* voices the Southern white opinion of such acquiescence when he says: "What other race would have submitted so many years to slavery without complaint? *What other race would have submitted so quietly to disfranchisement?* These facts stamp his (the Negro's) inferiority to the white race." The time to philosophize about the good there is in evil, is not while its correction is still possible, but, if at all, after all hope of correction is past. Until then it calls for nothing but rigorous condemnation. To try to read any good thing into these fraudulent Southern constitutions, or to accept them as an accomplished fact, is to condone a crime against one's race. Those who commit crime should bear the odium. It is not a pleasing spectacle to see the robbed applaud the robber. Silence were better.

It has become fashionable to question the wisdom of the Fifteenth Amendment. I believe it to have been an act of the highest statesmanship, based upon the fundamental idea of this Republic, entirely justified by conditions; experimental in its nature, perhaps, as every new thing must be, but just in principle; a choice between methods, of which it seemed to the great statesmen of that epoch the wisest and the best, and essentially the most just, bearing in mind the interests of the freedmen and the Nation, as well as the feelings of the Southern whites; never fairly tried, and therefore, not yet to be justly condemned. Not one of those who condemn it, has been able, even in the light of subsequent events, to suggest a better method by which the liberty and civil rights of the freedmen and their descendants could have been protected. Its abandonment, as I have shown, leaves this liberty and these rights frankly without any guaranteed protection. All the education which philanthropy or the State could offer as a *substitute* for equality of rights, would be a poor exchange; there is no defensible reason why they should not go hand in hand, each encouraging and strengthening the other. The education which one can demand as a right is likely to do more good than the education for which one must sue as a favor.

The chief argument against Negro suffrage, the insistently proclaimed argument, worn threadbare in Congress, on the platform, in the pulpit, in the press, in poetry, in fiction, in impassioned rhetoric, is the reconstruction period. And yet the evils of that period were due far more to the venality and indifference of white men than to the incapacity of black voters. The revised Southern Constitutions adopted under reconstruction reveal a higher statesmanship than any which preceded or have followed them, and prove that the freed voters could as easily have been led into the paths of civic righteousness as into those of misgovernment. Certain it is that under reconstruction the civil and political rights of all men were more secure in those States than they have ever been since. We will hear less of the evils of reconstruction, now that the bugaboo has served its purpose by disfranchising the Negro, it will be laid aside for a time while the nation discusses the political corruption of great cities; the scandalous conditions in Rhode Island; the evils attending reconstruction in the Philippines, and the scandals in the post office department—for none of which, by the way, is the Negro charged with any responsibility, and for none of which is the restriction of the suffrage a remedy seriously proposed. Rhode Island is indeed the only Northern State which has a property qualification for the franchise!

There are three tribunals to which the colored people may justly appeal for the protection of their rights: the United States Courts, Congress and public opinion. At present all three seem mainly indifferent to any question of human rights under the Constitution. Indeed, Congress and the Courts merely follow public opinion, seldom lead it. Congress never enacts a measure which is believed to oppose public opinion;—your Congressman keeps his ear to the ground. The high, serene atmosphere of the Courts is not impervious to its voice; they rarely enforce a law contrary to public opinion, even the Supreme Court being able, as Charles Sumner once put it, to find a reason for every decision it may wish to render; or, as experience has shown, a method to evade any question which it cannot decently decide in accordance with public opinion. The art of straddling is not confined to the political arena. The Southern situation has been well described by a colored editor in Richmond: "When we seek relief at the hands of Congress, we are informed that our plea involves a legal question, and we are referred to the Courts. When we appeal to the Courts, we are gravely told that the question is a political one, and that we must go to Congress. When Congress enacts remedial legislation, our enemies take it to the Supreme Court, which promptly declares it unconstitutional." The Negro might chase his rights round and round this circle until the end of time, without finding relief.

Yet the Constitution is clear and unequivocal in its terms, and no Supreme Court can indefinitely continue to construe it as meaning anything but what it says. This Court should be bombarded with suits until it makes some definite pronouncement, one way or the other, on the broad question of the constitutionality of the disfranchising Constitutions of the Southern States. The Negro and his friends will then have a clean-cut issue to take to the forum of public opinion, and a distinct ground upon which to demand legislation for the enforcement of the Federal Constitution. The case from Alabama was carried to the Supreme Court expressly to determine the constitutionality of the Alabama Constitution. The Court declared itself without jurisdiction, and in the same breath went into the merits of the case far enough to deny relief, without passing upon the real issue. Had it said, as it might with absolute justice and perfect propriety, that the Alabama Constitution is a bold and impudent violation of the Fifteenth Amendment, the purpose of the lawsuit would have been accomplished and a righteous cause vastly strengthened.

But public opinion cannot remain permanently indifferent to so vital a question. The agitation is already on. It is at present largely academic, but is slowly and resistlessly, forcing itself into politics, which is the medium through which republics settle such questions. It cannot much longer be contemptuously or indifferently elbowed aside. The South itself seems bent upon forcing the question to an issue, as, by its arrogant assumptions, it brought on the Civil War. From that section, too, there come now and then, side by side with tales of Southern outrage, excusing voices, which at the same time are accusing voices; which admit that the white South is dealing with the Negro unjustly and unwisely; that the Golden Rule has been forgotten; that the interests of white men alone have been taken into account, and that their true interests as well are being sacrificed. There is a silent white South, uneasy in conscience, darkened in counsel, groping for the light, and willing to do the right. They are as yet a feeble folk, their voices scarcely audible above the clamor of the mob. May their convictions ripen into wisdom, and may their numbers and their courage increase! If the class of Southern white men of whom Judge Jones of Alabama, is so noble a representative, are supported and encouraged by a righteous public opinion at the North, they may, in time, become the dominant white South, and we may then look for wisdom and justice in the place where, so far as the Negro is concerned, they now seem well-nigh strangers. But even these gentlemen will do well to bear in mind that so long as they discriminate in any way against the Negro's equality of right, so long do they set class against class and open the door to every sort of discrimination. There can be no middle ground between justice and injustice, between the citizen and the serf.

It is not likely that the North, upon the sober second thought, will permit the dearly-bought results of the Civil War to be nullified by any change in the Constitution. As long as the Fifteenth Amendment stands, the *rights* of colored citizens are ultimately secure. There were would-be despots in England after the granting of Magna Charta; but it outlived them all, and the liberties of the English people are secure. There was slavery in this land after the Declaration of Independence, yet the faces of those who love liberty have ever turned to that immortal document. So will the Constitution and its principles outlive the prejudices which would seek to overthrow it.

What colored men of the South can do to secure their citizenship to-day, or in the immediate future, is not very clear. Their utterances on political questions, unless they be to concede away the political rights of their race, or to soothe the consciences of white men by suggesting that the problem is insoluble except by some slow remedial process which will become effectual only in the distant future, are received with scant respect—could scarcely, indeed, be otherwise received, without a voting constituency to back them up,—and must be cautiously made, lest they meet an actively hostile reception. But there are many colored men at the North, where their civil and political rights in the main are respected. There every honest man has a vote, which he may freely cast, and which is reasonably sure to be fairly counted. When this race develops a sufficient power of combination, under adequate leadership,— and there are signs already that this time is near at hand,—the Northern vote can be wielded irresistibly for the defense of the rights of their Southern brethren.

In the meantime the Northern colored men have the right of free speech, and they should never cease to demand their rights, to clamor for them, to guard them jealously, and insistently to invoke law and public sentiment to maintain them. He who would be free must learn to protect his freedom. Eternal vigilance is the price of liberty. He who would be respected must respect himself. The best friend of the Negro is he who would rather see, within the borders of this republic one million free citizens of that race, equal before the law, than ten million cringing serfs existing by a contemptuous sufferance. A race that is willing to survive upon any other terms is scarcely worthy of consideration.

The direct remedy for the disfranchisement of the Negro lies through political action. One scarcely sees the philosophy of distinguishing between a civil and a political right. But the Supreme Court has recognized this distinction and has designated Congress as the power to right a political wrong. The Fifteenth Amendment gives Congress power to enforce its provisions. The power would seem to be inherent in government itself; but anticipating that the enforcement of the Amendment might involve difficulty, they made the supererogatory declaration. Moreover, they went further, and passed laws by which they provided for such enforcement. These the Supreme Court has so far declared insufficient. It is for Congress to make more laws. It is for colored men and for white men who are not content to see the blood-bought results of the Civil War nullified, to urge and direct public opinion to the point where it will demand stringent legislation to enforce the Fourteenth and Fifteenth Amendments. This demand will rest in law, in morals and in true statesmanship; no difficulties attending it could be worse than the present ignoble attitude of the Nation toward its own laws and its own ideals—without courage to enforce them, without conscience to charge them, the United States presents the spectacle of a Nation drifting aimlessly, so far as this vital, National problem is concerned, upon the sea of irresolution, toward the maelstrom of anarchy.

The right of Congress, under the Fourteenth Amendment, to reduce Southern representation can hardly be disputed. But Congress has a simpler and more direct method to accomplish the same end. It is the sole judge of the qualifications of its own members, and the sole judge of whether any member presenting his credentials has met those qualifications. It can refuse to seat any member who comes from a district where voters have been disfranchised; it can judge for itself whether this has been done, and there is no appeal from its decision.

If, when it has passed a law, any Court shall refuse to obey its behests, it can impeach the judges. If any president refuse to lend the executive arm of the government to the enforcement of the law, it can impeach the president. No such extreme measures are likely to be necessary for the enforcement of the Fourteenth and Fifteenth Amendments—and the Thirteenth, which is also threatened—but they are mentioned as showing that Congress is supreme; and Congress proceeds, the House directly, the Senate indirectly, from the people and is governed by public opinion. If the reduction of Southern representation were to be regarded in the light of a bargain by which the Fifteenth Amendment was surrendered, then it might prove fatal to liberty. If it be inflicted as a punishment and a warning, to be followed by more drastic measures if not sufficient, it would serve a useful purpose. The Fifteenth Amendment declares that the right to vote *shall not* be denied or abridged on account of color; and any measure adopted by Congress should look to that end. Only as the power to injure the Negro in Congress is reduced thereby, would a reduction of representation protect the Negro; without other measures it would still leave him in the hands of the Southern whites, who could safely be trusted to make him pay for their humiliation.

Finally, there is, somewhere in the Universe a "Power that works for righteousness," and that leads men to do justice to one another. To this power, working upon the hearts and consciences of men, the Negro can always appeal. He has the right upon his side, and in the end the right will prevail. The Negro will, in time, attain to full manhood and citizenship throughout the United States. No better guaranty of this is needed than a comparison of his present with his past. Toward this he must do his part, as lies within his power and his opportunity. But it will be, after all, largely a white man's conflict, fought out in the forum of the public conscience. The Negro, though eager enough when opportunity offered, had comparatively little to do with the abolition of slavery, which was a vastly more formidable task than will be the enforcement of the Fifteenth Amendment.

POST-BELLUM—
PRE-HARLEM

My first book, *The Conjure Woman,* was published by the Houghton Mifflin Company in 1899. It was not, strictly speaking, a novel, though it has been so called, but a collection of short stories in Negro dialect, put in the mouth of an old Negro gardener, and related by him in each instance to the same audience, which consisted of the Northern lady and gentleman who employed him. They are naive and simple stories, dealing with alleged incidents of chattel slavery, as the old man had known it and as I had heard of it, and centering around the professional activities of old Aunt Peggy, the plantation conjure woman, and others of that ilk.

In every instance Julius had an axe to grind, for himself or his church, or some member of his family, or a white friend. The introductions to the stories, which were written in the best English I could command, developed the characters of Julius's employers and his own, and the wind-up of each story reveals the old man's ulterior purpose, which, as a general thing, is accomplished.

Most of the stories in *The Conjure Woman* had appeared in the *Atlantic Monthly* from time to time, the first story, *The Goophered Grapevine,* in the issue of August, 1887, and one of them, *The Conjurer's Revenge,* in the *Overland Monthly.* Two of them were first printed in the bound volume.

After the book had been accepted for publication, a friend of mine, the late Judge Madison W. Beacom, of Cleveland, a charter member of the Rowfant Club, suggested to the publishers a limited edition, which appeared in advance of the trade edition in an issue of one hundred and fifty numbered copies and was subscribed for almost entirely by members of the Rowfant Club and of the Cleveland bar. It was printed by the Riverside Press on large hand-made linen paper, bound in yellow buckram, with the name on the back in black letters on a white label, a very handsome and dignified volume. The trade edition was bound in brown cloth and on the front was a picture of a white-haired old Negro, flanked on either side by a long-eared rabbit. The dust-jacket bore the same illustration.

The name of the story teller, "Uncle" Julius, and the locale of the stories, as well as the cover design, were suggestive of Mr. Harris's *Uncle Remus,* but the tales are entirely different. They are sometimes referred to as folk tales, but while they employ much of the universal machinery of wonder stories, especially the metamorphosis, with one exception, that of the first story, *The Goophered Grapevine,* of which the norm was a folk tale, the stories are the fruit of my own imagination, in which respect they differ from the *Uncle Remus* stories which are avowedly folk tales.

Several subsequent editions of *The Conjure Woman* were brought out; just how many copies were sold altogether I have never informed myself, but not enough for the royalties to make me unduly rich, and in 1929, just thirty years after the first appearance of the book, a new edition was issued by Houghton Mifflin Company. It was printed from the original plates, with the very handsome title page of the limited edition, an attractive new cover in black and red, and a very flattering foreword by Colonel Joel Spingarn.

Most of my books are out of print, but I have been told that it is quite unusual for a volume of short stories which is not one of the accepted modern classics to remain on sale for so long a time.

At the time when I first broke into print seriously, no American colored writer had ever secured critical recognition except Paul Laurence Dunbar, who had won his laurels as a poet. Phillis Wheatley, a Colonial poet, had gained recognition largely because she was a slave and born in Africa, but the short story, or the novel of life and manners, had not been attempted by any one of that group.

There had been many novels dealing with slavery and the Negro. Harriet Beecher Stowe, especially in *Uncle Tom's Cabin,* had covered practically the whole subject of slavery and race admixture. George W. Cable had dwelt upon the romantic and some of the tragic features of racial contacts in Louisiana, and Judge Albion W. Tourgée, in what was one of the best sellers of his day, *A Fool's Errand,* and in his *Bricks Without Straw,* had dealt with the problems of reconstruction.

Thomas Dixon was writing the Negro down industriously and with marked popular success. Thomas Nelson Page was disguising the harshness of slavery under the mask of sentiment. The trend of public sentiment at the moment was distinctly away from the Negro. He had not developed any real political or business standing; socially he was outcast. His musical and stage successes were still for the most part unmade, and on the whole he was a small frog in a large pond, and there was a feeling of pessimism in regard to his future.

Publishers are human, and of course influenced by the opinions of their public. The firm of Houghton Mifflin, however, was unique in some respects. One of the active members of the firm was Francis J. Garrison, son of William Lloyd Garrison, from whom he had inherited his father's hatred of slavery and friendliness to the Negro. His partner, George H. Mifflin, was a liberal and generous gentleman trained in the best New England tradition. They were both friendly to my literary aspirations and became my personal friends.

But the member of their staff who was of most assistance to me in publishing my first book was Walter Hines Page, later ambassador to England under President Wilson, and at that time editor of the *Atlantic Monthly,* as well as literary adviser for the publishing house, himself a liberalized Southerner, who derived from the same part of the South where the stories in *The Conjure Woman* are located, and where I passed my adolescent years. He was a graduate of Macon College, a fellow of Johns Hopkins University, had been attached to the staff of the *Forum* and the *New York Evening Post,* and was as broadminded a Southerner as it was ever my good fortune to meet.

Three of the *Atlantic* editors wrote novels dealing with race problems—William Dean Howells in *An Imperative Duty*, Bliss Perry in *The Plated City*, and Mr. Page in *The Autobiography of Nicholas Worth*.

The first of my conjure stories had been accepted for the *Atlantic* by Thomas Bailey Aldrich, the genial auburn-haired poet who at that time presided over the editorial desk. My relations with him, for the short time they lasted, were most cordial and friendly.

Later on I submitted to Mr. Page several stories of post-war life among the colored people which the *Atlantic* published, and still later the manuscript of a novel. The novel was rejected, and was subsequently rewritten and published by Houghton Mifflin under the title of *The House Behind the Cedars*. Mr. Page, who had read the manuscript, softened its rejection by the suggestion that perhaps a collection of the conjure stories might be undertaken by the firm with a better prospect of success. I was in the hands of my friends, and submitted the collection. After some omissions and additions, all at the advice of Mr. Page, the book was accepted and announced as *The Conjure Woman*, in 1899, and I enjoyed all the delights of proof-reading and the other pleasant emotions attending the publication of a first book. Mr. Page, Mr. Garrison and Mr. Mifflin vied with each other in helping to make our joint venture a literary and financial success.

The book was favorably reviewed by literary critics. If I may be pardoned one quotation, William Dean Howells, always the friend of the aspiring author, in an article published in the *Atlantic Monthly* for May, 1900, wrote:

The stories of *The Conjure Woman* have a wild, indigenous poetry, the creation of sincere and original imagination, which is imparted with a tender humorousness and a very artistic reticence. As far as his race is concerned, or his sixteenth part of a race, it does not greatly matter whether Mr. Chesnutt invented their motives, or found them, as he feigns, among his distant cousins of the Southern cabins. In either case the wonder of their beauty is the same, and whatever is primitive and sylvan or cam-

pestral in the reader's heart is touched by the spells thrown on
the simple black lives in these enchanting tales. Character, the
most precious thing in fiction, is faithfully portrayed.

Imagine the thrill with which a new author would read such
an encomium from such a source!

From the publisher's standpoint, the book proved a modest
success. This was by no means a foregone conclusion, even assuming its literary merit and the publisher's imprint, for reasons which I shall try to make clear.

I have been referred to as the "first Negro novelist," meaning, of course, in the United States; Pushkin in Russia and the
two Dumas in France had produced a large body of popular
fiction. At that time a literary work by an American of acknowledged color was a doubtful experiment, both for the
writer and for the publisher, entirely apart from its intrinsic
merit. Indeed, my race was never mentioned by the publishers
in announcing or advertising the book. From my own viewpoint it was a personal matter. It never occurred to me to claim
any merit because of it, and I have always resented the denial
of anything on account of it. My colored friends, however, with
a very natural and laudable zeal for the race, with which I
found no fault, saw to it that the fact was not overlooked, and
I have before me a copy of a letter written by one of them to the
editor of the *Atlanta Constitution*, which had published a favorable review of the book, accompanied by my portrait, chid-
ing him because the reviewer had not referred to my color.

A woman critic of Jackson, Mississippi, questioning what
she called the rumor as to my race, added, "Some people claim
that Alexander Dumas, author of *The Count of Monte Cristo*
and *The Three Musketeers*, was a colored man. This is obviously untrue, because no Negro could possibly have written
these books"—a pontifical announcement which would seem
to settle the question definitely, despite the historical evidence
to the contrary.

While *The Conjure Woman* was in the press, the *Atlantic*
published a short story of mine called *The Wife of His Youth*
which attracted wide attention. James McArthur, at that time

connected with the *Critic,* later with *Harper's,* in talking one day with Mr. Page, learned of my race and requested leave to mention it as a matter of interest to the literary public. Mr. Page demurred at first on the ground that such an announcement might be harmful to the success of my forthcoming book, but finally consented, and Mr. McArthur mentioned the fact in the *Critic,* referring to me as a "mulatto."

As a matter of fact, substantially all of my writings, with the exception of *The Conjure Woman,* have dealt with the problems of people of mixed blood, which, while in the main the same as those of the true Negro, are in some instances and in some respects much more complex and difficult of treatment, in fiction as in life.

I have lived to see, after twenty years or more, a marked change in the attitude of publishers and the reading public in regard to the Negro in fiction. The development of Harlem, with its large colored population in all shades, from ivory to ebony, of all degrees of culture, from doctors of philosophy to the lowest grade of illiteracy; its various origins, North American, South American, West Indian and African; its morals ranging from the highest to the most debased; with the vivid life of its cabarets, dance halls, and theatres; with its ambitious business and professional men, its actors, singers, novelists and poets, its aspirations and demands for equality—without which any people would merit only contempt—presented a new field for literary exploration which of recent years has been cultivated assiduously.

One of the first of the New York writers to appreciate the possibilities of Harlem for literary purposes was Carl Van Vechten, whose novel *Nigger Heaven* was rather severely criticized by some of the colored intellectuals as a libel on the race, while others of them praised it highly. I was prejudiced in its favor for reasons which those who have read the book will understand. I found it a vivid and interesting story which presented some new and better types of Negroes and treated them sympathetically.

The Negro novel, whether written by white or colored authors, has gone so much farther now in the respects in which it was criticized that *Nigger Heaven,* in comparison with some of these later productions, would be almost as mild as a Sunday School tract compared to *The Adventures of Fanny Hill.* Several of these novels, by white and colored authors alike, reveal such an intimate and meticulous familiarity with the baser aspects of Negro life, North and South, that one is inclined to wonder how and from what social sub-sewers they gathered their information. With the exception of one or two of the earlier ones, the heroine of the novel is never chaste, though for the matter of that few post-Victorian heroines are, and most of the male characters are likewise weaklings or worse.

I have in mind a recent novel, brilliantly written by a gifted black author, in which, to my memory, there is not a single decent character, male or female. These books are written primarily for white readers, as it is extremely doubtful whether a novel, however good, could succeed financially on its sales to colored readers alone. But it seems to me that a body of twelve million people, struggling upward slowly but surely from a lowly estate, must present all along the line of its advancement many situations full of dramatic interest, ranging from farce to tragedy, with many admirable types worthy of delineation.

Caste, a principal motive of fiction from Richardson down through the Victorian epoch, has pretty well vanished among white Americans. Between the whites and the Negroes it is acute, and is bound to develop an increasingly difficult complexity, while among the colored people themselves it is just beginning to appear.

Negro writers no longer have any difficulty in finding publishers. Their race is no longer a detriment but a good selling point, and publishers are seeking their books, sometimes, I am inclined to think, with less regard for quality than in the case of white writers. To date, colored writers have felt restricted for subjects to their own particular group, but there is every reason to hope that in the future, with proper encouragement, they will make an increasingly valuable contribution to literature, and perhaps produce chronicles of life comparable to those of Dostoievsky, Dumas, Dickens or Balzac.

THE STORY OF PENGUIN CLASSICS

Before 1946 . . . "Classics" are mainly the domain of academics and students; readable editions for everyone else are almost unheard of. This all changes when a little-known classicist, E. V. Rieu, presents Penguin founder Allen Lane with the translation of Homer's *Odyssey* that he has been working on in his spare time.

1946 Penguin Classics debuts with *The Odyssey*, which promptly sells three million copies. Suddenly, classics are no longer for the privileged few.

1950s Rieu, now series editor, turns to professional writers for the best modern, readable translations, including Dorothy L. Sayers's *Inferno* and Robert Graves's unexpurgated *Twelve Caesars*.

1960s The Classics are given the distinctive black covers that have remained a constant throughout the life of the series. Rieu retires in 1964, hailing the Penguin Classics list as "the greatest educative force of the twentieth century."

1970s A new generation of translators swells the Penguin Classics ranks, introducing readers of English to classics of world literature from more than twenty languages. The list grows to encompass more history, philosophy, science, religion, and politics.

1980s The Penguin American Library launches with titles such as *Uncle Tom's Cabin*, and joins forces with Penguin Classics to provide the most comprehensive library of world literature available from any paperback publisher.

1990s The launch of Penguin Audiobooks brings the classics to a listening audience for the first time, and in 1999 the worldwide launch of the Penguin Classics website extends their reach to the global online community.

The 21st Century Penguin Classics are completely redesigned for the first time in nearly twenty years. This world-famous series now consists of more than 1300 titles, making the widest range of the best books ever written available to millions—and constantly redefining what makes a "classic."

The Odyssey continues . . .

The best books ever written

PENGUIN  CLASSICS

SINCE 1946

Find out more at www.penguinclassics.com

Visit www.vpbookclub.com

CLICK ON A CLASSIC
www.penguinclassics.com

The world's greatest literature at your fingertips

Constantly updated information on more than a thousand titles,
from Icelandic sagas to ancient Indian epics, Russian drama to
Italian romance, American greats to African masterpieces

•

The latest news on recent additions to the list, updated
editions, and specially commissioned translations

•

Original essays by leading writers

•

A wealth of background material, including biographies
of every classic author from Aristotle to Zamyatin, plot
synopses, readers' and teachers' guides, useful Web links

•

Online desk and examination copy assistance for academics

•

Trivia quizzes, competitions, giveaways, news on
forthcoming screen adaptations